Adam Kennedy is nov... ... .
whose previous novels range from the highly successful thriller *The Domino Principle*, which inspired the
international hit movie of the same name, to *In A Far
Country*, an enthralling family drama set in the 1960s.
His most recent titles include *Love Left Over*, a collection of bitter-sweet love stories, and *Passion Never
Knows*, the first novel in the Kincaid Trilogy. He lives
in Connecticut with his wife, Susan.

All Dreams Denied

The Bradshaw Trilogy

Adam Kennedy

KNIGHT

First published in Great Britain in 1988
by W. H. Allen & Co. PLC

First published in paperback in 1989
by Star Books

Published in this edition in 1991
by HEADLINE BOOK PUBLISHING PLC

This edition published 1998 by Knight
an imprint of Brockhampton Press

10 9 8 7 6 5 4 3 2 1

ISBN 1 86019 6519

Printed and bound in Great Britain by
Mackays of Chatham PLC, Chatham, Kent

Brockhampton Press
20 Bloomsbury Street
London WC1B 3QA

I've had a rewarding life as a novelist. This book is dedicated to some of the people who helped me along the way.

Herbert Alexander
Mike Bailey
Richard Barber
Fredrick Bergmann
Clara Cedrone
Ross Claiborne
Digby Diehl
Paul Gitlin
Tom Guinzburg
Arthur Hadley

Barbara Hendra
Owen Laster
Tom Maschler
Bob Mills
Betsy Nolan
Jay Sanford
Cork Smith
Bob Tanner
Evarts Ziegler
Mike Zimring

It is also dedicated to my wife, Susan Adams, who helped the most of all.

Dwell in the past
and you'll lose an eye.
Forget the past
and you'll lose both eyes.

Russian proverb

Book One

Chapter One

[1]

In January 1964, Clara Bradshaw Causey died in her sleep at her home in Northumberland. As soon as the members of her scattered family had the news they hurried to railway terminals or airports and began the journey that would bring them back to Wingate Fields.

Her daughter, Nora, flew to England from Paris. Clara's adoptive brother, Jesse, and her niece, Helen, drove to Chicago from their home in Fort Beck, Illinois and flew from there to London.

Valerie, Clara's granddaughter, along with her husband, Floyd, drove to Dun Laoghaire from the house they were renting in County Mayo, boarded the ferry to Holyhead, then on from there by car to Northumberland.

Valerie's daughter and two sons, Clara's great-grandchildren, came home from all directions: Bill, the youngest, from Edinburgh; Polly from Heidelberg, where she had gone a year earlier to read German literature of the nineteenth century; and Rab, the eldest, from Sienna, where he had been living for several weeks in a *pensione* with a young actress he had captured in Brighton.

'She's quite gifted,' Rab said to his father when they met in Wingate. 'Dances. Sings. Juggles a bit. Has a future it seems to me.'

'Whether she's gifted or not,' Jesse said. 'She doesn't belong here. Not for Clara's funeral.'

'That's precisely what Gloria said. We discussed it between us, as a matter of fact. That's why I put her up at the inn in the village.

I did tell you her name, didn't I? Gloria Atwood. Theatrical family. Several generations, I'm told. Her mum and dad had a bird act. Parrots and cockatoos, that sort of thing. Did a command performance once for Princess Margaret. Little birthday celebration, I think it was.'

The two men, father and son, were alone in Jesse's study at Wingate Fields, the room he had worked in through all the years he lived there on the family estate. Jesse sat looking at Rab, a slender, expensively dressed young man in his early twenties. At last Jesse said, 'You're still going at it, aren't you?'

'What's that?'

'You know what I'm talking about. This clever programme of yours. Still trying to get even with me and your mother.'

'As I remember, that's what you said the last time we had a serious chat. When I decided to give up on rotten old Cambridge.'

'It was true then and it's true now. Ever since Valerie and I made a decision about divorce. Ever since we told you . . .'

'Common occurrence these days, Jesse. Divorce, I mean. I have chums from school who are married and divorced long since. Twenty-two years old, twenty-three maybe, a wee baby in the crib, and a wife come and gone. Domestic drama. Tears and heartbreak. Common stuff now. Coin of the realm.'

'You've got some notion in your head,' Jesse went on, 'that Valerie and I did you in. Shot you down. So you're determined to square things by turning yourself into a . . . God knows what.'

'A wastrel? How does that sound? I used to favour the word "bounder", but it's not used much these days. Call a man a bounder today and he doesn't turn a hair.'

'You really don't give a damn about anything, do you?'

'Ah-ha . . . that's where you're wrong. I give a damn about a great many things. *Secret* things. Private matters. All tucked away in a safe place. But at night when I can't sleep – I'm a restless sleeper, did you know that – at night I take them out, all those things I truly give a damn about, and I set them up in a line on the wardrobe beside my bed. Quite a display they make.'

Jesse walked to the liquor table and poured himself a drink. When he turned back to his son he said, 'It's obvious that you have no respect for me. I've resigned myself to that. But at a sad time like this, I expect you to at least show some respect for the occasion. And a bit of concern for your mother's feelings.'

10

'I've had no complaints from Valerie. Not a word. No complaints from anyone till you spoke up just now.'

'For God's sake, Rab, use your head. Everyone knows you're free and independent. You don't have to go on proving it. You don't have to advertise it. How do you think it looks to people when you come home for a family funeral and bring along with you . . .'

'I don't care how it looks. I don't give a damn about such things. Gloria may not be a certified lady of the county but she pleases me. Besides, the Bradshaws are rather a grab-bag lot in any case, aren't they? Chancy blood-lines here and there. Cloudy pedigrees. A bit of in-breeding from time to time. A whiff of incest in the air.'

'Is that what you think of your family?' Jesse said.

'Nothing negative intended. Judge not that you be not judged . . . that's my credo. In fact I'm bloody proud to be a Bradshaw. It's a colourful heritage. Bright escutcheon. Made me quite famous at Cambridge. I was called on very often to chart my family history. Very few chaps can claim that their father was once their grandmother's sweetheart. You're quite a story, Jesse. You must realize that. The stuff of legends. An odyssey. From Nora to Valerie, then back to Nora. And now you're living contentedly with my great-aunt while my mother is married to her cousin. It's a feast for the imagination, a challenge to your children. I've got a long way to go before I can begin to match your exploits. Or my mother's, for that matter. Polly and William and I are barely qualified to be Bradshaws. Our lives are so tame and ordinary.'

'But you're determined to change that. Is that what you're saying?'

Rab smiled. 'The apple doesn't fall from the tree. You see . . . I did learn something at university. Aphorisms, cynicisms, truisms. And a great number of pertinent quotes from Oscar Wilde.'

Jesse sat looking at his son. 'Is this something that will go on for ever or will it finally come to an end?'

'What's that?'

'This effort to get even with Valerie and me.'

'I wouldn't call it "getting even". "Emulation" would be more accurate, I suspect. You certainly can't be displeased if your children want to follow in your footsteps. Because that's what we're after. We want to disregard convention just as you've done. We don't want to play by the rules. We want to make up our own rules. Just as you did. You're a contented man, aren't you? Charted your own course, found your own way, and ended up with the golden fleece. Isn't that a fair description of you?'

'You've got a hateful streak in you, Rab. Valerie and I tried to raise you and Polly and Bill in the best way we knew how.'

'No complaints, there, Dad.'

'When we decided to separate we did everything we could to keep you from being hurt, to keep you from feeling it was somehow your fault.'

'You certainly succeeded,' Rab said. 'We don't blame ourselves.'

'You blame *me*.'

Rab shook his head. 'We admire you. That's what I said. You taught us an important lesson. You gave us courage. We've decided we don't have to programme ourselves. We can make it all up as we go along. Sweep our mistakes under the carpet and keep forging ahead. You'll be proud of us before we finish. I expect we'll show you a thing or two.'

[2]

Although Clara was eighty-eight years old, she had enjoyed good health all her life. Her family were surprised by her death. If they had known that she died not from heart failure, as her doctor concluded, but from a half-bottle of Seconal capsules she swallowed before going to bed that night they would have been shocked.

Clara's niece, Helen, if she had known the truth, would not, perhaps, have been so surprised as the others. She and Clara, from their first meeting when Helen was eighteen, had made a primal contact that had continued to grow deeper and stronger in the more than forty years they knew each other.

After their flight from Chicago landed at Heathrow, Helen and Jesse took a taxi to the railroad terminal and boarded the morning train to Northumberland. As they sat by the wide window of the dining car having breakfast, the fields and hills outside looking grey and umber through a screen of winter rain, Helen said, 'It's a long while since we made this trip the first time.'

'I was thinking the same thing.'

'After all those years . . .'

'What?' Jesse asked.

'You know what I'm saying. Do you think we realized then that we'd end up together some day?'

'*I* did but you didn't.'

'That's not true,' she said. 'You can't tell me you spent forty years longing for me.'

'Maybe not. But if I'd known then what I know now . . .'

She reached across the table and touched his hand. 'Sometimes when I look at you, when you're reading in bed in your pyjamas, or sleeping late in the morning, it's hard to believe that we knew each other and loved each other so long and still . . .'

'There are all kinds of love.'

'Maybe. But I like this kind the best.'

'A bird in the hand,' he said.

'Don't make jokes, you rat.'

'I wouldn't dare.'

'Sometimes it makes me angry that we spent all those years apart. And other times I tell myself that if we hadn't waited, if circumstances hadn't forced us to wait, it couldn't be so scrumptious now.'

'Scrumptious?'

'You know what I mean,' she said. Then: 'Do you think your children know how much we love each other?'

'Of course not. And they'd be damned annoyed if they did. They think they invented love and all the rest of it. They don't want obsolete creatures like us mucking it up for them.'

'Do you think they see us that way? Obsolete creatures?'

Jesse nodded. 'They're selfish little beasts. Totally self-involved. They define us only as we relate to *them*. Rab and Polly and Bill see me as a *father*. Period. That's *it*. To them I'm a one-cell animal. And Floyd sees you the same way. As a *mother*. We're not supposed to stay up late, drink too much or romp around in bed. Our children wouldn't like that sort of thing. It's all unseemly and a bit vulgar in their eyes.'

'Too damned bad about them,' Helen said.

'That's right. That's what *I* say.'

As they walked through the train corridor returning to their compartment, Helen said, 'I'm glad Clara knew how we feel about each other.'

13

'She knew it before we did, I suspect.'

'Of course,' Helen said. 'She knew what *everybody* was up to.'

[3]

Valerie lay on her bed and wept for more than an hour after the news came about Clara's death. As she and Floyd drove away from their lodge on Killary harbour the next morning and headed east for Dublin her eyes were still red and her face was mottled pink from crying. 'God, I feel awful,' she said. She'd tucked herself into the corner of the car seat with a lap robe folded round her. She looked like a wounded child.

'I've missed her so much these past two or three years. She kept urging me to come visit her and I kept making excuses not to go. So now I'm going. When it's too late to mean anything.'

'It means something,' Floyd said.

'Those years when Rab and Polly and Bill were growing up, Clara and I spent almost all of our time together. We ran Wingate Fields, the two of us. Whenever I wasn't looking after the children I was with her. We depended on each other. In those years it never occurred to her that I wouldn't take her place as mistress of Wingate Fields. She knew she could never count on Nora, so she counted on me. Helen was gone and Nora was gone and I was the only one left. Then all at once I was gone too.'

'It's nobody's fault, kid. You have nothing to feel guilty about.'

'Of course I do. I don't mean I want to change anything. I did the only thing I *could* do. You and I did what was right for us. But I can't make myself believe it was the best thing for Clara. Right or wrong, she saw Jesse and me as a new foundation for the Bradshaw family. The link between what had gone before and what was yet to come. A clan in residence at Wingate. But it all blew up or dissolved or whatever those things do. Helen and Jesse disappeared in America, you and I went into hiding here in Ireland, and Nora went back to Paris to whatever her life has become now. So there Clara sat, these last years of her life, like a fine old lioness left to fend for herself.'

'Don't underestimate your kids. I'm sure they don't want to see

14

Wingate Fields dry up and disappear. One of them will get married and raise a family there, just like you did. Maybe all of them will decide to settle down there. You never know.'

'I know, Floyd, and so do you. Rab is caught up in some strange whirlwind that no one can understand. He seems determined to drink himself to death or to be shot by a jealous husband. But whatever he has in mind for himself he certainly doesn't see it happening at Wingate Fields. And neither does Polly. God knows what she's up to. I have no more contact with her than Clara had with Nora. If I were a psychiatrist I'd say that she needs to associate with people she knows are inferior to her. You've seen some of those fools she used to bring home. Even when she was a little girl. I think Polly's ashamed of being a Bradshaw. She's ashamed of being what she is. She needs to prove to herself that she's as good as other people.'

'She's only twenty.'

'No matter. She hasn't changed since she was six.'

The ferry crossing from Dun Laoghaire to Holyhead was remarkably smooth for January. 'A great storm due to hit us tomorrow,' the steward told them. 'This is the lull before the nasty weather.'

They stood by the forward rail as the ferry moved out of the Dublin harbour into the Irish Sea. Bundled up in their winter coats, their arms around each other, they watched the gulls wheeling in great arcs, circling around the high deck, squawking and diving to beak up scraps of refuse from the water.

When the Irish coast was a pale shadow behind them, Floyd said, 'Are you cold?'

'A little bit.'

'Let's go inside and get some hot coffee.'

'With a little something in it,' she said.

'That's what I had in mind.'

They both sat in a booth in the corner of the lounge, eating soda bread and jam with their coffee.

'You look better,' Floyd said. 'The sea air must be good for you.'

'It's nice of you to say that, but I know what I look like. When I cry it takes my poor sad face several days to recover.'

'I've never seen you cry like that.'

'It comes hard,' she said. 'I don't cry if I can help it. But when I *can't* help it . . . you know what I mean.'

'Is the funeral going to be tough on you?'

15

'I hope not. I think the worst is over.'

'Are you going to be able to handle the other stuff?'

'Seeing Jesse, you mean?'

'Seeing everybody,' Floyd said. 'Your kids, Helen, Nora, the whole crowd. This'll be our first time at Wingate since we got married.'

'I haven't even thought about that. Only Clara. That's all I've had on my mind. How about you? Will it be awkward for you? Seeing Jesse, I mean.'

'That depends on him. I don't have a bone in *my* throat. If he behaves himself, I'll behave *myself*. We're all grown-ups, for God's sake. What's done is done.'

'Does it make you feel different about your mother?'

'Because she's living with Jesse now? I don't think so. And it's none of my business anyway. She's known Jesse since she was thirteen years old . . .'

'Nora thought Helen was always in love with him.'

'Maybe she was,' Floyd said. 'Or maybe she wasn't. It doesn't matter. They're both old enough to know what they want so if they decided they want each other, that's fine with me. You and I got what's best for us. Maybe they did too. At least I hope they did.'

'It's strange how we all got shuffled about. And when it was over only Nora was left out.'

'You always told me she was a survivor.'

'I always thought she was,' Valerie said. 'But now I'm not so sure. Nora had convinced herself she would never be older than fifty and never *look* older than thirty. And I *know* she thought she would never be without a man.'

'Maybe she isn't.'

'I hope she isn't but I have bad feelings about her. Some people you worry about when you don't hear from them. With Nora it's the other way around. For the past two years she's written me a letter at least once a week.'

'I'll bet you get a surprise when you see her. I don't think anything could keep her down for long.'

'I hope you're right,' said Valerie.

Karina Einhorn met Nora Bradshaw just after the war when Nora returned to Paris from New York. Karina, whose nationality at that time seemed to change from day to day – later it turned out that she was German, born in Cologne – came to Paris by way of Lisbon.

For years, these two women had the sort of wary friendship that only very beautiful women understand, and for a short time they shared, unbeknown to Nora, the same man, a fashion photographer from New York called Martin Vuko.

Karina had no other female friends except for a young woman named Dort, who shared her home in Neuilly and was identified sometimes as her cousin, sometimes as her stepsister. Because of Karina's flamboyant addiction to men – her husband lived in Estoril and never visited France – no one in Parisian society imagined that Dort was anything to Karina other than what she was presented as being: a relative.

Nor was Karina's friendship with Nora regarded with suspicion by their friends. They were simply two women of a certain age who had been friends for a long time. It seemed perfectly natural and acceptable that Nora, whose relationship with Jesse had ended after many years, would be more often than before in the company of her friend whose husband lived in another country. Each enjoyed free access to the other's house in the city and the changing groups of people who enjoyed weekends in Nora's country house in the forest north of Paris almost always included Karina.

The scene that was played in Nora's house on l'Ile St Louis as she prepared to go to England for her mother's funeral would have unquestionably altered all public assumptions about these two handsome and wealthy women. As Nora selected the dresses she would be taking with her it was Karina who was in tears.

'Stop it,' Nora said. 'I don't know what's come over you. You're acting like an absolute fool.'

'I can't help it. How do you expect me to act? You know why I'm upset. You know exactly what I'm talking about.'

'I understand the words you're saying but they certainly don't make a great deal of sense.'

'My God, Nora, let's not pretend with each other. You know very well what I'm saying. I'm not imagining things. I'm not *creating*

17

anything. We're talking about Jesse. Jesse Bradshaw. Not a phantom, not a stranger.'

'I don't even know if he'll be there.'

'He'll be there. You know it and I know it.'

'Then he'll *be* there – there's nothing I can do about it.'

'Yes, there is. I told you what you can do.'

'But that's an insane idea. My mother's dead. I received word only two hours ago. Do you think I can stay here in Paris and pretend that nothing has happened?'

'But there's nothing you can do for her now. It's just a matter of propriety. Can't you simply call and tell them you're ill? Or I'll call if you want me to.'

'I *don't* want you to. I don't want you to do anything.'

'Your family won't care. You've told me yourself they don't give a damn about you.'

'I'm not going because of them,' Nora said. 'I'm going because it's the right thing to do. Because I *want* to. Because I must.'

'But what about me?'

'This has nothing to do with you.'

'When I know that Jesse is there, when I know that the two of you will be staying in the same house . . .'

'What a mind you have. Do you think Jesse and I will be dancing down the landings to each other's bedrooms?'

'I don't know what you'll be doing. All I know is that I'll be going crazy.'

Nora went over and sat beside her friend. 'That's all over, Karina, and you know it.'

'I know it was over when he married Valerie. But it started up again, didn't it? What makes you think it won't start a third time?'

'Because it won't. He's with Helen now. He has been ever since Floyd and Valerie got married. He's not interested in me. I'm not interested in him.'

'Don't you think I know you? I remember what you were like when Jesse was married to Valerie. And I remember how it was when he came back. Don't tell me it couldn't happen again. I don't believe it. Everybody's somebody's fool, Nora.'

'And I'm Jesse's . . . is that what you're saying?'

'I don't have to say it. You know it as well as I do.'

Nora sat looking at her for a long moment. 'Look at me,' she said then. 'I'm not twenty-five years old any longer. I'm not even fifty.

18

Jesse and I went through a lot together. He meant everything to me. I've never tried to hide that. But it's over, Karina. We're not going to start up again. We can't. Don't you see that? Don't you believe me? My mother is dead. And I'm going home for her funeral. It's something I have to do. Something I need to do. It has nothing to do with Jesse or anyone else. I'll be back here in a few days and nothing will be different than it is right now.'

Karina sat slumped on the sofa, looking down at the floor.

'I don't believe you,' she said.

[5]

Polly flew from Frankfurt to Oslo, changed planes and flew across the North Sea to Newcastle. Her brother, Bill, met her at the airport, bundled her into his car and headed west towards Wingate Fields. As they manoeuvred their way out of the airport complex a light snow began to fall.

'Are you all right?' she said.

'Not very cheerful. It's an empty house without Clara.'

'When did you get home?'

'Yesterday early. Drove down from Edinburgh at night.'

'Is Rab here?'

'Arrived this morning. He's staying at the inn in the village.'

'Why's he doing that?'

'He brought a bird with him from London. Bleached hair and a science-fiction bosom. You can be sure of that.'

'Have you seen her?'

'No. But I know Rab.'

Polly smiled. 'What a bugger he is. Centre stage all the time. Is Dad here yet?'

'Due tomorrow. He called from New York.'

'And Valerie?'

'On the way. She and Floyd are driving across from Holyhead.'

'The whole cast assembled. How about our grandmother?'

'Nora's flying over from Paris today.'

Only a year apart in age, Polly and Bill had been close since childhood. 'It was a matter of survival,' she explained to her school

19

friends. 'We had to present a united front against our older brother. We loved him. We admired him. We idolized him. But he demanded more than that. Total worship was what he had in mind. Complete self-abnegation. So it was a struggle all the time we were growing up. Negative attention, the baby doctors call it. Rab was a master of that. Both our parents had their hands full with him; there wasn't much time left for Bill and me. So we plotted against him and told ourselves we hated him but all the while he had us hypnotized. And he still does. He never knows what he's going to do from one moment to the next so you can't help watching and waiting to see what will happen. His secret is that he's not afraid of anything. Full speed ahead . . . that's his only impulse. Makes himself over every day.'

'Bloody awful weather,' Bill said as the snow changed suddenly to rain and swept across the windscreen of the car. 'I thought Scotland had the worst weather but this is no better.'

'You should see Heidelberg in January. It's like living at the bottom of the ocean.'

'I still don't know why you went back for a second year.'

'Passion,' she said. 'The lure of the flesh.'

'You're still with that old man?'

'Jack's not so old. He won't be forty till next July.'

'Twice your age,' Bill said.

'Just for now. When he's eighty, I'll be sixty.'

'If he drinks as much as you say he does, he won't make it to sixty.'

'Some people think he won't make it to forty.'

'He must be crazy.'

'No question about it. He's brilliant and gifted and crazy. He doesn't know who he is. He was born in Karlsruhe, raised in Milwaukee, and now he's back in Germany, playing the cello, drinking himself to death, and giving political speeches on street corners. He speaks such flawless German the police keep arresting him for carrying an American passport.'

'He's not good enough for you.'

'Oh, yes he is. I'm not good enough for *him*. He's the wisest man I've ever met.'

'He sounds like a mess.'

'He is. But so's everybody else. He's just a different sort of mess.'

'I hope you're not going to marry him.'

20

'Not much chance of that. He wouldn't marry me if I begged him. And he couldn't in any case. He has a wife in Wisconsin. And a nine-year-old daughter.'

'What if he decides to go home to his wife?'

'I don't think he will but if he does, he does. I don't expect to have him for life. I'll just settle for as much as I can get.'

'How about you,' she said then. 'How's *your* love life?'

'Let me put it this way. There's a sign in the pub where I go that reads: "Lust is not a *must* in Edinburgh, not in the winter." And another one that says: "Beware of genital frost-bite. Don't fall in love till April." '

'They can't have duvets in Scotland.'

'Oh, they do. But under those duvets the Scots still sleep in their overcoats.'

Driving across the moors, the rain blowing in still from the west, as they topped a final rise and saw Wingate Fields in the distance, Polly said: 'Can we deal with this?'

'The funeral, you mean?'

'Not just that. I mean will it be awkward and terrible seeing Mother and Dad again?'

'I saw Jesse last summer in Illinois and I saw Valerie in Dublin in November,' Bill said.

'I know you did. But I'm talking about seeing them together in the same room. The two of them and Nora and Floyd and Helen. That could make for an uneasy dinner table.'

'Don't worry about it. Rab will probably make an ass of himself and all eyes will be on him.'

[6]

Rab, as it turned out, did not misbehave. Quite the contrary. Restrained, perhaps, by the hard-edged discussion he'd had with Jesse, he handled himself in an exemplary manner. Although his father, since Clara's death, was the senior living Bradshaw, he showed no eagerness to assume once again the head-of-household role he had accepted during his marriage to Valerie. Seeming to sense this hesitation on Jesse's part, Rab, as the elder son, took

21

over, albeit temporarily, as master of Wingate. Although he slept each night with his friend Gloria at the village inn, he spent most of the daylight hours during the five days that preceded and followed Clara's funeral helping to arrange the details of that ceremony and the burial in the crypt beneath the family chapel.

The discomfort that Polly and some of the others had anticipated did not materialize. It was as though Clara in death was the same stabilizing force she had been in life. All those present had resolved, it seemed, to relate to each other only as fellow mourners, only as Clara's descendants. If the warmth that often characterizes such family gatherings was absent, so were the tensions that might easily and understandably have displayed themselves. And there was no mistaking the fact that each individual felt an agonizing sense of loss. Even the staff members, who were accustomed to witnessing emotional reactions among the Bradshaws that were either larger or smaller than circumstances seemed to dictate, were aware that on this occasion, no fakery or simulation was required. The grief was heartfelt, the tears were real, the emptiness that existed now at Wingate because of the absence of one valuable person was clear and painful to all.

The Bishop of Newcastle, feeble and arthritic himself now, a man who had known Clara for most of her life, was close to tears himself when he closed the burial ceremonies with a personal reminiscence.

'We are born in pain, suffering is a part of all our lives, and death is a sorrowful occasion. It is not surprising that all of us at one time or another should find ourselves asking: "What does it all mean? Why must our lives be so cruel?" Even those of us who have devoted our lives to God, to Faith, to the life of the spirit, even the most dedicated of the Lord's servants cannot help but be shocked and pained by the senseless cruelties we witness every day. But just as those events make us question, so do they provide the answers we seek. Out of the swamp of suffering that we see all round us suddenly appears a remarkable person, an individual of unbelievable strength and patience and sweetness, someone who seems to have been created as an example, as a pattern, a person who demonstrates in countless ways that joy and triumph exist in every single life, that no pain or sorrow, not even death, can alter those joys or diminish those triumphs. Such a person was Clara Bradshaw. By sharing her life, each of us has enriched our own. We can't pretend that she will never leave us. This house, these

22

rooms, these gardens echo with her absence. But the marks she made on each of us are permanent. We are all changed by having known her. That is Clara's immortality. It's the only immortality any of us are allowed.'

[7]

From the time of their arrival at Wingate till the funeral service and the burial, each family member seemed under tight rein. Mealtimes were quiet and impersonal. When people spoke they spoke only of Clara, of her husband, Ned, of Angus and Louise, her parents. They gathered together in the library or the drawing-room with all the *politesse* of cordial strangers. Past relationships seemed forgotten or irrelevant. No future matters were discussed, not even the future of Wingate Fields itself, a subject that was surely in everyone's mind. The assumption seemed to be that the staff would maintain the property and the quality of life that many generations of Bradshaws had established. And some time in the future, present circumstances would somehow be altered and some unit of the extended Bradshaw family would again be in residence at Wingate.

Although there was no general discussion of these matters they were raised in the bedrooms of the house – not by the younger family members, who seemed either unaware or unconcerned that centuries of family continuity might now be in jeopardy, and not by Nora certainly, who in her own mind and in the minds of everyone who knew her was a permanent resident of France. Valerie and Floyd, however, in their upstairs suite, and Jesse and Helen, in theirs, returned again and again to the subject.

'It haunts me,' Valerie said. 'I can't get it out of my mind. I feel as if we're betraying Clara in the most cruel and unforgivable way. She had such plans and dreams about who would carry on in this house. From the time that Jesse and I came here to live she rejoiced in the belief that we would live here till the end of our lives. And since we had three children she felt sure that one of them, or all of them, would also stay on and raise their families here. Then it all exploded.

'I'm sure she must have realized before she died that things

23

would turn out exactly as they seem to be now. All of us rooted somewhere else, unable or unwilling to live here again, to be the centre of the family, to keep things stitched together the way Angus did and the way Clara has done since he died. It's sad enough that she's gone but this whole emptiness, this deserted house that we'll be leaving behind when we go back home, makes it seem as though she's dying for a second time.'

'Don't give up on Rab and Polly and Bill,' Floyd said.

'I'm not giving up on them. But I *know* them. The last thing that interests them is what they already *know*. They don't want what they have, they want what they don't have. If they saw some continuity here, as I did, that would be one thing, but what do they see? I'm living in Ireland, their father lives in America now, and their grandmother in France. Their money means freedom to them. They want to wander about and see new things and discover themselves. County life looks like no life to them. In twenty years it may seem different but by then it will be too late. Too late for them to change and too late for Wingate Fields.'

'So what's the answer?'

'There isn't one, I'm afraid. The only people who can do what needs to be done are either me or Jesse. But he's not going to move back here and neither am I.'

'Are you saying that because of me? Because if you are . . .'

'I'm not. I'm saying I couldn't come back now and live as though that other life I spent here had never happened. When I came to you I wasn't *escaping* from that life or this house. At least I didn't feel that I was. But now that you and I have found a life of our own as different as it could possibly be from what my life was here I could never transplant *that* life into this place. It wouldn't work. It couldn't work. I don't mean we couldn't survive living here but I don't want to risk losing one small speck of what we have now. If we need a Wingate Fields we'll build one somewhere but I don't want us to live here with all the Bradshaw ghosts and goblins.'

Helen's position, when she discussed the matter with Jesse, was even stronger than Valerie's. 'I couldn't do it, Jesse. I'll go anywhere with you. I'll live any place you like. But don't ask me to live here. That I can't do.'

'I wasn't asking you to. I just said that I remember all the talks I had with Angus years ago and I feel as if I'm violating everything he expected of me. I feel guilty and I can't help it.'

24

'I can understand that. But you left here before when you lived with Nora in Paris. You left again when you and Valerie were divorced and you came back to Illinois.'

'I felt like hell about leaving,' Jesse said. 'But at least Clara was here then. As long as she was alive there was no doubt about the state of Wingate Fields. But I look around me now and all the heart and vitality are gone. Clara died and the house died with her.'

'It's not just this place, Jesse. It's not just England. It's everywhere. Look at Fort Beck. All those fine old homes by the river are rooming houses now. They're filled with factory workers from Missouri and Kentucky, cooking on hot-plates and throwing beer bottles out the window. The good old stuff is being replaced with rotten new stuff. It's a pizza and hotdog world now. Blue jeans and rock music. Look at your own children. Do you think they give a damn about the Bradshaw name and the Bradshaw traditions?'

'I know they don't. That's all the more reason why I should. Why somebody should.'

'It's you or nobody, my love. I don't think Valerie and Floyd are about to take over the care and nurturing of Wingate Fields.'

After a moment he said: 'We could have a good life here, couldn't we?'

She shook her head. 'I don't think so. It's not us, Jesse. Too much has happened here. Too much *hasn't* happened. Maybe a long time ago we could have managed it. But not now.'

'It means a lot to me.'

'I know it does. Otherwise we wouldn't be discussing it at all.'

'What if I said I had to do it?'

'If you said you were coming here to live whether I came or not then I'd come with you of course.' She smiled. 'But I don't think you're going to say that.'

[8]

'You're making a big mistake, Bill,' Rab said.

'I don't think so. Seems like a sensible idea to me.'

'That's because you didn't ask me for advice. Take my word for

25

it, it's a dotty idea. A nice plan for Jesse perhaps, a little trick to help persuade himself he's a first-rate father, but no good for you.'

They were in Bill's room, just after breakfast, the morning of the funeral. Bill was changing his suit for the ceremony.

'You made a good decision by staying away from Cambridge. I'm an expert on that bee-hive. Nothing to be gained there. But you never should have settled for that mechanic's college in Edinburgh.'

'It's the best engineering school in Britain,' Bill said.

'Maybe it is and maybe it isn't. Either way it's no place for you. Industrial design . . . is that it? Is that what you're studying?'

'That's right.'

'Well, there you are. That's no profession for you, old cock. Struggling for four years to prepare yourself for a nine-to-five job at some dreary factory in the Midlands.'

'Come off it, Rab. Stop trying to dissuade me. I already told you I'm leaving Edinburgh.'

'That's true. But you're making another bad choice. Worse than the first one. America's no place for you.'

'How do you know? You've never been there.'

'Of course I have. Twice to New York. Once to Miami.'

'But I'm going to Illinois,' Bill said.

'Back to your father's arms. No good, laddy. A step back in time. A return to your nappies.'

'Go to hell, Rab. I'm switching to scenic design. University of Illinois. They've got a good department there.'

'I doubt it. That's corn country. What do they know about the theatre? And you mustn't trust Jesse on the subject. He'll tell you anything to have you close at hand. Salve the conscience. Staunch the flow of guilt. Restore his image of himself.'

'You're a bore, Rab. What have you got against Dad? He's never mistreated you. Too bad he didn't. Somebody should have given you an accurate assessment of yourself.'

'Ah-ha . . . mustn't defame your brother. We're allies to the death, you know. Damon and Pythias. Why would I spend so much time trying to put you straight if I weren't concerned about your future?'

'You're concerned about your own future. Nothing else.'

'Wrong again, Bill. My future doesn't interest me at all. I deal only in present matters. Present and pleasant. That's what I'm trying to impress on you. There's no need for you to pursue some

26

pedantic, time-wasting course in life. Your financial security is solid. You're healthy as a horse and reasonably attractive. You must take me as a model. Knock about. Amuse yourself. Sample the wine and make yourself available to both ladies and wenches. I'm sure you'll find, as I have, that the wenches are more amusing.'

'You didn't answer my question. What right do you have to attack Jesse at every opportunity?'

'Good question. It's simply a right I have assumed. I do not admire the man. I've read his articles and critical pieces and I do not admire those. I do not admire the way he sits a horse and I do not admire the way he treated Valerie.'

'He didn't abandon her,' Bill said. 'She left *him*.'

'Who told you that?'

'Polly.'

'Our sister is misinformed in all areas.'

'Besides,' Bill said. 'What difference does it make? We were practically grown up when they divorced. Do you think your life was damaged?'

'Not a bit. I simply don't, as I said, admire the man.'

'I don't admire you, but you're my brother . . .'

'Ah – but you do admire me. You know that I have your best interests at heart. You also know that I am both fearless and lucky so I'm a valuable ally. Because you are fearless but *not* lucky. So I suggest you hang on to me. *My* luck will get you further than either wisdom or industry. And when I tell you that a move to Illinois would be an unwise choice for you I expect you to follow my advice, not for my sake but for your own.'

'You're a royal pain in the ass. Do you know that?'

'I accept your use of the word "royal" but I reject all the rest of it.'

[9]

That evening before dinner, Rab visited Polly in her rooms.

'Your brother, William, thinks I'm too harsh in my judgement of Jesse. What do you think?'

'I try not to think about you at all. You can't be taken seriously.'

27

'You're trying to hurt my feelings,' he said.

'As a matter of fact, I'm not. But even if I made the effort, I couldn't bring it off. You're impregnable.'

'Does that mean I'll never get pregnant?'

'No. It means you have cast-iron skin and a concrete heart.'

'Odd that you should say that. The ladies I know tell me I'm unbelievably tender.'

'The ladies you know have my sympathy.'

'The poets say that all young women have a yen for their older brothers. Do you think that's true?'

She smiled. 'It's certainly true in my case. I spent a great deal of my time trying to find a man like you. At last I found an egocentric irresponsible drunk and I've been happy ever since.'

'You're still with him then?'

'You mean Jack? You were in Heidelberg in November. You know I'm still with him.'

'He's dangerous,' Rab said.

'No, he's not. He's sick and crazy but he's not dangerous. *You're* dangerous.'

'I can't imagine what attracts you to him.'

'He's selfish and mean and he's a sex maniac. What more could a woman want?'

'I don't suppose he thought much of me,' Rab said.

'He thought you were handsome and articulate. Why wouldn't he like you? You were charming that night. On your best behaviour. Almost unrecognizable.'

'I don't like *him* a lot. I thought he might have guessed that.'

'If he did he didn't mention it. In any case he's accustomed to not being liked. He doesn't try to be popular.'

'Neither do I.'

Polly laughed and said, 'Of course you do. You want everybody to love you. I've never met anybody who wanted to be loved as much as you do.'

'What a strange thing to say.'

'It's not strange at all. That's why you're so naughty. So people will be sure to notice you. Once you have their attention they're snared.'

'The spider and the fly.'

'Exactly,' she said.

'Do I have your attention?'

28

'Of course. I'm an easy mark. Bill and I were your early victims. We're caught for life.'

'Does Jack Dieter have you caught for life?'

'I hope so.'

'Does Valerie know about him?'

'Of course. We had a long talk about him.'

'Did you tell her that I don't like him?'

'Yes, I did. I said you hated him because he's smarter than you.'

'What did she say to that?'

'She laughed.'

'I'm not surprised. It's quite amusing.'

'Not really. It's true.'

Rab got up and poured himself a drink. When he sat down again he said, 'Did she say anything about Jesse?'

'You mean Mother?'

'Yes.'

'She asked if I was in touch with him and I said yes, he writes me long letters. I told her he also writes to Bill. I didn't know about you. Does he write to you?'

'Not very often.'

'Do you answer when he writes?'

'Not always,' Rab said.

'Have you ever answered his letters?'

'No.'

'That's why he doesn't write very often.'

'That's not the reason. He knows what I think of him.'

'What do you think of him?'

'I think he's a failure as a father.'

'Maybe he thinks you're a failure as a son.'

'I don't care what he thinks,' Rab said.

'We'll see about that.'

'What does that mean?'

'Just what I said. Maybe you'll discover that you care quite a lot about what he thinks. Maybe you'll find out you care more about that than anything.'

'Not bloody likely.'

'Since Valerie doesn't hate him and Bill and I don't hate him it's hard to figure out what terrible thing he did to you that he didn't do to us. You want to know what Jack says? He says you're not

29

mad at him for leaving Valerie. You can't forgive him for leaving you.'

'I don't give a damn what Jack says. What does he know?'

'He knows a lot. He knows a lot about everything. Jack's like Clara used to be. He can see inside people.'

'Well, he can't see inside me.'

[10]

The day after Clara was buried the temperature dropped sharply and the sky was clear. When Floyd walked out to the stables in the morning after breakfast, Jesse followed him. They stood in the tack room and talked, the first time they'd been alone together since arriving at Wingate Fields.

'Did Helen ask you to talk to me?' Floyd said.

'No. It was my idea.'

'Are you about to tell me we both love my mother so we should try to be friends for her sake?'

'No,' Jesse said.

'All right. Let's try this one. You used to be married to Valerie and now she's married to me, so some civilized accommodation should be made. For the sake of your children maybe. You're their father but I'm the stepfather so perhaps we should discuss their futures.'

'You really have a chip on your shoulder, don't you?'

'No. Nothing like that. Nothing's changed. You and I were never great friends from the start. So I'm wondering why we should go through the motions now.'

'No reason I can think of,' Jesse said. 'But it might make things a bit easier for Helen and Valerie.'

'Valerie never mentioned it to me. And you say Helen didn't mention it to you.'

'She didn't. But I know she'd like it if the situation could get smoothed out a bit. She'd like to see you more often than she has the past two or three years.'

'I'd like to see her, too. She's welcome at my house any time she can make it.'

'Good. I'll tell her that.'

'I think she already knows it.'

'Does that mean I'm welcome too?' Jesse asked.

'You'd have to ask Valerie about that.'

'I'm asking you. You must know the answer.'

'We've never discussed it if that's what you mean.'

'That's hard to believe.'

'Maybe so, but it's true,' Floyd said. 'Very little discussion in our home about the old days. Very little coming and going. We keep pretty much to ourselves.'

'No visitors welcome.'

'It's not a stated policy but that's how it seems to work out. Rab and Polly and Bill show up when they feel like it and Valerie pops off to see one of them from time to time. But aside from that . . .'

'Don't misunderstand,' Jesse said. 'I'm not trying to wangle an invitation, I just thought it might be possible for us to have a civilized arrangement.'

'That's what we have now. Helen's my mother and Valerie's my wife. Valerie used to be your wife and now you're living with my mother. So we all know each other pretty well. I don't see much point in our visiting back and forth so we can get better acquainted.'

'Neither do I. But I wish you could make an effort to see Helen once in a while.'

'I haven't heard any complaints from her,' Floyd said.

'You never will. It's not her style.'

'Well, I think that's something Helen and I will have to work out between ourselves. As I said, she's welcome any time.'

'I'm not sure she knows that,' Jesse said.

'Then why don't you tell her?'

'Maybe it would be better if you told her.'

'Maybe it would, but I'm not going to. Since you went to all the trouble of having this little talk with me I don't want to deprive you of the pleasure of reporting the result.'

'You're really a hard-nose, aren't you?'

'Not me,' Floyd said. 'I think of myself as a kind and gentle man. Gracious, considerate and fond of animals.'

Jesse stood looking at him in the bright-lit tack room. Finally he turned away and walked slowly back toward the house.

31

'I knew I was running a risk,' Valerie said to her daughter. 'Jesse knew it too. That's why we took such pains to explain matters to you and your brothers when we decided to proceed with our divorce plans. We were both surprised that you took it so well. All three of you in different ways. We congratulated ourselves that you were very grown-up and understanding. And later, when Floyd and I got married, although Jesse had already gone off to America, I didn't notice any secret resentments in you or Rab or Bill. I felt that you all wanted me to be happy. I was confident that you would have good relationships, each of you, with both me and Jesse, even though we weren't married any longer. Was I wrong about that?'

Polly shook her head. 'I don't think so. I accepted the situation. And I thought Rab and Bill did too.'

They were sitting, late morning, in a sunny corner of the breakfast room. Everyone else had gone back upstairs or had taken breakfast in their rooms.

'Now it seems clear to me that I deceived myself. That I simply believed what I wanted to believe. I know all three of you are older now, that you're busy with your own concerns and your own lives, but still . . . how can I explain it? I feel as if those warm years we spent together here at Wingate when you were growing up were simply washed off the slate somehow. I feel as though I'm being punished or banished or something.'

'We're all scattered about,' Polly said. 'That's part of the problem.'

'Of course it is. I know that. But there's more to it than that. There was a closeness before. We were a snug little family. That seems to be gone now. When I see you I feel as if we have to start all over each time, that I have to explain who I am, present my credentials. Do you feel that way, too?'

'I'm not sure.'

'You must. I can't believe this is something I'm imagining. It's certainly not a feeling that gives me pleasure.'

'As I said,' Polly said, 'it must be because we're all so far from each other.'

'Let me ask you this then. Do you think that if I still lived here in the old house, if Floyd and I had settled in here after we were married, that things would be different for all of us than they are now?'

'I don't know.'

'I don't know either,' Valerie said. 'But I have a strange feeling that things would be no better.'

'We know you love us. You must know we love you.'

'Of course I know that. But I also know that love needs to be tended. It feeds on impressions and perceptions and it must be fed regularly. I feel sometimes that if I didn't struggle to stay in touch with you I'd never hear from you again. I'm sure Jesse feels the same way.'

'Have you talked to him about it?'

'No. But I've talked to you and Rab and Bill. And none of you seems to have any real connection with your father. You write to him at least and Bill pretends to be involved. But Rab, as far as I can tell, wants nothing to do with him. Did something happen that I don't know about? Does he really hate Jesse?'

'You know how Rab is. He sees himself as the centre of every situation. He's always been that way. When you and Dad told us you were getting a divorce, both of you turned into different people all of a sudden. Rab pretended to think it was a great adventure but I'm sure it bothered him. In all the wrong ways. He's always seen himself as a star performer and the rest of us as supporting players. Then all of a sudden you and Jesse took over as individuals with lives of your own. In some way that diminished Rab. And he didn't like it. Then you got married and Dad was off in America with Helen and that gave Rab another jolt. He had to redefine people. His father had turned into a romantic figure and his mother was a happy bride with a handsome new husband. All the key actors had changed roles.'

'But if it didn't affect you and Bill, why did it make such a difference to Rab?'

'It did affect us. But not in the same way. Rab has it in his head that while he changes every second like quicksilver, everyone else in the world must stay the same. Besides, Rab has always had problems with Jesse. He hates him one day and worships him the next. Always has. But mostly he envies him. Wounded in the war, for example. Rab has no interest in joining the Army but he would love to have a glamorous limp like Dad has from 1917. He knows Jesse rides well so he goes out of his way to criticize his horsemanship. He doesn't want to write himself but it bothers him to see

33

magazines and books lying about with Jesse's articles in them. He thinks Dad can do all sorts of things he can't do and it bothers him. And the thing that bothers him most, because he's young and egotistical – he thinks Jesse is a great success with women.'

Valerie smiled. 'He does seem to have an impressive record. At least with the Bradshaw women.'

'All these things are difficult for Rab to come to terms with. So he solves the problem by telling himself he doesn't like Jesse anyway. Nothing he does or accomplishes is worthwhile. As long as Rab can make himself believe that, he doesn't have to compete with his father.'

'And Bill doesn't have that problem?'

'He has it but not with Jesse. His *bête noire* is Rab. He's smarter than Rab. He knows that Rab is like a rag-bag of acquired notions and characteristics. Nothing very deep or profound or even sincere about him, but all the same Bill would give his left arm to be a carbon copy of his brother. There's no logic to it. He just thinks Rab was born under a benevolent star. He sees him bluster and brag and blunder, lie and cheat and make an ass of himself. And always, in the end, he comes up with a rose in his teeth. It drives Bill crazy. Rab keeps talking about how lucky he is and Bill keeps believing it.'

'You're giving me an insight into my own children. How did you get so smart?'

'I'm not smart. I just pay attention. And in our family there are plenty of people to watch. Drama for one and all.'

'And how about you? What should I know about my newly grown-up daughter?'

'I always wanted to be like you but I found out I couldn't. So now I'm just trying to be myself.'

'Sometimes that's the hardest thing of all,' Valerie said.

'I know. I'm finding that out, too.'

[12]

If we are an amalgam of what we *are*, what we *think* we are, and what others think we are, where is the truth? Is it fair that we pass judgement on Rab Bradshaw based on his sister's conclusions about

34

him? Is he entitled to speak for himself? Most of us don't get such an opportunity but perhaps we should give it to him, keeping in mind as we do that his observed *modus operandi* seems to be composed of equal parts of deception and self-deception.

My name is Raymond Angus Bradshaw. I'll be twenty-two years old this year. I have a great deal of money in my own name, and unlimited self-confidence. Also, I have, in some quarters, a chancy reputation, some of it earned, some not.

Clara, my great-grandmother, believed that I am the way I am, *whatever* that is or may turn out to be, because my parents suddenly divorced when I was eighteen or nineteen, because my mother remarried soon after and because my Dad set up house in Illinois with my mother's second cousin who I think of as my Aunt Helen.

I loved my great-grandmother with all my heart and I respected her views but she was mistaken about my reactions to my parents' divorce. I didn't give a damn about that.

The facts are these: Polly and Bill and I were extremely fortunate. We had a fine time growing up at Wingate Fields. We were proud of our parents and we still are. At least I am.

Jesse and Valerie cared about what happened to us. They made us feel valuable. They taught us self-respect. And when the time came they bundled us off to excellent schools, a different school for each of us, so we'd have a chance to be individuals, away from whatever family identity we'd acquired through the years. They taught us to be grown-ups.

I admit I was surprised when they announced that they had decided to get a divorce. But then I thought, 'What the hell! They have lived together for twenty years and have known each other for almost forty years, from the time Valerie was a toddler.'

Who says a marriage must last for life? I don't. Two years with one woman seems quite long enough to me. A year ago I felt that two *months* was more than enough.

I have never attempted to make anyone proud of me. Nor have I tried to be proud of myself. I am content to move ahead, or backwards, or sideways, and keep my options open. Moment to moment. A strong horse to ride, a humidor filled with fine cigars, a decanter of port in every room, and a sweet-smelling young woman in bed at night. That's quite enough for me.

Having been fair and even-handed with Rab, must we deal equally with his sister, Polly? Of course we must.

I think about my mother every day. I think all sorts of things about her. But mostly I think about her mistakes. Her greatest mistake was getting married so young. Having children right away. Tying herself down as county matron when she was young and pretty and full of life. If she had enjoyed herself more when she was a girl, if she'd tested herself and taken a few risks, she wouldn't have fallen in love with Floyd when she was almost forty years old. She wouldn't have divorced Jesse.

Early commitments. Very destructive. Not for me. Not for me at all. I want to be like my grandmother. I want to live like Nora. I want to have it all. My father says that Valerie is like Clara, *her* grandmother, and I'm like mine. He's right. At least I hope he's right. Nora had the courage to take what she wanted and I'm going to do the same thing. I'm not cruel, but I don't want to be left behind either.

I'm not like Rab, of course. Nor do I want to be. He has a mean streak. There's something vicious about his detachment from everything and everybody. I like people and I want them to like me. Rab doesn't give a damn about anybody. Still people like him. They seek him out. I don't understand that but maybe I will later on.

I don't want to be like Bill either. He's all serious and dedicated but he's not quite sure what he's dedicated to. Whatever Rab is, Bill wants to be the opposite. Or so he tells himself. He can't decide if he loves Rab or hates him. He only knows that he envies him. A lot of people envy Rab and he knows it. Maybe that's why he's such a pill.'

Now, of course, Bill must have a turn.

My mother says I'm very much like my father but I don't see it. I don't think I'm like anybody. I'm certainly not like Rab. All that noise and self-confidence based on nothing. But still he manages to fool people. They figure anybody who's so monumentally impressed with himself must have something to back it up.

Rab and Polly insist that I'm Valerie's favourite but I don't agree. She never looks at me the way she looks at Rab. And even when she's angry with him he can make her laugh.

People think I'm mild and tame. But if they knew some of the things I feel, the thoughts that go through my head, they'd get a surprise. Polly's beautiful and wild and clever and crazy and Rab's a powerhouse but people only notice me because I'm quiet. I do my school work, run cross-country and I don't make trouble. But I know there's something inside me that will make people pay attention some day. I want to *do* something and I'm going to do something. I just don't know what it is yet. And even when it happens I suppose people will say: 'I can't believe that Bill did that.'

All the Bradshaws think of me as my mother's child because I look like her and because I was the baby of the family. But when they got a divorce it was my Dad I missed. I never knew how much I needed him till he went off to live in America when I was sixteen. I still miss him. It's funny how things change from year to year, how you find out things you didn't know before and all of a sudden everything gets switched around.

[13]

From the time of her arrival at Wingate Fields the day before Clara's funeral service to the hour of her departure the day after, Nora isolated herself, not in the rooms off the garden where she normally stayed but in the nursery suite on the second floor, where she and her brother, Hugh, had lived as children with their tutor and their nanny, Miss Jossy. Nora slept there, took her meals there, and encountered the rest of the family only in the chapel and at the closing of the crypt. When the service ended, when she went back upstairs to the nursery, her daughter followed her. When they entered the great sun-lit playroom, its old hobby-horses and stuffed toys ranged against the walls, Valerie saw stacks of photo albums and cartons of cards and letters near the chair by the window where Miss Jossy had sat each morning while the children played. Valerie followed Nora into the bedroom where her mother had slept as a child.

'Are you all right?' Valerie said. 'I've seen you so little these past two days.'

'I wasn't avoiding anyone,' Nora said. 'Certainly not avoiding you. I just didn't feel like talking. Couldn't bring myself to polite conversation. My mind was full of Clara and I didn't want those thoughts interrupted.' Her eyes filled with tears as she spoke. 'I've been crying a lot these past few days and that's something I needed to do alone.'

'I hate to think of you sitting here crying.'

'I don't like it either. But there are still a few private acts left in the world. And grief is one of them. At least to me it is.'

'Are you better now?' Valerie said.

'Not really. I can't undo all the things I've done in my life and maybe I wouldn't if I could. And it's too late to do all the things I failed to do. Jesse used to say that we are only able to tolerate ourselves because we have bad memories.'

Valerie nodded. 'I've heard him say that.'

'But occasionally something happens to jog your memory,' Nora went on, 'whether you like it or not. Since I had the phone call telling me Clara was dead, my memory has been working double time, reminding me of everything she did and everything I failed to do. At first I tried to fight it. But finally I decided to dive all the way in, to bury myself in this room and remember everything. From the beginning.'

'Did it help?'

'It almost killed me. All of us survive on self-deception, don't we? When you strip that away, for whatever reason, you see some very unattractive things.'

'It's not fair to compare yourself with Clara. Alongside her none of us would hold up very well.'

'I know that. That's what I tell myself. But what do you do when you compare yourself with *yourself*, when you examine what you are and measure it against what you might have been.'

'But you can't do that, Nora. None of us can. Nobody can stand up to that kind of scrutiny. It's not fair. It doesn't prove anything.'

'It proves something to me, my darling. But I don't want to talk about it any more.'

After a moment Valerie said, 'How are things in Paris?'

'Very busy. I keep myself very busy.'

'I don't like the way you sound. I wish you'd take a couple weeks off and come to see us.'

'In Ireland? I hate Ireland. I don't even like it in the summer when it's green and beautiful. At this time of year it's hopeless.'

'Then come see us in Portugal. We've been talking about taking a place on the Algarve.'

'The Algarve's no prize in the winter either. I don't like peasant countries. If you like peasants so much you should settle in Bulgaria. They grow white radishes bigger than carrots.'

Valerie smiled. 'I think you're coming back to life.'

'Just my mouth. Inside I'm all rust and corrosion.'

'Maybe so. But the outside looks wonderful.'

Nora smiled. 'People say that to me all the time. But I'm not taken in. I know they mean that I look wonderful for a woman of my age. That's quite a different matter. One thing I know for sure is how I look. I am a serious student of my own face. In the right light, at a proper distance, I can get by. Otherwise I suffer the same indignities and imperfections as any other woman my age. Whatever lies I manage to tell myself, my looking-glass tells me the truth.'

'I never thought I'd hear you question your own beauty.'

'The world changes. I never thought I'd sit in the nursery looking at old photographs and reading old letters and crying my heart out.'

'You talk like a woman who's about to make changes in her life.'

'I've already made changes in my life.'

'In what way?'

'In every way. A series of 180° turns.'

'You worry me,' Valerie said.

'I worry myself.'

'I think about you every day.'

'And I think about you,' Nora said.

'Good things?'

'You're my daughter. I love you.'

'You didn't answer my question.'

'Of course I did. I love you so I don't judge you.'

'I wish I could believe that.'

'Are we talking about Jesse now?' When Valerie didn't answer she said, 'I thought we settled all that a long time ago.'

39

'You left this nursery a long time ago too but that doesn't mean you forgot.'

'Nobody ever forgets anything. You don't forget. I don't forget. Jesse doesn't forget.'

'Does it seem strange to you, seeing him with Helen?'

'You know my quirks. I always thought they were crazy about each other. I thought it the first time I ever met them, when I was nineteen years old. All the time he and I were together, when you were growing up, I was still jealous of Helen. So I'm not surprised to see that they're together at last. Did it surprise you?'

'I'm not sure. I always thought she had a yen for him but I guess I believed him when he said he loved her like a sister. But . . . it doesn't matter now, does it?'

'Of course it matters,' Nora said. 'Anybody who hurt you once can keep on hurting you. It doesn't make sense but it's true. All of us try to survive by forgetting but sometimes all you forget are the unhappy times. All you remember is how good it was when it was good.'

They sat there in the small bedroom looking at each other. In this room too there were stuffed animals sitting in all the corners.

[14]

The day before she was scheduled to leave for Germany, Polly drove into the country with her father. They had lunch together in a sixteenth-century inn half-hidden in a clump of oak trees.

'This is the only family I know where everyone calls everybody else by their first name,' Polly said. 'We all called our great-grandmother Clara. Rab and Bill and I very seldom call you and our mother anything except Jesse and Valerie. Nora always called her father Ned and her grandparents Angus and Louise. That's unusual, isn't it?'

'Seems to be. But Helen called her father Raymond and at that time she didn't even know about the Bradshaws here in England. So I guess it's been going on for a long time.'

During lunch she asked him questions about his work and he told her in detail what he was writing and what projects he had in mind for the future. She told him about her studies in Heidelberg, described the town in some detail, and explained how it had been changed by the presence of United States Military forces.

At last, when they were having coffee and their conversation seemed to have lost momentum, she said: 'We both know why you drove me over here today so why don't we get on with it?'

'I wanted to have lunch with you. I don't see you enough. I thought it would be nice if we sneaked off for a couple of hours together.'

She shook her head. 'No good, Jesse. I don't buy it. You want to give me a lecture about Jack Deiter. Before you start, I want you to know it's a waste of time.'

'I've never lectured you, have I?'

'No, you haven't. But you're about to.'

'All right,' he said. 'Since you brought it up let's talk about it.'

'It won't do a bit of good.'

'Maybe not, but I feel obliged to make an effort.' Keeping his eyes on her he sipped from his coffee cup. Then: 'You're an intelligent girl, Polly, smarter than either of your brothers. Your mother's proud of you and so am I. There's no reason in the world why you shouldn't have a marvellous life.'

'I'm having one now.'

'Maybe you are. At least I'm sure you *think* you are. It's hard to be miserable when you're twenty. But you won't be twenty for ever . . .'

'Come on, Jesse, give me a bit of credit. This sounds like a father-daughter talk on the telly.'

'I want you to feel as good about yourself in ten years,' he went on, 'as you do now.'

'I don't expect any guarantees and you mustn't either.'

'Of course there are no guarantees . . .'

'Did you lay out your whole life-plan when you were my age?'

'No. But perhaps I should have done.'

'No, you shouldn't because it can't be done. Nora didn't do it, Helen didn't do it, Valerie didn't do it, and you didn't either.'

He sat looking at her for a moment. 'If you had something to say to me, do you think I'd listen?'

'You're manipulating me.'

'You didn't answer my question. It's a fair question isn't it?'

'Probably not. Nobody's fair when they're trying to get their way.'

'Would I listen . . . yes or no?'

'You would. Start the lecture,' Polly said.

'You're making a big mistake, honey.'

'You've never met him.'

'That's right. But Valerie did.'

'Did she tell you bad things about him?'

'No. She said he was nice to her and he's *very* nice to you. But . . .'

'But what?'

'But she thinks you're making a mistake.'

'I don't believe that,' Polly said. 'I don't believe you talked with her. When did you talk to her?'

'Last night. Before dinner.'

'I still don't believe it.'

'Use your head, Polly. What do you expect Valerie to think? Anybody would tell you the same thing. He's twenty years older than you. He's married. He has a daughter. He has no money, he's been a student all his life, and he drinks too much.'

'You're twenty years older than Valerie aren't you?'

Jesse nodded. 'More than that. Twenty-three.'

'So there you are.'

'Different circumstances.'

'Circumstances are always different. You're not saying that you and Valerie would still be together if you were the same age, are you?'

'I'm not saying it but some people might.'

'You don't give a damn about what other people say and neither do I.'

'What kind of future do you think you'll have?'

'How do I know? Nobody knows that.'

'What do you talk about, the two of you? What kind of plans do you make?'

'We don't make any plans. What kind of plans do you and Helen make?'

'You're not using my life as a model, are you?'

'I'm not using anybody as a model,' she said, 'but if I decided to, why shouldn't I use you? You don't think of your life as a wreck, do you?'

42

'No.'

'There you are. Neither do I. You don't think it was a mistake to marry my mother, do you?'

'No.'

'I didn't think so. And you don't regret all those years you lived with Nora, do you?'

'That's not the same thing.'

'Of course it's not. But you don't regret it, do you.'

'No, I don't.'

'Good for you. You're giving all the right answers. How about Helen? You're not living with her because you hate her. I mean you don't think she's a big mistake, do you?'

'Just because you're clever doesn't make you right.'

'I could say the same thing to you. The point is it doesn't matter to me if I'm right. I'm perfectly willing to make a mistake. I love every minute I spend with Jack. Can you imagine anything I could say to myself or anything you could say to me that would fill in those gaps if I decided that I shouldn't be with him any longer? Just because we may not have a future together. With Jack, the future is tomorrow morning. I know that. I've always known it. You're not the first person who's warned me about him. I used to warn myself. But I've stopped doing that. Now I just feel lucky. If I fly back to Germany tomorrow and he's not there I'll still feel lucky that I had him for as long as I did. And if there's any way to find out where he went, I'll follow him.'

'If you ask me, he's the one who's lucky,' Jesse said. 'But I still can't help worrying about you. What if you find out you're going to have a baby?'

'I pray for that. I've dreamed of it ever since I met him. Nothing would make me happier.'

'Is that what he wants, too?'

'No. Jack never wants to have another child. He thinks the world is a mess.'

'Would he feel that way if you were married?'

'We'll never be married. He thinks marriage is a joke.'

'But he's married now, for God's sake.'

Polly nodded. 'That's what convinced him it's a joke.'

'Don't you think if he cared about you, he'd want to get a divorce?'

'We're not talking about how he feels about me. We're talking

43

about how I feel about him. Jack's so crazy I'm not sure he can love anyone. I don't even know if he wants to. All I know is what I want and how I feel. That's enough for me. Why are you shaking your head?'

Jesse smiled. 'There's a school of Indian philosophy that says the only love we ever experience is the love we give.'

'I'm not a philosopher, I'm a victim,' she said.

'That's an odd choice of words.'

'Doesn't seem odd to me.'

Jesse offered her a cigarette and lit one himself. Then he said, 'This is a big jump. From the high plains of self-sacrifice to the marble floors of commerce.'

'I know what you're going to say. I have a great deal of money.'

'That's right. Does your friend know that.'

'Don't call him my friend. His name is Jack.'

'Does Jack know you're rich?'

'He knows everything about me.'

'How does he feel about that?' Jesse asked.

'I don't know.'

'You must have discussed it.'

'We didn't discuss it. I told him about it and that was that. We've never talked about it since.'

'Valerie says he has no money of his own.'

She shook her head. 'He has a scholarship at the university and an open airline ticket from Frankfurt to Chicago and that's it.'

'How does he support himself?'

'He doesn't. He lives with me.'

'How did he support himself before he met you?'

'He lived with a German woman who works at the Army PX in Heidelberg.'

'If you couldn't support him would he stay with you?'

'I think he would but I can't guarantee it.'

'You've thought about it then?'

'Of course I've thought about it. I think about all kinds of things. But it doesn't change anything.'

'It wouldn't hurt you if you found out he was with you just because you have money.'

'I wouldn't like it, probably, but as I said before it wouldn't change anything. If he needs money and I have money, why in the world shouldn't I give it to him?'

44

'You're very passive. Almost Biblical. I've never thought of you that way. You believe in turning the other cheek.'

'No, I don't. I've always thought that was a lot of nonsense. I don't trust people who are eager to be punished.'

'Is he faithful to you?' Jesse said then.

'You mean . . .'

'I mean are there other women who are as taken with him as you are?'

'It wouldn't matter. Because he wouldn't be taken with them. He's just with me.'

'But what if he isn't? What if you found out he had another lady friend? The woman from the PX maybe.'

'You mean if I knew about it. If I caught them together?'

'Yes.'

She smiled. 'I'd kill him. I wouldn't hesitate.'

[15]

The night before he left Northumberland to return to London, Rab swept Polly and Bill along with him to the inn in the village to meet Gloria Atwood.

'We've mourned with respect and genuine sorrow,' he said. 'Clara was a treasure to us all. But now it's time to snatch up the reins of our lives again.'

'I'm not in the mood for a drunken party,' Polly said, 'if that's what you've got in mind.'

'Nothing like that. Something more in the order of a proper Irish wake. An event our ancestor Angus would have advocated if the stories about him are accurate. We honour the dead by celebrating the living. Clara would have approved too, I'm sure of it. I've booked a private dining room at the inn. They've roasted some birds and a joint of mutton for us and I found some decent claret in their cellar so I think I can promise you an enjoyable evening. And of course you will meet Gloria Atwood. That in itself would be cause for celebration.'

Miss Atwood, it turned out, bore no resemblance whatever to the bosomy, peroxide-blonde creature Bill had envisioned. She was

45

a slender young woman, remarkably composed, with fair skin, green eyes that seemed almost yellow in certain lights, and brown hair pulled back in a soft bun. She had a rich, beautifully modulated voice that seemed like a central armature to her delicate body. She was one sort of creature when she sat in repose at the dinner table, quite another creature when she spoke.

'Rab says you come from a theatrical family,' Polly said.

Gloria smiled. 'Since you're his sister I'm sure you know that he seldom tells the truth about anything. I expect he's trying to make me seem more glamorous than I am. My family are sheep farmers actually. Our home is in West Dorset. Sherborne. Just east of Sherborne.'

'Oh, what a modest young lady she is,' Rab said. 'The truth is her family owns half the grazing land in Somerset, her father's in the House of Lords, her uncle's an admiral in the Royal Navy, and her brother is partner in a firm of solicitors in London.'

'Why did you say she's a juggler?' Bill said.

'Because she juggles the facts. As I've just demonstrated.'

'My mother studied to be a concert violinist,' Gloria said. 'But she gave it up when she and my father married. Perhaps that's why she's encouraged me to be an actress. She helped me to meet Sybil Thorndike and Edith Evans and they brought me to the Royal Academy of Dramatic Art. I've been there for the past three years.'

'So I was right,' Rab said. 'The Atwoods may not be a theatrical family yet but starting with Gloria they will be. She's already done Shaw at Chichester and a new play by Terence Rattigan at Birmingham so she'll be fully launched before long. She'll do two or three plays in the West End and by then my management office will be in operation and my television ventures as well, so I'll be able to present her in a series of motion pictures and television projects that will bring her recognition in America as well as Britain.'

'What's all this about?' Polly said. 'Are you planning to be the J. Arthur Rank of your generation?'

'Big plans,' Rab said. 'I've just invested in an off-shore radio station with a signal strong enough to reach every home in England.'

'How does the BBC feel about that?' Bill said.

'They don't like it at all. But we're outside their jurisdiction, Canadian money, a bit of money from America, a friend of mine and myself. A tight group. Aggressive. Our next step is an agency to represent talent. Actors, writers, directors. We've taken on a bright young chap who used to head up the William Morris operation in London. He'll bring in Ralph Richardson, Rex Harrison, Trevor Howard, and a whole group of promising young performers.'

'Do you think you can operate an off-shore television station as well?'

'Not off-shore. Independent. Commercial. We'll show American films and television series and sell advertising time to British sponsors.'

'Will the government permit that?' Polly said.

'Of course they will. Because it's profitable. We'll see commercials on the BBC before we're finished. The money's there just waiting for someone to pick it up. Lots of possibilities. Tie-ins with Canada and Australia. All kinds of ventures to explore.'

As they drove toward home later Polly said to Bill, 'What do you think of your brother now?'

'He's full of surprises, isn't he? One minute he advocates the dilatory life. Wine, women, and fur-lined overcoats. And the next thing you know he's working on a blue-print to capture the entire world of commerce.'

'He sounds serious, doesn't he?'

'He sounds convincing but that doesn't guarantee that he's serious. Rab's big talent is persuasion. Once he's persuaded everybody that he's wonderful then he's content to lie down in some cosy corner and take a nap.'

'This time he sounds different,' Polly said. 'He certainly seems to know what he's talking about.'

'Of course he does. That's his trick. He's like a strip of sticky paper. Facts and figures and scraps of history cling to him. But just because you know that there are three million more dachshunds alive today than there were in 1950, just because you know that the water level of the Nile has dropped four inches in the last six hundred years, none of that kind of scatter-gun information means you really know anything.'

'But as you said, he convinces people.'

'Not me. Tomorrow afternoon he could be sitting in the bar at the Savile Club telling people his plans for canning horse meat in Costa Rica.'

Polly laughed. 'You know him too well.'

'I don't know him at all. Neither do you. We just keep listening to him because we think that sooner or later it's all going to make sense. But it never will. Rab hears some kind of music that every-body else is deaf to.'

'What did you think of Miss Atwood?'

'Another mystery,' Bill said.

'How do you mean?'

'I mean she wasn't what I expected. Nothing like. When a young woman lets herself be shut away in a village inn and left there for hours and days while her boyfriend runs off to be with his family, when she is never taken to the house, never presented or introduced . . .'

'She's not a girl I'd expect to tolerate a situation like that.'

'Exactly. Not a little flower-girl from Piccadilly Circus. And she's not a juggler as he represented her as being before we met her. She's intelligent. No doubt about that. Comes from a fine family, it seems. So why do you suppose she lets Rab mess her around?'

'The pelvis has reasons that reason knows nothing of.'

'Is that it? Is it that simple?'

'Nothing simple about that. You're talking to an expert.'

Bill shook his head. 'Well, I'm not an expert but still you'd think that girls would see through him.'

'Maybe they do. Maybe Gloria does. That's a totally different matter. Whatever else Rab is, he's relentless. Most women like relentless men.'

'Does that mean I have to learn to be relentless?'

Polly laughed. 'Not at all. That's not your style. You've got something else.'

'What's that?'

'I don't have a name for it but I guarantee that once you decide to make yourself available you'll have young ladies falling all over you.'

'That's good news.'

'But first you have to make yourself available. As I said.'

'Should I put a sign on my shirt or place a little notice in the personal columns of the daily paper?'

'Think it over,' Polly said. 'You'll work it out.'

16

When they were in bed later in their rooms at the inn, Gloria said, 'Was I convincing? Did they believe me?'

'Totally convincing,' Rab said. 'You almost had me believing you.'

'I told you I was a good actress.'

'You've got a future. No doubt about it.'

'I thought I gave too many details. Or rather you did. My mum used to say, "If you're going to tell a lie, keep it general." '

'She's wrong. The details are everything. That's the clincher. The names and places and dates. That's what wins the day.'

'What if they find out there are no Atwoods in Sherborne?'

'There are. I went to school with one of them,' Rab said.

'But I'm not related to them. What if someone finds out I'm lying?'

'Then you smile and change your story. Tell them they misunderstood you. Besides, before we're finished, you'll be so bloody famous every Atwood in England will claim that he's related to you.'

She moved close to him and put her head on his shoulder. 'I'm not so keen on being famous, you know. I just want to be the best actress I can be. I want to do good work.'

'You do the good work and I'll make you famous.'

'I'm not sure I'd like it if I couldn't stroll round without having people follow me.'

'You'll like it. I promise you. You'll love it.'

Chapter Two

[1]

When Helen and Jesse returned to Fort Beck from England they found a letter from Clara waiting for them. It was post-marked January 19th, the day before her death.

> I haven't written to you for several weeks. I'm aware of that. And filled with proper guilt. But I have a good excuse. I've been in foul spirits, in a frame of mind that I was not eager to share with anyone. At last, however, I have resolved my dilemmas. More accurately, I have found a way to lose them. In fact, I have decided, after a great deal of thought, to lose myself.
>
> Seems an odd choice for me, doesn't it? Both of you will remember, I'm sure, how shocked and angry I was when Hugh shot himself. At that time it was beyond my understanding that any person, certainly not my son, could find himself totally without alternatives. I felt, as most people do, that any life is better than no life.
>
> Now I see things differently. Suicide always seemed to me a kind of cowardice, a confession that one is unable to handle the tears and pain and disappointments that come to each of us. Now I see it not as fear or cowardice, not as an inability to cope, but an unwillingness to do so. That conclusion came to me as a great revelation. There is such a thing as terminal weariness. We have all said, many times, 'I am very tired. I must sleep now.' What a normal and common feeling that is! It's the way I feel. I know no better way to explain it.

I have been very close to both of you. I'm writing this letter not to make you feel worse about my dying but to make you feel better. You know what great rewards I have had during my life. I've enjoyed robust health, I've been able to use myself in ways that had meaning for me, and I've been a part of a unique and vital family.

You remember, Jesse, that Angus said to you not long before he died that you would live to see the winds blow through the broken windows and empty rooms of Wingate Fields. I was shocked at the time to hear that he'd said those words. It was an ugly thought for me, an appalling prospect. Now I see it as an inevitability. It no longer shocks me but I have no desire to witness it.

Both of you have keen sensibilities so I don't have to tell you how fundamentally the world has changed in my eighty-odd years. There are no absolutes now. Our diplomats betray us, our children fight in the cities with police, your fine young President is shot in the street like an animal. In the name of dissent, any crime is possible, any sin is forgiven.

I won't go on. My own thoughts and convictions bore me now. In the hallway outside my sitting room two of the upstairs maids are arguing passionately about the carpet-sweeper. What is there about a household tool that can inspire such incipient violence? I can't find an answer for that. But I realize that if I stepped outside and saw one of them bleeding on the floor I would not be surprised. A man on the wireless last evening said that when they write of these times in future the title of the book will be *People Killing Each Other*. I believe that.

I know you won't dismiss me as an aged person who cannot absorb or accept change. Change is a principal part of our lives. But God help us when we can make no distinction between *change* and *deterioration*. God protect us from a world that insists on providing scientific or economic answers to spiritual questions.

I'm baying at the moon. I realize that. The world is no more interested in me than I am interested in it. So the only decent thing I can do, I believe, is withdraw, absent myself, before I find myself becoming what I detest.

This letter is not meant to be a burden or sorrow for you. Quite the contrary. But I'm vain enough to want someone to know that

51

I am acting for what I consider to be admirable reasons rather than sit here as an unquiet witness to chaos, wanting to be acted upon.

I'm giving you information that I'm giving to no one else. I hope people will believe I died of natural causes because that will surely make them more comfortable. I felt that you two, however, would be comfortable with nothing except the truth. If I'm mistaken, you must forgive me.

After each of them had read the letter silently, Helen said, 'What does it mean?'

Jesse didn't answer. He carefully folded the letter and put it inside the envelope. Then he said. 'It means she decided to stop living.'

'But the doctor said . . .'

'When a woman almost ninety years old dies peacefully in her sleep, heart failure is the simplest conclusion.'

'I'm so stunned, I don't know what to say.'

'I do,' Jesse said. 'I admire her. Angus once said she was the only person he knew who lived by her own standards.'

'Do you think any of that rubbed off on us?'

'I hope so.'

[2]

The following day, Jesse pretended that he had to drive to Urbana to do some research in the university library and Helen pretended she had to spend the day in Chicago to meet with her banker. Jesse did in fact closet himself in a small reading room in the library but he did no research. And Helen, when she arrived in Chicago did not see her banker. She met instead with Frank Wilson, her ex-husband. They had not seen each other or spoken for more than four years. She telephoned him at his office and they met for lunch at a restaurant on Walton Place. She was waiting there when he arrived.

'This is a surprise,' he said as he sat down.

'Yes. To me, too.' Then: 'Clara died.'

'I'm sorry.'

'She killed herself. I was in England for her funeral. We all thought she'd died of heart failure. I didn't know until yesterday that she'd . . .'

'That's a tough one,' he said.

'As soon as I found out I knew I wanted to see you. I don't know why. After that letter you wrote me I thought we'd never see each other again. I certainly didn't want to see you. But here I am.'

'I felt bad about that letter. I still do. People do strange things when they start feeling sorry for themselves.'

'I deserved it,' Helen said. 'I thought it was an accurate listing of my shortcomings. That's why it hurt. That's what you wanted, wasn't it, to hurt me.'

'Of course. I figured if I was wounded, you should be too. There was nothing rational about it. I knew you'd decided to get rid of me so I needed to strike back.'

'You got married again, didn't you?'

He nodded. 'About two months after I sent you that letter. How about you?'

'I'm living with Jesse. For several years now.'

'You mean living with him or *living* with him?'

'*Living* with him. In Fort Beck.'

'How did that come about?'

'He and Valerie got a divorce and she married my son, Floyd.'

'And what about Nora?' Frank said.

'You know all the good questions. But I don't have all the answers. Whatever she and Jesse had together, they don't have it any longer. I guess it's as simple as that.'

'I used to think about how much I knew about your family. But outside of Floyd I never met any of them. Do they know as much about me as I know about them?'

Helen smiled. 'Clara knew a little but no one else does. I always kept you to myself. You were my secret.'

'Are you and Jesse married?'

'No.'

'Planning to be?'

'No.'

'Just living together?'

'That's right.'

'Serious or casual?'

53

'Serious for me.'

'Not for him?'

'I hope. But you never know what's in someone else's head. Besides all these things look different when you're not thirty any longer. Or even fifty. The desperation goes away. A lot of things happen to you and you find out you can survive. When you're young you think you can't possibly live without a particular person. That's the way you want it to be. You need to believe that. But little by little you discover it's not true. And at last you realize it isn't true at all. You may not want to survive but you will. You take what comes to you and make yourself as contented as you can.'

'Doesn't sound like you,' Frank said.

'It's me, all right.'

'Sounds a little cold-blooded.'

'Not at all. When I was a young girl I was so much in love with Jesse it was painful. I didn't admit it to myself then but I certainly know it now. Then a lot of years went past. He wasn't available. I loved other people. Things changed. I was married to you. Then I was with Chet. Then later I was back with you again. And Floyd became a big part of my life. Parts of you get used up. You know that as well as I do. You learn to protect yourself. To hold back. Not to give everything. And the risk is that you end up with not much left to give. Time passes and adjustments are made. I'm tired of listening to myself. Tell me about your wife. What's her name?'

'Connie.'

'Constance?'

'No. Just Connie.'

'Sounds blonde and willowy. Champagne in a fluted glass and spike heels. Is she young and hateful?'

Frank shook his head. 'Not at all. She's smart and political and involved in all kinds of things. She has a 23-year-old son and a nineteen-year-old daughter. The daughter married a Cuban and lives in Havana.'

'So we don't see her much,' Helen said.

'We don't see her at all.'

'Where do you live?'

'We have a place on the Drive, about half a mile up from the Drake.'

'I thought you might be living in our hideaway on the South Side?'

'No,' he said.

'What happened to that place?'

'Nothing. It's still sitting there,' he said.

'You didn't give it up?'

'No.'

'What does Connie say about that?'

'She doesn't know about it.'

'Does she know about me?'

'Of course she does. Does Jesse know you came to Chicago to see me today?'

'Not yet. But he will.'

'You're going to tell him?'

'Sure. Won't you tell Connie?'

'No. I don't think so.'

'Why not?' Helen said.

'To tell you the truth I don't think she'd be interested.'

'I'm not flattered by that.'

'I didn't mean it the way it sounded. It's just that Connie doesn't think my life started when I met her any more than hers began when she met me. She's a grown-up lady. I'm not expected to report to her.'

After they'd finished their lunch, when they were having coffee, Frank said, 'I'm still not sure why you called me today.'

'Neither am I. As I told you, it had something to do with Clara, I'm sure. Some connection between you and me and the time when I saw her more often. I know you never met her but still I wanted to tell you what happened to her. No logic to it. Just a strong impulse I felt. And . . . something else besides. There was always something about Clara that made me want to try harder, to be better than I was. You know what I'm saying?'

'I'm not sure. Do I?'

'I always felt bad about the way things ended for you and me. Not just that letter you sent me, but the things I did to prompt you to write it. We were together a long time. When we were married and later when we weren't married. We meant a lot to each other. You still mean a lot to me. Maybe that's what I wanted to tell you. I'm delighted you're married to a nice woman and my life with Jesse is lovely and warm and peaceful. So we're both all right. But

55

all the same, I guess I needed to see you again, to have something more civilized pass between us, so we wouldn't just have some awkward vindictive things to think about when we were reminded of each other.'

'I don't think things like that,' Frank said.

'Neither do I. That's what I wanted to tell you, I suppose. That's what I wanted you to tell me.'

Frank lit a cigarette. 'So are we saying goodbye or hello?'

'Neither. We're just saying what we're saying.'

As she drove home she did not have the clear feeling of completion she had hoped for. She felt instead an unpleasant sense of guilt. Not for meeting with Frank but for the way she had described her life with Jesse.

Not long after he had come back to Fort Beck to be with her, she had sat alone in her bedroom one afternoon and tried to write down a description of her feelings.

How suddenly peaceful I am. I can't believe how calm and lovely my days have become. It can't simply be a matter of years passing, of the blood turning cooler, of problems solving themselves. It feels, very surely, like a process, not of subtraction, but addition.

Is it because Jesse is with me now, after all these years, in a new way? Have I fallen hopelessly in love with a man I've loved all my life as a brother? It must be so. There's no other answer, no explanation I know of for the warm and simple peace I feel. After all the trauma and disappointment and heartbreak, is Jesse my reward? And is it as good for him as it is for me? It doesn't matter. It can't matter. Nor do I care any longer about his years with Nora or his marriage to Valerie. When I think of them I simply tell myself that I knew him first and he's come home now to stay. Am I riding for a fall? Perhaps. But it doesn't matter. Nothing could be more right than the way things are now. If they change some time in the future I will deal with that some time in the future.

Remembering those words she had written down, and believing them now as much as she had then, she felt she had betrayed her relationship with Jesse in the way she had described it to Frank. Driving home, she was eager to see him again and to contradict,

56

by putting her arms around him, the words she had spoken to Frank across the luncheon table.

Everything proceeded according to plan. Or so it seemed. Jesse met her in the front hallway, helped her with her coat, and led her into the library for their pre-dinner cocktails. But after a few minutes, when he asked about her day in Chicago and she said she'd seen Frank he said, 'Why did you do that?'

'I didn't plan to. I called to tell him about Clara and he asked me to have lunch with him, so I did.'

'Why did you do that?'

'I guess I couldn't think of any way to say no. Are you mad at me?'

'No. I'm baffled. I thought you told me Frank had never met Clara.'

'He never had.'

'Then why was it so important for him to be briefed on the details of her death?'

'Maybe it wasn't. But he'd heard me talk a lot about her so I just thought it was a civilized thing to do.'

'Is this the first time you've seen him since I've been back here?'

'Yes, it is,' Helen said. 'What are you saying, Jesse?'

'I'm not saying anything. I'm trying to understand what you're saying.'

'I just told . . .'

'Did you tell him I'm living here now? Permanent resident. Man of the house?'

'Of course I told him.'

'What did he have to say?'

'I don't remember. What could he say? It's nothing to him. He's married again. You knew that. I told you that.'

'He was married when you two were playing house before, wasn't he?'

'Yes. But we're not playing house now.'

'I didn't say you were. I'm just trying to get the total picture.'

'You've got it,' she said. 'I had lunch with him. That's the total picture.'

'Any future lunches scheduled? A trip to the zoo maybe?'

'What's the matter with you? I've never seen you like this.'

'How did you think I'd react?'

'I didn't think you'd react at all,' she said.

57

'Then you don't know me very well.'

'Because there's nothing to react to.'

'There seems to be a difference of opinion about that.'

'What do you want me to say?'

'I don't want you to say anything. I want you to listen to what I have to say. I don't want you to have lunch with Frank. I don't want you to call him. I don't want him to call you. I don't want you to accidentally bump into him on the street. I don't want you to see him or talk to him at all.'

'I don't plan to see him.'

'That's good.'

After a long moment she said, 'Why are you talking to me like this?'

'Because there's something I want you to understand and I want to make absolutely sure you understand it.'

'I understand. But I don't know why you're using that tone with me. I've never heard you talk like that.'

'I've never had a reason to talk to you like that.'

'But now you think you do?'

'I know I do.'

She got up and refilled their glasses from the silver shaker on the bar table. When she sat down again she said, 'Are you upset about Clara? Is that it?'

'This has nothing to do with Clara.'

She leaned forward then, took his hand in hers and kissed it. 'I'm sorry if I did something to upset you.'

'I'm not upset. I'm mad.'

'But there's no reason . . .'

'There is a reason, Helen. And until you accept that, we're not going to get anywhere.'

'All right,' she said, 'I know you're mad. I can see that. I know you don't want me to talk to Frank again. So I won't. But I have to tell you I've never had anyone look at me the way you're doing now. No one has ever talked to me the way you've been doing. And I don't like it, Jesse. I don't like it at all.'

'If you want somebody who doesn't care where you go or what you do, you've picked the wrong guy.'

'That's not what I want.'

'Good. Then we understand each other.'

Jesse's relationship with Clara had been a singular one. After Angus adopted him in the early 1920s, when Jesse had first come to Wingate Fields to live, when his ambition to write something distinctive and personal seemed more a youthful desire than a possibility, it was Clara who took him seriously, who fitted out a fine private library and adjoining study for him to work in. And it was she who listened to his ideas and his plans in the days when talking seemed to be easier for him than putting words on paper. He could plan and theorize but he couldn't write.

Later, when he and Nora started a literary magazine in Paris, when Jesse lowered his sights and decided he was better fitted perhaps for criticizing someone else's efforts than for creating original work himself, Nora encouraged him, read his reviews and critiques carefully, and made him feel that what he was doing was valuable. Her confidence in him helped him to form some genuine confidence in himself, gave him the courage to go further and deeper in his criticism, caused him to trust his own judgement, enabled him to sharpen the edge of that judgement, and to steadily increase the scope of his knowledge of poetry, music, the novel and serious painting.

Although he worked closely with Nora as they struggled to make a success of *Icarus*, their magazine, it was always Clara's approval he was after when he sat down to write a new piece. It was her sense of worth that he tried to keep in mind as he worked. It was she he hoped to please. Although she was reliable in her support and generous with her praise, Jesse could never rid himself of the notion that he was doing pedestrian work. He was always conscious of the fact that his writing could not begin until some solitary artist had previously finished *his* work. Like an actor who is mute until someone provides him with a role, Jesse felt like a cultural post-script, an afterthought in the creative ferment of Paris. Always in his subconscious was the idea that some day a truly powerful concept would come to him, that he would snatch it up, hammer and mould and polish into a remarkable piece of writing. A book. A statement. A totality of all his experience, his intelligence, and his hunger to achieve would emerge and be admired. The longer this concept, this magical entity, evaded him, the more of a fixation it became. Through the years he filled notebooks with ideas, lists, first paragraphs, conclusions, and revisions of revisions of plans that had been abandoned and would be abandoned again. But that desire to please Clara, to drop something worthwhile at her feet, kept him going. Ironically, the fact that no subject seemed rich and rewarding enough or sufficiently distinctive or profound, could also be attributed to her, or at least to Jesse's assessment of her tastes. Each plan was abandoned because it wasn't up to the mark, because it wasn't good enough to bring to Clara.

When he left England and France at last, when he and Valerie were divorced and she was preparing to marry Floyd, when his life with Nora also came to an end, when he returned to Helen's house in Fort Beck, he felt as if he had left any small hope for greatness behind him. He resigned himself to his role as a rag-picker in cultural alleyways. He would sit behind Raymond's desk in that familiar old house and re-examine Klee, try to establish a link between Camus and Beckett, and put André Gide in his proper place.

As often happens, as quickly as he abandoned his search for a subject, he found it. More accurately it found him. As he flew west from Paris, crossing the Atlantic to New York, the sun burning orange ahead of him all through the flight, as he half-dozed by the window and watched the cottonwool clouds, as the years and their events moved forward and backward in his consciousness, he came to realize gradually that his subject, his *only* subject, was the Bradshaw family. That whole canvas of triumph and tragedy, of wealth and lunacy, passion and power and idiosyncrasy contained every colour, every brushstroke and tone and texture he would ever need. By telling their story he could put down everything he felt, everything he'd ever learned, everything he knew. The family and his relationship to it . . . that was all he needed to tell. No plotting, no construction was necessary. He only had to start at the beginning and tell the simple truth.

When the plane was still an hour or more east of New York he asked the steward for paper and a pen and began to write.

I pride myself on my ability to see behind the façades people build around themselves. I can see what fires them and what frightens them. At the same time I have found that my secret is visible to no one.

I have been called arrogant, cruel, selfish, perceptive, gifted,

60

insightful, and destructive. No one has noticed that I am distinguished, if I'm distinguished at all, by my guilt.

I feel guilty that I left my parents when I was sixteen and saw them only one time after that, guilty that I lost contact with my brother and sister, and guilty that I took more from Raymond Bradshaw, Helen's father, than I gave in return.

Although I did not set out to use people, I became skilful at it. I used Helen certainly. And Angus and Clara and all the Bradshaws. An argument could be made that Nora used me, but I used her as well. And I feel guilty about that. Guilty, too, because I left her and married her daughter. Perhaps I did not use Valerie but I was unfaithful to her. And I was not the exemplary father to my children I would like to have been.

My present guilt is simpler on the one hand, more complex on the other. I regret the lost years. I regret that I scattered myself so widely and squandered resources that can't be replenished. I feel thin and diaphanous and insubstantial. I'm racked with guilt.

Jesse folded the piece of paper neatly and put it inside his passport case. He promised himself he wouldn't read it till he was sitting behind Raymond's desk in the house at Fort Beck. When he sat there, however, late that night, when he read what he'd written on the plane, he saw that it was not what he had intended. Trying to begin an intimate examination of the Bradshaw family, he had revealed nothing except himself.

That single page had been put away among his papers and almost forgotten. But as he sat quietly in the University of Illinois Library the day after learning that Clara's death had been suicide, the words he'd written came clearly back to him. With equal clarity he saw that the only way he could write about the Bradshaws was to tell the truth about himself. And now he knew he would be able to do that. At least that's what he told himself.

[4]

'Child of privilege,' Jack Dieter said. He and Polly were sitting in her apartment on Ulmstrasse, at nearly midnight, the day after she had returned to Heidelberg from England. 'What was it like being at home in the land of milk and honey, steeped in wealth, ministered to by lackeys and blackamoors, champagne and pheasant for breakfast, string quartets playing in every corner?'

Polly smiled. 'Nothing like that, my dear. We're simple country folk.'

'Don't tell me that. I've seen photographs of that pile of stone you live in. All flying buttresses and parapets, drawbridges over the moat.' He had a mop of dark hair, flat cheeks and a wide agreeable mouth, but his face seemed pale and puffed. His upper body carried a bit more flesh than needed and his hands when he drank from his glass or brought a cigarette to his lips were not steady.

'No moat, sweetheart. No drawbridge. And it was a sad occasion. Clara was the only one in the family that *everybody* loved.'

'They all love you. I'm sure of that. Strangers in the street love you, barmaids and pork butchers. You have the gift of tenderness. You attract all kinds of odd buggers. If you tell me that certain members of the Bradshaw family disapprove of you then it might make me question my own judgement. I wouldn't like to discover that I've chosen flawed merchandise.'

Polly came over and sat beside him. 'You didn't choose anything. You didn't have a chance. I chose you. Remember? I put you under my arm and brought you home.'

'I must have been drunk and helpless.'

'You were. You were very drunk. You were trying to sell your belt with the silver buckle so you could buy a bottle of aquavit. But every time you unbuckled the belt to take it off, your pants began to slide down. You were very skinny then.'

He pinched his middle between thumb and forefinger. 'But now I have a spare tyre like a proper German burgher.'

'That's because I treat you right. Feed you a proper diet.'

'You also keep me in schnapps and lager. *That's* what keeps me healthy.' He took a long drink from his glass. 'But don't get me off the subject. I want a full report on the Bradshaws. You saw your mommy and daddy surely. Along with your mommy's husband and daddy's paramour. How did all that go?'

'Fine. There wasn't as much time to be with them as I'd hoped . . .'

'A bit awkward, I should think. Sorting out the real parents from the pretenders.'

'It wasn't that. We were all very occupied with the occasion.'

'But you surely managed a few hours alone with mommy. Ladies' secrets whispered behind your fans. And a serious down-to-earth talk with your father, the stud. Did he counsel you about the pitfalls of your life with a cello player who drinks too much?'

'No,' she said.

'No conviction in that denial, young lady. Don't lie to an expert. I invented lying. Tell me what papa said.'

'Not much really. You know what fathers are like.'

'I'm a father and my daughter is allowed to make her own decisions as long as they don't affect me. Just as my mother is allowed to make any decision that doesn't include me. Come on, Miss Polly, don't withhold information. You're not good at that. You're an open-hearted lass. Tell us what your profligate father had to say about your profligate lover.'

'I told you. Nothing interesting. Very boring stuff. Standard concerned parent. You know how it goes.'

'No, I don't. I never had a concerned parent and I've never been one.'

'He frets about the fact that you're older than I am, that you're married and have a child. Things like that.'

'Does he know that I have no money and no prospects? How does he feel about that, bless his heart?'

'I guess that worries him too.'

'He thinks I'm after your money?'

'I don't know what he thinks,' Polly said, 'and I don't care.'

'Maybe you should listen to your papa. I am after your money, you know.' He took in the room with a sweeping gesture. 'You've spoiled me with all this splendour. Clean sheets, hot coffee, cold beer, and toilets that flush dependably. I'm enslaved by your money. You've destroyed my ambition. All I'm good for now is playing the cello and living the good life. Have you ever thought what would happen to me if you turned me away?'

'I think about it all the time. And I know what would happen to you. You'd be back in Pietra's bed without missing a beat.'

'What a cynical young person you've become. Do you honestly think I could go back to Frau Wessen after knowing you?'

Polly smiled and snapped her fingers. 'Like that,' she said. 'Not only are you a musical genius and a sexual acrobat, you're a survivor. You were quite content with chubby Pietra before I kidnapped you. I'm sure you could make do with her again.'

'She's lost a bit of weight, I hear. Has a new man in her residence. Krause is living with her.'

'Donny Krause? What does she want with him?'

'The regular everyday things, I suppose.'

'I've never even seen him with a woman,' Polly said.

'Perhaps not. But don't be deceived by that. There are certain pleasure houses opposite the public gardens where Krause is a loyal customer.'

'Don't give me that. He's queer, isn't he?'

'Let's just say he has catholic tastes.'

'And now those tastes include Pietra?'

'So they say. The fact is I saw them together while you were away. At that beer hall on Ludwigstrasse. All lovey-dovey. Tangled together in a corner. Quite a handsome couple.'

'I'm sure of it. Two fatsos together.'

'Shame on you. Unkind.'

'I'm not trying to be kind, Jack. I think she's a tramp and Donny's a disgrace. And they both have their eyes on you.'

'Wrong again, sweetheart. As I've been telling you, they have eyes only for each other. It's a touching sight.'

'I'll bet it is. Like mating season at the crocodile farm.'

He touched her cheek with his fingertips. 'I thought you might like to invite them over for supper some night.'

'There are very few things I wouldn't do for you. But you've just suggested one of them.'

'My poor stumbling father, whose only triumph was kindness, used to tell me that when you have good fortune you must share it with others. Otherwise the gods will be angry.'

'Your father didn't know Donny and Pietra. I'm perfectly willing to share my good fortune with you but not with them. What they really want to share with me is you.'

'What a fine fellow I must be if everyone wants to nibble at my ears.'

Polly kissed him and placed her hands on each side of his head. 'That's the mystery,' she said. 'You're not a particularly fine fellow but all the same people seem to be attracted to you.'

'But I'm attracted to no one but you.'

'I count on that. Your physical safety depends on it.'

He pulled her close to him and kissed her. Then: 'It's important to remember, however, that whatever his shortcomings and quaint habits, Donny Krause is an old friend of mine from Wisconsin. He's also a gifted linguist and a brilliant organist. Brings Bach to life in an extraordinary way.'

'He's weird, Jack. He gives me the creeps.'

'He speaks well of you.'

'I doubt it.'

[5]

For all the steel-ribbed certainty she had demonstrated when she discussed Jack Dieter with Jesse or Valerie or Rab, Polly, not long after returning to Heidelberg following Clara's funeral, began to sense a change taking place either in Jack or in herself. Her efforts to label that change or even to define it properly proved fruitless. She told herself repeatedly that there was no true cause for her unquiet. But still she was uneasy and watchful. She noticed that he seemed to drink less than before, that he seemed more responsible about his fellowship duties at the University, that he played the cello almost constantly now when they were alone in her apartment.

Any one of these developments she would have expected to feel good about. Any sign that Jack had begun to see himself in a new way should have delighted her. But this sudden turning away from his normal pattern of casual self-destruction was too mysterious and arbitrary. Telling herself that everything she observed was positive and encouraging, she found herself, nonetheless, feeling apprehensive.

As though some strange virus had wafted up from the cellars and underground storage bins of Wingate when the Bradshaws were assembled there for Clara's funeral, each family member, upon returning home, discovered, as Polly had, that some delicate internal transformation had taken place. Words and thoughts and attitudes that had previously been clear and accepted slowly took on alternative and contradictory meanings. Treasured possessions seemed less valuable than before. Familiar rhythms and rituals

65

became too familiar, too repetitive and commonplace. Strongly held convictions became subject to review and rejection. Past choices became regrettable, clear avenues seemed suddenly shrouded with fog, and self-esteem itself demanded reassessment. Most alarming of all, the symptoms of this persistent virus were so subtle as to be almost unrecognizable. One only felt ennui, dissatisfaction, unease, and a lack of patience, suddenly perceived, with one's self and one's life.

Since no one knew how to react to these unfamiliar but oddly disturbing stimuli, since they could neither diagnose their symptoms nor prescribe for them, since there was no pattern of logic to explain their various states of mind, they decided that action, any action, was the answer. Within days of returning home from Wingate, each of them had made an abrupt turn. For some the change was internal, for others it involved a change of place, a new country, a new domicile.

Valerie and Floyd went ahead with their plan to spend the winter and spring in Portugal but, before going there, Floyd travelled alone to America to visit his stepdaughter in California. Valerie was to go alone to Portugal, to take over the house in Praia da Rocha and wait for him there. And she was indeed waiting when he arrived three weeks later. As they told each other in detail what they had done while they were separated, Valerie did not mention that she had stopped off in Zurich for five days on her way to Portugal. For his part, Floyd left out a great deal of what he had said to Betsy, his stepdaughter, and what she had said to him.

In Helen and in Jesse, the changes following Clara's funeral were subtle. Each of them told themselves that those altered feelings had nothing to do with the other person, that they would quickly disappear and have no lasting effect on how they were together. Because they were both intelligent and mature and because they truly cared about each other, they made specific efforts to ensure that no damage was done. In most areas they succeeded. In other critical areas, where success was impossible, they failed.

Bill, whose decision to go to America had been trashed and ridiculed by his brother, gained further resolve from Rab's opposition and began to make specific plans for that change as soon as he was back in Edinburgh. A few months later, however, four days before he was scheduled to fly to Chicago, he received a telephone call from Gloria Atwood. She desperately needed his help. When his flight to America left Heathrow, Bill was not on the plane. A few days later he was headed in the opposite direction, by himself, to a town called St Raphael in the south of France.

Rab, it seemed, was least susceptible to the forces of change, whatever their nature, that followed Clara's death. Because he had so thoroughly compartmentalized himself, because he was able to close and lock any door, keeping inside whatever he valued, keeping outside everything else, he was spared the subtle sea-changes that seemed to affect the other members of his family. Nonetheless, in the same period, at the same time that the other Bradshaws were being somehow redirected, Rab met Herman Mullet, a man he truly detested. Then he met Dorsey, Mullet's wife. From her Rab learned humility, for the first time in his life. Later she taught him all she knew about humiliation.

[6]

Clifford Woodburn, one of Rab's associates in the funding of an off-shore radio station, mentioned to him as they sat at lunch one day, that he had met Herman Mullet.

'He seemed interested in what we're doing,' Woodburn said. 'Asked me who was involved in our operation, and when I told him he said he'd like to meet you.'

'Why would he want to meet me?'

'Said you sound like a bright chap.'

'What's that to him?' Rab said.

'He didn't say. Just said he'd like to talk to you.'

'I thought he never left California. What's he doing in London?'

'Just bought a home in Knightsbridge. Going international he says.'

'You'd better tip off Scotland Yard. He'll be pinching the globes from streetlamps.'

'Doesn't need to. He has a lot of money.'

'All stolen,' Rab said.

'Stolen or not, he's got it. I watched him playing roulette the other night. He dropped five thousand pounds in twenty minutes.'

'Feaster told me he was involved in a co-production deal with

Mullet in Toronto. The picture went broke when they were half-way through shooting and Mullet walked away with a million-two. Bad news, Feaster said.'

'Maybe he said that, but they acted like long-lost brothers at the Embassy Club the other night. That's how I met Mullet. Feaster introduced us.'

'Feaster's a crumb.'

'Maybe he is,' Woodburn said, 'But he's *our* crumb. He's in for thirty percent of our operation.'

'Not for long. I'm planning to buy him out.'

'What if he doesn't sell?'

'He'll sell,' Rab said. 'He and that brother of his would sell each other if the price was right.'

'What shall I tell Mullet?' Woodburn said then.

'About what?'

'I told you. He wants to meet you. I said I'd set it up.'

'Why'd you tell him that?'

'I was a little drunk, I guess. Besides I thought you might want to meet him. He's made some big pictures.'

Rab shook his head. 'Goldman over at MCA told me Mullet has never made a picture. He flies around like a buzzard looking for independent projects in trouble. He comes in with completion money in exchange for half the action and executive producer credit. He's not in the movie business. He's in the money business.'

'Well, it's his money. If he wants to invest it . . .'

'It's *not* his money.'

'Whose money is it then?'

'Use your head, Cliffie,' Rab pushed his nose slightly to one side with the tip of his forefinger.

'What does that mean?'

'You know what I mean.'

'Who told you that?'

'Nobody told me that. I've got a brain. I use it. I can add two and two together and get four.'

'I still don't know what to tell him. He said he'd call me some time this afternoon.'

'Tell him I'm in the last two weeks of a difficult pregnancy. Tell him I'll call him in July after the baby's weaned.'

A week later, Woodburn called Rab at home one evening and said, 'I think you'd better see Mullet.'

'Did you tell him what I said?'

'No. I told him you were in Brussels but he didn't believe me.'

'What's he want now?'

'I think he's got what he wants. He's about to become our partner. The Feasters gave him a first refusal on their stock.'

'That doesn't mean anything. They can't sell anything if I don't agree to the sale. It's all in the corporate agreement.'

'Do they know that?'

Rab nodded. 'One thing they're good at is reading the small print. But that doesn't mean they told Mullet. Can you reach him tonight?'

'If I can't, I can leave a message. He gave me his number.'

'Good. Tell him I'll be in my office tomorrow afternoon if he wants to ring me. Then get in touch with the Feaster brothers and tell them I want to see them in my office at ten tomorrow morning.'

The following day, when he met with Leo and Harold Feaster, Rab said, 'What sort of game are you playing with Oscar Mullet?'

The younger brother, Leo, said, 'Not us, Rab. As I told you before, we've had bad experiences with Mullet.'

'Once burned, twice shy,' Harold said.

'Now you're playing games with me,' Rab said. 'Are you saying you didn't offer to sell him your shares in our off-shore project?' When the two brothers looked at each other, Rab went on. 'I knew the answer to that question when I asked it, so don't waste time denying it.'

'He did approach us,' Leo said, 'but we told him we weren't interested.'

'Did you tell him that your agreement with me doesn't permit you to sell your shares without my approval?'

'There was no need to tell him anything because we never considered his offer.'

'Did you tell him that I have a contractual right to buy you out any time before November?'

'We don't want to sell, Rab.'

'We told you when we came in,' Harold said. 'We like the project. It's a permanent partnership as far as we're concerned.'

'I did a bit of research,' Rab said. 'Mullet offered you twenty-five percent above the amount you invested. My option gives me the right to buy you out at seven percent more than you paid in.' He opened a leather folder and handed it across the desk to Leo. 'Here

69

is your termination agreement signed by me and Mr Woodburn. And this is a cheque for the total amount due you. When you've signed the agreement, I will sign the cheque.'

'But we don't want to sign it,' Harold said. 'We only agreed to that termination clause because we . . .'

'Suit yourselves,' Rab said. 'The termination agreement went into effect when Clifford and I signed it. You know the terms as well as I do. No one's forcing you to sign. But until you do, your money won't be released.'

'I thought we had a good working relationship,' Leo said. 'Harold and I have made a real contribution to this project.'

'No, you haven't. You've been along for the ride and you know it. Because I'm half your age you thought that somewhere along the line you'd find a way to out-manoeuvre me.'

'Looks to me as if we're the ones who've been out-manoeuvred.' Harold said. 'When you needed our money, you sang a different song.'

'I never needed your money,' Rab said. 'I needed a Canadian partner. I still want a Canadian partner. But this time I'll pick one I can trust.'

'You're not being fair,' Leo said. 'What could we have possibly worked out with Mullet?'

'I'm not sure. And I don't think you know either. But when a man like Mullet enters the picture, I'm not willing to wait to see what may happen next.'

Later that day, when Rosalind, his secretary, rang through to say that Oscar Mullet was calling, Rab said, 'Tell him I'm on my way to Stockholm.'

'Do we know when we'll be back in London?' Rosalind asked.

'No, we don't.'

'Are we anxious to talk with Mr Mullet?'

'No, we're not.'

[7]

When Bill went to London the day after Gloria Atwood telephoned him in Edinburgh, he met her at the house in Sloane Square that had been owned by the Bradshaws for two hundred years. The butler showed him into the library and a few minutes later Gloria came in to greet him.

With only her telephone call to go by, Bill had not known what to expect. The Bradshaw women were not given to shedding tears so he'd had little experience in dealing with that sort of emotion. He hoped, as he sat in the library waiting for Gloria to appear, that she would not enter weeping. As it happened, she was neither solemn nor tearful. She swept into the room, gave him a sisterly hug, and said, 'Are you hungry? I'm starving.'

As she led him up the staircase she said, 'I've ordered up some tea. We'll have some sandwiches while I'm sorting myself out and later on we'll go out and I'll treat you to a fine supper.'

Several pieces of half-filled luggage were scattered around her upstairs sitting room. As they talked she took articles of clothing out of drawers and closets and packed them carefully.

'I'm sorry about that frantic call yesterday,' she said. 'I wasn't truly frantic. But I was very confused. Now I'm better. I had dinner with an old girlfriend last night, someone I've known all my life. I told her in gruesome detail what a bastard your brother is and I woke up this morning feeling a great deal better.'

'Didn't you tell me on the phone that Rab went off somewhere?'

'Geneva. At least that's where he said he was going. He might be in the house across the street watching me through binoculars. Rab never tells the truth except by accident. But he said he was flying to Switzerland, that he'd be back tomorrow or the next day, and he wanted me and all my things out of here before he got back.'

'What's that all about?'

'I'm not sure. I only know what he says it's about. He says I deceived him. Told me he'd never be able to trust me again. Don't get the wrong idea. It's not the way it may sound. I wasn't sneaking about with another man. Nothing like that. He says I deceived him because I accepted a job. Can you believe that?'

'What sort of job?'

'A three-month tour of Canada. We're doing Ibsen and Strindberg in repertory. A fine company of actors. A lovely opportunity for me.'

'And Rab wants you to turn it down?'

'I'm not sure what he wants. I think he was angry because it's something he didn't have a hand in. You heard him that night we all had dinner together in Northumberland. He had a notion, I think, that he was going to repeat the Pygmalion experience. He was going to mould me and launch me and see to it that I developed my potential. I thought he'd be delighted that I'd been offered such a fine opportunity. But I was mistaken. He couldn't have been more angry if he'd caught me in bed with the gardener.'

Later, when they were having dinner, Bill said, 'I'm not sure what you expect me to do.'

'There's nothing you can do,' she said. 'I think I knew that almost as soon as I put the phone down after talking to you. No one can bring Rab round once he's made up his mind. And now that I've had time to think about it I'm not sure I want to win him over, even if I could. I'm certainly not going to give up the tour just to make him happy. And even if I agreed to do that it might not do any good. He's such a devious bastard, perhaps he was just looking for an excuse to dump me. He may have gone to Geneva to celebrate. One thing I'm sure of. As we're sitting here, Rab is not having a solitary dinner somewhere. Some little Swiss dumpling will be in his bed tonight.' She sipped from her wine glass. 'Does it surprise you to hear me talk like that? I'm sure you know your brother as well as I do. He has a great deal to offer a woman but fidelity is not among his gifts. I doubt if he even knows the meaning of the word. If he does know it, he simply ignores it.' Then: 'What's it like to be his brother?'

Bill felt uneasy suddenly, as though he was being nudged into some dark area of betrayal. Finally he said, 'He's my brother. He's not perfect, I suppose, but neither am I. Rab has a lot of energy. He likes to win. He needs that. So when you accept that about him, it makes it easier to understand some of the other things.'

'Are you putting me in my place?'

Bill shook his head. 'Not me. Besides, you probably know him better than I do.'

'I doubt it.'

'At least you know him differently. You can evaluate him in ways that I can't. And you can walk away from him the way you're getting ready to now. I can't do that. I don't want to do that. But even if I wanted to, I couldn't.'

After a moment she said, 'You don't think I want to walk away from him, do you?'

'I'm not sure. But I could understand it if you did.'

'I don't,' she said. 'That's why you and I are talking like this. That's why I spent half the night last night talking to Enid, my girlfriend. I was trying to find some way to stay with Rab, if he still wants me, without just handing myself over to him like a piece of fruit.'

'Is that the way you see it?'

'There's no other way,' she said. 'I've thought about nothing else for the past two days and I keep coming to the same conclusion. Rab has to have everything or nothing. Every drop of my blood. Every minute of my life. He has to own me. If I'm not willing or able simply to turn myself over to him, then he's not interested. And if I did do that – and this is the most frightening thought of all – he still wouldn't be interested, not for very long.'

'Then I guess you've got nothing to lose.'

Gloria smiled. 'Oh, yes, I have.'

[8]

'You're a real bastard,' Bill said. He was sitting in Rab's office the morning after he'd had dinner with Gloria.

Rab laughed. 'No, I'm not. I'm the legitimate elder son of Jesse and Valerie Bradshaw. Registered, documented and christened. And the proud brother of Polly and William.'

'You know what I'm talking about. Gloria's a nice girl. You don't have to spend your life with her but if you're breaking up, why not be decent about it?'

'I hope you made this same speech to her. She's the one who announced that she's flying off to Canada for a few months.'

'So what? She's an actress, isn't she? You can't blame her for taking a good job when it's offered to her.'

'Ah, but I do blame her. While I've been making important plans for her, it seems that she's been offering herself around town for other projects. This is not some petty misdemeanour she's committed, no flirtation. It's a form of professional adultery.'

'Oh, for Christ's sake, Rab. She's crazy about you. She thought you were crazy about her.'

73

Rab held up one forefinger. 'Trust, William. That's the important word. When that goes, everything goes.'

'Do you think she trusts you? Do you think she ever trusted you? She knows you fall into bed with anybody who's breathing.'

'That's right. She does know that. Because I never tried to deceive her about it. That was part of our understanding.'

'Not the way I heard it. She may have accepted it, but she didn't understand it.'

'Let me tell you something about women, Bill. Most of them don't give a damn if their man is having a bit on the side. What they care about is if other people find out. If it's not common knowledge, if other women don't giggle about them in the powder room, they can make the adjustment. Women aren't nearly so concerned with rules as men are. That's why they're so nice. They're soft and flexible. Able to make adjustments.'

'How about you? Do you make adjustments?'

'All the time. You have to give a little and take a little.'

'But some people take more than they give,' Bill said.

'I keep hearing that but I'm not sure it's true. Things balance out, it seems to me.'

'So you're glad to be rid of Gloria, is that it?'

'No, that's not it. But she made a choice and it's not a choice I would have advised her to make. She decided to go ahead on her own, so I have no choice but to let her do that.'

'You're talking about her career,' Bill said. 'I'm talking about how you feel about her. You've been living with her. You must at least like her. Now you sound as though you're never going to see her again. You've cut the cord. How do you feel about that?'

'I feel rotten about it.'

'Like hell you do. You talk as if you're sending a suit back to the tailor because the trousers don't fit.'

Rab smiled. 'Let me tell you something, Bill. Maybe you're a kinder man than I am. Maybe not. But you'll find out, if you haven't already, that you can't marry everybody you sleep with. And women aren't little flowers. They may smell good but they're not delicate. They're tough, resilient little beasts, most of them. When marriages break up, it's not the wives that suffer. Most of the time it's the men.'

'Who says so?'

'God says so. And I agree with him.'

'Clever isn't smart, Rab. Just because your mouth works . . .'

'You're right. That's why I've chosen the entertainment business as my *métier*. It's the only field where vocal cords serve as a substitute for brains.' He lit a cigarette. 'Let me tell you something else before you get such a low opinion of me that I'll never be able to fix it. Gloria is a fine and attractive and talented young woman, but she's just as intricate and self-serving as you think I am. Matter of fact, she's worse than I am. I like people I love to love me back. Gloria wants that, too. But she also wants to be loved by *strangers*. That's the actor's curse, the need to be worshipped by people they've never laid eyes on. Politicians have the same germ. They need *general* love, love from the masses. I'm no genius, Billy, but I'm smart enough to know that that sort of love is no love at all. But all the same, once you're hooked on it, you're hooked. The bad stuff drives out the good. Gloria's going to travel round the western hemisphere for a few months, seducing great faceless audiences, and I'm going to stay here in London and seduce a few carefully selected individuals. I'm not asking you to decide which one of us is behaving splendidly. I'm merely suggesting that you mark the difference in our behaviour patterns and agree with me that if we weren't separating now we would certainly separate later.'

'What happens when she comes back from Canada?'

'How would I know?' Rab said.

'Do you think you two will get together again?'

'Are you asking for yourself or as an emissary from Gloria?'

'For myself. She doesn't know we're having this talk.'

'Is it possible that you have a little yen for her yourself and you're checking to see if the decks are clear?'

Bill shook his head. 'It's tricky enough just being your brother. I'm certainly not eager to follow you into somebody's bed.' He paused. 'You still haven't answered my question.'

'About my future with Gloria? Let me put it this way. If she returns unspoiled from Canada, not diseased or pregnant, and if she is willing to accept me as the all-powerful and omniscient figure that she secretly knows me to be, if she is willing, with good grace, to put her life and her destiny in my hands, then I suppose anything is possible.'

'In other words, you don't expect that the two of you . . .'

'Not likely,' Rab said. 'Not bloody likely.'

'Are you telling me,' Rab said, 'that Oscar Mullet had something to do with Gloria's being hired for that tour in Canada?'

He was sitting in Amelia's, a Mayfair restaurant, having lunch with Clifford Woodburn. It was almost a month since Gloria had left London for Montreal.

'That's the way it was told to me,' Woodburn said. 'Reliable source. Number two man in Mullet's office.'

'Coincidence or something else?'

'Something else, I should think. Mullet had his heart set on buying those shares from the Feasters.'

'And I outmanoeuvred him,' Rab said.

Woodburn nodded. 'He also got the idea you were playing a game with him when he tried to contact you by telephone.'

Rab smiled. 'I'm a busy man. You know that. Mustn't spread myself too thin. Bad policy to be available to everyone.'

'Mullet's not stupid. He knew you were messing him around. So it seems he mounted a counterattack.'

'But why Gloria?'

'Why not? Everybody knew you two were living together. Most people know she's an actress. Ambitious. Eager to get ahead. So he must have decided to toss a few pebbles into your electric fan.'

'Was he the producer for that tour?' Rab asked.

'I don't think so. But he pulled some strings with whoever is the producer. She got the job and you lost a lady friend. At least temporarily.'

'How did he know I wasn't anxious to get rid of her?'

'He didn't. He was playing the percentages. Were you anxious to get rid of her?'

'That doesn't matter,' Rab said. 'The important thing is he thinks he got the better of me. Is that correct?'

Woodburn nodded. 'That's the impression I got from the chap in his office.'

'In that case I think I'll have to do something about that.'

'If you're even, why not let it go at that?'

'*Even's* not good enough for me, Clifford. You know that.'

When they had finished lunch and were heading for the exit,

76

Woodburn said, 'Looks like you're going to meet Mullet whether you want to or not.'

'I want to. Where is he?'

'See that stocky fellow with ginger hair just inside the entrance? That's Mullet. The tall lady with dark hair is his wife.'

'What's her name?'

'Dorsey.'

'She's something to look at. What does she see in him?'

'You'll have to ask her,' Woodburn said.

'Not a bad notion. Maybe I will.'

[10]

Three days later, Rab invited Oscar Mullet to have lunch with him at his club in St James's. As soon as they sat down together, Rab said, 'I believe I owe you an apology. I realize you've tried to contact me several times through my office and I haven't been as conscientious as I might have been in getting back to you.'

'No reason to apologize. I'm told you're a very busy man.'

'It's my own fault. I haven't learned to delegate authority. Feel I have to do everything myself.'

Mullet's expression changed in a way that was intended perhaps to be a smile. 'I learned to delegate authority when I was a very young man,' he said. 'Ever since then, I've been learning that it's a mistake to delegate too much authority. Whenever there's an important decision, I find I have to make it myself or suffer the consequences. Details are everything. If I don't stay on top of the details, the details end up on top of me.'

'I'll remember that,' Rab said. Then; 'They tell me you plan to make your home in England.'

'That's a story my wife's spreading. She thinks if I read it in the newspapers often enough I'll be persuaded. The fact is it's hard for me to think of any place as a permanent home. I'm in a gypsy occupation. I go where the business takes me. For now, my associates and I think that Italy and Spain will be important production centres. At least for the next few years. And since I've lived in Rome and Madrid, where they have never heard of delicatessen, I

77

decided that this time I'd give London a try. There's a man in New York who sends me a food package once a week.'

'Did I read somewhere that you bought a place in Knightsbridge?'

'That's right. At a good price, the broker tells me. Overlooks the park. And there's a garden in the back for Dorsey to fiddle with. She was born on a farm in Nebraska and she never got it out of her system.'

'Is she an actress?'

'Dorsey? Not a chance. She hates a camera like a snake. If somebody shows up with a home-movie outfit she hides under the bed with the dog. She was a model in New York when she was a kid. Worked in showrooms in the garment district, but never gave a damn about being a cover girl or getting into the movie business. Like I said, she's a farm girl. She's got her eye on a place in the Cotswolds. An old rectory that somebody remodelled. A little stream running beside it and forty acres of pasture and apple trees. I'm afraid if I buy it I'll never get her into London again. She'll be wearing rubber boots and corduroys and chasing after a herd of sheep.'

'Do you have children?'

'A son and a daughter. They're grown-up. And Dorsey has a boy who goes to a private school in Virginia. But we don't have kids together. How about you? Are you married?'

Rab smiled and shook his head. 'Men marry late in my family. It's a tradition.'

'Whether it's a tradition or not,' Mullet said, 'it's a damned good idea. I've been married four times, the first time when I was nineteen. Nothing wrong with my wives. They were all decent women. But if I'd been as smart as I like to think I am, I would have waited till I was thirty-five to get married the first time. When you're driving to be the richest man in the world it's hard to be the world's greatest husband. I'm still not the richest man in the world and I'm sure as hell not the world's greatest husband but I'm closer than I used to be.'

When they sat in the club library later having coffee, Mullet said, 'I heard a lot of talk about you when I first came to London, about the radio deal you set up and some of your plans for independent television programming and I thought you sounded like somebody I should meet. I've met a lot of mavericks in the picture business. Most of them go broke but a few of them do damn well. D. W.

Griffith was a maverick. People don't remember that now. So were Von Stroheim and Barrymore and Garbo and Orson Welles. Some of those people died broke, too, but they set the tone for the whole business. First, somebody has to take a chance and later a lot of second-rate bozos reap the harvest. Anyway, people told me you were young and full of ideas and you knew how to raise money. They also said you'd gone out of your way to bring in Canadian and Australian partners so you'd have a broader base for your company. That interested me too because that's exactly what my partners and I are doing.'

'Who are your partners?'

'Money people for the most part. New York investors. Venture capital. No film people except for myself and Ben Eisler, who was Columbia's man in Europe for twenty years. What we didn't have when I was trying to get in touch with you was a British partner. I thought you might be interested. But when I didn't hear from you I decided you were too busy so we made inquiries elsewhere. Do you know Hugh Mayberly?'

'Very well. He ran Korda's operation for many years.'

'Am I supposed to call him Sir Hugh?'

'*You* don't have to, but most of us do.'

'Since he left Korda he's been trying to set up a production and distribution operation of his own. We've had several meetings and he seems to make sense. What do you think of him?'

'He's honest and respected and experienced. I think his work with Korda was more in distribution than production. He knows the market, here and in Europe, but he's not known as a creative genius. If you give him the product he can sell it as well as anyone. Whether he can attract picture-makers is a question I can't answer. I know you're not offering *me* anything, and if you did I'd have to turn you down, but if you're still trying to make up your mind I'll tell you that Sir Hugh may be conservative but he can give your company a foundation here in England that nobody else can. All kinds of regulations and restrictions and bureaucratic red tape disappear when Hugh's in the picture.'

The following day, a hand-delivered note from Mullet arrived at Rab's office.

Thanks for the lunch. We had a meeting last night and decided to go forward with Mayberly. I appreciate the nudge.

And since you and I can't do business together, at least for the moment, I want you to know that I'm available for any help I can give you in your projects. Also, I'd like to feel free to call on you for advice when I hit snags in *my* operation. Such an arrangement will benefit us both, I'm sure. I'll call you soon to ask you to join my wife and me for dinner. No refusals accepted.

Rab reread the note, then folded it twice and dropped it into the wastepaper basket beside his desk. His impulse to meet Dorsey Mullet seemed to have diminished. Having expected to have a negative reaction to her husband, he had found him almost sympathetic. Rab had prepared himself to hear a recital of triumphs. He hadn't heard it. He had not been treated to the display of self-confidence he had anticipated. He had sensed, instead, a whiff vulnerability. He would not have been surprised, towards the end of their luncheon together, if Oscar had suddenly disclosed a list of his frustrations and failures. Having approached the meeting as a David confronting Goliath, he had come away feeling no difference in their stature. Rab's sense of competition was not stirred. His need for vengeance, if indeed that was what he had felt before, seemed to have subsided. And Dorsey, the imagined instrument of that vengeance, seemed to have disappeared from his thoughts altogether.

When Rab agreed to have dinner with them, therefore, two weeks or so after his luncheon with Oscar, it was with no feeling either of anticipation or uneasiness. It was simply a dinner with casual acquaintances, with no thought that they would ever become more than that.

The evening's conversation concerned itself with the motion-picture business almost exclusively, discussions of financing, above and below the line, listings of which directors were likely to come in under budget and which performers would surely extend the production schedule. Dorsey stated at the outset that she was a total ignoramus about her husband's business and thereafter sat radiant and exquisite in the candlelight and, to a large degree, silent. Although he couldn't keep his eyes from returning often to that remarkable face, Rab had concluded by evening's end that she either had no intellect and no vocabulary or was totally mesmerized by her husband.

She came to life, however, in a most unexpected way as they

80

prepared to leave the restaurant. When they claimed their coats at the cloakroom, as Mullet turned away to give some money to the attendant, Dorsey slipped a folded piece of paper into Rab's hand. As soon as the Mullets pulled away from the kerb in their car, Rab opened the note and read it.

I'll be at the Hampshire Hotel tomorrow, behind Victoria station, registered as Agnes Dorsey. Meet me there at three. I'm desperate to talk with you.

[11]

'Does anybody with a brain believe those stories that are cominjg out of Washington?' Jack Dieter said. 'Did anyone ever believe what we were told went on in Dallas that day?'

'Everybody in the States believes it now,' Donny Krause said. 'My brother wrote me from La Crosse and said that Walter Cronkite went on television with a blackboard and a pointer and convinced everybody that Lee Harvey Oswald did it all by himself.'

'That's right,' Jack said. 'With a sling-shot. Standing on his head in a canoe. Marine Corps records say this idiot couldn't hit a bear in the ass with a banjo but that morning in Dallas he couldn't miss. He cranked up that mail-order rifle and blew Kennedy's head off from a third-storey window a hundred yards behind him. Nobody wants to hear that at least one shot came from the front, nobody listens when eye-witnesses say other shots came from the overpass and the parking lot, nobody gets disturbed when twenty eye-witnesses suddenly get dead within a few months of the assassination.'

They were sitting in the beer hall that looked down on the Heidelberg Gardens, late one night. Jack and Donny, Pietra Wessen and Polly.

'It's over now,' Pietra says. 'No one cares any longer.'

'That's right,' Donny said. 'That's what's sick about it. Nobody gives a good goddamn.'

'No records of what Oswald said when they questioned him in the Dallas police station. How does *that* grab you? No explanation

81

for how a small-time hood strolled into the police station and shot Oswald in the gut. Was Oswald being paid by the CIA? Was he on the payroll? Nobody can remember. Maybe it was Army Intelligence that paid him. Maybe it was the tooth fairy,' Jack said.

'We know the Republican Party didn't shoot him,' Donny said. 'They can't even piss straight.'

'That's right,' Jack said. 'So who else hated him? The mob hated him. Didn't like his old man. Don't like his brother Bobby, don't like anybody named Kennedy. But it's not their style to use a ding-dong fruit-cake like Oswald for a hit man. But on the other hand they were like eight-in-a bed with Jack Ruby, and Jack Ruby was like eight-in-a-bed with the Dallas Police department. So what does that tell us? It tells us to keep looking. Who else hated Kennedy? How about the oil guys in Texas? Kennedy was about to shoot down their off-shore oil-lease scam.'

'And as soon as Johnson came into office, *that* got straightened out.'

'Right. Millions of dollars at stake. Billions. And they were about to have the President visit on their home turf. So why not include a little accident on the menu? But Texans wouldn't come up with a bird like Oswald either. Not their style. They'd drive him to the Oklahoma border, tie a tin can to his tail and drop him off. Plenty of crack shots in Texas. They don't need a pinko like Oswald.'

'But if Oswald didn't do it, why did he shoot the policeman on the street later?' Pietra said.

'Who says he did? Or if he did, who says the cop wasn't in on the trick and came to shoot *him*?' Donny said.

'Let's stick with the enemies' list,' Jack went on. 'How about the Cubans? Kennedy let them down on the Bay of Pigs invasion. And if it's true that he gave the green light for the CIA to send a mob guy to pick off Castro, then the *other* Cubans were sore at him too. Besides that, he called Kruschev's bluff and got the missiles pulled out of Cuba. Lots of Cuban sharp-shooters ready to take a crack at him if they got a chance. So what have we got? The mob, the oil men and the Cubans – a lot of arms and legs but no brain. I mean nobody with the know-how to put together an assassination of the most important man in the world, in broad daylight and not get caught with their fingers in the pie.

'So who could organize an operation like that, keep everybody clean, finger the fall guy, and then get him killed before he can tell

82

anybody what happened? I mean that's a big order. A complicated scenario. You hear that word? *Scenario*. That's what they'd have to work from. But nobody uses a scenario except people who make movies and television programmes. Is that what you say? Well, you're wrong. There's a department of the government that hires men for just that purpose – to write scenarios. That department is called the Central Intelligence Agency. When they plan an operation, they take every possible event into consideration, they anticipate everything that can possibly go wrong. At least they try to. Then they compensate in advance, plot their moves, plan their reactions. There's a different scenario written for every set of circumstances they can imagine. They do the same thing when they're looking for somebody. Martin Bormann, for example. They find out where he was last seen and go on from there. They try to imagine every possible choice he could have had and how he would have reacted. If they come up with fifty separate scenarios they play out each one to the end till they find the man they're looking for. So the key word in the Kennedy killing is that word . . . scenario. It couldn't just happen. Somebody had to write it.

'Does that mean the CIA helped kill Kennedy? Maybe. Maybe not. It could have been an ex-agency man if there is such an animal, or it could have been a maverick inside the agency. But I say it was somebody who knew how to write a scenario for that kind of operation. And it just so happens there was such a guy. This man knew the CIA routine backwards and forwards and he knew Oswald's record, Russia and all the rest of it. Not only that, he knew Oswald personally. Remember when Oswald was clowning around in New Orleans, after he came back from Russia, this CIA bird, Donnelly or Connelly or Lipschitz, whatever his name was, had an office in the same building with the pro-Cuban group that Oswald was attached to. So they knew each other. No question about it. Not only that but the CIA guy was involved in the whole Cuban invasion nonsense; he's thick with both sets of Cubans, pro-Castro and anti-Castro, and he knows who does what to whom in the mob. Not only that, this guy was the king of the scenario writers for the agency. He's so good at it he even writes mystery novels under another name. So assuming that somebody, *anybody*, wants Kennedy dead, who would be able to put it all together better than this guy? He can deliver the mob, the Cubans, CIA techniques, and a paranoid fall guy who once defected to Russia and has a Russian wife. A false lead for everybody. Did Castro order the hit, did the Kremlin order it, or was it some Cosa Nostra weirdo from Brooklyn? Or did Oswald simply dream it up and carry it out on his own? The more complicated and amateurish the whole thing looks, the more people will be willing to accept it as a one-man job.'

'But what about the Dallas police?' Donny said. 'How do you explain that whole mess? Are you saying they were in on it from the start?'

Jack shook his head. 'That part bothers me. I don't have an answer for that. My instinct tells me they weren't in on it before the fact. But once Oswald was picked up, somebody put the pressure on them to keep him in a box. Only some high-powered Texas politician could pull *that* off. Or if the mob had the Dallas police in their pocket. The way the police behaved is the big tip-off. The scenario probably read that Oswald would be killed by the police. If for some reason that didn't come off he had to be sealed up tight till something else could be worked out. Maybe the reason there was no record of the interrogation was because he wasn't interrogated. Maybe they just kept him on ice till he could be led out in the open where Ruby could shoot him.'

'You're just guessing,' Pietra said. 'Anyone can do that. If other men fired at Kennedy that day, people would have seen them.'

'People did see them,' Jack said. 'But they were either discredited or scared off or bought off. Or they died mysterious deaths.'

'So what happened to those other men? Did they just disappear?'

'No. This is the best part. They didn't disappear. They were arrested in the parking lot that overlooks Dealey Plaza. A few minutes after Kennedy was shot, there was an announcement on the radio that three vagrants had been arrested as suspects. Those men were never identified or mentioned again. No follow-up on the radio, no newspaper stories.'

'That doesn't mean anything,' Pietra said.

'Yes, it does. Somebody took photographs of those three men when they were being arrested, quite a few photographs as a matter of fact. And a couple of months ago some little printing company in Texas published those photographs in a book. The men didn't look like bums at all. They wore old clothes and hats because they were trying to pass themselves off as bums. But it turned out that one of the men looked very much like the CIA man from New Orleans, the second one looked like a man named Gutierrez who helped plan the Bay of Pigs fiasco, and the third man looked like a twin brother of Oswald.'

'Where did you see this book?'

'An orderly at the Army hospital showed it to me. His brother lives in Austin. He sent it to him.'

'Are you saying that people in the government know why President Kennedy was killed and who did it, but they're keeping it a secret?'

'That's it. That's what I'm saying.'

'Do you think President Johnson knows?' Pietra asked.

'Yes.'

'Do you think Robert Kennedy knows?'

'Yes.'

'Then why wouldn't he tell the people?'

'I don't know.'

When they were at home later, Polly said, 'You're upset about all that Dallas business, aren't you?'

'Not upset. Mad. The whole thing makes me sick.'

'I thought you didn't give a damn about what goes on in America.'

'I don't.'

'You always say you don't feel any connection with the United States.'

'I don't.'

'Then why . . . ?'

'I don't know, Polly.'

Later, when they were lying in bed with the lights off, she said, 'Don't let it get you crazy, Jack. It has nothing to do with us. We don't live there. We live here.'

For a long time he didn't answer. She thought he'd gone to sleep. At last he said, 'I don't live here. I'm stuck here. I hate this bloody country.'

[12]

'I think you're wrong, Jesse,' Helen said. 'What could be nicer than to have Bill spend a year or two here with us? I should think you'd be happy to have him around.'

85

'I am. That's why I suggested that he come here and finish his schooling at the University of Illinois. That was our deal. That he'd live in Champaign and go to school there.'

'But now he's decided he wants to go to Foresby and live with us here in Fort Beck. What's wrong with that?'

'Nothing maybe. I'm just surprised he wants to. And I can't figure out why he wants to. He was keen on Illinois because of their theatre department. Lighting, set design, all that. He can't get any of those courses at Foresby.'

'That doesn't seem to matter to him. He knows he can get a fine education there. Maybe that's more important to him now.'

'It doesn't make sense to me.'

'He's only twenty years old, Jesse. He may change his mind half a dozen times before he decides what he wants to do with his life.'

'Do you really want somebody living here in the house with us?'

'Of course I don't,' Helen said. 'but this is different. This is Bill we're talking about. It would never occur to me to make him feel he wasn't welcome here. And even if it did occur to me, I wouldn't be able to tell him.'

That evening, when they were sitting in the library after dinner, Helen said, 'What's the real reason you don't want Bill to live here?'

'I don't know what you mean.'

'Yes, you do. I know you pretty well. You always make perfect sense except when you're trying to hide something. Then everything comes out lopsided.'

'Sorry to spoil your moment of fantasy but I have nothing to hide. Nothing that I'm aware of at any rate.'

'If you saw Bill every day would it remind you of Valerie?'

'You know better than that.'

'No, I don't,' she said. 'You haven't spent much time with your children since you and Valerie divorced. You certainly haven't lived under the same roof with them. It seems perfectly logical to me that living with one of them now might remind you of your life when you saw them all the time. And Valerie was a big part of that life.'

'If your father were alive and he heard you make that speech he'd send you to the dictionary to look up the word "sophistry".'

'No, he wouldn't. Raymond realized that I knew the definition of sophistry by heart.'

86

'Then you know you've just practised it. You've followed an apparently valid process and reached an invalid conclusion.'

'That's what you say.'

'I'm the one who knows,' Jesse said.

'Maybe not. Just because you don't want something to be true doesn't mean it's not true.'

'This is the side of you I don't see very often. Hypothetical questions and fairyland answers.'

'I'm not trying to trap you,' Helen said. 'Why shouldn't Bill remind you of Valerie. She's his mother and you're his father. That's a permanent connection.'

'No, it's not. My connection with Valerie ended when we stopped living together. My connection with Bill or Rab or Polly is another matter altogether.'

'Raymond's been dead since 1918. You still feel connected to him, don't you?'

'No question about it. And so do you.'

'That's right,' she said.

'Do you still feel connected to Frank?'

'No.'

'Why not? You were married to him as much as I was married to Valerie.'

'No, I wasn't. Frank and I didn't have children.'

'You and I don't have children. We're not even married. Do you feel connected to me?'

She nodded. 'Since the first day I met you.'

'Whatever your theory is,' Jesse said, 'You're slowly destroying it.'

'No, I'm not.'

'Of course you are. Hugh was Floyd's father. Do you feel a connection with Hugh?'

'No. But if I'd lived with him, if I'd known him, if we'd raised a child together, I'd certainly feel connected to him.'

'Maybe you would and maybe you wouldn't,' Jesse said. 'You're smothering yourself in hypothesis. Trying to redesign the world to fit your theory.'

'Even when I know I'm right, I never can win in a discussion with you. But that doesn't mean I'm wrong.'

'This time you're wrong. If you think I see Valerie dancing in front of my eyes every time I look at one of my kids, you are totally mistaken.'

'You win,' she said. 'I lose. But I still can't see why you're so horrified at the thought of Bill living here in the house with us.'

'I'm not horrified. I just don't think it's a grand idea. Either for him or for us. And I'll give you a specific reason. This is a small town. You and I are not married . . .'

'This is 1965, Jesse. Nobody gives a damn about that any more. I certainly don't.'

'Maybe you're right. But in case you're wrong, I wouldn't want Bill to be embarrassed by people gossiping about us.'

'For God's sake, Jesse. He's a Bradshaw. He doesn't have to come to Illinois to hear outrageous stories about his family. If people in Northumberland stopped gossiping about the Bradshaws they'd surely end up as mute as stones. I promise you the fact that you and I are living together in middle-aged sin will be no embarrassment to Bill. And if you're still hesitating I hope you'll remember how much it meant to you when you were Bill's age, living in this house with Raymond. You still remember those years, don't you?'

Jesse smiled. 'Only about twenty times every day.'

[13]

Before he left for America, Bill went to Germany to see Polly. He landed at Frankfurt and she drove up from Heidelberg to spend the day with him. As they had lunch at his hotel, she said, 'Are you quite sure you know what you're doing?'

'No. But I'm doing it anyway.'

'I couldn't believe it when I got your note. Jack couldn't either. He thinks you're crazy to go there.'

'I don't give a damn what he thinks.'

'Sorry I brought him up. I know you don't like him.'

'Nobody likes him except you. He's a great one to call somebody else crazy. He and his bloody cello will end up in a padded cell one of these days.'

'Don't say that, Bill.'

'Why not? It's the truth and you know it.'

'No, I don't know it,' she said. 'I know he's not like other people, but he's not had a happy life . . .'

'Oh, come on, Polly.'

'I mean it. He had a tough time in Korea.'

'I know. I've heard all that. Every drunk in every pub in England will tell you a sad story about why he drinks day and night. Bad wars, bad wives, bad luck. I don't buy any of those stories. A drunk's a drunk.'

Polly looked away. When she turned back, there were tears in her eyes. 'What do you want me to say? Jesse says the same things to me. So does Rab.'

'That's because they care about what happens to you. So do I.'

'Nothing terrible is going to happen to me.'

'It's already happening, Polly. You just don't see it. Or if you do see it, you won't admit it.'

'I admit all kinds of things to myself but it doesn't change anything. The sun comes up every morning and I have to deal with the day. That's what everybody has to do.'

'No, they don't. That's just some lie you keep telling yourself. You're a young woman, Poll. You're smart and you're kind and you're so beautiful people can't stop staring at you. You don't have to sit here and rot in Germany just to prove something to yourself.'

'That's not what I'm doing. You and Jesse seem to think I'm a doomed creature, but I'm not. I came here to Heidelberg to go to school, I fell in love with a man and I'm still here.'

'Still going to school?' Bill asked.

'Of course.'

'When was the last time you attended a lecture?'

'I do a lot of independent reading,' she said.

'When was the last time you attended a lecture? When was the last time you took an examination?' When she didn't answer Bill said, 'You're not going to school and you haven't been for more than a year. You're acting as housekeeper and nursemaid to somebody who's not good enough for you. Next thing you know, you'll be thirty years old and Jack will be off in the Himalayas somewhere, living with a goat.'

Polly began to laugh, still with tears in her eyes. 'I know you're trying to help me but you can't. And I can't help myself. I'm not even trying to. I made a commitment, Bill, not to Jack but to myself, and I have to stay with it. I want to stay with it. And I'm going to.' She dabbed at her eyes with her napkin. 'Now we have to talk about something else because I'm all talked out about Jack.'

He told her about his travel plans then. When he would leave for New York and when he expected to arrive in Illinois. 'I have a friend in Easthampton who wants me to spend a few days with him. And another one in Connecticut. And I want to take a bus from New York to Illinois to see what the country and the towns look like. So it will be mid-August before I arrive in Fort Beck.'

'What did Jesse say when you told him you want to live with him and go to school at Foresby?'

'He was surprised.'

'What did Valerie say?'

'She was surprised too.'

'That makes three of us.' Polly said. 'How about Helen?'

'She wasn't surprised at all. She thinks it's a great idea. At least that's what she told me on the telephone.'

'Most people our age want to get as far away from their parents as possible.'

'I know they do. But I don't feel that way. That's why I'm going there. So I can spend some time with Jesse.'

'You're a strange bird, Bill.'

'I don't think so. We all went off to school when we were twelve years old. Then, when I was sixteen or seventeen Jesse and Valerie got a divorce. And since then, I don't know, I just feel as if I lost touch with him, and I don't like that. I don't want things to just peter out between us.'

'How about Valerie? You feel the same way about her?'

'Not exactly,' Bill said. 'How about you?'

Polly shook her head. 'A few years ago I never would have believed I could say that. She meant everything to me when I was growing up. And it makes me feel wonderful to know she's happy now. But all the same I feel as if some connection was broken. Maybe it's *because* she's so happy. Does that sound terrible?'

'Not to me.'

'She's so good about writing. I love to get her letters. They're always positive and cheerful and encouraging, full of details about what she's been doing and what she and Floyd have seen. It sounds as though she's made a perfect life for herself. And then I start thinking, "nothing's *that* perfect." It's all very confusing. I'm not

90

sure if I should envy her or feel sorry for her. Do you feel that way?'

'Not exactly. When I see her I get the feeling she's trying very hard to be the same woman she was when we were growing up. I want to tell her that nobody expects her to be the way she used to be. But I don't know how to say it. So she just keeps trying and it makes me uncomfortable. And I see Floyd looking at her as if he doesn't know what she's up to. I mean, she doesn't expect *me* to be the same as I was when I was ten years old so why should I expect it of her. Maybe she feels guilty for some reason but if she does I don't like to see it. I want her to feel good about herself but when I see her I'm not sure she does. I feel as if she's trying to say something to me and I keep trying to say something to her but neither one of us says anything. We just keep telling each other how good we look and we say we have to work out some way so we can see each other more often. Then we say goodbye and go tootling off in separate directions and that's that.'

'I was always closer to her than I was to Jesse. Now for some reason I feel closer to him. Why is that?'

'Because he's the same now as he always was. And she's not.'

[14]

Valerie's decision to divorce Jesse had been a balanced and reasonable one. Her choice of Floyd had been reckless and fired by passion. In neither instance, however, had she felt guilt. In neither instance had she believed that her children would suffer from her actions. Choices that were so right for her, she concluded, could not possibly be wrong for them.

Nothing in the succeeding years had caused her to change her mind. Her maturing children, she persuaded herself, were everything she had hoped they would be. Clear-headed, unmarred, fuelled by a healthy supply of self-esteem, warmly devoted to their parents even though those parents were no longer devoted to each other. She had risked everything and had lost nothing. Her rich life with Floyd had not been paid for with the discontent of her children.

91

How can it be, then, if she had overheard the conversation in Frankfurt between Polly and Bill, she would not have been surprised? As her children grew up, Valerie's secret belief was that her strong connection with each of them was a sensory one, a matter of touch and scent and vibrations of the voice. She had always sensed when they were unwell or disappointed or discontented. They had sensed when she was displeased or unquiet. Her warmth had taught them more than her words, she believed. Her presence had moulded them in a final and permanent way. This realization, these convictions, had been a source of strength to her at the time she decided to separate from their father. She truly believed that nothing could weaken or sever the strong link between herself and her children.

No incident occurred to make her question those beliefs she held. There was no sudden halt or sharp corner. Rather, in the months following her marriage to Floyd, as they redefined pleasure and passion, as they recast the world in terms of themselves, as they dawdled and dozed, loitered and lingered and travelled from the loveliest corners of France to the flowered hills of Tuscany, she carried with her the permanent fact of her children, their flesh, their feelings, their attachment to her. They were a constant, an area of absolute assurance and certainty. Until suddenly, or perhaps it was a gradual thing, she realized that this precious absolute in her life had disappeared. She quickly hastened to reassure herself then, with letters, telephone calls, and visits to all three children. And she was reassured. She detected no change in them, no coolness, no lack of concern. She had hurried back to Sestri Levante to rejoin Floyd feeling that all her fears had been groundless. In the days ahead, however, as she reviewed her days with Rab and Polly and Bill she discovered remarks and questions and fleeting expressions that she had glossed over at the time. New details continued to present themselves like tiny thorns. When Floyd met her in the railway terminal at Genoa, when he said, 'What's the matter? Did something terrible happen?', she said, 'No. Everything was wonderful. I'm just horribly tired, and I missed you so much.'

The months that followed were a torment to her. Some part of her insisted that she must measure her happiness with Floyd against that dreadful unquiet she felt whenever she thought of her children. She refused to make such a measurement, refused to question or condemn herself. Having made her choice she knew that she could never choose again. She had neither the will nor the desire for any change. Nor was she able to acknowledge and accept that one joy had been irrevocably traded for another. She refused to see herself as the person who had made, albeit innocently, such a choice. So she floated somewhere in the middle distance between sin and absolution, resisting, as much as she was able, any final conclusions, refusing to make connections between actions and consequences, and absolutely refusing to disclose her tortured state of mind to anyone.

At one time she would have turned to Nora. Always, during Clara's lifetime, Valerie would have turned to her. But now she had only Floyd. And Floyd, she knew, although he was an active participant in her quandary, would be able to offer her no solution except himself.

At last, however, she couldn't keep it from him any longer. He had sensed, since he'd met her that evening in Genoa, that something was disturbing her. He had tried to question her but she had turned him away each time with a smile or a kiss. Finally, as they were having breakfast in bed one morning he got up, locked the bedroom door, and put the key into the pocket of his robe.

'Well . . .' she said. 'Now what? Am I in danger?'

'Not for the moment. But you could be.'

'What does that mean?'

'It means you've been carrying some secret around in your head for weeks now and I'm tired of watching you suffer.'

'I don't know what you mean.'

'Yes, you do,' he said. 'Something went wrong when you went to visit your kids, didn't it?'

'No. Not the way you mean.'

'I don't know what I mean,' he said. 'I'm waiting for you to tell me.'

'I told you . . . I saw them and . . .'

'I know what you told me. Now I want you to tell me the truth.'

After a moment she said, 'It seems so . . . I don't know . . . I don't know where to start.'

'It doesn't matter where you start. Just start some place.'

'I'm afraid, Floyd. I'm afraid you'll think I mean something I don't mean at all.'

'I can't think anything till you tell me what's in your head.'

'You know how I was with my children. You saw me with them

93

when they were tiny. When you and Helen first came to Wingate Fields.' She paused. 'From the time when I played with dolls, a day never passed when I didn't think about what it would be like to have a family of my own. I never thought about a career, even when I was at college, because I thought raising a family would be my career. And Jesse felt the same way I did. I used to think that perhaps that was what brought us together. Anyway, after we got married we had three children in four years. I used to say that I wanted ten children and I thought I meant it. I was only twenty-four when William was born and he was baby number three. But Jesse was almost fifty then and he started talking about the problems of a twenty-year-old boy having a seventy-year-old father. So we talked and discussed and postponed and time went by and finally we decided to settle for the three children we had. I had my hands full with Rab and Polly and Bill so I didn't really mind. And the way things turned out I'm glad we had just the three. But I was determined to give them everything a parent can give. Love, discipline, a sense of structure, a sense of joy, strength, tenderness, patience, tolerance. I wanted to make sure they were exposed to all the good things. And I was selfish, too. I wanted to be as important to them as they were to me. I had visions of myself as a white-haired lady living at Wingate, grandchildren and great-grandchildren all around me, each of them raised the same way I'd raised mine. A real continuum, that was what I saw. A connection. My children when they were fifty in close touch with me just as they had been when they were five. It sounds crazy maybe but that's what I wanted. That's what I thought was important. And by the time I divorced Jesse and married you I knew I had it. I didn't think I had perfect children – I hadn't reached for that – but I thought we were a strong and permanent unit, locked in place, unbreakable. I knew we would always be able to communicate, to understand, to empathize. We were together. That wouldn't change.'

She poured some coffee into her cup, then set the silver pot on the bedside table. 'Well . . .' she said, 'I was wrong. Either I was always wrong or I'm simply wrong now. In any case, the result's the same. There are three handsome grown-up people named Bradshaw who call me mother but beyond that it's just old baby-clothes in straw hampers and leather photo-albums. They don't know who

I am and they seem determined that I shouldn't find out who they are.'

'You're exaggerating,' Floyd said.

'No, I'm not. God, how I wish I were.'

Those feelings Valerie had expressed to Floyd did not diminish as time went; they became instead a familiar part of her emotional larder. The original sharp pain of recognition became instead a continuing ache. At last she tried to persuade herself that the deterioration she felt in her relations with the children was simply a result of their growing up and finding independent lives, not an indication of her having failed them or their having failed her. The news that Bill had decided to go to America, however, to live with his father, brought her former anxieties to full flower again.

'It has nothing to do with you,' Floyd told her. 'Why shouldn't he finish school in America? And if he's going to be there, why shouldn't he be where Jesse is? Ford Beck's a nice town and Foresby's a terrific college. If I'd had any sense I'd have gone there myself after I got out of the Navy.'

'There are all kinds of nice towns in the States,' she said. 'The only reason Bill's going to Fort Beck is so he can live with Jesse.'

'All right, maybe he is. What's wrong with that?'

'Nothing, I suppose. But it makes me feel strange.'

'You're making something out of nothing, Valerie. Bill's not rejecting you and choosing Jesse. There was never any discussion about his living with us.'

'Maybe there should have been,' she said.

'Why? He's a young man. He has his own life to lead.'

'Then why is he going to live with Jesse?'

'We already went over this.'

'I know we did but we didn't come up with the right answer. I say Bill wants to have some connection with his family and since he doesn't have a strong tie with me any longer, he wants to be closer to Jesse.'

'Maybe he does. But why shouldn't he?'

'No reason, I suppose. But you can't expect me to feel good about it.'

'Why not? It's not a contest. You're not in competition with Jesse.'

'Of course I am. Whether I like it or not. I'm not a saint. If Bill's having the time of his life living with Jesse and Helen I don't see that as a cause to rejoice. It makes me feel inadequate. Makes me feel like a failure.'

'I swear to God, Valerie, I don't know where you get these ideas. You have better instincts and more common sense than any human being I know. But when you're trying to deal with Rab or Polly or Bill you have all the logic of a witch doctor.'

'I admit it,' she said. 'I'm envious. I'm jealous. Where they're concerned I don't want to be second-best to anyone.'

'Jesse's not the enemy.'

'I know that. But when they choose him over me, I don't like it. I don't think I deserve that.'

'Maybe they think you chose me over them,' Floyd said. 'We've talked about that before.'

'I know we've talked about it but I've never accepted it.'

'If you're jealous of their father, why shouldn't they be jealous of me?'

'I don't know. But it would kill me if I thought they were.'

'Why?'

'I don't know. It just would.'

'Would it make you think you'd made a mistake by leaving Jesse and running off with me?'

'Never,' she said. 'Nothing could ever convince me that was a mistake.

[15]

From the moment Helen mentioned her father, as soon as she brought Raymond's name into the conversation, Jesse saw Bill's coming to Fort Beck in a different light. He cast Bill as himself many years earlier. And *he* would play a role he had long identified with, that of Raymond.

'This house meant a lot to me,' he told Bill a few days after his arrival in Illinois. 'I was your age then, actually a few years younger, when I met Raymond Bradshaw. He was Helen's father and Clara's brother. If he were still alive he'd be your great-uncle. Angus was Raymond's father. He was the one who adopted me and made me a Bradshaw after Raymond died.'

96

'Clara told us a lot about Angus when we were little,' Bill said, 'but I don't know much about Raymond.'

'He taught English Literature here at Foresby and I came to live with him in this house when I was sixteen. Raymond was divorced and Helen was living in New York with her mother. After I'd been here for a year, Helen came here to stay with her father.'

'Just like I'm doing.'

'That's right. So Helen and I have known each other since she was thirteen years old and I was seventeen.'

'I guess Valerie wasn't even born then.'

Jesse shook his head. 'She was born after the war. In 1920.'

'What happened to your real parents?'

'They're dead now. But before I came here I lived with them in Chicago. My dad was a musician when I was born.'

'What sort of musician?'

'Dance band. He played the banjo. But then he started working in restaurants and he ended up as a restaurant manager when we were in Chicago. His name was Thomas Clegg. My name was Jesse Clegg before I became a Bradshaw.'

'How did all that happen? Why did you leave your own family?'

'I never got on too well with my father. He had strong ideas. My mother was a nice woman but she always sided with my dad. So when they told me they were moving to San Francisco I decided I didn't want to go. I went downtown one day, traded in my San Francisco railroad ticket for a ticket to Oklahoma City, and the next day I left Chicago.'

'Why Oklahoma City?' Bill asked.

'I was born there. I had no place else to go so I decided to go back to Oklahoma.'

'How'd you end up in Fort Beck?'

'I'd written an essay for a high-school contest the year before. I didn't win a prize but I had a nice letter from one of the judges. That was Raymond. He said he was a teacher at Foresby and when I was ready to go to university I should consider it as a school. I looked it up in a catalogue of colleges and saw it was located here in Fort Beck. So when the Oklahoma City train made a station stop in Fort Beck, I got off, looked up Raymond Bradshaw's address in the phone book, and went to see him. He took me to dinner and we talked a lot and I ended up staying all night at his house. I never really decided to stay on, I just never got around to leaving.

I finished high school in Fort Beck. Then I went on to school at Foresby. And after I came back from the war Raymond helped me get a job teaching there. Then Raymond died, he died the night Armistice was declared, and later Helen and I went to England to visit the Bradshaw family. After that my whole life changed.'

'It must be a funny feeling, leaving your own parents and being taken in by another family altogether, changing your name and everything.'

'I agree with you,' Jesse said. 'It was certainly not what I intended to do. But when I met Raymond I felt as if I was related to *him*. I'd never felt that way with my own family. Nobody ever laughed in my house. No one had any fun. There was a lot of tension and suspicion and scheming to make money. No kindness. My father thought the world was a battlefield. And that's the way he lived. I always had stomach-aches when I lived in Chicago. The first thing I noticed when I came to live in Fort Beck was my stomach stopped hurting and my skin cleared up. I don't mean that Raymond was always an easy man to live with. He expected me to do my best. And Helen too. 'Nothing else is good enough,' he used to say. 'If you don't push yourself a little, you'll never know how good you could have been.' But he was fair. And he always knew how to make me laugh. I guess that's what I remember most about those years with Raymond, the three of us sitting at the dinner table laughing so hard we couldn't eat.'

'You used to make us laugh a lot,' Bill said, 'when we were little.'

'I tried to. But I wasn't in Raymond's class. Not in any way. He had style. At least that's what we used to call it. Knew how to handle himself. Never seemed out of control. When he died the way he did, all of a sudden, his friends were sad, but mostly they were angry. They felt cheated, like someone had swindled them out of an important part of their lives.'

'Did you feel that way, too?'

'I did then but I don't now. I'm just glad I stumbled off that train and looked him up that day.'

16

After he'd seen Polly in Frankfurt but before he flew to New York Bill had stopped in Paris and spent three days with Nora.

'*Grand-mère*,' she said. 'A beautiful word actually. I hate *grandma* or *granny*. Ugly words. Bad images. Spotted aprons and great brown liver-spots on wrinkled hands. But *grand-mère* is another item altogether. I have no objections whatsoever to being called *grand-mère*.'

'I don't think of you as *grand-mère*,' Bill said. 'You're just a sexy lady named Nora who lives in France and has the same last name as I do.'

'Ahhhh . . . *qu'il est beau parleur*. And only twenty years old. If you stay in Paris, a dozen lovely women will be fighting over you.'

'Haven't had that problem so far. I'll settle for an acceptable girl with straight legs and blue eyes.'

'You've been underselling yourself. That's your problem. If Karina and I start promoting you, all the straight legs and blue eyes in Paris will be lined up outside your door.'

'You start that promotion and I'll stop again when I come back from Illinois.'

'You're really going there then?'

Bill nodded. 'Against the advice of everyone I know.'

'Apart from saying you're making a mad decision, I won't try to dissuade you. I won't tell you that Illinois is the dreariest possible section of a hopeless country. I won't remind you that the weather is intolerable and the food inedible or that the women wear rubber girdles and padded brassieres.'

'Have you been to Illinois?'

'No,' she said. 'Nor have I been to Bulgaria. But I don't hesitate to give it a bad report. So far everyone, including Bulgarians, agrees with me.'

'Jesse thinks Fort Beck is a fine place.'

'Your father is the only human being I've ever met who likes Bretagne in the winter. If I remember right he said it reminds him of Illinois. I think it's admirable of you to want to spend time with your father while you finish your education but I think your purposes would be better served if you spent two weeks with Jesse motoring about looking at the cows and the swine and then hurried back here. You could take up residence on my *quatrième étage* and enrol at the Sorbonne. Or I could arrange to have you taken on as an apprentice in the school for stage design of the Comédie Française.'

'If Illinois is as bad as you say, I'll be back in two weeks.'

'It's an open offer. Two weeks from now. Or two years. I expect to live till I'm a hundred and my *quatrième étage* will always be at your disposal.' Then, 'How does your father feel about your going there?'

'The truth?' Bill said.

'Only the truth.'

'A bit cool on the idea at first, I felt. But I persisted. And his last two letters were downright enthusiastic.'

'That's good. Your father always wanted to have children. Has he been a good father?'

'I'm no judge of that since he's the only father I've ever had.'

'My mother once said he was the most decent man she'd ever known. From someone else I might have thought that was damning with faint praise. From her I felt it was a high compliment. What do you think?'

'I'm more interested in what you think. Rab says you know Jesse better than anyone.'

'What does Rab know?'

'Rab knows everything,' Bill said. 'He says so himself.'

'I agree he knows a lot. Did I tell you I saw him last week?'

'No.'

'No, of course I didn't. He called and invited me to supper Chez Allard. A last-minute invitation.'

'That's Rab.'

'Of course. I scolded him for giving me no notice but I accepted. When I met him at the restaurant it turned out that he had travelled from London with a lady he introduced as Agnes Dorsey. About thirty I should judge. But a truly exquisite woman. Yellow eyes, Bill. Not for you. Flecked with green. And thick lashes that any woman would kill for. Tall and slender, the body of a mannequin, but very much a woman inside her clothes. Composed. At ease. A lovely voice like butterscotch, and unless I can no longer read the signs, hopelessly in love with your wastrel brother. Oh, yes, she wore a wide ring of baguette diamonds with emerald guards. Is it possible that Rab is married?'

100

Bill shook his head. 'Not possible.'

'In that case, there's a wealthy gentleman somewhere in London who's sitting up nights waiting for his wife to come home.'

'Rab's a rake, don't you know that? He's determined to be the world's most notorious rake.'

'I suspect he's off to a good start.'

'We were talking about my father,' Bill said then, 'the world's most decent man. Was *he* a rake?'

'He could have been but he wasn't.'

'What does that mean?'

'The thing that made Jesse attractive to women was the fact that he didn't believe he was attractive to women. He was not a fop. He looked well in his clothes but he dressed conservatively. He never tried to dominate the conversation or attract attention to himself but in spite of that, perhaps because of it, he did attract attention. He had presence. People noticed him. He was self-conscious about the fact that he walked with a cane but because he was tall and slim and athletic-looking, the cane only gave him an air of vulnerability. And that made him doubly attractive. He was at ease with women and at ease with men but I never saw him flirt or present himself as an available object. Jesse and I were together for a long time. Did you know that?'

Bill nodded. 'That's part of the family history, isn't it?'

'Scandal is a better word for it perhaps. But whatever one calls it, we were happy together. I loved him very much and he loved me. And in all those years, as I say, he never made me feel as though he was interested in other women. The only person I was ever jealous of was Helen. I'm not sure why. Perhaps because when I met them they arrived at Wingate Fields together. They were young and handsome, *tous les deux*, and I suppose I assumed they were sweethearts. In any case, whatever that original assumption was, it stayed with me for a long time. It's only since your mother and Floyd got married that I've changed my mind about Jesse and Helen. They're certainly together now but I don't think they were before. All those years before I think they were just close friends as they said they were. Anyway, your father was the great love of my life. Does it make you feel strange to hear that your grandmother was mad about your father?'

Bill shook his head. 'We've known about you and Jesse ever since we were old enough to understand such things.'

'There was a time, a long time, when I thought I couldn't live without him. And if I'd been smarter, or less selfish, perhaps I wouldn't have had to. But if that had happened, we wouldn't have had you and Rab and Polly in the family. So it's all worked out for the best.'

'Do you think Jesse's a happy man?'

'Oh, my dear, what a question. After a certain age I'm not certain that anyone is wildly happy. There's too much to remember. And for some perverse reason, the bad memories seem to crowd out the good ones. If you're asking whether Jesse feels good about himself I suppose the answer is yes and no as it is for most of us. He and Valerie had a good life together and I know he's extremely proud of his three children. But all of us have locked rooms in our lives. As well as I know Jesse, I can't say what secrets he may have tucked away in corners. I know he's always struggled with his work and perhaps he always will. I've spent most of my life with painters and poets and I know they very seldom manage to do what they set out to do. And the very best ones are usually the most dissatisfied. They're always reaching for something they can't touch. Perhaps that's what makes them great. Jesse is not a great artist. Perhaps he's not an artist at all. He's too civilized and too careful. He could never dissect himself and use himself in his work the way a serious writer must do. But all the same the desire is there. And it always will be there, I'm sure. In his lifetime he's known fifteen or twenty absolutely worthless, selfish, despicable men who have the gift of art. That's all they have. In all other respects they're not fit to sit in the same room with your father. But what they have is what he wants. He has turned himself into a respected craftsman but he'll never be able to soar. He can't lose control. His hand and his heart will never be allowed to take charge of his mind.'

'Is that good or bad?' Bill asked.

'It's bad for any of us. For an artist it's death. The mind has some value, I suppose, as a housekeeper or accountant, but all the music in our lives comes from somewhere else. The mind can only put a label on joy. It cannot produce it.'

17

The week before, after the dinner with Nora that she had described to Bill, Rab and Dorsey Mullet flew back to London together. 'Well, I'm waiting for a report,' Rab said. 'You haven't told me what you thought of my sexy grandmother.'

'I can't believe she's anybody's grandmother. She's gorgeous. I can't imagine what your mother must look like if Nora's your grandmother.'

'Not much resemblance. Valerie looks more like *her* grandmother, Nora's mother. The longer you look at her, the prettier she gets. But she's not a shocker like Nora. No bright lights and bongo drums. Nora's a star and Valerie's a pretty supporting player.'

'How about you?' Dorsey said. 'Are you a star or a supporting player?'

'What do *you* think?'

'Big noise. Major star.'

Rab shook his head. 'Compared with my mother and father, I'm definitely a supporting player. Compared with some of the other Bradshaws, I'm a spear-carrying supernumerary. Lots of larger-than-life folks in my family. You just met one. My great-great-grandfather was another one. His name was Angus. He was the last pirate of the clan. He took all the land and all the money he'd inherited and doubled and tripled and quadrupled it. Since then, since Angus died, we've all just sat back and watched our inheritance multiply by itself. And his wife, Louise, managed everything in Northumberland that Angus didn't have time for. Including the Church of England. Their son was a piece of work, too. So I'm told. His name was Raymond and he was a renegade. He fell crazily in love with a married woman when he was still at university. And she was just as crazy as he was.'

'Like us,' Dorsey said.

'Not so crazy as us, I'm sure,' he said. 'Anyway, his father, Angus, decided he'd better break it up. So he sent Raymond off to Ireland to school while his lady-friend's husband took *her* for an extended tour of Italy.'

'Shame on him.'

'But they managed to meet again, the following spring, at a hotel in North Wales. Emily's husband, however, found out about it –

that was her name. Emily – and followed them there. There was a fight in the hotel room, a revolver went off, and Emily was accidentally shot and killed. Her husband then walked downstairs, crossed the street to a park opposite the hotel, and shot himself. Not long after that, Raymond left England and went to America. His family never saw him or heard from him again.'

Dorsey put her hand on his. 'Why didn't we stay overnight in Paris?'

'Because you said you couldn't. You said you had to get back.'

'I know what I said. You shouldn't have listened to me.'

'Next time I'll remember that.'

'We could have been in the Crillon right now. On those soft white sheets.'

'Don't start something you can't finish,' Rab said.

'Don't talk about it or I'll die.'

'I didn't bring it up. You did.'

'Don't remind me. Talk about something else.'

'Nora's brother, Hugh, was another renegade,' Rab went on. 'He was in trouble from the time he was fourteen years old. Finally he went to Scotland and bought a big hunting estate. He never came back to Wingate Fields except for short visits. He drank and fished and shot stag and finally he married a second-rate woman who had five children. And one day when he was still in his thirties he shot his favourite stallion and then killed himself. Do you want to hear more?'

'God, no. What have I let myself in for?' she asked.

'You've nothing to worry about. I am neither violent nor suicidal.'

'You may not be suicidal but you're certainly violent.'

'Are you complaining?'

'Not at all. I'm longing for you.'

'Did you notice this plane is almost empty. And no one has used that first-class restroom just ahead for more than twenty minutes. Don't you notice these things?'

'You lovely bastard.' As she stood up she trailed her fingers along the top of his thigh.

As soon as she disappeared behind the restroom door he stood up and followed her. He opened the folding door and squeezed in beside her, then closed the door and locked it behind them.

'Not as roomy as the restrooms on Air France,' she said.

104

As she opened the front of his trousers he raised her skirt. 'Where are those beautiful panties you bought in Paris?' he said.

'Safely packed away in the . . . oh . . . oh, God . . .'

'What are you saying?'

'Don't talk. Please . . .' she said. 'Please . . .'

He wedged her tight against the sink and her legs went round him.

'Oh, Rabbie . . . I can't wait . . . I can't stop . . . I can't . . .'

'You're not meant to.' He drove up inside her until she jerked and trembled and went limp. As she moaned and whimpered he kept her pinned against the sink until a light blinked on by the door and a crewman's voice said. 'We're preparing to land at Heathrow. Will all passengers return to their seats please and fasten their seat belts?'

Holding her close against him, Rab whispered in her ear, 'Would you like to return to your seat?'

'I can't move.'

'I'll help you fasten your seat belt.'

'Oh, God, Rab. You're going to kill me. You're killing me.'

Chapter Three

Rab and Dorsey, from the beginning, had carefully designed their time together. As their emotions had tried to drive them as far from Oscar Mullet as possible, reason had persuaded them that he must be included. More accurately, a pattern had to be created whereby Oscar would believe that he and Dorsey were including Rab. 'The more we're seen together, the three of us,' Dorsey had said to Rab, 'the more often you and Oscar are seen together, the less conspicuous it will seem if you and I are occasionally seen in public.'

Certain circumstances already in place worked in their favour. Others had to be added, neatly and judiciously. Oscar's previous interest in a business relationship with Rab was further encouraged and stimulated. 'The more involved I become in the television film area, the more I'm convinced that there are great opportunities there,' Rab told him. 'Electronics will certainly revolutionize the film business. Home viewing is sure to increase in one way or another. At last we'll see films made not for theatres but for individual homes. The technology's not there yet but it will be. I expect to be in on these developments from the start and you should be too, Oscar. The business will be international then, in a way that nobody ever dreamed possible. When that happens you and I could have a world-wide organization.'

Mullet, whose whole life had been one of deception, felt a surprising, almost fatherly, interest in Rab. Having no wish or need, at least for the moment, to deceive him, it didn't occur to him, certainly not at the outset, that he, himself, might be a target for deception.

Rab also played his Gloria Atwood card with skill. 'Just because you don't see me with a woman on my arm doesn't mean I'm celibate or diseased,' he told Mullet. 'The fact is I'm secretly engaged to a young actress named Gloria Atwood and she's gone off to Canada, on tour with a fine company of actors.'

Oscar, of course, knew about the tour and about Gloria Atwood but he suspected that Rab did not know he knew. Not wanting to risk being caught out, however, Oscar decided to tell the truth. 'Of course,' he said. 'I'm aware of that tour. Sam Borck and Lewis Darling put it together. I've done a great deal of business with them in Canada.'

When this brought no response from Rab, Mullet went on to say, 'The fact is I gave them a bit of help when they were putting together that company and I was at the theatre when they chose Gloria Atwood. A striking girl and a fine actress. Seems to me that someone mentioned she's a friend of yours.'

'More than a friend,' Rab said.

'So you're telling me that you're a man of principle, that while your fiancée's away you're not making yourself available to the available ladies of Mayfair.'

'That's correct. I'm socially acceptable now only to people who are willing to include an odd single man.'

'My wife tells me single men are never odd. To the contrary, they are very much in demand. They certainly are at our home. So you have an ongoing blanket invitation to join us any night you're free. We're not nesters, Dorsey and I. We have a dinner party at home or go out to dinner every night of the week. Dorsey enjoys being with you and so do I. So I expect you'll get tired of us before we get tired of you.'

Dorsey's views on the matter had been carefully composed and rehearsed in her mind. 'You know how tired I get of hearing film people babble on about grosses and saturation-booking and four-walling and all the rest of that mindless gobbledegook, but at least Robb . . . is that his name?'

'Rab,' Oscar said. 'Raymond Angus Bradshaw is his full name. *Rab* for short.'

'At least he talks about something else once in a while.'

107

'He's a cultured young man. Went to Cambridge. And he has more money than Randolph Scott and Joel McCrea combined.'

'He's too young to be really interesting,' Dorsey said. 'You know that as well as I do. But if he fascinates you . . .'

'No one fascinates me. I think he has a good head, I know he has money, and he's British. All those things are in his favour as far as I'm concerned.'

'Then I assume we're going to see a great deal of him. Correct?'

'I expect to see him but you needn't if you don't want to.'

'I'm certainly not going to turn you two loose and unattended in London.'

Several weeks and several dinners with Rab later on, Dorsey said one evening to Mullet, 'I know how happy you are when I can get somebody else to take me to a concert or the ballet . . .'

'That's true.'

'Do you think I might persuade Rab to take me now and then?'

'Why not? It wouldn't hurt to try.'

So the pattern was set, one of those rare circumstances where each individual benefited, either in fact or in fantasy. The Mullets and Rab were seen everywhere together, Rab and Oscar were often seen having lunch at Tarchers or Francesca's and when Oscar was in New York or Madrid or Rome or when the programme at Albert Hall appealed to Dorsey she was seen in the proper and circumspect company of Rab Bradshaw. When they were *not* seen, they were naked and laughing together in a shades-drawn apartment in a narrow street just adjacent to the British Museum.

In order to fill in every possible area on this new-painted backdrop of his life, Rab asked his secretary to call for a copy of Gloria's itinerary in Canada. When he had it before him, he began to write to her once a week. Without apologizing for his behaviour before she left London, he made it clear, and with each letter made it more clear, that he was looking forward to her return to London.

For her part, once she'd left Montreal and had begun her tour to the west, Gloria had slipped into an affair with her leading man, a near obligatory routine for touring actors. But since she knew that arrangement would end when the tour ended, she began to answer Rab's letters, first with *politesse*, then with awakening interest, and at last, as her tour neared its close, with real affection.

108

Rab had not responded to Dorsey's invitation to meet her at the Hampshire Hotel. He had been mystified, in fact, by her note, pressed into his hand the first night they met. Though he was seldom cautious in his sexual arrangements, some instinct told him that reasonable caution was required in this instance. All the same he was eager to see her again. But when he invited the Mullets to lunch with him the following week, Dorsey did not show up. 'She asked me to apologize for her,' Oscar said. 'She'd made a date with a woman friend for lunch and a matinée today and hadn't marked it in her calendar.'

When Rab did see her again it was by chance. One late afternoon as he was hurrying down Jermyn Street he saw Dorsey and her driver come out of a men's shop with a number of packages; they were loading them into her car when she saw Rab.

'Sorry you couldn't make lunch the other day,' he said.

'So am I. I'm such a fool. I have a calendar at every telephone but that doesn't prevent me from making duplicate social dates every now and again. As it happened we had a dismal lunch and saw a dreary play. I'd have been better off with you and Oscar.'

They chatted at the kerbside for a few minutes while the driver carefully stored her packages away.

'I'm going to my club,' Rab said. 'Just down the way here. Why don't you come and have a drink with me? Or tea if you prefer.'

She glanced at her watch. 'How sweet of you. But I'm afraid I can't.'

'Of course you can. It's just a quarter past four. I'll turn you loose in half an hour and you'll be home by five.'

'All right,' she said. 'Why not?'

They sat in a great bow window looking out on St James's. Rab ordered a whisky and she had a sherry.

'Tell me about the play you saw the other day,' he said.

'*Punctuation* it's called. Have you seen it?'

'No, I haven't. With Denholm Elliott, I believe.'

'That's right. And Kenneth More. Both marvellous actors, I think. And they were *good*. They always are. But the play did them in. They played journalists. Stranded for some reason that was never made clear in some drab city in Cameroon.'

'Yaounde?'

'No. I kept thinking they were calling it "elbow".'

'Ebolowa,' Rab said.

'That's it. Have you been there?'

'No, I haven't. But I had a strict geography tutor at prep school. He left me with a mind like a world map. I may be the only man in England who knows the population of Terre Haute, Indiana.'

'I'm impressed,' she said.

'You were telling me about the play.'

'Oscar detests plays that are all talk and no conflict. I don't mind that. But in this case the talk was meaningless. I felt as though the playwright was depending on the actors to show him what his play was all about.'

'But they failed.'

'Tried hard but failed,' she said. 'Doomed from the start.'

'After I saw you the first time, I asked Oscar if you were an actress. He said no.'

'He's right. I have no gift for it and no interest in it. I have no desire to exhibit myself. Even when I was a child I hid behind the furniture a lot. Just the thought of walking on a stage makes me nervous.'

'Oscar said you were a model in New York.'

She nodded. 'When I was too young to know my limitations. But I didn't do it very long. I couldn't. I've always felt awkward and self-conscious. Parading around in designer clothes only intensified those feelings. I was sick to my stomach for three years.'

'That's how long you did it?'

'About that. Since then I've found other things to feel sick about. I'm not a great mountain of security, you see. Self-esteem is not my distinguishing feature. A fluttery stomach and shaky knees . . . that's me.'

'No one would ever guess that to look at you.'

'That's because I'm tall and have no expression on my face. The truth is that tall people are nowhere near as secure as short people think they are. And almost all the beautiful woman I've met are painfully self-conscious.'

'Did Oscar tell you I have a son?' she said then.

'Yes, he did.'

'Named Charlie. After my father. He's a good kid. I'll tell you about him some time. Or maybe I won't.'

Rab looked at his watch. 'I promised I'd get you home by five.'

'Not necessary. My schedule's not that tight. Let's have another drink.'

After the waiter put fresh drinks on the table in front of them Dorsey said, 'I made an ass of myself, didn't I?'

'What do you mean?'

'You know exactly what I mean. When I handed you that note the other night. What did you think when you read it?'

'I'm not sure,' Rab said.

'I know what you thought. Some lecherous married woman was trying to get you into her bed. Am I right?'

'No. I don't think so. You said you were desperate to talk to me. I had no reason to doubt that.

'But you didn't show up,' she said.

'Did you think I would?'

'I didn't know what to think. I wanted you to and at the same time I didn't want you to.'

'That's the way I felt when I read your note. I wanted to meet you but I didn't want to . . . I don't know what I thought . . . you must have a lot of men sending *you* notes.'

'I'm very adept at discouraging people. I learned that when I was seventeen working in the garment centre in New York.'

He took a drink from his glass. 'I probably shouldn't tell you this,' he said, 'but the first time I saw you I had a very specific reaction. I knew you were married but I didn't care. I wanted to find some way to make contact with you. I wanted to sit down with you somewhere, the way we're doing right now. I wanted to put you under my arm and take you home.'

'I don't believe you.'

'It's the truth. So when you gave me that note, when I read it, I felt as if I'd written it and handed it to *you*.'

'But you didn't come.'

'God knows I wanted to,' Rab said. 'But I wanted to see you on my own terms, I guess. I didn't want to run the risk that maybe you really did just want to talk to me about something. I wanted to talk to you too, but the only thing I wanted to talk about was us, the way we're doing now. I didn't want you to start thinking of me as a platonic friend before I'd had a chance to tell you I had something totally different in mind.'

She smiled suddenly. 'Like what?'

'You know what I'm talking about. What about you? What did you have in mind?'

'I don't know. I just didn't want to shake hands and step into a car and run the risk of never seeing you again. I decided to do something reckless to show you . . .'

'To show me what?' he asked.

'To show you what I'm showing you now. That I care about who I am and what happens to me. That I *am* desperate to talk to you as I said in the note.'

'Can you meet me tomorrow afternoon?'

'Yes,' she said.

'Three o'clock?'

'Yes.'

'How about Green Park?'

'No.'

'Brown's Hotel for tea?'

'No.'

He took a card out of his pocket and wrote on it. 'This is the address of a building I own on Grantham Place, just north of the British Museum. There's a doorman there. He'll bring you in.'

[3]

'Is this where you bring aggressive women who pass notes to you in restaurants?' Dorsey said the following afternoon.

'I'm sure that's not a serious question,' Rab said. 'But I'll give you a serious answer anyhow. The fact is that nobody comes here except me. It's not my home and it's not my office. It's a place that nobody knows about, where I can come and work. Or read a book. Or do nothing.'

'When the doorman brought me in I thought I was in the wrong place. The building looks deserted.'

'It is. Except for this apartment. The building next door is empty too, and we've almost finished relocating the tenants in the third building. When that one's finally empty, we'll demolish all three and put up a ten-storey office block. That will be the headquarters

112

for Bradshaw Productions. We hope to have it ready for occupancy a year from now.'

'Then what?'

'Then we'll start making some money.'

'You act as if you already have money,' she said.

'I do. But now I'm going to *earn* some.' He got up, crossed the room, and took a bottle of champagne out of an ice bucket. 'How about a glass of champagne?'

'Sorry. I hate champagne.'

He started to loosen the cork. 'I didn't ask you if you liked it. I asked you if you'd like to join me in a glass of champagne. Or a bottle? or five bottles.'

She started to laugh. 'Sure. Why not?'

The cork popped and he poured the wine into two glasses. He handed her one, lifted his own glass, and said, 'Here's to the serious conversation we're about to have.'

She sipped from her glass and set it on the table beside her.

'No good?' he asked.

'What?'

'The champagne. You don't like it?'

'I told you . . . I hate champagne. But this tastes good.' She picked up her glass and took another sip. 'It tastes *very* good.'

'Then what's that expression on your face?'

'Just thinking about what you said. About the conversation we're going to have.'

' "I'm desperate to talk to you". That's what you wrote in your note.'

'I know what I wrote. But I have no idea what I intended to say to you if you'd showed up at the Hampshire Hotel that afternoon. I've no idea what I'm about to say to you now. I just know that I felt some need to make contact with you, that first night we met. I'm not sure if it was desperation to talk to you or just a desire to talk to *someone*. However it began, by the time we finished dinner, after sitting there watching you and hearing you talk with Oscar, I had some odd feeling that I'd known you for a long time and an even stranger feeling that *you* knew *me*. It was a very pleasant, very unusual sensation for me and I didn't want it to go away. That's why I quickly scribbled that note and gave it to you. Does all this sound like the ravings of a crazy woman?'

'No.'

113

'You're a lot younger than I am. How old are you?'

'Twenty-three,' Rab said.

'That's what I thought. But you seem older. Did Oscar tell you how old I am?'

'No.'

'I'm thirty-two. And that son of mine that we tell everyone is nine years old is really almost thirteen. I was a child bride.' She sipped from her wine glass. 'I don't have a thing about age, incidentally. My thirtieth birthday was not a trauma for me and I don't expect any painful reaction whem I'm forty or a hundred and twenty if I get that far. If I had a problem with people's ages, I guess I never would have married Oscar. He's twice my age. He was sixty-four in October. And you talk about age phobia . . . he really has it. Every birthday's like a cyanide pill to him. He tells people he's only fifty so don't tell him I told you his real age. Oscar was never a gorgeous man – I'm sure that's obvious to you – but the way he carried on, you'd think the most beautiful face and body that God ever created were in danger of deterioration. He's had plastic surgery half a dozen times. No major face lift, thank God. Just little tucks here and there. Over the eyes, under the eyes, behind the ears, under the chin. And two years before I met him he had a dimple put in one cheek. The surprise is he doesn't mind losing his hair. Yul Brynner told him that baldness is a sign of virility and Oscar believed him. Quotes him all the time.'

Rab got up for the bottle and poured more wine in their glasses. After he sat down she said, 'Where was I?'

'You were telling me about Oscar.'

'I know I was but that wasn't what I intended to do. I wanted to tell you how I was feeling that night I met you, why I reacted to you the way I did. I think it started when we came here to England. Of course it didn't *start* then but it intensified. And after we bought the house and I realized we'd be here for a long time, it got worse.'

'Oscar said you like England.'

'I do. I love it. It's not that. It's just that being in a new place, in different surroundings, brings everything into sharp focus. You start to see yourself and everything and everybody around you in a strong white light. Sometimes that can be good, sometimes not so good. For me these past few months have been very bad. All the lies I've told myself since I was twenty came tumbling down

114

on me like an avalanche of rocks. I started to examine what I was doing, how I felt, how I *am*, and I felt as if I was turning into powder. I tried to remember when I'd last done a positive thing, when I'd made a difficult decision, when I'd done something I could be proud of. It was a short list. Having my son, giving birth to Charlie, was the only medal I could pin on myself. So I had to go back thirteen years. Between then and now, there were no triumphs to remember. Plenty of compromises and rationalizations and promises to do better but nothing to feel really good about. I can't even take pride in raising Charlie. When I married Oscar, whatever else was included or left out of our marriage contract, it was clearly understood that he wanted his wife to travel with him. And as everybody knows Oscar travels a *lot*. So I turned over my kid to a series of governesses, tutors, and expensive private schools and let them do the job I should be doing. As I say this I realize that all those people have probably done a better job with him than I would have done. But that doesn't console me. It only makes me feel worse. And it's nothing I can fix. Not now. I lost all those good years with him. Now he's almost a man. I think he loves me. God knows I love him. But I'm a visiting parent, a sort of vacation mother. I show up at his school, he introduces me to the headmaster and to his teachers, we have a lunch or two together and a dinner and I'm off to meet Oscar in Miami or New Orleans or Chicago. The last few times I've sensed that Charlie's glad to see me but relieved when I go. He's happy to get back into his school routine with his friends. Do you think I'm weeping and wailing on you?'

'No.'

'I don't mean to. I don't feel sorry for myself. I really don't. I'm just trying to tell you how things are with me, how they've been, and how they are now. If I'm boring you to death, stop me. Will you do that?'

'Yes.'

'Promise?'

'I promise. You're not boring me.'

'I try to think of how I could have handled things differently, other choices I might have made, but that doesn't help much either. When I'm totally honest with myself I have to admit that if I were faced with the same choices today I'd probably make the same decisions I made before.'

'That means you were right, doesn't it?'

'No. It means that if I was a coward before I must be a coward now.'

'That's a word that doesn't mean much,' Rab said. 'Everybody's a coward some time or other and most of us are cowards more often than we like to admit.'

She smiled. 'I know all that. But I'm not talking about what I've done or how I feel about what I've done. I'm talking about what I *am* and how I got to be this way and if it's possible for me to be some other way.'

They sat there facing each other, talking but not touching, till it got dark outside. Finally she said, 'What time is it?'

'Almost six-thirty.'

'I have to go.' Her voice sounded small and pale and tired.

'Are you sure?'

'Yes. I'm worn out. I feel as if I've been nailed to a board in the bright sun.'

When they walked to the door she said, 'Don't come downstairs with me.'

'I want to. I'll get you a cab.'

'*I* can do that,' she said. 'I'm good at things like that.' At the door she turned to him.

'I hope you don't think I'm a helpless shipwreck.'

'Nothing like that.'

'I wanted you to know something about me. But I didn't expect to go so far.'

'You didn't go too far,' he said. 'When can I see you again?'

'Whenever you want to.'

'Tomorrow.'

'Tomorrow I can't. Thursday. Can we come here again Thursday?'

He put his arms around her. 'Thursday's fine.'

'Don't kiss me,' she said. 'I'll crumple up like tissue paper.' She touched his mouth with her fingertips. 'Let's save everything till Thursday. On Thursday I promise I won't talk at all. I won't say a word.'

He went to the window after she'd gone. As soon as she walked out of the building a cab pulled up and she got in. Rab watched the driver ease out into the early-evening traffic. After the cab disappeared at the corner he stayed there at the window looking

116

down at the street. At last he turned back to the room and switched on a lamp. Then he finished the champagne that had gone warm in the bottle.

[4]

When Valerie said, and she said it often, that she'd never had a choice when she decided to leave Jesse and go with Floyd, it was the simplest, most irrevocable truth she knew about her own life. She was neither sentimental nor romantic by nature but she believed without question that she and Floyd had been crafted as matching halves of one single and beautiful unit. Although she had no patience with theories of predestination and paths of fate she was convinced nonetheless that some master-plan had ticketed them for each other. She was certain too that Floyd shared these feelings.

It had never occurred to either of them, once they were together, that anything could ever separate them. They saw no shadows in their future together, no storms or roadblocks. Their contentment and fulfilment were foregone conclusions. They started their life together, both at age forty-two, with the expectation that they would be occupied henceforward only with pleasant flavours and rewarding details. Several days after they were married, Valerie had said, 'We have a critical problem. How do we improve on perfection?'

'We don't,' Floyd said. 'We don't even try. We just enjoy it.'

So they had done that. Floyd continued to feel an attachment to his stepdaughter, Betsy, who was married now and living in California with her husband and two children, but he knew the decisions of her life were out of his hands now. And Valerie accepted the same truths about Rab and Polly and Bill. So she and Floyd were free to travel where they chose, to change directions without consulting or informing anyone, and to indulge themselves in any way that appealed to them.

They spoke often of their contentment. 'The greatest part of being lucky,' Floyd said, 'is knowing you're lucky. Most people don't recognize joy till it's over. They define it by its absence.'

'Not us,' Valerie said. 'We know what we have.'

117

In addition to everything else they shared, they were splendidly flexible and amenable. Their natural rhythms did not conflict in any way. They could stay up all night or go to bed at ten. Each of them loved to drink and they were not afraid of drinking too much. But they would sometimes go for ten days or two weeks and not taste so much as a glass of wine. They smoked expensive Turkish cigarettes and were outrageously intolerant of people who didn't smoke at all. They often put on their finest clothes and gambled in the casinos of the Algarve or the Côte d'Azure but they took equal pleasure from dining in workmen's cafés or sailors' bars near the wharves.

'We have no rigid pattern to our lives, do we?' Valerie said.

'Of course we do. Our pattern is that we have no pattern.'

'We're free and floating,' she said.

'Exactly. Drops of mercury on a slanting table-top.'

One day she asked him, 'What would you like to have that we don't have?'

'There's nothing we don't have or can't get if we want to.'

'There must be something.'

'Yes, there is,' he said. 'I'd like more hours in the day.'

'I'd like more hours in the night.'

'*Evidemment*. That goes without saying.'

'Can it really be like this for ever?'

'It must,' he said. 'You promised me it would.'

'Can we be sybarites and hedonists and not feel guilty?'

'Of course we can. Hedonists never feel guilty.'

'No good causes. No charity work?'

'None of that. We're too happy for such things. A truly sad person can sacrifice himself for a cause. All martyrs have low self-esteem. We, on the other hand, serve by example. People look at us and say, "*That's* what I want. I want to be like them." '

'But that's impossible. No one can be like us.'

'That's true. But it gives the poor buggers something to work for.'

'Can we really be solitary and selfish?' Valerie asked.

'We're not selfish. We're extremely generous.'

And they were. To employees, to friends, to acquaintances, to organizations, to communities, to family members, to their children. Openly on occasion, more often anonymously, they gave freely.

118

'But it's only money,' Valerie said. 'We give nothing of ourselves.'
'That's right. We're very protective of our persons. We save ourselves for ourselves.'

Valerie, of course, was as devoted to the course she and Floyd had chosen for themselves as he was. She cherished their aloneness. Reason told her it was not only the best way of living for them but perhaps the only way. The ugly death of Floyd's first wife and the slow lingering demise of Valerie's marriage had pointed both of them in similar directions, toward simplicity and silence, toward fresh new scenes and unfamiliar faces, toward an atmosphere of tranquillity where they could relate to themselves and to each other in an uncluttered way.

All of this Valerie applauded. It was a kind of renaissance she both needed and wanted. But the rhythms of her previous life could not be easily discarded. Since her marriage to Jesse when she was twenty-one years old the key element in her daily pattern had been *responsibility*. Rab had been born less than a year after her wedding, Polly eighteen months later, and Bill a year after that. It was during the war, they had lived in a large house in Boston and servants had been impossible to find. So Valerie had cared for her three children, cared for her husband, and managed their house, to a large degree, by herself. What would have been burdensome to many other young women was in no way a burden for Valerie. The work from dawn till bedtime did not demean her, it *defined* her.

When they returned to England at the end of the war, when they became residents, she and Jesse and the children, of Wingate Fields, Valerie's physical tasks were taken over by a corps of skilled servants. But her other responsibilities increased enormously. On the one hand she refused to relinquish supervision of her children to governesses and tutors. She saw to it that Rab and Polly and Bill were in daily contact with herself, with Jesse, and with Clara. So her duties, if less arduous, were extremely time-consuming. Furthermore, she began to take on some of Clara's work. The two of them shared the supervision of the great house and the domestic staff, while Jesse gradually took over management of the lands, the livestock, and the tenant farmers.

Those years with Clara were foundation years for Valerie. The two women shared their work, their thoughts, their lives, in a way that was new to Valerie. Her relationship with her own mother had

119

seemed like a bond between sisters. Nora had been very young when Valerie was growing up, she had been barely forty when her daughter was twenty, so the sharp separation of generations had not been a part of what they shared.

In Clara's case, however, just as daily exposure to Valerie made her feel younger than her years, the time Valerie spent with her grandmother gave her wisdom and warm tolerance that were unusual for someone her age. And most important, she began to see herself as a functioning part of Wingate Fields, as a cog in the machinery that drove that enormous and complex entity. In those first years she felt she was taking over a lifetime task, just as Clara had done. What had been passed on to Clara by Louise would be passed on by Valerie to Polly. Love and property, sacred and indivisible.

Those were secure and fulfilling years, then. Studded by present rewards and the promise of rewards to come. Clara's world was solid and structured. The routine of her days served as a model, it seemed, for the pattern of her thoughts. Her values, her habits, her activities were all of a piece. Or so it appeared to Valerie. And she strove to achieve that same peaceful balance in herself.

She succeeded too well, her mother thought. Nora believed that Valerie had deliberately become older than her years, had gone much too far in her efforts to transform herself into a responsible *county* woman. 'My God . . . she'll be older than Jesse if she's not careful. She seems determined to create a life without surprises. I hope she fails. Because if she succeeds she might as well be dead.'

Valerie had failed of course. Her decision to divorce Jesse, her subsequent revelation that she planned to marry Floyd were two of the most remarkable surprises in Bradshaw family lore. Even Nora, who was seldom astonished, was, in this instance, *thoroughly* astonished. Valerie had suddenly exhibited an independence and a disregard for family approval that made even Nora's past transgressions seem tame.

To Valerie, who had traced these rebellious steps one by one in her consciousness, all seemed wonderfully inevitable and right. The process of engineering such a total turn-around in her life lifted her out of herself. She felt like a beautiful iridescent serpent shedding its skin. The physical change amazed and fascinated her. Mistaking all her cosmetic transformations for fundamental ones, she felt an inner power that was new to her, and a sense of security that was not new but radically altered. It was as though she had

120

stood to one side to watch herself perform tricks she hadn't known herself capable of. No longer just a fourth-chair instrumentalist she had become suddenly both composer and conductor. People marvelled at her. She sensed it. Or they were scandalized by her. Equally thrilling. She knew only that she had taken indisputable command at last of her own life. That was enough. Beyond that intoxicating horizon she didn't try to go.

This fresh assessment of herself, this new evaluation would be a durable one. Or so she told herself. She gave herself up to it and to the changes that resulted from it, the random, perfumed, itinerant idyll that developed for her and Floyd. She found her new life not only acceptable but irreplaceable. Its brilliant colours and changing rhythms, new scents, and foreign flavours kept her firmly fixed in the present tense, rooted in the moment. No slippage allowed, no soft renewals of other scenes or older values. Nothing lost, everything gained, memories denied, the world in her hand.

It couldn't last, of course. The gods who reward and wreak vengeance would not allow it. The consciousness is composed of loops. Abandoned objects return newly wrapped. Scents drift back on returning winds. One day without warning the looking-glass shows you the person you used to be and will become again. All this quite gradually happened to Valerie.

One day as she sat in a café in Portimão waiting for Floyd she found herself scribbling almost illegibly on a paper table covering.

What is the matter with me? Is it possible that *everything* is not enough? Why is my mind wandering so? What am I after? What have I lost?

It was several months later, in their house on a cliff overlooking Praia da Rocha, that Floyd repeated the question she had asked herself. 'What's the matter with you?' he said.

'Nothing, darling. I'm fine.'

'No, you're not.'

'Are you angry?'

'No,' he said.

'Yes. You are. I've never seen you angry with me.'

'I've been waiting for weeks for you to say something. I thought it would come out finally. I thought you'd tell me what was bothering you.'

'Why do you think something's bothering me?'

'Because I know you,' he said. 'I know you better than anyone else. At least I thought I did. And then one day you faded out, like the dye running out of a piece of cloth. The first time I noticed it, it only lasted for a few minutes. Then it began to happen more often and last longer each time. Now it seems as though you disappear for days at a time.'

'That's silly, Floyd. How *could* I disappear?'

'I don't know. But you do. You go out of focus. Your arms and legs work. And your voice. But your eyes give you away. Instead of looking at me they seem to be looking inside. And they don't seem to enjoy what they see. Is something happening to you that I don't know about?'

'Of course not. What *could* be happening?'

'I don't know,' he said. 'That's what I'm asking you.'

'I'm the happiest woman in the world, Floyd.'

'I didn't say you're not happy. I said you're not here. You're missing.'

After a moment, she said, 'Anybody's mind can wander a bit, can't it?'

'I don't know. You tell me.'

'Don't you ever think of anything except what we're doing or saying at some particular moment?'

'Of course I do.'

'Well, there you are. So do I.'

'Let me ask you another question,' he said then. 'Do you know what I'm talking about and you just don't know how to deal with it? Or do you just not know what I'm saying?'

'I understand the words you're saying but I'm not at all sure what you're talking about.'

'In that case I guess we'd better change the subject.'

'You really are angry, aren't you?'

'No, Valerie, I'm not.'

'When you say "Valerie" in that tone of voice, I know I'm in trouble.'

He put his arms around her. 'You're never in trouble with me.'

Some time later, two or three weeks perhaps, when they'd driven to Albufeira for lunch and were on their way home, Valerie said, 'I've been thinking about what you said to me.'

'What's that?'

'That day when you were very serious and cross. When you told me I'd been going out of focus. Do you remember?'

'I remember. But we don't have to beat it to death.'

'I know we don't. But it bothers me when we leave things unfinished. Up in the air. That's not our style.' When he didn't answer she said, 'Remember a long time ago when I asked you how we could improve on perfection?'

'What did I say?'

'You said we should just enjoy it and not try to improve on it.'

'That makes sense.'

'I know it does,' she said. 'But maybe that's what we've been trying to do.'

'Not me. I know when I'm well off.'

'So do I. But maybe that can be a problem too. I've told you before . . . I feel guilty because things are so perfect for us. We can live in our cocoon and know we have nothing to fret about. But I can't pretend that I don't think about Rab and Polly and Bill and wonder what they're up to. And I'm sure you must worry about Betsy. Also I feel guilty sometimes because we've all left Wingate Fields unloved and unattended. So maybe when you catch me in those moments that's when I seem to have disappeared. But I haven't. Not from you. Clara told me once that when you really love someone you wish you could have known them and been with them from the time they were born. You don't want them to have had any life before you. That's the way I feel about you and maybe you feel the same about me. But there's no use pretending that we weren't alive before we met each other. And there's no way to prevent your memory from nudging you once in a while. But when it does it has nothing to do with us, Floyd. We have all the luck there is and we're not going to lose it.'

[5]

It was a watershed moment in Jesse's creative life when he realized at last that if he was ever to write something of value it would require a kind of self-exposure that he had previously taken pains to avoid. As he spent long hours in Raymond's study in the house

123

at Fort Beck, as he scribbled and deliberated and quarrelled with himself, as he tried to find ways to blunt or to avoid this new challenge he had flung at himself, even as he tried to take refuge in old work-habits, he knew that he had reached a point in his consciousness where he must deal with the truest facts he knew or stop writing altogether.

When he began at last, when he wrote the critical first sentence that turned him loose, he was not sitting comfortably behind Raymond's desk by the garden window. He was waiting in the car for Helen, in the parking lot of a Fort Beck food market. As though he was not trying to attach too much importance to this work which, as it turned out, would occupy him and obsess him for the rest of his life, the first words he wrote were scribbled on the back of an envelope he found in the car's glove compartment. He sat behind the wheel on a crisp and golden October day, the wind swirling brown leaves across the tarmac of the parking lot and wrote, 'How difficult it is to tell the simple truth.' He sat there looking down at those few words he'd written. Then he read them aloud in a quiet voice. The dog had been asleep in the back seat; he woke up and began whimpering for attention. Jesse reached back and patted him on the head. Then he folded the envelope and slipped it into the pocket of his leather jacket. But the words, as though he'd recorded them, repeated themselves over and over in his head.

When they got home, after he'd carried the groceries from the car to the kitchen, Helen said, 'I'm chilly. I think I'll make a nice pot of tea. Are you interested?'

'I'm interested but I think I'll pass. I have a couple letters I've been postponing. I think I'll take a crack at them now.'

As soon as he was inside the study, he took a clipboard from the desk drawer, sat in a comfortable chair by the window and began to write.

How difficult it is to tell the simple truth. As a writer I've spent my entire life searching for a subject. I became a critic at last because in that field a subject was always provided for me. Any book, any play, any painting can provide a starting-point for an article or a critique.

As a result I spent my most productive years writing monographs, analyses and aesthetic judgments. I read and studied, probed and interviewed, spent my hours in galleries and ateliers and libraries, seeking always to get to the heart of other men's work, to discover what was real and lasting and to point out what was synthetic and without value. These activities I pursued with dedication and full vigour. I told myself that I had found at last my true *métier*, that a responsible critical voice was as rare and necessary as pure creativity. I did not allow myself to consider that my dedication to the work of other artists was a way of avoiding whatever responsibility I had to develop my own abilities and my own view-points.

I continued to question myself, of course. I continued to believe that one sonnet was more valuable than twelve volumes of literary criticism. But my carefully worked-out answer blunted all questions. I simply told myself, and I continued to believe, that my failure through the years to find subjects that were grand enough, or penetrating enough, was proof that I was a craftsman, perhaps, but not an artist. Something, unquestionably, held me back. I needed guarantees that art can never provide. Safe solutions. Predictable results. Acceptance.

A gifted painter said to me, 'When I start a new picture I know it will be an endless process of mistakes, of trial and error. Some of the mistakes can be fixed or painted over. Some cannot. They stay there, captured in the paint, mocking you. The mistakes always keep the work from being what you intended. But without the mistakes the picture would be worthless. A man doesn't make a picture or write a poem to explain to the world who he is. He does it to find out who he is. That's the only reason to work. It may be the only reason to be alive.'

He was an old man when he told me this. He was small and bent over and largely unrecognized except by other painters. Talking with him changed the way I looked at paintings. I tried to see them with his eyes. And though at last I began to understand, I found no way to turn his truth into my truth. I could accept the thesis that the flaws in a masterpiece are essential to its final worth but I could find no foundation of self-confidence that would allow *me* to work that way. The *process* would not sustain me. I needed to foresee, as accurately as possible, the *result*. Magnificent failures were beyond me. I needed to sustain myself with inconsequential successes. I had taught myself to be

125

careful, to conceal or eradicate the flaws in my work, to conceal the flaws in myself. I needed to be perfect so I tried to be.

There was no sudden revelation. No shattering event, no blinding light. It was rather a gradual pattern of altered circumstances. Relationships changed. Winds shifted. People redefined themselves, changed costumes, took on new roles. I did not, however, redefine myself. I simply left Europe where all the triumphs and follies of my adult life had taken place and returned to America, to its centre, to the house in Illinois where I'd lived with Raymond and Helen and where I would now live with Helen in circumstances which each of us had perhaps envisioned through the years but which had seemed unlikely to come to fruition. It caused me to refer to the past, that move, brought the far past, the near past, and the present into an unquiet relationship, like painted screens moving silently back and forth in a dim-lit room. Easy moves, soft transitions, but everything blurred a bit, voices indistinct, faint music from colliding decades making an evocative but disturbing blend of elusive sound.

Details keep us honest. All conclusions are deceptive. Being back in Raymond's house, I found, stripped away the conclusions I had reached about myself since I'd left there. Sitting in his chair in his study, I began to peel away multiple layers of self-delusion and self-deception that I had used for armour in all the years since his death. I realized that if he were there to ask me questions about the years since we'd seen each other I would tell him a different story than I had persisted in telling myself. Whatever I had become, whatever I imagined I had become, would have been subject to close scrutiny and fair but objective assessment if Raymond had been there. Only the truth would have been good enough and I would have been expected to provide it.

I had no impulse, however, to create a fantasy conversation between Raymond and me, no need to absolve myself by a full confession of my sins and shortcomings. But all the same, being in that ambience, remembering, in spite of myself, details from that long-ago time, I began to find a tolerance for the painted-over mistakes in myself, began to hear voices I had silenced long ago, to open doors I had bolted shut, to look without flinching at cruel behaviour and selfish choices. Years before, when I was at Foresby as a student, I had copied down a line from a psychology text: 'It's painful to hate yourself. It's more painful not to know yourself.'

Does all this, does *any* of this make sense? Perhaps not. The problem may be that I am not trying to present a case. The process is inductive rather than deductive. I cannot give you the whole truth. I am only trying to find small pieces of the truth, and allowing them to be what they are. Not structural devices or supporting arguments but simply tiny crumbs on a very large platter.

I am not about to announce a discovery. What I'm dealing with, although it is very exciting for me, can more accurately be called suspicion. I suspect that I have found, at last, the subject I sought for many years. I always told myself that only the great themes were worth writing about. Love and war, death and betrayal, God and fate, evil and self-sacrifice, faith and hope and vengeance. Now I believe that a man is permitted to know only one subject in his lifetime . . . himself. If he can tell that story truthfully, painful as the process may be, he may find that he has become the most complete man and the finest artist he is capable of being.

[6]

In moments of high hilarity, Nora had often described herself as a witch. 'I can put a spell over you,' she boasted. 'I can turn your pet cat into a cobra, take away your canary's song, and make your hair dead straight, even on a humid day.' No one took her seriously, of course, but it amused them to accept as a truth her supernatural qualities. They also accepted her claims that she had penetrating insight in sexual matters. 'I can look at a man across the room and tell you much more than you perhaps wish to know about his sexual proclivities. All sorts of excess and deviation are at once clear to me. *Une bête* I can spot in a moment. The same with *une femme vicieuse*. And there is no *pédéraste* alive who can deceive me. It's my gift, a minor one, I concede, but a special gift all the same. I can spend five minutes with any married couple and tell you precisely what they do to each other in the bedroom. Or in the kitchen, as the case may be. White-haired ladies who make sexual demands on their poodles can't fool me either. One needn't see lip rouge on a dog's forehead to know that things are not as they should be.'

She had known, of course, from the beginning about Karina's true relationship with Dort, the young woman-cousin or half-sister – however she was described – who shared Karina's house in Neuilly. When they first met, just after the war, when Karina was in her early thirties and Nora just past forty, Nora, once she had been introduced to Dort, said to Karina, 'I'm a woman of the world, my dear. There's almost nothing I disapprove of. Which is not to say that I indulge in everything that I witness. I experimented with hashish and cocaine when I was quite young. And I used to own an opium pipe that was of museum quality. But none of those things interested me so I don't take part. Nor do I seduce young boys or young girls for that matter. I met a young woman when I was first divorced, when I had come to live in Paris with my daughter. And this woman, this girl, her name was Elise, was convinced that she and I should become lovers. I thought she was amusing and she was extremely attractive. So when we met on social occasions, as we did often, I sat with her and allowed her to explain to me in extravagent detail what she proposed to do to me and what my reactions would be. I was not persuaded, however, and I told her so. But she was not easily convinced. She persisted, pleasantly but tirelessly, for months. Sent me flowers and great boxes of Belgian chocolate – really bizarre behaviour. But when she finally realized that I was having none of it, she turned vicious. Cut me cold in public, gossiped about me, and sent me truly outrageous letters. Finally we met one evening in the ladies' lounge at Maxim's and before she could speak to me I struck her several times with my open hand and left her half-stunned where she'd taken refuge under a table. Oddly enough I never saw her after that evening. The following year she was found floating face down in the Marne with her throat cut but I didn't grieve for her. She was a truly nasty young woman.'

'Why are you telling me all this?' Karina said.

'I'm not sure. We were talking about sexual freedom, I believe. And I was saying to you that there's no necessity for you to make explanations about Dort. In the first place I can *see* how things are and in the second place it doesn't matter to me. The fact that I am endlessly fascinated with the marvellous differences between men and women does not mean that I rule out all other activities for other people.'

'You're mistaken about me. I am married, as you know, and I am as appreciative of men as you are.'

'I don't doubt that. But you have catholic tastes. You are what Americans call a "switch hitter".'

'What does that mean?'

'In baseball, it means a batter can hit the ball either right-handed or left-handed.'

'I don't know anything about baseball.'

'In that case, we'll pretend you're not a "switch-hitter",' Nora said.

'Whatever you think, Dort is my cousin.'

'That's all right with me. And Jesse's my uncle.'

'I don't believe that,' Karina said.

'Then we're even.'

Through the years they had become, not intimate friends, but constant friends. They gossiped and shopped and had lunch together like schoolgirls. They quarrelled and didn't see each other for months. Karina, who was notorious for her inability to keep a secret, never passed along anything that Nora told her. For her part, Nora treated everything that Karina told her about herself as privileged information although she knew that Karina had already confided the same facts to everyone she knew.

If people are normally loved and revered for their best qualities, Karina attracted people by her flaws. She was flagrantly untruthful but she was always touchingly apologetic when reminded that she had lied. All women's husbands were fair game to her but her conscience often forced her to confess her transgression to the betrayed wife. In at least one such instance, Karina could only placate the angry husband by offering him a continuing relationship. Under those new circumstances, Karina felt no guilt and saw no reason to confess a second time to the man's wife.

In fairness to Karina, it must be said that her failings were all in relation to sexual matters. She had simply severed the nerves that connected her brain with her pelvis. Her mathematical skills, on the other hand, were astounding. She was a canny investor on the Bourse and she was brilliantly informed about the political climate in every European capital. 'I detest de Gaulle because I'm German,' she said. 'I detest him because he's a conceited fool. He's still living

129

in the thirteenth century. If the French people love him so much, they should make him King of Brittany and force him to stay there. They must never elect him President.' About Franco she said, 'He's there because the people want him. When they don't want him any longer, they'll kill him. Franco understands that. Why is it such a mystery to the rest of the world?' About the United States she said, 'Americans talk about freedom as if they invented it. They don't realize that most people don't give a damn about freedom. They want to be rich. And if they can't be rich they want to be safe!'

Through the years, during the post-war time in Paris, the casual relationship between Karina and Nora came to resemble a true friendship. Since they were both beautiful women they never trusted each other. Still . . . as time passed, their investment in each other bound them together by volume if not by intensity. But the quality of their friendship improved, too. When Nora and Jesse renewed their long love affair which had ended at the beginning of the war when Jesse married Valerie, the only person in Paris who knew about it was Karina. Only she knew the address of the house in Montparnasse where they met every day. She was key witness, also, to the mixture of joy and heartbreak that Nora felt when her daughter and Jesse divorced.

'It's not your fault they divorced,' Karina said. 'Valerie told you that.'

'I know she did. I wish I could believe her.'

'You have to believe her. Why make yourself miserable? Why would she lie to you?'

'Everybody lies to everybody.'

'Not always,' Karina said. 'I believe that things will work well now for you and Jesse. He will come to Paris to stay. You'll live together in your fine house and work on your magazine together. In a few weeks you'll tell me how happy you are.'

Jesse did come to Paris. He lived in Nora's house on the Seine. But in a few months he was gone. 'He went to America,' Nora told Karina. 'He didn't want to be in England for the wedding, when Valerie marries Floyd.'

'I can understand that. But couldn't he stay here?'

'I'm sure he felt I wouldn't go if he didn't. And he knows Valerie will be disappointed if I'm not there.'

She hadn't told Karina the truth. She hadn't described how silent the house had been when Jesse came back. They had tried to be cheerful, had talked about the new life they would live now, better even than the time before the war. And when the conversation flagged they took turns assuring each other that they were not responsible, the two of them, for Valerie's decision to get a divorce. 'After all, she told you that,' Jesse said, 'and it's also what she told me. In no uncertain terms. I know you didn't believe her at first and I guess I didn't either. But when everyone found out about her and Floyd things took on a different sheen. I don't know how long they've been making their plans but we know Valerie doesn't do anything on impulse. So there's no doubt in my mind that the two of them had come to some decision long before you and I got back together. I know you detest being innocent but in this case you are.'

It all made sense to them. They nodded and smiled. But in the days that remained before Jesse departed for New York the silence between them persisted. They were extremely kind and considerate to each other. They both sensed it and they both hated it. When they parted at the airport, however, they were in good spirits. Or at least the people who saw them together assumed they were in good spirits and in love. They'd had a long lunch at La Coupole, sampled all the wines offered to them, and shared a bottle of champagne from the proprietor's private cellars.

Jesse held her close and kissed her at the entrance to the tunnel leading to the plane. 'I love you, kid,' he said. 'You take good care of yourself.'

'It's only a wedding. What can happen to me?'

'Weddings are dangerous affairs,' he said.

'Only for the people who are getting married.'

'We were smart. We avoided all that.'

'That's right. *Smart*. That's the word for us.'

'Nothing better than *smart*. That's the best.'

'Wrong, Jesse. *Lucky* is the best.'

'If that's true, you can't lose. You're the luckiest woman in France. Everybody knows that.'

She nodded but didn't answer. Then she said, 'How soon will you be back?'

'Two weeks. Three at the most.'

She carried it with her, that airport parting, when she went to Northumberland for the wedding. She blocked out the silences, the

131

guarded looks, the sense of disquiet she had felt and sensed in him those days before he left. She simply erased all that and focused instead on their misty and tender airport farewell. That told her all she wanted to know. And it masked out all the things she refused to believe.

When she returned to Paris after the wedding, however, there was no room for self-deception. She found a letter waiting from Jesse, a short letter. By telling her nothing, it told her everything. It was postmarked Fort Beck, Illinois.

Still standing in the foyer of her house, her luggage sitting on the floor beside her, Nora called Karina. 'The son of a bitch is returning to the womb. Back to where he came from, a place called Fort Beck, whatever that is.'

'I can't believe that. What did he say in the letter?'

'Nothing. There's nothing he can say. I know he's moved in with Helen and he knows I know it.'

'Wasn't Helen at the wedding?'

'Of course she was. She treated me like a long-lost friend. So I knew I was on shaky ground.'

'I'm sorry, Nora.'

'To hell with it.'

'What are you going to do?'

'I'm going to chill three thousand bottles of champagne and drink them all. How does that sound to you?'

'It sounds wise and wonderful.'

'Good. I'll see you here at about seven.'

With short interruptions for food and sleep, the two of them drank together for three nights and two days. They sang and danced and excoriated men, *all* men. They stumbled about Nora's bedroom in their dressing-gowns and collapsed in great chairs before the fire. And when they were too drunk to sit or stand, they folded down softly on the bed, like creatures without skeletons, and slept.

Late in the morning of the third day, when Nora woke up, she said, 'Am I dead?'

'I don't think so.'

'But we can't drink any more, can we?'

'I don't think so,' Karina said.

'We drank a lot, didn't we?'

'We did everything a lot.'

132

After a moment Nora said, 'I thought maybe that was something I dreamed.' When Karina didn't answer, she said, 'No dream, huh?'

Karina shook her head. 'Maybe I'm supposed to say I'm sorry but I'm not sorry. Are you?'

'I'm just hung over. If I'm going to be sorry it will have to be later.'

'I don't think you'll be sorry,' Karina said, 'and I don't think you were as drunk as you say you were.'

Nora turned her head on the pillow and looked at Karina. Finally she said, 'We're two grown-up women. We know everything that we'll ever know. I'm not in love with you so don't fall in love with me.'

'I don't promise anything,' Karina said.

'That's fair enough. Neither do I.'

[7]

After Bill had been living with them for three months, Jesse said to Helen, 'Well, he's been here for a while now. What's it like having a strange young man living in your house?'

'*Two* strange men. You and Bill.'

'But you're accustomed to me. If you're not by now, you never will be.'

'I'm accustomed to him, too. He's very easy to live with. The only surprise is we don't see him as much as I'd expected.'

'He's taken up. School work. Soccer team. And it looks as if he's turning out to be cat-nip for the coeds.'

'Takes after his father,' Helen said.

'Not the way I remember it.'

'Then you don't remember correctly. When you were at Foresby, Raymond used to say you only come home to change your shirt.'

Jesse smiled. 'That does sound vaguely familiar.'

'Of course it does.' Then, 'What's it like for you, having him here?'

'Very good. Easy and good. After all the commotion with me and Valerie I wasn't sure how he'd come out of that. I thought he might have some strange grudge against me. We haven't seen each

133

other much for the past three or four years. But now I don't see any problem. He acts as if he's lived here all his life.'

They weren't deliberately deceiving each other. They were just leaving out vital facts. Helen, like Jesse, had tried to draw a parallel between Bill's living with them and Jesse's living with Raymond and her. She reasoned that she, as Jesse's unmarried mate, could function much the same in the triumvirate as she had as Raymond's daughter, whereas Jesse, rather than being a kind of foster father as Raymond had been to him, would be living under the same roof with his own son. She would not even be burdened with the title of stepmother. 'Maybe he'll introduce me as his stepmistress,' she said to Jesse. 'I doubt it,' he said. 'The fact is you will be put in no category. So you two will have a good chance to be friends.'

Oddly enough, in practice, Helen's unease had come from just that unusual circumstance. She had no clear role. She found it difficult to label herself in relation to either Jesse or Bill. When they were alone, before Bill's coming, she and Jesse had simply been two attractive, mature adults who lived in the same house together, slept in the same bed, and neither advertised nor denied this domestic arrangement. Since his arrival nothing had altered between her and Jesse; she felt neither shame nor embarrassment. But she found she was constantly aware of the situation. She began to indulge in that most unrewarding of human activities, trying to see herself as others might see her. Not 'What am I?' but 'What do people think I am?' Of course she wondered what Bill secretly thought of her, how he explained her away to his friends or if he referred to her at all. Having never considered her role or her reputation in the community, she went so far now as to dwell on it. And farther along that path, she asked herself if Jesse regarded her differently now that his son was in the house. Neither these questions nor the substantial range of possible answers alarmed her. But they made her self-conscious in a way that was new to her, made her feel at times like a vagrant in her own home, an alien in her own skin.

There were no incidents to substantiate these anxieties she felt or imagined or anticipated. There were no supporting details. Everything was abstract and filmy and therefore indestructible. At the end of Bill's first month with them she told herself the most difficult part was over. At the end of the third month she had stopped making herself any promises whatsoever.

134

Jesse's unease was of an altogether different nature. Nothing abstract or theoretical about it. From the moment he met Bill at the airport in Chicago, when he saw this mature young man striding toward him, he felt an empty and ugly sensation of failure, of time lost that couldn't be recovered. Standing there with his arms around his son, no inner voice saluted him for what he'd accomplished. Rather a long list of assets he'd squandered unfurled before him.

That sensation left him of course. The details of getting Bill settled in occupied him totally for a time. The two of them then went off on a week-long driving tour, looping west through Iowa, south into Missouri and across southern Illinois to Indiana, then finally back to Fort Beck. Bill's curiosity and enthusiasm, his involvement with the new things and places he was seeing left no space for reflection or redirection on Jesse's part. Seeing things through his son's eyes steered him away from his own ruminations.

Back in Fort Beck, however, he sank again into the vat of *mea culpa* he had managed to avoid temporarily. His self-criticism took on different shades and colours now. He began to measure himself against Raymond, began to compare the things Raymond had given him with the things he felt he was able to give to Bill. If he'd been in a different, more rational frame of mind he'd have known it was an unfair contest. He had concluded, as a sixteen-year-old boy, that no one he had ever known could measure up to Raymond Bradshaw. That admiration had grown through the years after Raymond's death to iconic dimensions. Once, in anger, Nora said to him, 'Do you know what Raymond is to you? He's your excuse for keeping yourself detached, for staying aloof from everybody and everything. You've decided that if you love and adore and worship *him* enough, it classifies you for ever as a loving person, relieves you of any emotional responsibility towards anyone else. All utopians are scary but people who hide behind a utopian love are really killers.'

Jesse had ignored and forgotten that attack from Nora. It played no part in the current struggle he was having with himself about Bill. This was a struggle with facts. His memory of the years he'd spent with Raymond was encyclopedic in its detail. He remembered, or believed that he remembered, every nudge, every direction, every word of advice he'd gleaned from the older man; he remembered, too, that almost every guidepost had been wrapped in a heavy cloak of humour. There were no life-and-death choices

135

in Raymond's lexicon. One-hundred-eighty-degree turns could be made, splints could be applied to broken bones, mistakes could be corrected or forgotten. Choices were only choices, he seemed to believe, not shackles. He counselled the art of living, not the cruel science of prevailing.

All these memories echoed in Jesse's mind as he spent long hours with his son, as they strolled the autumn streets, drank beer in a workmen's tavern by the Boone River, or sat in the library of Raymond's house, talking about books and soccer and the endless mysteries of mid-western college girls. As Jesse heard himself speak, it all sounded hollow and memorized to him, words coming in some reasonable order from a place where they had been stored, to be fished out as needed like minnows on a string.

Jesse tried so hard to be something he was not that he lost all chance of being simply what he was. He saw doubts and uncertainties on his son's face which were not in fact there. They were simply magic lantern projections of his own reservations about himself.

None of these subliminal tides had any effect, however, on the day-in, day-out functioning of Helen's house in Fort Beck. The currents that truly existed as well as those that were only imaginary stayed well beneath the surface. Bill moved ahead briskly with his new life. The rhythm that had existed before he arrived seemed unchanged. But the metronome had ceased to function.

[8]

'I'm not prying into your business,' Polly said to Jack. 'I'm not checking up on you. But I worry about you.'

'You are not to worry,' Jack said. 'After many months with me, years now, you are still miraculously unscarred and unspoiled. No worry lines are permitted on that lovely forehead.'

'I'm serious, Jack.'

'But you mustn't be. That's what I'm saying.'

'You're not saying anything. You're putting me off, as you always do.'

'Not at all. I'm protecting you from anxiety.'

136

She crossed the room and sank down on the floor by his chair. Leaning her head against his legs she said, 'How did I end up with a maniac like you?'

'Very easy, as I remember it. You reached into the grab-bag and pulled me out. I think you felt sorry for me, like a small dog at a pet shelter. You took me home, cleaned me up and put me on a leash. So here I am.'

'You've never been on a leash in your life. And you never will be. You're like a timber wolf who only comes close to the village when he needs something to eat.'

'I wish that were true,' he said. 'I think of myself as a lap-dog that gets bathed every day and has pink bows tied to his ears.'

'I know. I've heard those stories before.'

'Am I wrong?'

'One hundred percent,' she said. 'Your visions of yourself are very different from what other people see.'

'But what do *you* see?'

'If I pulled you out of a grab-bag, as you say, I certainly got my money's worth. Instead of one man I got a dozen different ones. I never know which one I'm living with from one day to the next.'

'Multiple schizophrenia . . . that's my gift. A quilted person. Scraps from here and there. Fold it once and you see a certain pattern. Fold it again, the pattern changes. Rumple it up on the bed and something altogether different emerges. Infinite variety . . . that's what Shakespeare said about Cleopatra. Meant it as a compliment, I think. What do you think?'

'I think *you* have infinite variety and it scares me to death.'

'Nothing wrong with that, is there? Boredom is the real threat. I'm eager not to bore you. Mustn't let you get tired of me.'

'That will never happen,' she said. 'You know that.'

'Then you're happy . . . is that what you're trying to tell me?'

'Not, it's not. I told you I'm scared and worried. I have no idea what's going through your head. For weeks we haunted the beer halls. Every night with Donny Krause and Pietra. Sleeping all day and drinking all night. Then you were off on a bus to Bad Stolz. Gone for three weeks.'

'The Bavarian Alps. Cleanses the soul, that country. High in the mountains. Snow on your shoe-tops. In touch with God. Eternal truth.'

'You don't believe in God or anything else.'

137

'Careful. As I told you, I was in Oberammergau for three days. Saw the Passion show every day I was there.'

'Why? You're an atheist. What could possibly . . . ?'

'Pageantry.' he whispered. 'Crown of thorns, blood sacrifice, stigmata. A lot of high-powered stuff. Great imagery. Those men who sat there smoking their pipes and dreaming up the Bible really knew what they were doing. They knew their audience. Sex and violence. That's what it's all about. Smell the perfume. See the blood. Pontius Pilate, the Jews, the thieves, virgin births and harlots in the street. Miracles and betrayals and tablets of stone. A masterpiece, the Bible.'

'You're impossible, Jack.'

'Improbable maybe. Not impossible.'

'I mean impossible. As soon as you came back from Bavaria you went into another phase and never left this house for a month. Played the cello night and day. Sat in a corner on the floor with that book of Van Gogh drawings . . .'

'There's a Christ figure for you. If you're looking for the saviour, you don't have to look any further than Vincent.'

'He couldn't even save himself,' Polly said.

'Of course not. All of us saints are vulnerable. Targets for destruction. That's our value. Nobody notices us till we're destroyed.'

'You think Van Gogh was a saint?'

'I don't want to joke about the man. Is that a serious question?'

'Yes, it is,' she said.

'Let me answer you this way. He was a unique embodiment of the human spirit. Forget his painting for the moment. Let's just concentrate on his drawings and his remarkable letters to his brother. I'm talking about *revelation*. No one has ever revealed himself in that way. Not before. Not since. Anyone who takes the time to study those drawings, to read every word of those innocent and tortured letters, any person with even basic sensibilities can never look at a tree or a hand or a workman's face in the same way again. It's not a pleasant experience to look inside another human being with all the protective layers pulled away. Vincent had no protective layers. None. That was his genius. It wasn't a tragedy that he died the way he did. It was a blessing. He'd converted his own misery into a haunting legacy of beauty so there was nothing left for him to do. Nothing he wanted to do or needed to do.'

138

'If you want to know what scares me,' Polly said, 'it's things like that. When you say things like that.'

'This has nothing to do with me. We're talking about a poor miserable man who transformed himself. There's nothing scary about that. Vincent's an inspiration. And we're wrong when we say he couldn't save himself. He saved himself all right. He turned himself into a cathedral.'

She looked up at him and smiled. 'Is that your ambition? Is that what you're planning to do?'

'God, no. I can think of nothing worse than being immortal. People thumbing through your life and examining the remnants of your mind long after you've flaked away in your coffin. The greatest gift life has to offer is anonymity. Fame and notoriety are in fact previews of Hell. In the Devil's house everyone is famous. Can you imagine anything more painful or obscene than being recognized in the street by a stranger? I can't. I sometimes duck into alleys to avoid meeting close friends. Not eager for social congress. No decent person is. Only politicians, public performers and whores are compelled to be seen, to be stroked, to be popular. The rest of us, those who are wise, are not anxious to be residents of any province larger than our own skin. If you were willing to bring in sugar buns, knockwurst, and a bit of lager every day I would be content to spend the rest of my days in this chair, contemplating the infinite.'

'If that's true, why is this the first day I've seen you in that chair for more than two weeks?'

'Busy, busy.'

'Once you put down the Van Gogh book, you strolled out the door and have only been seen on rare occasions ever since.'

'Not true, my love. Home in my bed every night.'

'Very *late* every night.'

'Unavoidable. There's a lot to be done and never enough time to do it.'

'I saw Pietra at the flower market and she said Donny is as absent as you are.'

'Joint project,' Jack said. 'Rather a large and important work that requires full attention from both of us.' He paused. 'I speak German almost all the time, as you know. Apart from you and Donny, I have no English-speaking friends. But someone the other day heard me speaking English, a young woman who works at the University library, and she said I have a strangely formal, almost literary way of speaking…'

'That's because you think in German now and translate it into English as you speak.'

'Exactly. That's the precise information I gave to the young librarian.' Then, 'Where was I?'

'You were talking about a project.'

'Right. More than a project. A mission, actually. One might even call it a crusade. I'm not political, as you know. But I have never forgotten my childhood lessons about right and wrong.'

'You also tend to speak in a formal, almost flowery fashion when you've had a lot to drink,' Polly said.

'You're right.'

'Did you mention that to the librarian?'

'No, I didn't but I should have. In any case she seemed satisfied with the other explanation I gave.' He gave her a questioning look.

'Right and wrong,' Polly said. 'You've never forgotten your childhood lessons about right and wrong. Is that what you said?'

'Exactly. Fairness. Equity. Reasonable behaviour. All those principles were drilled into me by the Jesuits. I can't say I've allowed them to guide my life but, on the other hand, something comes up occasionally that spurs me into action.'

'And that's what's keeping you away from home all day and most of the night.'

Jack nodded.

'But you're not going to tell me about it,' she said.

'Of course I'm going to tell you. I have no secrets from you. But I can't tell you right now. Other people are involved. Not just Donny.'

'Are you about to do something crazy?'

'Not at all. In fact I think you'll be proud of me.'

'If it's something crazy or something dangerous, I *won't* be proud of you.'

'No risk at all,' he said. 'Just an element of secrecy at the moment. When the time comes you will know everything there is to know and, as I say, I expect you to be proud.'

'I'm always proud of you. Almost always.'

'Ah, but this is different. You're proud of what I am. I know I'm physically presentable at least. And I'm an affectionate animal.

140

Good sense of humour – I get that from my mother's side – and an unusual desire to please. Is that an accurate description?'

'You left out your cello.'

'I know I did,' he said.

'Surprised you didn't mention that first of all.'

'Normally I would. But I'm not satisfied with the way I've been playing lately. Struggling with Haydn for the first time in my life. You've been listening. You must have noticed.'

Polly shook her head. 'You're too hard on yourself.'

'*Can't* be. Another thing I learned from the Jesuits. Baseball, too, they taught me. Did I ever tell you I was an excellent player when I was sixteen years old. Later, too. I played for my company team in the Army. But I was never better than when I was sixteen. Played first base. Very fancy with the mitt. Dig the ball out of the dirt, handle the drag bunt with the best of them, stretch for the wild throws, hold the runner on the bag. You don't know anything about baseball, do you?'

'My brother told me it's like cricket.'

'In my judgment, your brothers know very little about anything. About baseball they know nothing.'

'Don't be nasty.'

'I take it back. Your brothers know how to be rich. Beyond that, they know nothing. In Korea we used to say a friend is a guy who sticks with you when you get in a street fight; I wouldn't have faith in your brothers in a street fight.'

'You might be surprised.'

'Maybe I would. Anyway, I was telling you about my baseball days. Ask Donny, he's seen me play. He'll tell you I was a hot shit when it came to playing baseball. No home runs. That wasn't my style. I was a contact hitter. Spray the ball around. Hit to all fields. Lay down the bunt, hit behind the runner going to second, bloop singles just over the infield. I had the eye and a smooth swing. Hit almost four hundred one season. You don't know what that means, but I do. Damned proud of my baseball days. I'm probably the only cello player in the world who can say he hit four for four, seven different times.'

'Sounds good to me.'

'That's because you're a dope,' he said, 'but like I told you before, I want you to be proud of me.'

'I am.'

'For things I do,' he said. 'Just remember that.'

He came home very late that night. Morning light was bleeding in around the window shades when he slid under the blankets. She turned over and lay against him with her head on his shoulder.

'Are you awake?' he said.

'No. Are you?'

'No.'

'You smell like cigar smoke.'

'You want me to get up and take a bath?'

'No. I'll kill you if you get up.'

A few minutes later he said, 'Are you still awake?'

'I think so.'

'I was thinking about you tonight. I wanted to tell you I'm sorry.'

'For what?' she said.

'General principles, I guess. I know I act like a horse's ass most of the time. But that has nothing to do with the way I feel about you.'

'I know that. If I didn't, I wouldn't hang around.'

'Every time I come up the stairs I tell myself you might not be here.'

'Not a chance. I'm not doing you any favours. I'm here because you're the most interesting man I know. In fact you're the only interesting man I know. Multiple schizophrenics are hard to find.'

[9]

When Floyd flew to California to visit Betsy and her family he drove south to Ojai one day to see his friend, Abe Rettberg.

'You look pretty good for an old gent,' Abe said. 'How old are you now?'

'Last time I looked I was forty-five.'

'You're a baby. Wait till you're my age.'

'You don't look a day older than you did the first time I saw you in that bar in San Diego.'

'Don't try to bull-shit me, sailor. That was 1941. I was thirty-seven years old then. Lots of wear and tear on the old chassis since then.'

Abe was working as resident manager of an old four-storey apartment building near the tennis courts in the centre of Ojai.

'One day I made a list of all the jobs I've had,' he said. 'Forty-seven I came up with. Isn't that something? Forty-seven different ways to keep a little bread and sausage in your gut and a bottle of tequila on the floor by the bed. One thing I'd never done was look after an apartment building. So I decided to give it a try.'

'Doesn't sound like you. You're not what I'd call a diplomat. How do you handle the complaints?'

'Don't have any,' Abe said. 'The women tenants all have the hots for me and the men are all scared shitless that I'll lay one on 'em with my good arm. This is the life. I'm telling you. Wait'll you see the pad I've got. Two bedrooms. Two bathrooms. Can you believe that? And a big desk where I can sit and smoke and get half-bombed and smell the roses in the garden.'

'Sounds like you're going soft, Abe.'

'No doubt about it. I took my social security early and they pay me off the books here. Under the table. No taxes. So I've got the world by the tail. The way I see it this is my last stop.'

'I don't believe it. A year or two and you'll be off some place in a pickup truck with two bad tyres.'

'Don't kid yourself. I've already seen every place I'm curious about. I've been here for almost five years and I never had it better in my life. Nobody looking over my shoulder, all kinds of middle-aged pussy hanging around, and nothing much to do besides cool my heels and give orders to a couple of wet-backs who do the work for me.'

'I thought you didn't like Mexicans.'

'Don't know where you got that idea. I love Mexicans. The real ones. The Indians. They're great people. If you're talking about that crowd of Sonora hustlers that you used to hang out with in Culver City, I admit I had no time for them. Those monkeys almost got you shipped off to Chino for a few years. Walking around with leg irons on your ankles.'

'Don't remind me,' Floyd said.

'What was that lawyer's name, the guy who got you off with a suspended sentence?'

'Rosenthal. Mike Rosenthal.'

'Are you in touch with him?'

'No. No reason to be.'

'What do you mean? A rich jaybird like you. You ought to send him a big cake with a naked hooker in it every year for Christmas.'

'He doesn't want anything from me. Never did.'

'I remember. You told me. Never understood it then. Don't understand it now. When a lawyer keeps you out of the pen and doesn't even send you a bill that's front-page news.'

'He did it as a favour to my uncle,' Floyd said.

'And then your uncle did you a favour. Right? Did a little mating dance with your wife.'

'That's ancient history, Abe. I never think about that stuff any more.'

'I don't blame you. If somebody's gonna put horns on me I sure don't want it to be a member of my own family. Your mother's half-brother, wasn't he? Paul, wasn't that his name?'

Floyd nodded. 'Paul Buscatore.'

'Poor bastard. If anybody was gonna kill him it should have been you, not your wife's first husband.'

'Nobody should have killed him. I never blamed Paul. Nobody ever put a move on Jeannette if she didn't want them to. She was trying to use him to put a few dents in me but it didn't work out that way. They both took the heat.'

'Well, like you say, it's old news now. You're living the good life, rich and lazy. Sitting around in your underwear drinking cocktails. Any kids?'

Floyd shook his head. 'Valerie had three from her first marriage.'

'Why do all your wives have kids but not you?'

'Bad timing, I guess.'

'Maybe you're shootin' blanks. You'll end up like me. With nobody there to throw roses on your grave.'

'I don't think so. I think of Betsy as my daughter. We went through a lot together when Jeannette got killed.'

'Must be a rough trip for a girl when her old man signs off her mother and then kills himself.'

'She handled it damned well,' Floyd said. 'Better than I did.'

'But you ended up smelling like a rose. Am I right? Wandering around from one country to another, scattering money in the streets, sending picture postcards to your friends. A life like that would drive me nuts. You really like it?'

'It's so perfect it scares me.'

'Does your wife like it too? What's her name again?'

'Valerie.'

'That's right. Does she like it?'

'We have a great time, Abe. She misses her kids sometimes but that's normal. I miss seeing Betsy, too. That's why I'm here.'

'Don't give me that crap. You came to California for one reason. To see *me*. If you don't check in and get some serious advice from me every year or so you fizzle out like a wet firecracker. God knows where you'd have ended up if I wasn't keeping an eye on you.'

[10]

Floyd stayed in an old Spanish-style hotel in Santa Barbara for the ten days he was there. It fronted on the ocean, only a twenty-minute drive from Betsy's house. When he'd written from Portugal telling her of his plans he'd said, 'It was very nice of you to invite me to be your house guest but I would never consider disturbing your privacy with Taylor and the children. I expect to spend as much time with you as you can manage, day and evening. But I don't want to be underfoot. So I will tuck myself in every night at the Biltmore.'

Betsy's two little girls, Julie and Jenny, were two and three years old but they were already skilled swimmers. They spent a good part of each day in the family pool just outside the sliding glass doors at the rear of the house. It was a time of warm and pleasant weather as Floyd and Betsy sat in sling chairs on the decking beside the pool while the children swam and played in the shallow water.

'Taylor had them in the water when they were only a few months old,' Betsy said. 'He was a champion runner and swimmer at Northwestern when we were in school and he's a fanatic on the subject of diet and exercise. Insisted that I breast-fed both girls for a full year. Wasn't interested in the pediatrician's views on the matter. And since they've been weaned he's had them drinking goat's milk. As you can see we have a little army of goats down the hill there among the oak trees. He's a wonderful father. He cuts their hair, gives them massages and bathes them every night before he puts them to bed. If I hadn't put my foot down when we were first married, he'd do the cooking too. He knows all there is to know about nutrition. Reads everything he can find on the subject. And he's written several articles himself. He measures his waist every morning and if it's more than twenty-nine inches he fasts for three days. He's proud of the fact that he weighs exactly the same now, at twenty-six, as he did when he was sixteen and running cross-country in high school. He runs five miles every morning before breakfast and swims sixty laps every evening when he comes home from work. I hope you don't mind if we don't eat out when you're here. Maybe you and I can sneak a lunch but we mustn't tell Taylor. He detests all restaurants. We buy nothing but organically grown vegetables and fruit and chicken. We used to eat fish too but Taylor's reading has convinced him that the ocean fish are poisoned and fresh-water fish are worse. We eat well, of course, but it's not an exotic menu. We grow our own herbs and we season with those. Since you don't smoke I know that wouldn't be a problem. Taylor's a fanatic about smoking. He's even worse on the subject of alcohol but I told him weeks ago that drinks would definitely be served while you were here. He struggled for days with that idea but we finally laid in some gin and dry vermouth and a few decent bottles of wine. So a few of the evils of the outside world will be permitted while you're with us.'

Taylor, in person, was indeed as slim as a reed. When he appeared late afternoon in his tank briefs to do his rain-or-shine sixty laps, each bone, muscle and tendon in his body seemed prepared for inclusion on a medical chart, ready for labelling. When he swam his body knifed through the water making scarcely a ripple. Later when he had showered and dressed, he seemed like a man who had never in his life been exposed to dirt or grime. Indeed his skin had a sheen to it as though it had been starched or varnished.

At dinner Taylor presided over the table like a resident surgeon. Each item of food was served from his station at the head of the table. Carving knife, fork and ladle were handled like the instruments in an operating theatre. The nasty wine service, however, was left to other hands. Betsy, at the opposite end of the table served herself and Floyd, a communion-size sip for herself and a proper robust glass for her stepfather. Taylor, when the wine was being poured, busied himself with other matters, averted his eyes, and carefully dabbed at the corners of his mouth as though drops of the hateful wine had somehow managed to leap across the table and stain his thin lips.

He seemed incapable of simple social conversation, speaking and listening in turn, give and take. Taylor either lectured at length on some area of his extended expertise, inviting no opinions or outside contributions and ignoring those that came uninvited, or he simply withdrew. He carefully dissected the vegetables and shreds of pale chicken on his plate and lifted them in small bites to his barely opened mouth, his eyes glazed over; while Betsy and Floyd conversed he seemed far away, returning to table only when there was a gap in the conversation which permitted him to begin an enlightening discourse on the potential damage posed to human intestines by the sand in an oyster.

Betsy seemed not to notice her husband's social pecularities. She moved ahead steadily through the evening meals, the only times when she and Floyd and Taylor were all together, kept herself and the conversation afloat and smilingly ignored the advice from the head of the table that she must chew each bite sixty times. Otherwise, she was loving and attentive to her husband and gave little indication that his views were not identical with her own.

Floyd noticed, however, as the days of his visit went by, that she spoke much less frequently of Taylor when they were alone in the afternoon with the children. And twice, during the last evenings that Floyd was in Santa Barbara, she insisted that she be allowed to take him to local restaurants while Taylor stayed home and massaged his daughters with a mixture of buttermilk, goat urine and eucalyptus oil.

For his part, Floyd never made the slightest reference to any of Taylor's rather specialized characteristics. When they were together, the three of them, he took his cue from Betsy and simply forged ahead, offering up no contradictory opinions, and failing to hear, by choice, much of the instruction that was offered to him from his host.

During one of his two restaurant evenings alone with Betsy he asked her if she thought very often of her mother.

'Every day,' she said. 'Usually several times a day. How about you?'

'I think about her a lot.'

'Sad thoughts or not sad.'

'Not sad for the most part.'

'The same with me,' Betsy said. 'At first it used to surprise me. I told myself I was just editing out the bad stuff, especially the rotten way she and my dad died. But finally I realized that the stuff I remembered was the real truth, the way she was. So now I think of her that way all the time, almost all the time. It's a pleasant experience for me. I don't try to fight it. I sit by myself watching Jenny and Julie play, and all sorts of things about Jeannette come into my head. She was an interesting woman. Lots of electricity in her that most people weren't aware of. Am I right?'

Floyd nodded. 'Sometimes I think she should never have left Crawfordsville, Indiana. And the next moment I decide she should have left when she was sixteen years old.'

'When you left.'

'I was a little older than that. But I often think that if I hadn't left, if Jeannette and I had got married when we were kids, the way we wanted to, that neither of us would ever have left that nice little town.'

'And?'

'And what?'

'Would it have worked,' Betsy said. 'Would you have stayed married?'

'Who knows? Most people who get married in those towns stay married, don't they?'

'Mom and Dad didn't.'

'I know they didn't.'

'Can I ask you a tough question,' she said then, 'one that's none of my business?'

'Shoot.'

'After Jeannette and my dad got a divorce, when you and she got married, did it work? I mean did it really work? If she hadn't been . . . I mean if Dad hadn't gone crazy the way he did and run her over in that parking lot, do you think the two of you would have stayed together?'

'We'd had our problems. I won't lie to you about that. But she was heading for New York to meet me the day she died. I think we would have stayed together. What do you think?'

'I always thought you would have. But then when you married Valerie, I wasn't sure. I knew you'd met her a long time before and I thought...I don't know what I thought.'

For a moment Floyd was tempted to tell Betsy the whole story about himself and Valerie but he decided against it. Instead he said, 'The first time I met Valerie she was married and had three little children. As I remember we didn't even like each other very much in those days. But after Jeannette died and Jesse and Valerie got a divorce, we ended up together. After all those years.'

'And you're happy together, aren't you?'

Floyd nodded. 'We're very lucky. And we know it.'

After a long moment Betsy said, 'I had an adviser in college who said the key to contentment is acceptance. He said you can't keep changing directions and second-guessing yourself. He said all of us make bad decisions and bad choices sometimes. And some of them can't be changed. At the time I thought he was mistaken. Now I'm not so sure. What do you think?'

'I don't know, Betsy. That's a tough one to answer. I've certainly made my share of mistakes. But I can't be sure I've learned anything from them. If I make a bad choice next week, I have a hunch I won't handle it any better than the bad choices I made twenty years ago. Most people don't really learn anything during their lives. They just build up scar tissue so the bumps and bruises don't hurt so much.'

She smiled. 'Taylor thinks everything can be learned and everything can be managed. He'd go crazy if he heard us talking like this.'

'Then it's a good thing he's not here,' Floyd said.

[11]

'Almost every woman I've met is like a walking autobiography,' Rab said. 'As soon as the introductions are over they begin talking about themselves. It's quite remarkable. I've heard the most astounding confessions from ladies I'd met only a quarter of an hour before.'

'I know,' Dorsey said. 'I hate that. But you must realize that men are no different. Oscar has friends who can make or break whole corporations with a single telephone call, but they sob and whimper like babies about their bedroom and bathroom secrets to any woman who will listen.'

It was the third afternoon she had come to meet Rab at the house in Grantham Place. They'd been asleep but were awake now, pale light slanting through the shutters, her head on his shoulder.

'Shall I tell you my intimate bedroom secrets?' Rab said.

'Not necessary. I already know them.'

'What I started to say a moment ago,' Rab went on, 'was that I know very little about you. Do you realize that?'

'You know everything that means anything. You just don't know historical facts. We don't need historical facts, do we?'

'No. But it's normal for a few things to come out, isn't it?'

'Maybe. But we've been busy with more important things. Eating and sleeping and running back and forth to this marvellous secret place in this empty building. Have you scheduled it for demolition yet?'

He shook his head. 'Not yet. I'm waiting to see how you behave. If you're prompt and obedient and cheerful, if you continue to perform your duties well, I may be able to postpone demolition indefinitely.'

She touched his face with her hand. 'It doesn't matter,' she said. 'I'm very happy here but when this building comes down we'll find another place.'

'What if I get tired of you?'

'Then I'll do ugly things to you with a sharp knife.'

'What if you get tired of me?'

'I won't. I'm accustomed to you now.'

'In such a short time?' he said.

'It seems like a long time to me. I can't remember what I did with my afternoons before I knew you.'.

'Lunch with boring ladies. Trips to the National Gallery.'

'Not me,' she said. 'Not often at any rate. I'm a loner. Very capable of spending the day by myself.'

'Before you met me.'

'That's right. Before I met you. Independent before. Very dependent now.'

'How long have you been married?' Rab said then.

'Historical facts?'

'If you like.'

'What makes you think I *am* married?' she asked.

'Because you said you were, Oscar said he was, and you were introduced that way.'

150

She smiled. 'I am married. But I don't feel married. Especially since I met you. Actually Oscar and I have been married for twelve years. Since my kid was a year old.'

'What's his name – your son?'

'Charlie Larkin Mullet. Oscar adopted him officially when we got married.'

'What about his father?'

'His father and I weren't married. We weren't much of anything. He was a photographer's model trying to become an actor and I was a farm girl from Nebraska trying to survive in New York. His name was Sam Shriner, at least that was the name he used for work. He came from St Petersburg, Florida, and he was so beautiful it made your eyes hurt to look at him. But somewhere along the line he'd been spoiled rotten. He said his family were poor people – his mother was a Seminole Indian, he told everyone – but he acted like a spoiled rich kid. Sweet and polite to everyone, but never thinking about anything except what *he* wanted and what *he* needed. Did you ever meet anyone like that? Soft-spoken and reasonable, almost apologetic. But underneath there's a layer of steel – or scrap-iron in Sam's case – and you know that nothing will budge that person an inch off the course he's selected for himself.'

'What did he do when he found out you were going to have a baby?'

'He didn't do anything,' Dorsey said. 'I wasn't surprised. I didn't expect him to do anything. I almost didn't tell him because I knew there was no point. But finally, when I did tell him, he was very sweet about it. Like he was about everything. He was so touched I thought he was going to cry. But a couple of days later I had a letter from him. Special delivery, delivered to the place where I was working. He wrote that he was already married to a girl in St Petersburg. And he said he'd send me some money as soon as he got back to Florida. But I never heard from him again. I didn't expect to. And it was just as well. I'd never thought of Sam as a man I could spend my life with. He was just beautiful and I was stupid.'

'So what happened after he left?'

'The two girls I lived with – they worked at the same place I did – told me I was crazy to try to have the baby. They arranged something with a doctor they knew about in Queens and I was all

151

set to go through with it. But when the time came, I couldn't. I thought I'd go back to Nebraska and stay with my folks till my time came but my dad wouldn't hear of it. As soon as he found out I was pregnant and wasn't going to get married he gave my mother her orders and she had to listen because that's the way things are at our house. My dad's a strict Swedish Lutheran and he's a deacon in the church there at North Platte so there was no way to reason with him. And I didn't want to reason with him anyway, once my mom told me how he felt. So, I stayed in New York. I worked as long as I could. Then I sat at home in the apartment and waited. Charlie was very co-operative. He was six weeks premature so I didn't have to wait too long. Not long after he was born, two or three months later, when I saw he was fat and healthy, eating like a little animal and sleeping through the night, I found a nice Ukrainian lady to look after him and I went back to work. I'd never looked so well in my life and I'd never felt so miserable. I loved my little boy but I felt as if my life was over. Then I met Oscar. I hadn't been going out with men at all and I certainly wasn't interested in going out with *him*. I'd heard about him, of course. I knew he was connected with the motion-picture business. And I'd seen stories about him in the newspapers, but there was nothing about him that appealed to me. One of my room-mates said, "He has a face that looks as though it's worn out three bodies." And that's true. But my other room-mate thought he had the most beautiful hands she'd ever seen. And he does have nice hands. Anyway, he kept after me so finally I did go to the theatre with him one night and we had supper later. Oscar's a good talker, as you know, and he had a lot of funny stories to tell about his Hungarian relatives. And he knew all the gossip about the film people he'd worked with. So I can't say it wasn't a pleasant evening. But when I said good-night to him that evening I had no intention of seeing him again. I knew about his reputation with women but to me he was like a man my father's age. Actually, he's three years older than my father.'

'So what happened then?' Rab asked.

'All sorts of things happened. All at once. One of my room-mates decided to get married and the other one decided to go home to Toronto. When I spoke to the landlord about taking over the lease for the apartment he said his son was entering graduate school at Columbia and he needed the apartment for him. That meant when

152

my room-mates moved, I would have to move, too. I knew I couldn't afford to rent a place by myself and I also knew I'd have trouble finding room-mates who'd want to live with a little baby. But I started looking anyway. And the longer I looked, the more desperate I got. Finally I reached a point where I had ten more days before I had to vacate the apartment. Just then Charlie started running a high fever and I had to take him to the hospital. He had some sort of bronchial infection and two days later it turned into pneumonia. It was early December in New York and already very cold. When the doctor at the hospital took me into his office to talk about Charlie he said, "I don't want you to think that you don't have a strong little boy. You do. The X-rays don't show any organic weakness in his lungs." But then he talked about how bad the winters can be in New York and said I should be especially careful that Charlie didn't catch cold because he could have a recurrence of the bronchial trouble and if that became a pattern at his age it could be a serious problem. Can you imagine how I felt when I walked out of that hospital that night? As if I didn't have enough grief, an icy rain was falling. I couldn't find a taxi, and I walked fourteen blocks, cold and soaked through, crying my eyes out. And when I got home finally and stripped off my wet clothes to take a bath there was no hot water. So I started to cry all over again. I wasn't feeling sorry for myself. I was just trying to think what I would have done if I'd been trying to bring Charlie home that night. And how I would manage in a few days when I did bring him home. None of the questions had any answers. When the phone rang I was sobbing too hard to answer it. It stopped ringing but a few minutes later it started again. As soon as I answered, Oscar's voice said, "What's the matter with you?" and I said, "Nothing. I can't talk now." After I hung up the phone rang again, for a long time. Finally it stopped. Twenty minutes later my downstairs doorbell rang. When I answered the intercom, Oscar's voice said, "This is Oscar Mullet. If you don't open the door I'll be back in ten minutes with the police and they'll open it."

'I let him in,' Dorsey went on, 'and I managed to pull myself together. I put on dry clothes and we went downstairs to an all-night café. Oscar drank coffee, I ate soup and a chicken sandwich, and we talked, or rather I talked, for almost two hours. When I finished he just sat there looking at me for a long time. Finally he said, "All right. Here's what we're going to do." He told me he

153

was leaving for Egypt in three days and would be gone for six months. "But before I leave," he said, "I'm putting you and your son on a plane to Phoenix. I have a house there in Scottsdale. I'll arrange to have you met at the airport and taken there. There's a cook and a gardener to look after things and a car for you to drive. You'll be under no obligation to me. You can stay there as long as you like or you can leave after a week if you want to." '

'What did you say?' Rab asked.

'I said I couldn't do it. But Oscar said I couldn't do anything else. And I knew he was right. I didn't have much choice.'

'So you went to Arizona?'

'That's right. All the way there on the plane I told myself I was making a mistake. And when the driver met us at the airport and drove us to Scottsdale I still felt as though I'd made a bad decision. But after a week had gone by, as I saw the marvellous change in Charlie, as I watched him playing in the sun every morning and splashing in the wading pool, I knew I'd done the only thing I could do. I stopped feeling strange and out of place. I just felt lucky and wonderful.'

'And how do you feel now?'

'Right here? With you?'

'No. How do you feel about the choice you made?'

'I told you. I didn't have a choice. I did what I had to. And you may not like the sound of this, but under the same circumstances I would probably do the same thing again. When I was truly desperate Oscar gave me something I needed. And when the time came I felt obligated to pay my debt.'

'Very businesslike.'

'Not at all,' she said. 'It's not as cold-blooded as it sounds. I've never been in love with Oscar and he knows it. But if I hated him I couldn't have stayed with him on any terms. I've heard people say he's the cruellest man in the movie business but he's never been cruel to me. They say he's vengeful and he is. I've seen him spend twenty thousand dollars on legal fees to win a five-thousand-dollar judgment. He's capable of firing an actor even if he knows the film they're working on will be a failure without him. He's a crazy man in all kinds of ways. Untruthful and dishonest and deceitful. But in relation to me and Charlie, he's been at his best. That doesn't make me love him but it's allowed me to live with him and be married to him without hating myself.'

154

When Floyd stopped in Fort Beck on his way back to Europe from California neither Bill nor Jesse were there. Bill was on a school break and had gone to New York to see Rab, who was there on business. Jesse had gone to Berlin to meet with an editor of *Der Spiegel*.

'Later he's going to stop off in Heidelberg to see Polly,' Helen said.

'How's she getting along?' Floyd said.

'You and Valerie probably know as much as we do. Polly's good about writing letters but you always feel as if she's being careful to include only the good news. According to her nothing in her life could be improved.'

Floyd nodded. 'Sounds familiar. That's pretty much the way she writes to Valerie. Champagne and rose petals.'

'Does Valerie believe her?'

'Of course not. She's met that self-styled genius Polly's living with and so have I.'

'Jesse's never met him. Maybe he will this trip. What's he like?'

'It's hard to say. He's a reasonable-looking guy. Not handsome but a lot of vitality bubbling beneath the surface. Not a big talker, at least not when I met him. Very quiet. But if he was a stray dog you'd never let your kids play with him. Polly says he's brilliant and I don't doubt that. But there's something strange in the mix. At least that was my reaction. Something that makes you wary.'

'Does Valerie feel the same about him as you do?'

'Not exactly. She wants to like him. She tries to see him as Polly sees him. And Valerie's a woman, so of course she reacts to him differently than I do. But all the same, there's something about him that scares her. So we don't discuss him very much. She just stays in touch with Polly and hopes for the best.'

'I'm glad I don't have a daughter,' Helen said. 'I think I'd worry about her constantly, whether she was married or not.'

Floyd smiled. 'Does that mean you don't worry about your son?'

'I think about you a lot but I don't worry. You've been in charge of your life since the first day I met you.'

'In charge maybe, but not in control. You were lucky. Most of my escapades were behind me by the time we found each other.'

'That's a nice way of putting it,' Helen said.

'How's that?'

'You said, "By the time we *found* each other." That's a gentle way of saying it. I know it's a long way behind us now but does it ever bother you still that I gave you up when you were a baby, that I let someone else take you and raise you?'

He shook his head. 'I'm a lucky guy, Helen. I don't mean I haven't had problems but most of them I brought on myself. I was raised by nice people. They did the best they could for me. And ever since you found me again, it's been one good thing after another.'

'Not exactly,' Helen said. 'You had some problems in California.'

'That was nobody's fault but mine,' he said. 'But even there I was lucky. If it hadn't been for you and Paul I could *really* have been in trouble. And the bad stuff with Jeannette was something that nobody could have foreseen. When I count my blessings I just ignore all that.'

'How does Betsy handle it now? Has she managed to put it behind her?'

'I doubt it. But she's not tortured by it. She's a terrific young woman. Out of all that chaos between her mother and father she turned out calm and smooth.'

'And now she's married with two daughters of her own.'

'That's right,' Floyd said.

'And what's her husband like?'

'Don't ask.'

'What does that mean?'

'It means he's a consummate jackass.'

'You're kidding. That was a college romance, wasn't it? I thought they'd been together since she was nineteen or twenty.'

'They have. He was a great athlete and a scholarship student. The works. But I can't believe he wasn't different then from the way he is now.'

'How do you mean? What's he like?'

'He's a martinet. When the computer age finally comes, they'll be able to use him as a model. He's against social security but in favour of war. Politically, he lines up just to the right of Calvin Coolidge. He thinks every word of the Bible is literal truth. He thinks any physical ailment can be cured by a high colonic. He is eager to do the laundry and the cooking but he's violently opposed

156

to all forms of contraception. He worships the music of Wagner and thinks Mussolini was the most misunderstood man in history. He takes a laxative every day and his favourite food is jellybeans.'

Helen was laughing. 'I don't believe you. You're making it up.'

'I wish I were. I'm only hitting the high points.'

'Does he work? What does he do for a living?'

'Very successful. Started his own insurance company when he was still in school at North-western. Perfect business for him. All statistics and actuarial tables. Owns three insurance companies now. And two years ago he started a real estate development firm. Bought fifteen miles of ocean-front property north of Santa Barbara. He told me one evening as he was sipping Kool-aid that he never discharges an executive once he's hired him. He simply has the telephone and all the furniture and files removed from the man's office and replaced with a card table and a folding chair. He says one man stayed on for a month but most of them leave in a few days.'

'My God,' Helen said. 'He sounds like a monster.'

'He'd be shocked to hear you say that. Betsy says he thinks of himself as a kind and benevolent man. She says he's very sentimental.'

'My father used to say that sentimentality and cruelty come in the same package.'

Floyd nodded. 'I couldn't very well say that to Betsy.'

'Of course not. But how does she handle the situation?'

'I think she handles it by looking the other way. She concentrates on her children and the Santa Barbara weather and doesn't permit herself to make judgments. And I imagine she remembers the young man he used to be and tries to ignore the self-righteous idiot he's become.'

'She can't keep that up for ever, can she?'

'Hard to say. Seems to me that Betsy is determined to have stability in her life. She's not like her mother, and doesn't want to be. So I think she's prepared to ignore a great many things. She'll sacrifice whatever it is she may have to sacrifice.'

'For the rest of her life?'

'Who knows?'

The first night Floyd spent in Fort Beck, he and Helen went to a restaurant just outside town that overlooked the Boone River.

'A few years have gone by since you and I came here the first time. I was fresh out of the Navy.'

'Looking very cute in your sailor suit,' Helen said.

'Jesus, I hated the Navy.'

'I know you did.'

'Wasn't cut out for that life. I'm not big on regimentation. Never was, even as a kid. Never felt great about taking orders from people. Especially when I could see that the guy giving the orders was an idiot. If you hadn't handed me a silver spoon I think I'd have been in trouble. Walking down the road. Sleeping in the fields.'

'I doubt that.'

'When I was a kid bumming around, after I ran away from home, I used to get fired from every job I tried. I really had a chip on my shoulder. I got to the point where I was ready to punch a guy as soon as he hired me.'

'And now you don't want to punch anybody.'

'That's right. Now I'm a pussycat. Friend to mankind.'

'Except Betsy's husband.'

'That's right. He could use a couple of good whacks. But he's probably a judo fanatic. He'd beat me up and then I'd have to get a gun and kill the bastard.'

After they'd placed their order Helen said, 'I'm sorry you missed Jesse.'

'I'm not. It's good to see you by yourself. We have to check in once in a while to make sure we still like each other.'

'You and Jesse never really hit it off, did you?'

'Is that what he says?'

'He doesn't say anything. He certainly never says anything bad about you.'

'That's nice.'

'I mean, he doesn't resent it that you and Valerie ended up together. At least I've never seen any sign of that.'

'He can resent it if he wants to,' Floyd said. 'It doesn't matter to me.'

'What I meant was that you two weren't wild about each other from the beginning, when you went with me to Wingate Fields that first time, isn't that true?'

'Is that what he says?'

Helen shook her head. 'I told you, he doesn't say anything. It's just a feeling I had then. And I still have it.'

'I don't know the answer. We were always like a couple of fighters feeling each other out. He didn't know what to make of me and I didn't know what to make of him. When I first met him he made me feel like a trespasser. I'm not saying he did it deliberately . . .'

'I'm sure he didn't,' Helen said.

' . . . but the effect was the same. Every time I saw him I always felt as if we were sparring with each other. There seemed to be something at stake but I was never quite sure what it was. It certainly wasn't Valerie, not at the beginning. Maybe it was you. Anyway, all that's beside the point now. Jesse and I are never going to be warm good friends any more than he and Frank Wilson are going to be warm good friends.'

'I suppose you're right. I wish it could be different but I guess it never will.'

'If we all lived in the same town maybe we'd work out some civilized arrangement but since we live on separate continents Jesse and I can dislike each other as much as we want to.'

'That's true. But you can't blame me for wishing.'

'I mentioned Frank Wilson,' Floyd said then. 'Or did you mention him?'

'You did.'

'What's happening with him?'

'I don't know,' Helen said. 'I haven't seen him or talked with him for a while. He's married again, perhaps I told you that, and I guess he's semi-retired now. But he's always negotiating some sort of deal. He used to say that when he's buried he wants a telephone in his coffin. Just in case someone's trying to reach him.'

Floyd smiled. 'I never figured out what you and Frank were all about.'

'Neither did I.'

'A long time after you got a divorce, you got together again.'

'That's right. Some people get along better when they're not married.'

'Like you and Jesse maybe?'

'I wasn't talking about Jesse,' Helen said. 'I was talking about Frank.'

'Have Jesse and Frank ever met each other?'

159

'No. There's no reason why they should.'

'I suppose not.' Then, 'Do all families have the kind of tangled lives the Bradshaws have?'

'I don't know. That sort of thing doesn't matter much to me at any rate. I've never been much good at making charts or drawing conclusions. I have to live my life in little pieces. One small section at a time. That's all I can handle.'

Chapter Four

On plane trips, however long the flight, Jesse had always made it a practice never to write, or to plan, or to think about his work. He considered such flights a kind of musical rest, an opportunity to let his thoughts wander or to have no thoughts at all, a chance to sleep or dream, or drink champagne or watch a mindless movie. Or simply to sit with his eyes closed and allow his subconscious self to direct him along any path it might choose.

On this flight from Chicago to Berlin, however, Jesse took out a pen and a pad of paper and began to write almost as soon as the plane was airborne.

Is it dangerous for a man to contradict or redefine a lifetime of self-deception? Or is it beneficial perhaps? Is it possible to look at yourself naked, in full light, when always before you had permitted yourself to be seen only when bewigged, disguised, and in shadow?

I believe, I choose to believe, I have forced myself to believe, that at last all the *maquillage* must be taken away and the padded costumes put aside. What might have been or what might still be, cannot be substituted for what is. You are what you are, you must be *seen* that way, or you're nothing.

It is clear to me now that I was always skilled at deception. From the start I had a talent to deceive. A genetic gift from my father? Perhaps. Or in saying that, am I continuing to pass to him responsibilities that are not properly his? Probably. That's a habit I formed many years ago. Also, many years ago, I remember that I carefully studied the behaviour of my brother, Leo, and my sister, Doris. I noted and remembered what sort of pranks and oversights and falsehoods got them into trouble with our parents. Observing the resultant reprimands and punishments, I fashioned my own actions in such a way that I would under all circumstances appear guiltless. When I was in danger of being found out, I found a way to shift the blame to Doris or Leo, or I simply lied. I became a master at lying. When I was obviously innocent, however, I tried to take the blame for transgressions which were clearly those of my brother or my sister. Not only did it confuse the two of them but it caused my mother to think of me as a saintly child. The day I overheard her saying to my father, 'Jesse would rather be punished himself than to see his sister punished,' I realized – I was perhaps eight years old at the time – that I had fashioned a coat of moral armour for myself that, if properly maintained, might protect me for ever from parental discipline.

My mother, in those years, was totally persuaded by my guile. My father, less so. His instinct, perhaps, was keener than his intelligence, and that instinct told him, I believe, that I was shamming. Because of that, I see now that he never trusted me. That lack of trust surely put a stamp on our father/son relationship. The tales of neglect and insensitivity that have characterized my descriptions of my father through the years may not have been totally inaccurate but they were certainly incomplete. Somewhere along the line I concluded that my own shortcomings could best be concealed or justified by the existence of a certain kind of parent. I then carefully constructed that creature and passed him off to strangers as my father.

The same technique that I employed at home I carried along with me to school. Loud-mouth and rough-and-tumble in the Chicago schoolyards to impress my peers, and quiet concentration in the classroom to ensure the approval of my teachers. Also occasional hints that my life at home was not what it might have been. In those years, in Chicago, teachers were not surprised when parents failed to visit the schools to enquire about their children's progress. But in my case, because I carefully explained, always, why my mother and father were unable to visit school on parents' night, their absence was always noted by my teachers. Certain conclusions were then drawn which enhanced my image.

By my twelfth birthday, bolstered by my imagination, my reading, and my weekly attendance at Saturday movies, I had come to believe that I was destined for a future that was in no way indicated or guaranteed by my family background. I simply believed there would be *developments*, that certain things would happen. Since I had no inkling of what I wanted to happen or how it might come to pass, I simply waited with full confidence for the genie to appear.

By the time I was fifteen I was still waiting. My unique qualities continued to be invisible to my family and to the rest of the world. My brother, Leo, on the other hand, was not only working and wearing a made-to-measure suit, he was in the process of buying his own automobile. Even Doris, whom I thought of as pretty in a cheap way but barely literate, had found a job selling bon-bons and glazed fruit in the lobby of a near north-side variety theatre and, if one was to believe Leo, had caught the eye of the gentleman who owned that theatre.

When an essay I had written for a city-wide contest received only an honourable mention, it seemed no honour at all to me. Seeing my name in such a listing was only humiliating evidence that my work did not deserve a prize. And when a letter came later from Raymond Bradshaw, who identified himself as one of the judges for the essay contest, that, too, meant nothing to me. After reading the complimentary things he had written, my reaction was, 'If he liked the damned thing so much, why didn't he give me a prize?'

I kept his letter, however, and hid it in my bureau drawer at home. And while I waited for more dramatic developments I occasionally fished it out and read it over. With nothing else to fuel my fantasies, that letter began to take on greater importance and Raymond Bradshaw began to increase in stature until at last he seemed like a gateway to the future. When my father announced that his employer would be opening a new restaurant in San Francisco and had invited him to come along, to bring his family and settle there in the west, I made another choice: Fort Beck and Raymond Bradshaw.

From the time he opened his front door, when I identified myself and he let me in, I knew I'd found a place where I wanted

165

to stay. I had been inside schools and libraries built of stone but never a private house. I had no idea how much crystal chandeliers cost, or Chinese urns, or Persian carpets, but I knew I was in an atmosphere that was new to me. New but not foreign. I knew that very first day that I wanted to be a Bradshaw. If I'd been closely questioned, if I'd had the courage to be truthful I think I would have said, 'I don't want a house *like* this. I want *this* house.' Did Raymond know what was going through my mind? Perhaps he did. But if he did, it didn't matter. Or if it mattered, it didn't matter so much that he thought less of me.

Does this mean, does *all* this mean, that my devotion to Raymond, my admiration of him, were constructed and contrived as covers for a newly discovered sense of greed and acquisition? Did I foresee from the beginning that a kind of life, a kind of munificence, I'd never even dreamed of might open up for me? Of course not. But the need to be something I had never imagined I could be, the need to have things, own things, possess things, that need which grew and spread inside me like a tumour surely began during those first days in Raymond's house in Fort Beck.

These facts, these feelings that I acknowledge freely now, were not of course so clear to me at the time. And if they had come clear then, I would never have acknowledged them, even to myself. I was so occupied with trying to earn the position and the rewards that I longed for that I was blinded to any motive or impulse that could have labelled me unworthy. As the months went by, as I could feel myself becoming a part of the household, as the servants and the neighbours, Raymond's colleagues at the school, and then Helen, came to accept me as openly as Raymond did, I was tortured still at times by the thought that I was deceiving myself, that a day would come when I would realize, or be bluntly told that what I had mistaken for reality was in fact an elaborate charade. Long after Raymond's death, after I had been adopted by his father, Angus, after I was legally and permanently and unquestionably a Bradshaw, even then I had searing suspicions that someone, some day, some white-wigged court official perhaps, would bring it all to a peremptory close. Now that circumstances have taken me away, and will undoubtedly keep me away, from my beloved Wingate Fields, perhaps the thing I feared has already happened. I'm back where I began, in Fort Beck. With Helen, with the Bradshaw name, and the Brad-

166

shaw money. But I'm struggling to find out what I traded away for all that. And if there's any way I can get back what I gave up.

[2]

'How's your love-life?' Rab said. He and Bill were having dinner at an Italian restaurant named Verdicchio in Greenwich Village.

'None of your business, big mouth. I wouldn't tell you anything unless I wanted it in the London tabloids.'

'Naughty, naughty. I'm your brother. Your only brother. it's important that we both remember that. I have a great number of business friends and business enemies and well-tailored sycophants who think I may throw a few thousand pounds their way, but I have only one brother.'

'This is odd. I'd never realized what a tender fellow you are.'

'*Responsible* is the word, as I see it. I'm the eldest. Family obligations and all that. In addition to my other activities in the world of commerce, I see it as my job to hold the family together.'

'A little late for that, isn't it? The Bradshaws exploded in a dozen different directions when Clara died. Bodies flying everywhere. Taking root wherever they fell. Last time I checked my address book, you were the only Bradshaw left in England. And judging from the postmarks on those cards you keep sending me, you're abroad more often than you're in London. I'm surprised you haven't turned Wingate into a film studio, or an animal park.'

'I don't know if you're being educated at that dreary school you've found but you've certainly taken a sudden turn for the clever. I remember you as basically dull but sincere. Instead you've gone rotten clever on me.'

'I've turned American. All Americans are clever.'

'Not the ones I deal with. Dead serious chaps for the most part. They all speak like solicitors. I never trust that lot. Most men with a legal turn of mind seem to be planning something that's not legal at all.'

'Never mind that. I'm more interested in this mission of yours to hold the family together. What sort of plans have you made?'

167

'No immediate plans. Just planting a few seeds here and there. Reminders. Keeping the pot boiling.'

'I don't know what the hell you're talking about.'

'Of course you do,' Rab said. 'This is a bit of a transition period in the family. People scattered here and there. Doing things they feel must be done. But all that will get sorted out. And at last there will be a great pilgrimage back to Wingate Fields.'

'Are you serious?'

'Extremely. This is vital business. Vital to all of us.'

'Who do you expect to be the first pilgrim to go back?'

'Hard to say. It wouldn't surprise me to see our mother back there before long. She loves the place. And continuity means something to her. Tradition. Keeping things together.'

'Valerie giving instructions to the staff and Floyd clumping about the box stalls in rubber boots. Is that it?'

'Why not?'

'And maybe Jesse will come back and take over the west wing. He and Helen can have Valerie and Floyd in for tea on the odd Thursday.'

'Not impossible, old cock. They all have strong ties with Northumberland.'

'And strong ties with each other. And some of them *used* to have strong ties with each other but don't have them any longer. What about Nora? You see her taking up residence in her old rooms, pruning roses in the garden? Breeding spaniels to kill time?'

'Odd sense of humour you've developed over here. Is this the frontier humour I've read about? Tying a man's feet together with his shoelaces . . . that sort of thing?'

'I don't see much humour in *this* subject,' Bill said. 'This is obviously something that's important to you so I'm taking it seriously. Since we have a limited number of people available who might qualify as lord and lady of the manor I was just trying to go through the list with you. With all due respect to your suggestions so far, I think *you're* the logical choice. Eldest son, a head for business. Certainly a logical candidate for a sensible marriage to a lovely county girl. Or maybe you could persuade Gloria Atwood to give up the theatre and live the bucolic life with you at Wingate.'

'Odd you should mention Gloria. She's just back in London.'

'And back in your bed?'

'Not a delicate question,' Rab said.

'Not meant to be. You enquired about my love-life. Now I'm enquiring about yours.'

'It's obvious you're not being serious but I will give you a serious answer all the same. Before Gloria went off to Canada some months ago we made changes in our arrangement.'

'Does that mean you broke up?'

'Not exactly. We simply tried to make some adjustments. She was going off on a new adventure, doing exciting work, so I thought it wasn't fair for her to be tied to a man four or five thousand miles away.'

'*You* thought that or *she* did?'

'We agreed.'

'I see,' Bill said. 'But now she's back and life goes on as before.'

Rab shook his head. 'Not precisely. After all, several months have gone by.'

'So she's not back in your bed.'

'We're not living together if that's what you mean. She's back in the mews house in Talley Lane, and I'm still in the house in Sloane Square. We've seen quite a bit of each other, actually. But I'm busy night and day and she has her career to look after so it's a difficult time to make long-term plans.'

'What about all those plans you were talking about two or three years ago? Gloria was going to become world-renowned and you would be her Svengali. Motion pictures, West End productions, and a distinguished series of masterpieces to be presented on the telly.'

'Nothing's changed. Just a matter of priorities. I've been acquiring a great number of theatres, some in London, others all over Britain. A few of them will be converted to multiple cinemas. That's the future – five films being shown in a building where there was only one screen before. But most of those theatres we'll just board up and hold on to. They're all in prime locations, valuable land, so they'll be profitable for demolition or resale later. Office blocks, that's where the profits will be in ten years or so.'

'You're a tycoon, Rab. I'm impressed.'

'Not at all. All round me men are scrambling to make money. I already have money so I'm just amusing myself. And in the process I'm making more money than anyone. Swelling the Bradshaw coffers.'

'I'm proud of you. But let's get back to Gloria. If you're giving

169

up on her maybe I'll let her know that I'm available. How does that strike you?'

'Are you serious?'

'Sure. Why not? I like her. I never thought she was your type at all.'

'That's not the question,' Rab said. 'The critical question is whether or not I'm her type.'

'That's what I'm trying to find out. Are you two still connected or not?'

'You *are* serious.'

'Of course I'm serious.'

'Then I'll give you a serious answer. If I were forced to wager a thousand pounds on whether or not Gloria and I would be together a year from now I would bet against it. But because of certain other matters that have nothing to do with her and me it's important that we continue to give the impression that we're together.'

'Important to you or important to her?'

'Important to me. Gloria knows nothing about the real situation.'

'What is the real situation?' Bill asked.

'The real situation is extremely tricky.'

'That means you're not going to tell me.'

'Not at all. It just means I can't tell you all the details,' Rab said. 'The truth is I'm involved with a married woman.'

'The first time you told me that was six years ago.'

'That was a dust storm, Billy. This is an earthquake.'

'Does her husband know about it?'

Rab shook his head. 'I wish he did.'

'Then why don't you tell him?'

'If I did I'd never see her again.'

'What does that mean?'

'It means the situation is complex. I always think I can fix anything. But this is something I can't fix. I feel as if I'm bleeding at every aperture.'

'I can't believe what I'm hearing. What happened to all that advice you used to give me? "No woman is indispensable" – wasn't that what you said? "Find 'em, fuck 'em and forget 'em." *That* was your motto.'

'Don't rub it in.'

'I still can't believe it. How does Gloria fit into all this mess?

'This woman is married to somebody I have business dealings

170

with. So I see him and his wife two or three nights a week. It's important that he associates me with Gloria. That way he won't get suspicious about me and his wife.'

'How does Gloria feel about all this?'

'She doesn't know about it. I think I said that before.'

'Does that mean you're still playing slap and tickle with her while you're waiting for your married lady to have a free afternoon?'

'I can't just kiss her goodnight and leave her at the bloody door.'

'You poor bastard. You're really suffering, aren't you?'

'*That* part's not difficult. I like Gloria. I always have.'

'Then why don't you walk away from this other mess?'

'I can't. You know me. I'd get out of it in a minute if I could. But I can't. There's something so fucking tragic about this woman. Death and transfiguration. I get inside a room with her and I forget who I am and where I come from. I'm locked in. It's like a knife in my gut. I used to have fun with women but this is no fun. It hurts like hell. Still, when I'm not with her, I can't wait to see her again.'

'You're sunk, Rab. She's about to turn you into a warlock.'

'Let's get drunk. I don't want to talk about it any more.' He signalled to the waiter and ordered another bottle of wine.

'I think I'd better take you back to Fort Beck with me. There's a thirty-year-old widow at the school who teaches zoology. I think she could get you back on track again. Or if you don't like her you could pick and choose among the girl students. They like men with British accents. If they heard you talk they'd fall right out of their clothes and start to vibrate.'

'Sounds like they're keeping you busy as well.'

'Not me. I don't slip around. I stick with one lady. Found her the first week I was here. We're in the same art history class. Her name's Bernadette. Comes from Cleveland. We had coffee a few times after class and finally she told me she was engaged to be married to a fellow she knows in Ohio. They've been getting it on since she was fourteen. "Neither one of us has ever cared about anybody else," she said, "but when I'm away from him for months at a time he doesn't expect me to live like a nun." '

'That's what she told you?' Rab said.

Bill nodded. 'That was it.'

'Can't make it any plainer than that.'

'That's right.'

'So you're provided for?'

171

'No doubt about it. I go up the fire escape to the attic of her dormitory seven nights a week. There's a big mattress on the floor there, underneath the eaves, and the floor is insulated so nobody downstairs can hear us. That's the best part for Bernadette. She likes to moan and squeal a lot.'

'How about you?'

'I'm the silent type.'

'So your education's not being neglected?'

'Not at all,' Bill said. 'I'm learning a lot.'

[3]

'I'm going to have a chance to meet your outstanding father,' Jack said. 'Isn't that true?'

Polly shook her head. 'Not if I can help it. I wouldn't subject either one of you to that.'

'You mean you wouldn't subject him to me?'

'No. I meant it the way I said it. I love both of you but you're not required to love each other.'

'I thought you said he wanted to meet me.'

'I did say that. But I told him it was impossible. I told him you were very busy with whatever it is that you and Donny are so busy with and you didn't have time to meet miscellaneous American fathers.'

'Do you think of him as American?'

'I didn't when I was growing up in England. But he was born in America and now he's gone back there. So he's an American by choice as well as by birth. Or so it seems to me.'

'A bit of resentment there, I think. Suppressed anger perhaps.'

'Not at all,' Polly said. 'Why should I be angry at Jesse?'

'Ah-ha, who knows? A woman's anger can flourish in the rockiest soil. You could be sore at him for abandoning your mother.'

'He didn't abandon her. She left him.'

'Can't imagine anyone leaving Valerie. She is a singular woman. Did she think I was a singular man?'

'We don't want to go over all this again, do we?'

'Did we go over it before?' he asked.

'Several times.'

'Slipped my mind.'

'No, it didn't. Nothing ever slips your mind.'

He got up from his chair, walked over to her chair, knelt down and put his arms around her. 'Are you edgy with me?'

'No.'

'Maybe that's the wrong word. Are you impatient, intolerant, or unquiet?'

'None of those things,' she said.

'If you let me meet your mother, why shouldn't I meet your father?'

'Because I know how you'll behave. You'll say and do every outrageous thing you can think of.'

'Unfair,' he said. 'I can't believe your mother gave a bad report about me.'

'She didn't have to, Jack. I was there. You did whatever you could to make an ass of yourself. I know you weren't deliberately trying to humiliate me but if you had been trying you couldn't have done a better job of it.'

'It's almost two years since I met Valerie. Why is all this coming out just now?'

'Because you've been asking why you couldn't meet my father.'

'Good question. Why can't I?'

'Oh, give it up, Jack. I can't understand you when you go on these odd binges just to upset me. What's the point?'

'What exactly did your mother say about me?'

'I told you at the time.'

'I've forgotten.'

'I don't believe you.'

He held up his right hand. 'On my honour.'

'Why are you home tonight?' she said then. 'For three weeks, four maybe, you haven't been at home one single night.'

'Now, I'm home. Turned over my duties to Donny so I can stay home and . . .'

'What duties?'

'Miscellaneous meetings and errands. Donkey work. Freeing the minds of better men. Allowing them to concentrate fully on the job at hand.'

'If I guess what you and Donny are up to, what these weeks of meetings are all about, will you tell me if I'm right?'

173

'If you guess wrong I'll tell you you're right. If you guess correctly I'll tell you you're wrong.'

'In the Frankfurt paper yesterday it said that Albert Speer and Baldur von Schirach will be released from prison soon. Did you know that?'

'I don't read the newspapers. Remember I told you on my birthday I've taken a vow never to read another newspaper.'

'It also said that young Communists at all the universities would be demonstrating against their release. Do you know about that?'

'I'm not political. You know that.'

'I know you say you're not political. But nothing escapes you. You're certainly not going to tell me that Donny isn't political. He's so far left they wouldn't give him a visa to go to East Berlin.'

'That's true. Donny thinks Stalin was a Fascist. And Donny's right. Stalin was a Fascist wearing Socialist pyjamas.'

'You didn't answer my question,' she said.

'Forgive me.' He held up his right hand. 'I am not now nor have I ever been, a member of the Communist party. I have advocated the overthrow of every American President since Roosevelt but I've never advocated the overthrow of the American government.' Then: 'What did your mother say about me?'

'She said you must have received a great deal of negative attention when you were a child.'

'I detest all that psychiatry lingo. Is Valerie a psychiatrist?'

'No.'

'Has she undergone deep analysis, either Freudian or Jungian?'

'No.'

'Are you sure?'

'Yes. She just meant that you're too smart and gifted and basically nice to behave the way you do. She thinks you deliberately alienate people.'

'She's right. That's exactly what I do. Valerie's a perceptive lady. She's cut straight through to the core of my philosophy. It's my credo. You try very hard to alienate everyone you meet. The ones who cannot be alienated are your true and reliable friends. The others can all be discarded.'

'That's sick, Jack. And you know it.'

'Maybe it is sick. Most things are sick. But that doesn't mean it's not true. You should invite your mother up to see us again. Or maybe we'll take a run down to Portugal. I'd like to talk to her

174

in some detail about negative attention. Where does Jesse stand, incidentally, on that subject?'

'Doesn't like it, I'm sure. Most grown-ups don't.'

'But, you see, I don't like most grown-ups. So it evens out.'

'That's another reason why you two should never meet. Because whatever else he may be, Jesse is definitely a grown-up.'

'Then we must meet. As I understand the principle of negative attention it is most often associated with those of us who, for whatever reasons, are locked in our childhood. In my case, I'm sure that any exposure to a bona fide grown-up can only be beneficial. And, who knows, Jesse may benefit from meeting an aging child. Fennellosa said, "Look for the child in the man. It exists in all of us." Rilke said, "Genius is the ability to re-enter childhood at will." And *I* say, "Everything is innocent till someone calls it evil." '

'Please don't make a scene, Jack. I haven't seen Jesse for almost two years. He'll only be here for a day or two. Just give me a chance to spend some time alone with him.'

'Of course I will. I'll sleep out while he's here. When I meet Jesse I'll see him at his hotel. In a public room. People all around. A civilized exchange. Soft voices required. No antipathy or contentiousness. No show of temper.'

'Please, Jack.'

'Wait a minute. I haven't finished. You say I am not able to behave like a grown-up. I plan to prove that I can. I promise to discard my normal procedure of deliberate alienation. Don't look at me like that. I mean it. I guarantee you there will be a report from your father that will astonish you. I think I can predict what he will say. He'll use words like amenable, gracious and reasonable. I'm sure he'll make some reference to my intelligence and my knowledge of world affairs and he'll certainly take notice of the fact that I'm well groomed. I've read quite a number of his critical pieces so I'll be knowledgeable about his work and I will not dwell on my own minor achievements at all. I will compliment him, and defer to him in all things. Without becoming maudlin, I will make sure he understands how much I love and respect his daughter and how much I believe your fine qualities are a result of your training at home. I will also be humble. Can you believe that? It's the truth. I will tap reservoirs of humility that haven't been disturbed in years. Furthermore, I will borrow a packet of marks from Donny so I can

175

pay for Jesse's drinks. It's important that he sees me as not only a civilized and cultured man but a generous one as well. You know me better than anyone else in the world. You know I can do this if I set my mind to it. Whatever his preconceived notions may be I will be able to replace them. And when I've completed the process of self-abnegation and presented him with a courteous and well-scrubbed young man without flaws, do you know what his reaction will be? I can guarantee precisely what his reaction will be. He will *hate* me.'

[4]

When Rab returned to London from New York, Gloria drove to Heathrow to meet him.

'What a fine surprise,' he said. 'How did you know what flight I'd be on?'

'I have a chum at British Airways. She checked the passenger lists for me.'

At the baggage claim area Rab said, 'Where's Russell?'

'I gave him the night off. I'm driving.'

'You're full of surprises, aren't you?'

'A young woman has to be alert,' she said.

Halfway into London she pulled off the motorway into what had once been a small village before the sprawl of the city had absorbed it. 'I'm going to buy you dinner,' she said. 'How does that sound to you?'

'Sounds fine. I'm quite hungry as a matter of fact.'

'I know you never eat airline food. I thought you might enjoy a nice joint of venison.'

She turned into the yard of an old coach house that had been converted into a small and exclusive restaurant.

'Have you eaten here?' she said.

'Twenty times.'

'I don't believe you.'

'More than twenty times actually. And I love it.'

They sat by an open fire, drank a great deal of claret and ate everything that was set before them. She talked about actors and

176

the theatre, what plays were failing and what plays would open in the coming weeks. Rab told her about his business meetings in New York and his dinner with Bill.

'I like Bill,' she said. 'How is he?'

'He's become quite a chap. All angular and filled with self-confidence. Drawing a bit of attention from the ladies in the restaurant. Hair brushed back, tall and lean.'

'I remember him as quite shy.'

'Shy no more. He asked about you quite specifically. I suspect he'd like to lure you into a quiet corner.'

'I'll keep that in mind,' she said. 'I will definitely put that down in my futures book.'

While they were having coffee and cognac Rab said, 'Why do I have the feeling that something's about to happen that I didn't expect?'

'Because you're a perceptive gentleman. Nothing escapes you. Is that correct?'

'Not exactly. Quite a number of things go right past me.'

'Don't fret,' she said. 'It happens to all of us. I've just learned, while you were away, that something strange has been happening to *me*.'

'What's that?'

'I've discovered that you've been making a bloody fool of me.'

'I have? It's news to me.'

'Don't do a dance for me, Rab. This time it won't work. I know about you and Dorsey Mullet.'

'Dorsey Mullet?'

'That's right.'

Rab smiled. 'I can't imagine what you think you know. There's nothing *to* know. You and I have spent several evenings with the Mullets. It's a business relationship. Dorsey's the wife of a man I might do business with.'

'And now you're doing business with *her*. I thought there was something strange in the air the first time I met them. It was all very cordial and friendly. Everyone being dreadfully nice to everyone else. But halfway through the evening I noticed that you and she didn't talk to each other. No contact between you at all. When she talked she spoke to me or her husband but not to you. When you talked, you also spoke to me or to Oscar. But not to her.'

'That's the way she always is. Very little to say. So I don't find much to say to her. She's like an ornament.'

'A beautiful ornament,' Gloria said.

Rab nodded. 'No question about that.'

'Do you know an actor named Abner Swift?' she said then.

'I don't think so.'

'He does character roles. Shakespeare mostly. Came from Birmingham. Still works a lot up there. Also in Edinburgh and Glasgow. In his forties, I suppose. Incurably homosexual. But very bright and gossipy. Fun to spend an evening with. I met him through his cousin, Jocelyn. She was on tour with me in Canada. Anyway, he rang up last week while you were away and asked if I wanted to see Trevor Howard and Coral Browne in *Waltz of the Toreadors*. So I met him at the theatre. After we were seated I noticed Oscar Mullet and his wife seated several rows ahead of us. I thought perhaps I'd see them in the lounge at the interval but they apparently never left their seats. And when the final curtain came down and the lights went up I saw them leaving by a side exit. Abner and I struggled through the crowd to the street. Abner steered me to a spot near the actors' entrance and said, "Let's wait till Coral Browne comes out. I'm a great admirer of her work. Did a Shaw play with her at Bristol three years ago." As we waited there, we could see a line of limousines slowly edging ahead to pick up their owners who'd seen the play we saw. Suddenly Oscar Mullet and Dorsey came out of a small wine bar just beside the theatre and walked to the kerb. As soon as Abner saw them he said, "Ah-ha, there she is . . . the mystery woman."

I almost told him I knew her but for some reason I said nothing. We stood watching from the head of the alley that leads to the performers' entrance and then a most peculiar thing happened. As the Mullets' car pulled up and their driver hurried round to open the door for them, Oscar, who had been smiling and talking with Dorsey, suddenly brought his arm up and struck her in the face. Not a slap. He struck her with his fist. She stumbled back against the car and would have fallen if the driver hadn't caught her and helped her into the rear seat. Oscar stood there calmly as though nothing had happened. Then he also got into the car and the driver closed the door behind him.

'A bit later, when we stopped for a coffee, Abner said, "Drama. Inside the theatre and out. God, how I love it." When I asked him

178

why he'd referred to Dorsey as "the mystery woman", he told me that a chum of his has a flat on Grantham Place. Abner stops there whenever he's in London. Just opposite, he said, is an empty building and several times a week, in the afternoon, he'd seen Dorsey arrive there and go inside. Then a few hours later she'd come out, hail a taxi, and leave. Love in the afternoon.'

'You mean your friend thinks she's meeting a man there?'

'He knows she is. He's seen the man. He described you exactly. Including the dimple in your chin. And that war surplus ski-trooper weather coat you wear when it rains.'

'It wasn't my dimple he saw,' Rab said. 'I'm not ducking into deserted buildings with Oscar Mullet's wife. If I'm to be seduced I prefer a comfortable bed in a proper flat.'

'There is a comfortable bed there,' Gloria said. 'I thought it rang a bell when Abner mentioned Grantham Place. So I strolled round there the next morning to see for sure. You took me there once, Rab. When I first knew you. We'd been to the British Museum and you said, "Come along the street here and I'll show you some buildings I own." It's your building, Rab. It's vacant now, as it was then. With just a uniformed guard outside. And you and Dorsey inside, on selected afternoons.'

'Innocent,' Rab said. 'I plead innocent. Tell your little twat of an actor friend that it's a case of mistaken identity. You can tell him also – and if you don't tell him, I will – that if he spreads any gossip about me, I'll give him a chance to repeat it in court.'

'You're bluffing, my darling, and you know it. It's what I expected. So I rang up Dorsey three days ago. When she invited me to tea, I accepted.'

'You told her what you've just told me?'

'Of course not. I learned my fencing technique with a foil not a broadsword. We chatted about gowns and hairdressers and the latest fragrance from Lancôme. And little by little I eased into the subject of men. From there it was very easy to bring you on stage so to speak. She seemed quite curious about our relationship, especially since I came back to London from Canada.'

'What did you tell her?'

'I didn't actually tell her anything. I was very discreet. I just complimented you in a general way. Mentioned your sensitivity, your patience, your unselfishness. I implied that you are physically attentive – I think I used the word *ardent* – in ways that are inde-

179

scribable. I even managed to blush. I told her you had taught me that nothing is forbidden or indelicate between a man and woman in the privacy of their bedroom. I can't tell you how thoroughly I captured her attention. She sat there at the tea-table like a stone figure, her eyes fixed on me, her lips slightly parted. And while I was blushing slightly from the things I was revealing about you and me, there was no colour in her face at all. Even her lips grew pale, it seemed, as she listened to me. I knew exactly what she was feeling because I felt the same way. I realized that everything I described to her was something *she* had experienced with you. But now she was discovering, as *I* had, that it was a *shared* experience. I'm sure she felt *used*, just as I did. You seem to have nothing to say, Rab. Does that mean you're admitting that I'm right?'

'Not at all. I'm admitting nothing. It's simply not true.'

'That's all right. It doesn't matter what you *say*. When you see Dorsey again you'll know that our little tea party was exactly as I described it. You'll see that she knows about you and me just as I know about you and her.'

'I can't understand what you're up to,' he said. 'What do you hope to accomplish by all this?'

'That's very simple, my darling. Vengeance. I'm getting even.'

[5]

When Jesse called Nora from Berlin, Karina answered the telephone. 'I'm sorry, Jesse. *Pour le moment, elle n'est pas ici.* I'm not sure where she's gone or when she'll be back.'

'All right. As soon as she comes home, ask her to call me. I'm at the Kampinski in Berlin. But I'm flying to Heidelberg this evening. So I'm anxious to talk to her before I leave.'

'I'll do my best. But I can't promise. It's difficult to know when she'll return. Perhaps not till tomorrow. So if you don't hear from her..' Karina looked up and saw Nora standing in the door of the library. 'I promise I will do my best to locate her.' She returned the phone to its cradle and turned to face Nora. 'There you are,' she said. 'I thought you'd gone out.'

'I was just upstairs. Who was that on the telephone?'

180

'What?'

'I said who called just now?'

'A silly man I met last week at a party. You don't know him. I pretended I was a servant.'

'You're playing the same games with men you played when you were twenty-five.'

'It's necessary,' Karina said. 'One can't be straightforward with a man. If he's not abused, he's not interested.'

'Depends on the man, doesn't it?'

Karina shook her head. 'They're all the same. When they get what they want they're arrogant and hateful. When you spank them, they're pitiful and apologetic. Only brutes are worthwhile but they're hard to find these days.'

'Is Helmut a brute?'

Karina made an ugly gesture with one hand and said, 'Helmut's my husband. Husbands are never proper brutes. Marriage turns men into geldings. Once he's domesticated a man can be vicious, and he usually is. But he'll never be a brute again. Helmut and I have the same tastes now. We both prefer ten-year-old girls.'

'I've never heard you admit it.'

'It was a pleasantry, not to be taken seriously. I mean it's true of Helmut but not of me. I love children but not in my bed.'

'You only love other people's children.'

'That's true. I was not designed to be a *maman*. The Lord did not intend me to be a parent.'

'What did he intend?'

Karina smiled. 'I think I was meant to be a luxury item and a source of divine inspiration. Do you agree?'

'You're a luxury item,' Nora said. 'That's as far as I'll go.'

At seven that evening, when they were dressing to go out to a dinner party, Jesse called again. This time he reached Nora.

'Did you get my message?'

'No. When did you call?'

'About four.'

'I was here all afternoon.'

'I talked to Karina. She said you were out.'

'She was mistaken,' Nora said. 'Where are you?'

'Berlin. Leaving in five minutes for the airport. I'm going to Heidelberg to see Polly.'

'And then you're coming to Paris to see me.'

181

'That's right. Will you be there?'

'Of course. Let me know when you'll arrive and I'll meet you at the airport.'

'That's a deal,' he said.

As soon as she hung up the receiver, Nora walked down the corridor to Karina's room. Karina was dressed, ready to leave, touching her ear-lobes with cologne.

'Jesse just called,' Nora said.

'That's nice. Where is he?'

'You know where he is. He's in Berlin. He says he talked to you when he rang here this afternoon.'

'He's mistaken,' Karina said. 'He must have talked with one of the servants.'

'He talked to you, Karina. You know it and so do I. For someone who's only told the truth two or three times in her life, you are an extremely clumsy liar.'

'I swear to you . . .'

'Don't swear to me. Just tell me the truth.'

'I don't know what to say.'

'The truth. Why didn't you tell me he called?'

'I was afraid,' Karina said.

'Afraid of what?'

'I was afraid he'd say he was coming here.'

'He is coming here.'

'Oh, God . . .'

'What's the matter with you?' Nora said.

'Do you have to see him?'

'I want to see him. And he wants to see me. That's why he's coming here.'

'You promised me . . .'

'What are you saying? What did I promise you?'

'Maybe you didn't promise but I . . . I thought it was all over between you. He's with Helen now, isn't he? What do you want with him?'

'I don't want anything.'

'Yes, you do. I know how things were between you two. Things like that don't just go away.'

'You just said it was all over between us.'

'That's what I want to think,' she said. 'That's what I need to

182

think. But every time I hear his name my stomach turns over. I have to take a drink and sit down.'

'It sounds as if you're the one who's in love with him.'

'Not me. I could never love a writer. They have too many secrets. I don't want to have to read a book to discover what kind of man I'm sleeping with. But you're different. I know what you like. You like mystery and insecurity. You don't mind at all if a man changes completely between *jeudi* and *dimanche*.'

'Of course I mind. Jesse hasn't changed in any fundamental way in the past thirty years.'

'Then why can't he change? Why doesn't he sneak off somewhere and change completely? Why can't he leave us alone?'

'He's not coming to see us. He's coming to see me. And I can't understand what's come over you. What is it?'

'For God's sake you know what it is. I'm jealous. I'm so jealous I can't see straight. I hear his voice on the telephone, all calm and under control, announcing what he's doing and what he plans to do, and all I want to do is hang up. Or tear the phone off the wall and throw it out into the street. Of course I didn't tell you he called. I didn't want you to know. I don't want him to come here. I don't want you to see him.'

'We're grown-up women, Karina. You're talking like a fifteen-year-old girl. We don't own each other. I don't want to own you. When you go to Lisbon to see Helmut, what would you say if I told you not to go?'

'That's altogether different.'

'No, it's not. He's your husband.'

'I'm married to him but he's not my husband. You know what my arrangement is with Helmut. It's all about money. Basic economics. He has millions of marks in Cologne and he can only get his hands on them through me. I'm a courier to him and that's all I am. I haven't been in his disgusting bed for more than twenty years.'

'Do you expect me to say I feel that way about Jesse? If you do you'll be disappointed. You know how things were between him and me. I'm not trying to tell myself they're still the way they once were. Too much time has passed. Too many things have happened. But all the same when I think of him, when I remember the times that we were together, I don't have a bad taste in my mouth. I don't think how rotten it all was. I was a crazy woman when I was

183

young. Jesse had to put up with a lot of that lunacy. But I wasn't so crazy that I didn't know how well off I was. I've never told myself that I'd have been better off if I'd never met him. I don't know what I would have been like without him. I'm just glad I never had a chance to find out. I think I made good things happen for Jesse. I don't think he would ever have become the kind of person he is without me. And he certainly made good things happen for me. He gave me a centre. My impulse was to fly off in ten directions at once. He kept me concentrated on what I did best.'

'I understand everything you're saying. And it makes sense to me. I mean in my head it makes sense. But all the same every time you say something good about him it's like sticking a knife in my side.'

'Karina, you have to stop this. You and Jesse are not competing for me. If you were, you would lose. You must know that. I've never deceived you about that. You and I are friends. We've been friends for a long time. Now something else has developed between us. It was a surprise to me. It's still a surprise. But it's not a major part of my existence. I don't feel as if I've finally discovered the meaning of life. I'm too old to redefine myself. I mean I'm not Gertrude Stein and you are not my Alice B. Toklas. This is no surprise to you. We've discussed it before. I love you as a dear friend but I am not able to fall in love with you. So you mustn't try to make us into something we're not. We're perfectly fine as we are. Whatever I've given to Jesse in the past, however I feel about him now, those things have nothing to do with you and me.'

[6]

'What about Camus?' Jack asked.

'What about him?' Jesse said. 'What do you mean?'

They had just sat down in the corner of a dim-lit wine *Stube* in a narrow street by the castle gardens in the centre of Heidelberg.

'I know you interviewed him just after the war. Sartre, too. I read both those interviews. I think he's an important voice. *La Nausée* is the best fiction I've read. But I'm not sure about Camus. Did you take him seriously?'

184

'Everyone takes Camus seriously. Sartre certainly takes him seriously.'

'You're probably right. But when an important man dies in an automobile accident it's hard for me to take him seriously. Somebody like Aly Kahn . . . OK, that's as good a way as any for him to go. Race horses and expensive whores and fast cars, champagne in an ice bucket on the front seat, live by the sword, die by the sword, you know what I mean? But a man with brains and sensibility, what's he doing racing around the highways at two in the morning? What's he *after*? What the hell is he *looking* for? Jackson Pollock's another one. A guy I know in New York said he was present at a party at Peggy Guggenheim's one night when Jackson Pollock took a crap in the fireplace. That's all right with me. The man's an eccentric, I don't mind. But when he screws around and gets himself killed in a car, then he loses me. Lost me right there. His paintings don't look the same to me as they used to. They'll never look the same again. What do you think about Pollock?'

'Overrated. I've always thought that. But not because he died in an automobile accident.'

'Camus was too smooth for me. I always had the idea he had some cocked-up image of himself. Black neck-tie, raincoat over his shoulders, freedom-fighter, all that stuff, and everything he wrote was designed to support that image. Good talker, I'll bet. Never met him, of course, but I'm sure he's a man who could talk your leg off. Sartre, on the other hand, I see as a silent bird. Cock-eyed and intellectual. Head-music. No sense of an audience. No public self. "I am what I *think*" – that kind of thing. Am I right? No big speeches or monologues from Jean-Paul. Right?'

'The fact is that Sartre talked all the time and Camus had very little to say. At least that's the way it was when I interviewed them. And of the two, Sartre was more of a public man. At least he thought of himself that way. Had no doubt about his importance. Liked to be seen and recognized. Liked to hold forth. He didn't go to Café Flore every day and Les Deux Magots just to drink coffee. He was a celebrity in the fifties and he knew it.'

' "*L'homme est une passion inutile*," ' Jack said then. 'Heavy stuff. If that's not the slogan of the century, what is? That's the answer. That sums it up. "There is no choice" – that's what Sartre says. "There is only being useless and knowing it and being useless and

185

not knowing it." With that statement he wiped out three hundred years of constipated philosophy.'

'Only if you're an existentialist.'

'If a man has a brain it's hard to be anything else, isn't it? We're all jerked around with the idea of freedom as if it was something to be discovered or earned or handed out as a gift. But Sartre's not fooled. He says that man is never free. Man is simply too stupid to recognize that fact. So he's a sitting duck for any ideological marmalade that the Pope or the professors or the politicians want to spoon on his head.'

Jesse took a drink from his great balloon glass of white wine and said nothing.

'I admire you,' Jack said then. 'Know quite a lot about you as a matter of fact. That's why I wanted to meet you. Polly's told me what it was like growing up there in England and everything she says makes me think you've been a terrific father. I have a daughter, you know. Did you know that?'

Jesse nodded his head. 'Polly told me.'

'Thirteen years old now and I haven't seen her since she was five. Elinor. That's her name. Not much of a name if you ask me but her mother liked it, so what the hell?'

'Why haven't you seen her for such a long time?'

'That's what I started to tell you. I admire anybody who's a good parent because I'm such a lousy one. No gift for it. Never did have. Some gypsy in a carnival read my palm once and she said, you must have been shut up in a room by yourself when you were a kid, and I said no, that wasn't true. Then she asked me if I'd ever been in prison, and I said no, that wasn't true either. So she just sat there and shook her head. Then she gave me back the half-dollar I'd paid her when I sat down. Now that's a world record for gypsies. Very seldom see a gypsy woman give a customer a refund. The reason I brought that up is because when I was married to Thelma – that was my wife's name – I used to think about what that palm-reader had said and I decided maybe something had happened when I was little and that's why I felt trapped all the time I was married. And then when the baby was born I felt twice as trapped. So I just bailed out. I packed up and left. Put my cello in the back seat of my Plymouth coupé and away I went.'

'Who takes care of your wife and daughter?'

Jack shook his head. 'I don't know anything about Fond du Lac,

186

what's going on back there. And I don't care. Because I can't care. I can't make myself feel guilty about something I can't change. I mean, it's great to have noble thoughts and be willing to sacrifice yourself for somebody, but what does that signify? In practical terms, I mean. What good would it do Thelma and Elinor if I journeyed back to Wisconsin, got myself a job in the tractor factory and tried to behave like all the other dingbats I went to grade school with? If I could stick it out, then it might mean something to somebody else, even if it *ruined* me. But I couldn't stick it out, you see. Endurance is not what I'm good at. The sprints, the short events – that's my style. Always has been. Always will be, I suppose. So it's important for me not to fool myself. And not to fool anybody else either. You see what I mean?'

'I'm not sure. Are you trying to tell me something about you and Polly?'

'No. Nothing like that. I just mentioned that I envy people who have a talent for parenthood. Then I went on to say that I don't have that talent myself. Put shackles on a man's legs and he can't walk. Put shackles on me and I can't even breathe. I mean I don't mind having responsibility. But I like to choose it. I don't want it forced on me. That gets me crazy. Another six months in the Army and I'd have ended up in a looney bin.'

'How did you happen to get married if you felt that way?'

'I didn't feel that way then. I was a dumb kid from the Midwest. Everybody I knew was getting married so I decided I'd better get in line. And that's what I did. But it didn't take me long to find out I'd taken a bad turn. So, like I said, I took off. Didn't know where to go, didn't want to work, so I bummed my way down to Iowa City and enrolled in the university. The Army was paying for it, so I thought why not? I'd learned to speak German from living with my folks so I decided to go on with that. Then I went from German to the Slavic languages. All that came easy to me. So I stuck with it. Been going to school ever since. Berkeley, University of Chicago, the Sorbonne. Always on scholarships. I'm a professional student. Found my way of life. Here in Europe they don't care how long a man goes to school. In Wisconsin I'm a bum no matter how many degrees I have. In Europe I'm a scholar.'

'What about the cello? Polly says you're a cello player.'

'Since I was five years old. My mother's father taught her to play the violin in Bremen and she taught me to play the cello. We lived

187

in Dowagiac, Michigan, and I gave a cello concert in Detroit when I was eight years old. By the time I went in the Army I'd played all over Michigan and Ohio. After I came back from Korea I never played in public again.'

'Why not?'

'Didn't want to. Actually, one time I did play. Got half-bombed in Iowa city one afternoon and played for an hour on the front steps of the library. After that they were after me to play with the school orchestra but I told them to take a flying screw at the moon. Since then I just play for myself, usually when I'm drunk. And I play for Polly.'

After a moment, Jesse said, 'Since you brought up Polly, I'd like to ask you a couple of questions.'

'Go ahead.'

'What kind of future do you see for her?'

'I've never thought much about it. But it seems to me she can do just about anything she wants to. She's smart and she's beautiful and she has a lot of money. So how can she miss?'

'Are you pretending you don't know what I'm talking about?'

'You were asking about Polly.'

'That's right. Do you have any plans for her?'

'I'll tell you the truth. I don't live like that. I don't think like that. And neither does Polly. We just skate along from one day to the next. If a problem comes up we try to handle it. Otherwise it's German beer, schnitzel and strudel, and watching the seasons change.'

'How much longer to you expect to be in Heidelberg?'

'I can't answer that. I do independent study. I can work almost any place I want to. Warsaw's after me. And the University of Prague.'

'You said "work". Does that mean you plan to teach?'

'Not me. I hate teaching. When I said "work" I meant "study". That's my work. And I don't get paid, if that's what you're getting at. The schools try to be generous but money's always short. It's a tight squeeze.'

'So it's helpful that Polly has money of her own?'

'No doubt about it. Thanks to her we live very nicely.'

'And you have no problems with that?'

'You mean, do I feel guilty because Polly has money and I don't? God, no. I've lived on next to nothing most of my life but I wouldn't want her to have to do that. She doesn't have the background for it.'

'Do you and Polly ever talk about getting married?'

'There'd be no point to that conversation. I'm already married.'

'People get divorces.'

'Not me. To do that I'd have to get in touch with my wife and I don't want to get in touch with her. I don't want her to know where I am and I don't want to see her.'

'What about your daughter?'

'What about her?'

'You don't care to see her either?'

'I wouldn't recognize her if I saw her in the street. And she wouldn't recognize me.'

'Have you thought about having children with Polly?'

'Sure, I've thought about it, but I'm not going to do it.'

'Does she know that?'

Jack nodded. 'We hashed *that* out the first week we were together. She knows me. She knows how I am.'

'So what you're telling me is that the way things are now for you and Polly is the way they're going to stay.'

'No. I'm not saying that. All kinds of things could happen. Maybe she'll get tired of me. I don't expect that to happen but it might. Or I might get tired of her. I really don't expect that to happen, but who knows? We're talking about human beings. When I was Polly's age I had no idea I'd ever meet her. When she's the age I am now, she may not even remember that she knew me. So how can I tell you what's going to happen tomorrow? Or next week. Or next month. I don't know and I don't give a damn. I never expected to win the lottery. And just because I feel as if I've won it since I met Polly doesn't meant I expect it to last. You might sit down with her tomorrow morning and convince her I'm a worthless son of a bitch. Her mother might write her a twelve-page letter that would turn her whole head around. I'm skating on thin ice here and I know it. But don't expect me to chop a hole in the ice so I'll fall in quicker.'

'Let me ask you another question,' Jesse said then. 'If you can imagine me in your position and you in mine what do you think you'd say to me?'

Jack grinned. 'I'd tell you to stay away from my daughter or I'd cut off your nuts.'

'And what do you think I'd say to you?'

'You'd tell me to go screw myself.'

Three days later, after Jesse had gone off to Paris, Polly said to Jack, 'You're a big fake.'

'Who says so?'

'I do. You told me you were going to look up Jesse at his hotel so you two could meet each other.'

'What makes you think I didn't?'

'Because I didn't hear an explosion downtown. And because he didn't mention that he'd seen you.'

'Are you sure?'

'Of course I'm sure. I was waiting for the sword to come down and it didn't happen.'

'What if I told you I did see him? What if I said we sat in a wine *Stube* around the corner from his hotel and talked for an hour?'

'*Is* that what you're saying?'

'Yes.'

'I don't believe you.'

'Why would I lie? I said I was going to do it and I did it.'

Polly shook her head. 'You said you were going to do it and you didn't do it. Now you don't want me to think you're a fake. And you certainly wouldn't want me to think you didn't see him just because I asked you not to. Isn't that true?'

'I'll have to think about it.'

She put her arms around him and kissed him. 'You see . . . you *are* a fake. Am I right?'

'You're right.'

[7]

After she said goodbye to Floyd at the airport in Chicago, after he'd boarded his plane, Helen stood by the wide windows of the passengers' lounge watching the lumbering bird-like plane pull away from the terminal and roll slowly to its position in the departure line. At last it sped along the airstrip, lifted off, made a great climbing circle to the east and disappeared in the cloud cover.

Helen stayed there at the window long after the plane had

vanished, looking out across the runways at the service vehicles scurrying back and forth and the great heavy planes moving into departure positions. At last she turned away, crossed the arrival area and went into the cocktail lounge. She tucked herself into a booth in a dark corner and sipped a brandy and soda.

She sat there for more than an hour, silent and still. It was mid-afternoon when she finally went to the parking lot, located her car, manoeuvred her way through the tangle of airport access roads, and turned south on the highway that would take her home to Fort Beck.

Each time she saw her son, she was reminded that their relationship had been characterized by arrivals and departures. In the more than twenty-five years since she'd found him at last at the naval base in San Diego, in all that time, although they had seen each other at fairly regular intervals, they had never spent more than three months together. And more often it was three days. Or two weeks. Many breakfasts and luncheons and cocktails and dinners in airport lounges. Helen had come to accept it as the unchangeable fabric of their life together.

Since Floyd's marriage to Valerie and since Jesse's coming to live in Fort Beck, Helen had seen her son even less frequently than before. While she and Jessie had remained, to a large degree, stationary, Floyd and Valerie had chosen a pattern of unusual mobility. They were often in the west of Ireland, or in Portugal at Praia da Rocha, but it was never surprising to have cards from them postmarked St Raphael, Venice, Corsica, Ronda, Barcelona, Sestre Levanti, Siena, or Dubrovnik. For reasons of their own they were seldom in cities such as Paris or Rome or Madrid or Lisbon and almost never in London. Having chosen isolation, they continued to transport their cocoon of privacy from one isolated spot to another.

Driving home from the airport, Helen realized that she would be alone in her house now for the first time in several years. She and Jesse had gone to England only once, for Clara's funeral, and he had gone off by himself rarely, to visit for two or three days with one of his children. Since Bill had come to live in Fort Beck and since Jesse almost never met with Rab, those solo trips had become rare indeed.

As she sat in her upstairs bedroom that night, no sound in the house other than faint rustling from the servants' quarters, she realized how much of her life had been spent in this house. And

191

much of that time by herself. Until Jesse had come here to stay after Valerie's wedding to Floyd, Helen had never been with a man here, had never shared her lovely bedroom. When she'd been married to Frank Wilson they had lived on Lake Shore Drive in Chicago. During the precious tortured time with Chet Comiskey they had lived in Maine, in their tiny house in the woods near Hedrick. And long after their divorce, when she and Frank had discovered each other again, they'd lived on the south side, near the University of Chicago campus. But now Jesse was here in Fort Beck, not in the third-floor bedroom where he'd lived when Helen was a schoolgirl and Raymond was still alive, but with her. Fulfilment of a contract that had been silently negotiated perhaps many years before but had only recently been activated.

For many years, for all of her adult years, Helen had thought of herself as a collage, an assemblage of ill-matched *objets trouvés*. Nothing, under close inspection, was what it seemed to be. Anna, her mother and Raymond's wife, had never truly come to life for her, either as a mother or as Raymond's wife. Her aunt Clara, on the other hand, had seemed a *mélange* of older sister and mother to her ever since their first meeting when Helen was eighteen. Whatever she knew, she wanted Clara to know. Everything she *felt*, she wanted to share.

Raymond did not fit neatly into his paternal niche either. He'd been an exemplary father certainly, but he'd also been endowed by his daughter with a number of god-like qualities. She loved and admired and adored and worshipped him. The shock of his sudden death when she was seventeen was intensified by the aftershock when she learned that his life had been a lie, that the stories he'd told his wife and his daughter about himself, where he came from, who his relatives were, were all fabrications. At last, however, that imperfection only increased his value to her. After she'd gone to England with Jesse and met Raymond's family, after Nora had told her the details of his early life that Raymond had concealed, Helen treasured him in a new way, mysterious and smoky and intense.

No one, it seemed, fitted neatly into Helen's pattern. Hugh, Clara's son, whom Helen had barely known, had been the father of her child. Frank, to whom she'd been uneasily married, had after their divorce become in some way a constant in her life. And Chet, when he died, had carried away some tender part of her that she knew could not be replaced.

192

And what about Floyd? And Jesse? Why couldn't she simply define them, accept them and be grateful for them? She lived now with Jesse in loving intimacy. He was her lover – that label always made her smile – in the world's definition of the word but he had been too long a brother, had related to her as a brother for so many years, that the act of love in itself could not totally redefine him. She had always loved him. Now she loved him differently. Or did she? At times she simply felt as though she was twined in passion with her brother. At other times she concluded that she had always wanted what they had now. But if that was true, why had they waited so long? Occasionally she asked herself, 'Did we spoil it by waiting?' But even as she asked the question she shook her head and told herself that nothing was spoiled, that nothing *could* be spoiled. All the same, she longed for Clara, or someone like Clara, to talk with.

As she rejoiced in Floyd's happiness, she resented it. She admitted to herself that she resented it. And she resented Valerie. She had known her first as Nora's daughter. Then, surprisingly, as Jesse's wife, as the mother of his three children. Now Valerie was married to Floyd. And each time she changed course she took something away from Helen. Or so it seemed to Helen. The fact that Jesse came to Helen after his divorce from Valerie was blunted in Helen's mind by her conviction that Valerie had sought the divorce and if she hadn't sought it, Jesse would still be in residence at Wingate Fields. Still, Helen had learned to deal with all that, to put it behind her, just as she'd painted over the years Jesse had been with Nora. Her present discomfort was more recent, more difficult to rationalize. She felt as if Floyd had been abducted, isolated, and imprisoned. And by the same young woman who had isolated and imprisoned Jesse. Helen was wise enough to realize that she had not been selected as a victim in either instance, but she felt victimized all the same.

Sitting up in her bed that night after Floyd's departure, she held a book on her lap but she read none of the words. Her thoughts wandered and floated, sling-shotted back and forth, settling nowhere, and continued to return to Clara. At last Helen felt herself organizing her thoughts as though she was writing to Clara or talking to her as she had so many times in the morning room at Wingate Fields.

193

Do you ever feel that you don't know yourself at all? 'This above all, to thine own self be true.' Nothing wrong with that advice, I suppose. But how can you be true to a self you're not sure of, one that keeps changing shape from day to day, or certainly from year to year.

I know what people said about me when Raymond died. They said I'd loved him too much, that I would measure every man I might meet against him and wouldn't be pleased with any of them. I thought that idea was ridiculous, of course. I still think that. But I'm not absolutely certain that I haven't done what they predicted I would.

Nora once said that I care about Jesse because he's the closest thing I could find to Raymond. Is that possible? If so, maybe that's why all the Bradshaw women seem to have been drawn to him. Nora, Valerie, and me. And you, too, in your own way. But now he's back here with me. So I know that's what he wants. Or do I know that? There are times when I tell myself he's here by default. There are other times when I think I only have him for a little while, that he and Nora are cut from the same cloth and eventually he'll go back to her. If that happened I think it would kill me but a small voice inside says no, that I would survive. And I would of course. Just as I survived Raymond's death and Chet's death.

People have told me I'm a survivor and I took it as a compliment but I'm not sure it was intended that way. If you truly feel the pain is it possible to survive? Or is it that I'm too wise, too experienced, maybe too old now, to really suffer? Is it possible that there's nothing I really want? Maybe after Raymond died there was nothing I ever truly wanted.

By asking these questions, by appearing to go along with the theory that I was attached to my father in a disproportionate way, I feel that I will refute all such arguments. But perhaps I protest too much. Perhaps I should be more concerned with living my life and less concerned with either understanding or defending it. with you, of course, no defence is necessary, is it? If you don't accept me as I am, whatever I am, then surely no one does.

Enough of all that. Here is the leitmotif. At my age – not old but exasperatingly mature – I am delighted to tell you that I am able to scandalize this community where I live. At first when

Jesse came back here to live, the neighbours simply averted their eyes. The ones who are too young to remember Raymond were told that Jesse was a sort of foster son to my father and therefore a sort of foster brother to me. But the servants in Illinois gossip just as servants do in Northumberland, so it wasn't long before the natives knew that the mistress of the house was also the mistress of her house guest. Since Jesse and I act like married folks, or sweethearts, or like any other couple who are living together and enjoying it, there was no shortage or corroboration of the servants' stories. So Jesse has a kind of local fame now as a grey-haired seducer while I must be content with sleazy notoriety. But in any case we are not ignored. All eyes turn when we stroll through the grocery store. And we are invited *everywhere*, a triumph of curiosity over morality. Since we turn down most invitations we are doubly in demand.

But I'm off the track. Freud said, 'What does a woman really want?' And I say no one knows. It's certainly not a question that one can ask a woman because none of us have the answer. All men, on the other hand, *believe* they have the answer. *Unless* the question is asked about a man's own wife. Then all wires go dead.

My concern is, as I said, that I want nothing. Did I want Jesse more before he came to me? I think not. I certainly hope not. But in my state of mind these days, these months, these years, all possibilities are possible. I now accept more theorems than I reject and I'm proud of that.

Helen put her book aside at last, unread, turned off her bedside lamp, and tried to sleep. But her thoughts kept niggling. Reviewing Floyd's visit, she tried to discover for herself his true state of mind, tried to chart for herself the changes that had taken place in him during the more than twenty years that had gone by since they'd met that first time in San Diego.

He was remarkably unchanged physically. Hard and lean, sun-bleached hair, and an easy manner. And slow as always to talk about his own problems. Had the shock of Jeannette's death left scars on him? Was his life with Valerie as serene and fulfilling as it seemed? Was he truly fond of the nomadic life they lived together? All these questions had no answers. At least Helen could find no answers.

When Jesse edged into her thoughts she had, she felt, more specifics to deal with. When he left for Germany they had not discussed whether or not he would stop in Paris on his way home. They had not discussed it because there was no need to. Helen knew he would stop there and she knew he would see Nora. Perhaps his only reason for going to Paris would be to see Nora. The thought disturbed Helen but she accepted it, perhaps because she had no choice, perhaps because such thoughts had been a painful fact of life for her since she was eighteen years old. She had learned, just as Valerie and Clara had learned, that acceptance was the key word, perhaps the only word when one considered how to deal with Nora. Clara had once said to her, 'She's like a virus that no one can find a cure for.'

Having floundered badly in trying to examine her own state of mind in the hours since Floyd's departure, Helen was no more successful in her efforts to plot Jesse's emotional curve. Like Floyd, he seemed never to change, not at least in any substantial way. The winds never came up. The danger was not in being capsized, the risk was in being becalmed. He left the house to fly to Germany exactly as he left to drive to Urbana to use the university library. When they were at home he worked every day in the study and reported each night at dinner that the work had gone well. They laughed and drank and danced together and seemed to enjoy the moments of their life in ways that made their friends envious. 'People envy us,' Helen said to him and he answered, 'Of course. There's a hell of a lot to envy here. We're a world-class couple.'

And they were, of course. She believed it and she was convinced that he believed it also. But sometimes, very rarely, as she watched him, his eyes lost their sheen, his concentration seemed to blur, and she felt responsible. She told herself she was to blame.

[8]

Rab and Dorsey had devised elaborate and fool-proof schemes for contacting each other. The day after his arrival home from New York he put those schemes into motion. Rosalind, his secretary telephoned the Mullets' home, identified herself as Miss Foster, a salesperson at Fortnum and Mason, and asked if Mrs Mullet could ring her back as quickly as possible. After such a message, Dorsey always telephoned Rab at his office within an hour. On this day, however, after three hours had passed, there had been no response from her. Rosalind then placed another call. This time she left a message that Mrs Mullet's order could be picked up at Beckwith's in the linen department at four that afternoon. This was the signal to meet Rab at the apartment on Grantham Place at four. Rab went there at three and waited till six but she didn't come.

After several days of futile attempts to reach her, Rab made a luncheon date with Oscar. As they ate Rab suffered through the details of Mullet's latest film project. Three westerns to be made in Spain. 'Money from Switzerland, actors and director from Italy, and two stars from Hollywood. The Spanish government will give you their shirt they're so hungry to get production down there. They're even throwing in completion money if we need it.'

'That means you'll *need* it, whether you need it or not,' Rab said.

'Exactly. I'll make a co-production deal with the devil as long as I furnish the accountant.'

When coffee and port arrived at their table Rab said, 'If you're free tomorrow night, why don't you and Dorsey have dinner with me?'

'Only if you promise to bring Gloria. I don't mind looking at her when I'm having a nice plate of scampi.'

'I'm afraid you'll have to settle for me. Gloria can't make it.'

'Not having a spat, I hope. You mustn't drop a thoroughbred like her on the open market.'

'She's not mine to drop. We've never had any sort of formal contract with each other. No guarantees. That's the problem, I suppose. You know women better than I do. They like a great deal of security. Need things they can depend on, that sort of foolishness. Want a chap they can count on. You know what I mean?'

'Of course I do,' Oscar said. 'Bad timing. It happens to all of us. Does that mean you two are calling it off entirely?'

Assuming that at least part of this conversation would be carried home to Dorsey, Rab had planned his answer carefully. 'Not much to call off as far as I'm concerned. Since Gloria came back from Canada, you and Dorsey have seen her as much as I have. I mean those several dinners we all had together were the only times I've been with her.'

'What a waste. Two young colts like you. I had it figured differently. X-rated, all the way. Champagne and silk sheets and nobody sleeps a wink.'

Rab shook his head. 'Not with Gloria.'

As they waited at the kerb for their cars to come round, Rab said, 'Are we on then for dinner tomorrow night?'

'Afraid not. I'm off to Barcelona and Madrid for two weeks. Flying down tomorrow morning first thing. But we'll do it as soon as I get back. You could ask Dorsey, of course. Under normal circumstances I'm sure she'd be delighted to have dinner with you. But at the moment she's hiding out from the world.'

'Is she ill?'

'Nothing clinical. Just a sudden attack of vanity. She had an accident in her bedroom a week or so ago. Struck her head on the door of the armoire. A nasty crack. Didn't break the skin but there was a welt on her cheekbone and her eye was black and blue. Now it's turned a nice lavender and pale yellow but she's very self-conscious about it. Before I leave tomorrow she'll be off to hide in the Cotswolds.'

'Well, that should be pleasant for her. Beautiful there this time of year.'

'Dull as hell if you ask me. Nothing but the sound of the stream rippling by. All that does for me is make me want to take a leak.'

'Did you buy the place you told me about? The old rectory?'

'No,' Oscar said. 'Too close to the village she decided. So she latched on to another place, a stone cottage by a river. Roses and vines and a lot of grass to mow. And a field of sheep across the river. Dorsey likes to look at sheep for some reason. I don't mind a sheepskin waistcoat or a couple of lamb cutlets for dinner but a four-legged sheep walking around is a bore.'

Back in his office after lunch, Rab again asked Rosalind to leave a series of messages for Dorsey. That afternoon at four he went to the apartment in Grantham Place and waited there till eight.

The following morning as soon as he arrived at his office he called Rosalind in and said, 'Ring Mullet's secretary and tell her you're calling from Lew Grade's office. Tell her you have some contracts that Mullet wanted sent to his country house in the Cotswolds.'

Rosalind smiled. 'We've misplaced the address and we'd appreciate it if they could give it to us again.'

'That's right.'

A few minutes later she called through on the intercom and said, 'Upton-on-Severn. South of the village. Just beside the river. On Locust Lane. They also said that Mr Mullet left this morning for Spain. Or did you know that?'

'I knew that,' Rab said. Then, 'You're very intelligent, you know, and very attractive. But if you get too intelligent, I'll have to declare you redundant.'

'You can't do that. No other secretary would rub your neck the way I do. My ex-husband was a masseur and he taught me all he knew. Young women like me are hard to find.'

'That's true. You don't miss a thing. When Oscar Mullet was in my office a few weeks ago he told me he would hire you in a minute and pay you considerably more than I do.'

'I know,' she said. 'He told me the same thing.'

'So if I sacked you, you could go straight to him.'

'But I don't want to work for him. I'm happy where I am.'

'Still . . . if you had no other choice?' Rab said.

'If I had no other choice, what else *could* I do?'

'I pity your ex-husband. You must have led him a merry chase.'

'I did. But he had a jolly time. He'd take me back in a minute.'

As soon as Rab switched off the intercom there was a light knock on his office door and Rosalind stepped in. 'Fun is fun,' she said, 'but I just want you to know that I'm not interested in working for Oscar Mullet or anyone else but you. If you ever decide to discharge me I will wait for you in the car-park some evening and flog you to death.' She smiled sweetly, stepped back through the door and closed it behind her.

[9]

Rab drove north-west out of London just after dawn the next day. He stopped for breakfast in Aylesbury, drove on west through Oxford and Gloucester, then followed the river north to Upton-on-Severn. In the village he asked for directions to Locust Lane and just before eleven in the morning he turned into the long driveway of the Mullets' cottage. Far back from the road, just by the bank of

199

the Severn, he stopped at the end of the drive and got out of his car.

Dorsey, wearing trousers and a sweater and dark glasses, was working in the garden. When she looked up and saw him she stood perfectly still. He walked along the drive and crossed the lawn to where she waited.

'Why do I have the feeling you've been trying to avoid me?' he said. Trying to be light.

'Please go away. I don't want to see you.'

'But I want to see you.'

'It's too late,' she said. 'I've made up my mind.'

'You've made up your mind about what?'

'I don't want to talk to you. I don't want to see you.'

'You already said that.'

'That's all there is to say. I want you to leave. We can't stand out here talking like this.'

'Then let's go inside.'

'We can't do that either. I don't want to do that. I don't want to do anything or say anything. I just want you to go away.'

'But I'm not going to do that,' Rab said. 'I drove out here to see you because I haven't been able to see you in London. So I'm not going to get back in my car and drive away.'

'You have to. That's exactly what you have to do. There's nothing to talk about. It's all over, Rab.'

'No, it's not. It's not over for me and it's not over for you. It wasn't over before I left for New York so why should it be over now? What happened while I was gone?'

'We can't stand out here like this. I told you that.'

'Why not?'

'I always feel as if I'm being watched.'

'Then let's go inside.'

'I'm afraid to.'

'Afraid of what? What in God's name is the matter with you?'

'I don't know.'

'Is there somebody inside the house?'

'No. I came here by myself.'

'You're not afraid of Oscar, are you? He's in Spain.'

'Are you sure?'

'That's what his office says.'

'That doesn't mean anything. I never know where he is.'

'Are you telling me you're afraid of Oscar?'

'You just asked me that,' she said.

'But you didn't answer.'

She looked down at the cut flowers she was carrying in a basket. At last she said, 'Of course I'm not afraid of him. Why should I be?'

'Then let's go inside. We can't just stand out here.'

Inside the cottage she sat down in the kitchen, the first room they came to. The shutters were closed against the sun but she didn't take off her dark glasses. 'I ran into something,' she said. 'I bruised my face. I have a black eye like a clown.'

When Rab sat down at the table across from her she said, 'I'm not offering you tea or a drink. The house isn't stocked yet.' When he didn't answer she went on. 'The truth is I don't want this to be a social occasion. I don't want you here but I can't make you go away. So please ask me whatever questions you have in your head and let's get it over with. Then if you won't leave I'll call the constable in the village.

He sat looking at her for a long moment. Then, 'What in the name of God is the matter with you?'

'I can't believe you don't know. Have you talked to Gloria since you came back?'

'Yes, I have. She met me at the airport.'

'Of course. I should have known that. Did she tell you we had tea together?'

'Yes, she did,' Rab said.

'And did she tell you what we talked about?'

'No. I didn't ask her.'

'I'm surprised she didn't tell you. But if she didn't then I don't suppose I should.'

'What am I supposed to say? If you don't want to tell me, then don't tell me.'

'You asked what's the matter with me. That's what's the matter. Gloria spent a great deal of time explaining to me what you've done to her in bed.'

'Oh, for God's sake. Then she's stupid. Is that what this is all about? You knew we lived together. I told you that. I can't take back everything that happened before I met you.'

'She wasn't talking about before you met me. She was talking about now. Since she came back from Canada. According to her,

201

you've been fucking her night and day. She was quite eloquent on the subject.'

'She's an actress. What do you expect? She gets paid for being eloquent.'

'But it's true, isn't it?'

'No, it's not true, but what if it were? How do you think I feel about your going home to Oscar every night? Do I quiz you about what goes on in your bedroom?'

'You don't have to. I've told you. I sleep in one room and he sleeps in another. He hasn't come near me for years.'

'I know you've said that. And that's what I want to believe. But you can't expect me not to have some doubts now and then. You know Oscar's reputation. He's supposed to be the wildest woman-izer in the film business. There's an old joke that even Lassie, the dog, wouldn't work for him. So you can't be surprised if people believe he notices his own wife from time to time. Especially when she looks the way you look.'

'I don't care what people believe. I told you the truth.'

'And I lied to you . . . is that it?'

'Can you imagine how I felt? Sitting there listening to her.'

'Of course I can. But I just told you she was lying to you.'

'Why would she do that? Why would she think I'd even be interested in hearing about you two?'

'She knew you'd be interested. Because she knows about us.'

'You mean you told her?'

'Of course not. I'd have to be crazy to tell her when I've been using her as a stalking horse to throw Oscar off the track.'

'Then how . . .'

'A friend of hers stays in a flat just opposite the entrance to my building in Grantham Place. He's seen you coming and going. And he's seen you with me.'

'Oh, my God. Then he knows who I am.'

'No, he doesn't. He doesn't know Oscar and he doesn't know me. He was at the theatre with Gloria one night when you and Oscar were there. He pointed you out as a lady he'd seen on Grantham Place. And when he described me, Gloria made the connection.'

'And now she'll tell everybody in London.'

Rab shook his head. 'Not Gloria. That's not her style. She went to tea with you and told you a sexy story about herself and me.

202

That's her style. If I've been making a fool of her, she wanted to make sure that you suffered a little, too.'

'A little? I've never felt so miserable as I did that afternoon. But now I feel worse. I feel as if I'm sitting on a powder keg. If some fool I've never met knows about you and me, if Gloria knows, how long will it be before Oscar finds out?'

'What if he knows already?'

'Why do you say that?'

'I thought maybe he'd found out somehow. I thought that might be the reason I haven't been able to see you or talk to you since I got back from New York.'

'I told you . . .'

'I know what you told me but it's hard for me to believe. You and I both realized what we were up to these past few months. We were taking a hell of a chance and we knew it. But it didn't matter. We didn't let it matter. We stumbled and ran and schemed to be together every minute we could. It's some kind of craziness. Something new to me. Something I can't explain. And it's not over, not at all, not for me. And I don't believe it's over for you. I don't believe that Gloria could sit you down and tell you a few bedroom stories and make you decide you never want to see me again. That doesn't add up. There has to be something else in your mind.'

'I don't know what you mean.'

'Yes, you do. Something must have happened between you and Oscar. Did you think he had suspicions about us? Does he know something? Does he know everything maybe? When you said you were frightened, when you said you feel as if you're being watched, was that what you meant?'

'I don't know what you're trying to say. If Oscar had some suspicions about me, he certainly wouldn't go off to Spain for two weeks and leave me alone in London.'

'But you said you're not sure he is in Spain.'

'I didn't mean that the way it sounded. I just meant that he travels around so much it's hard to remember where he is from one week to the next.'

'That's not what you said when we were outside in the garden.'

'Maybe not, but that's what I meant. I was so upset to see you here I didn't know what I was saying.'

'But now you're saying that nothing has changed between you and Oscar. No arguments, no revelations, no suspicions?'

'No. Nothing like that. He didn't let on to you that anything was going on, did he?'

'When?'

'Didn't you have lunch with him the day before yesterday?'

'Did he tell you that?' Rab said.

'I don't remember. I thought you mentioned it.'

'No. I didn't.'

'Then he must have said something about it. My head's in such a state I don't know where I am these past few days.'

'You asked if he said anything about you,' Rab said. 'He didn't. I told him I'd like to take the two of you out to dinner and he said he had to go to Barcelona. Then he said you probably wouldn't want to go out anyway because you'd run into an armoire door and bruised your face.'

'That's right. We haven't gone out at all since that happened.'

'You know I've been trying every way possible to talk to you and see you. If I hadn't driven up here today and cornered you in your garden, would I have heard from you?'

'I don't know,' she said.

'You don't know or you don't want to say?'

'I don't know.'

'All right, let me ask you this. If I get back in my car now and drive back to London, is that the end of it? Will I hear from you? Or will we pretend that nothing ever happened between us?'

'I don't know, Rab. I don't know anything.'

'You know what that means to me? You know what an answer like that sounds like to me? It sounds like "no".'

'I don't know.'

He reached across the table then and took off her dark glasses.

'Don't do that,' she said. She covered her face with her hands. 'Please. I don't want you to look at me.'

'But I want to look at you,' he said. He got up, walked round the table and gently pulled her hands away from her face.

'All right, *look*, damn it.' She looked up at him. 'See how pretty I am. A purple bruise on my cheekbone and my eye still swollen and every colour of the rainbow.' There were tears in her eyes. 'Have you seen enough? Can I have my glasses back now?'

He handed her the glasses and she carefully put them on again. At last he sat down across the table from her. Then he said, 'Why did he hit you?'

204

'What do you mean?'

'You know exactly what I mean. Why did Oscar hit you with his fist outside a theatre on Shaftesbury Avenue?'

'I don't know what you're saying.'

'Yes, you do. Oscar hit you and you know it.'

'That's ridiculous. He didn't hit me. He's never hit me. If he did I'd leave him and he knows it.'

'It's a good try, Dorsey, but it won't work. I know what happened.'

'That's right. Because I told you.'

'I know. You said you hit your head on the door of the armoire in your bedroom. Oscar told me the same story. But it's not true.'

'You were in New York. How do you know what went on in London?'

Rab tapped his forehead with one finger. 'Because I'm brilliant. I'll tell you precisely what happened and you tell me then if I'm mistaken.'

'I already told you . . .'

'Just listen to me. *Waltz of the Toreadors*. Trevor Howard and Carole Browne. You and Oscar were there.'

'That's right. I told you that.'

'When the play ended you left by a side exit. While you waited for your car to come round, you popped into a wine bar just beside the theatre. A few minutes later, when your car stopped at the kerb, you and Oscar came out of the bar and walked across the pavement. Just before your driver opened the rear door so you could get in, Oscar struck you in the face with his fist and you fell back against the side of the car.'

'That's nonsense,' Dorsey said. 'Where do you get such ideas?'

'It happened, Dorsey. I told you Gloria was there at the theatre that night. She saw it happen.'

'Why do you believe anything *she* tells you? You said yourself she's trying to get even with me. She'll tell you anything.'

'Her friend saw it, too, the young man who's been staying in the flat on Grantham Place. The street was crowded, Dorsey. A lot of people saw it happen.'

She sat very still by the table, looking down at her hands. Finally she said, 'What do you want me to say? What am I supposed to say?'

'I don't expect you to say anything. But if *you* know the truth and *I* know the truth . . .'

'What's the difference? What does it matter?'

'It matters a lot,' Rab said. 'I'm trying to find out why you suddenly decided to walk away from me.'

'I told you . . .'

'I don't believe that nonsense about Gloria and neither do you. I think there's a connection between what happened between you and Oscar that night and what's been happening to us ever since. Does he know about us, or doesn't he?'

Her voice was very soft when she answered. 'I don't know, Rab. I honestly don't know. He was very angry that night. He pretended it was . . . I mean he never mentioned your name. He kept talking about another man, a screenwriter we used to see a lot when we lived in Beverly Hills. He's in London now writing a screenplay for Ronald Neame.'

'So what?'

'That's what I said. But Oscar has some odd notion that . . . you know . . . he got it into his head that there was something between Bob and me. That's his name – Robert Gingrich. He wrote a play that did well in New York in the early fifties. They made a film of it with Widmark and Dana Andrews and some other good people, so Bob went to California and became a hot screenwriter for five or six years. Then it petered out like everything else peters out in California and he started to drink too much and slip around on his wife and make a general ass of himself.'

'And Oscar thought he was slipping around with you?'

She nodded. 'Strangest thing. The only time it's ever happened since I've known him. I thought Oscar didn't know what jealousy meant. He gave me a long lecture on the subject before we got married. Fidelity was not a part of marriage, he said. That was his theory. When I said it *was*, as far as I was concerned, he said that was my business but that I mustn't expect him to change his ways. So that's the way things went with us. I behaved myself but he didn't. And before long it became a marriage in name only. I've told you that before.'

'So why did he get a fix on . . . what's his name?'

'Bob Gingrich. I'll never know. If I were *looking* for a man it certainly wouldn't be Bob. He's pale and overweight and when he gets drunk he cries a lot. But when he's sober he's very smart and

206

very funny, so he was fun to be with. And mostly I liked his wife, Jeannie. She was watching her life fall apart and she didn't know what to do about it. So I used to spend a lot of time with the two of them, always the two of them. They'd come over and spend the day with me and Bob would get pleasantly soused. Or I'd go out and see them in their little beach-house at Zuma. And somehow, from that, Oscar got the idea that I had something going with Bob. It wasn't an ugly thing. In fact he used to tease me about it. And on the rare occasions when he and I would see Bob and Jeannie together, he'd tease them about it too. He'd say, "Jeannie, you and I had better make some plans about what we'll do after Bob and Dorsey run away together and leave us holding the bag." And then Bob would say, "I wish that was true, Oscar, but it's not. If Dorsey runs away with anybody, it'll be Jeannie." '

'You said "rare occasions". Was that because Oscar had suspicions about you and Bob?'

'I don't think so. I think it was because Bob was out of work. Producers don't like to waste time with people who aren't working, don't like to be seen with them in public. Nobody wants to be mentioned in a newspaper column with a loser.'

'Let me get this straight. Did Oscar think you were involved with this guy or not?'

'I don't know. As I said, he used to bring it up all the time but in a teasing way. And that was a long time ago. We haven't lived in California for almost six years.'

'And neither of you has seen Gingrich in all that time?'

'Maybe Oscar has, but I haven't. I heard his wife left him and went home to her family in Oregon. And then I heard that Bob had moved back to New York and was trying to write plays again. But I had no idea he was here in London till Oscar mentioned it to me that evening we were going to the theatre.'

'He thinks you've been seeing Gingrich?'

She nodded. 'He accused me of all kinds of things.'

'What did you say?'

'I tried to laugh it off. But Oscar wouldn't let up. At the interval during the play we stayed in our seats while everyone else went to the bar in the lobby and all the time he was telling me what I'd been up to in London. At first I couldn't take it seriously. But then I began to feel that he wasn't talking about Bob at all. He was talking about you and me.'

'Why would he do that? If he knows about us why wouldn't he come out and say so?'

'Because he wouldn't. You don't know Oscar. He doesn't do anything in straight lines. He's Hungarian. All I know is that when he hit me and I almost fell down in the street, there was only one thought in my head. I was convinced he'd found out about us.'

'But what good does it do him to go around in circles?'

'It might do him a great deal of good. I'm sure he doesn't want to go head-to-head with you. As long as he's producing films and using London as home-base, he thinks you're a great ally. And you are. So he can't very well call you up and tell you to stay away from his wife. On the other hand if he can make such a fuss with me that he scares me off . . .'

Rab shook his head. 'It doesn't make sense. No matter how smart you are he can't expect you to guess that when he's talking about Gingrich he's actually talking about me.'

'If we were talking about someone besides Oscar I would agree with you. But he's a negotiator. He doesn't behave the way other people do. He just picks a spot he wants to reach and then figures out all the possible ways to get there. He goes down the list until something finally works.'

'Are you telling me,' Rab said slowly, 'that there's nothing in the world we can do except what this freak you're married to wants us to do? Am I supposed to be trembling because he may have found out I'm in love with his wife?'

'Love has nothing to do with it. Oscar knows nothing about things like that. He deals in properties. He buys them, owns them, and controls them.'

'He hasn't bought you.'

'Maybe not. But he certainly thinks he owns me.'

'What do you think?' Rab asked.

'I don't know what I think. I can't think straight.'

Rab got up from his chair, leaned over and gently took off her dark glasses.

'Don't' she said. 'Please. I look so horrible.'

'No, you don't.' He held her head in his hands and kissed her bruised cheekbone. Then he gently kissed the discoloured swollen spots around her eye. 'There you are,' he said. 'All cured.' Then, 'Are there any other bruises on your body that need attention?'

When she shook her head he said, 'I don't trust you. I think I should look you over.' He pulled her to her feet and held her against him. 'I'm going to take you into the examination room. In cases like this, one can't be too careful.' He put his arms around her waist and led her through the house and up the stairs till he found the bedroom.

[10]

They lay beside each other in the bed, the late-afternoon sun slanting in through the window shades. 'God, but it's silent outside,' Rab said. 'I always forget how brilliantly quiet it is in the country.'

'I'm asleep,' she said.

'No, you're not. We had a fine tea an hour or so ago. You were quite awake then.'

'Now I'm asleep.'

'In that case, so am I.' He pulled her close to him and felt her body fit itself to his. She slipped into sleep almost at once. He could feel her breath against his neck. He lay on his back as his thoughts tumbled slowly back and forth and at last he, too, went to sleep.

When they woke again it was almost dark.

'I died and went to heaven,' she said. 'I never want to leave this room.'

'Then we won't.'

'I wish we never had to talk, or think, or worry, or be concerned with other people.'

'We don't. We'll just disappear.'

'Can't be done,' she said.

'Of course it can. My mother divorced my father, married another man, and to a large degree, disappeared. She's seldom been seen since then.'

'Why can't we do that?'

'We can,' Rab said.

'No, we can't. I can't. I have my son to think about.'

'My mother had two sons. And a daughter besides.'

'But she didn't have Oscar.'

'Neither will you when all the pieces are in place.'

209

'You don't understand. He'll never divorce me.'

'Maybe not. But there's no law that can force you to live with him.'

'I know that,' she said. 'I've thought of that a thousand times. That's the easy part. The difficult part is Charlie. Oscar adopted him when we got married. He's his legal father.'

'That doesn't matter. After a certain age a child can choose the parent he wants to live with.'

'That's the hardest part,' she said. 'I'm not sure Charlie would choose me instead of Oscar. Oscar has him mesmerized. He's given him all kinds of things other boys his age don't have. Not material things necessarily although, God knows, we've both smothered him in those. Oscar's gift is the gift of himself. It's worth everything or nothing depending on your viewpoint. The public relations people who represent Oscar's company, for example, have Charlie on their mailing list. A copy of every press release, photograph or brochure they send out goes to him. All his classmates are movie and television freaks and Charlie's their source of inside material. He's been on movie sets all over the world, Oscar gave him screen credit when he was ten years old as third assistant director and when he was eleven, as casting consultant. He gets Christmas presents from Hollywood people he's never heard of because he shows up on their gift list as Oscar's son. And on his birthday he gets cards from Henry Fonda, Paul Newman, Steve McQueen, and Charlie Bronson. All his heroes. They don't *know* him but a card goes out from them anyway because he's Oscar's kid. His teachers tell me Charlie doesn't lord any of this over his friends. They say he's very matter-of-fact about it. But all the same, he knows that Oscar gives him an importance he wouldn't have otherwise.'

'Do you think all that stuff is good for him?'

'Of course I don't. But he does. And I can't blame him. I'd have felt the same at his age. And there's no stopping Oscar. I've tried and it doesn't work. That's his business . . . selling himself. And he's certainly done the job with Charlie.'

'Are you telling me you're tied to Oscar for life because your son likes him?'

'No. I'm saying it's a difficult situation. I'm saying I don't want to lose my kid. And it could happen.'

'In seven years he'll be twenty years old,' Rab said.

'Seven years is a long time.'

'You're painting a gloomy picture.'

'I don't mean to. I'm just trying to tell the truth.'

'All kinds of different things are true.'

'Tell me about it,' she said.

'Answer a question for me,' he said then. 'What do you want from me?'

She didn't hesitate. 'Everything.'

'When do you want it?'

'Now. How about you?'

'I feel the same.'

'You'd better.'

'Now all we have to do is work out the details.'

He could see her smile in the dim light. 'That's it,' she said. 'That's all we have to do.'

Chapter Five

[1]

'It's a long time since we sat down to a fine dinner together,' Nora said.

'That's true,' Jesse said.

'Since you're living with the redskins on the frontier now, it must be a long time since you've had a really decent meal with *anyone*.'

They were sitting in a restaurant on the Quai Bourbon looking across the Pont Louis-Philippe. Jesse had arrived in Paris that afternoon.

'You're right,' he said. 'Where I live, if you can't shoot a deer or a rabbit you simply go hungry. You can always make a slap-up meal of hominy grits or flannel cakes but if you want meat on the table you have to go out with your rifle and hunt for it.'

'*Chacun à son goût.*'

'Exactly,' he said.

'I remember the first time Hugh and I saw you. All arms and legs and your hair combed straight back. We decided you looked like those American cowboys we'd seen in silent movies.'

'I'm glad you didn't tell me that. I was trying to look British.'

'Impossible, my darling. You were too relaxed to pass yourself off as an Englishman.'

After Jesse ordered the wine she said, 'How many dinners have we eaten in this restaurant? At this table?'

'Eight thousand.'

She laughed. 'Less than that, I suppose, but a great many, all the same.'

'That's because you're a creature of habit.'

'Not at all. It's because I have become a Frenchwoman. An American always searches for something *new*. The French look for something excellent and once they find it they stick with it.'

'What about the English?'

'They cling to what they know, whether it's good or not.'

They ordered their dinner then and drank Sancerre while they waited for the first course to arrive.

'I get the feeling that we're going to talk about old times,' Jesse said.

'Why not?'

'You once told me that you are only intrigued by where you're going, that you have no interest in where you've been.'

'I was younger when I said that.'

'You said it's the first sign of old age when the past is more attractive than the future.'

Nora smiled. 'I was mistaken about that. The first sign of old age is arthritis, especially for those of us who live by the Seine. Besides, since you and I have no present and no future, it's the past or nothing for us.'

'Not necessarily. There are all kinds of things we could discuss besides ourselves.'

'Too boring,' she said. 'What could be so interesting as us? Now . . . tell me what you're working on these days.'

Jesse had considered whether or not he would tell her about the project he was trying to bring to life, a candid memoir of his life with the Bradshaws. On his way to Paris from Heidelberg he'd decided that he would tell her. But now that the direct question had been asked, some instinct for privacy took over. 'Nothing major. Nothing world-shaking,' he said. 'Researching a Kirchner piece for *Der Spiegel* and thinking about something on Schmidt-Rottluff.'

'The Germans don't interest me any longer.'

'They never did, did they?'

'Not much. Too cruel for me. But I like Klee.'

'He's Swiss.'

'Maybe that's why I like him. He pleases me but he never frightens me.'

'You're not conservative about anything in your life – but you're conservative about painting. I've never understood that.'

213

'Neither have I. I guess I have some Victorian notion that a painting should stay on the wall. I don't want it to jump out of the frame and strangle me.'

'You certainly used to show some wild painters in your gallery.'

'Of course I did. Because I wanted to make money. I soon found out that if I really hated and detested a painting, if it was something I would never hang in my own home, some collector would buy it from my gallery as soon as I put it up.'

'You're perverse.'

'Of course. I have contempt for commerce but commerce is my only gift.'

'You'd be very offended if someone else said that.'

'Only because it's true. Nobody wants to hear the truth from somebody else's mouth.'

'How is *Icarus* doing?'

'It's a very successful magazine. People buy it and quote from it and take it seriously.'

'And do they take you seriously?'

'Very. They think I'm a latter-day Sylvia Beach. College students come knocking on my door to ask if I still hold my weekly salons.'

'Do you?'

'No,' she said. 'I'm a legend now. And legends must never be seen in public. You're a legend, too, did you know that? Since you stopped writing for *Icarus* people think you're dead. One young chap said he was doing his master's thesis on you. Did you know that?'

Jesse nodded. 'Thanks to you he tracked me down in Illinois. I talked with him for an hour but I haven't heard from him since. I think he liked me better dead than alive.'

While they ate dinner he told her about his visit to Polly in Heidelberg.

'Did you meet the young man she's living with. Jack . . . is that his name?'

Jesse nodded.

'What do you think?' she said.

'It's hard to say.'

'Rab hated him, Bill hated him, and Valerie said he frightened her to death.'

'I know,' Jesse said. 'Bill gave me a full report. They all think

214

he's a bad guy for Polly. And so do I. But she doesn't feel that way at all. And Polly's not stupid.'

'Love is blind. Do people still say that?'

'I doubt it, but even if they do it doesn't apply to Polly. She knows Jack Dieter better than any of us. And the longer she's with him the more attached she becomes.'

'Does that mean you gave her your blessing?'

'Christ, no. But I didn't try to give her a lecture either. There's no point to it. She doesn't try to hide his faults and neither does he. He doesn't pretend to be anything he isn't. But what he *is* is something that..I don't know how to describe it. He's like a ragbag full of little scraps of cloth. All colours and patterns, some of them faded and torn and dirty. But you get the feeling that all of a sudden those rags could be turned into a warm quilt. I'm not saying that such a thing will happen in Jack's case but I'm also not saying that I don't know what Polly sees in him. Because I *can* see it and I think Valerie sees it too. But to Rab and Bill he's just an American drunk who's smarter than they are and who goes to bed any time he wants to with their beautiful sister.'

'Sounds as if you like him,' Nora said.

Jesse shook his head. 'I'd like to strangle the bastard. But I'm sure as hell not going to let him know that. Or Polly either. Because I know that neither one of them gives a damn how I feel about him. I can like him or not like him and it won't change a bloody thing.'

When they ordered dessert, Nora asked the *patron* to bring them a bottle of champagne.

'Sancerre, St Emilion, and now champagne,' Jesse said. 'I thought you believed in moderation.'

'Never,' Nora said. 'I'm told that after a certain age, our tolerance for alcohol is sharply diminished but I reject that theory. I insist on obeying my appetites. Furthermore, if you don't walk me across the Pont Louis-Philippe after dinner for an armagnac *Chez Claudine* I will stamp my foot and scream.'

'Mustn't have that. Of course we'll visit Claudine. How is she?'

'Old and cranky and arthritic. But she opens her café every morning at six and closes it at midnight. Her only concession to her age is a midday nap but she admits it to no one. When she leaves the café at three she says, 'Now I have work to do at home.''

After the patron poured the champagne and left the table Nora

215

said, 'We've known each other too long to lie. I want to tell you a simple truth and then we'll go on from there. How does that strike you?'

Jesse smiled. 'However it strikes me, I know that if you've decided to tell me a simple truth, then that's what you'll do.'

'Not necessarily. You could stab me in the throat with a steak knife. Or you could run downstairs and throw yourself in the river . . .'

'But short of that . . .'

'Short of that I'm going to say what I have to say.' She picked up her wine glass, sipped from it, then put it down again. 'Just as I have refused to give up on wine,' she said, 'I refuse to give up on you, my friend. I refuse to give up on us.'

When Jesse didn't answer she went on. 'When you left me and married Valerie I knew that some day you'd come back to me. And you did. After you and she were divorced and you left again, after you went to America to be with Helen, I wasn't so sure you'd come back. I know your leaving the last time was more complex. It seemed suddenly that everyone in the Bradshaw family was involved somehow. And most important, both of us felt guilty. You know I'm right. You remember the discussions we had. No matter how much Valerie denied it, we believed that she had divorced you because she'd found out about us, because she knew we were living together whenever you were in Paris. Isn't that true?'

'I certainly remember those discussions we had.'

'After all the years we'd known each other, after all the time we'd been together, I suddenly felt ill at ease with you. And I could sense that you felt the same when you were with me. Am I right?'

He nodded his head and she went on. 'I understood your wanting to be somewhere else when Valerie and Floyd got married. I knew you wanted to be away from me for a while, too. And I understood *that*. And once I got over being hurt, after I realized you were living with Helen in her house, I tried to understand that as well. At that time I believed you and Helen had always had a little romance going so it wasn't as if you'd discovered someone new. She was there and you were there, so what the hell? I don't mean to say I wasn't angry. I was. Helen has always been a knife in the heart to me and you know it. I cried a lot and got drunk a lot and called you every foul name I could think of. But I never said to myself, "Now it's over. Put it all behind you" – because I didn't believe that. And I don't believe it now. Because whatever that life is that you've invented for yourself, it's not enough to feed you and nourish you and carry you through from now till the end. Whatever you thought you were getting into, whatever nostalgia you may have had for that place where you lived with Raymond and went to school and came back to after the war, whatever scenario you may have written and cast yourself in, it simply won't work for you. For a few years maybe but not for ever. You're not a nester, Jesse. You need places and people and problems and conflicts and ideas. You need all kinds of things, *different* things, to stimulate you and keep you alive. Maybe you have nothing but rotten memories of those years we were together, but if that's true then your memory's playing tricks on you. Because we *invented* ourselves then, we invented *each other*. Every idea and impulse and value that either of us has was planted during that time, in those wild years. I used to tell myself there weren't enough parts to go around so we only managed to create one person. That person had two heads and two bodies and two names. That person was *us*. And it's still alive. Just because the two halves are living on separate sides of the ocean doesn't mean the creature is dead. We didn't use up everything we had together. We didn't get tired of each other. We didn't betray each other. We didn't love each other too little. We loved each other too much. But when other people got mixed up in the stew, people we both loved, we couldn't sort out the pieces and figure out which piece belonged to which puzzle. So we tossed *all* the pieces in the dustbin. Am I right?'

'I don't know,' Jesse said.

'Yes, you do. You may not want to admit it. Maybe you didn't want to face up to it. But you know I'm right.'

'I never contradict a beautiful woman who's just ordered a bottle of fine champagne.'

'Don't try to joke your way out of this. It won't work and you know it. You're one of those people who thinks your brain will never let you down. Use your head, be logical and wise, and everything will turn out right. What nonsense. The main activity of the brain is self-deception.'

'Is that what this lecture is all about? Are you telling me I'm deceiving myself?'

'I don't have to tell you. You already know it. I'm just reminding you,' she said.

217

'First you're going to diagnose my condition, then you'll recommend a cure, is that it?'

'No, that's not it. I know you too well to prescribe anything. No one can *tell* you anything. Everyone knows that. I just thought I might open you up a bit, let a little light shine through, give you a chance to take a fresh look at yourself.'

Jesse smiled. 'I do that every morning when I'm shaving. It's a ritual. With every stroke of the razor I ask myself a significant question.'

'No, you don't,' Nora said. 'If you did you wouldn't be crumbling away in some damp corner of Middle America.'

'Crumbling away? Now you're getting my attention. I thought I was in pretty good shape for a chap my age. Bill says his girlfriend is quite taken with me.'

'God, you are tiresome,' she said. 'I'd forgotten how tiresome you can be. You absolutely refuse to enter any contest you can't win.'

'Is this a contest? I thought of it as a sort of reunion.'

'You know very well what I'm saying. It's not a contest between the two of us. But it's very much a battle between what you *are* and what you've decided you're going to be.'

'Am I winning or losing?'

'You're losing, my darling. But you don't want to face it. So let's drop the whole subject, please. I will toddle home and you can wander back to your hotel on Place St-Sulpice and think about what a pleasant dinner we had and what a top-notch person you are.'

'You're really angry, aren't you?'

'Not angry. *Sick* is the word.'

He sat back in his chair and lit a cigarette. 'Why don't we start over? I think I must have missed something.'

She shook her head. 'You didn't miss anything. And no, I don't want to start over. I have a headache. The champagne wasn't a good idea after all.'

'What about that armagnac you promised me? Coffee and armagnac at Claudine's.'

'It was a lovely notion at the time but now I think not.'

'I'd forgotten how spoiled you are,' he said then.

'*I* haven't forgotten. You used to remind me of it all the time.'

'You've been sitting here trying to manoeuvre me into some kind

218

of statement, some admission of guilt or bad judgment and since I
can't figure out what I'm suppose to say . . .'

'You're wrong,' she said. 'I've been trying, in some sort of clumsy
way, to tell you that I care about you, that it matters to me what
you do, that it hurts me when I think you're hurting yourself, that
you're not thinking straight, not acting correctly, not using yourself
well. If I were twenty years old I would simply put my arms around
you and tell you how much I love you. I'd have confidence that
everything else would work out then, that all the other questions
would be answered. But we've come too far for such innocent
gestures to have any meaning. All we can do now, it seems, is
make each other angry or resentful or guilty. Your solution is to
make jokes and my solution is to get a headache and go home. I
should have known that words wouldn't solve anything. They
never did for us.'

[2]

On the day that Albert Speer and Baldur von Schirach were released
from prison, students demonstrated at colleges and universities all
over Germany. School guards and local police had been fore-
warned, so the demonstrations, for the most part, were orderly
and non-violent. At Heidelberg, however, after the university chancellor asked the city to send riot police to the school grounds, a
bloody battle developed. When it ended at last, a school guard and
two students were dead, an historic building was half-burned and
several students were in hospital. One of the dead students was
Jack's friend, Donny Krause, and Jack himself, with a fractured
skull and a broken arm, was carried unconscious to the university
infirmary.

The government at Bonn and local officials in Heidelberg did
what they could to minimize the affair and the West German press
was co-operative but within hours of the incident an East Berlin
paper carried the story on its front page. Under a headline that
read *Two Students Dead in Heidelberg*, they described a peaceful
demonstration by Socialist students led by two American war-
veterans. The demonstration had been broken up by a neo-Nazi

student group and riot police. Two students had been beaten to death, and many had been hospitalized.

Before leaving Paris for Germany, Jesse visitcd both the British and American Consulates in Paris and when his plane landed in Frankfurt, he went directly to the American Consulate there. He was taken to the office of Harold Kinsman, an Associate Consul.

'We've been talking to our people in Bonn,' Kinsman said, 'as well as officials in Heidelberg. Because of our military presence there, we have good relationships with the local government. They know we're damned upset about the way this whole thing was handled. I'm sure they'll co-operate in every way as far as Jack Dieter is concerned. We've already asked to have him transferred to the US Military Hospital.'

'We want to make sure he gets the best possible care,' Jesse said.

'He'll get it there. He needs some patching up but I understand his condition isn't critical.'

'Will he need a lawyer?'

'I wouldn't think so. No criminal charges have been mentioned and I don't expect that any will be. I suppose you could bring a damage suit against the university or the City of Heidelberg but I wouldn't recommend it.'

'The British Consul in Paris thought it might be a good precaution for us to engage a German lawyer.'

Kinsman looked for a moment at an open file-folder on his desk. 'Yes, I see we've had a call from the British people here. May I ask why you went to them?'

'My daughter's a British subject.'

'But you're an American, aren't you?'

'I have dual citizenship.'

'I see.' Another glance at the folder. 'Polly Bradshaw's your daughter?'

'That's right.'

'And she's married to Jack Dieter?'

'No. They both go to school in Heidelberg. And they live together.'

'The people at the British Consulate seem to think they're married.'

Jesse shook his head. 'I told them exactly what I told your Consul in Paris. And what I'm telling you now. He's not a family member but we are very concerned about his situation, we want to help out ' any way we can, and we will appreciate whatever help we can get from you.'

'I understand that and I don't foresee any problems. It might have been simpler however, just from the standpoint of logistics, if we hadn't involved the Brits.'

'Why is that?'

'Nothing serious. It's just that their methods are usually different from ours. They have their own peculiar relationships with the locals. Just a matter of style, I guess you'd say. When they're in the picture, things tend to drag on a bit if you know what I mean.'

'You can be sure that our family wants to keep this as simple as possible. And I explained that to the British people as well. You say you foresee no problems for Mr Dieter. Neither do we. But we want to be prepared in case a problem does arise.'

'That's our position exactly. We'll stay on top of this. I assume you're going straight ahead to Heidelberg.'

'That's right. As soon as I leave here.'

'We sent a man over there yesterday. Dale Tunstall. I'm sure he's in touch with your daughter by now.' He handed Jesse a card. 'Here's where you can reach him. But I expect he'll be waiting for you at the hospital.'

It was late afternoon when Jesse arrived in Heidelberg. He went directly to the hospital at the US Army installation. The sergeant at the reception desk had no record of a patient named Jack Dieter. When Jesse insisted that he see the Resident-in-Charge, the sergeant sent him along to Colonel Echols. 'We did hear from the Consulate in Frankfurt,' the Colonel told him. 'They said Dieter would be transferred here early this afternoon but so far he hasn't come in. Let's run a check on him.' He pressed a buzzer on his desk and a corporal appeared from an adjoining office. 'Call Dr Herzfeld at the University infirmary. Find out what happened to a transfer patient named Jack Dieter.'

When the corporal left the room, Jesse said, 'The Consulate in Frankfurt sent a man down here. I'm supposed to contact him. May I use your phone?'

'He's probably at the Schamberg. That's where those guys usually stay. You have the number?'

Jesse read him the number from the card Kinsman had given him. 'That's the Schamberg,' Echols said. He dialled the number and handed the phone to Jesse.

221

The young man at the hotel desk spoke excellent English. He said Mr Tunstall was out but would return between six and seven. 'Tell him I'll telephone him at seven this evening. My name is Jesse Bradshaw.' He dialled the number at Polly's apartment then. No answer. He hung up, dialled again, and let it ring seven times. When he hung up this time he wrote Polly's number on a slip of paper and gave it to Echols. 'Here's where I'll be. It's my daughter's apartment. Please let us know when you get some information about Dieter.'

He went to the university then, located the infirmary, and went inside. The grey-haired woman at the reception desk was extremely polite and thorough. 'Our discharge records show that Herr Dieter was transferred early this afternoon, at half after one to be precise, to the hospital of the US Army installation.'

'I just came from there,' Jesse said. 'He's not there.'

'Perhaps they made an error.'

'I spoke to the Chief of Staff. He knew of the transfer but he said the patient never arrived.'

'Let me check downstairs,' she said, 'for verification.' She made three telephone calls, grim-faced, speaking in no-nonsense German. When she hung up she turned to Jesse and said, 'The paperwork is all in place. It is exactly as I have said. The patient was transferred this afternoon. The ambulance left at half after one.'

'There must be some mistake.'

'There is no mistake. We keep careful records.'

'May I speak with your Dr Herzfeld?'

'Dr Herzfeld is not in the hospital today.'

'This is most important. Who is your supervisor?'

'Dr Mittag is our resident manager. He goes home at four o'clock. He'll be in tomorrow morning at seven. If you insist on seeing him I suggest you come back tomorrow.'

Jesse tried to call Polly again from a phone box outside the infirmary. Again there was no answer. By the time he reached her apartment it was a quarter past seven. As he walked into the downstairs foyer a grey-haired woman in a brown uniform appeared in a doorway beside the elevator. In laboured English she asked, 'Is it that you are being papa to Fraulein Bratshaw?'

'Yes, I am.'

'I am to give you some latch-key. Apartment four-zero-six.' She

222

handed him the key, stepped back out of sight, and closed the door behind her.

As soon as he was inside Polly's apartment, Jesse called the Schamberg. 'Yes, sir, Mr Bradshaw. This is Dale Tunstall. You just caught me. I have to run up to Frankfurt. I'll be back by noon tomorrow. Meanwhile everything seems to be in order here. The patient was transferred and he's on the base where we can keep an eye on him.'

'No, he's not. He's not at the Army hospital and he's not at the university infirmary.'

'My information is that he was transferred at one-thirty this afternoon.'

'That's when he left the infirmary but he never showed up at the Army hospital.'

'I don't know who you've been talking to but . . .'

'I talked to the Chief of Staff, Colonel Echols. At *five* this afternoon. He told me Dieter's not there.'

He heard Tunsall lighting a cigarette. Then: 'All right. Here's what we'll do. As soon as I get back here tomorrow I'll get this all straightened out. Meanwhile I'm sure there's nothing to be alarmed about.'

'I'm not alarmed, God damn it. Kinsman told me to check in with you and that's what I'm doing. I'm trying to locate Jack Dieter and you know less about him than I do.'

'Here's my problem,' Tunstall said. 'I'm on a tight schedule here. So let's sit down and review all this tomorrow. Why don't you meet me for a late lunch here at the hotel . . .'

'Go to hell,' Jesse said and hung up the receiver.

[3]

Polly came home at nine o'clock that night. 'I'm glad you're here,' she said. 'I am *very* glad you're here.'

'I came as soon as I could after I found out.'

'I was going crazy when I called you in Paris. I didn't know if Jack was alive or dead.'

'Did you call Valerie?'

223

Polly nodded. 'Right after I talked to you. I didn't want her to read about it for the first time in the paper or hear it on the radio.'

'Is she coming here?'

'She wanted to but I told her not to. There's nothing she can do really, except feel sorry for me and feel terrible herself. So I hope she won't come.'

'Did you call Rab?'

'Yes, I did. He's a madman but he always comes through when you need him. I hope I won't need him but if I do he knows a lot of people in London.'

'I called Helen and Bill and told them I was coming back here. Before I left Paris, Helen called back and said the story was on the television news there.'

'All that publicity scares me to death. They're trying to twist it around into something it wasn't.'

'How do you mean?'

'There's a lot of anti-American feeling in Germany. Particularly here in Heidelberg. This has been a United States military centre since the war and now it looks as though it's a permanent thing. Even non-political people are tired of seeing American uniforms on every corner. So that's the ferment. And the politicians take advantage of it. Both sides of the fence. You can see it very clearly at the university. There's a student leftist group. They call themselves Socialists but everyone else calls them Communists. And on the other side there's a crowd of baby Fascists who think Hitler lost the war because he was too soft on the Jews.'

'And Jack was involved in all this?'

'Jack's never been really involved in anything except music. But Donny was involved. He wasn't the ringleader, as they're saying he was, but he went to the meetings and made a speech once in a while. But when the business about Speer and von Schirach came along, when it was announced that they were to be released from prison, he really got excited. And so did Jack. Nothing like Donny but I knew he was steamed up about it. I even had a suspicion that they were involved in some sort of demonstration that was scheduled to take place around the time those two prisoners were let out. Jack was very mysterious about it, didn't say anything to me about where he was spending his evenings, but I knew he was with Donny and I guessed they were up to something. It didn't disturb me because in the first place I was against the Speer and von Schirach release myself. And besides, political demonstrations at the university are an every-day affair. Posters and speeches and people shouting at each other. And another thing, Jack had just gone through a long period – a few weeks, but it seemed like months – when he never left this apartment. He slept and ate and drank and played the cello and never went outside. So when he started going out at night with Donny I thought it was a good sign, no matter what they were up to. But I was wrong, I guess. Because the next thing I knew, Donny was dead and Jack was being patched up in the hospital.'

'How long has it been since you've seen him?'

Polly looked at her watch. 'About three hours. I stayed with him till they threw me out.'

'You mean you know where he is?'

'Why wouldn't I?'

'Because nobody else does. I've been trying to track him down ever since I got to Heidelberg. I knew you weren't at home so I decided if I found Jack I'd find you. But he wasn't at the US Army hospital.'

'Why did you go there? What made you think he was there?'

'Because the American Consul in Frankfurt told me that was where he'd been transferred to. They'd arranged it. But when I got to the university infirmary all they knew was that he was gone. But they didn't know where. Or else they didn't want to tell me. The lady at the reception desk said he'd been taken to the Army hospital.'

'The grey-haired lady. Sweet voice but a steel spine.'

'That's the one.'

'Ah-ha. Now it's starting to come clear. She told me the same thing when I asked where they were taking him. But I decided not to take a chance. When they took him downstairs to the ambulance I waited in my car in the street and followed the ambulance. They took him to the Bavarian State Hospital on Ulmstrasse.'

'And he's there now?'

'Yes, he is. And now I know why they were so surprised to see me turn up. At first they said he wasn't there but I said I knew he was there because I'd seen him delivered in an ambulance. I speak German like a native now, you know, including good old profane street German, so when I turn it loose it takes the natives by surprise. Finally they admitted he was there but they said I couldn't

225

see him. So I located a supervisor and started screaming all over again, told them I was pregnant and they were keeping me away from my child's father, told them my grandfather was a high official in Bonn, and at last they let me see him. Twenty minutes. When I left they said I could see him twenty minutes each time, twice a day. But if I told anyone else he was there I would not be allowed to see him at all.'

Polly fixed some supper then and they sat in the kitchen eating.

'What sort of shape is Jack in now?' Jesse asked. 'Have you been able to talk with him?'

'A little bit. He's on pain-killers and he's a bit fuzzy about details but the nurses told me he should recover quickly. There was no serious damage from his head injury and the break in his arm was a clean one. Halfway between the wrist and the elbow. So it won't affect his cello playing. That was the only thing he was worried about.'

'What did he say about the demonstration?'

'He doesn't know much about it. He must have gone down as soon as the baby Fascists and the riot police moved in. He doesn't know that three people were killed. He doesn't know that Donny's dead. The first time he talked to me in hospital he said, "I guess we had a hell of a fight, didn't we?" So that's how he sees it. A demonstration that got a bit out of hand.'

'How do you see it?'

'I'm not trying to draw any conclusions but I've been hearing some of the radio reports and I'm afraid it's being blown up into a major thing. The good Germans versus the bad Germans. They see a Communist behind every tree here in Bavaria. The local people think that all of us students at the university are in daily contact with Moscow. It's a paranoid community. They see themselves as hostages, caught between the radical students and the American military. Enemies all round. As soon as they moved Jack to the Bavarian State Hospital they stationed a soldier outside his door. When I asked what that was all about they said, "Just a courtesy. Request from the mayor's office." '

'Have you talked to a man named Tunstall from the American Consulate?'

'For about two minutes,' she said. 'I told him to leave me alone and leave Jack alone. Those bastards are so busy protecting their own fences they get everyone in trouble.'

'I didn't realize that. I talked to their people in Frankfurt because I thought we might need their help.'

'We do. But that doesn't mean we'll get it. And if we do get it, it doesn't mean we'll like what we get.'

Later when he was in bed trying to read himself to sleep, Jesse heard Polly's telephone ring in her bedroom down the hall. A few minutes later there was a light tap on his door and she said, 'Are you asleep?'

'No. Come in.'

She came and sat on the edge of his bed. 'Rab Bradshaw strikes again,' she said.

'Was that him on the telephone?'

'No. That was a man named Kendall calling from the Foreign Office in London. He asked if I was Rab Bradshaw's sister and then went on from there. He said a man named Noel Barber will be coming to see us tomorrow morning. He's from their office in Frankfurt. Then he told me they've notified the West German government in Bonn that they were concerned with Jack's situation. And they've filed formal papers with the Heidelberg authorities demanding that they be kept informed about Jack's whereabouts. If he's moved from the hospital where he is they want to be told exactly where he's been taken.'

'Well, that's a good development, isn't it?'

'I suppose it is. But it frightens me to death. I thought all we had to do was get him well and bring him home. Now I don't know what to think.'

[4]

Noel Barber was a neat and precise man. Close-cropped hair, tweed suit, and a navy-blue tie. He arrived at Polly's apartment at nine the next morning and sat in the kitchen with her and Jesse while they had tea and toast.

'I stopped on the way for coffee and a sausage roll. Looked at the newspaper and made my plans for the day. It's my habit. I'm an early riser. Take a bit of abuse from my family about it. Even on holiday I'm up and going not long after sunrise.'

227

He quickly came to the matters at hand. 'Clumsy business here. Five young people with misdirected energies. Proper impulses perhaps, students of government and politics, eager to be heard, to make their feelings known, very important to enlist the young people in our national doings, but in this instance everything carried too far. Ideology carried too far is a dangerous affair. And violence is no ideology at all, is it? This is not to say that the students were necessarily at fault. It's unthinkable that the university leaders and the mayor of the city should see fit to send in a riot squad to silence a student demonstration.'

'When did the fighting start between the two groups of students?' Polly asked.

'That's an interesting point,' Barber said. 'Our local people tell us that the people who came to break up the demonstration were, for the most part, not students at all, but young men from the town who fancy themselves as a new generation of storm-troopers. Also, if our information is correct, this group arrived at the scene of the demonstration precisely when the riot police came. The demonstrators had no weapons other than the sticks their placards were fastened to, so they were no match for the clubs and truncheons used against them. There may have been some knives as well.'

'But how was the university guard killed?'

'He was an unarmed man doing his routine patrol of the university grounds. When he tried to stand between the students and the riot police he was struck on the head and killed.'

'The newspapers are saying the demonstrators killed the guard.'

'Of course. The local authorities did not expect that things would go so far as they did. They need a scapegoat.'

'I hope you're not saying they're trying to blame this on Jack.'

'We're not sure yet what they're planning. We just know that all at once a lot of attention is being directed here. From every corner. So certain officials are scrambling to clear their skirts. It's clear that the young American who was killed . . .'

'Donny Krause,' Polly said.

'It seems clear,' Barber went on, 'that he is the focus of their attention. Since the Soviet press has come out so strongly in defence of the demonstrators, it's a near certainty that Krause will be identified as a Communist and the ringleader. They're saying now that it was he who threw the petrol bomb that started the fire in a university building. And we're told there is a deposition from one

228

of the riot police who swears that Krause was the one who struck the university guard.'

'There were so many students there,' Polly said. 'They saw what happened. The officials can't just say anything they want.'

'Let's hope not. But it's a complex situation. And the political ramifications seem to get more intricate every hour.'

'Is Jack under arrest?' Polly said. 'Is that why there's a guard outside his hospital room?'

'When we asked them that early this morning they said no. They said he'll be able to come home as soon as the doctors release him from the hospital.'

'Do you believe them?'

'Let's say I have no good reason to disbelieve them. Not yet.'

'But if they're trying to blame the whole mess on Donny, what makes you think they won't include Jack? Everyone knows they were close friends.'

'That's what we're trying to prevent. So we've arranged secretly for a local solicitor to intercede on his behalf. His name is Speicher. He is preparing the papers that Mr Kendal told you about last night. But they can only be filed on your behalf. Those papers will prevent the authorities from whisking him away somewhere so we won't know where he is.'

'Do you think that's likely?'

'I hope not. But when petty officials are protecting their jobs all sorts of things are possible.'

'Do you trust this solicitor?' Jack asked.

'We're all strangers here,' Barber said, 'in a difficult situation. We have to trust somebody.'

Early that afternoon, Polly and Jesse met for an hour with Heinrich Speicher. He asked a great number of questions about Jack and Donny Krause and took careful notes as Polly spoke. His clothes were expensive but rumpled. He looked more Irish than German. His English was slow and careful. 'I have one sister in Claremore, Oklahoma,' he said, 'and another in Santa Rosa, California. They're quite happy in America. One grows orchids, the other breeds small dogs. I don't like small dogs.'

Finally he said, 'All this will be helpful to me. Now let me gather as much information as I can from the local officials. We will have a better idea then about how to proceed.'

'Why do we have to *proceed*?' Polly said. 'Jack's a victim, a patient

229

in hospital. They've said he can come home as soon as he feels well enough.'

'Then I'm sure that is the case. But all the same we should have all the information we can get.'

As Polly and Jesse stood up to leave, Speicher said to her, 'I feel that you're disturbed by something I've said.'

'No, it isn't that. I'm just concerned that . . . I mean do we give the impression that we think Jack is guilty of something when we take on a solicitor?'

'In some people's minds perhaps. But I believe that's an acceptable risk. One you must take.'

[5]

'I don't know what you're talking about,' Jack said. 'Who gives a damn about the British Consulate? I'm an American citizen, for Christ's sake, whether I'm proud of it or not. And why are you talking to a German lawyer? Was that your father's idea?'

'No.'

'I don't need a lawyer. I needed a doctor. And now I've got doctors coming out of my ears. I mean, let's not make this into an international mess.'

'That's what it is, Jack.'

'What do you mean? We had a little student demonstration, somebody sent in the goons, and I got my head caved in because I didn't duck fast enough. But it's over. Let's not dwell on it. I've got other things to think about. Like getting home and sitting in my corner.'

'It's serious, Jack. It's not the way you remember it.'

'Sure it is. I told you all about it.'

'No, you didn't. Tell me now. Tell me exactly what happened. What really went on at the demonstration?'

'It never got started. We came marching into the common grounds there at the centre of the school, thirty or forty of us, yelling the slogans we'd make up and carrying signs. But before we got to the spot where people make speeches, a whole squad of those riot police bastards, swinging clubs and carrying shields in front of them, with half a dozen attack dogs on leashes, came whipping around the corner of the administration building and ran straight for us. At the same time a crowd of roughnecks from the town came at us from the other side. We were caught in the middle with no place to run to. I remember getting cracked on the arm with a club when I tried to protect my head and then I guess somebody made a direct hit on my skull. Next thing I knew I woke up in the hospital with splints on my arm and a bandage on my head. I was just in the wrong spot, I guess. The rest of the guys probably got off easy.'

'Is that all you remember?'

'That's it.'

'And nobody at the infirmary or here at the hospital has talked to you about it?'

'Nobody talks to me at all,' he said. 'Except you. And you don't stay long when you come.'

'I stay as long as they'll let me.'

'What does that mean?'

'It's not the way you remember it, Jack.' She paused. 'I didn't want to tell you this before. I don't want to tell you now.'

'Tell me what?'

'Three people got killed. When you were already unconscious two students and a university guard were beaten to death.'

'What kind of a story is that?'

'It's the truth.'

'I don't believe you. Somebody would have told me if something like that happened. Donny would have been in here like a shot.' When she didn't answer he said, 'Did Donny get hurt? Is that why he hasn't been in to see me?'

She started to cry suddenly. As she brought her hand to her mouth, she felt the tears on her cheeks.

'Hey . . . what's the matter with you? Cut it out. I'm the one who's all banged up . . . not you. What are you crying about?'

'Donny's dead, Jack. He didn't make it to the infirmary.'

'What are you telling me?'

'They flew his body home to Wisconsin yesterday.'

After a long moment he said, 'Jesus . . .'

'I didn't want to tell you. But I didn't want you to hear it from somebody else either.'

An orderly came to the door of the room and spoke to them in German. 'Visiting hours are finished. Your time is up.'

'Please . . .' she said.

'You're six minutes over the limit now.'

She leaned over and kissed Jack, one hand on each side of his face. 'I'm so sorry Jack. I didn't want to tell you.'

'*Bitte*,' the orderly said, stepping into the room. 'You must leave now.'

'I can't stand to see you look like that,' she said. 'I'll be back tomorrow. We'll talk about it then.'

'*Fraulein! Bitte*,' the orderly said.

She turned and left the room. The orderly followed her and carefully closed the door behind him. He said something to the guard standing by the door and the guard laughed.

[6]

Heinrich Speicher's expression was grim when Polly and Jesse sat down in his office two days after their first meeting with him. 'The situation has changed, I'm afraid, since we last spoke together. The outlook at the moment is not bright. You mentioned that you had been in contact with the American Consulate. Have you heard from them since we talked?'

'I've tried to contact Kinsman in Frankfurt,' Jesse said, 'and Tunstall here at the Hotel Schamberg but I haven't been able to reach them.'

'They may have called the apartment when we weren't there,' Polly said.

'I don't think so,' Speicher said. 'I don't think you will hear from them again.'

'What does that mean?'

'It means that a great deal of pressure is being put on a great many people. First of all, both the guard and the German student who was killed were local people. Certain groups here in Heidelberg are demanding an explanation from the school and from local authorities. Bonn is also asking for details that will help them explain to the world what took place at the school the night of the demonstration. People are asking why such force was necessary to suppress a student demonstration. If the authorities support the police action that was taken they many be accused by the world press of supporting neo-Nazi groups. If they back the students they run the risk that they may be seen as siding with the Soviet press. The mass of German people, including the leaders at Bonn, have a great fear of Communism. The politicians know that any suspected association with Soviet ideology means political suicide.'

'I'm sure they're not forgetting either that an American citizen was killed. And another one badly injured. That won't go unnoticed in the United States,' Jesse said.

'Of course not. That's another part of the problem. At least it would seem to be. But from what I've learned in the past two days I'm afraid the authorities, both here and in Bonn, see the two Americans as a *solution* to their problems.'

'What does that mean?' Jesse said.

Speicher turned to Polly. 'I met with the Commissioner of Police today. He told me that both Donny Krause and Jack Dieter have police records here in Heidelberg. Is that true?'

'They drank a lot sometimes. And I know they've had some problems with the police.'

'The Commissioner says Krause has been arrested and detained six times, Dieter five times.'

'What does "detained" mean?'

'It means they spent time in the Heidelberg jail.'

'That's not true,' she said. 'I think they kept Donny overnight one time when he was too drunk to tell them where he lived but Jack has never been in jail, not since I've known him.'

Speicher held up a sheet of paper. 'This copy of the police record shows that he was incarcerated for ten days a little more than two months ago.'

'That's simply not true.'

'I see. Well, that's what we're up against.'

'What are you saying?' Jesse asked.

'I may be mistaken. I hope I am. But from what I've learned, I think they plan to use Krause and Dieter as scapegoats in this matter. Krause in particular, they say, has a record of leftist associations and radical activities that dates back to the time of his military service in Korea. Do you know anything about that?'

233

'No,' Polly said, 'and I don't know how the police in Heidelberg would know about it either.'

'They say the US Army installation here provided them with certain service records for both men.'

'Is that why you said we won't get any help from the American Consul?' Jesse said.

'I suspect there may be a connection.'

'Listen,' Polly said. 'Donny was an outspoken man. He spouted off about all sorts of things. He was against the Church and against the military and after he came home from Korea he didn't like the United States a great deal. But he wasn't political, not in the way you mean. If he was anything he was an anarchist. He didn't like *any* rules or guidelines. I'm sure that's why he got in trouble in the service and it was undoubtedly why he had problems with the Heidelberg police. Jack doesn't like to be told what to do either but, if anything, he's less political than Donny. He thinks all governments are dishonest and destructive and horrible, and so do I. Jack thinks Stalin was the worst bastard who ever lived. Donny's dead. So nobody can ask him now what he believes but anybody who talks to Jack for ten minutes will know he's not a political leader or a leader of anything else. Mostly he's a musician. Almost everything else, in his mind, is just a way to kill time.'

'I believe you. But the people we're talking about don't want to believe you. They've made up their minds about Krause, and seeing that Dieter was his friend since they were schoolboys they have also made up their minds about him.'

'Guilt by association?' Jesse said.

'I'm afraid so.'

'But what do they want from Jack? Donny's already dead. What more do they want?'

'I believe they want a trial. Public exoneration for themselves.'

'They're going to put Jack on trial?' Polly said.

Speicher nodded. 'He's still in hospital and he will be as long as it's necessary, but as of this morning he's also in police custody.'

'How can they do that?' Jesse said. 'What are the charges?'

'I have not seen the arrest order. But from what the Commissioner said, I believe he'll be charged with conspiracy, destruction of property, disorderly conduct, and manslaughter.'

'Manslaughter?'

'They say they have a witness who saw him strike the guard.'

'I can't believe what I'm hearing,' Jesse said.

'These things happen,' Speicher said, 'even in your country. When the trial takes place it will be a politician's dream. The Socialist Germans who hate Americans will be satisfied, the conservative Germans who hate Socialists will be satisfied, the Americans, by not trying to block the trial, will please *all* the Germans, and the officials will present themselves as militant enemies of Communist activities inside Germany. Even the Soviets will be happy. They'll have a fresh propaganda tool. They can tell the Americans that their young men are turning to Socialism even if it means death or prison and they can broadcast to the German people that their leaders are returning them to the days of the Third Reich.'

'My God . . .' Polly whispered.

'Are you saying there's nothing that can be done?' Jesse said.

'No, I'm not. We have open courts, just as you do. I'm sure you will see to it that Dieter is properly defended. But I would not be fair with you if I didn't say that there are large issues involved here, crimes have been committed, and so far as I know, Dieter is the only person who has been charged.'

When Polly went to visit Jack that afternoon the guard outside his room had been replaced by two uniformed police officers. As soon as she came in the door, Jack said, 'Don't look so gloomy. I already know everything that's going on. A couple of birds in double-breasted suits came in this morning and told me all about the plans they have for me. I told them if I don't have a double bed in my jail cell I'm not going, but they didn't get the joke. One of them said to the other one in German, "Make sure his bed will be of an adequate size." '

He told her then what the men had said and she repeated everything that Speicher had told her and Jesse. When she finished he said, 'So there we are. Painted into a corner.'

'No, we're not,' she said. 'A lot of people are aware of what's going on here. They can't just do whatever they choose to. Heinrich Speicher is going to defend you and we'll have a lawyer from American too. The best one we can find.'

'Save your money, sweetheart. The boat sailed. They need a patsy and I'm elected. There aren't five people in the German Republic who would vote to let me off the hook. I'm an American, I was demonstrating against two German war heroes, they have every reason to believe I'm a bomb-throwing Socialist, and there's a chance they can prove I killed somebody. That's quite a parlay. Also, I have a local reputation as a drunk and a street-fighter. Lots of strings to my bow.'

'Don't talk that way. That's what they want. They'd like us to give up and take whatever comes. But we're not going to do that.'

'Maybe I should function as my own lawyer. What do you think of that strategy?'

'This is serious business, Jack. Don't toss it off. I'm worried sick.'

'But I'm not, you see. I refuse to let these silly bastards take control of my life.'

'But if they send you to prison . . .'

'Listen to me, Polly. Come sit here on the bed and listen to me.' He reached out and took her hand, pulled her to the bed and kissed her. Then he said, 'Look at me. I'm lying here in splints and bandages with two jackass guards standing outside the door. They're worrying about me but I'm not worrying about them. That's what I'm talking about. I *own* myself and I'm going to continue to own myself.'

'But . . .'

'No buts about it. You mustn't kid yourself. You mustn't tell yourself that everything depends on my being turned loose when the trial's over. That's not going to happen. It's all choreographed. Just like *Swan Lake*. I fulfil a need. Nobody else can do what I'm going to do. I'll go to jail for a few years and a whole lot of people will feel a lot better. That's what jails are for. Not to make people inside feel *bad*. But to make the people *outside* feel *good*.'

'You're impossible,' she said. 'You're an impossible man. Are you trying to make me believe that none of this bothers you?'

'No, I'm not. It bothers the hell out of me. But if I tried to kid myself, it would bother me more. Besides, there's nothing that anybody can take away from me, nothing that really matters.'

Suddenly she was crying. He pulled her close to him and said, 'Stop it. You'll get my night-shirt all wet. Do you think I'm talking about you? Do you think anybody can take *you* away from me? Not a chance. You're tattooed on the back of my eyelids. When I'm an old cocker slobbering on my tie you'll still be there.'

'I don't want to be on the back of your eyelids. That's not where I want to be.'

236

'There you go again. I've turned you into a sex maniac. You've lost all your appreciation for the finer things in life.'

'I love you so.'

'Good. Let's talk about that for a while and forget about all this other stuff.'

[7]

Late that night, Jesse sat in the chair in the guest bedroom and wrote a letter to Helen.

I told you most of the crucial facts when I talked to you on the phone this afternoon but now it's late, Polly finally gave up and went to bed, so I feel like writing a letter. This is the first chance I've had. It's been a hectic few days.

This evening after we ate a bite — neither of us was particularly hungry — the door-bell rang and it was Noel Barber, the man I mentioned to you who came to us from the Foreign Office. He's an interesting fellow. Although he mentions his family a lot I have a feeling he doesn't get to see them very often. They live in Gloucestershire, he says, but I believe that in his line of work he spends a great deal of his time *away* from Gloucestershire.

Anyhow, he didn't come to us tonight on business. 'More of a social call,' he said. But he meant, I think, that it was a condolence call. He knew that Jack has been taken into custody.

Barber told us that his office had received a request from the United States Embassy in Bonn, to make no further efforts on Jack's behalf. He said, 'And that's a proper course to follow, I suppose, since we work for Her Majesty and Jack Dieter is a bona fide citizen of the United States.' Although he said that, I don't think he fully believes it. I would bet, in fact, that he doesn't believe it at all.

He also said, 'If you repeat that I said this, I will deny it but a young woman I know at the US Consulate in Frankfurt told me that they have also been called off Dieter's case. Too sensitive for the moment, they were told.' He said that order also came from the American Embassy in Bonn. Since neither Polly nor I have

237

heard from the Consulate for several days we were not much surprised by Barber's news.

I haven't seen Jack of course since I've been here. So I've been exposed to him only through Polly's eyes. I'm not sure if it's that fact or my involvement in his predicament but I find myself thinking of him very differently now. Polly says the circumstances, which could hardly be worse, seem to have changed him hardly at all. But I guess they've changed me. It makes me mad as hell that I can't do more than I'm doing. I keep expecting Polly to fall apart but she just gets tougher and stronger. A direct descendant of Angus.

It's hard to say how long I'll be here but I'll stay till this whole matter has crystallized one way or the other. Then, if things go the way they seem to be going, if they take Jack away, I'll have to see what Polly's plans are and take it from there. I'm sure she'll make up her own mind in whatever way seems best to her but I want to be here to give her a lift in case she needs it. Meanwhile, I miss you and I miss Bill. Give him a hug for me. I'll call again in a few days, probably before you get this letter.

He undressed and got ready for bed then. He propped himself up with two pillows and began reading from an English translation of a Hermann Hesse novel that Polly had given him. After a few minutes, however, he put the book down and switched off the lamp. He lay very still on his back. The light from the street below filtered through the window shutters and made a soft geometric pattern on the ceiling. At last he turned on the lamp again, sat up in bed, took a pen and a pad of paper from the bedside table and began to write.

Dear Nora,

It's very late in Heidelberg. Black and silent. But I can't sleep. I know that Polly telephoned you earlier today, so you know most of the details. Since then there's been no improvement. All the news is bad. We'll keep you informed as things go along. It seems that there will be a trial and I have a feeling it will be very soon. Probably as soon as Jack is able to leave the hospital.

As you can imagine I have been fully occupied with Polly's problems. There's a good chance she may have to give up someone who's very precious to her and she knows it. But she's

238

functioning damned well. She's a lesson in courage and I'm proud of her.

Amidst all the chaos here I've been thinking about some of the things you said to me when we had dinner in Paris. You're a wise bird and you always were, underneath your bright plumage.

Last night, Polly was reading some poems by a young German poet she admires. She read aloud parts of one poem to me. My German as you know is sketchy at best. When she repeated one particular line several times and I asked her to translate it into English she sat looking down at the page for a moment. When she looked up she said, 'I don't believe in love that stops.'

That line has been ringing in my head ever since. I suspect it will also dance around in your brain for a while.

[8]

'I can't believe this,' Valerie said. 'You and I don't quarrel. We've never had a serious argument. Are we really having a silly fight over my going to Germany to be with Polly?'

'That may be what you're talking about but I'm not. I thought the question of your going up to Heidelberg was settled when Polly told you not to come,' Floyd said.

'I never thought she meant that.'

'Yes, you did. You were all ready to leave till you talked to her. Then you unpacked your bags and said you were staying here.'

'But now I think I should have gone. I still think I should go.'

'I know you do. But not because you think Polly *needs* you there. She's told you she doesn't. You want to go because you have some crazy sense of guilt that's hanging over you like a black cloud.'

'It's not guilt. It's not that.'

'Yes, it is and you know it is. It bothers you that Jesse's with her, that apparently Polly wants him to be there, but she doesn't need you.'

'That's not true. I think it's wonderful that Jesse was in Paris when all this happened. So Polly could call on him.'

'But you can't stop telling yourself that if he hadn't been in Paris, she would have called on you. Isn't that right?'

'Perhaps she would have. I'm not sure.'

'Of course she would have. At least that's what you believe.'

'I'm not an idiot, Floyd. I'm not stumbling around in a world of fantasy.'

'I didn't say you were. I said you've developed some over-powering sense of guilt about your kids. It really bothered you when Bill went to America to live with Jesse. It still bothers you. You see it as some sort of contest. And you're not winning.'

'You're wrong, Floyd. At least I think you're wrong. But what if you were right? What difference would it make? How am I supposed to feel about my children?

'I'm not making the rules,' he said. 'You're supposed to feel the way you want to feel. But nobody likes feeling guilty, do they? That's what I'm talking about. I'd hate to see you spend the rest of your life thinking about all the things you should have done that you didn't do. Nobody holds up under that kind of pressure. Walking backwards never got anybody anywhere.'

'Now I feel terrible,' she said. 'I feel as though I've been making you miserable.'

'We're not talking about me. We're talking about you in relation to yourself. At least, that's what I'm talking about.'

'But if I'm as mixed up as you seem to think I am, that can't be very pleasant for you.'

'Are you mixed up? Does everything I'm saying make sense to you or do you think I'm just looking for a fight?'

'Of course I don't think that. And I do know what you're talking about, but I don't know how to fix it. I *have* been worried about Polly. How can I not be? It's hard for me to accept the fact that there's absolutely nothing I can do, even if *she* believes that. And yes, it does bother me that she feels she can depend on Jesse and she doesn't depend on me or need me there when she's in trouble. It bothered me when Bill went off to live with his father, too. That still bothers me. I know there's no logic to it. It doesn't mean that he's choosing Jesse and rejecting me. But all the same it hurts my feelings in some silly unexplainable way. I tell myself that there's something I should have done that I didn't do. Sometimes I think they feel that I abandoned them and now it's their turn to abandon me.'

'Oh, for God's sake, Valerie, what's happening to you? I've never met anyone in my life who has her feet on the ground the way you do. You've always been able to fix everything for everybody. Clara said you were able to do what had to be done, no matter what it was. Waterproof, weatherproof, solid as stone.'

'I know that,' Valerie said. 'I know what she said. And she meant it. And I always felt that way about myself. But now it's hard to . . . lately, for some reason, it's difficult. Sometimes I feel as if the ground is washing away from under me. As if my body's in one room and the rest of me has floated off somewhere.'

'When I said that a few weeks ago, you said you didn't know what I was talking about.'

'I know,' she said. 'When I'm feeling tentative and foolish it's not something I'm eager to pass along to someone else.'

'Why not?'

'I'm not sure. I guess I don't like you to know when something's troubling me. These years we've been together have been so perfect I'm afraid sometimes . . .'

'Afraid of what?'

'I don't know, Floyd. Afraid you'll think things have changed maybe. Changed for us, I mean. If you find out there are things in my life that aren't perfect, if you see I'm troubled by things that have nothing to do with us, you might start to believe that I've edged away from you in some way, that the crazy, happy, irresponsible time we've had together has to change now or has already changed without our knowing about it.'

'Everything changes, Val. Nothing's ever exactly the same on Tuesday as it was on Monday.'

'I realize that. But you know what I'm saying. We made everything over just to fit *us*, to *please* us. We've been like barefoot children in the rain, and I don't want that to go away. I don't want to lose anything we have. Or give up anything. Or see it diluted or painted a different colour. I *want* us to be selfish. I want us to have it all. I revel in that, I'm proud of it. No pangs of guilt at all about us and our headlong, sexy life together, but . . .'

'But what?'

'I don't know. It's just that . . . sometimes, not often, there's some little troll inside me that says I can't have it all, that I mustn't, that I can't simply continue to count my blessings when . . . I know this won't make sense to you . . .'

'Try me,' Floyd said.

' . . . when other people, people I know and love, are wrestling

241

with their lives, trying to put square plugs into round holes, and making a bloody mess of it.'

'You're talking about your kids?'

'I don't know. Am I? I suppose I am. Not Rab so much. He's never seemed to need anything from me since he learned to walk. But Polly and Bill and I were another matter. We were very close. They were close to each other and close to me. We counted on each other in a thousand small ways. Not a desperate need, not a sick kind of dependency, just a good feeling that things were nicer and better when we were together than they were when we had to be apart for some reason. I always knew they'd grow up. I encouraged them to be independent and self-sufficient. But I knew the closeness we shared was a permanent thing. I was convinced of that. I carried it in my coat pocket like a warm chestnut. I didn't have to touch it or see it every day. I just knew it was there. Then one day I discovered it *wasn't* there and it gave me a jolt. And it hasn't been there since. Lately, however, I've begun to think it's still there for them. They're still close to each other. But the other part, the part that was mine, has been transferred to Jesse. That hurts.'

'You mean you're jealous?'

'Damned right I'm jealous. I'm human. It's bad enough to lose something. It's even worse to find out it wasn't lost at all. It was just given away to somebody else and you can't have it back.'

'You blame Jesse?'

'I'd like to but I can't. I blame myself. I left my property untended and someone took it.'

'Bill and Polly are his property, too, aren't they?'

'Of course they are. But I'm not talking about that,' she said. 'I'm talking about a particular little flowering plant that was growing on that property. That was mine. I neglected it and I lost it and I regret it. You say I'm shrouded with guilt and maybe I am. *If* I am, *that's* what I feel guilty about.'

'When you say that, do you know what I'm hearing?' Floyd said.

'It has nothing to do with us, if that's what you're about to say.'

'It has everything to do with us, whether you admit it to yourself or not. You're saying that by going off with me you lost something that was precious to you and now you want it back.'

'Don't try to trap me, sweetheart. It's too easy. I don't know what I'm saying. I admit that. I've just been trying to describe something that can't be described, trying to explain something that

242

I can't explain. But don't try to make it into something that diminishes us in any way. Because it doesn't. It can't. Nothing can. You know that as well as I do. When I divorced Jesse and married you there were no consequences that would have prevented me from doing that. If everyone I knew, everyone in my family, including my children, had told me they would never see me again or talk to me, I still would not have hesitated. And I feel exactly the same now. All I have, all I need, is us. You and me together. I wouldn't trade away the tiniest portion of what we have. But if I can have other things without losing that, that's all right, isn't it?'

'Anything's all right, Valerie. This discussion didn't begin with my finding fault with you. We've been talking about your dissatisfaction with yourself. As far as I'm concerned that's what we're still talking about. And if it will make you feel better, we can stop talking about it. If it will make you feel better, I'll drive you to Faro tomorrow morning and you can fly to Germany. You can also continue to feel guilty if you want to, but I hope you won't. It fogs up all the mirrors in the house.'

She smiled and came to sit beside him on the couch. 'Don't let me turn into a pest. Don't you think I know how lucky I am, how lucky *we* are. I never forget that, even when I'm fogging the mirrors. I admit I've been in a state about Polly but that won't last for ever. She will solve her problems somehow, just as all of us do, and I'll get older and wiser. You'll be proud of me when I'm an old lady. I'll let my hair go white and pull it back tight in a bun. I'll wear severe black dresses and spike heels like the fine cultured ladies of Lisbon.'

She lay back on the couch then and rested her head in his lap. 'If I've developed character flaws it's your fault, you know. You've turned me into an indolent woman. I was a *hausfrau* from the time I was twenty-one. When the children were babies during the war, servants were impossible to find. I cooked and cleaned and did the laundry, mopped floors, and tended our little vegetable garden. And later, when we were back at Wingate Fields, Clara and I were busy from breakfast till bedtime keeping that great museum of a house in working order.'

'Are you telling me your self-esteem is dependent on how much physical labour you can do in any given day?'

'No. I'm saying you've spoiled me.'

'An idle mind is the devil's workshop,' Floyd said.

243

'That's it.'

'I think as a first step we should sack the laundress. That will give you a chance to wash and iron my shirts and underdrawers.'

'Don't think I couldn't do that. I can.'

'I'm sure you can. Shall I discharge Maria or will you?'

'I couldn't bear to do it. She needs the money.'

'But *you* need the activity. Isn't that what you implied?'

'Not exactly. I just said you've spoiled me.'

As they lay down together later that afternoon in their cool bedroom she said, 'I'm sorry.'

'Did you do something bad?'

'You know what I'm saying, don't you?'

'I guess so.'

'I'm going to be very good and stop feeling guilty.'

'I can't believe it. How will I recognize you?' Floyd said.

'By my usual cry and distinctive natural markings.'

[9]

When the date of Jack Dieter's trial was announced in Heidelberg a television station in Milwaukee did an interview with his wife, Thelma, and their daughter, Elinor. At the close of the programme the manager of the station presented Thelma with two round-trip tickets to Frankfurt so that she and her daughter could be in Germany at the time of Jack's trial.

Portions of that interview were repeated on other television stations during the next two days. As soon as Bill Bradshaw heard the news he called his sister in Heidelberg. That afternoon when Polly visited Jack and passed the information on to him he said, 'Jesus Christ. That's all I need right now.'

'That's what I thought you'd say.'

'Why can't people keep their noses out of things that don't concern them?'

'Bill says the German-American communities in Illinois and Wisconsin have become very involved in this story because of you and Donny. A great many articles in the papers. So when they found out that you have a wife and daughter in Fond du Lac that gave them an entirely new subject. That's why the television station put up the money so they could come here for the trial.'

'What a bloody farce.'

'Just because they've raised the money, that doesn't guarantee they'll come. Maybe your wife's no more anxious to see you than you are to see her.'

'Oh, they'll come all right. No doubt about that. Give them a little notoriety and that idiot family will take off their clothes and jump in the public fountain. They're all amateur tap-dancers. All the women. Even Thelma's grandma was a tap-dancer. Cocktail waitresses and tap-dancers, that's their speed. Pick up a drink at the bar and shuffle off to Buffalo. Oh, Thelma will be here all right, and with the kind of luck I've been having she'll probably bring her mother along. She's the eighth wonder of the world. Went to California when she was nineteen years old, had an operation to make her boobs bigger. Then, about twenty years later when they started to fall, she had another operation to make them smaller. Bleaches her hair and wears ankle-strap shoes like Joan Crawford. From across the street she looks like Debby Reynolds, close up she looks like Lyndon Johnson. And her mother dresses the same way she does. Same shoes. Same hair-do.'

'How old is she?'

'Old enough to know better but not as old as you think. They all have a kid when they're sixteen. One kid and then they stop. And it's always a daughter. A whole clan of women. Thelma, Lily, her mother, and Garnet, the grandmother. And now they've got Elinor warming up.'

'How old was your wife when Elinor was born?'

'Sixteen, like I said. I thought she was twenty when we got married. That's what she told me. But it turned out she was only fifteen. Garnet had fixed up a fake birth certificate for her.'

'So she's twenty-nine now?'

'That's right. Her mother's forty-five. And racy old Garnet's sixty or sixty-one. But I guarantee you, she's passing herself off as forty. She owns a cocktail bar and short-order café on the interstate just west of Fond du Lac. Open twenty-four hours a day. Pretty waitresses, a card game in the back, and two or three rooms for truckers who want to get a back-rub from one of the waitresses.'

'What about her husband?' Polly asked.

'No husbands for the Richter women. Richter. That was Garnet's maiden name and she still uses it. And so does Lily. And I'll bet Thelma does too by now.'

'You mean they don't get married?'

'Oh, they get married all right. They just don't stay married. Once the breeding function is performed, the husband gets his walking papers. I was the only husband who left before he was thrown out.'

Polly smiled. 'You're terrible. I never know if you're telling the truth or if you're making up a preposterous story just to amuse yourself.'

'No story I could make up about the Richter tribe could sound more preposterous than the truth does.'

'You think she will come here then?'

'If they gave her a ticket she'll come.'

'How will we handle that?' Polly asked.

'Nothing to handle that I can see. Certainly nothing for you to fret about. She's not your responsibility and she's not mine either. I had nothing to do with her coming here and I want nothing to do with her once she arrives.'

'Maybe the authorities will grant her marital visiting rights. Move her right into the cell with you.'

'Not a chance. If they move her in, they'll have to move me out.'

'What about your daughter?'

'I hope Thelma's got enough horse-sense not to bring her.'

'But you think she will?'

'Not much doubt about that. Not if there's the chance for a little melodrama.'

'How do you feel about seeing your daughter?'

'It's been a long time. You know that. I guess I assumed I'd never see her again,' Jack said. 'But if she's here I'd like to see her. I liked her when she was little. She was fat and cute and she never cried. Strange thing. You'd put her in the crib at night, pat her on the bottom a couple times, and she'd go right to sleep. Sleep through the night. In the afternoon I used to take her to the neighbourhood pool hall. She'd sit there in her stroller and watch me shoot pool for an hour or so and never let out a peep. And she liked to hear me play the cello. But that was a long time ago. After thirteen years with the Richter witches, God knows what she's turned into. If I could see her without Thelma sitting there picking at her cuticles, I would. But I don't want to play some big scene with her mother. I also don't go for the idea of Elinor seeing me here in the visitor's

246

room. Or sitting in a court room and listening to people accuse me of all kinds of bad stuff. I just wish she wouldn't come.'

'So do I. But it looks like she's coming. And the newspapers will crucify you if she travels all the way from America and you won't see her.'

'I don't give a damn what the newspapers say.'

'Neither do I,' Polly said. 'At least, I try not to. But I hate to have people thinking rotten things about you even before the trial begins.'

'It doesn't matter what people think. The trial will only last about twenty minutes anyway. It's all prosecution and no defence.'

'That's a ridiculous attitude, Jack. That's not what Streicher says.'

'What does he know? He's just a lawyer. Lawyers aren't paid to think. You wind him up and he keeps saying, "My client's not guilty," till the judge tells him to sit down and shut up.'

'God, you're impossible. I'm surprised you don't tell them you're guilty of any charges they want to make and get it over with.'

'I've thought about that,' Jack said. 'But why should I make it easy for the bastards?'

'Jesse's been on the phone a lot to New York trying to line up a good American lawyer to work on your defence with Streicher.'

'No takers?'

'Everybody's very interested in the case. It's had a lot of publicity in the States. But some of the people are reluctant to try to defend an American in a German court. They know there's a lot of political foolishness mixed in with the facts. But the real problem is time. Since the trial date is so close it's a back-breaking job, they say, trying to prepare a proper defence.'

'I have a perfect defence,' Jack said. 'I was unconscious all during the demonstration. I was the first man to go down.'

'Let me finish. Now it looks as if we have the man we want. Jesse's talked with him twice on the phone. He's talking to him again today. His name is Rosenthal. He's a brilliant criminal lawyer. When Floyd got into some trouble in California twenty years ago this man defended him and kept him from going to prison.'

'And now he's going to do the same for me?'

'It looks that way.'

'Don't hitch your hopes to a miracle, kid.'

'Why not?' she said. 'Miracles happen all the time.'

'Not to me. Not this time. Not in Heidelberg.'

While Polly was visiting Jack, Jesse was indeed talking on the telephone to Mike Rosenthal in New York. They talked for forty minutes. When he hung up at last Jesse called Floyd in Praia da Rocha. 'I couldn't sell him,' Jesse said, 'but I still think he can be sold. Did you mean it yesterday when you said you'd help out?'

'Sure I did. I'll be in New York tomorrow.'

An hour later Floyd was on his way to Faro. Late that afternoon he flew from Lisbon to New York, and at noon the next day he met Rosenthal at the Century for lunch.

'It's good to see you,' Rosenthal said. 'I'm like an old obstetrician. Always happy to meet the babies I delivered.'

'Delivered from jail, you mean.'

'That's right. The only problem is all my clients seem to have short memories. Arthur Miller told me one time – and this is a quote – "Actors never remember *anybody*." Same thing happens to me. Once they're out of that courtroom they don't remember me. I'm dogmeat. Most of them don't even remember my name next time they get collared and need a lawyer. So they end up in prison. Or I read their names in the New Jersey obituaries.'

'Why New Jersey?'

'Don't ask me. All my old clients seem to end up in New Jersey. A few of them even live there. But most of them just go there to die.'

When they were sitting at their table upstairs, Rosenthal said, 'It's not fair. Here I am, a hard-working man, friend to the needy, contributor to good causes, a true benefactor of mankind, and what do I get in return? Falling hair, a pot-belly, a ruptured disc, and an incipient case of gout. Not only that, but I have an eighty-year-old mother who calls me twice a day to tell me what I have to do and what I have to *stop* doing if I want to live till next Thursday.'

'You look healthy to me,' Floyd said.

'Don't kid yourself. The timbers are falling. Now you, on the other hand, sit there with a twenty-thousand-dollar suntan. No grey at the temples, no pouches under your eyes, no liver spots on your hands, and no gravy stains on your silk tie. Haven't met your wife but I'm sure she's a winner too. And all your kids have soft curls and blue eyes.'

'I don't have any kids.'

'There you are. Lucky in everything. I have two kids. A daughter who married a cement finisher and lives in Hudson, New York, and a son who works at a reptile farm in Silver Springs, Florida. He's queer for snakes. Their mother hated herself and hated me because she had thick ankles. She figured I was to blame for that somehow. From the knees up she was Lana Turner but the ankles were a dead loss. So when she gave up on me, she gave up on the kids as well. She married some runt who makes porno films in his garage in Cleveland and she's happy as hell. Not only did she find a man she could feel superior to but it turned out that his uncle is a chiropodist. He operated on her ankles and trimmed enough meat off so her legs look pretty good. She limped for a couple of years but finally that went away and now she's in heaven. Now she doesn't think about her kids, or me, or New York, or anything. She just sits out there in Cleveland drinking Southern Comfort, watching dirty movies, and stroking her pretty ankles.'

Rosenthal lit a cigar and said, 'Something else I'm not supposed to do. I had a doctor who took me off cigars and my blood pressure went sky-high. So I went to another doctor and he asked me if I'd changed any of my habits lately. I said I'd stopped smoking and he said, "That's it. Start smoking again." So I did. And my blood pressure went back to normal. Incidentally, both those doctors I went to are dead now. One of them was fifty when he died. The other was thirty-eight.'

The waiter came to take their order then. When he left, Rosenthal said, 'You seem like a serious young fellow now. When I met you in California, when most guys in your shoes would have been climbing the walls, you didn't seem to be rattled about anything. Everybody around you was sweating blood and you looked like a man without a care in the world. Roll the dice and who gives a damn.'

'That's the way *you* act *now*,' Floyd said.

'Exactly. Took off my serious suit about three years ago, sent it to the cleaner and threw away the claim cheque. I told people not to depend on me so much. I said, "Call me if you've really got a problem nobody else can solve. Otherwise, let me sleep late and count my blessings." '

'You talk like a man who's trying to retire. You're not old enough for that.'

'I'm as old as the world,' Rosenthal said. 'I was nineteen yesterday. You know who wrote that line? George Bernard Shaw. You know who said it and in what play? Marchbanks in *Candida*. I saw Marlon Brando play that part. No good. You think I'm not smart? You think I'm not cultured? Think again.'

'I have a hunch you're trying to answer my question before I ask it. You know why I came here, don't you?'

'Of course I do. When Jesse Bradshaw calls me three times from Germany and then Floyd Bradshaw shows up at my office in New York I can make that connection in no time at all.'

'All right. You made the connection. Now you're telling me in a roundabout way what you told Jesse, that you can't help us.'

'That's right.'

'You mind telling me why?'

'The same answer I give most of the people who call me: I turn down cases all the time.'

'This means a lot to us,' Floyd said.

'This guy Dieter lives with Jesse's daughter, I know that. What relation is she to you?'

'She's my stepdaughter. I married Jesse's ex-wife.'

'I see. So everybody feels as if Jack Dieter is a member of the family.'

'Not at all. Nobody in the family likes him. Except Polly.'

'She's the daughter?'

'That's right. And she's in love with him.'

'Let me get this straight,' Rosenthal said. 'If everybody thinks this guy's a loser, why not let nature take its course? If he's convicted and locked up somewhere in Bavaria then he's out of the picture as far as the girl is concerned.'

'That might help somebody but it wouldn't help Polly. And it sure as hell wouldn't help Jack. Besides, we're convinced he's innocent. He doesn't belong in prison even if it might be convenient for the Bradshaw family.'

'Is there a scent of altruism in the air? I hate altruism. Don't trust it.'

'No. A scent of justice maybe. But mostly we want things to be good for Polly.'

The waiter brought their food then and poured wine into their glasses and the two men ate in silence for a few minutes. Finally, Rosenthal said, 'I am not going to keep you in suspense. I will tell

250

you what I told your relative on the telephone. I am not going to take this case. I happen to like you, so I'd do you a favour if I could. I also know that I would make a great deal of money if I said yes. But I can't say yes. For three very good reasons. Number one: I would be deceiving you if I led you to believe that this case can be won. It can't. I have taken some cases that I thought I might lose. I've never taken one that I knew I would lose.'

'What makes you so sure about this case?'

'After I talked with Jesse the first time, I had my office gather up all the newspaper clippings they could find about Dieter and his friend Krause and the demonstration. I read them all. Then I talked to a couple of Washington journalists I know. After that I talked with Lewis Cobb, chief legal counsel to the State Department in Washington. Lew was my clerk when he came out of law school. We've been close friends ever since. He listened carefully to what I had to say. Then he said he'd call me back the following day. And he did. That was the day before yesterday. He told me then what I had suspected and what I'm telling you now. This case is closed, my friend. It has been negotiated in Bonn and a decision has been reached. Testimony will be heard that will satisfy every pressure group. Something for everyone. But mostly a message will be sent to the Soviets, especially the East Germans, that any activities that have a whiff of Communist shenanigans about them will be cracked down on hard. Riot police will be called out. Blood wil be shed if necessary, and the courts will support the government.'

'Jesse said a man from the British Consulate told him something very similar to that.'

'Of course. They know how the game is played. But all the same he was just guessing. I am giving you the final box score. I can even tell you what the sentence will be. Twenty years. Because they will prove that Dieter led the demonstration and that he was suspected of Communist connections when he was in Korea. And there will be testimony that he was responsible for the death of the university guard.'

'Twenty years,' Floyd said. 'That's rough.'

'Here's chapter two. He won't serve the full term. After ten years, there will be some new evidence that will cast doubt on the manslaughter charge and he'll be released.'

'Are you telling me they're going to orchestrate somebody's life just to . . .'

'This is the big league,' Rosenthal said. 'The international jack-asses playing chequers with each other. I say chequers because most of them are too fucking dumb to play chess. All they know is that something has to be fixed. So they fix it any way they can.'

'You said you had three reasons. I guess I don't need the other two.'

'Yes, you do. I gave you the clincher first. But the other two are important, also – because I'd have to say no to you for these reasons even if I didn't know the case had already been cooked. Reason number two is about me and the way I practise law. I said a while ago that I've taken cases I thought I might lose. That's true. But I've never gone into court without every card I needed to win. Between taking the case and actually defending it I put together every single piece I needed. That's the way I function. In a criminal case it's the only way to go. I've always defended important people. Big crimes, big money, everything at stake. You can't win cases like that with sincerity and brains and hard work. You have to find the guarantee. If it's not in the evidence, if it's not in the case itself, then you have to go *outside* the case. You know without my telling you that I never would have defended you if Paul Buscatore hadn't been your uncle. You *knew* that, didn't you?'

Floyd nodded.

'In one respect it was like this case. Only the reverse. I took one look at that Mexican operation and I knew I could blow them away. In forty-eight hours I had the tools and the testimony to do it. But for insurance I went *outside* the case. Some phone calls were made and the prosecutor's office put a man on to prosecute who my people knew. He was a man you could communicate with. But things can happen to a prosecutor. He can get sick. Or he can chicken out and *pretend* he's sick. And all of a sudden you're up against a sharpshooter you don't know. So I needed some insurance. I found a way to speak to the judge. Not personally of course. Someone spoke to him at a dinner party in Beverly Hills. It all sounds complicated. Right? It took me three days, a total of four hours' work maybe. You understand what I'm saying? This is the way to practise criminal law. Nobody with any brains wants to take a chance with a jury of his peers. You never know what you might run into. You may not like to hear this, but I could have got you off with a straight acquittal. But when the prosecutor and the judge are making me look good I find a way to make *them* look good. If I'm smart I do. So instead of pushing for acquittal I give them a watered-down conviction. But you walk out whistling. Not one day of time to serve. I could do that because you already had a record. Since you weren't clean anyway, one more line on the sheet didn't mean much. If you hadn't been nabbed before, I'd have played different cards and you'd have strolled out of there like a virgin. You see what I'm saying? That's the way I work. That's why I'm rich. It's also the reason I won't die in Jersey in a parked car.'

'Are you saying you can't practise your kind of law in Germany?'

Rosenthal shook his head. 'Don't think the things I'm describing to you don't happen there. They do. But I'm not the guy who can *make* them happen. Not there. I'd have no edge there. No way to even *look* for an edge.' He took a drink from his wine glass. 'And now I'll tell you the third reason. And this one also would convince me even if the other two didn't. I'm a Jew. My mother and father were born in Germany. In a town called Remscheid, not far from Essen. As far as I know I didn't have any relatives killed in gas chambers, I never stuck a dagger in a map of Germany and said, "I'll never set foot in that country." I don't hate German music or German food or German art. But the fact is I've been to Europe a dozen times and I've never gone to Germany. I haven't planned it that way. At least not consciously. But I know when I die, whenever that happens, I still will have never seen that country. And as far as practising my profession there is concerned, I could never do it. A trial lawyer must always present his defence as though victory was a foregone conclusion. If I ever stood up in a German court I would feel as if *I* were on trial. Not a victor at all. I'd feel like a victim.'

[11]

Before he left Portugal to fly to New York, Floyd had said to Valerie, 'I never thought I'd be making a fast flight to New York just because Jesse asked me to. Why am I doing him a favour?'

'You're not doing it for him,' she said. 'You're doing it for me. And mostly you're doing it for Polly.'

'Good. I'll try to remember that. But since he's the last man in the world I'd ask for a favour it's a bit of an adjustment for me to feel as if I'm doing one for him.'

'I remember when I first met you, when *all* of us met you for the first time, when Helen brought you to Wingate Fields, I thought you and Jesse would be great friends.'

'It didn't work out that way, did it?'

'I never really understood why.'

'It's pretty simple. Jesse had something I wanted.'

'You mean me?'

'What else?'

'But you didn't give a damn about me then.'

'Don't kid yourself.'

'You were barely civil to me.'

'I know. I didn't want to run the risk of becoming your friend. I didn't want you to think of me as a relative. I had other things in mind.'

'You were naughty.'

'Not at all. I was angry. I just *wanted* to be naughty.'

'Are you telling me you envied Jesse? I've never heard you say you envy anyone.'

'I wouldn't call it envy. I just thought he wasn't good enough for you. Or maybe I decided he was *too* good and *I* wasn't good enough. Whatever it was I didn't like him much. And I still don't. I used to dislike him because he was married to you and now I dislike him because he used to be married to you.'

'You're a funny man,' she said. 'Full of surprises. Just when I think I know you I find out something new.'

'This is nothing new. It's just something I never told you before.'

'Are there many other things you've never told me?'

'Millions. I'm like a grab-bag at a kiddie party. When you reach in you never know what you'll pull out.'

When Floyd and Valerie were first married, she had said to him, 'I can't believe that I have so little recollection of the years I spent with Jesse. If I concentrate, of course, I can remember details of that time but almost all of them involve the children. Apart from them the things I remember seem to have no emotional zing, past or present. I feel as though I was a mother through those years and nothing else. Oddly enough, my clearest memories of Jesse are when I was much younger, when he was living with Nora and we

254

were all together in Paris. Sometimes I think I always thought of him as my mother's property even when I was married to him.'

Floyd thought about that conversation with Valerie as he flew west towards New York. Tilted back in his seat with a glass of scotch in his hand he tried to imagine, as he had many times before, how he would have reacted to Jesse if he'd met him under different circumstances, how he would have evaluated him. But no answers came to him.

As odd and senseless as it seemed, Floyd had to acknowledge that just as Valerie thought of Jesse only in relation to her mother, he thought of him only in relation to Valerie. There was no jealousy in that conclusion. He certainly did not see Valerie as Jesse's wife. But Jesse, it seemed, was indelibly defined in Floyd's mind, as Valerie's husband. That fact had disturbed Floyd when he first met Jesse. The memory of it disturbed Floyd still.

[12]

After his meeting in New York with Mike Rosenthal, Floyd flew to Frankfurt. When he met with Jesse and Speicher there, he told them in detail what Rosenthal had said.

'Do you think he knows what he's talking about?' Jesse said.

'I know he knows what he's talking about. When he doesn't know he doesn't say anything,' Floyd said.

'Every time I hear an elaborate conspiracy theory I think someone's imagination is working overtime,' Jesse said.

'Rosenthal doesn't operate that way,' Floyd said.

'Maybe he was just looking for a good excuse to turn us down.'

'He doesn't need an excuse. He's an expert at saying no.'

Jesse turned to Speicher. 'Does it make sense to you?'

'I'm afraid it does. And if you remember, what this man Rosenthal says is not so different from the British gentleman . . . I don't remember his name.'

'Noel Barber,' Jesse said.

Speicher nodded. 'Barber indicated that something complex was going on in Bonn and Washington. This scenario we've just heard must be the result of that.'

'Are you saying there's nothing we can do?' Jesse said. 'These government idiots have prejudged the case and all we can do is sit by and listen?'

'No, I'm not saying that,' Speicher said. 'What I am saying is that the odds are very difficult now. It is good that we know what we're up against but it is bad also. Because we cannot use any of this information.'

'Why not?' Jesse said.

'Because there is no hard evidence of collusion between the governments involved. And even if we found such evidence, it would not be permitted.'

'I don't understand that.'

'They have been clever,' Speicher said. 'In spite of all the publicity they have kept this a local matter. Heidelberg courts and Heidelberg officials. So any implication we might make that state officials or officials of another government have taken a hand in the affair would be branded as irrelevant and not admitted in the proceedings.'

'Don't you think we should still bring in a lawyer from American with some international court experience?' Jesse turned to Floyd. 'Don't *you* think so?'

'I thought so when I went to see Rosenthal,' Floyd said. 'Now I'm not so sure.'

'What changed your mind?'

'I didn't say I've changed my mind. I said I'm not sure. After what Rosenthal told me, I think you'd have a difficult time finding a man who might be effective.'

'The United States is full of good trial lawyers,' Jesse said. He turned back to Speicher. 'Isn't that true?'

Speicher nodded. 'I'm sure it is. And if you're determined to find one, then that's what you must do. But there is a severe problem of time because the trial date was set so early. Now some days have passed and the time has grown even shorter. If I were asked to enter a case on such short notice, for example, I would refuse.'

'I'm a stubborn bastard,' Jesse said. 'I hate to be told that nothing can be done.'

'When a private citizen goes against a government he discovers very often that nothing can be done. It appears that Jack Dieter is being forced to deal with *two* governments.'

256

'Why bother with a trial?' Jesse said. 'Why don't they simply announce that he's confessed and put him in prison?'

'They want the trial,' Speicher said. 'They need it. It's necessary to show the world how fair they are.'

Floyd did not tell Jesse and Speicher everything that Rosenthal had told him. He did not tell them that the time of Jack's sentence had been pre-determined. Nor did he tell them that, after having served ten years, he would be released.

[13]

When Jack's wife and daughter arrived two days before the trial was scheduled, he refused to see them. When Speicher tried to persuade him to change his mind, Jack said, 'Not me. Just because some television station in Wisconsin wants to create a sad-assed story, that doesn't convince me that I should play a part in it. If I wanted to be with my wife, I'd have stayed there in Wisconsin. But I didn't want to so I left. I wasn't trying to get away from my daughter but she was part of the package so I had to leave her too. And I've never regretted it for a minute. So now people expect me to crank up a *mea culpa* serenade to make a bunch of reporters happy? Not a chance.'

'The publicity could make you look very bad just before the trial.'

'Who cares? The outcome of this kangaroo court doesn't hang on whether or not I'm a dandy husband and father, and you know it.'

When Polly arrived at the jail later that day she said, 'I think you should see her, Jack. I think you have to. Things are bad enough without making them worse.'

'They can't be worse.'

'Yes, they can. If everybody in Germany thinks you're a bastard by tomorrow night, that hurts you. It helps the prosecutors to do or say anything they want because they know people will believe that you deserve whatever punishment they give you.'

'They'll believe that anyway.'

'Maybe they will. But it's a certainty they will if everybody thinks your wife and daughter came all the way over here and you refused to talk to them.'

257

'I don't care about that.'

'But I care. Do you think I want everybody to think you're a miserable son of a bitch? You're not like that so why should people be allowed to think you are?'

'They can think whatever they want to.'

'You're driving me crazy, Jack. You're like a man who wants to commit suicide but you're looking for someone else to hold the knife so you can fall on it.'

'Don't go theatrical on me.'

'I'm not theatrical. That's your wife's department. When she arrived at the airport she told reporters that you abandoned her when your child was only two years old but she has never tried to divorce you because she believes that marriage vows are for life.'

'Oh, my God.'

'The papers said she was crying.'

'I'll bet she was,' Jack said. 'She was good at that. Extremely gifted in the boo-hoo department.'

'She said she's sure you're innocent of all charges but even if it turns out you're guilty she felt that she and Elinor should be here with you.'

'Did she say "at my side"?'

'I think she did as a matter of fact.'

'It figures. She's a great reader of romantic fiction. Thought Errol Flynn's autobiography was the best book she'd ever read. And the truth is it probably is the best book she's ever read.'

'I don't understand how you two got together in the first place.'

'Neither do I,' Jack said. 'I'd like to be able to say it was a sexual attraction but that's not true. She wasn't very good at that either.'

Just before she left him, Polly said, 'What are you going to do?'

'About what?'

'About meeting with your wife and daughter.'

'I told you. I'm not going to do it.'

'I want you to, Jack. I think you're doing your case a lot of damage if you don't.'

He shook his head. 'Can't hack it. I'd like to see Elinor in a way but I can't face the two of them doing some wounded-bird performance.'

'What if you could see them separately?'

'I don't want to see Thelma at all.'

258

'But couldn't you manage it for a few minutes if it meant you could see Elinor by herself?'

At last he capitulated. He agreed to see them separately. And he insisted that he see Elinor first. When Thelma was told of this proposal she turned it down but after a tense meeting with the reporters from Fond du Lac who had accompanied her and who were determined to send back a story – second-hand though it might be – of the long-awaited meeting between Jack, his wife, and his daughter, Thelma reconsidered and agreed to Jack's proposal.

Elinor was tall for her age, almost as tall as Jack, and solidly built, like her mother's father. She looked like a young person who was accustomed to wearing jeans and a sweat shirt but when she came into the bare room with a table and two chairs where Jack was waiting for her she wore a tight-fitting rose-coloured dress and a maroon corduroy jacket. When she sat down across from him, she glanced over at the guard sitting against the wall and said, 'Boy, it's just like the movies, ain't it?'

'I'm sorry,' Jack said. 'He has to be in the room whether we like it or not.' When she didn't answer he said, 'That's a nice dress. Is it new?'

'Yes, but I don't like it much. I have a blue one that I like better but Mom wanted me to wear this one so I gave in.'

'It's very pretty,' he said. Then, 'I guess you can't remember me, do you?'

'I was awful little when you left. I was two, wasn't I?'

'That's right. I wouldn't expect you to remember.'

'But I've looked at all those snapshots of you and Mom. She loves picture albums. We've got them scattered all over the place. Enough pictures of me to paper a couple rooms, I bet.'

'Are you still living in the same house?'

She nodded. 'Same place we've always had. Lily and Garnet downstairs, me and Mom upstairs. Grandma says it's like a sorority house. We have all kinds of fun. Mom and I have our own kitchenette but as often as not the four of us eat together downstairs. Lily's some good cook, I tell you. We all have to go on a grapefruit diet every month or so. Otherwise we'd be as fat as the four little pigs.'

'Where are you in school now?'

'I got kept back a year so I'm just starting ninth grade. I should be in tenth but like I said, they held me back.'

'What happened?' Jack said.

259

'Nothing *happened*. I just flunked some courses, that's all. Mom said I'd better not talk to you about school or you'd give me a lecture.'

Jack shook his head. 'No lectures. Sounds as if you don't like school much.'

'Hate it. Detest it. Can't wait to quit. The day I'm sixteen I'll be long gone. Toot, toot, tootsie, goodbye. Garnet has a friend named Harley Winch, an older guy, sells ready-mix concrete all over Wisconsin, and he told me he thinks it's a waste of time for a girl to go to school after she's sixteen. He says after that, some practical work experience is worth more than studying Europe history or geometry or something. And I agree with *him*, I'll tell you that. I want to get out there and earn some money. Be independent. Am I right?'

'Well, I guess that depends on what you want.'

'I know exactly what I want. Lily took me down to Milwaukee a couple years ago and we ate in a donut shop. *Mister Donut* it's called. It's a franchise deal. You know about stuff like that?'

'A little bit,' Jack said.

'I knew as soon as I saw it that it was the business for me. There's no other donut shop in Fond de Lac except for a restaurant out on the highway north of town that makes a few donuts and sweet rolls just as kind of a side line. Once we're in business we'll blow that joint right out of the water, Garnet says. And she ought to know. She knows the food business backwards and forwards, from one end to the other. *Mildred Pierce*, Mr Winch calls her. That was a movie with Joan Crawford, about a woman who baked pies for a living and got very rich doing it.'

'You want to be rich?'

'Sure I do. Doesn't everybody?'

'I don't.'

'I know you don't. That's what Mom says. I guess that's why you're still going to school. It's funny, ain't it, you liking school so much you're still doing it and me hating it like a snake. Garnet says nobody in our family ever liked school so I guess I come by it natural.'

Jack sat quietly for a moment, looking at this stranger who was his daughter. He had not known what to expect so he had constructed in his imagination a facsimile of Thelma as he remem-

260

bered her. Studied fragility, aggressively feminine, tender voice, soft curls, and ruffles on her petticoat.

Elinor, however, bore no resemblance to that mother model. There was a frontier brashness about her that was appealing, an unwillingness to compromise, a confidence in her own judgments that seemed to be her only genetic inheritance from him. For an instant he allowed himself to wonder whether she would be very different if she had grown up with him in the house. He asked her then how she liked Germany, what little she'd seen of it.

'I was just going to bring that up,' she said. 'I was going to ask you why you've stayed here so long. It's a mystery to me what you see in this place. I mean, I don't have anything against the Germans. I know your folks were German and I guess Mom's half-German, and God knows there are tons of German families in Wisconsin, but all the same this place really ticks me off. I mean, I'm not stupid, I didn't expect people here to speak English but I'll tell you one thing, when you hear nothing but that German lingo for twenty-four hours it really gets old. I mean you get your can full in a hurry. It's an ugly sound. And did you ever notice the way people here walk? *Heavy*. Clumping along like they're marching in a parade, even the women and little kids. And nobody's smiling, I'll tell you that. There was a drunk man in the hotel restaurant last night and he was laughing and carrying on but you look for a smile in the streets and you've got a long wait in front of you. A place like this makes me sad. That's what I mean. When I think about how much laughing the four of us do in our house this is a sour-apple place. Is it all right if I say that?'

'Of course it's all right. Why not?'

'Mom said I should be careful what I say to you. Tricky questions and things like that. She told me you have a bad temper, that you can fly off the handle over nothing. So she thought I'd better take it easy on the questions.'

Jack smiled. 'I don't think you have anything to worry about. If I start to hit you with a chair I'm sure that guard over there would come to your rescue.'

Elinor glanced at the guard. 'I'd hate to have anybody standing around watching over me. Doesn't that drive you crazy?'

'I don't like it much but it doesn't drive me crazy.'

'I'd be nutty as a fruit-cake if somebody locked me up in a little

261

room. What if they decide to keep you in jail for a long time, won't that make you wacko?'

'I hope not.'

'These are the kind of questions Mom told me not to ask you. Are you getting mad at me yet?'

Jack shook his head. 'Not yet.'

'What's going to happen to you? After the trial, I mean.'

'I don't know. You'll be there. You'll find out as soon as I do.'

'I know that. But you already know lots of stuff I don't know.' She looked over at the guard, then lowered her voice. 'Did you really kill that guy like they say you did?'

'No. I didn't kill anybody.'

'Mom said she's seen you mad enough to kill somebody.'

'Well, I hope she doesn't say that at the trial,' Jack said.

'She wouldn't. She wouldn't say that to anyone but me. She's not out to get you. She's not mad at you or anything.'

'That's good. I'm not mad at her either.'

Elinor sat silent for a long moment. Then, 'If you didn't kill that guy then you might get off easy. They might even let you off altogether. Isn't that right?'

'I suppose that's possible but I'm not counting on anything. We'll just have to see what happens.'

'If you got off, if you didn't have to stay in jail, is there any chance you might come home with us? That's another question I'm not supposed to ask.' When he didn't answer she went on. 'You could help me run the donut shop. When you call a place *Mister Donut* it's good to have a man around, don't you think?'

'I guess so. It's certainly something to think about.'

Suddenly she said, 'Why did you go away and leave Mom and me the way you did?'

'I don't know,' Jack said.

'I told you Mom's not mad at you and I don't think she is. And I'm not mad at you or I wouldn't be here talking to you like this. But I'll tell you the truth, I've asked myself that question a thousand times. "Why did he leave?" '

'I told you, kid, I don't know.'

'Mr Winch calls me *kid*. I used to hate it but now that I'm getting older I kinda like it.' Then: 'Are you telling me you didn't know then or you don't know now?'

'Don't know now and didn't know then.'

262

'That means you don't want to tell me, I guess.'

Jack shook his head. 'It means I don't know.'

'That's hard to swallow, that you'd do something as important as that and not have any idea what you're doing.'

'A lot of people don't know what they're doing.'

'I know that,' she said, 'but you're smart. Most people aren't.'

'Sometimes smart people do dumb things,' Jack said.

After a moment she said, 'Do you think it was a dumb thing to go off and leave like that?'

'I never thought of it that way. It was just something I felt like I had to do. So I did it. You said before you'd go crazy if you were locked up. I guess that's what was happening to me. I felt closed in. Locked up.'

'Because of Mom, you mean?'

'Because of a lot of things. Because of me mostly. Either I had too much of something or I didn't have enough of something.'

'You mean you didn't like yourself?'

'No, I don't mean that. It's hard to explain it to you. All I can say is that it wasn't something I planned. I just woke up one day and I knew I had to leave. So I went. I don't know if it was the right thing to do. I didn't feel guilty then and I don't feel guilty now. I didn't belong in Wisconsin. Maybe I don't belong here either. But I knew, sure as hell, I didn't belong there.'

'You don't think much of Mom, do you?'

'When we were kids I loved her,' he said.

'But you don't like her.'

'I guess we didn't have time to get around to that.'

When the guard signalled the visiting time was up, she said, 'I'm glad I got to talk to you by myself.'

'Yeah. Me, too.'

'I hope they don't dump on you at the trial. I'll be rooting for you.'

'Thanks.'

'Just in case you're wondering, I'm not planning to tell Mom everything we talked about.'

'It's all right. You can tell her if you want to.'

'I don't want to.' Just before she turned to leave she said, 'Take it easy with Mom. She's not out to get you.'

'Hi, darlin',' Thelma said when she sat down across the table from Jack. 'I know you're not dying to see me so we can make this as short as you want to. What I really wanted was for you to see Elinor and for her to see you. Now she's got something to go on besides a black-and-white Kodak snapshot. Did she give you a hug?'

'No,' Jack said.

'That doesn't mean anything. She's not much for lolly-gagging. But she's got it inside where it counts. If she likes somebody they can hit her on the head with a stick and she'll still like them. She's a good kid. I'm proud of her. She's not great beauty and I guess she never will be but she doesn't give a damn. It's kinda nice to have a girl who doesn't stand in front of the looking-glass night and day.'

'I like her looks.'

'So do I. Don't get me wrong. I just meant she's not a typical Richter female. I guess she takes after your side of the family.'

Jack smiled and said, 'Maybe she'll outgrow it,' and Thelma laughed.

'You're acting pretty nice,' she said. 'I figured you'd start to yell at me as soon as I sat down.'

'I don't yell at anybody.'

'You sure used to. You were a world-champion yeller.'

'I used to do a lot of things I don't do any more.'

'My mother and my grandma think I should be sore at you. They've got no patience with me because I'm not mad as hell. But I just don't feel that way. Never did. Oh, I suppose I was mad right at the beginning. It was embarrassing trying to explain things to people. And my feelings was hurt, I won't lie to you about *that*. But I never hated you or wanted to get even. And I never said bad things about you to Elinor. If you ask her she'll tell you that's the truth. But I have to be honest with you. There's one thing I never understood. I never knew why you'd just leave the country when you did and never let anybody know where you went to. I wouldn't have come tagging after you. I've got some pride, you know. I don't want to make a pest of myself to somebody who don't want me hanging around. But still . . . we was still married. And Elinor *is* your daughter. You'd think a person would let us know where they could be reached in case of a death in the family or something.'

'I didn't tell *anybody* where I was going. I didn't want to be reached.'

Thelma nodded. 'I figured that out. But I still don't understand it.'

'There's nothing to understand. I just thought that was the best way to handle it.'

'I figured sooner or later you'd want a divorce and I'd hear from you then.'

'I don't want a divorce,' he said.

'But what if I want one? Did you ever think of that?'

'If you want one, go ahead. I won't stand in your way.'

'One of the reporters told me you're living with a woman here in Heidelberg.'

'That's right.'

'What if she decides she wants to get married?'

'She knows I'm already married. She knew it from the beginning.'

'But if we got a divorce you could do anything you want to.'

'I do anything I want to now,' Jack said. 'And one of the things I don't want to do is get married again.'

'Do you ever remember what it was like when you and I were together at the beginning? Before Elinor was born?'

'That was a long time ago, Thelma.'

'I know it was but a person can't help remembering once in a while. At least I can't. Can't help wondering whatever became of you . . . you know what I mean.'

'It's not going to make either one of us feel any better to go over everything now. You don't want to do that, do you?'

'No, I don't,' she said. 'I know what you're saying. But I just wanted you to see what a jolt it was for me, after all this time, to read about you in the Milwaukee paper. And see your picture on the television screen. I'd made up my mind that I'd never see you or hear from you again, then *bang*, all of a sudden, there you were. And the next thing I knew, two men from the television station came to the house and said they'd pay for Elinor and me to fly all the way over here to see you and be at your trial. At first I said no. For several days I told them I didn't want to go. Since I'd never heard from you I knew you didn't want to see me, so I thought, "Why should I stick my nose in? If he wants to be left alone, then

265

I'll leave him alone." But then I got to thinking about what was best for Elinor. And the more I thought about it, the more I decided she had a right to see her dad. So, like I said before, that was what clinched it for me. The next time they called from the TV station I told them we'd go. You may not think I did the right thing but I do. Anyway, it's done now. You can be mad at me if you want to but don't take it out on Elinor. It's not her fault.'

'I'm not mad at her. I'm not mad at anybody. I'm glad I got to see her. I like her. She's a good kid.'

'Did she tell you how she wants to run a donut shop?'

Jack nodded. 'She told me all about it.'

'All excited about it. And she'll do it, too. Once she makes her mind up to something, she's a go-getter. Loves to work. Loves to make money. Doesn't give a damn about books and school work but she's a whip with figures. Figured up how much coal we should be burning at the house just by pacing off all the rooms and measuring how high to the ceilings. After she fiddled around with a calculator for a few minutes, she told Garnet exactly how much money it should cost her to heat the house if she kept the thermostat at seventy. She's a crackerjack, I'll tell you. She'll never have to count on a man. Nobody worries about her being able to take care of herself.'

'Good for her,' Jack said.

They sat silent then, Thelma glancing over at the guard stationed in the far corner. 'I think she'd like it if you wrote to her,' she said then. 'Did she mention that to you?'

Jack shook his head. 'I'm not much for writing letters.'

'I know you're not. That's what I told her. But all the same I know she'd like to hear from you.'

'Well, let's see what happens. The way things look I should have a lot of time to write letters.'

'What about that?' Thelma said. 'What's gonna happen to you?'

'God knows.'

'Do you feel funny about Elinor being at the trial?'

'Everybody else will know what's going on. Why shouldn't she?'

'I hate for her to hear people saying bad things about you.'

'You should have thought of that before you brought her here.'

'I did think about it. I told you. That's why we almost didn't come.'

'Well, don't worry about it. Like I said, it's a public carnival. She might as well see it first-hand as read about it in the papers. I'm sure your newspaper friends from Wisconsin will want to interview her about it, get all her reactions.'

'She won't talk to *anybody* from the press. She's really hard-nosed about that. Doesn't like to be photographed either, not if she can help it.'

'Good for her. That means you'll have to earn your travel expenses all by yourself.'

'Don't be snotty, Jack. What good does that do?'

'It's true, isn't it? That's why they paid to bring you over here, wasn't it? I mean, it wasn't a humanitarian gesture. They expect something from you. Like a full report on this conversation we're having. Who said what to whom? A few tears for the camera.'

'I'm not crying,' she said. 'I haven't shed a tear since I came in here, have I?'

'From what I hear, you're all cried out from the scene you played when you landed at the airport.'

'I couldn't help that. I admit I cried when I was still at home. When I first found out where you were and that you were in trouble. But then I promised myself I wasn't going to fall apart. No more crying, I decided. But when I got off the plane here in Germany, everything seemed so strange and foreign to me. And then all those reporters got us into a corner at the terminal and started asking questions and I was so upset I didn't know what to do or what to say. If you think that's an easy situation to be in, just try it some day. Those people get you so crazy, they keep putting words in your mouth, and you don't know what you're saying.'

'Don't worry about it. I don't give a damn what you say.'

'Yes, you do. That's what we're talking about and that's why you're sore at me. I was hoping we could have a talk for a few minutes and you wouldn't fly off the handle.'

'I told you. It doesn't matter.'

'Oh, yes, it does. Don't you think I *know* you? That's when you're really mad. When you say it doesn't matter. When you clam up and refuse to say anything, that's when I know I'm in trouble. That's when you hide in some corner with your viola.'

'It's not a viola, Thelma. It never was a viola. It's a fucking cello.'

'You see what I mean. Don't tell me you're not mad. You're mad as hell. You're mad because we came over here. You're mad because we wanted to talk to you like civilized people. We're not strangers, Jack. Even if you hate me, I'm still your wife and Elinor's your daughter. I can remember, even if you can't. I can remember when you liked me. You liked me a lot.'

'OK. Whatever you say. Let's not make a big thing of it.'

'Why not?' she said. 'Why save anything up? I used to think I'd never see you again. But I am seeing you again and when you get that look in your eyes I know that this is the last time I'll see you. And you know something? I don't care. I've been blaming myself for years, trying to figure out what I did wrong, what I could have done differently, how I could have *been* different, so you wouldn't have wanted to run away. I was crazy about you, you know that. It almost drove me nuts thinking that I was the one who'd spoiled things for us. But now I know that it wasn't something I did or didn't do. What you decided you didn't want was me. On any terms. I wasn't good enough for you.'

'Oh, for Christ's sake, Thelma.'

'You may not like the sound of it but it's true. I know what you think of my mother and my grandmother. Lily and Garnet, the two man-eaters, the two jokers. We both used to laugh about them. But then you started to lump me together with them and after that it was all over. And you know something . . . you're right. I am like them. They're my family. We're related. And chances are, you daughter will be a little like us, too. So I guess she won't be good enough for you either.'

'I never said that. I never said anything *like* that.'

'You didn't have to. Actions speak louder than words. Everybody knows that. Maybe we started too young, you and me. Maybe that was it. But all I know is that by the time we got married you already had me riding in the back of the truck. To me, we were still two wild kids who couldn't wait to get into bed with each other and to you . . . I don't know what was in your head. But it certainly wasn't me. You had your eyes on some other life, some other place, some new way of living. And I was so happy and dumb I couldn't see it. But, oh, God, do I see it now! You're sitting here talking to me as if I'm somebody you've never seen before, some chippie who wandered in off the street. No wonder you didn't want to see me. You have nothing to say to me. You don't even know who I am.' She stood up. 'Anyway, I'm glad Elinor got to see you. I think it was important for her. And I guess when it stops hurting I'll see

268

how important it was for me.' She turned and walked across to the
guard. He opened the door and let her out.

Chapter Six

[1]

Jack's trial lasted only two days. Very late, the night of the second day, when it was over, Jesse wrote a letter to Helen.

The trepidations I felt when I called you last night, the trepidations I've felt ever since I got here, all turned out to be well-justified. The scenario that Rosenthal gave to Floyd after he talked with his friend at the State Department was played out here as though it had been rehearsed. Jack was found guilty of conspiracy and manslaughter, and sentenced to twenty years in a German prison.

As you know the whole family is here. All of us, those of us who thought we knew what to expect – Floyd, Speicher, and I – and those who had no idea of how the trial would turn out, are stunned. How strange that a group of people, only one of whom, Polly, has any love for Jack Dieter, and several of whom truly detest him, should be so upset by what has happened to him.

As you know, I had serious reservations about Jack, even before I met him. And mixed feelings later. But when he was sentenced, perhaps because I had become so involved in his defence, and perhaps because I have begun to almost *like* him, I felt as if it was Bill or Rab being sent off to prison.

Whatever else he is, Jack is not a common type. At first we marvel that an iconoclast like him can manage to survive in a conforming world, then quite often our original feelings, whatever they were, become a kind of admiration, and at last this

craggy, difficult and unique creature takes on an aura of inde-
structibility. We start to believe that his survival skills have
become so formidable that nothing can bring him down. A man
who seems to fear no consequences will appear to be justified in
his fearlessness. No bad consequences will come to him.

My attitude toward Jack had begun to follow that pattern. Since
he obviously doesn't give a damn, I began to believe that his
attitude alone might give him a kind of invulnerability. Why flog
a man who doesn't feel the pain? So, for all my fore-knowledge
of the probable outcome of the trial, I was as unprepared as
anyone for the result. All of us were quite shattered, Valerie in
particular. I have known her, as you know, since she was a child,
but I have never seen anything affect her as this has.

I have not seen Jack, of course, since he left the courtroom but
Polly, who was allowed to see him this evening, says he was
concerned for her but not for himself. He said to her, 'Bad news
never surprises me and it mustn't surprise you either.' Whatever
the secret formula may be for his remarkable composure, Jack
seems to have shared it with Polly. All of us had a quiet, almost
silent, dinner together after the trial closing and later Polly and
I came home alone to her apartment. We sat up quite late, drank
a bottle of wine, and talked. We didn't dwell on the subject of
Jack, nor did we avoid it. She seems to have made some sort of
peace with the situation. She plans, it appears, to keep her feelings to herself. She did say two things, however, that stuck in
my memory. One – 'I never deceived myself that life with Jack
would be peaceful. He promised me that trouble and torment
seem to follow him and he was correct. I've always had to
measure the joy against the sadness and I've never felt cheated
by the proportions.' And two – 'I've lost things I wanted before
and I've cried and cursed my fate as everyone else does. Now I
feel as if I've lost everything and there's nothing in my experience
that tells me how to react. So I'm simply waiting.'

Because of the difference in time, you have heard already the
details of Jack's trial on your television news. And tomorrow you
will have it all in the Chicago papers. So this written report will
come to you late. But still, until I come home and we can talk
about it at length, I thought you should have some sort of
personal briefing from me.

You know what the charges were against Jack. They were

271

heavy. The fact that he was the only person indicted as a result of the demonstration and the violence was like an additional charge. The case presented by the prosecutors was devastating. They produced witnesses who swore that Jack was the leader and the instigator of the student revolt, that he had planned the burning of the university building, that he was a Communist sympathizer, and that he had struck the blows that killed the university guard. The prosecution conceded that Donny Krause and the other student who died that night had been accidentally killed by the riot police as they performed their duty of breaking up the demonstration.

I have great respect for Speicher. He is a resourceful lawyer. In cross-examination he tried every device he knew to discredit the prosecution witnesses. But the court blocked his way whenever he came close to scoring a critical point. When the time came to present his defence, Speicher could see that he had no real weapons to use against the mountain of evidence the prosecution had put up. Even Jack's fellow students who had participated in the demonstration testified against him. They said he had radicalized and politicized what had originated as a peaceful demonstration against the release of Speer and von Schirach. Other students who had promised they would attest to Jack's innocence changed their minds and did not appear at the trial.

Jack refused to testify in his own defence. Nor would he allow Polly to appear as a witness. His music teacher and the Dean of the Department of Slavic Languages testified that he had remarkable musical gifts and a genius for languages. Both admitted, however, under cross-examination, that they knew nothing of either his personal life or his political beliefs.

Speicher's principal defence witness was a young German woman named Pietra Wessen. She had lived with Donny Krause for some time before his death and previous to that had lived with Jack before he met Polly. She had presented herself to Speicher and said she would testify that Krause, in fact, was the one who had been an avowed and active Communist. She said he had conceived of and organized the demonstration, had planned the throwing of gasoline bombs into the university building, and had personally made anonymous phone calls to Heidelberg city officials saying that the demonstration on the university grounds would be a violent and destructive one. Jack,

272

she said, was not political at all. He had only gone along with the demonstration because he was Donny Krause's friend and because he sincerely believed that Speer and von Schirach should not be released.

When Speicher told Jack about his meeting with Pietra Wessen, Jack conceded that what she had said was true but he was disturbed by the prospect of her testifying and appearing to put all the blame on Krause. 'If what she says is untrue I will not allow her to testify,' Speicher told him, 'but if it's true then she must testify. She is our strongest witness.'

I'm not saying that the court decision against Jack would have turned out differently without Pietra's testimony. Perhaps it would not have. But once she had spoken from the witness chair there was no question but that he would be found guilty. In testimony she completely reversed the story she had previously told Speicher. When he asked her in front of the judge who had planned the demonstration, she said Jack had done it. She said he had put together the gasoline bombs in her kitchen and that Krause had been an innocent dupe in the whole affair. He had, indeed, made telephone calls to Heidelberg officials warning them of the potential violence but Jack had carefully written out on a card what Donny was to say. Apart from that single act, she said, Krause had taken no part in the planning of the demonstration and had only gone along because Jack insisted. She cried and said, 'Donny would be alive today if it weren't for Jack Dieter.' She went on then to say that she had been frightened of Jack, that she had only broken up with him because of his leftist politics and his violent temper. Under cross-examination she was asked by the prosecutor if she had ever imagined that Jack was capable of killing anyone and she said, 'He told me about the people he had killed in Korea and I never doubted that he could do it again. I was afraid it might be me. That's why I left him.'

You can imagine the kind of wave that sent through the courtroom. The guilty verdict and the sentencing were almost anticlimactic after that. Even people in the courtroom who had assumed from the start that Jack was guilty were stunned by Pietra's testimony. Only she seemed calm and unperturbed. When Speicher asked her later why she changed her testimony she said, 'I wanted to help him because he was Donny's friend so I lied to you. But when I thought about Donny, already in his grave back in America, I realized I had to tell the truth.'

'You lived with Jack Dieter for two years. Then he left you to live with another woman,' Speicher said to her. 'Are you sure that had nothing to do with your testimony against him?' 'Of course not. What sort of woman do you think I am?' 'I can see what sort of woman you are. I hoped you might be willing to admit it.'

As I say, the case against Jack was made before Pietra's testimony. But any hope for a defence was destroyed by the things she said.

All the Bradshaws seem to have been struck dumb. They'll be slowly pulling themselves together now and heading back to where they came from. I'll stay here with Polly for a few more days, then I'll finish up what I started in Paris and come home. But I will telephone you before then. Probably several times. I'm glad you weren't here. It wasn't a triumphant occasion for the Bradshaws.

[2]

Rab had to return to London the day after Jack's trial. Polly had agreed the day before that whatever the outcome of the trial she would have a private luncheon with him and Bill before Rab had to drive to the airport. When they sat down at table as planned Rab said, 'Seems a long time since the three of us sat down together without being chaperoned by a gaggle of tiresome adults.'

Polly smiled. '*We're* tiresome adults now, Rab.'

'Adult perhaps, but never tiresome,' he said. 'Matter of fact, I'm not sure I want to be an adult just yet.'

'I'm not sure you'll ever want to be an adult,' Bill said.

'Respect,' Rab said. 'You're the youngest, William. Very important that you treat Polly and me with respect.'

Bill grinned and lifted his water glass in Rab's direction. 'I've always given you the respect you deserve and I always will.'

'Meaning no respect at all.'

'That's it.'

'No insult can touch me,' Rab said. 'No man's a hero to his butler. No man's a prophet in his own country, to say nothing of his own family.'

Bill turned to Polly. 'How are you doing today?'

'Just about as you might expect.'

'Did you sleep at all?' Rab said.

She nodded. 'Sat up late with Jesse. We talked and he plied me with wine. And at last I went to bed and slept.'

'When's Mother leaving?' Bill asked.

'Tomorrow, I believe. I expect I'll have some supper with her and Floyd tonight. Nora's already gone. Left first thing this morning for Paris.'

'Quick exit,' Rab said.

'I asked her to,' Polly said. 'I appreciate the fact that all of you came here to be with me. But now that it's over, it's too awkward for people just to wait around in hotels. I don't need that and I don't want it.'

'You're a tough old bird,' Rab said.

'No, I'm not. I wish I were. I feel like cold porridge inside. But I've told myself that if Jack can hold himself together the way he has, then it's not proper for me to fall apart. So I'm not going to.'

'It's one thing to say that,' Bill said, 'and another thing to do it. I have a feeling you're just waiting for all of us to leave. Then you'll crawl in a corner and collapse.'

'Is that what you're planning to do?' Rab said.

'No,' she said. 'I can't guarantee anything but that's certainly not what I'm planning.'

'What are you planning?' Rab asked.

'I don't know. Maybe I'll know more after I see Jack. I hope they'll let me visit him this afternoon.'

'Jesse said Speicher doesn't plan to appeal.'

'No, that's not what Jesse meant. Speicher does plan to appeal. At once. But he feels certain it will be turned down. There's no fresh evidence or new testimony to be presented.'

'Wouldn't it help if Jack testified?'

'I don't know,' Polly said. 'He doesn't think so. So that's all that matters.'

'Maybe he wants to go to prison.'

'Don't be stupid, Rab. Nobody wants to go to prison.'

'Then I just don't understand him,' Rab said.

'You don't have to understand him. He doesn't give a damn whether you understand him or not, and neither do I.'

'Rab's right, though,' Bill said. 'Why wouldn't he try to defend himself?'

'If there'd been a chance that his testimony would have made a difference, maybe he would have. But after the prosecution finished presenting its case and after Pietra sat there and nailed him to the cross, I guess Jack knew there was no point to his speaking up. And I knew it too.'

'I thought that German woman was supposed to be his friend,' Rab said.

'Pietra's not his friend at all,' Polly said. 'She's in love with him.'

'Then why would she turn on him like that?' Bill said.

'You don't know much about women, Bill.'

'You'd be surprised how much I know. I just don't know any women like her.'

'Have you thought about what you're going to do now?' Rab said.

'No,' Polly said.

'I know we didn't find out till yesterday what would happen to Jack. But I thought perhaps you'd made some contingency plans.'

She shook her head. 'I don't plan to do anything except what I've been doing.'

'Does that mean you expect to stay here?'

'Of course. Where else would I go? First I have to find out where they're sending him. If it's not too far I'll stay on in Heidelberg. If the prison's a long distance from here then I'll have to move.'

'You mean you're staying in Germany no matter what?' Bill said.

'What else can I do? What else do you think I'd want to do? Can you see me relaxing with a good book at Wingate Fields? Or walking on the beach at Praia da Rocha with Valerie?'

'I think it might be good for you to come spend some time in London,' Rab said.

'Or fly back to America with me. Dad would like it and so would I.'

'I know you're trying to be helpful,' she said, 'and I appreciate it. But can you imagine me writing long letters to Jack describing the plays I've seen in the West End? Or the splendours of the National Gallery? Do you think I could spend one day in some marvellous place while he's being slowly introduced to the pleasures of prison life? If you think that, you don't know me very well. You don't know me at all. I can't give one thought just now to what's best for *me*, what might make *me* comfortable or happy.'

'But when he's locked away somewhere, what can you do for him?' Rab asked. 'I know what you're saying. I admire the way you feel. But in a practical sense, what can you do for him?'

Suddenly there were tears in her eyes, for the first time in a great many days. 'There is no practical sense. We're not talking about practical matters. Maybe you're right. Maybe I can't do anything for him. But I can be here. I must be here. Since everything else in his life is going to change, at least one thing has to stay the same. And that one thing is me. I have to stay here, whether he wants it that way or not. It's my obligation to myself. It's also what I want. Just now it's the only thing I want.'

[3]

Although Helen had never met Jack Dieter, and although most of the descriptions of him she'd heard had been negative, she felt real compassion for him. And although she had never had an opportunity to get to know Polly well she sensed the pain of her present situation.

Both Jesse and Bill had asked her to come to Germany when the family was gathering before the trial. She had said no, then yes, and had decided at last that her presence might provide more hindrance than help. She knew that Jesse was deeply involved, working long hours with Speicher to try to pull Jack's defence together, and for reasons that were clear to her but which she had no urge to explain to someone else she did not want to be an object of *politesse*, she did not want to be left in the care of Valerie and Floyd, nor did she want to be assigned as companion to Nora. Also, quite apart from what might be called these selfish motives, she genuinely believed that Polly's problems might be increased rather than diminished by the sudden appearance of a great horde of relatives.

Helen's choice, then, to stay in Fort Beck rather than fly to Germany, had been her own. She had carefully explained it to Jesse and Bill and in notes to Floyd and Polly. All the same, when she received Jesse's letter about the trial with references to 'all the family' being assembled in Heidelberg, she felt a twinge that made no sense to her but which gave her discomfort all the same.

Sensing that she was on unstable ground, she tried to put the whole matter out of her mind, reminding herself that the only reason she was not in Germany was because she'd chosen not to go. But none of these reassurances worked.

The fact was that Floyd's marriage to Valerie had begun long since to isolate Helen from the rest of the family. Jesse's decision to return to Fort Beck to live with her seemed to have accelerated the pace of that isolation. And Clara's death had completed it.

Polly's situation in Heidelberg, then, had not created a new condition in Helen's life but it was a disturbing reminder of conditions that had already been locked into place. Apart from Jesse and Floyd, who had become Bradshaws only because of her and whose true roots were more American than British, she realized that she no longer had a true or rewarding connection with her father's family.

On the other hand, and ironically, she knew that both Floyd and Jesse were fully enmeshed in the Bradshaw fabric, Jesse through his children and Floyd by his marriage to Valerie.

Although Helen had not planned or ever wished that it should happen, she had assumed, when Jesse came back to Fort Beck after his divorce from Valerie, that he would somehow take up his life as it had been before the two of them, Helen and Jesse, had gone to England for the first time so many years before. Living together with him in the house where they had spent their young years with Raymond, it was easy for her to define her present life as a lovely and logical continuum of that other time, with all the years and events involving the Bradshaws of Northumberland seen as a kind of parenthetical chapter of her personal history.

Whether she had willed it so or not, that period was concluded now, she felt, and she was back at the beginning, before Angus and Clara and Nora and Hugh had stepped on stage with her and played such critical roles. They were dead now, along with Raymond and Louise and Ned. Of the family she had met on that first visit to Wingate Fields, only Nora remained. And Nora, from the first time they met, had been a symbol of mystery and antipathy and misunderstanding to Helen. Their relationship had been made

278

bearable through the years only because their distrust of each other was so totally mutual.

Jesse, as always, was the key to Helen's unease and confusion. Just as his total involvement with Helen's new-found family in the years just after Raymond's death had made her feel neglected and abandoned, so did her present realization that his connection to Nora and Valerie and Rab and Polly and Bill, and that strange and singular place, Wingate Fields, was as strong and permanent as ever, make her feel once again, like a family of one. Clara had once said to her, 'Jesse became a Bradshaw even before Angus adopted him. He told me it was as though he'd had a lifetime nostalgia for a place he'd never known or seen. Also, if he's honest with himself, he must admit that he's only loved three women in his life, you and Nora and Valerie. All Bradshaw women. And I think he loves me, in a very different way. So you see, he's created an emotional cocoon for himself. If he were a Bradshaw by blood rather than adoption it would be alarmingly incestuous. As it is, he is merely selective in an unusual way.'

Since she had known Jesse all her life, and known him well, Helen realized that Clara's observations about him were true. She knew also that his Bradshaw fixation had begun some years before his arrival at Wingate Fields. Helen believed that Jesse had imprinted on Raymond as a sled dog imprints on his master. His desire to emulate Raymond in all things had led him to believe in some childlike way that he *was* Raymond or that he had a mandate from someone, from himself perhaps, to *become* Raymond. This drive in him had only increased after her father's death. When they learned by chance that Raymond had been born not in Maine but in England, when Jesse had secretly begun to correspond with Helen's relatives, it was he who had insisted that she must go there to meet them and, when she resisted, had said that he was going, whether she went or not.

Although Helen believed that in his role as Raymond's extended self Jesse was acting on her behalf, she also knew, or believed strongly and had so believed for many years, that while Jesse had no selfish ambitions and was not attempting to serve himself by going to England, there was all the same a strong personal need that fired him, an urge to see all what he had never seen and to be what he had never been.

As a young woman, as she watched these pell-mell developments

279

in Jesse, Helen had felt betrayed and cast off. But through the years the things they had shared became more telling than the things that divided them. During her marriage to Frank and her love affair with Chet Comiskey she found levels of tolerance inside herself that had not been there before. The brother-sister relationship she had shared with Jesse came alive again then and evolved, after his divorce from Valerie, into what it was now, something they told themselves it was destined to be from the beginning.

As she waited for Jesse to return from Paris, however, Helen began to think she had deceived herself. She began to suspect that she and Jesse had not *come* together, as they assured themselves, but had been *thrown* together by a chain of circumstances. Convenience and passion had merged and had been accepted as destiny. Or so she told herself as she spent the days alone in her house and went upstairs to bed by herself.

There were more lucid and reasonable moments, too, as she waited, when she said to herself, 'For God's sake, Helen, he went off for two weeks to do some business and see his daughter. Then something totally unpredictable happened and he was delayed in coming home. Don't build it into something it isn't. Don't make it into a Wagnerian opera. He'll be home in a few days, you'll meet him at the airport in Chicago, and everything will settle into place again. It won't matter then that the people you loved at Wingate Fields aren't there any longer. And it won't matter that you don't have much connection with the Bradshaws who are left. You're in Raymond's house, where you belong, and Jesse will be here, too.'

She began to rely on that litany she had created. She put herself to sleep with it every night. And with admirable self-control she kept herself clear of the shoals that frightened her most. She didn't allow herself to think about Nora.

[4]

'You have to find a way to get hold of yourself,' Floyd said. 'You'll make yourself sick.'

'I'm sick already,' Valerie said. 'I feel as if I've been exposed to some nasty virus and all I can do is wait for the symptoms to start showing.'

They had just flown from Frankfurt to Faro and were driving west in their car to Portimão.

'Never in my life,' she went on, 'have I had such strong feelings that there's something I must do. And I've never been so unable to think of one single thing I can do.'

'Sometimes there isn't anything to do. Nobody likes it but it happens. Sometimes you can't do anything but feel lousy.'

'But I can't stop thinking about Polly. She's barely past being a child and it seems she has no place to go. Every way she turns, a door slams shut. She's lovely and gifted and wise for her years. I always believed there was nothing she could want that wouldn't be available to her. Now all of a sudden nothing is available to her. God, how I wish she'd never gone to Germany.'

'So do I,' Floyd said. 'But I don't think Polly feels that way.'

'I wish she'd never met that strange young man.'

'The last time you went to visit her in Heidelberg you came home saying how happy she was.'

'She was happy. She adores that fool. But look what it's got her into. She talks as if she's been hypnotized. She acts as though she has no choices.'

'You may not like what she's doing with her life. But you can't say she doesn't know what she's doing,' Floyd said. 'She's more in control than anyone else in the Bradshaw family.'

'I know she is. Or at least she seemed to be when we were there in Heidelberg. But that's what scares me. Her mind hasn't stopped working, has it? Doesn't she realize the kind of future she's laid out for herself?'

'I'm sure you asked her that question. What did she say?'

'She didn't say anything. Nothing at least that made sense to me.'

'Did you offer any advice?' Floyd asked.

'I tried to but she wouldn't listen.'

'What do you think she should do?'

'I don't know. That's what I said before. I just know that she can't just sit there where she is. Do you realize that when Jack gets out of prison Polly will be forty-three years old and he'll be almost sixty?'

281

'Polly's the smartest one in the family,' Floyd said. 'Anything we can think of, I'm sure she thought of a long time ago.'

'That's just it. She hasn't. She hasn't used her head at all. She just feels and reacts.'

'She's in love, Val. That's the way it works. Do you think we were using our heads when we ran off together? When Helen told us we mustn't get married and have children do you think we made a *sensible* decision?'

'I tried to,' she said.

'No, you didn't. You just ran off and hid in Italy till neither of us could stand it any longer. Then we got married.'

Valerie sat silent, looking out the window for a long time. Then she said, 'It still haunts me that we couldn't have a family. I hated to deprive you of that.'

'You didn't deprive me of anything. And don't start feeling sorry about us. You've got your hands full with Polly.'

Again she was silent. Then, 'If we made a bad decision it was so we could be together. Polly's making a decision that means she'll be spending a great deal of her life by herself.'

Floyd was tempted then to tell her what Rosenthal had told him in New York, that Jack might be released in ten years. But he held up for the same reason he hadn't told her before. He didn't trust the information enough to hold it out as a hope for either Valerie or Polly. Instead he said, 'They must have a parole system in Germany as we do in America. Or maybe he'll get time off for good behaviour.'

'I mentioned that possibility to Polly,' Valerie said.

'What did she think?'

'She says Jack doesn't know the meaning of "good behaviour". She says he'll be lucky if they don't keep him longer than twenty years.'

'She's a hard-nosed kid, your daughter.'

'Maybe she is, but I'm not. Every time I think of her sitting in some dreary apartment by herself just so she can journey once a week or once a month to the prison to visit a man who wasn't good enough for her *before* he went to jail, every time I think of that future for her, all I can do is cry.'

'All kinds of things might happen,' Floyd said. 'Maybe Speicher will be granted an appeal after all. Some new evidence could come up. Jack might have a new trial or he might even be pardoned.'

282

'You don't believe all that sunshine talk and neither do I. There won't be any miracles for Jack. Because if one turned up, he'd wreck it. And there won't be any miracles for Polly either because she doesn't have good luck. She's just not lucky. Sometimes I think the Bradshaws have used up all their luck.'

'You know what I think? I think you need a drink. I'm going to take you home and get you drunk.'

'It won't work,' she said, 'I'll still feel rotten tomorrow.'

'We'll worry about that tomorrow.'

[5]

'Do you ever think about abandoning that dismal country where you live and coming back to France?' Nora said.

'I *am* back in France,' Jesse said. 'I'm sitting in the Bois du Boulogne having an excellent lunch.'

'I'm talking about something of a more permanent nature. Do you ever think about coming back to me?'

'Nope.'

'I don't believe you.'

'All right,' he said. 'What if I tell you I think about that all day every day?'

'I wouldn't believe that either.'

'You don't trust me. I can't win.'

'I trust you except when you're agreeable. That makes me think you're lying.' Then: 'I don't mean that. Whatever faults you may have, lying has never been one of them. If anything you were always too truthful.'

'A man of honour.'

'Not at all. You simply said you were too lazy to lie.'

'That's true.'

'If you don't think of coming back to me,' she said, 'you should. We've separated and got back together more than once. You remember those occasions, don't you?'

'I suppose I should but I have a bad memory.'

'Only when it serves your purpose,' she said. 'Only when it's convenient. The truth is, the most remarkable thing about your mind is your memory. And you're fortunate because you've chosen to live in a country where a good memory is always mistaken for intelligence.'

'Then you approve of my living there.'

'Not at all. The day you left France you left your soul behind.'

'As I recall we left France together. The Germans were poised at the Maginot Line.'

'That's true. But I came back. As soon as I could. While you went off to moulder in Northumberland, returning to Paris only briefly, from time to time, to try to find tiny pieces of your soul. What you don't seem to realize is that if you came home now to this magnificent city your soul would re-enter your body completely intact, that young and healthy soul you left behind when we went off to New York.'

'As I recall you didn't want to go.'

'Not at all. And if I had it to do again I *wouldn't* go. It was a dreary Occupation, no doubt of that, but all the same, people stayed on. Picasso was here. Many of the painters stayed. And those little English ladies who lived at the Liberia and ate every evening Chez Rosalie, they never left. I'm sorry I didn't stay on. I lost a lot by going to New York. I lost you, of course, but I lost other things as well. I forgot who I was. I let other people define me. Americans like to do that. They love to tell you what you like and what you think, and when they've finally convinced you they say, "There you are . . . I told you so," and one never sees them again. I thought they were all frightfully attractive, and they were. I also thought the people I knew were first rate but they weren't. They weren't even third rate. They were simply quick and clever. Americans have never learned the difference between change and progress. Or between success and achievement. They truly believe that any problem can be solved by moving from one apartment to another, by buying a new automobile, by having one's nose bobbed. They worship the superficial and castigate anything they don't understand. And since they truly understand so little, a great deal of time is spent in castigation.'

'Don't you realize it's out of style to criticize Americans? No one does it any more,' Jesse said.

'Of course they do. Here in Paris no one has a good word to say about America.'

'Ah, but you're different. At least you should be. Your daughter has been married to *two* Americans. Your grandchildren are half-American.'

'Not true, Jesse. My grandchildren are totally English since you are the most English of all the Bradshaws. Only Floyd is unchangeably American.'

'Just as you are unchangeably French.'

'Not at all,' Nora said. 'I am simply an Englishwoman of a certain age who has spent her life in France.'

'And when you die you'll be carried to the Cimetière Montparnasse.'

She shook her head. 'If I die, which is unlikely, I may very well be put to rest in the family crypt at Wingate Fields.'

'I don't believe my ears.'

'Why not? Just because I've spent my life as a free spirit doesn't mean I have no sense of tradition. I have always detested the thought of living in Northumberland but I have no objection to being there when I'm dead. That may be the future of Wingate Fields. We'll all go there to die.'

'Like a herd of elephants seeking their burial ground.'

'Just so,' she said. 'And I will request that my coffin be placed close beside yours. Do you have any objections to that?'

'None whatsoever. I think it's quite touching.'

'No, you don't. But that doesn't matter.' Then: 'You steered me away from my central theme. In my subtle and ladylike way I was trying to persuade you to come and live with me again. Seems like a simple procedure to me. We could sit down together and write Baby Helen a sweet letter of explanation. Ask her to send your things along, unless of course there's nothing there in Illinois you really need. In that case the letter could be even shorter. How does that strike you?'

'Sounds awfully abrupt to me. Damned difficult letter to write.'

'You're humouring me, of course. I expected that. But I'll move right along anyway and pretend you're as serious as I am. The letter as I see it would be no problem at all. You're a writer, skilful at fitting words together. But if you feel too personally involved, too close to the situation, I could help you out. I'm a publisher, remember, accustomed to working with writers. I'm sure I could make constructive suggestions. Might even tap out a first draft for you if that would make it easier.'

'I see.'

285

'No, you don't. You're still humouring me. You think I'm an impossible ignoramus but I don't mind. The truth is that I see this matter with total clarity and you don't. But at last you will. And the sooner, the better for both of us. You see, the difficulties are all in your mind. The simple approach is the answer. The simpler, the better.'

She opened her shoulder-bag and took out a folded sheet of writing paper. 'After I left Heidelberg, while I was waiting here for you to come back, I made a few notes and studied them carefully. Then I jotted down this letter, which I think would be a perfect message for you to send to Helen. Shall I read it to you?'

'Of course.'

Nora adjusted her reading glasses, cleared her throat softly, and read from the sheet of paper. 'Dear Helen. It is difficult for me to express the things I need to say to you. But I will do my best. You know that I spent more than twenty years of my life here in Paris. I came to think of it as my home. I've discovered that I still think of it that way. So I've decided to stay on here.' Nora looked up at Jesse. 'How do you like it so far?'

'You're quite a writer.'

'My theory is that it's best not to beat about the bush. You simply say what you're going to do. Then you say why you're doing it. You explain in a decent civilized way but you don't apologize.' She read from the page again. 'I know this will surprise you. It surprises me too. But when you think it over I'm sure you'll agree with me that I have no alternative. I feel as if I belong here. The years I spent in Paris were happy and productive ones and I think I owe it to myself to have that kind of experience again.' Nora folded the letter and put it back in her bag.

'Is that it?' Jesse asked.

Nora nodded. 'The briefer, the better.'

'Seems awfully impersonal to me.'

'You could always add a few words at the end.'

'Like what?'

'You could say that this decision is no reflection on her. If you're afraid of hurting her feelings you could say you're not choosing a person you're choosing a place.'

'What if she says she'll come here to Paris to live with me.'

'Then you'll have to tell her you're choosing a person as well as

286

a place,' Nora said. 'Because if she came here to live I would murder you both.' She smiled. 'You think I'm outrageous, don't you?'

'Yes, but I'm accustomed to it.'

'It's not nearly so outrageous as you think. Since you've been gone, since you came to Europe a few weeks ago, do you think it's never occurred to Helen that you might not come back to America? Of course she's thought of it. She thinks of it every day. And she should. Those years you and I spent together were the happiest years of our lives. Whether you admit it to yourself or not, it's true. I've seen pictures of that grey stone house you live in with vines crawling up the sides. Do you expect me to believe that anything that takes place inside that cold place can begin to match the life we had together? I dare you to tell me that such a neat little buttoned-up person as Helen can take you to places where we went together. It's not possible, Jesse. I may be crazy but I'm not a fool. I know what we had and so do you. And I don't mean when we were twenty-five or thirty years old. I mean just a few years ago when Floyd and Valerie got married. There was no reason for you and me to separate then. There was every reason in the world for us to stay together. We had nothing to feel guilty about. Valerie didn't divorce you because she found out about us. If we didn't realize that then we certainly know it now. Don't you see what I'm saying? If we didn't let your marriage to Valerie stand in our way, why should we let Helen keep us apart?'

After a moment Jesse said, 'You're right. We've known each other for a long time. I know you as well as I know anyone, I suppose. But for all that, I'm never sure when you're serious and when you're not.'

'You know I'm serious now, don't you?'

He shook his head. 'Of course not. How would I know that? We're sitting here drinking wine and smoking cigarettes and you're disposing of people like used paper-cups.'

'You mean Helen? Is that who you're talking about?'

'Of course.'

'All right,' Nora said. 'Let's talk about her. But let's tell the truth about her for once. Let's take off the ribbons and gold foil she likes to wrap herself in. Let's see how she's mucked things up for me through the years.'

When Jesse started to protest she held up her hand and said, 'No, let me finish. And if I'm wrong you can have as much time

287

as you like to point out my mistakes. First of all, you and I became engaged that first summer we met. But when Baby Helen found out about it and ran back to America you had to follow her to make sure she was tucked up safely at university. Before leaving, however, she slipped into my brother's bed and managed to get herself pregnant. When she disappeared somewhere on the great American frontier, you broke our engagement so you could wait there in Illinois for her to come back. And I married Valerie's father.'

'I didn't break our engagement.'

'Oh, yes you did. Not in so many words perhaps. But you knew how I felt about Helen. You knew how I would react if you kept postponing your return to England. By the time you came back I was married to Edmund and Valerie was three years old. And the next time we broke up, you and I, after I had left Edmund, after you had spent all those lovely years with me here in Paris, it was Helen at work again.'

'Not at all.'

'Not in your mind perhaps but very definitely in mine. If she hadn't sent out a cry of distress to you, if you hadn't trotted off to help her locate her long-lost son, you and I would never have fought the way we did, we would never have said the things we said to each other, and we wouldn't have broken up.'

'We broke up because of Valerie.'

'I've never believed that,' Nora said. 'I think you married Valerie because you and I broke up, not the other way around.'

'Jesus, Nora . . .'

'Let me finish. You promised. The last time Baby Helen did me a favour was after Valerie and Floyd got married. When I saw Helen at the wedding I didn't realize that when she went back to Illinois you'd be waiting there for her.'

'It wasn't planned that way and you know it.'

'Not in your mind, perhaps. But very definitely in hers. It took her a long time. She planned it since she was fifteen. But she finally got you back in her daddy's house and into her ruffled bed. I'll bet you ten thousand pounds her bed has ruffles on it.'

'No bet,' he said. 'I don't remember.'

'Of course not. Men don't notice such things.'

After a moment, Jesse said, 'Are you finished?'

'Yes.'

'Good. Now tell me what the point was. What are you trying to prove with that distorted history lesson?'

'Not distorted,' she said. 'Selected facts but no distortion.'

'For what reason? Am I supposed to run out on the Boulevard de la Grande Armée and burn Helen in effigy?'

'Not at all. You could never bring yourself to do that in any case. What you are meant to do is to admit for the first time in your life that Helen is not made of spun sugar, that she's made as many selfish choices and done as much damage as any of us have. I mean you are not endlessly in her debt, Jesse. You need not feel that because you're living with her now you're bound to her for ever.'

'Is that the way I feel?'

'Something very like that, I expect.'

'The last thing I want to do is hurt your feelings,' Jesse said, 'But what if I told you that I'm with Helen by choice, that I'm not indebted to her or bound to her, would that surprise you?'

'Not at all. That's the sort of thing I'd expect you to say. You see yourself as an honourable chap. Clara thought you were the most honourable fellow she'd ever met. But she was a little bit in love with you herself, I suspect, so her judgments were not crystal clear where you were concerned.'

'How about yours?'

'Not clear at all. Not meant to be. Muddied by love and resentment and experience and frustration. I see you as a flawed human animal, just as I see myself. Just as I see everyone I've ever known, including Helen. But she's something of a special case. Her greatest flaw is her belief that she has no flaws. And you've spent much of your life sharing that belief with her.'

Jesse smiled. 'You'll go to your grave hating her, won't you?'

'Not at all. I simply believe she is not what she pretends to be and that disgusts me. That kind of silly pretence is a waste of one's life and a frustration to everyone who shares that life.'

'How about you? Are you what you pretend to be?'

'I don't know. You would be the best judge of that. I try not to pretend at all. But there again you should ask *yourself*. You've seen me revealed in ways that no one else has or ever will. I admit that I'm never completely certain what I'll do till after I've done it and I'm sure I've been as careless and cruel as the next person. But I don't believe I've presented myself as someone I'm not. I never seem to have time for all the planning and preparation that entails.

289

God knows, I did terrible things to you. And I said cruel things. But I never plotted against you. I never felt an ounce of malice towards you even when I wanted to kill you. And if I had killed you it would have been a *crime passionnel*. I wouldn't have known I'd done it till it was over. Then I'd have killed myself.'

After a moment Jesse said, 'I'm getting all sorts of conflicting messages from you today.'

'You're only meant to get one,' she said. 'I'm telling you how much I love you. I'm throwing my heart over the wall and saying that I want to spend the rest of my life with you. I want you to spend the rest of your life with me. As I said before, I am a woman of a certain age. The waiting game no longer fits into my plans.'

'What are your plans?'

'You must know by now. I have no plans that don't include you.'

'I don't know what to say. You make things difficult for me.'

'No, I don't. You are not obligated to say or do anything. I expect nothing from you. I want everything and expect nothing. What could be more benevolent than that? I'd like to slip inside your brain and plant flowers there that smell like me but I know that's impossible. I know what I want and now you know, too. But I'm not trying to wreck your life. All I can hope to do is jog your memory. I hope when you think of me you'll remember it all fresh, the way it really was. Sometimes I force myself to think of the worst possible things I can remember about us and, God, how unimportant they seem now. If I never see you again I like to think you'll remember some of the good stuff and if you do, if you let yourself remember it straight, then I think I will see you again. But *if* you come back you'd better expect to be chained up. Because next time I won't let you leave. When the tourist boats go up and down the Seine the guides will point to my house and say, "There's a man kept in chains in there. Pampered and feasted and treated like a king, they say. But he's never let out of the house." '

[6]

After his trial, Jack was kept in the Heidelberg city jail for five days before being transferred to the regional prison at Wurzburg. Polly was allowed to visit him for half an hour every afternoon. On the

290

last day before his transfer, when they sat down across the table from each other in the guarded room, he said, 'Pietra Wessen came to see me this morning.'

'I don't believe it.'

Jack nodded. 'The guard brought a message to my cell just after breakfast. It was from the director's office. It said Frau Wessen had requested permission to see me and it had been granted. If I wished to see her she would be brought to the visitor's room.'

'You didn't see her, did you?'

'Yes, I did.'

'Why, for God's sake?'

'Curiosity, I guess.'

'Curiosity? She did her best to get you convicted. And she succeeded. What more do you need to know about her?'

'I guess I wondered why she did it.'

'What's the difference, Jack? She did it. That's all that matters.'

'They didn't need her testimony to convict me.'

'Maybe not. But *she* didn't know that.'

'That's right. She didn't. That's what she said. She thinks it's all her fault that I was convicted. She told me she wants to go to the judge and tell him she lied. She thinks if she does that I'll get a new trial.'

'What did you say?'

'I told her to forget it.'

'Why? Maybe she's right. Maybe it would make a difference.'

'Not a chance. You know it and so do I. They're sending me over to Wurzburg no matter what anybody says or does. So why should Pietra go to jail too?'

'Because she deserves to. She sat there in court and lied about you. Are you saying that doesn't matter to you?'

'It mattered then,' he said. 'I sure as hell didn't like to listen to it. But it didn't change anything as far as the final verdict was concerned.'

'How do you know that?'

'I just know it. So does Speicher. And so do you if you're being honest with yourself.'

'But why do you want to protect her? Of all people?'

'It's not a question of protecting her.'

'What is it then?'

291

'Like I said . . . why should she go to jail? Who would benefit from that?'

'I would,' Polly said. 'I'd slam the cell door myself if they gave me the chance.'

Jack smiled. 'I'm seeing a new side of you. Maybe I should get you a job as a guard over at Wurzburg. Then I could see you every day, walking down the cell corridors with a whip and a gun.'

'Don't try to make a joke of it. This is the worst day of my life. Starting tomorrow everything's going to change for us. And you're trying to . . . I don't know what you're trying to do.'

'I don't know either. Maybe I'm just trying to keep myself from falling apart.'

'Why did she do it?' Polly asked.

'We don't want to keep talking about Pietra, do we?'

'You brought her up. I didn't.'

'But now I think we should drop the subject.'

'But I don't. I want to know why she did it. Didn't she say anything?'

'She was crying a lot. Saying all kinds of things. She was upset about Donny.'

'So were you. So was I,' Polly said. 'But that wasn't the reason. She didn't give a damn about Donny when he was alive and you know it. Donny was gay and Pietra was still crazy about you. She just lived with him because he was your friend, because it gave her a chance to see you. Isn't that right?'

'I don't know.'

'Yes, you do. Why do you think she said all those things about you on the witness stand? She wanted you to be convicted. If she can't have you, she doesn't want me to have you either.'

'Then why would she come here and offer to retract her testimony?'

'Because she's crazy. And because she doesn't want you to hate her. And most of all she wants you to notice her. I guarantee you she'll be coming to Wurzburg to visit you. Every day if they'll let her.'

'I don't want her to visit me.'

'Why not?' Polly said. 'You saw her today.'

'She took me by surprise.'

'She'll take you by surprise again. She's good at that.'

'You're really sore at me aren't you?'

292

'No. I'm stunned. I thought I knew you. You're the most vengeful, angry, vindictive bastard I've ever met. An eye for an eye and a tooth for a tooth. Now all of a sudden you're being reasonable and benevolent about an idiotic woman who did her best to destroy you.'

'Maybe I'm St Francis of Assisi and this is the first time you've noticed.'

'Oh, Jack . . .'

'Don't cry, baby. We've struggled through this whole mess and I haven't seen you cry.'

'Just because you haven't seen me doesn't mean I haven't done it. I cry at night. By myself. In my bed. That's where I cry.'

'I've been watching you,' he said then, 'watching you closely. And I've come to a decision. It seems to me that if I make you angry enough, if I can keep you angry and frustrated and convince you that I'm a hopeless waste of time then maybe I can persuade you – better still, you might persuade yourself – that you should leave Germany, forget about me, and go back to England. Or go live in Portugal with your mother. Or in Paris with your grandmother.'

Polly reached across the table and touched his lips with her fingertips. 'Hush,' she said. 'Just forget all that. I'm not going anywhere. You've always been impossible. You've always been a hopeless waste of time. But since I've never left you before, chances are I won't leave you now.'

[7]

Flying from Paris to London, Jesse wrote a letter to Helen.

Bill must be back with you now so he has undoubtedly filled in all the details of what went on in Heidelberg. And whatever he leaves out I will supply as soon as I'm back. When will that be? Very soon. I have to stop in London for a day or two so that the solicitors and bankers realize there are still one or two Bradshaws keeping an eye on family affairs. Then a fast trip to Wingate Fields to check on matters there. Since I'm the senior Bradshaw I feel an obligation to the family and to the home property. Even

293

the best managers and staff need to be reviewed from time to time. They need it and welcome it. Angus said that when staff are neglected for long periods of time they think less of their employers and at last they begin to think less of themselves. 'When that happens,' he said, 'they are of no value whatsoever.'

Here, in capsule version, are the individual reactions, as I saw them, to Jack's trial and conviction. Jack himself seemed fatalistic and resigned to whatever may come. Polly is quietly and privately heart-broken. Floyd was stunned and silent and Nora kept her feelings to herself, which makes me believe she was profoundly disturbed about Valerie, who seems shattered in a way that none of us has witnessed before. Rab was angry and frustrated, as I was, that every device, every pressure and manipulation we could bring to bear came to nothing, and poor Bill, who is closer to Polly than anyone else in the family, seemed almost physically sickened by her situation. It would not surprise me if he left school and went to Heidelberg to stay with her for a while. Perhaps for a long while. But don't mention to him that I said this.

I will drink a silent toast to you in London. And another one (or two) at Wingate Fields, and I'll be back in Fort Beck wearing my cap and bells and bringing you lovely English gifts before you know it.

Jesse had not planned to keep his presence in London a secret from Rab. He told himself what he had told Helen, that he would be there for only a day or so, that he would be fully occupied with family business, and would have little time for anything else. He decided, however, that he would contact his son as soon as he had a moment's free time. If Rab's schedule permitted, they would have a drink or a meal together.

Rather than use one of the Bradshaw apartments in London, Jesse checked into the Stafford. He met with the bankers and solicitors the next day, made whatever decisions were necessary, and explained that he would be at Wingate Fields the following week if further discussions were needed.

He did not, however, go north to the family estate as quickly as he'd planned. Rather, he found himself pleasantly involved in the rhythms of London. Each morning, after breakfast in the Stafford dining room, he walked in St James's Park or Green Park. He visited the National Gallery, the Tate, and the Museum of Natural History. He attended performances at the Haymarket, the Savoy, the National Theatre and the Albert Hall. And he prowled the familiar streets of Belgravia, Mayfair and Covent Garden. He visited public houses he had known for thirty years and dined in restaurants he had frequented during his marriage to Valerie.

Having been away from London for a number of years, he quickly came to believe that he had not been away at all. While he did not measure his daily experiences against the life he led in Fort Beck, Illinois, he could not ignore the adrenalin in his veins, or the spring in his step, or the flood of ideas that coursed through his brain as he strolled along the Strand, or entered the dress circle of a theatre, or studied the matchless paintings of Bellini or Uccello. He found himself reading the listings of estate agents in *The Times* and carefully examining bright new automobiles in their showrooms. At last, one morning at breakfast, when his stay in London had extended itself to eight days, he said to himself, 'Let's not lose control here. Tomorrow morning you're off to Wingate Fields and a week from today you'll be snugly back in Fort Beck.'

That afternoon when he returned to the Stafford he found a note from Rab in his letter box.

As I drove past the Stafford this morning I thought I saw you walking out through the courtyard. But when I wheeled back round the square you were gone. I rang up the hotel and they told me you were indeed staying there. Are you avoiding your magnificent son? Let's have dinner tonight at our club. If I don't hear from you at the number just below I will meet you tonight at half past seven.

[8]

When Nora returned to Paris from Germany she had found a wire from Karina in Lisbon: *Chaos here. Agony and Torment. See you soon in Paris.*

Two days after Jesse left for London, Karina telephoned.

'Where are you?' Nora asked.

'In Paris. At my house. Is Jesse still there?'

'Jesse was never *here*. He stayed at his hotel at St-Placide.'

'You know what I mean. Has he gone?'

'Yes. Day before yesterday.'

'Thank God. I need to see you,' Karina said.

'I have to go out this morning. Why don't you come about four?'

'No. Please. I have to see you now. I'll be there in twenty minutes.'

When she arrived in Nora's drawing room half an hour later, Karina said, 'I was frantic. I was afraid you were still in Germany. I was afraid I might have to leave again without seeing you.'

'Where are you going?'

'I don't know. I mean, I'm not sure what I'm doing. That's why I needed to talk to you.'

'When did you get back from Lisbon?'

'Last night. I wanted to telephone you then but the plane was delayed and I got home too late.'

'Why are you so upset? What's this all about?'

'I don't know where to start,' Karina said.

'Why don't you start at the beginning?'

'My husband has sold all our property in Portugal. He's going to live in Brazil. He's flying to Rio tomorrow.'

'Does that mean you have to go there too?' Nora asked.

'I didn't think so. As you know, we've never really lived together since we left Germany. He's been in Estoril and I've been here in France. But when I got home last night I found some legal papers waiting for me. My charming husband has also sold my house here in Paris, the furniture, the paintings, our two cars. Everything but my clothes.'

'I thought all that was in your name.'

'It was. But Helmut's not only my husband, he's my legal guardian. I thought it was amusing at one time but now I'm not amused. Also, his French lawyer had power of attorney over all my property here. They told me it was all designed to protect me but now I see it was for another purpose.'

'But he's always been very generous with you.'

Karina nodded. 'He has. Because he truly loves me. But he also depended on me. I was the conduit for money flowing to him from Cologne. But since Kiesinger became Chancellor, Helmut's friends

296

have worked out other arrangements. They set up a company in São Paulo and they're gradually transferring all his funds to Brazil.'

'Is he trying to force you to go there with him? Is that why he sold everything here?'

'That's a part of it, I'm sure. But he also wants to own nothing in Europe. He wants no records with our names on them, his or mine. He's determined to disappear and he wants me to disappear with him. I was supposed to fly to Rio with him tomorrow. I slipped away and came here instead.'

'Why does he have to disappear?'

'I'm not sure he does. But he thinks he does. He's in a panic. He thinks he's being watched. He's afraid he'll be kidnapped, taken to Israel and tried as a war criminal.'

'But you told me he was not involved in the war.'

'I told you he was not in uniform and he wasn't. He was not a military man. His family owned the largest chemical plants in Europe. They furnished every sort of fuel and gas and chemical substance that the German war effort required. Helmut escaped to Portugal before the war ended but he always expected to go back to Cologne when things stabilized. Certain factions in Adenauer's government, however, called him a war profiteer and his friends, including Adenauer, convinced him it was wiser for him to stay in Portugal. Meanwhile his factories continued to operate and prosper and great amounts of money were funnelled to him through me. He lived like a sultan in Estoril with a great staff and bodyguards and an endless supply of sixteen-year-old girls to keep him amused. He had no urge to return to the icy winters of Cologne. Then, about three months ago, Simon Wiesenthal made a speech in Vienna. It was not widely reported but it caused a stir in Israel.'

'What did he say?'

'He reported on the progress that he and his staff had made in tracking down German war criminals. With the help of the Israeli secret service a great number of former Nazi officers and concentration camp administrators had been located and brought to justice.'

'How did that affect your husband?'

'He was mentioned by name in the speech. Along with three other German industrialists. Wiesenthal said that the time has come to list as war criminals the men whose companies had provided fuel for V2 rockets, chemical weapons that were used on the

Russian front, and the gas that was used to murder concentration camp victims.'

'And do they know where your husband is?'

'He believes they do. I don't believe it.'

'But if they know his name . . .'

'Einhorn is not our name. All evidence that links us to his family was destroyed many years ago. He has no children, no parents, and no living relatives. And his plants are operated by a faceless corporation. Also, my husband's family had a fetish about being photographed. There are no existing photographs of him from all the years he lived in Germany. And even if there were he looks totally different now. When I married him he was quite large, with a moustache and a great mane of hair. Now he is thin and bald and clean-shaven. He's brown from the sun, the colour of mahogany. He wears black suits and black ties and looks like a Portuguese nobleman. He has no German friends in Portugal and only French and Portuguese are spoken in his home.'

'Then why does he believe . . .'

'He is totally paranoid about the Israeli agents. He believes they are superhuman. He thinks they know or can find out the identity of every German living outside Germany. There's nothing rational about his fears but they are very real to him. Whatever his other flaws, Helmut does not lack courage. But since Wiesenthal made that speech in Vienna, my husband has been trembling with fear. And now so am I.'

'What do you have to be afraid of?'

'If they're looking for my husband and they can't find him then they'll surely come looking for me, won't they? They'll think I know where he is and they'll be right. That's why he sold everything here. Without my home in Paris I'm sure he believes I'll follow him to Brazil.'

'Will you?'

'How can I?' Karina said. 'My life is here. I've lived here for twenty-five years. But on the other hand I don't want a bodyguard with me twenty-four hours every day. I don't want to have to look behind me every time I walk down the street. I don't want to be kidnapped and, God knows, I don't want to be drugged or tortured. I'm a physical coward. If someone frightened me or hurt me I'd tell them anything.'

298

'But you said you don't think they know who your husband is or where he is.'

'That's true. But on the other hand I can't be certain. In Lisbon it's difficult to know about such things. It was the spy centre of the world during the war and there's still that atmosphere there. So while I feel Helmut is safe there, I wouldn't risk his life on just that feeling.'

'It does sound risky the way you describe it. But maybe you could find a place in the *banlieu*. Or you can move into my country house if you want to. Marcel and Henri are there full-time. They'd be delighted to look after you.'

'But I'd go insane living there alone. Would you come along?'

Nora shook her head and smiled. 'I hardly ever go there now. You know that. Too many bad memories. I spent the first twenty-three years of my life in country houses. A country house wants a man about.'

'You said Henri is there.'

'I don't mean a servant. I mean a man,' Nora said.

'But it would be all right if we both were there.'

Again Nora shook her head. 'I can't think of anything that would pull me away from this place.'

After a moment Karina said, 'If I have to leave Paris, and I don't want to go to Brazil, does that mean you wouldn't come with me?'

'What do you mean? Where are you going?'

'I don't know. Anywhere. There are all sorts of wonderful places in Italy. In the hill towns. We could find a lovely villa and no one would even know we were there.'

'But I don't want to disappear like that, like a mourning widow or a school teacher in retirement.'

'I don't want to do it either but if we were both there . . .'

'If we were both there we'd be *twice* as miserable.'

'I have a wonderful aunt in Switzerland, my mother's sister. She lives in a place called Schaffhauser, north of Zurich, near the German border. She's very nice but she detests Helmut so I haven't seen her much these past years. She was married to a lumberman, a wealthy Canadian. She has a house like a castle with stunning gardens. Nothing would please her more than to have us come there to stay.'

'But I don't need a place to stay. I have a perfectly delightful place to stay.'

299

'But I can't stay here with you,' Karina said. 'Don't you see that?'

'Yes, I do see that, now that you've explained the situation to me. I think Paris is too risky for you. I'm not even sure my country house would be a good idea.'

'Don't you know what I'm doing?' Karina said then. 'Don't you understand what I'm trying to say?' She stood up and walked to the window. Standing there with her back to Nora, she said, 'I'm trying to work out something so you and I won't be separated. Trying to make some arrangement so we can be together. And I feel as if all you want to do is hustle me off to Rio.'

Nora crossed the room and stood beside her. 'Karina, darling. I'm not trying to hustle you off anywhere. You came here because you have a problem, not an easy one, and I have been trying, perhaps in a clumsy way, to help you solve it.'

Karina turned to face her. 'But there must be some solution other than my going to Brazil on the next plane.'

'Perhaps there is but you haven't found it yet. And you're not making things easier by trying to include me in your plans.'

'I'm not *trying* to include you. You *are* included.'

Nora shook her head. 'No, I'm not, Karina. I can't be. We've talked about this before.'

'No, we haven't. You've talked about it and I've listened.'

'You may have listened but you haven't heard me. I care about you. You know that. Over the past few years you've become my dearest friend. Sometimes I feel as though you're my only friend. And I love you.' She touched Karina's cheek with her hand. 'But I'm not *in love* with you. I never have been and I never could be. I have no guilt or regret over anything that's happened between us. If you think I've committed a terrible sin by going to bed with you when I wasn't in love with you then I accept whatever low opinion you may have of me. But I don't believe you do think that. Should we have asked each other for guarantees before we took off our clothes? I don't think so and you don't either. Your body has always had a life of its own and it always will.'

'I'm not as clever as you are,' Karina said. 'All I can say is that I have a heart. It never explains anything to me. It just hurts. It's happened to me before and it's happening now. And this time I'm afraid it's going to last for a long time.'

Nora stood looking down at the floor. Finally she said, 'I don't want to talk about this any more. Either you leave now or I'm going to leave.' She turned and walked across the wide room.

'What's the matter?' Karina said. She followed her across the room. 'What did I say?'

'I said I don't want to discuss it.'

'Please, Nora. Don't cut me off like that.'

'That's exactly what I'm trying not to do. I'm trying to be as honest and as open as I can. I know that words are empty and stupid when they don't match up with another person's feelings but I was doing the best I know how. So it doesn't help matters when you try to make me feel guilty.'

'I wasn't doing that,' Karina said. 'I mean, I wasn't trying to do that. I just feel disappointed and lonesome and rotten. And I keep thinking that things would be different if Jesse hadn't just been here.'

Nora shook her head. 'The thing you and I are talking about would not be different. No matter what might happen between me and Jesse.'

'Is he coming back? Is he going to live here again?'

'Do you want the truth?'

'Yes.'

'He's coming back,' Nora said.

'When?'

'I don't know when. Neither does he. But he is very definitely coming back. Does that make you feel better or worse?'

'It makes me feel terrible. But not as bad as I felt a few minutes ago. I never fooled myself I could win if it was a contest against Jesse.'

[9]

Long silences. An atmosphere of unquiet. Tentative questions and vague answers. These were the characteristics of the early part of the evening that Jesse and Rab spent together at White's. Each of them had several whiskies before going into the dining-room, and as they drank they discussed large issues. The Common Market, Tito's relationship with Russia, Peron's destruction of the Argentine economy, the role of Sweden's king in a Socialist state. Both men showed respect for contrary viewpoints. Neither took a strong position that might offend the other. It was a conversation that might have taken place between two business associates whose economic ties prevented them from being either genuinely warm or totally candid.

Once they were at table, although the tone did not change, their subjects became more personal. They discussed Polly and Bill and Jack Dieter's trial, but only in general terms like politicians who were leery of being quoted. They touched lightly on Jesse's current projects and even more lightly on Rab's maverick approach to the world of entertainment. And they worried a bit together about the future of Wingate Fields. Here, too, however, they stopped short of defining particular problems or of providing even tentative solutions. They glided smoothly across the surface of each subject they dealt with, raising no dust, disturbing no stones, leaving no tracks.

Their conversation managed to limp along through the soup, the pâté, and the asparagus. But they spoke sparingly as they picked at the whitefish, and after the roast venison arrived at their table they ate in silence. When the Stilton was served, however, and the port, Rab opened up an area that quickly transformed what had been a civilized if impersonal evening into another sort of encounter altogether. 'I have a feeling I shouldn't have left that note at your hotel this morning. Am I right or wrong?'

'Dead wrong,' Jesse said. 'I'm surprised you even ask a question like that.'

'You can tell me the truth. My feelings won't be hurt.'

'Why should they be? I don't know what you're trying to say.'

'I'm saying that if I hadn't happened to see you in the street I wouldn't have known you were in London. True or false.'

'Nonsense. Do you think I'd come here and not try to see you?'

'That's what I'm trying to find out. You said you've been here for a week. Isn't that right?'

Jesse nodded. 'The time went very fast.'

'And you're going up to Wingate Fields tomorrow?'

'That's the plan.'

'And from there back to New York.'

'I'll leave from Heathrow, of course,' Jesse said.

'But you're not planning to come into London again.'

'I shouldn't think so.'

'That's my point. Then I wouldn't have seen you if I hadn't left a note for you.'

'I have a feeling I'm on the witness stand and I'm not sure what I've been indicted for.'

Rab smiled. 'How about child neglect?'

'I plead innocent. And I'm glad to see you're smiling. I thought perhaps I was in for a good scolding.'

'Not likely. That's not the pattern. Children commit the sins and the fathers do the scolding. *That's* the pattern. Can't be reversed.'

'Of course it can. In the first place you weren't brought up according to a rigid behaviour code. And in the second place you're not a child and you haven't been for quite some time. After a certain age a father and son are either friends or they're nothing.'

'Which category do we fall into?'

'Friends. No question about that. Male adults with equal rights.'

'It has a nice ring to it, Dad. But it's easier said than done.'

'Not at all. It's a natural condition.'

'When I was a schoolboy,' Rab said then, 'one of the subjects I excelled at was psychology. I was taught there are no "natural conditions" within family units. Each case is different, depending on the individuals involved. Father-son relationships are particularly tricky, the textbooks say. Patterns of emulation all tangled together with subtle competitions. The old bull and the young bull . . . that sort of thing. A parent can dislike a child on sight and vice versa.'

'That's a lot of rot. You don't believe that, do you?'

'I have no way of knowing. I've never been a parent. Only a child.'

'Well, I've been both. And I say it's rot,' Jesse said.

'You weren't too keen on *your* father, were you?'

'This really is an inquisition, isn't it?'

'Not in my mind. I see it as a philosophical discussion over a glass of port.'

'Maybe so. But all the same I think I'd better be careful with you. When you were twelve years old your headmaster told me you have a first-class mind. He also said you have a tricky mind. Thought you might have a future as a barrister.'

'You're pretty tricky yourself. You didn't answer my question about your father.'

'What did you want to know?'

'I know you left home when you were fifteen or sixteen, and you told me a long time ago that you only saw your parents once after that. So I concluded that you weren't too keen about your dad. And maybe he didn't think of you as his best friend either.'

'That's a long time ago, Rab. At my age it's difficult to see things exactly as you did when you were sixteen.'

'I know it. That's true even at my age. But since you and your father weren't too eager to live together . . . I mean, it's like the textbook said. Every case is different. You said after a certain age a father and son are either friends or they're nothing. With you and your father is was nothing, right?'

'I don't like the sound of that,' Jesse said. 'And I certainly never thought of it that way.'

'Maybe not. But facts are facts. And the fact is, once you were grown up, the two of you couldn't have been friends because *you never saw each other*.'

'Are you trying to make me feel rotten because I didn't ring you up as soon as I arrived in London?'

'Not at all. You don't feel rotten, do you?'

'No, I don't,' Jesse said.

'Then nothing I could say would make you feel rotten. And I wouldn't even try. I'm not trying to say that you have the same relationship with me that your father had with you. I was just trying to work out the transition that takes place when two people go from being father and son to being friends. Male adults with equal rights . . . I think that's what you said. I'm sure it doesn't happen overnight just because a son leaves home or finishes university or reaches a certain age. I mean, it's probably a gradual transition, wouldn't you say?'

Jesse nodded. 'A transition's a process of change. That's what the dictionary says. So that must mean it takes some time to happen.'

'That's what I thought. So the problem is to know when it starts and when it ends. And the ideal thing is for both people, the father and the son in this case, to be on the same timetable. When the son wants the father to be a friend and the father is still working full-time at being a father, that could present a problem.'

'That's right. Some transitions are smoother than others.'

'I'm sure of it.' Rab concentrated on his wine and cheese for a few moments. Then: 'Do you remember when Clara died, when all of us came home to Wingate for her funeral . . . you and I had a serious conversation.'

'I remember it very well.'

'It wasn't really a conversation actually. I believe I'd call it a lecture. You said some ugly things to me. I assume you were talking to me as a father that day.'

'It was a difficult situation for all of us. There was some things I felt I had to say to you.'

'As a father?'

'Yes.'

'I was twenty-one years old then. Almost twenty-two. But I assume we were still in transition. A bit past father and son. Not quite friends.'

'I was acting as head of the family. I felt you were behaving in a way that was detrimental to all of us.'

'But if I'd been your brother or your nephew would you have spoken to me in a different tone of voice perhaps?'

'Probably. The fact that you're my son made me particularly conscious of what you were doing.'

'You're talking about my bringing Gloria to Northumberland with me?'

Jesse nodded. 'As I recall we got into some other areas but that was certainly what started the conversation.'

'So you spoke to me the way you did because I'm your son. And I only allowed you to speak to me that way because you're my father. Just a good old family argument. None of the obligations of friendship involved. Is that correct?'

'I suppose so.'

'What if I told you that by that time in my life, when you and I hadn't lived under the same roof for several years, I regarded myself as a fully fledged, self-governing grown-up? A male adult with equal rights.'

'That wouldn't surprise me.'

'Then I'm sure it won't surprise you when I say that I was offended and humiliated by the way you talked to me. I couldn't get the things you said out of my mind. I still can't. I kept asking myself what right you had to pass judgement on me and why I don't have the same right to judge you.'

'I'm sure you do,' Jesse said, 'if that's what you want.'

'You mean, I have the right now but I didn't have it that day?'

'You had it that day, too.'

'No, I didn't,' Rab said. 'You left no doubt about who was in charge. There was no easy flow of conflicting opinions, as I recall. It was a case of corporal punishment without the whip. No mention whatsoever of male adults with equal rights.'

'I have a feeling I'm supposed to apologize.'

'Not at all. This is a discussion, not a contest. But I can't help wondering, by your standards, whether I, either as your son *or* your friend, have the right to list your shortcomings the way you listed mine that day.'

'As I recall, you did pretty well. Spoke your mind very clearly.'

'I was defending myself. Trying to at least. But you scored all the major points. You said I don't give a damn about anything. Not a killing blow, I suppose. But in this case you said it with such conviction that I started to believe it myself. Took me quite some time to convince myself that your evaluation of me was not the final and definitive one.'

'Is this a side of you I've never seen, or are you playing some elaborate game with me?'

'Neither. I am being direct and truthful. And not, as you might imagine, for the first time in my life.'

'Have you somehow convinced yourself that I don't like you?'

'No, I haven't. Should I concern myself with that?'

'That depends on what you're after. Are you asking for permission to dissect me and lay out all my faults and shortcomings the way you think I've done with you?'

'I don't need permission. We now have equal rights.'

'Then slice away.'

'I'll admit I've considered doing that,' Rab said. 'As recently as five minutes ago. But breeding prevails. Let's just say that I value you as a friend and respect you as a father, so I rest my case.'

As they waited in the foyer for their coats Jesse said, 'Your headmaster was right. You do have a tricky mind. Our involved conversation this evening had as its theme your suspicion that I don't like you very much. But the real message you're sending out is that you don't care for me at all. Isn't that true?'

'When I was a child I used to worship you. I wish I still did. But I don't.'

'Is this something I can fix? Is there some penance I'm supposed to do?'

'Not at all,' Rab said. 'I think the best solution for us is to stay away from each other.'

The attendant brought Rab's coat first. Carrying it over his arm he went outside to his car and drove north toward Piccadilly. When Jesse's coat came a moment later he put it on, went outside, and walked slowly along St James's to his hotel.

[10]

Jesse flew to Newcastle the next morning. The chauffeur from Wingate Fields met him at Newcastle airport and brought him home.

For the next four days Jesse drove himself tirelessly. He got up at dawn, had breakfast and rode out, either alone or with the estate manager. He talked with all the herdsmen and tenant farmers, all the stablemen and gardeners and gamekeepers. He reviewed the ledgers, inspected recent repairs and approved projected ones. He spent hours in the cellars with the wine steward, took long drives in each of the five cars and spent every hour he could spare on horseback galloping across the moors. He ate sumptuous meals every day, sometimes in nearby inns, usually at home. The kitchen staff, delighted to have the master in the house again, devised extravagant menus for him. Every night he spent two hours at table, alone in the great dining hall, crystal and silver gleaming all round, claret glowing red in his goblet. After dinner he played billiards and drank brandy by himself until he was too tired to stand. Then he climbed the wide staircase to his room and slept like a dead man.

All this to occupy his mind, to deaden his senses and turn off his memory. Details and fatigue and activity. No time allowed to reflect or consider or remember. He avoided his library and his writing room, did not touch or sit down behind the magnificent oak and leather desk Clara had found for him. He made no notes, wrote no paragraphs, allowed no projects to ferment in his consciousness. Eating, drinking, sleeping, he functioned in those days, as much as he was able, as a mindless animal, forced himself to lead a physical life – sights and sounds and scents and textures.

307

Thick grass to walk on, fine fabrics against his back, bird-calls and wind songs and water rushing in the narrow river beside the deer park.

Only once, early in the morning of the day when he left for America, did he allow himself to sit behind his desk. When he wrote then it was as though Helen and Nora and his children did not exist, as though the events of the past days and weeks had never taken place.

God, how I love this place. I feel as if I was born here. I know my body will refuse to die until it's carried here. If I have less love to give than I would like to it's because so much of it is squandered here. Is it possible to love a place like a person, *more* than a person? If so, I've done it, I'm doing it, I will continue to do it.

Book Three

Chapter Seven

[1]

'I guess I ought to apologize for just dropping in on you like this. I know there's a big difference between the way things operate here in London and the way they operate in Burbank or Beverly Hills. When Oscar Mullet gave me your phone number and office address he told me to be sure to call you first and I said I would but I was strolling through Shepherd Market this morning and next thing I knew I was on your street, so I thought, "What the hell. The worst thing that happens is he throws me out." '

Rab smiled and said, 'None of that here. You caught me at a good time. I'm glad you stopped by.'

'Oscar said he'd give you a call before he went to Barcelona but I'm not sure if he did.'

'It doesn't matter. I'm sure he mentioned that you were here doing a screenplay for Ronald Neame. Or maybe Mrs Mullet mentioned it.'

'Beautiful woman, isn't she? Haven't seen her since I've been in London. I always tell Oscar she's too good for him but he says nobody's too good for him.'

When his secretary had told him that Robert Gingrich was waiting to see him, Rab had not made the connection. But when she mentioned that he was a friend of Oscar Mullet, Rab remembered in detail the conversation he'd had with Dorsey about Gingrich. 'I told him it would be better if he made an appointment to see you next week,' Rosalind said.

Rab's reactions were mixed. Gingrich, the friend of Oscar Mullet, did not interest him. But his curiosity had been aroused by the Gingrich Dorsey had described.

'Since he's here,' Rab said, 'let's bring him in. If he's still here in half an hour, interrupt us and tell me I have to go somewhere to a meeting.'

When he came into Rab's office and they shook hands, Gingrich said, 'I know I look like I've been on a two-week drunk but that's the way I always look. My mother has pictures of me from the time I was born till I was thirty. In every picture I look like I've been on a toot. The fact is since I left California and moved back to New York I've been pretty much on the wagon. And since I hit London all I've had are a few pints of Guinness.'

He sat down across the desk from Rab. 'The main reason I look the way I do is because I can't sleep. My eyes aren't worth a damn either so I try not to read at night. So there's not much left to do except prowl the streets. That's what I've been doing here in London. And I do it in New York. But all those years in California they had me in a box. You can't take a walk there at night. The police catch you strolling on the streets after dark, they collar you. They figure anybody who's not driving a Mercedes deserves to be in jail. Adlai Stevenson took a walk one night when he was staying at the Beverly-Wilshire and the police were all ready to lock him up. You can drive drunk out there but God help you if you try to walk sober. How about you? You ever have trouble sleeping?'

Rab smiled. 'Have trouble getting to bed sometimes but no trouble once I get there.'

'That figures. Young and healthy. You look about twelve years old. Doesn't make you mad when I say that, does it?'

'No.'

'Half the studios in Hollywood are being run by guys your age now. Agents and businessmen, most of them. Don't know a grip from a juicer. But they know how to read a budget. At least they think they do. Numbers, that's all they do. They smoke dope, eat breakfast together in the Polo Lounge, and talk about numbers. And that's it. These guys don't even want to get laid. Can you imagine that? When I first went to Hollywood that was the only reason to go there. A man can write a screenplay anywhere. But the action is all out there between La Cienega Boulevard and Ocean Avenue.' He lit a cigarette. 'Anyway, I put all that behind me. My wife ran off with a carpenter, or a juggler, or whatever the hell he is, and I moved back to New York.'

'How long do you expect to stay in London?'

'I don't know. I like it here. I may stay on for a while.'

'How about the screenplay you're writing for Neame?'

'It's just a polish. That's all I'm doing. The story was written by two fags and an eighteen-year-old girl. And the screenplay was written by *five* people. And after I'm finished and paid off they'll probably have a few more hacks redo what I'm writing.'

'Doesn't sound like Neame,' Rab said.

'It's not. He's a good film-maker. But he's caught in a crack. Like anybody else who tries to put together an independent film these days. Too many partners. By the time you dig up all the money you need to shoot your picture, you find you've got two executive producers, a couple more associate producers, and somebody's wife is contributing additional dialogue.'

Rab studied Gingrich as he talked. He looked pretty much as Dorsey had described him. Pale and overweight, she'd said. He was indeed pale. Clean-shaven, thinning brown hair, and shell-rim glasses with tinted lenses. He did not seem overweight but his suit fitted him as though it dated from a time when he had been.

'Neame made a couple of great films,' Rab said. '*The Horse's Mouth* and *Tunes of Glory*.'

'Right,' Gingrich said. 'Terrific stuff. Those two pictures would never have been made in America.'

'They'd never have been made here except for Guinness.'

'Yeah, I know. Ronnie told me the story. It's all a crap-shoot. George Jessel said, "Show business is *no* business." '

'You say you may be staying in England. Will you be doing some projects with Oscar?'

'Not at the moment. He's up to his ass in westerns and that's not my field. But there are some other notions we might get together on a bit later. He mentioned that you have some things in the planning stage that I might be able to help with. That's why he suggested we have a talk.'

'That's a possibility,' Rab said. 'But we're not angling for the big screen yet. We're thinking in terms of films for television. Based on classics mostly. Films we can sell all over the English-speaking world. Maybe television doesn't interest you.'

'I'll be candid with you. I'm a theatre man. Only writing for the

313

stage really interests me. But, as you may know, I've written quite a few films. It's a craft I'm good at. And at this stage in my life, a film is a film. It doesn't matter to me whether it's destined for big screen or little screen.'

'The problem is,' Rab said, 'that we are in our very early stages. Our first three projects are being scripted now. All based on plays. One by Strindberg, one by Shaw, another by Ibsen. We're in the process of trying to select six more. Until we do, we won't be able to think about writers or directors or actors.'

'No pressure,' Gingrich said. 'No rush. Oscar just thought we should meet. Now we've met. When you're ready to talk, if you're interested in me, we'll get together. If I'm back in New York by then we'll talk on the telephone. If I'm still here, that will make it simpler.'

Some instinct told Rab that the sooner he ended this interview, the better it would be. There was something about Gingrich that disturbed him, something below the surface, he sensed, that was quite different from what it seemed to be. At the same time he was curious about the story Dorsey had told him, that Oscar was suspicious of her friendship with Gingrich. Wanting to know and *not* wanting to know, his curiosity triumphed at last. When Rosalind called in to tell him he was due to leave for a meeting he said, 'Mr Gingrich and I are still having a chat. If I'm a bit late for the meeting it will be all right.'

When he hung up the receiver Rab said to Gingrich, 'How long have you known Mullet?'

'A long time. I met him when I first went to the coast. He and Dorsey were married by then. She introduced me to him. I'd met her when she was just a kid, when she first came to New York. If you think she's beautiful now, you should have seen her then. I thought I was quite a ladies' man in those days and I was all ready to make a move on her till her room-mate told me she was only sixteen. I was about thirty then, a little older maybe, and I'd been around the track a few times. I didn't know much but I knew trouble when I saw it. I mean this was a few years back and a man could get into serious trouble in New York on a delinquency charge. Jail-bait they called girls that age. So I steered clear. But I was crazy about her. Couldn't stop looking at her. Christ, she was beautiful. So I used to see her a lot. Took her to lunch and baseball games and stuff like that. We became friends. She thought it was great but I hated it. I used to just sit there and stare at her. What was I up to? Damned if I know. Waiting for her to get to be eighteen, I guess. But I waited too long. Next thing I knew she was goggle-eyed over some beautiful kid from Florida. I never met him but she used to show me his pictures that she'd cut out of magazines. He was a model. Posed for photographers. Swimming trunks, underwear ads, he was a real jock. When she told him about me he said he didn't want her to see me any more. Isn't that a hot one? True-blue Gingrich, the maidens' friend, and her hot-shot boyfriend thought I was competiton. What a joke. So . . . I didn't see her any more. I started getting some action as a playwright and two or three years later I saw in the paper that she'd married Oscar.

'Later, when I went out to the coast, she called me at the hotel where I was staying, and I met her and Oscar for a drink. So that's how I met him. There you are . . . a long answer to a short question. A director I worked with once, a real asshole, incidentally, used to tell me I should have been a novelist. "Too many words," he said, "you're in love with language." He's right. I am. This guy was like most of the directors I've worked with. Illiterate. They think actors should be mute and writers should be shot. They're queer for *cameras*, all those bastards. They'll shoot thirty cover shots of anything that's moving and tell themselves they're making cinema history.'

Gingrich made a move to go then. 'Listen,' he said, 'you don't have to hear the sad story of motion pictures from me. I've taken enough of your time already.'

'Not at all,' Rab said. 'I'm not pressed for time. The fact is I'm a beginner in this business. I've never even been inside an American film studio so this is an education for me, talking with someone who's seen first-hand how things work there.'

'Right at the moment it works like this,' Gingrich said. 'Everybody's trying to decide whether to do a rip-off of *Easy Rider* or *Butch Cassidy and the Sundance Kid. Easy Rider*'s winning because the geniuses out there figure all they need are two motorcycles, two hill-billy kids who can ad-lib dialogue, and a truck with a camera mounted on it.'

'How about Oscar as a producer? You must have worked a lot with him.'

'Not too much as a matter of fact. That's why we're still friends. Or maybe I should say, that's why we're as friendly as we are.'

'What does that mean?'

'Nothing. I got off the track. Personal stuff. In answer to your question, Oscar and I never went all the way through a picture together. I used to doctor screenplays for him. He'd throw a fast twenty-five grand at me and I'd stay up for three nights with two secretaries and try to turn a script he'd paid two hundred and fifty thousand for into something his director could shoot. In a situation like that you can never make it good, you can only try to make it better. My wife, I was married to my third wife by then, thought I was crazy. She told me if I didn't have the guts to write plays I should at least try to write movies that were worth something. She was probably right. At least half right. Nobody can make a living by trying to write movies that are worth something. On the other hand nobody can live with himself if he turns out mindless crap year after year just so he can go to screenings once a week at the Motion Picture Academy.'

'Is your wife here in London with you?'

'She's not my wife and she's not here. The last I heard she was on her way to Oregon with some clown she'd met in a parking lot. We got a divorce by mail. Oscar and Dorsey played a part in that little drama, too, but that's a story you'll never hear from me. I almost ended up with Dorsey, after all. But I didn't. Oscar ended up with her but I'm not sure he feels good about it.'

Late that afternoon, Dorsey met Rab at his apartment on Grantham Place. Later that night when she returned to her own house she called Bob Gingrich at his hotel. When he answered she said, 'This is Dorsey. Are you sober?'

'Like an angel,' he said. 'I don't sauce any more.'

'Good. Now listen to me. There's an all-night restaurant in Victoria Station. I want you to meet me there in half an hour.'

'It's midnight, for Christ's sake.'

'What do you care? You never sleep anyway. Everybody knows that.'

He was waiting for her in the restaurant when she arrived. When she sat down he said, 'What's all the cloak-and-dagger business?'

'No jokes, Bob. I'm not in the mood. I'm mad as hell at you.'

'Couldn't you be mad at me in the daytime?'

'Yes, I could. I expect to be just as mad at you tomorrow. But tomorrow you have to give a performance. Tonight you are going to rehearse.'

316

'Rehearse what? What's all this about?'
'You know damned well what it's about.'

[2]

The following afternoon at five Gingrich joined Dorsey at a corner table in the lounge at Claridges. As soon as he sat down, Rab came in from the bar and joined them.

'Well, this is a nice surprise,' Gingrich said. 'It's good to see you again.'

'Good to see you,' Rab said.

After they ordered drinks, Dorsey smiled at Gingrich and said, 'How long is it since we've seen each other?'

'When did you and Oscar leave California? It must be six years?'

'You've been in London for weeks and you've seen Oscar half a dozen times but you haven't been to the house. Shame on you.'

'Busy,' Gingrich said. 'You know how it is.'

'Yes, I do. I'm very busy myself. Anyway, it's nice to see you looking well. You've lost weight. And it's a pleasant surprise to see you ordering Perrier.'

'Having drunk all the Bombay gin in California I saw no reason to go for the national championship when I moved back to New York.'

As soon as they had their drinks Dorsey said, 'If I gave you the impression that we were meeting for a pleasant social drink I deceived you. We've got serious business to deal with. That's why I invited Rab to join us. I have a few comments to make and then I have some questions for you, Bob. I'm going to tell the complete truth and I insist that you do the same.'

'Are we playing charades?'

'We're not playing at all. As I said, this is serious business. Rab and I are in love and we're going to be married. As soon as Oscar comes back from Spain, I'm going to ask him for a divorce. I hope we can do it peacefully but I plan to divorce him one way or the other. Outside of Rab and me, you're the only person who knows our plans.'

'I'm not sure what I'm supposed to say.'

317

'We'll come to that in a moment. Our problem is this. When you sat with Rab in his office yesterday, you said some things that surprised him, things that seemed to contradict what he'd heard from me. You lied to him, Bob, and I want to know why. Did Oscar ask you to go see Rab?'

'Of course he did.' He turned to Rab. 'We discussed that as soon as I sat down in your office.'

'I don't mean that,' Dorsey said. 'I'm not talking about business. I'm talking about me. Did Oscar send you there to say things about me?'

'I'm not a messenger boy, Dorsey. Nobody sends me on errands.'

'You're a bad liar, Bob. Remember that. Jeannie said she could always tell when you're lying and so can I. If you can't tell the truth, or if you won't tell the truth for some reason, then let's say goodbye and get out of here. And I mean goodbye, Bob. This is extremely important to me. It's vital. Rab means everything to me. And if you sit there and lie the way you did in his office you could ruin things for us.'

Gingrich took a long drink from his glass. 'All right. Oscar did ask me to do a little number. He thinks the two of you are up to something and he wants to break it up. The way he put it, it sounded like you were having a six-week fling so I didn't take it seriously. He said if I gave the impression that I'd had a little *do* somewhere along the line with Dorsey, it might cause enough trouble between you two to break things up.'

Dorsey turned to Rab. 'Now we're getting somewhere.' Then back to Gingrich. 'Tell Rab where we met for the first time.'

'We met at a party at your house in Bel Air when I was doing some work for Oscar.'

'And did we see each other after that?'

Gingrich nodded. 'The four of us, you and Oscar and Jeannie and I, used to have dinner together once in a while.'

'Did you and I become close friends?'

'I wouldn't say so. You and Jeannie used to see each other in the afternoons, and you came to see us at Zuma a few times, but that was about it.'

'Did you and I ever have a drink together, or lunch, or dinner, when Jeannie or Oscar weren't there?'

'No.'

318

'Did we ever even have a five-minute conversation when nobody else was there?' Dorsey asked.

'Not that I can remember.'

'I remember,' she said. 'We didn't.'

Rab said, 'You told me that when you and your wife separated, you and Dorsey almost ended up together. What was that all about?'

'All crap. That was Oscar's idea. Like I said before.'

'And all that stuff about knowing me in New York before I married Oscar?' Dorsey said.

'That was my contribution,' Gingrich said. 'That's what I get paid for, you know, making up stories.'

After Gingrich left, Rab and Dorsey stayed at the table. 'I told you he was lying,' she said. 'Are you satisfied?'

'I'm still trying to sort things out. That was like a scene from a Noel Coward play. Except nobody would believe it if they saw it on stage. He didn't even try to defend himself. Once you went at him he just reeled off answers as though he was in the witness box.'

'He's a coward,' she said. 'Bob's not in a business that builds courage and integrity. I'm surprised he didn't shed a few tears.'

'But how will he cover himself when he sees Oscar?'

'He won't. As far as Bob is concerned this little meeting we just had never took place. I'm sure he's already put it out of his mind.'

'But what if you tell Oscar what happened?'

'Bob knows I won't. Why should I? I don't need to make Bob look bad in front of Oscar. And I don't give a damn what Oscar thinks about me. All I care about is what you think. That's why I had to take on Bob with you here as witness.'

When they walked out through the lobby Dorsey said, 'What would you say if I told you I want to go home by myself, sit in the bathtub for an hour, turn off the telephone, and go to bed early?'

'What am I expected to say?'

'Speak your heart, my darling.'

'I'd rather have you come home with me.'

'I'd like that. But this whole business with Gingrich has given me the creepie-crawlies. I feel dirty. The way I used to feel after an evening with Oscar's friends in California. I'll clean up good, though, you'll see. Tomorrow I'll be a new woman.'

When Rab put her in a taxi in front of Claridges he gave the driver her address in Knightsbridge. As soon as the car turned off Brook Street into Regent Street, however, Dorsey told the driver to take her to the Abingdon Hotel on Hill Street. When they reached the hotel she took the lift to the seventh floor and walked along the corridor to room 728. When she knocked, Bob Gingrich opened the door and let her in.

'Well done,' she said.

'Was it a good audition?'

'Better than that. A star performance.'

'He seems like a good guy,' Gingrich said. 'I like him.'

'I *adore* him. I hate to deceive him like that.'

'All in a good cause. It wouldn't have been necessary if I hadn't talked too much in his office.'

'No apologies required. We covered that last night. You screwed things up because Oscar asked you to and now you've straightened them out because I forced you to.'

'We convinced him? No doubt about it?'

'No doubt at all.'

Standing by the foot of the bed then, she slipped out of her shoes and unfastened the waist buttons of her skirt.

'Are you staying for a while?' he said.

'What's it look like?'

'It looks like I'm going to be rewarded.'

'Not at all. We made no arrangement. I asked you to help me, as a friend, and you did. I don't pass myself around in payment for favours.' She smiled. 'But everyone knows a friendly gesture very often stimulates a friendly response.'

She quickly took off the rest of her clothes. Just before she walked across the room and put her arms around him she slipped her bare feet into her high-heeled pumps. 'You see,' she said. 'I haven't forgotten what you like.'

[3]

As he came home to Fort Beck from England, Jesse prepared himself for a flood of questions from Helen. During every telephone call to her, and in every letter, he had said that the details could wait till he was back. So he had every reason to believe that the trial of Jack Dieter, Polly's troubles, his stays in Paris and London, and his trip to Wingate Fields, would be the topics of conversation and enquiry for several days after his return.

Helen surprised him, however, as they drove home from the airport when she said, 'Bill has told me everything about the trial and the family so there's no need for you to rehash it. I'm sure it was an awful time for you so the sooner we put it behind us the better.' She leaned close to him on the front seat of the car and kissed his cheek. 'I'm just happy to have you back here where you belong. I know you want to do everything you can for Polly and so do I. But you have to think about your own life as well. You're important too.'

Having pondered what exactly he would say to Helen about the weeks he'd been away, having tried with some diligence to imagine what sort of information she might be eager to hear, this unexpected attitude from her switched him full round. Rather than being pleased by her seeming lack of interest in what he had thought and seen and done in Europe, he saw it, to his surprise, as a stimulus. He felt free suddenly, almost obligated, to tell her *exactly* what had happened and how he felt about it; that impulse helped him to see things more clearly than he had before and to speak of them with candour.

About Polly, he said, 'I don't go along with the family's conclusions about her, about what she's done and what she should do. It's too late for any of us to make a qualitative judgment of Jack Dieter. Much too late to wonder about what might have been. Polly's a gifted young woman who is capable of making decisions about herself and her life. She was eighteen years old when she chose to attend university in Germany. Since then most of her choices have been extremely personal ones. She seems to go with her instincts. I'm sure she considers the advice and experience of other people, or at least she pretends to, but when the final decision comes it's always *her* decision, based most often on her feelings rather than on what we refer to as common sense.'

'That's the surprise,' Helen said. 'Because she has a great deal of common sense.'

'Exactly. But she doesn't let it rule her. God knows, she flew in the face of every guidepost known to God or man when she chose Jack. All of us predicted chaos and now it seems that chaos is the

321

result. But Polly saw it differently. She let her senses decide for her.'

'Love works that way, doesn't it?'

'So we're told,' Jesse said, 'but no matter what the poets say, a great number of people still try to use their heads.'

'But not Polly.'

'No, indeed. She gambled everything. And she knew when she did it that when you take that risk you can also *lose* everything. Has she lost everything now? It's hard to say. But it seems that she's lost the things she valued most.'

'Are you saying she regrets it?'

Jesse shook his head. 'She regrets nothing. She concedes nothing. She expects nothing. Given a chance to repeat her choices, she would do exactly what she has done. She has a stubborn determination that is both miraculous and heart-breaking.'

'Maybe you're right but it all sounds terribly hopeless. I can't accept the fact that she's forced to tie herself for ever to one unhappy choice.

'She's not *forced* to do anything. That's my point.'

'But I can't believe that she'll . . . do you believe she really intends to spend all these wonderful years of her life living alone in Heidelberg with nothing but occasional visits to some dreary prison to keep her going?'

'Yes, I do.'

'Did you try to reason with her?'

'Not at all,' Jesse said. 'That's not a decision for me or anyone else to make. It's Polly's choice and she made it some time ago.'

'Bill said he and Rab tried to talk some sense into her but it didn't work.'

'Of course it didn't work. Polly has more sense than Bill and Rab rolled together. They'd like to find a sentimental solution to her situation but there is none. It might make them feel good but it would be of no value to Polly.'

'That's hard to accept. I can't believe there's nothing any of us can do.'

'I didn't say that. We can pay attention and we can wait. And if she asks for help we can give it to her. But if she doesn't we have to be kind enough and perceptive enough to let her alone.'

Jesse had always been considered outspoken by his family and by the teachers and editors and publishers he had dealt with in his

322

professional life. It was an attribute he was proud of. It was one of the many characteristics of Raymond he had tried to emulate. He concluded early on that speaking forcefully helped a man to be taken seriously. At the same time he was conscious of the fact that his father, Thomas Clegg, was a man who spoke total nonsense with a great deal of authority. So, although Jesse accepted the principle of positive and informed speech and had attempted to put it into practice from his first week in Raymond's house, he always suspected, because of his father perhaps, that he was shamming, that each time he opened his mouth he was in danger of being contradicted or ridiculed by someone better informed or simply more self-confident than he. This lack of confidence had been a key factor in Jesse's success as a student, a teacher, and later as a researcher, a critic, and author. He was always scrupulously prepared because he was afraid not to be. Needing to speak with true authority, he took pains to make sure that he was genuinely authoritative on any subject, in any area of art or literature, where he might be challenged.

With all this preparation, however, with all this careful attention to scholarship, his fear of being caught out still made him cautious. He tended to use only half of his genuine knowledge, to take refuge in, and draw conclusions from, only irrefutable facts. In situations where he was fully capable of being both daring and enlightening he settled for being solid and dependable.

Now, however, and suddenly, in his conversations with Helen, he found himself drawing conclusions and making projections that were based on conviction and instinct rather than experience and research. And surprisingly, as he heard himself speak, he felt a sureness that was new to him. He no longer needed to say, 'I know.' He found himself saying, with total authority, 'I believe.' Raymond had often said, to both Jesse and Helen, 'If you're wrong, if you make a mistake, you can always fix it. If you're tentative, that's a condition, a frame of mind, that's almost impossible to fix.' Jesse had always understood this theorem. Now suddenly he was able to practise it. If he had attempted to codify it he would perhaps have said to himself, 'To hell with the words. I'm not afraid any more.'

This new impulse, once it hit him, spread like a benevolent virus. When Helen asked him about the writing projects that had taken him to Berlin and Frankfurt, the original reasons for his trip to

Germany, he said, 'Everything went well. I saw the people I wanted to see, talked to my sources, visited the libraries and museums I needed to visit, and gathered all the material I needed for the articles I was planning to write. And some time between the time I left Berlin and the time I came back here I decided I wasn't going to do those particular articles, or any other articles that remotely resemble them. I put all my notes and photocopies in a big envelope and dumped them in a trash container at Heathrow.'

'I don't believe you.'

'Straight truth. Do you realize that I've already written about every subject that *really* interested me as well as a hell of a lot of things that didn't interest me at all. I've dissected Shaw and Camus and Kierkegaard, Stendhal and Maurois and Wright Morris and Gertrude Stein. And everybody else who's written anything new or startling or original in this century. I've examined and reconsidered and evaluated every painter from della Francesca . . .'

'Della Francesca,' Helen said. 'That was your springboard. You had him on the brain before you even knew how to write.'

Jesse nodded. 'And I still do. But I've written everything I know, everything I suspect or guess or *think*, about him and his work. And the same for Rembrandt, Giotto, Uccello, Matisse, Leger, Klee and Mondrian. There's nobody you can name that I haven't flayed or celebrated. And I loved every minute of it because each paragraph I wrote told me something about myself, mostly about my own limitations.'

'Are you saying you've learned all there is to know?'

'No. I'm saying I've learned all I want to know. And in the process I have angered, enlightened and instructed as much as I care to. My new credo is from an anonymous philosopher who said, "Anything that can be learned is worthless." If I write any more at all, and I may not, I will simply put down what I know. That way I will find out if I know anything at all.'

'And who will be allowed to read these simple truths?'

'No one. Having devoted all of what might loosely be called my creative life writing a specific number of words about preselected subjects or persons, I will now devote myself to the *process*. If I write at all, I will simply write. If I've accumulated anything at all as I've stumbled about during my lifetime I will let it come out.'

'Autobiography?'

'Not if I can help it. Making mud-pies with language. That's more like it. How does that sound to you?'

'I suggest two aspirin, warm soup, and early to bed.'

'Ah-ha,' Jesse said. 'That's a prescription for a sick child. I am a very healthy, silver-haired grown-up.'

'Maybe yes. Maybe no. How does Nora feel about this new direction in your life?'

'Haven't told her. Don't expect to tell her. Haven't told anyone but you. It's an extremely personal matter. Nobody's business but mine. In the larger scheme of things, such a decision is about as important as choosing a pack of razor blades in the market.'

When he left London, Jesse had no intention of confiding in Helen or anyone else about the evening he'd spent with Rab. The memories were too clear, all the dialogue was too fresh, still, in his mind. It was a subject he had avoided dealing with during his stay at Wingate. He hadn't wanted to come to terms with it, hadn't wanted to draw conclusions. He decided that time was the best solution, that the situation would sort itself out only if it was left alone. Then, perhaps, he or Rab, or both of them, would find a way back from the wreckage they'd scattered that night at dinner.

When Helen asked him, however, about Rab, when she asked whether they had been able to spend time together in Heidelberg and if they had seen each other in London, Jesse said, 'We hardly saw each other in Germany. I was too busy with Speicher and Polly. But we did meet in London. We had a disastrous dinner together.'

He then told her in detail what he and Rab had said to each other, reporting their conversation, as much as he was able, word for word.

'My God,' Helen said when he finished, after he'd told her the last words Rab had said to him, 'did he really *say* that?'

'Yes.'

'Did he mean it?'

'Time will tell, I suppose. But he certainly convinced me that he meant it.'

'Have you talked with him since then?'

'I left for Wingate Fields the next morning.'

'You haven't talked on the phone? You didn't try to call him from Heathrow?'

Jesse shook his head. 'No point. It would have been a hopeless conversation. If you'd had dinner with us that night, you'd know what I mean.'

'I can't imagine what you could have said to him that would make him respond that way.'

'I told you exactly what I said. It's not that simple in any case. Whatever's in his head about me has been there for a long time. He just chose that particular time and place to let it out.'

'Do you think he's still angry at you because of that discussion you had at the time of Clara's funeral?'

'I don't think so. He seems to have made a final judgment of me some time ago. Since then he's just been collecting impressions and incidents to shore up the conclusion he's already reached.'

'But what happens now? Can you just leave things like this?'

'Why not? Suspended animation is a common human condition.'

'Don't you care, Jesse?'

'Of course I care. Rab was my first kid. That's not an experience you tuck away in a book and forget about. But it's not daddy and the baby any longer. Hasn't been for a long time. Parents are the last ones to know sometimes when their children have grown up. And I'm no exception to that. I can talk till I'm blue in the face about "adult males with equal rights" but when I look at him, or at Polly or Bill, my eyes play tricks on me. No matter how smooth and independent and self-reliant they've become I can't help seeing them as they used to be. Trying to walk, trying to talk, trying to feed themselves. And no matter how clever you are at disguising that, children sense it, they expect it, they feed on it. It gives them another cord to cut, another reason to break away.'

'But not like this. If Rab really feels that way, if he said what you say he said . . .'

'He said it,' Jesse said.

' . . . it sounds so final. Biblical almost. A great clap of thunder and two people never see each other again. And you, the world's most structured man, seem willing to accept the situation.'

Jesse smiled. 'In the first place I'm not the world's most structured man. If I ever wanted to be I don't want that any longer. But in the second place I'm structured enough, I'm *smart* enough, to know when I'm outgunned, when I don't have the cards to justify a bid.'

'I don't know what you're saying.'

'Yes, you do. Have you ever had somebody you don't give a damn about tell you they adore you and can't live without you?'

326

'What does that have to do with what we're talking about?'

'Everything. Think about it.'

After a moment she said, 'Yes, I suppose I have.'

'What was your reaction?'

'I don't remember. No reaction, I suppose. If you're not interested in somebody, it doesn't matter much how they feel about you.'

'Exactly. I just got a clear message from Rab. He wants to be left alone. So in these circumstances it doesn't matter too much what I want, does it?'

'It just seems so cold-blooded.'

'Maybe not. Rab reminded me that I never saw much of my folks after I left home. And as I remember, I never felt as if I was cold-blooded.'

'So you're saying there's nothing you can do.'

'It's not a question of what I'm saying. There really isn't anything I can do. And I'll tell you something else. There's nothing I want to do. I'm too old to play games with people, even my own kids. At this stage of the game I'm not interested in trying to sell myself.'

'In other words you can get along without anybody if you have to.'

'I wouldn't put it that way. But if somebody doesn't want me around I'm not anxious to make a pest of myself.'

Helen smiled. 'What if I said *I* didn't want you around?'

'I'd take you to the doctor and have your head examined.'

Several days after Jesse came home to Fort Beck, Helen said to him, 'Something happened to you between the time you left here to go to Germany and the time you came back. What was it?'

'Nothing world-shaking,' he said. 'Just a lot of odd scraps stitched together.'

'Are you sure you didn't wander into one of those weird German cabarets and get yourself hypnotized? No exotic drugs? No truth serum?'

'What are we getting at?'

'You've gone through a metamorphosis. A dramatic turn-around.'

'How so?'

'You know what Raymond used to say about you. He said you were the best person he'd ever met for keeping a secret. He said you didn't mind answering a question now and then but you *never* volunteered information. Remember his saying that?'

327

'That was a long time ago,' Jesse said.

'Yes, it was. And we've both changed a lot since then. But the thing that hasn't changed in your case is that reluctance to volunteer information. God knows, you've become articulate and informed and socially adept, not hesitant at all about saying what you *think*. But how you *feel* is something else again. That hasn't changed through the years. Very slow to let people know what's going on inside.'

'And you're saying I'm a changed man now, willing to confess all my guilty secrets to the world. Is that it?'

'You tell me,' she said. 'Am I wrong? I have a feeling that you suddenly have nothing to hide, that you've turned into a truth machine. Is that possible?'

'I don't remember lying to you.'

'We're not talking about lying. At least I'm not. I'm talking about a remarkable reluctance to divulge information. Isn't that a characteristic you would admit to?'

'Probably.'

'Then what's changed? When you talked about Polly, about your work, about Rab, that was a new Jesse I was hearing, new to me, and if I don't know you, after all these years, who does?'

'*You* does,' Jesse said. He stood up from the chair where he'd been sitting, struck a theatrical pose, and declaimed, 'I am a simple man of the fields, not given to deep analysis or self-searching. You may draw whatever conclusions you wish about me but don't ask me to help you do it.'

It was true. He did not draw conclusions about himself. Or if he did, when he did, he put another label on the process. But all the same he did feel a new freedom that seemed to coincide with Helen's assessments of him. One thing was remarkably clear: there was an ease to their relationship that was new to both of them. Both of them welcomed it. But beyond occasional musings by Helen, they made no effort to dissect or understand it.

One afternoon, quite casually, they began to talk about Nora. In all the years since they had met her – they had met her on the same day when they arrived for the first time at Wingate Fields – they had seldom discussed her. And the few discussions that had taken place had been early on, before the ill-defined battle lines had been drawn between Helen and Nora.

328

'Bill said Nora was in Heidelberg for the trial. Did she create havoc as usual?'

'Not at all. She didn't present herself publicly as Polly's grandmother but on the other hand she didn't slink about on spike heels trailing her sable coat behind her. She did nothing to attract attention to herself.'

'Well, that's progress, isn't it? Am I being bitchy?'

'Probably. But it doesn't matter. There's never been any love lost between you and Nora. Why should that change now?'

'Is she ageing well?' Helen asked.

'You saw her at Clara's funeral. It's not that many years ago.'

'She looked gorgeous then.'

'She still looks pretty much the same.'

'I'm envious. Do you think she has a Dorian Grey portrait of herself tucked away somewhere, a picture that's ageing for her as she goes along looking the same as she did twenty years ago?'

'You're a great one to talk. I don't see people offering to help you across the street.'

'That's true,' Helen said, 'but since I've never deceived myself that I'm the same variety of peacock as Nora, I certainly shan't begin to do that now. She's simply a divine-looking creature. Every time you see her I expect you won't come back.'

'I knew you first. Remember?'

'That's true. That means I have first claim on you.'

'She said something that surprised me,' Jesse said then. 'She plans to be buried at Wingate Fields.'

'What did you expect?'

'I'm not sure. We'd never discussed it before. I guess I thought she'd insist on being buried just beside Balzac in the Montparnasse cemetery.'

'Do you think she might go back to England to live?'

'No. She doesn't mind being there when she's dead but she has other plans for her life. I don't think she'll ever leave Paris.'

'Does she have a gentleman in residence at the moment?'

'I don't know. She didn't tell me and I didn't ask.'

'Did she make you any attractive offers?' Helen asked.

'What do you mean?'

'You know precisely what I mean. Whatever else she may be, Nora is not shy about stating her wishes. If she wanted to lure you back to Paris on a permanent basis I'm sure she'd be able to find the words to tell you that.'

Jesse smiled. 'We don't really want to discuss that, do we?'

'Of course we do. Why not? This isn't an inquisition. We're simply discussing the foibles of our close relative. Since she had you loitering about the house for a good many years one is naturally curious about her present wishes. Perhaps she'd like you to loiter there once again.'

Still smiling, Jesse said. 'At the risk of seeming to praise myself I think it's fair to say that I would be welcome in her home.'

'Of course you would. But surely she has no unkind words to say about me.'

'Not at all. She just has a very sketchy idea of what it's like to live in America. Having seen only New York and Boston, she's persuaded herself that everything between the Atlantic Ocean and California is cowboys and Indians. And red-necked peasants tilling the potato fields. She can't imagine that anyone could make a proper life in such surroundings.'

'Did you straighten her out?'

'No. Nora needs her fantasies.'

'All of us do.'

'That's true,' Jesse said. 'But she more than most. It's no accident that she lives on a tiny island in the Seine. For all of her conception of herself as a reckless, adventurous, liberated woman, she's in desperate need of a controlled environment. Who she is and where she is are inseparable. Her house in Paris is a precise reflexion of everything she needs and wants and loves. It's her biography and she knows it. Those years in New York during the war were agony for her. She lost all definition. Didn't recognize herself. England, too, is a mine-field for her. Only when she has French soil under her feet does she come alive. Only on that small island, inside the walls of her historic house, does she breathe deep and inhabit her own skin.'

'And only with the splendid Jesse Bradshaw . . .' Helen began.

'As I said,' Jesse broke in, 'she's dependent on her fantasies. All sorts of words and images come tumbling out of her mouth. But we only accept what we want to accept. We believe what we choose to believe.' He put his arms around Helen. '*We* know that her perception of frontier life in America is not accurate. Don't we know that?'

330

'I know that. But when we travel, sometimes we forget.'

'Not me,' Jesse said. 'I don't forget.'

[4]

Several days after Dorsey's meeting at Claridges with Rab and Gingrich, Oscar flew to London from Madrid. The first evening he was at home she told him she wanted a divorce. She had rehearsed in her mind every possible way she could tell him. She had also tried to foresee what his reaction would be. When the moment came, however, she said it the simplest way she knew how. 'I wish I knew some easy way to say this, Oscar, but I don't. So I have to be blunt. I'm in love with someone else and I want a divorce.'

He sat looking at her for a long moment. Finally he smiled and said, 'Is that any way to greet your hard-working husband when he comes home after a rugged three weeks in Spain?'

'I'm sorry. I said I was sorry.'

'Are we allowed to enquire who the lucky man is?'

'Don't be cute, Oscar. I'm trying to be as honest as I can. Let's not play games with each other. You know who I've been seeing.'

'How would I know that?'

'I had a long conversation with Bob Gingrich the other evening. I assume he reported to you about it.'

'Why would he report to me?'

'He told me you'd asked him to do you a little favour.'

Oscar shook his head. 'You know Bob. Loves to gossip. Loves to make up stories. Some of them are almost good enough to turn into screen-plays.'

'You're going to make this difficult, aren't you?'

'Why do you say that?'

'Because I can see it. All right, I'll go along with you. I'll pretend I'm giving you fresh and wonderful information. Rab Bradshaw. That's the man I want to marry.'

'A little young for you, isn't he?'

'He doesn't seem to think so.'

'Let me get this straight,' Oscar said then. 'You said you had a conversation with Gingrich. Was Rab there too?'

331

'Yes.'

'Very cosy. Does that mean your husband-to-be knows the tender story of you and Robert Gingrich?'

'No, he doesn't. And I don't plan to tell him.'

'I can understand that. But I wouldn't trust Gingrich if I were you.'

'He's already dropped a few hints in Rab's office. But Rab paid no attention. And if you're planning to tell him . . .'

'Why would I tell him?'

'I'm not sure,' she said. 'But if you do . . .'

'I don't plan to. That's not my style.'

'I'm glad to hear you say that. It has nothing to do with us anyway.'

'That's true. You and Gingrich are ancient history.'

'I tried to imagine how you'd react when I told you,' she said. 'But I . . .'

'I'm the man of a thousand faces. You know that.'

'You're not surprised, are you?'

'No,' he said.

'How long have you known?'

'Since the beginning.'

'That's why you hit me that night at the theatre, isn't it?'

He nodded. 'That's right.'

'You were so angry then and you're not angry now. What happened?'

'I made an adjustment. I forced myself to remember the first law of marriage: you can't stay married to someone who doesn't want to stay married to you.'

'I'm not saying there's something wrong with you. That's not what this is all about.'

'I know that. It's about young love in the springtime. Youth speaks to youth.'

'You are still angry, aren't you?'

'Not at all. Didn't you ever read what Walter Winchell said about me? And Louella Parsons was even nastier. She said I shed wives like a snake sheds its skin.'

'I hate that. I've heard you say that before.'

'No offence,' he said. 'Not applicable in this case anyhow. Because it's you who's shedding me.'

'I don't think of it that way and you shouldn't either. There must

332

be a way to end a marriage without the two people trying to wreck each other. I certainly have no urge to hurt you.'

'That's good.'

'So how shall we handle it?'

'Don't ask me. I've been divorced four times and I've never got the hang of it. So I try to stay out of the whole process. That's what I have lawyers for.'

'I'm not talking about the divorce. I'm talking about us. How do we handle that? I want us to be civilized about it.'

'Well, that may not be possible. But we can try if you want to.'

'Why isn't it possible?' she said.

'You know how lawyers are. They're paid to resolve conflicts. If there is no conflict, they create one. Then they resolve it.'

'Then let's do it without lawyers. People do it all the time.'

'Not people like us,' he said. 'We're famous folks. In the public eye. We can't just get a divorce. We have to get a *divorce*. Besides, a woman has to have a high-powered lawyer to protect her interests, to see that she's well-provided for.'

'That's what I'm trying to say. I don't need to be provided for.'

'Of course you do. And even if you don't need it, I have to provide it. People expect it from me. A man as successful as I am has to pay through the nose when his wife divorces him.'

'Then you divorce me,' she said.

'Whatever you say. But then it will cost me more.'

'You're not taking this seriously at all, are you?'

'Of course I am. More than you are. You've given me the best years of your life. That's worth something. It's an insult to women everywhere if you place a low value on yourself. You're a valuable item, Dorsey. Attention must be paid. Property must be divided, depositions taken, agreements must be made and broken. This is serious stuff. My reputation's at stake here. If you let me get off cheap I may never work again. If I don't give you the moon, people will start to think I don't own it.'

'I don't like the sound of this,' she said. 'We've had discussions like this before. I try to be serious and all you want to do is joke around. Then all of a sudden you cut me off at the knees.'

'No such thing. Nothing like that intended.'

'All right,' she said. 'I'll make one more try. Whether you believe it or not, I feel awful about this. I've never been divorced before. It makes me feel terrible just thinking about it. So don't make it worse by telling me what you're going to give me. I don't need anything. If we're going to separate I want us to do it without a lot of wrangling about property and money. I don't want us to have terrible memories of each other. Can't we manage that?'

He shook his head. 'Difficult. You see, we're wrangling now about property and money. I want to give you what you deserve and you're telling me you deserve nothing. If you're going to be bull-headed about this it may take us five years to reach a property settlement. Also, we have to think about Charlie.'

'What about Charlie?'

'We have to think about his welfare. There are all kinds of questions we have to consider that affect Charlie.'

'I'm not sure what you're saying,' she said.

'Nothing complicated. Just what it sounds like. Since a child is involved, we have his welfare to consider.'

'Are you saying we're going to have a custody battle over Charlie?'

'Not at all. Is that what you're saying?'

'God, no. I'm counting on your having enough class not to drag him into all this.'

'I'm afraid he is in it, whether we drag him in or not. You're his mother and I'm the only father he's ever known and now we're not going to be married any longer. So we can't expect him not to notice.'

'That's not what I mean and you know it. I just got a terrible sinking feeling. You're going to try to take him away from me, aren't you?'

'I said nothing at all about it. I'm saying he must be provided for. That has to be a part of any agreement we sign.'

'No court in the world would take him away from me if that's what you're thinking.'

'I have no intention of trying to take him away from you. It would be a pointless exercise even if I did. He's old enough to choose who he wants to live with. If he told a judge he wanted to be with you, no court would give him to me. You're right about that.'

'And if he said he preferred being with you, no court would give him to me. Is that the other side of the coin?'

'I hadn't thought about that,' Oscar said, 'because it never occurred to me that it could happen.'

334

'But if it did?'

'If I were you I wouldn't waste time thinking about that.'

'If you were me,' she said, 'you wouldn't think about anything else.'

[5]

'I don't know what you're so upset about,' Rab said. 'It sounds to me as though he's trying to be reasonable.'

'He doesn't know what that word means,' Dorsey said. 'He only pretends to be reasonable while he's planning what he really intends to do.'

'Why should we borrow trouble? You'll know soon enough if he's going to be difficult. So we'll deal with it then. When it happens. In the meantime you should be grateful that he didn't scream and yell and start to throw things.'

'I'd feel better if he had. You don't know him the way I do. Everyone knows that when he's amenable you'd better look out, some kind of trouble is brewing.'

'Let's be logical about it,' Rab said. 'What can he do to you? He can't force you to live with him. If he makes it difficult to have a divorce, who gives a damn? You and I will live together and he can do whatever he likes. Your secret weapon is that you want nothing from him. He has nothing to use against you.'

'You're forgetting about Charlie. That's what he has to use against me.'

'But you said you settled everything about Charlie.'

'Nothing's ever settled when you're dealing with Oscar. He knows I'm vulnerable where Charlie's concerned. Just because Oscar nods his head and agrees to something doesn't mean he'll agree tomorrow. Also, I have no idea how Charlie will react. He thinks Oscar's a world-class father.'

'So what? What's wrong with that?' You're not trying to prevent the two of them from seeing each other. Charlie will be in school for the next five or six years anyway. You'll have legal custody and Oscar can go see him any time he wants to. Isn't that all right with you?'

335

'It's all right with me but it won't be all right with Oscar. I guarantee it. He doesn't like to be told what he can do. He likes to make all those decisions himself.'

'It doesn't matter what he likes. The court will decide about Charlie. You gave birth to him, you're his natural mother, and you'll have custody of him.'

'I wish I was as confident as you are.'

'You will be once you get out of this muddle you've got yourself into.'

'But what if Charlie decides he wants to live with Oscar?'

'Why should he do that?' Rab said.

'I don't know. I don't know anything. But nothing would surprise me.'

'Listen to me. You're flying to Virginia in a week or so. You and Oscar agreed that you would tell Charlie about the divorce. I'm sure half the kids in his school have divorced parents. He's way ahead of the game, I promise you.'

'I don't know,' she said. 'I don't know what to think. I used to be afraid of nothing. Now all of a sudden I'm scared of my shadow. All I think about are consequences. What will happen if I do. What will happen if I don't. You're sure of everything. You don't know what it's like. I'm scared of my own kid.'

'Then don't tell him. Let Oscar tell him. He offered to.'

'Of course he did. He'd love to do that. But that's one thing he mustn't do. Thank God he had to go back to Barcelona. He'd have been on the first plane to the States otherwise. That would wreck me if he got to Charlie before I do. It's just that I'm such a bloody coward. I hate doing things like this. It was bad enough talking to Oscar about it. It will be ten times worse talking to Charlie.'

'That's the part I don't understand.'

'You know how kids are. If you tell them something they don't want to hear they just sit there and look at you. No reaction. No expression on their faces. Makes you feel like a bug. I'm just no good at giving people bad news. I want to run and hide instead. You'll probably have to tie me up and carry me to the plane next week.'

'Wouldn't it be simpler if I went with you?' Rab said.

'Don't even mention it. Of course it would be simpler. I'd give anything if you could come along. But I told you before, I think

336

it's too dangerous. I don't want to give Oscar anything to use against us.'

'But he told you he's known about us from the beginning.'

'Maybe he has and maybe he hasn't,' she said. 'But knowing is one thing and having proof is something else. If we fly to Washington together, stay in a hotel together, there's a documentary record that we've been naughty. Not a smart move when you're about to sue your husband for divorce.'

Rab put his arms around her. 'You're being too careful,' he said. 'I think you should risk everything. Fly in the face of caution and respectability. Ride the current. Have your picture in the tabloids. Become a scarlet woman. Forsake everything except me. Abandon your friends. Throw away your jewellery. Give away your clothes. Become totally dependent on Raymond Angus Bradshaw.'

'I am totally dependent on you. I have given up everything.'

'Then you have nothing to fret about. You have nothing left to lose.'

'Yes, I do,' she said.

[6]

Jesse's reassessment of himself when he returned to Fort Beck from London extended to the last piece of writing that he retained some faith in, his subjective history of certain members of the Bradshaw family. Although it still stayed alive in his mind as a project, he no longer deceived himself that it was a profound subject, one that might touch or enlighten people other than himself. He concluded, to the contrary, that however successful he might be in putting his thoughts and his recollections into the best prose he could provide, the result would have significance only for him.

This conclusion did not, however, turn him away from the subject or lessen his enthusiasm. In a way, as it became in his mind smaller and more private, it also became more compelling and gave him even greater freedom to think with clarity and write with candour, to explore and reveal the recesses of his mind and memory.

This new courage, this fresh determination to follow his thoughts and judgments to wherever they might take him, pushed him

337

forward to a subject he had always avoided even in his most private musings, to a person he had never had the courage to examine – Raymond. From the moment he picked up his pen he sensed that he was about to learn things about Raymond, and about himself, that he had neither suspected nor admitted before.

Now that I'm older, appreciably older, than Raymond Bradshaw was when he died, is it possible that, for this reason alone, I see him differently now than I did before. I worshipped him when he was alive and idolized his memory through all the years since he died. But now I find myself asking questions about him that seem to have no answers. At least they are not the answers I would have expected.

Was he the heroic figure I believed him to be or was he in fact a failure? Was there more cruelty than kindness in him? Was his apparent concern for others a shield to conceal the fact that he was concerned only with himself? Was his façade of courage a mask for cowardice? Did he love Helen and me as he seemed to or does a close examination of his life reveal that he was unable to love? Was he brilliant or merely clever? Was he, in any way at all, what he seemed to be? Was his early death a tragic loss or was it a blessing that he died before he revealed himself as a charlatan?

Cruel and difficult questions. But they lead me to attempt a biographical portrait of him which is markedly different from the one I have accepted and revered through most of my life.

Raymond was a child of privilege, a soft and beautiful boy who was adored and spoiled by his parents and grandparents, by his sister, and by the family servants. He was carefully shielded from any exposure to hardship and crisis. So when he fell in love, at age twenty, with a married woman, with someone he couldn't have, he found himself in a frustrating no-exit situation. When her husband took her away, then when Raymond's father sent him away to finish his schooling in Ireland, his only resources, his only weapons, were anger and resentment. Did he say to himself, 'How could such things happen to someone like me?' It's very probable that he did.

When he met the young woman again, some months later, at a hotel in Holyhead, when her husband surprised them, when the young woman was accidentally shot and killed in the struggle

338

that followed, once again he found himself enfeebled. Resentment and humiliation kept him away from his family. Either he needed to be detained in a clinic for emotional disorders or he pretended such a need.

Resisting his family's efforts to help him, he chose to concentrate all the blame for his unhappy situation on Angus, his father. He brooded in his bare white room, refused to see visitors, and at last, like a child who holds his breath to attract attention, he disappeared, leaving no message, no hint as to where he had gone.

Like a miser who practises vengeance beyond the grave by denying relatives and leaving his entire estate to the cat, Raymond visited a cold and senseless cruelty on his parents and his sister by simply cutting himself off from them for ever.

In America he created a new identity for himself, retaining only his name. He carefully acquired a New England accent, learned to dress, move and behave like an American, and invented a new family background. Born in Maine, no living relatives.

In New York City he married an Italian girl from a working-class family. Did he consciously marry beneath him? Did he need to do that for some reason? Could he shore himself up only by being with someone who surely felt inferior to him even though she was not? And did he deliberately transport her to rural Illinois to further accentuate her feelings of isolation from her roots? Perhaps not. Perhaps he was merely careless.

When his wife left him and took his daughter with her did he make a genuine attempt to bring them back? Did it really matter to him? Or did he simply accept it, as he seemed to accept other events? And what was his reaction to his daughter's return? Was Helen truly a daughter in his eyes, or was she a tantalizing mix of disciple and platonic woman of the house? Did he allow her to love him too much, encourage her perhaps, because he loved her too little? Or was she, perhaps, the only thing he could love, because he had created her, because she was a part of himself?

Can any flawed human being hold up under such scrutiny? Could I? Surely not. On the other hand, Raymond, it seems, had some unique and particular gift for cruelty. All of us, in anger or on impulse, can be unkind. Sustained punishment is another matter. Running away, getting even, making other people suffer for real or imagined transgressions, all these are classic reactions to pain. But in most of us those impulses lose their fuel. Forgiveness takes place. Or as the pain subsides so does the need to punish.

Raymond's case, however, is unusual. Having selected his family as targets for vengeance, he was content, it seemed, with nothing short of *lifetime* vengeance. Had he not died a comparatively young man, his parents would have gone to their graves with an aching emptiness, not knowing what had become of their son.

Surely this was the result he had in mind. Not only his parents but everyone else in his family would have been totally and permanently ignorant of his whereabouts if Helen and I had not happened on those old locked-away clues in his strong-box.

Why did he take me in? Was that a kindness as it seemed to be, or was it in response to some need that he felt? Did he need a son? Did he want to experience something of what Angus had experienced with him? Is it possible that it was an elaborate extension of his cruelty to his father? Did he tell himself that whereas Angus had lost a son, he, Raymond, had found one? Borgian and unlikely, one would think, but possible when one studies the total evidence.

Other possibilities are these: he needed someone to mould and advise and instruct, someone to admire him and emulate him. He needed an audience. Having abandoned his parents and having been abandoned by his wife and daughter, perhaps he longed to create a family of one, some needy person like me who would stay with him no matter what. If these suppositions are true, if any of them are true, then those years when Raymond had both Helen and me under his roof must have been, without question, the finest years of his life, just as she and I have always felt they were the finest years of our lives.

So what was he, our Raymond? More than he seemed or less? And does it matter? Was he so much a father to me, perhaps, that I must destroy him now before I can become what I always imagined he was. Or is that the last thing in the world I want to be? Christ knows.

When Bill Bradshaw made his final decision to go to Heidelberg to be with Polly, he discussed it first with Helen. After he'd explained his plans, Helen asked him how Jesse felt about it.

'I haven't told him yet,' Bill said.

'I'm surprised you're telling me first.'

'I guess I wanted to ease into it. Pick up a bit of support. Sometimes women see things differently.'

Helen smiled. 'Almost always, I think.'

'I suppose I'm just testing the water. If you tell me I'm a raving maniac then I'll know I'm in for trouble with Dad.'

'Not necessarily. Jesse and I often have different points of view. Also there's no reason for him to know that we're having this talk if you don't want him to.'

'Oh, no,' Bill said. 'I wouldn't put you in that position. I plan to tell him I've already discussed it with you.

'Well,' she said, 'it sounds like a serious step and I'm sure you've given it serious thought. But it's your decision after all.'

'I realize that. But all the same I don't want to burn my bridges. I don't want to leave here with you and Jesse thinking I'm some sort of ungrateful idiot.'

'I don't see what gratitude has to do with it.'

'Quite a lot, I think. You were very kind to take me in here when I decided I'd like to come to Foresby to finish school. Now I'm leaving with still a year of classes unfinished and I realize that's not exactly a responsible move.'

'There's no reason why you can't come back and finish school later. I'm sure you don't plan to stay in Heidelberg for ever.' When he didn't answer she said, 'Or do you?'

'I don't know. That depends on Polly. It's hard to know how long I'll stay.'

'How does Polly feel about all this?'

'You want the truth?'

'Of course.'

'She thinks I'm crazy. Doesn't want me hanging about, she says. Wants me to stay here and finish my schooling.'

'Then why . . .'

'That's what I expected her to say,' Bill said. 'Polly thinks she doesn't need anything from anybody. But she's wrong. I'm not saying that I'm the solution to all her problems but at least I'm somebody she knows and trusts. She'll have somebody to talk to and fuss over. Polly needs that. And maybe I can look after her a little bit.'

'What do you think she plans to do with herself now?'

'I know what she's going to do. Rab and I had a long talk with her after the trial. She's going to bury herself in Heidelberg, like an animal in a cave. She'll only come out when she drives to Wurzburg to see Jack on visiting days.'

'That doesn't sound like Polly,' Helen said. 'She must have made friends there. And she can go on with her work at the university.'

'Polly doesn't care about school. She hasn't gone to a lecture for more than a year. And whatever friends she'd made, she abandoned them after she met Jack. The only people they saw were that friend of his who was killed during the demonstration and the German woman who crucified him during the trial.'

'There's something else to consider,' Helen said. 'Maybe this is a time when Polly needs to be alone. Have you thought of that?'

'Of course I have. But I don't think that's the answer. I know Polly better than anybody knows her. She needs to believe that she's independent and self-sufficient. And she is. But only superficially. Inside she's all cream pudding. She's afraid to admit to me that she wants me to come there because then she'd have to admit it to herself. If there's no one to watch her suffer then she won't suffer. That's her theory. But that's madness.'

'What if Jack is in prison for twenty years and Polly stays there in Germany till he gets out, are you saying that you expect to stay with her for all that time?'

'Nobody can see that far ahead,' Bill said. 'I just plan to stay as long as it's necessary.'

The next day, after Bill talked with his father about his plans, Jesse telephoned Polly in Germany. That evening after dinner Jesse and Bill talked again.

'She doesn't want you to come, Bill. I think it's a damned generous and unselfish thing you want to do and Polly thinks so too, but it's not necessary, she says, and she doesn't want you to do it. She'd love you to come visit her during school breaks but she doesn't need anyone to stay with her.'

'I know what she says. She's said the same things to me.'

'Do you think she doesn't know what's best for her?'

'That's exactly what I think. She's telling us what she believes we want to hear. But it's not what I want to hear. I don't trust her assessment of the situation. I don't think she's the best judge of what she needs right now.'

'But *you* are. Is that it?'

'I'm not a doctor, Dad. Or a faith healer. I'm not saying that. But I love Polly more than anybody else in the world does. In some ways we're like one person. She senses things about me that nobody else knows anything about. And I do the same with her. We've always been like that. So when I say she needs me there, I know it's true. It doesn't matter what she says. Because I know the same things she knows.'

[8]

Not long after Jack's trial, Floyd and Valerie closed their house in Portugal and drove northward through Spain and France, Belgium and Holland and Denmark. Floyd had arranged for them to rent a house in the south of Norway, in a fishing village called Larvik. One evening, en route, as they were having dinner in their hotel in Copenhagen, Valerie said, 'Do you realize that you've given me a thousand reasons why you want to go to Norway and you never mention the real reason. You act as if I don't know what it is.'

'I don't know what you're talking about.'

'Of course you do. I'm the reason we're going. You think I need to be distracted. So you're providing an elaborate distraction. New places, new things to see.'

'Not true. I only do things for selfish reasons. The fact is I'm going to Norway to please myself. I've never been there and I hear it's a great country. Brave people. Tough Resistance fighters during the war. Drove the Occupation troops crazy. The Germans hated long-haired men so every man in Norway let his hair grow. Everybody wore red-knit caps as a symbol of defiance. When the Germans closed the theatres, the actors put on plays in people's homes, in church basements, and gymnasiums. And a lot of German soldiers ended up in Oslo harbour with their throats cut.'

343

'Don't try to get me off the subject when I'm saying something nice to you. You knew how upset I was about Polly so you decided to get me away from Praia da Rocha before I threw myself off the cliffs.'

Floyd shook his head. 'You're not the type. You're too vain to mess yourself up on a bunch of sharp rocks.'

'Never mind that. It's true, isn't it? Isn't that why we're going to Norway? To get my mind off Polly?'

'Let me put it this way. I thought it would be good for both of us to have a change of scenery.'

She smiled. 'Whatever you tell yourself, I know what you're doing and I appreciate it. Next time you're depressed *I'll* bundle *you* up and take you somewhere.'

'I never get depressed.'

'That's true. Is it because you're married to such an extraordinary woman?'

'It must be.'

'I'm going to be good now,' she said. 'You'll see. Every morning when I wake up and every evening before I go to sleep, I'll count my blessings. I'll eat a nutritious breakfast, I won't drink cognac at night because it keeps me awake and I will discharge the laundress if she puts starch in your shirts.' She reached across the table and put her hand on his. 'And I will do my very best to think good thoughts about Polly.'

It had been a pattern with them since their first days together. Valerie had said early on, 'We have a marvellous secret, an excellent device. We have a light-hearted approach to serious matters and we're deadly serious about nonsense.'

To some degree what she said was true. They believed that their most important concern was the care and feeding not of themselves but of whatever it was that they shared together. Both instinct and reason told them that if *they* stayed on course all other unpredicted storms could be weathered. They had come to believe that most problems can be solved and those that can't must be ignored.

Both of them realized, however, that for some time before Jack's trial, during it, and after it, Valerie had begun to take refuge in private corners of herself. A new kind of silence existed suddenly in their house. While no conflict or disagreement had in fact taken place there was all the same an ambience that suggested such an event. Valerie sat alone in the library, walked alone on the beach.

344

She was sleepless at night and she wept behind closed doors when she thought Floyd couldn't hear. There was a sense of unease that had no name, only a quiet and persistent presence.

Out of this condition, and quite abruptly, came Floyd's plan to drive to Norway.

The house in Larvik delighted them. It sat on high ground back up from the harbour, a great square bourgeois pile with dark woodwork, heavy carved doors, leaded windows, and an eight-foot stone wall surrounding house and garden. The kitchen and the bathrooms were new and gleaming but the rest of the house and its furnishings were from another century. Their bedroom jutted out from the second floor with windows on three sides and a wide veranda that overlooked the garden, and their bed was like a great ship at anchor with sculpted oak cornerposts, down pillows and duvet, and heavy drapes all round to keep out the cold and the morning light.

'What a lovely spot,' Valerie said as they toured the house with the estate agent. When he asked what staff they would require, she said, 'We'll need a gardener. And two people to come in and clean one day a week. that's all, I believe.'

'There's a cook available, of course. As well as a laundress and a housekeeper,' the agent said.

'I think not,' Valerie said. 'I'll be doing all that myself. If I find it's too much for me, we'll call on you later.'

When they were alone in the house after the agent left, Floyd said, 'You can't take care of this place by yourself.'

'Of course I can. That's what I'm good at. We can lock ourselves in behind these beautiful walls, the butcher and the baker and the greengrocer will make daily deliveries, and there'll be no sounds in the house except the sounds that *we* make.'

'You're going to clean up the kitchen and do the laundry?'

'Of course. I'm not helpless. I'll keep your bathroom sparkling as well, and the parlour dusted, and your shirts and pyjamas sweetly pressed and folded in deep drawers.'

'I'll never see you,' he said. 'You'll have a kerchief round your head and soap suds up to your elbows from morning to night. And by the time dinner's over you'll want to go straight to bed.'

'Exactly. What's wrong with that?'

'What about our indolent life? Breakfast in bed and someone to draw our hot baths. What about all that?'

'You won't feel deprived, I promise you.'

'Will you have callouses on your hands now and burn marks on your forearms?'

'Probably. But all the rest of me will stay exactly the same. You'll see. Remember when I came to meet you in Dublin and we went to our lovely Hotel Russell and closed the door behind us and never went outside for all those sweet days? Remember how fine it was to be alone? That's the way we'll be now. No footsteps in the house but ours. No voices. No discussions in the pantry. I'll take care of you and you'll take care of me and we'll be snug and warm and happy in this stuffy old neighbourhood of burghers' homes.'

'Isolation. Utopia. Escape from reality. Dangerous ideas,' Floyd said.

'Not dangerous at all. *Wonderful* ideas. Just right for us.'

[9]

Dorsey flew from London to Washington, DC, where she took a local flight to Waynesboro. There she rented a car and drove south to her son's school just outside the village of Cornwall. At the residence where Charlie had been living when she'd visited him last she was told that he had moved to another dormitory. 'The headmaster, Mr Seabury, asked me to send you to his office when you arrived. He'll take you to your son.'

There was nothing of the academic about David Seabury. He was compact and muscular. He had been a conference champion pole-vaulter in his undergraduate days and he still had the look and the movements of an athlete. Many parents who sent their boys to his school did so as a direct result of their meeting and talking with Seabury. Dorsey was one such parent. She'd had numerous discussions with him about Charlie and each one had left her with the feeling that her son was in good hands. This day, as soon as she sat down in his office she said, 'They tell me he's been moved to a new residence. Is there some problem?'

'No, I don't think so. He hasn't actually moved. He's just been spending a few days with Mr Rubington and his wife. Arthur Rubington is Charlie's history teacher.'

346

'I don't understand. You mean, he's moved to his teacher's house.'

'It's not a permanent thing. Mr Rubington's his faculty adviser and they've become friends. So we thought . . .'

'There is something wrong, isn't there? This isn't something you do ordinarily.'

'Not frequently,' Seabury said. 'But in some circumstances we've found it can be helpful.'

'Please tell me what's going on.'

'It's hard to say. Charlie doesn't seem to be eager to talk about it. As you know, your husband came to see him a few days ago, and since then . . .' He studied Dorsey's face for a moment. 'You knew Mr Mullet was here, didn't you?'

'Yes,' Dorsey said after a slight hesitation. 'Of course I know he was here. But they're shooting one of his films in Spain. He must have come straight from Madrid and flown back there. I haven't actually spoken with him since he came back.'

'I see,' Seabury said. Looking at him, she realized she hadn't reacted quickly enough. She knew he didn't believe her. 'Then you wouldn't know what they talked about,' he went on, 'that might have upset your son?'

'How is he upset? What did he say?'

'He hasn't said much of anything, I'm afraid. He's just ceased to function as a student. He refuses to attend classes. He's left the school grounds twice and gone into Lexington. He doesn't eat and he's been fighting with his schoolmates. So we thought a short spell with the Rubingtons might calm him down.'

'And has he calmed down?'

'We thought so until yesterday.'

'What happened yesterday?' Dorsey asked.

'He started a fire in a rubbish container in their garage.'

'My God. Where is he right now? I must see him.'

'That's another problem, I'm afraid. As soon as I got your message saying you were arriving this afternoon I walked over to the Rubingtons' to tell him. But when I saw him, he said . . . I'm sure he didn't really *mean* this . . . he said he didn't want to see you.'

'I can't believe that.'

'As I said, I don't think he means it. But he thinks he means it.

347

Are you sure you have no idea what he and your husband may have talked about?'

'No, I don't. But I'll find out as soon as I see Charlie. Is he still at the Rubingtons'?'

Seabury shook his head. 'He was quite agitated when I told him you were coming so Arthur and I put him in the car and drove him to the infirmary. Dr Bellson gave him a mild sedative and put him to bed.'

'He's in the hospital?'

'Just for a day or so. Till he settles down.'

'I can't believe we're talking about the same child. You make it sound as if he's out of control. Charlie's a sweet little boy. I've never heard of giving tranquillizers . . .'

'He was very upset. And I think you'll discover when you talk with him that whatever it is that's disturbing him has no connection with his teachers or his schoolmates.'

Charlie was sitting up in a chair, fully dressed, when Seabury and Dorsey walked into his infirmary room. As soon as he saw them he said to Seabury. 'I told you I didn't want to see her.'

'But she wants to see you. You'll have to straighten all that out with your mother.' He turned and left the room.

'Are you all right, sweetheart?' Dorsey said.

'I'm not sick if that's what you mean. I just don't want to talk to you.'

'That's the silliest thing I've ever heard. Why in the world are you acting this way?'

'I told you I don't want to talk about it.'

'Well, I want to talk about it. And I'm not going to leave here till we do.'

'That's up to you.'

'I flew all the way over here from London . . .'

'I didn't ask you to come. If you'd asked me I'd have told you not to come.'

'I can't understand what's come over you. And I don't like the way Mr Seabury's acting. Is there something wrong here at school? Something you haven't told me about?'

'No.'

'Because if there is, I'll take you out of here today and we'll find a new school. Is that what you want?'

'I don't care. Do whatever you want to.'

348

'What is it?' She took a handkerchief out of her bag and dabbed at her eyes.

'Don't start crying,' he said. 'What's the use of doing that?'

'I've known you all your life and I've never seen you like this. Can't you tell me what's the matter?'

He looked out the window and didn't answer. Finally she said, 'The headmaster told me your father came to see you.'

'Didn't you know it till he told you?'

'Oscar's been spending a lot of time in Spain. You know that.'

'Sure, I know it. I like Spain. I was there when he was making *Tarantula*. Remember? It's a great place. I wish I was there right now.'

'Well, maybe we can work it out so you can go there after your school term's over.'

'I'd rather go now. You just said you were taking me away from here.'

'Only if you don't like it. I mean, if they're not treating you the way they should . . .'

'They're treating me OK. Mr Rubington's a good guy. And I like his wife, too. She cuts her own hair and makes great pancakes.'

'What's wrong, Charlie? What did Oscar say to you when he was here?'

'Nothing.'

'What does that mean? You must have talked about something.'

'Why don't you ask him?'

'I'm asking you. Was he saying bad things about me?'

'Why would he do that?'

'I don't think he would. I'm just trying to find some reason why you're treating me like your worst enemy.'

'Think it over,' he said.

'What does that mean?'

'You're a smart lady, Mom. I'll bet if you really sit down and think about it you'll be able to figure it out.'

'Did Oscar tell you that he and I are having trouble?'

'Are you having trouble?' he asked.

'I wouldn't call it that exactly.'

'What would you call it?'

'I don't know. It's grown-up stuff. Nothing I'd want to dump on you.'

'You mean it doesn't concern me?'

349

'It *concerns* you. Of course it does. But it's nothing for you and me to talk about.'

'Why not?'

'It just isn't.'

'Then what makes you think Dad was talking to me about it?'

'I didn't say he was. I just asked what he said.'

'I don't want to talk about it, Mom.'

'Damn it, Charlie, we have to talk about it. You look at me as if you never want to see me again. Is that what you want me to think?'

'Maybe it's the other way around,' he said.

'What does that mean?'

'What do you think it means?'

'I don't know. That's what I want you to tell me.'

'Never mind. It's not important.'

'It is important. Nothing else is important. Stop playing games with me.'

'You're the one who's playing games,' he said. 'You said it's all grown-up stuff. Something you and I can't talk about.'

After a long moment she said, 'All right, let's start over. Did Oscar tell you we're talking about getting a divorce?'

'Is that what you're doing?'

'Yes.'

'You're talking about it or you're going to do it?' he asked.

'We're going to do it.'

'Is that what you came here to tell me?'

'Yes.'

'Well, you wasted a trip because Dad already told me.'

'Why in the world didn't you tell me that before?'

'I thought maybe he didn't get it straight. I wanted to hear it from you. Now I've heard it.'

'Is that the reason you told Mr Seabury you didn't want to see me? Is that the reason you've been cutting classes and leaving the school grounds and getting into fights?'

'I'm tired of talking about it, Mom.'

She started crying again. 'Jesus, Charlie, you could drive a person crazy. What are you trying to do to me? Do you think I'm happy about breaking up with Oscar? Do you think I'm doing it to make him feel bad? Or make you feel bad? Is that what you think?'

He sat looking at her, no expression on his face, and didn't answer.

'All kinds of things happen to people. Good stuff and bad stuff. Nobody gets married with the idea that they can always get a divorce if it doesn't work out. Nobody wants to fail. Not if they can help it. Because that's what a divorce is. Both people fail when a marriage breaks up. But it happens all the same. It happens quite a lot. You know that. Just because something ends, that doesn't mean that everything that went before was no good. Oscar and I haven't had a terrible life together. We haven't been mean to each other. And we've tried to give you the things you wanted and needed. I'm not sorry I married him and I'm sure he's not sorry either. But most things, even good things, don't last for ever. People change. Their ideas change. Their needs change. You'll see. Ten years from now you'll have friends your own age, maybe quite a few friends, who've been married and divorced already. You could even be one of them.'

'Oh, come on, Mom, don't hand me that philosophic stuff. I know why you want a divorce and so do you. You found another guy you like better than Dad.'

[10]

A few days before she left London to fly to Washington, DC, Dorsey had said to Rab, 'I don't know if I can go through with this.'

'Of course you can. You're going to visit your son at his school. That's all. You've done it many times before and you'll do it many times in future.'

'It's not that simple, Rab, and you know it.'

'Of course it's not simple. Because you're afraid to tell your son what you know you have to tell him. But you said it was important that he should have the news from you. So you should be happy you'll be seeing him before Oscar does.'

'I am. But I'm still paralysed by the thought of going there. I wish you could go with me.'

'So do I. But you said that's out of the question.'

'It is. We talked about it before. I can't take the chance. If Oscar found out about it he could use it against me. God knows what he might do.'

'You told me you weren't frightened of him.'

'Did I say that? I guess it's true. I mean, I'm not afraid to be in the same room with him. But I'm always wary of him. I never know what to expect. He's a manipulator. He does it in his business and he does it in his life. He keeps people off balance. He certainly keeps me off balance. When he's in Spain and I'm here, when I don't hear from him for a few days I always think he's cooking up something. I always expect a bad surprise. And especially now. I just wish you could be with me. I know you can't but I still keep wishing.'

When they met the next day, Rab said, 'I made your reservations at the Castle Rock Inn at Charlottesville. Two nights. I also made a reservation for John White at the Olde Forge Motel three miles west of Charlottesville.'

'What's all that about?' she said.

'I'm John White.'

'You can't be. We can't do that.'

'Yes, we can. I have some business to attend to in New York. I'm going over two days before you do. On the day you go to visit Charlie I'll fly down to Charlottesville and check in at my motel. Later, after you check in at your hotel, you can drive over to where I am.'

'Can we do that?'

'Of course we can. If someone wants to check up on me, I'm still registered at the Sherry-Netherland in New York. And you're staying at the Castle Rock in Virginia.'

'But what about when we go home?'

'I'll be leaving from New York and you'll be leaving from Washington.'

'You're so smart,' she said. Then she put her arms around him. 'But I can't spend the night in a motel with a stranger named John White. You'd never forgive me.'

'I'll never forgive you if you don't.'

It was late when she arrived at Rab's motel after leaving Charlie, driving to Charlottesville and registering at her own hotel. When he opened the door he could see she'd been crying.

'What happened?' he said.

'God, I'm glad you're here. I'm going crazy.'

They sat in his room and she told him everything that had happened that afternoon at Charlie's school, everything she'd said, everything he'd said.

'How was he when you left?' Rab asked.

'The same as he was when I arrived. He's so angry I couldn't believe it. He wouldn't tell me what Oscar told him but whatever it was it must have shook him up terribly. He just kept looking at me and not saying anything. Everything he did say I had to prise out of him.'

'Is he trying to keep you from divorcing Oscar? Is that it?'

'I don't know. I have no idea what's in his head. And the thing that really scares me is that I don't know what's in Oscar's crazy head either. It looks as if he's going to fight me for custody.'

'We talked about that before. You knew it was a possibility.'

'But now I'm sure of it. Why else would he race over here to see Charlie after we'd agreed that I should tell him we're breaking up? There's no other answer, is there? He wants Charlie. He wants to keep me from having him.'

'That may be what he's trying to do. But getting it done is another matter altogether.'

'What if Charlie tells the authorities he *wants* to live with Oscar? Then what?'

'He hasn't done that,' Rab said, 'and there's no guarantee that he will, no matter how nasty he seemed today. At his age, if he's not a little bit in love with his mother, there's something wrong with him. He doesn't want to hear that you're in love with somebody he's never heard of before. In his head you're not just leaving Oscar, you're leaving him. But that's a first reaction. He'll get used to the idea. Once he knows that he'll be seeing Oscar as often as he ever did he'll settle down and get on with his own life.'

'I hope you're right.'

'I went through this when my folks were divorced. It didn't affect me so much because I was a little older but my brother Bill was mad as hell. Didn't like the idea of his mother falling in love with a handsome young chap he barely knew. But he got over it.'

'Isn't he the one you told me was living with your father in America?'

'That's right.'

'Then maybe he didn't get over it after all.'

'I know what you're saying. But that's another matter. There are no hard feelings between Bill and our mother now.'

'I know you're trying to make me feel better and I know you're telling me the truth. Don't think I didn't tell myself all these things when I was driving up here tonight. I'm not looking for trouble, God knows. I do believe I could straighten things out between me and Charlie . . .'

'That's what I'm saying.'

'You didn't let me finish. I mean I could straighten things out if I didn't have Oscar to deal with. Oscar's a fanatic when he thinks someone may be getting the better of him. I've seen him in action. There's only one thought in his head . . . getting even. If he wants to get even with me, he knows the best way is through Charlie. He knows he can't stop me from divorcing him but if he can make me miserable in the process, that's what he'll do.'

Rab telephoned the bar then and had sandwiches and beer sent to the room. As they ate he turned on the television set and watched the ending of an old American film with the sound turned off.

'Is this a silent movie?' Dorsey asked.

'It is now. I just turned it into one.'

'If it's not worth listening to, why are we watching it?'

'I'm waiting to see a weather report. In New York they told me the weather might be bad tomorrow.'

'You're flying back to England tomorrow night?'

He nodded. 'That's what we agreed on, wasn't it?'

'I guess so. I just hate to have you leave.'

'You said you wanted me to be waiting for you when you come home.'

'I do. But I also want you here. You know me. I want everything.' Then: 'Why don't I fly back tomorrow too. Then we can meet each other in London. We can meet at Heathrow.'

'Sounds good to me. But I thought you were going back to the school tomorrow.'

'I don't think I can. I don't know if I can face it again.'

'Then you might as well go back to London.'

'I know that tone of voice,' she said. 'You think I *should* go back to the school tomorrow.'

'I think you should do whatever you think is best.'

'You're no help. I think it's best if I go back there and see Charlie again. But that's not what I want to do. What I want to do is run

354

away and hide with you.' When he didn't answer she said, 'So I'm going to stay. I'll fly back to London the day after tomorrow.'

When they were lying in bed later she said, 'Do you know I've never stayed in a hotel with anybody except Oscar? You notice I didn't even bring a toothbrush.'

'I brought you a toothbrush.'

'Do you always carry an extra toothbrush in case some strange lady tumbles into your bed?'

'A gentleman never answers a question like that.'

'If you were really a gentleman, you'd have brought me a night-gown, too,' she said.

'Count your blessings.'

Late that night, very late, the motel bar closed long since, no engines purring in the parking lot, the Virginia darkness soft and black and heavy. Rab woke up suddenly. It seemed he'd heard the click of a door closing. He sensed there was someone in the room. As he reached to turn on the bedside lamp a flashlight snapped on, its strong beam blinded him, and a muffled voice said, 'Don't make a sound. Don't get out of that bed and you won't get hurt.'

Rab felt the sheet and blanket being ripped off the bed then, and flashes from two cameras began to pop and crackle. In the hot light Rab could make out four people in ski masks, one on either side of the bed, two at the foot of the bed with cameras. When he tried to get up, something heavy hit him on the wrist and he was shoved back on the bed. When Dorsey screamed and tried to retrieve the blanket to cover herself, the man on her side snatched it away, struck her across the face and said, 'Shut your mouth or I'll put you to sleep.'

It ended as suddenly as it had begun. The flashes stopped, the door clicked shut and the men were gone. Outside, car doors opened and closed and tyres squeaked on the tarmac as a car pulled away.

'Oh my God,' Dorsey whispered. 'Oh, my *God*.' She lay face down on the bed, trembling, her fingers clutching the brasswork of the bedstead.

Chapter Eight

[1]

At the Charlottesville Hospital the young doctor in the emergency room told Rab his left wrist was broken. 'Not serious,' he said. 'It's just *above* the wrist actually. I'll put a light cast on it and it should heal up with no problem. You play golf?'

Rab nodded. 'But I'm not a fanatic. Don't have time to be.'

'Well, when you do find the time, you'll discover you can play as well as you ever did.'

He got back to his motel at nine o'clock in the morning. He'd been gone for an hour and forty-five minutes. When he unlocked the door and went inside, Dorsey wasn't there. He called her hotel then, and the switchboard lady said, 'Mrs Mullet asked us to hold her calls. She's sleeping. If you leave your number I'll have her get back to you.'

'You can ring her room,' he said. 'It's all right. She's waiting to hear from me.'

'I'm sorry, sir. Mrs Mullet said no calls whatsoever.'

Rab's first impulse was to drive directly to the Castle Rock Hotel. But remembering the state Dorsey had been in earlier that morning he decided it would be best to give her an hour or two to herself. He took a bath, shaved and put on fresh clothes. Then he ordered coffee and eggs to be sent to his room.

After he ate, he lay back on the bed and allowed himself to review the events of a few hours before. He couldn't bring things into sharp focus. The flash bulbs in the dark of the room, the masked figures, Dorsey's scream, were all cinematic and unreal to

356

him. Only the pain in his wrist gave it sharp reality. And Dorsey's near-cataleptic reaction after the men had gone. Her hands had fastened to the brass bars at the head of the bed. They seemed frozen there. She began to lose sensation in her hands and feet then, and she had difficulty breathing. Her face was flushed but her body was trembling and cold to the touch.

Rab was able at last to disengage her fingers from the bedstead. He carried her into the bathroom and put her into a tub of warm water. He forced her to sip some cognac, then he massaged her feet and hands and the back of her neck. When she began to breathe normally, when she stopped shivering, he rubbed her dry with a towel, wrapped her in a warm blanket, and carried her back into the room. 'Not in that *bed*,' she said. 'Let me sit up in a chair.'

She was very pale now, sitting straight and still in the upholstered chair, her hands hidden inside the blanket, her feet tucked under her. 'You look cold,' he said. 'Are you still cold?'

'No.'

She seemed, still, like a child who had lost her way. She avoided making eye contact. She looked down at the floor or raised her eyes slightly and stared at a blank space on the wall. Rab sat in another chair a few feet away. At last she said, in a low scratchy voice he could scarcely hear, 'When there's a war, sometimes a whole bunch of soldiers rape one poor woman, one after the other. I've read those stories. That's the way I feel. I feel dirty and ugly. I feel as if something was ripped out of me. I feel dead.'

'Why don't you lie down and try to sleep?'

'I can't. I couldn't. I couldn't lie on that bed.'

He sat there with her, both of them silent, until the first light began to edge in around the window shades. A radio went on softly in a room across the court, a car engine started. He hoped she would go to sleep but she didn't. She sat motionless in her chair staring at nothing. Finally, she began to talk.

'It was Oscar,' she said. 'You know that, don't you?'

'No, I don't know that.'

'I don't mean he was here in the room with us but he was behind it, no question about that. He put them up to it.'

Rab shook his head. 'One chance in a thousand, Dorsey. There are crazy people all over. We were just unlucky. Three or four of them focused on us.'

'Not a chance,' she said. 'Why would perfect strangers want to take pictures of us? What could they do with them? Those pictures are no good for anything except to prove that you and I were in bed together in a motel in Virginia.'

'I know you think Oscar can do anything he wants to but this is a little elaborate even for him.'

'Oh, no, it's not. That's his speciality . . . doing things nobody thinks he can do.'

'But what's the point?'

'You know the answer to that as well as I do. Do you think I can go into court to divorce him when I know he has those pictures in his hands.'

'You don't know that.'

'I know it, Rab, as surely as I know anything. But even if I didn't, even if I just suspected it, I'd be in the same fix. I should have known he wouldn't take it lying down when he found out about us. But, God, I didn't expect this.'

'It was an ugly thing to go through,' Rab said. 'I know how you feel. But it's not the end of the world. It isn't something we can't get past.'

'It isn't? How do I get past it? How do I get it out of my mind? How do I stop myself from wondering when those pictures are going to turn up? What do I say when they do?'

'Why would they turn up? What if you're right? What if Oscar did pay somebody to break in and take pictures of us in bed? What if the pictures are in the mail to him tomorrow? Do you think he plans to show them to all his friends or sell them to some naughty magazine?'

'No, I don't think that. It's not what he will do that scares me. It's what he might do. If he has the pictures he'll never even tell me he has them. He doesn't have to and he knows it. He's planted something in my head that will stay there till I die.'

Rab knelt down beside her chair and put his arms around her. 'In a few months we'll be married and none of this stuff will matter to either one of us.'

'God, how I wish that were true. All I want is for the two of us to run off and hide somewhere. But that's what we can't do. I can't do anything now except . . . I don't know what I can do. Yesterday at this time I thought my only problem was Charlie. Now I feel as if I don't even own myself any more. I feel as if those cameras swallowed me up and when they get ready they'll spit me out and I'll just be a dirty stain on some dirty sidewalk.'

Rab gave up trying to reason with her. Just before he went off to the hospital she said, 'I'll order some coffee and try to pull myself together. I'm ashamed of myself. You're the one who got hurt and I'm the one who's feeling sorry for herself.' But when he came back to the room she was gone.

When he drove to her hotel he didn't stop at the desk. He went straight up to her room. But when he tapped on the door, it eased open. The room was empty. No luggage, no toilet articles in the bathroom, no clothes in the closet. He picked up the phone and called the desk. 'I'm a friend of Mrs Mullet's. She asked me to meet her in room 234. That's where I am now but this room's empty. Can you tell me if she's moved to another room?'

A woman's voice said, 'Just a moment, sir. I'll check the registration desk.' A moment later: 'Mrs Mullet checked out earlier this morning.'

Rab went down to the lobby then, found a telephone booth, and called information for the number of Charlie's school. When he located the headmaster at last he said, 'This is the manager's office at the Castle Rock Hotel in Charlottesville. One of our guests, Mrs Oscar Mullet, left word with us that she could be reached today at your school. Can you tell me how we can locate her?'

'I'm afraid she's not here,' Seabury said. 'We had expected her but she called early this morning to say she had to fly back to London today.'

He called his office in London then. Rosalind said, 'I was just leaving for the day. Where are you?'

'Officially, I'm in New York. Actually, I'm in Virginia.'

'Actually, I knew that,' she said. 'Officially, I didn't.'

'I need some information. Call one of your chums at BOAC and check on their flights from Washington to London today.'

'Only one, I think. Eight o'clock tonight.'

'Well, check and see if Mrs Mullet's on the passenger list. I'll hang on.'

When Rosalind came back on she said, 'She was booked for the eight-o'clock flight but she cancelled. BOAC show her as transferred to TWA flight 400.'

'Leaving when?'

'Eleven-thirty a.m. Washington time. What time is it there now?'

'Eleven forty-five.'

'She must be on her way,' Rosalind said. Then: 'Is everything all right with you?'

'Nothing is all right. I've got a headache and a broken wrist and an urge to kill. Otherwise, all goes well.'

'You'd better come home.'

'I agree. Get me on the BOAC flight from New York tonight. And call Lord Hinson's office and make a date for me to see him on Tuesday.'

[2]

Ten days later in Madrid, Rab finally located Dorsey. Late one morning he went to the Hotel Alfonso and took the elevator to her apartment on the fifth floor.

'La senora no está aqui,' the manservant at the door said. He tried to block the entrance but Rab pushed past him. 'If the senora *no esta aquia,'* he said, 'then the senor will wait for her.'

'Pero no es posible, Senor.'

'Es posible,' Rab said. Then he called out. 'Senora . . . you have a caller. A guest. A friend.'

When Dorsey appeared in the doorway of the reception room she said to the servant, *'Todo va bien, Miguel. Gracias.'* As soon as the man left the room she said, 'You can't come here like this.'

'Of course I can. And unless you want Miguel to hear everything I have to say, you'd better find us a room with doors we can close.'

'What in the world are you doing?'

'What the hell do you think I'm doing? I'm trying to bring you back to your senses. Did you think I'd just roll over and play dead after you skipped away from Virginia like a gypsy?'

'Can't I meet you somewhere?' she said. 'Away from here. So we can talk?'

'I don't trust you. Let's say what we have to say right here.'

She led him down a long hallway lined with flowers to a bright sunny room that looked out across the Retiro gardens. When she closed the door behind them she said, 'How did you know Oscar wasn't here?'

'I didn't. I was hoping he would be. It would save me a trip to Montehormoso.'

'He's not there either.'

'Yes, he is. I talked to his office in London. They even gave me his phone number.'

'What is happening to you? What are you trying to do to me?'

'That's not the question. The question is, "What are you doing to yourself?" '

'I'm doing what I have to do. I've made up my mind. If you care anything about me . . .'

'Spare me *that*, for Christ's sake. I've already seen that movie.'

'I mean it,' she said. 'You can't accomplish anything. You can't change anything. All you can do is hurt *me*. Make things impossible for *me*.'

'Are you telling me things aren't impossible for you now? Did you suddenly change identity?'

'No. I suddenly realized that I couldn't win. That we can't win. I was crazy to think we could.'

'What are you talking about? What does that mean?'

'It means that Oscar won. He always wins.'

'Are you telling me that you've decided to settle down and spend the rest of your life with that son of a bitch? Are you saying you have no choice?'

'I didn't decide anything. I just did what I had to.'

'You said that before. Who says you had to? I say you don't have to. I say you can do what you like. What have you and I been talking about these past few months?'

'We were dreaming. And it was my fault as much as yours. More. Because I know Oscar. I should have realized . . .'

'Will you stop talking about that bastard as if he were some kind of all-powerful being? He's not. He never was. He's a second-rate movie producer who knows how to chisel and manoeuvre and make money. Nobody in the business thinks he's important. Nobody takes him seriously. Nobody even trusts him. Nobody but you. You, of all people.'

'You can talk as much as you like. You can say anything you want. But it won't change anything.'

'Are you telling me to get back on a plane and fly back to London?'

'Don't make it tougher on me, Rab. Do you think I like things

361

the way they are? Do you think I've lied to you all this time we've been together? It kills me to have to give you up.'

'Then don't do it. You don't have to. We don't have to. What do you think I've been talking about? What do you think you accomplished by leaving Virginia without telling me you were going? Was that supposed to be some message you were sending me?'

'I was too miserable to send any message. All of a sudden I couldn't bear to see you and talk to you when I knew . . .'

'When you knew what? You're talking like a crazy woman. You're not a prisoner. You didn't sell yourself into bondage for the rest of your life. You got married. So what? A lot of people get married. Some of them stay that way and a lot of them don't. Nobody your age says, "All right, I made a mistake. Now I have to live with it." '

'I'm not saying that. I'm not saying anything. There's nothing I can say. Don't act as if you don't know what I'm talking about. We went over it all before we left London. And we talked about nothing else when we were in Virginia. Do you think anything's changed since then?'

'Of course I do. The big change is that you've given up on us and gone back to your husband.'

'Not by choice, Rab. You know that.'

'No. I don't know that. That's why I'm here. Look . . . I know what a jolt it was, that whole crazy business in Charlottesville. I know how you felt. I know how you still feel. But that will go away . . .'

'Never.'

'Yes, it will. I mean it won't disappear completely but the edges will wear off. It won't hurt so much. And after a while it won't hurt at all. I promise you.'

She stood by the window looking down at her hands and didn't answer.

'Do you think you make it better – that night with those freaks and their cameras – by trying to stay with Oscar? Do you still think he was responsible for that?'

'Don't you?'

'It doesn't matter what I think. The point is this. How do you think you can go on living with him when you know that he

362

humiliated you like that? Can you just forgive him and forget the whole thing?'

'No, I can't. You know I can't. It makes me sick just thinking about it. I mean it makes me physically ill. If I were capable of killing anyone, I'd kill Oscar. But I'm not capable of that. There are all kinds of things I can't do. I never told you I was strong. I'm not strong at all. I'm scared to death of almost everything.'

'You told me once you weren't afraid of him.'

'I'm not. But I'm scared of what he can do.'

'How in the name of God can you live with someone like that?'

'You're not dumb, Rab. You know the answer to that question. I have no choice.'

'He has a hold on you?'

'God, does he have a hold on me.'

'For life? Is that what you're saying?'

'I never use that expression. I'm afraid of that, too.'

'What we're talking about is your son. Isn't that right?'

'You know that's what I'm talking about. I've never lied to you about that.'

'That's right. You haven't. You've always told me how much you love him and how important he is to you.'

'It changed my whole life, having him.'

'I'm surprised you don't keep him with you. It must be tough for you, having him away at school most of the time.'

'I hate it. I've always hated it. But in the beginning, when I was first married to Oscar, when I was grateful to him for giving Charlie and me a nice secure life, I felt as if I owed him something. I didn't think I could just stay home with my kid while my husband always had to be off somewhere, away from home a good part of the time. So we fell into a pattern of nurses and governesses and housekeepers and tutors. Charlie was healthy and happy and did well with his school work so it was easy for me to think I was doing the best thing for him. But if I had it to do over again I'd never be away from him. Either I would stay home or I'd take him with me.'

'Let me ask you something,' Rab said then. 'Do you think you have to do what's best for your son even if it's terrible for you?'

'Yes.'

'When he's twenty-five years old, if you told him you'd sacrificed your own happiness for his, if he knew you'd stayed married to Oscar only because of him, how do you think he'd react?'

363

'I don't know. And I'll never know. Because I would never tell him. Besides, this isn't his problem, it's mine. I have to do what I think is right.'

'All right. Let me ask you something else. All the time you and I have been together, did you know what you're telling me now?'

'I didn't know anything. I didn't think or remember or plan anything. I was afraid to. All I knew was that I loved you. I didn't want it to end. I still don't want it to end. Do you think it's easy for me to say the things I've been saying to you? All I want to do is kiss you so much we can't talk. All this talk is like a knife in my throat. It's not hard for me to know what I want. But I want two things. I want two people. And I can't have them both.'

Rab smiled at her. 'You are really strange, do you know that? You get an idea in your head and you repeat it a few times and pretty soon you start to believe it's God's law. Do you think I'm just going to sit here and nod my head and agree with you? If you do, you don't know me at all. I've got too much time invested in you to let you get away now.'

'I wish you'd get angry,' she said. 'If you're sweet to me I'll collapse on the floor and bawl my eyes out.'

'Go ahead. It might be good for you. Get those wax-museum ideas out of your head.'

'Maybe I am getting a little crazy. I think that sometimes.'

'You're not crazy. You're just like a dog that can't be trusted off its leash. Every time you see a shadow you run off and hide.'

'I told you. I'm scared of everything.'

'You're not afraid of me. And you have to get the idea out of your head that Oscar's real name is Svengali. He's no match for you, in any way, if you'd just take hold of yourself.'

'God, how I wish that were true.'

'Trust me. It's true. What did he say when you came down here to Madrid?'

'He said he was glad to see me.'

'Was he surprised?'

'Didn't seem to be. He's never surprised. That's his trick. Very few things get a reaction from him.'

'Did he tell you he'd been to Virginia?'

'No.'

'Did he ask what happened when you talked to Charlie?'

'No.'

'He didn't say anything about me or the divorce?'

She shook her head. 'He acted as if we'd never talked about it.'

'And you didn't say anything either?'

'Nope.'

'Two ghosts in the spook house,' Rab said. 'What did you talk about?'

'It was as if we'd planned all along that I'd come down here. I called before I left London and he called back and said he'd have somebody meet me at the airport.'

'No mention of the four crazies breaking in and taking pictures of us?'

'God, no. I'd never give him the satisfaction of mentioning that.'

'And no conversation about Charlie?'

'Of course we talked about him.'

'But no mention of the fact that Oscar had seen him just a few days before?'

She shook her head and Rab said, 'How do you play games like that? The last time you saw him you told him you were in love with me and wanted a divorce.'

'He knew when I showed up in Spain that the situation had changed.'

'Without talking about it?'

'I didn't want to talk about any of that stuff and neither did he. When a situation's really terrible, the less you talk about it, the better.'

'What is that – the Gospel according to Samuel Goldwyn?'

'Maybe. There are lots of odd people in California. Strange habits develop. Unquiet drifting.'

'So where do you go from here? Second honeymoon? A mature understanding?'

'Don't be nasty. We go nowhere. We're simply back where we started. Status quo. He knows what I think of him. But he also knows I'm stuck. Charlie's *my* son but he's Oscar's trump card.'

'Let me ask you something,' Rab said then. 'What if Oscar came to you next week and said *he* wanted a divorce? What if he said he wanted to marry some young actress? What would you do?'

'I'd put a carnation in his lapel and call him a taxi.'

'I'm serious.'

'So am I. Since I don't give a damn for him anyway, why would I want to keep him if he wanted to leave?'

365

'You mean you'd agree to a divorce?'

'Of course.'

'What about Charlie?'

'What about him?'

'You've been telling me that you can't divorce Oscar because of your son. Are you saying now that if he divorces you it's all right?'

'It might not be all right but it's very different. Oscar, when he wants something, is not at all the same as when someone wants something from him. When he's trying to win he can be almost kind. Even generous. In those circumstances I'm sure he'd give me anything I asked for.'

'But how about Charlie? Wouldn't it be just as bad for him no matter who wanted the divorce?'

'Not at all. Because Oscar would present it to him in a way that would make it sound wonderful. I'm sure he'd tell him that I'm an angel and he's not good enough for me. Then he'd offer him a summer job on one of his pictures and pretty soon everything would be arranged.'

'Charlie wouldn't worry that you might be upset?'

'He'd know I wasn't upset. He'd be able to tell by looking at me. Besides, Charlie's a male chauvinist like most little boys his age. He's trying very hard to be a man so he sees everything from a male point of view. I'm sure he thinks that if I divorce Oscar, he might lose his father. But if Oscar divorces me it would be another situation altogether. Charlie would then be spoiled by both of us.'

'Is that what he wants, to be spoiled?'

'That's what everybody wants. But we don't think it's nice to admit it. Children, however, don't worry about being nice. They use their full energies trying to get what they want. And Charlie's no exception to that.'

'Don't you think you and I could give him anything Oscar can give?'

'Of course I do. But Charlie doesn't know that.'

'Why don't you tell him?'

'I can't. I don't know what Oscar's said to him and I don't know what he'll say in the future. I never know what he'll say or do. And I couldn't go through anything like those crazy men in Charlottesville . . . I mean even the thought of something like that happening again is . . . it makes me shiver just to think about it.'

'So we're locked in a room with no doors or windows. Is that it?'

'You're not. But I am.' She slumped down in a chair then and put her face in her hands. Rab took a step toward her, then stopped. He stood there looking at her for a long hollow moment. Then he turned and left the room, closing the door behind him. An hour later he was driving through the outskirts of Madrid, heading south-west toward Montehormoso.

[3]

'Too bad you can't drive out to the set with me tomorrow,' Mullet said. 'We've built a western town that would knock your eyes out. A dead ringer for Tombstone, Arizona, in 1860. We've got an Italian art director who's a miracle-worker. I had to cough up a lot of money to get him and pay a bribe to Fellini besides, but the guy is worth it. When he puts a set together you've got something you can shoot. He's saved me ten times his salary already on production costs and camera time. You sure you can't stay over and see how we shoot a twelve-million-dollar picture on a two million-dollar budget?'

Rab shook his head. 'Afraid not. I have to be back in London tomorrow.'

It hadn't been an unexpected visit. Before leaving London, Rab had called Mullet's office and asked them to tell him he'd be in Montehormoso the following Tuesday. All the same he was surprised by the way Oscar greeted him. It was like an open and friendly meeting between two business associates whose activities had prevented them from seeing each other for some time.

'When I was your age,' Oscar said, 'I used to think all a producer had to do was find properties, hire a director and a writer, raise money, make deals for actors, get the picture made, and sell it. What a mistake that was. I'm out there in the dust and the mud and the horse manure every day like a two-bit wrangler. And you know something? If I wasn't there, every picture I've ever done would have gone fifty percent over budget. I don't yell at people. I don't have to. I'm just there. Standing around. Making a few notes, talking to the crew. And believe me, everybody's concentration is immensely improved.'

367

They'd met for a drink, late afternoon, in the hotel bar. Rab had carefully planned what he would say to Mullet and how he would say it. But only when Oscar said, 'My people in London said you were flying down here to talk to me about something important,' did Rab make his opening remarks.

'I'm not sure that I should be doing this,' he said. 'The fact is I have some information I probably shouldn't have, based on a conversation with a government official, a director of the Exchequer.'

'That sounds like an income-tax man to me.'

'They refer to themselves as collectors of national revenues.'

'I hope you're not saying they were asking questions about me.'

'It didn't start out that way. I asked for the meeting, as a matter of fact. The gentleman in question is an old friend of my family. I needed some information about the international aspects of my own company. My accountants and solicitors normally handle these matters but sometimes I like to get more direct information. We examined some pretty intricate details about structure and liability and how the tax codes for the different countries try to accommodate each other. I don't have to tell you, it's a complex set of rules and guidelines and headaches. The more you learn, the less you know. At least that's the way it seems to me. I suppose that's why solicitors claim such high fees.'

Rab was deliberately taking his time, trying to lure Mullet into the conversation, waiting for him to ask a question. He was careful that the facts he was giving should not sound like a rehearsed narrative. At last, Mullet responded. 'Did I understand you to say he was asking questions about me?'

'That's what I was coming to. After he'd examined some of the problems I'd brought up about my company, after he'd made some specific suggestions as to how we should proceed, he started telling me, in some detail, about what we should avoid. He said that there are all kinds of loopholes, legal and financial, in international business codes, that some companies make a practice of finding those loopholes and exploiting them. He says it's not unusual for an organization to set up a branch in England, or Ireland, or almost any country other than their own, for the sole purpose of taking advantage of loan programmes, guarantees against loss, and tax credits that they are technically, but not legally, entitled to. In three or four years, these operations, if they're clever, can fleece their home governments as well as a host government, out of hundreds of thousands of dollars. Millions sometimes. He mentioned my business, the film business, as a prime offender. A great deal of money involved, no heavy assets, units of production that begin and end in a comparatively short time, and clever bookkeepers. While certain branches of the British government encourage foreign film units because of the production moneys they bring in, the people in the Exchequer are always alert against being fleeced. And they are fleeced, my friend said, with great regularity. He was mentioning several examples of companies who had taken advantage of British residence, who had profited and were continuing to profit in illegal ways and he mentioned a film of yours, that love story you shot in Wales a couple of years ago. What was it called?'

'*Water's Edge*.'

'That's it.'

'Did he say anything specific about me? Did he mention my name?'

'No. Not at first. But when I said I knew something about the company that made that film he asked if I knew you and I said yes, I did. I told him you were a well-known producer and that you'd made pictures all over the world for quite a few years.'

'Then what?'

'This is the part you won't like,' Rab said. 'He said they're starting an investigation of you and your company, that they're planning to freeze all your funds in British banks and subpoena your financial records.'

'Jesus Christ.'

'He also said they'd be sending an investigator to interview me.'

'What can you tell him?'

'Nothing. I explained that to him. But he said he's been ordered to question all your business associates and friends.'

'Ordered by whom?'

'His superior, I expect.'

'What the hell is going on here? Who is this guy?'

'I can't tell you his name. It wouldn't help you if I did.'

'Why not?'

'He wouldn't talk to you or any of your representatives. He only told me because he thought he could trust me. I'm violating a confidence in telling you.'

'Yeah, well, I appreciate that,' Mullet said.

'I didn't decide to tell you because I think you're vulnerable. I just thought it might be helpful if you had some lead time to get your accounts in order.'

'How the hell do these things get started? Do they just pull names out of a hat?'

'I asked him that. He says they're constantly examining tax records, especially for international companies or Americans in residence in England. But in the biggest cases, it's usually someone in the company who gives them inside information.'

'Bookkeepers?'

'Usually someone more important. Has anybody in your firm resigned lately. Someone in a position to see financial records?'

Mullet nodded. 'Hugh Mayberly. Six weeks ago.'

'I'm surprised to hear that. How did I miss that news?'

'We didn't spread it around. We had a disagreement about policy. Nothing serious, I thought. But he resigned.'

'Sorry to hear that,' Rab said. 'Hugh's a good man.'

'A little too deliberate for my operation. Sometimes we have to make fast decisions.'

'He comes from a family of solicitors. He doesn't like to make mistakes.'

'He made a big mistake if he turned me in to the authorities. I'll take his ass to court.'

'It doesn't work that way,' Rab said. 'Any direction the Exchequer gets from an outside source is totally confidential. They don't accept allegations of guilt. They only investigate suggestions that some company may be in violation of a statute. Any decision they make is based entirely on their own investigations.'

'What am I supposed to do now?'

'There's not much you can do except wait. They'll get in touch with you. I'm not telling you this because I assume you have something to hide. But one always likes to bring the ledgers up to date when someone's going to inspect them.'

'I can't get my mind off Mayberly. He's the last guy I'd expect to pull a trick like this.'

'I agree. It's not his style at all. You say he resigned? You didn't discharge him?'

'Hell, no. He just quit. He never really approved of me. I paid him a lot of money but he didn't like my way of doing business.

370

He used the word "principle" a lot. He'd spend half a day going over a contract.'

'Well, whatever reason he had for leaving, I don't think he would have tried to cause you trouble. How about the Feaster Brothers? Have you had any dealings with them lately?'

'Not if I can help it. I don't even like to be seen with those two.'

'Have you ever told them that?'

'Worse than that. Lots of times. But those birds couldn't do me any damage. Any deals I made with them were cash and carry. They don't know beans about my business.'

'They don't have to. All they have to do is turn you in. Then the burden of proof is on you.'

'Jesus, I thought this was a civilized country. All of a sudden I feel as if I'm back in Los Angeles.'

'I hope you don't think I'm interfering in your business. I just felt this was something you should know.'

'No question about it. I appreciate it. Nobody wants a joker in a derby hat showing up at the office unannounced. I mean, I'm an honest guy but we all bend the rules once in a while. I'm going upstairs now to call my people in London. They'll get the books in order in no time.' He stood up and said, 'I'm buying dinner tonight. You'd never guess it but there's a pretty good restaurant in this burg. Great beef. And shrimp the size of your fist. I'll meet you here in the bar at seven-thirty and we'll walk to the restaurant. After we eat, we'll go look at the dailies.'

[4]

When they'd finished eating dinner, when they were having cognac and a cigar, Rab said. 'I didn't fly all the way down here just to tell you that you're going to be examined by the Exchequer. I'm sure you figured that out.'

'I admit it occurred to me.'

'I want to talk about Dorsey.'

'That occurred to me, too.'

'We both know that a lot has been going on. But I'm not good at playing peek-a-boo. I like to know where I stand.'

371

'So do I.'

'I thought it might clear the air if I tell you what I want and you tell me what you want.'

'What about what Dorsey wants?' Mullet said.

'We'll get to that later. We'll start with you. What do you want?'

'I want what I've got.'

'That figures. What I want is for Dorsey to get a divorce. I love her and I want to marry her. I guess she told you that, didn't she?'

'Yes, she did.'

'And she said you agreed.'

'Not exactly. But it's hard to have a reasonable discussion with a woman who's decided she doesn't want to live with you any longer.'

'What made you change your mind? About the divorce, I mean.'

'I didn't,' Mullet said. 'She changed her mind.'

'Did she tell you that?'

'She didn't have to. When she flew down here after she came back from America I figured it out for myself.'

'You know why she came back, don't you?'

'I didn't ask and she didn't tell me.' He smiled like a benevolent fox. 'I guess she decided she couldn't live without me.'

'Let me ask you something,' Rab said. 'Why did you go see her son?'

'Our son,' Mullet said.

'Dorsey said you'd agreed that she should tell him about the divorce.'

'We did agree. But I changed my mind. Nothing sinister about it. I fly over to see Charlie every chance I get. I see him more often than Dorsey does. I always have.'

'But you did tell him about the divorce.'

'I didn't plan to,' Mullet said. 'That's not the reason I went to see him. But I've always tried to be honest with Charlie. So I didn't feel right about keeping it to myself.'

'Dorsey said he was upset about it.'

'I'm surprised to hear that. He took it pretty well when I told him.'

'Very angry with her. Blamed her for the whole thing, she said.'

'He's very close to his mother,' Oscar said.

'She says he's very close to you.'

'I hope she's right. He certainly means a lot to me.'

'You told him about me, I take it.'

Mullet made a limp gesture with one hand. 'He asked me why we were getting a divorce so I told him the truth.'

'Have you asked yourself why Dorsey had a change of heart suddenly?'

'When something good happens to me I don't question it. Bad stuff is something else. I do everything I can to change *that*.'

'You never asked yourself any questions when she suddenly showed up in Madrid?'

'Not really. I suppose I thought that something had gone wrong between the two of you.'

'Not exactly,' Rab said. 'The truth is Dorsey's afraid she'll lose her son. She thinks you'd fight her to get custody.'

'She's right about that. I would. I can't keep her from doing whatever she likes but I don't intend to give up Charlie.'

'She feels the same way.'

'I'm not surprised,' Mullet said.

'So in a situation like that, divorce looks impossible, doesn't it?'

'I don't think so. Couples have custody battles all the time.'

'But if one takes place between you and Dorsey, you're confident you'd win. Isn't that true?'

'Let's just say I would try very hard to win.'

Rab took a sip of cognac. Then: 'Did she tell you what happened when she went to Virginia?'

'No.'

'And you didn't ask her?'

'No.'

'No curiosity?'

'I have curiosity about everything,' Mullet said. 'I'm a curious man. But, as I think I told you, I was married several times before Dorsey. And I learned a few things. Most important, a man should never ask his wife a question if he doesn't already know the answer.'

'Did she tell you I was in Virginia when she was there?'

'No.'

'Does that surprise you?'

'No.'

'Dorsey said nothing ever surprises you,' Rab said.

'Did she mean that as a compliment?'

'I don't think so.'

373

'I suppose not.' Then: 'I assume that Dorsey knows you and I are having this heart-to-heart talk.'

'No, she doesn't.'

'Am I supposed to keep it a secret?'

'That's up to you,' Rab said. 'I plan to tell her in any case. You can do whatever you like.'

'I'm not sure how I'm supposed to respond. What brought all this on, this notion that you and I should confide in each other?'

'You and Dorsey seem to feel that a lot of things are better left unsaid.'

'Almost everything is better left unsaid.'

'I don't agree,' Rab said. 'In a situation like this it's important for people to know where they stand.'

'It's simple, isn't it? Dorsey and I are married and you want her to be unmarried so she can marry you.'

'It's not quite that simple. She wants to be unmarried, too, but she's afraid of the consequences.'

'Dorsey's afraid of a great many things. If she has a weakness, that's it. You should have known her when I met her. It was almost clinical. Fear. She was crippled by it. She had the same symptoms even when she wasn't quite sure what it was she was frightened of. New York was a nightmare for her. It still is. She hates to go there. She was much better after I took her to California. But before we left there, she had a whole new set of fears. She saw a rat in a palm tree one day – that's a common occurrence in a place where they grow palm trees – and she was ready to move and sell the house.'

'I don't blame her. Who wants to see a rat in a palm tree?'

'Nobody, I suppose. But when the condition exists, it's something you have to adapt to.'

'And if you're in danger of losing custody of your child, you may have to adapt to . . . you know what I'm saying.'

Mullet smiled his fox smile. 'If you're comparing me to a rat in a palm tree, I object.'

'If she didn't tell you I was in Virginia, then you don't know what happened to us while we were there.'

'No, I don't. But I have a feeling you're about to tell me.'

Rab turned back the cuff of his jacket to show the light cast on his left wrist. 'What happened to you?' Mullet asked.

'Some men broke into our hotel room in the middle of the night.

One of them cracked me on the wrist with a steel rod. While he was doing that, his friends were busy taking flash photos of Dorsey and me. You didn't know about that?'

'How would I know if she didn't tell me?'

'Dorsey thought you might have some independent knowledge of the event. So did I. We couldn't imagine who else would want photographs of us in bed.'

'Why would I want pictures like that? I certainly know what Dorsey looks like and I'm sure you won't be surprised to learn that I have no curiosity at all about how you look in your night-shirt. Do you wear a night-shirt?'

'No.'

'What happened after these guys left? Did you call the police?'

'No.'

'If somebody broke in on me in the middle of the night and cracked a bone in my arm, I'd have had the police there in five minutes.'

Rab shook his head. 'No, you wouldn't. Not in our situation.'

'It must have scared the hell out of Dorsey.'

'She was in a bad state.'

'Well, it sounds pretty awful to me. I'd hate to go through something like that myself. But I'm still not sure why you're telling me about it.'

'I told you. I think it's time we put things out in the open.'

'And I told you what I think about that. What good does it do? What's the point?'

'The point is this. I want you to know why Dorsey came back to you. She did it because she's frightened. She's afraid she'll lose her son and now she's afraid of what you might do with those pictures that were taken of us.'

Mullet chuckled. 'You don't believe that, do you?'

'I believe Dorsey. She knows you better than I do.'

'I wouldn't even put a scene like that in a film, let alone set it up in real life.'

'I'm telling you what she thinks and how she feels. It's real for her whether it's real for you or not.'

'So you're telling me I have a wife by default?'

'That's right. She's so mixed up she doesn't know where she is right now. But she'll get over it.'

'You think so?'

'I'm sure of it.'

'Then what?'

'Then we'll see what happens,' Rab said.

As they walked out of the dining room, Mullet said, 'I'm still not quite sure why you flew all the way down here to see me.'

'Friendly gesture. When a man's going to be investigated by the Exchequer the least you can do is give him a bit of warning.'

'Don't think I don't appreciate that. I do. But I can't help thinking that was a secondary reason for the trip.'

'No question about it. I wanted to talk to Dorsey and I wanted to talk to you.'

'Another friendly gesture?'

'Not at all. Where Dorsey's concerned, you and I are adversaries.'

'I thought you might say "enemies".'

'Not yet,' Rab said. 'It depends on how you behave.'

When he got back to London, he wired two dozen roses to Dorsey in Madrid. He enclosed a note.

As far as I'm concerned the war is on. You can stop playing games and dodging shadows now. I told Oscar everything there is to tell. Now it's up to you. You can't spend your life with him just because you're frightened. I know you need some time and I'll give you all the time you need. Within reason. I love you and I'm impatient for us to start *our* life.

Rab.

[5]

'I always thought you were the sane and steady one in our family. Rab and I were the lunatics,' Polly said, 'Now it turns out that you're the dottiest Bradshaw of all.'

'Not true,' Bill said. 'I'm just a smashing good Samaritan and a loving brother.'

'But I don't need a good Samaritan.'

'Maybe not. But every woman needs a loving brother.'

I didn't believe you when you said you were coming here to live with me. When I told Jack he didn't believe it either. Then before I knew it, there you were, on the doorstep.'

'A foundling,' Bill said.

'That's it. Rosy cheeks and swaddling clothes.'

Bill's instincts, it turned out, had been correct. Although she didn't admit it, even to herself, his presence made a great difference to Polly. Without trying, he pulled her outside herself. He was a living reminder of where she'd come from and what she'd been, what her life had been like before coming to Heidelberg from England. By simply being there, being in residence, he changed the rhythm of her days, forced her to be engaged in a world apart from Jack, apart from her own anxieties.

Polly was, had always been, a positive and good-humoured young woman. Her unpredictable life with Jack, more sorrow than joy, accompanied, even symbolized perhaps, by the mournful sounds of his cello, had fundamentally altered those original characteristics, obliterated them, she sometimes felt. Laughter had not been a major part of Jack's life or of her life with him. The world according to him was dark and dank indeed, and his views, to a marked degree, became her own. All this had been brought into painfully sharp focus by his arrest and trial. And his removal to the grey prison at Wurzburg had made that colour, *grey*, a screen through which she viewed everything about her.

She did not feel sorry for herself. Her upbringing did not permit that. The women she'd grown up with, Valerie and Clara, had presented no such pattern to emulate. The pain she felt was for Jack, not for herself. But that pain was real and omnipresent and gave no sign of being diluted by either time or philosophy. Her situation, she felt, her frame of mind, were things that could not be changed. There was no masochism in her, however. She did not delight in her no-exit future. She simply accepted and endured it and, continually measuring her own situation beside Jack's, felt guilty about her comparative good fortune.

It was a cocoon life to which she had assigned herself, parenthetical and walled away from everything that had gone before, a kind of weightless suspension over a deep gorge, one that she expected never to explore. Not allowing herself to think about what might come or what had gone before, she also took no pleasure from the present. Like the co-operative patient of a sensible and responsible psychiatrist, she structured daily routines for herself that would occupy her totally. Dismissing the cleaning woman she had employed before, and the laundress, she took on those duties herself. Scheduling herself, she made an elaborate chart of her tasks and her hours, filling every day with physical activity. She put up a time-plan on the wall of her kitchen and studied it each morning as she had breakfast.

In this new work-scheme she had devised, there were no insignificant duties. Each task was approached with the attitude that it was critical. She used all her energy and skill, and where new skills were required, she learned them. After breakfast each morning she tidied up her kitchen, bathed, and dressed herself. Then she went out, did her errands, and shopped for the grocery items she needed for her lunch. She tried, weather permitting, to shop twice each day, buying each time the precise amounts she would need for the next meal.

Her apartment was large, six rooms, so she developed a routine of cleaning one room each day. Each room was thoroughly scrubbed, dusted and polished every week. And there was always time scheduled for laundry, pressing and mending, and polishing silver. Late in the afternoon, on the way home from shopping for her dinner, she stopped every day for five o'clock mass in the Catholic church just down the street from her home. She had not attended church since she was a schoolgirl in England. Jack had been ferocious on the subject of all organized worship. But since he'd been taken to Wurzburg she had sat, for a few minutes each day, in the cool darkness of her neighbourhood church.

She had described her routine to Jack when she'd visited him in prison, leaving out her church visits; he had found it hugely amusing.

'What are you doing, turning yourself into an automaton? Is that all you learned from me? I mean, is that the way your pendulum swings once I'm out of the house? You're betraying me, you baggage. I'm the prophet of profligacy. Do nothing that doesn't give you pleasure and do that a lot. You'll find no hair shirts in my wardrobe. You're rich, for Christ's sake. You're filthy rich. You should surround yourself with servants, smoke expensive Turkish cigarettes . . .'

'I don't smoke.'

'So you'll start. That's my point. Guzzle Dom Perignon and Lafitte Rothschild. Sleep under a sable duvet. Drive a Jaguar. Or better still, hire some Kraut to drive you. I know you're killing time, waiting for me to die . . .'

'Don't say that.'

' . . . or get out of prison. You know how I feel about that. I thought you were crazy to live with me but to live like a nun by yourself while I rot here in jail is lunatic behaviour.'

'I don't want to discuss it,' Polly said. 'You've told me your views before. I'm not interested.'

'I know you're not but you should be. I know you'll never find another man like me but at least you should find somebody.'

'Very boring, Jack. I'm not amused.'

'Lunacy. Like I said. I can't accept it.'

'You have no choice.'

'I don't accept that either. But I'll win that debate later. For now, I'm insisting that you break out a little.'

'I have. I go to the cinema twice a week, to a concert once a week, and I eat in restaurants. Lunch on Tuesdays. Dinner on Thursdays and Sundays.'

'That's what I mean. You're turning yourself into a fucking robot. Every minute accounted for. I'm surprised you can find time to visit me once a month.'

'Not funny, Jack. I'd visit you twice a day if I could. I'd move into your cell if they'd let me.'

She had expected that Jack would be pleased when she told him Bill had come to live with her. Instead he said, 'God, what a weird tribe you Bradshaws are. All you seem to do is marry each other, break up, and get back together. There's a whole green world out there and you people keep nailing yourselves in boxes. I mean, it's crazy enough for you to spend your life visiting me in this crummy prison. Now you're telling me your brother's going to join you. You're doing nothing and he's going to help you.'

'Don't say mean things,' she said. 'It's a waste of time. If you think you'll make me angry or hurt my feelings and I'll go off somewhere and leave you alone, you're wrong. Be nice to me or I'll stop bringing you cookies and dill pickles.'

'You be nice to me or I'll marry Pietra Wessen. Then they won't let you come visit me any more.'

'You can't marry her. You're already married,' she said.

'Then I'll be a bigamist. What can they do . . . put me in jail?'

'I never thought of that. So why don't you marry me?'

379

'I can't. You're too good for me. It's bad enough being in this joint. I don't want to make it worse by feeling guilty.'

When she told Bill some of the things Jack had said about her regimented work schedule Bill said, 'He's right. I know all about the therapy of work and self-denial. I was a crackerjack student in clinical psychology. But there's such a thing as overdoing it. You don't help Jack or yourself or anybody else by grinding yourself into the dirt. You've got a big enough problem. There's no point in making yourself a few additional ones. If you ask me, the best thing you can do for Jack is to have some life of your own. Doing something for yourself doesn't deprive him of anything.'

'I haven't even been able to think about myself. Not for months now. All I can think of is . . .'

'Then it's time you got started. Maybe that's what Jack's trying to tell you. Jesse said a smart thing to me not long ago. He said the first law of life is: *use yourself*. Pretty good, huh?'

'It's good if it works, I guess.'

'It only works if you try it. But it's also good to remember that it's no sin to have a little fun and laugh once in a while. You can't make life better for Jack by making yourself as miserable as you think he is.'

'You're my baby brother,' she said. 'I taught you everything you know. What makes you think I'll take advice from you?'

'I don't think that. Otherwise I'd advise you to get the hell out of here.'

'You already did. You *and* Rab. Remember?'

Bill nodded. 'Bad timing on our part. And not such a good idea in any case. I admit it. I think you're better off staying here. But you can do that without turning yourself into a maid-of-all-work with callouses on her knees.'

The thing that Bill brought her was a sense of balance. She had swung from the extreme point of her life with Jack to the extreme opposite position of solitary isolation. Now she slowly edged back to some more comfortable centre, some sense-memory recall of who she had been and how she had functioned before Jack. The operative word is *slowly*. From a world of schedules and timetables, she gradually allowed herself to be governed less strictly, to respond to demands of the moment, to react to unexpected events. She re-hired the laundress and the woman who came to clean twice a week. She went more often to the university library, she and Bill

380

ate in restaurants at least once a day, and they took long drives in her car. Through the Black Forest to Karlsruhe, along the Necker valley to Stuttgart, or following the Rhine northward to Mainz or Wiesbaden. And one day she announced to Bill that she was thinking about taking some classes again at the university.

'Not a bad idea,' he said. 'I may do that myself. If I wear a student cap maybe the neighbours won't think I'm your fancy man.'

That choice, which she had considered before but had always rejected, came easier now because the entire atmosphere of her home was easier now that Bill was there. By making no demands on her, he allowed her to make new demands on herself. More accurately, she was reminded, bit by bit, of what her days had once been like and was able to bring that pattern to life again. Inside herself she knew that what Bill had predicted was true. By beginning to nurture herself again, she had taken nothing from Jack. As for him, his reaction when she said she might go back to school was black and funny but only to him. 'That's a fine idea. Long overdue. That means that if one of these cretins I'm locked up with decides to cut my throat some morning, you'll have your studies to console and distract you.'

When she told Bill what Jack had said, he said, 'Jesus. What a thing to say. What's wrong with that guy?'

'All sorts of things. But not the things you might imagine. What's inside him is not what comes out. I'm the only one who knows what he's really like. And that includes him. His entire life has been devoted to concealing himself from himself.'

'Has he succeeded?'

'Not at all. That's why he doesn't really mind being in prison. He's felt locked up all his life.'

[6]

One day at lunch in their dining room, Helen said to Jesse, 'How's the work going?'

He made a face, 'Sometimes I think I should have followed my father's advice and become a head waiter.'

381

'Are we permitted to ask what you're working on?'

'Of course you are. And maybe some day I'll be able to answer.'

'Last time we discussed it you had just set yourself free. No more critical pieces, you said.'

He nodded. 'Big talk. It's always easy to stop something. Starting something new is a whole different matter.'

She poured more coffee into his cup. 'I have total faith in you. I've seen you in these quandaries before. I expect you'll come floundering out of it before long.'

'Floundering is the correct word. No doubt about that.'

'I don't know if you're aware of it,' she said then, 'but when you spoke about your father a moment ago, I realized that I haven't heard you mention his name in a long time.'

'I'm surprised I mentioned it now.'

'Do you think about him very often?'

Jesse shook his head. 'I didn't think about him much even when I lived with him.'

'I'm serious.'

'So am I. I was like one of those kids that hack writers used to make up stories about. Little boys who thought they'd been kidnapped by gypsies and raised by a shoemaker who had one leg shorter than the other.'

'Is that what you thought?'

'Not exactly. I just thought I was part of a family I wasn't actually related to. I suppose I felt some connection with my mother when I was little but she turned out to be such a clone of my dad that it was embarrassing just watching her trying to answer a question if he wasn't there to put words in her mouth. My brother and sister were a couple of foreign exhibits too. I've struck up warmer relationships during a ten-minute ride on the New York subway than I ever had with them. And as far as Dad was concerned, he was in the restaurant business, you know, after he gave up playing the banjo. He always made me feel as if I was a starving kid and he owned the only place to eat in town. Except he never had a vacant table.'

Helen smiled. 'You exaggerate.'

'Not at all. Actually, I make him sound better than he was.'

'It all seems so strange to me. So hard to understand. You know how I felt about Raymond.'

'You know how I felt about him. I never realized what a total

382

loss my dad was till I came to live with Raymond. That seems like a century ago.'

She made a face. 'Not quite.' Then: 'Your father's dead now, isn't he?'

'I imagine so but I'm not sure. The last word I had from him was when my mother died.'

'And how about your brother and sister?'

'Vanished. My sister disappeared in the fleshpots of New Orleans years ago and the last I heard about my brother was a strong hint from my father that he was in prison in Michigan.'

'Maybe he'll turn up some day,' Helen said.

'I hope not. An accident of birth doesn't make somebody your brother. It takes a lot more than that to stitch a family together.'

'It doesn't matter, anyway, does it? You're a Bradshaw now.'

'I felt like a Bradshaw the day I moved into your father's house.'

'Lucky for me,' she said.

'Lucky for me, too.'

Before they left the table, she slid an opened envelope across the table to him and said, 'I got this funny note today. I don't know what to make of it.'

Jesse picked up the envelope and reached in his sweater pocket for his glasses. 'Who's it from?'

'Connie Wilson. She's Frank's wife.'

'Number three . . . right?'

Helen nodded. 'Very few men have been married only once, like you.'

He pointed his forefinger at her like a dagger. 'Also very few women,' he said. Then: 'I left my glasses on my desk. You read it.' He handed the envelope back to her. She took out a lavender card and read the message to Jesse.

Dear Mrs Bradshaw,

You don't know me. I'm Connie Wilson. Frank's wife. Don't be alarmed by this note. It's not an announcement of calamity. It's more in the way of an invitation. As you can imagine, I've heard a great deal about you, all of it positive. And since I'm a social and inquisitive creature I thought it might be pleasant for us, you and me, to have a ladies' lunch some day. If such a notion seems ridiculous to you, simply drop this note in the fire.

383

But if it doesn't seem ridiculous, please call me at my office 927 9413, and we'll pick a time and place.

Helen looked up at Jesse and said, 'What do you make of that?'

'Sounds as though she's a social and inquisitive creature who wants to see who her husband married the first time round.'

'Why would she want to do that?'

'I guess you'll have to ask her.'

'I don't want to ask her.'

'Why not? It might be entertaining. You could take turns picking the bones of old Frank.'

'I don't happen to like ladies' lunches, as you well know. And I certainly have no impulse to sit down for a gossip session with a woman I don't even know.'

'Ah, but you have something in common. It's rather like being alumna of the same college.'

'You seem very amused. Why am I not amused?'

'Maybe you feel threatened.' Jesse said.

'Why in the world would I . . .'

'Classic reaction. Here's a woman you've never met who very probably knows a great deal about you, things you wouldn't like to be in the public domain.'

'That never occurred to me. I don't know what you're talking about.'

'Of course you do. Little household hints, anecdotes from your marriage, souvenirs from the past.'

'I'd be surprised if Frank has given her a detailed account of our marriage.'

'If he hasn't that would make her twice as curious.'

'If I'm not curious about her, why should she be curious about me?'

'Maybe he talks about you in his sleep. Maybe he does needlepoint with your name concealed in a geometric design. Maybe he compares her with you, makes her feel inadequate, tells her your roast chicken is superior to hers.'

'Are you saying I should go up to Chicago to see her?'

'That's up to you. But if I were in your position, I'd be extremely curious. Does that surprise you?'

'Yes, it does. The last time you and I discussed Frank Wilson you had some strong views on the subject. You gave me very firm instructions about him.'

'Doesn't sound like me,' Jesse said.

'I know. That's what I told you at the time. But you persisted. I was not to see him, telephone him, or write his name on my grocery list. Do you remember that conversation?'

'Vaguely. As I recall, you thought I was being severe with you.'

'You were. I didn't enjoy it. It wasn't like you.'

'I agree. Live and let live. That's my credo. Let sleeping dogs lie. Neither a borrower nor a lender be. Sufficient to the day is the evil thereof.'

'You're an odd duck, Jesse.'

'But sincere and well meaning. I'm trying to tell you, in my clumsy, sophomoric way, that I regret my behaviour that other time. I must have been thrown off by something else. As you know, you are free to come and go as you wish.'

'No, I'm not,' she said, 'and I don't *want* to be.'

'I mean that if you want to have a chat with your ex-husband or have a meal in a well-lit restaurant that is entirely your affair.'

'But I have no desire to see Frank. I never said I did. I just resented the way you talked to me that day.'

'I know that. And I take it back.'

'It's not serious, Jesse. This is not a serious conversation. I just read that note to you because I thought it was odd and amusing.'

'And it is.'

'I had no intention of actually calling her.'

'Don't decide too quickly,' he said. 'I have a feeling there might be more to this note than meets the eye. If it were me I'd be very tempted to find out what's on her mind.'

Helen got up, walked around the table, and sat on his lap. She put her arms around him and said, 'But I don't want to, you dunce. I don't care what's on her mind.'

She did care about Jesse's reaction, however. If she had been surprised and hurt before by his insistence that she should have no contact whatsoever with Frank, she was equally disturbed now by his light-hearted attitude toward Connie Wilson's letter. She had difficulty getting their conversation out of her mind. She concluded that if Jesse had once been jealous of Frank he had either forgotten about it or the feeling had disappeared. And as always, when

385

anything about Jesse confused or upset her, she soon found herself
thinking of Nora.

[7]

Betsy had always been a faithful letter-writer but not a frequent
one. Her letters to Floyd arrived usually every four or five weeks.
From the time he and Valerie settled in Norway, however, the
letters became more frequent. She wrote twice a month. And soon
he was receiving a letter from her once a week.

'How nice that she's writing so often,' Valerie said. 'Do you think
that means something?'

'It probably means that since Julie and Jennifer are in nursery
school, Betsy has more time to herself.'

'I hope so.'

'What does that mean? You read her letters. What do you think?'

'I don't know. Usually when a mother starts getting a flood of
mail from her child, that child is either concerned about her
mother's state of mind or very concerned about her own.'

'I don't see that in what she writes,' Floyd said.

'Neither do I. But there are all sorts of ways of saying "Help".'

'Betsy doesn't beat around the bush. If there's something on her
mind it usually comes out in a hurry.'

'You know her much better than I do. You're probably right. But
from the way you described that husband of hers . . .'

'You're right. I keep telling myself that she sees him differently
than I do. But at the same time I don't think she'll be mesmerized
for ever.'

In her next letter, as though they had willed it, Betsy wrote to
Floyd:

You're a smart guy. You've probably been reading between the
lines of my letters. But in case you haven't, I tell you now that
things are not good here. The only bright spot is that Taylor
doesn't know how bad things are. The situation is very, very
complicated and it promises to get much worse. But as of now
things are under control. I'm trying to be wise and careful so the

386

world doesn't blow up in my face. I'm doing fine. I'm telling you this because I need to tell you but I can't put all the details in a letter. When we sit down and talk about it everything will be clear to you. But now is not the time for that. Please don't write to me about all this. I suspect that some of my mail is not getting to me. Don't worry. I'll keep you posted. And when there's something you can do to help, I will let you know. Guaranteed.

'I think I should go there,' Floyd said.
'She says this is not the time.'
'I don't trust her.'
'I think you have to trust her,' Valerie said. 'It sounds like a delicate situation. And she says she's in control.'
'That's what everybody says. Then all of a sudden they're not in control.'
'This is the first letter where she's brought it up. I think you have to give her a chance. She said she'll let you know when you can help.'
'She also said we have to talk face-to-face before I'll understand.'
Valerie picked up the letter and looked at it. 'And she said not now. She makes it very clear.'
'The worst thing that happens is I waste a trip.'
'That's not the worst thing. She's obviously walking a fine line with her husband. We must be careful not to . . .'
'Her husband's a maniac. I hate the thought of her being in the same house with him, even when things are going *well*. If there's some trouble between them . . .'
'If there's some trouble and it's as complex as she says, you can only make it worse by barging in on them.'
'I'd rather take that chance than find out later that I should have been there when I wasn't. There's a plane from Oslo at noon tomorrow. I think I should be on it.'
'You're making a mistake, Floyd.'
'Maybe I am. But I can't just sit here and drive myself nuts worrying about what her letter was all about. She had enough grief from her own mother and dad. If I can keep her from having some more, I have to try.'
'I understand that. But we're talking about timing. Before you start making plane reservations, do me a favour. Telephone her.

Don't ask her any specific questions. Just get a feeling of how things are. Please.'

Floyd went into the study and called Betsy in California. When he rejoined Valerie ten minutes later he said, 'I don't know any more than I did.'

'What did she say?'

'Not much of anything. It was as though she'd never written that letter.'

'Was her husband there?'

'I asked her and she said no. But it didn't sound as if she was alone.'

'Did she sound upset?' Valerie asked.

'Not at all. All smiles and cheerful reports about the children. Asked about you. Asked what we were doing. I expected her to tell me what they had for dinner last night.'

'Her husband must have been there.'

Floyd shook his head. 'He's never home at this time of day. It's mid-morning in Santa Barbara. He's run five miles, had a high colonic, and closed three real estate deals by now.'

'Well, maybe it's not as serious as we thought. You'd think she'd give you some hint about something. Did you say anything about her letter?'

'No. I just said I had to fly out to Los Angeles on business in a day or so and I thought it would be a good chance to drive up to see her.'

'What did she say?'

'Said they were leaving tonight for a camping trip in the Sierras. Said they wouldn't be back for ten days.'

'Well, that takes care of that,' Valerie said.

'No, it doesn't. I'm going anyway. As soon as I hung up the phone I called SAS and made a reservation for tomorrow.'

'But she won't be there.'

'Yes, she will. Betsy's a terrible liar. I didn't believe that camping trip story for a minute.'

After dinner, when they were having a cognac in their second-floor sitting-room, Valerie said, 'I don't think you should go tomorrow. I don't think it's a wise time from Betsy's standpoint but we've already discussed that. Now I'm being selfish. I'm talking about me. I'm sure you've noticed that I've been a bit shaky lately. I try not to burden you with all my stupid anxieties but the fact is

388

I've felt very odd for some time now. I thought I'd be able to throw off that whole ugly time in Germany but I haven't been able to. And it isn't just that. As you know, it bothered me when Bill went off to America to live with Jesse. Now it bothers me in a different way that he's gone to live in Heidelberg with Polly. It's as though he has no centre and he's trying to plug into somebody else's life. That disturbs me. And Rab disturbs me. Not because of anything he's doing but because I have no idea what he's doing. I feel totally separated from him. We couldn't be farther apart if he'd gone to New Zealand to live on a sheep station. I'm not a sentimental fool or a hypochondriac – you know that – and I'm not suggesting that I should become a psychiatrist's patient. I hate all that rot. But I am telling you, as simply as I can, that I'm very dependent on you just now. I'm always dependent on you. We're dependent on each other. But these last weeks I've been waging some wars in my head and they only simmer down when you take charge of me. You can always make me laugh, even at myself, and you can make me feel that I have some value even when my self-esteem has shrunk to nothing.'

'We'd better get out of Norway before you go into a deep Norsk depression.'

'It's not Norway. I love it here. It's just the sort of new place I wanted to see and spend some time in. It's not our home, or this country, or you, or our life I'm finding fault with. It's me. I'm the faulty part in the machine.'

'Two days after I met you I said to Clara, "Valerie's not afraid of anything, is she?" and Clara said, "Never has been and never will be." '

'For once Clara was wrong. I used to be in full command. Now I'm in need of a commander.'

'You don't have to stay here while I'm gone,' Floyd said. 'Come with me. After I've seen Betsy we'll hire a car and drive through northern California. All the way to Seattle if you like.'

Valerie smiled. 'That would only work if I could leave my head here in Norway. Otherwise I'd be a poor travelling companion, I'm afraid.'

The following morning Floyd called to cancel his plane reservation. He was still concerned about Betsy; he felt guilty because he hadn't gone to see her. Valerie also felt guilty because she'd persuaded him not to go. But neither of them blamed the other. Each of them assured themselves that the other was blameless.

After Rab's return from Spain, he and Lord Hinson had several brief telephone conversations, but nearly a month went by before they were able to see each other. At last they met for dinner one evening at the Reform Club.

'Any new developments since we talked on the phone last week?' Rab asked.

'Quite a number, actually. Plus a few earlier revelations that I couldn't discuss in detail from my desk at the Exchequer.'

Alfred Hinson's father had been a school friend of Ned Causey, Clara's husband, and a financial adviser to the Bradshaw family. And Alfred himself had been a school chum of Hugh Causey, Clara and Ned's son. He had also been a short-time suitor of Nora before she met Jesse and before she married Edmund Bick, Valerie's father. Alfred had known Rab since he was born and when Rab was in his teens they had frequently fished and shot grouse together.

'The fact is,' Hinson went on, 'this has developed into an extraordinary exercise. A bit more exciting than the routine investigations our chaps are normally involved with.'

'I gathered that from our telephone conversations.'

'You remember I was a bit hesitant when we talked just before you went off to Spain. Your suggestion seemed harmless enough. I mean it's not uncommon for us to receive a hint from one place or another that someone may be playing fast and loose with our department, fiddling with their ledgers, that sort of thing. And we do follow those leads, of course. We quite appreciate them actually. But in your case I sensed a vendetta, thought you might be trying to throw a scare into Mr Mullet.'

'You're right. That's precisely what I wanted to do.'

'I also suspected you had no real evidence of his wrongdoing.'

'I didn't. I believe I told you that. But I know his reputation. He's a man who takes advantage of all his opportunities. So I had strong suspicions, I still have those suspicions, that he might be trying to benefit financially from his residence in Britain. Whether it was strictly legal or not.'

'Have you had business dealings with him?'

Rab shook his head. 'I was warned off him long ago. My involvement is more personal. I'm in love with his wife. There's some difficulty about a divorce. So I would be happy to expedite it if I could. I have no desire to see him in prison but I certainly wouldn't be unhappy if he left England.'

'And left his wife behind?'

'Something like that.'

'Well, you may not have wished him in prison but there's a chance it could happen. This is all in the strictest confidence, you know.'

'Of course.'

'Even from his wife. Perhaps I should say, *especially* from his wife.'

'I understand.'

'After our luncheon, as I've said, I was a bit hesitant to proceed. I was finding reasons to delay action, which is unusual for me. But at last, one day when I was having tea in my offices with Robinette, my number two, I asked him quite casually if he'd heard the name of Oscar Mullet, an American film person now living in Knightsbridge. He said, "Of course I have, and the investigation against him is proceeding very well." It seems our people have been keeping a watch on Mullet's activities ever since he arrived in London. I'd like to credit it to our energy and expertise but in this case, according to Robinette, we were helped along by a tip from the Internal Revenue Service, our counterpart in America. It appears that the motion picture business is something of a sideline for Mullet, a means to an end if you will. His primary function, we suspect, is manoeuvring money about. From America to England to Switzerland to the Bahamas. One reason he came here from America, it seems, was to relieve himself of the pressure he was beginning to get from the United States Government. Transferred all his funds out of that country, we're told. Millions of dollars. So in addition to income tax problems, he may be violating international currency regulations. All sorts of loose ends hanging about.'

'Are these personal funds we're talking about?'

Hinson shook his head. 'Most of his personal funds seem to be in the Bahamas. The money we're talking about is money that floats through his various production companies. I understand he has a reputation for producing films at a very low cost.'

'So I'm told,' Rab said. 'He's an expert at cutting corners. They say he can make a ten-million dollar picture for three million.'

'According to the American chaps his books tell another story. They say a picture that was budgeted for ten million but produced for three still shows in his records that it did, indeed, cost ten million.'

'And he keeps the seven million?'

'Not all of it. Only his percentage. The rest he funnels back to the original investors. In cash. Untraceable. Since he often produces three or four films in a year, those tax-free kickbacks can amount to a great deal of money. As much as thirty million in one year, we suspect.'

'If he's chiselling on costs why wouldn't he keep the money for himself?'

'I'm sure he'd like to but that could be dangerous. The Americans tell us that his investors are a crime family that operates in New Orleans and Phoenix. He legitimizes their gambling profits for them and they support his film productions. The tax people became suspicious when they discovered how many of his films are never released, and of the ones that *are* released, how few of them ever show a profit. And all the while, Mullet gets richer and richer. His underworld friends, one assumes, get richer still.'

'Does he know yet that he's being investigated?'

'I believe he only knows what you told him,' Hinson said. 'We've been proceeding cautiously. Almost all his employees here are Her Majesty's subjects and we've restricted our inquiries and depositions to them so far.'

'Will this become a public matter?'

'That's never our intention but sometimes it can't be avoided.'

'What sort of time frame are we discussing?'

'Impossible to say. We tend to move ahead rather deliberately in these matters. We like to be sure of our facts. Saves a lot of trouble later on. And in a situation like this one, where it appears there has been a sophisticated and long-term process of deception, a great deal of time can be consumed. We know that Mr Mullet is represented by a clever group of solicitors so if he decides to contest our findings we could be in for a bit of a struggle. But we'll win out in the end. We always do.'

392

'So he could be in for a great deal of trouble.'

'Almost certainly. One way or the other. We're also suspicious that his friends in America may have links with a nasty criminal organization here in London. If it turns out that Mullet has financial ties with British citizens as well, he could end up with a very full plate indeed.'

'All this was not what I had in mind when I mentioned him to you that day at lunch.'

'I realize that. And as it turned out, as I've explained to you, that conversation had nothing to do with this investigation our people are doing. In fact, I'm not sure I would ever have mailed that letter you'd asked me to write. I didn't know then about your interest in Mrs Mullet but I had a feeling there were things you hadn't told me.'

'I deceived you, Alfred, I confess. My instincts were selfish but harmless, I thought. Many businessmen have something to hide from Exchequer, especially promoters like Oscar Mullet. So I thought a routine letter from you, a request to examine his financial records, might shake him up a bit.'

'And how did you think that would benefit you?'

'I wasn't certain it would. I knew it was a long chance. If he was really in a difficult position I thought he might come to me for help. Quite apart from the awkward situation with his wife, he trusts my business judgment. And he thinks I have some influence in the ministries.'

'And then what?' Hinson said.

'This may cause you to raise your eyebrows but I will risk telling you all the same. I had a notion that perhaps I could use his perception of my influence as a bargaining tool. Since, on the basis of my agreement with you, I knew there was, in fact, no pending investigation, I planned to tell him, after a proper period of reluctance, that I could arrange to have the examination of his records called off.'

'I suspected something of the sort.'

'But I would not provide that service,' Rab went on, 'unless he agreed to divorce his wife promptly and painlessly.'

'I'm delighted to see the Borgian instincts have not been bred out of the Bradshaws,' Hinson said.

'Nothing Borgian about it. As I saw it, only minor deceptions

393

were involved, and those to a good end. Do you feel betrayed, Alfred? Should I feel guilty?'

'Not at all. Perhaps I'm the one who should feel guilty. It seems I've taken away your bargaining tool.'

'Biblical vengeance, Alfred. Hubris rewarded.'

[9]

'You know the history of the Bradshaws as well as I do,' Bill said. 'The same old problem. Back through the centuries female children in quantity. But always a shortage of males. The dynasty always in danger of extinction. The death of the Bradshaw name. So when a male child did come along there was formidable pressure for him to reproduce himself, to keep the pot boiling, to have two sons, three sons, a dozen sons. But it never seems to work out that way. With rare exceptions the Bradshaws produce magnificent women and chancy males. Am I right?'

'Of course not. My brothers are second to none.'

'That's true. But Rab and I are yet to be proved as breeding stock. We might be producers of nothing but girl babies. As you know, the sex of the child is determined by the father. Even you might be a producer of females. Time will tell.'

'I see you and Rab as stern and sullen fathers of great flocks of boys. Rowdy and ill-smelling. Guns and fishing-rods all round and dogs sleeping on the sofa.'

Bill shook his head. 'Rab perhaps, but not me. That's the point of this whole discussion. I have withdrawn from the paternal sweepstakes. I plan to be the first Bradshaw bachelor in memory.'

'Not you, my dear. Not in a million years. I walk down Friedrichstrasse with you and I see you looking over the frauleins. And they're looking at you as well. Are you telling me that all those vibrations are the prelude to a life of celibacy?'

'I said nothing at all about celibacy. I said I had no plans to be a husband or a father.'

'Ah, that's something else again. Most men don't make elaborate plans about fatherhood till some cute little bird makes those plans for them.'

394

'It's possible, I suppose, but I don't think so. This is something I've given a great deal of thought to. I feel about the institution of marriage the way you've told me Jack feels about the institution of the church. Too many rules. Too much structure. Too much organization. And too little passion.'

'You do sound like Jack. But even Jack got married once.'

'And he's still trying to figure out why.'

'That's true,' she said. 'But you're not Jack. You grew up in a different atmosphere. You learned different things.'

'So did you. But all your friends from home are married now. Most of them have a child or two. That life was available to you but you didn't choose it. You dashed off to Heidelberg in search of culture and adventure. And here you are, lecturing me on the sweet inevitability of married life. I'll tell you what – the day you get married, I'll get married.'

'That's not fair. You know my situation.'

'Of course I do. But you had no plans for marriage even before Jack got into trouble. Isn't that right?'

'It's right but it has nothing to do with you. Jack and I never even talked about being married. Never considered it.'

'He's talked about it. You told me so. He said he'd never get married.'

'That's not what I meant. I meant we don't need to be married.'

'Neither do I. You said it for me. Don't want to. Don't need to. Don't plan to.'

'Jesse told me you were having a serious encounter with that girl at college. What was her name?'

'Bernadette.'

'That's right. Wasn't that something monumental? Jesse thought it was.'

'It was terrific. We had a great time. Because we knew we weren't planning ahead. No obligations. No guarantees. The first time we ever slept together she said, "Listen, I've got this guy from home. I've known him since I was five. Our folks decided we were going to get married when we were in kindergarten. So I can't screw up everybody's plans. Just thought I should tell you." '

'What did you say?'

'I said that was fine with me. And it was. From then on we had a splendid time together.'

'How about her friend at home?'

395

'He goes to college at Williams, a school in Massachusetts. So she only sees him during school holidays.'

'So you share her. Is that it?'

'Not the way you think. She doesn't sleep with him.'

'Is that what she tells you?'

'It's true,' he said. 'She was a virgin the first time with me.'

'I don't believe it. And then she gave you that little speech about the young man she plans to marry?'

'That's right.'

'Odd young woman you picked. I don't think I'd like to meet her.'

'Of course you would. She's a remarkable girl. Reminds me of you, as a matter of fact. Not as pretty as you. But she has a nice spirit about her. A bit of courage. Speaks her mind.'

'How'd she feel about your deserting the cornlands of America and coming here to live with me?'

'Angry as hell about it. She surprised me. She's a young woman who's always in control. Or seems to be. Puts great store in that. She says anyone who can upset you owns you. So almost nothing makes her angry.'

'What did she say?'

'Said I was a damned fool. Tried to put it on a practical level at first. Only a few months from completing school, she said. Seven, to be exact. Thought it was foolish for me not to hang on and get my degree.'

'She's right about that, isn't she?'

Bill shook his head. 'Not at all. She's dead wrong. I don't give a damn for degrees and all that. That's not why I was going to school. I don't plan to pursue a profession or explore the world of commerce. I don't have any plans, actually, that require a guarantee from some university that I'm a first-rate and dependable chap.'

'Stage design,' Polly said, 'wasn't that your goal?'

'For a moment. When I was young and insecure. When I felt I needed a specific answer to questions about my future plans. But now nobody asks me and even if they did I no longer feel obliged to answer. When I said goodbye to my faculty adviser at Foresby he said, "What do you expect to do now?" And I told him I was coming to Heidelberg to spend some time with my sister.'

'Did that answer satisfy him?'

'Of course not. He looked at me as if I'd just told him I never take a bath. Then he said, "I mean after you leave Heidelberg," and I said, "I have no plans beyond that." '

'Is that what you told Bernadette also?'

'That's what I told everybody. It's the truth.'

'You didn't tell me that,' Polly said. 'What if I get tired of having an untidy brother hanging about?'

'Then I'll move down the street and tag along after you when you go to the market.'

She bent down and kissed him on the forehead. 'You're not untidy and I'm not tired of you. No wonder Bernadette didn't want you to leave. You're an acquired taste.'

'Like an olive?'

'More like an anchovy.' Then: 'How about you? Did you mind leaving her?'

'Of course I did. We spent a lot of time together. Practically all the time except when we were in class. We had fun together in bed and we had fun when we weren't in bed. There was no pressure on us. We knew it was all going to end the day we graduated. She'd made that clear from the first. Her family had started planning her wedding a year before. We used to joke about it. Once she said to me, "I really should invite you to the wedding. You're the one who should give me away." '

'But all the same she was angry when you left. Why was that?'

'That's what I asked her. But she had no answer. I guess she thought I'd changed the rules of the game. Or maybe she liked me more than she'd planned to. I was certainly crazy about her. I wasn't looking forward to the automatic goodbye that would take place the day we were scheduled to graduate.'

'The whole arrangement sounds dreadfully cold-blooded to me.'

'I know it does. But it didn't play out that way. After that very first time when she explained her situation we never talked about it. We just went along, day to day, as if it was going to last for ever. She had a car at school and we covered a lot of territory. We drove to Chicago and St Louis and over to Indiana and there was a pretty motel in the woods about thirty miles from Fort Beck. We used to spend a great deal of time there. She drove like a maniac, smoked like a chimney, loved to play poker, and swilled down great schooners of lager like a lorry driver. She was sweet and warm for all of that, and extremely affectionate. Awfully fond of making love, too, once she'd discovered it.'

397

'Sounds as if you were a well-matched couple.'

'We were. We talked about that a lot.'

'But she never had second thoughts about this young man her family had picked for her to marry?'

'Never.'

'Extraordinary. She sounds like the last person in the world who would let someone choose a husband for her.'

'It wasn't as simple as that. She had chosen him too, I expect. As I told you, the two of them had been great chums since childhood. The assumption that they'd get married had been hers as well as her family's.'

'But whether she admitted it to you or not, it's clear she was having second thoughts. Otherwise, why would she react as she did when she found you were leaving?'

'She'd set a timetable, I suppose. She knew we were going to give each other up on a certain date but she wasn't at all prepared for changing that date. She's an odd mix. She likes to pretend that she lives moment to moment, instant choices, snap decisions. But inside her there's a little clock ticking. She likes to know where she is and where she's going.'

'Sounds like an interesting bag of contradictions. I'm sure you were never bored.'

'Not for a moment.'

'I suggest you go back to Illinois and claim her. I have a feeling she could be persuaded to change her mind about the young man she grew up with.'

Bill shook his head. 'Not likely. She's programmed. But even if she could be made to change her mind, I'm not interested.'

'Why not?'

'I'm not sure. All the time we were frolicking about together, I think I resented her somehow. You used the words "cold-blooded". That doesn't describe her, of course, but there was a matter-of-fact quality about her that made me think that nothing could alter any course she'd set for herself. She has beautiful eyes. Grey, I suppose you'd say. A bit on the greenish side in a certain light. And little yellow flecks. I'd look in those spectacular eyes and she'd cling to me and tell me how much she loved me and I'd think, "Jesus, I'm lying here in bed with two separate women." And that's the way I felt. One of them was all instinct and fun and affection, and the

398

other one was like a neat piece of machinery that turns on and off with a switch.'

'But she did love you . . . she told you that?'

'Never stopped telling me. But it was a special sort of love. Love as a part of our original understanding. Love with restrictions. Love with a stop-date.'

'Maybe she didn't like the situation any more than you did.'

'Maybe not. But if that was true, she took great pains to conceal it from me. Even when she knew I was leaving, when she made it very plain that she didn't want me to go, even then, through all the tears and the anger, I could sense that once she'd had her say, she'd be very safe and solid again behind that wall of self-determination she'd built round herself. I felt like a household gadget that she didn't want to throw away but that she knew she could do without when the time came.'

'Maybe it's *you*, Mr Bill. Maybe you're the tough one.'

'Not me. Somebody told me once that it's better to give too much than to give too little. I believe that. Once I knew what the ground-rules were I simply pretended there were no such rules or restrictions. One time, not long after we started up together, she thought she was pregnant. She missed two periods, drove to Urbana for a frog test, and sure enough, the doctor told her she was going to have a child. I guess I knew what her answer would be but I said, "Let's get married. If you don't think it's working out between us after the baby's born I'll give you a divorce and I'll guarantee you full support for the child." Told her I'd sign a firm contract to that effect.'

'What did she say?'

'She cried. She knew I was trying to do something nice but it never occurred to her to go along with it.'

'What happened?'

'She went to a high-class gynaecologist in Chicago. He told her he couldn't abort her but he called a reputable clinic in Puerto Rico and arranged for her to go there. She made a plane reservation for the following week. She let me pay for the ticket and give her money for the clinic but she wouldn't let me go with her. She kept saying, "It's my fault it happened so I have to take care of it." I couldn't budge her.'

'So she went alone?'

'She didn't go at all. One of her sorority sisters gave her some pills to take, then she drank a great deal of gin and sat in a hot bath for ten hours, and finally, the morning of the day I was going to drive her to Chicago to take the plane for San Juan, she got her period. Her friends at the sorority had a big party that night. They finished the gin that was left and another bottle as well.'

'How were things after that? For the two of you, I mean.'

'Same as before. She simply put it behind her. Or so it seemed to me.'

'But it bothered you,' Polly said.

'The Puerto Rican trip bothered me. Even though it never took place. I was worried about her. But when things turned out the way they did, I just accepted it, I guess, as she did.'

'You didn't run out and buy a soccer ball the day she told you she was pregnant?'

He shook his head. 'I didn't let myself get involved in any father fantasies. I knew from the beginning that she'd decided not to have the baby.'

'Is that when you decided to come over here?'

'No. No connection. As I said, I came here because you're here.'

They were sitting in an historic beer hall in the oldest section of Heidelberg. It was late in the afternoon. People from nearby offices and students from the university were arriving in groups of three or four, also couples, and an occasional white-haired man by himself. At last Polly said, 'I hope these stories you've been telling me haven't poisoned your mind against all women.'

'Not at all. My decision to become a plaything for thousands of women rather than husband to one preceded my relationship with Bernadette.'

Polly smiled. 'Ten years from now I'm going to remind you we had this discussion. At the same time I'll inform your wife, whoever she may turn out to be.'

[10]

Helen and Connie Wilson met for lunch at the Drake Hotel. They sat by a wide window looking north across the lake. Connie was a large woman, beautifully but simply dressed, who looked as though

400

she had once been an athlete. She was waiting at the table when Helen arrived. Helen reported later to Jesse that she was the most disarming woman she'd ever met. 'I'm not sure what I expected. Someone all stuffy and proper, I suppose. But she's anything but that. As soon as I sat down she started talking about her feet.'

'I always try to get to the table first when I meet someone in a restaurant. I'm tall as you can see so I don't wear high heels very often. My first husband was four inches shorter than I am and though Frank isn't a short man exactly, I'm a bit taller than him, too. So I've spent most of my adult life in low-heeled shoes. When Chip and I were married – he was my first husband, Clifford Clinger, but no one called him anything but Chip – we practically lived on tennis courts or on his boat – we were in San Diego then – and all I ever wore were tennis shoes or deck sneakers. Very comfortable but through the years they played havoc with my feet. Did something dreadful to my Achilles tendon. So now I'm not really comfortable in any shoes. I hobble and limp around, and people think I'm ten years older than I am. So that's why, when I meet someone I've never met before, I try to arrive early. They get a chance to know me a little before they see what a miserable walking machine I've turned into.'

After they had ordered drinks, Connie said, 'Frank says you and I are about the same age but I don't believe it. You look at least fifteen years younger. That's what comes from my spending my life in the sun, I guess. Or maybe it's in the genes. I'm a great believer in genetics. I think it's the answer to everything. I have six children – Chip believed in big families – and they're all so different you wouldn't believe they're brothers and sisters. One boy is a little like me, and Virginia, our oldest girl, resembles Chip, but the rest of them look nothing like us and nothing like each other. All throwbacks, I guess. You have any kids?'

'Just one. A son.'

'Where does he live?'

'Right now he's living in Norway. He and his wife travel a lot.'

'Seems as though nobody stays at home these days. My kids are scattered all over the map. I've even got one in Buenos Aires. Works for Sears-Roebuck down there. And a daughter in Copenhagen. She's married to a Dane. Another daughter's divorced and lives in Windsor, Ontario, and the rest of them have settled one place or another here in the States.'

While they had lunch she told Helen her first husband had died in a boating accident when her youngest child was only three. 'Chip had been successful at his work but we spent every dollar we made so things were a little tight for a year or so. The kids and I lived on his life insurance till I got myself in gear and started to make money on my own. As soon as I built up a good line of credit, I got into everything. Real estate, interior decorating, wallpaper manufacturing, and franchise restaurants. When I was thirty-eight I started a bank in El Centro, California. I never had so much fun in my life. By the time I was forty-five I could have retired but by then all my kids were long gone so I kept on working. And I haven't stopped yet.'

'Sounds like Frank,' Helen said. 'That's the kind of pace he used to set.'

'No more. I wish he did.'

'Is he all right?'

'He's healthy, if that's what you mean. Plays tennis and swims every day. But I think he's bored. He's not a spectator. If he can't be in the middle of things he's liable to sit back and do nothing at all. And there's nothing wrong with that if a person enjoys it. But I'm afraid Frank doesn't.'

'When I knew him,' Helen said, 'his problem was not in finding things to do. He was always trying to find time for all the things he felt he had to do.'

'Of course. But circumstances change. They change for all of us. But some of us bend better than others.'

When they'd finished their lunch and were having coffee, both of them sensing that there was some central topic hovering over them that hadn't been addressed yet, Helen said, 'Does Frank know we're having this little visit together?'

'Of course.'

'You told him you'd written to me and that I'd called you back at last and that we made this luncheon date?'

Connie smiled and nodded. 'All the details.'

'What was his reaction?'

'Several reactions. When I told him I'd written you a note he thought it was an idiotic thing to do. He said I wouldn't get an answer from you and, as you know, for several weeks I didn't. Although that's what he'd predicted I had a feeling he was disappointed somehow that you hadn't responded. But when you did call and I told him we'd made a date for today, I sensed that it disturbed him in some way. I knew he would never forbid me to come here any more than I would forbid anything to him, so I said that if the idea bothered him I would get in touch with you and cancel. But he wouldn't hear of that. So here I am. Here we are.'

'Did you tell him why you wanted to see me?'

'Not at first. Because I didn't know. Not precisely. As I told you in my note I'm like a cat. Inquisitive and harmless. Frank knows that about me. Also, it's not my nature to hold things back. Certainly not from my husband. Chip used to say, "A bedroom's no place for secrets" and I agree with that. So Frank knows what I think and what I feel. He knows all about Chip and my little platoon of kids. He knows about my work. He knows everything. At first I think it was a burden for him. Sometimes it's easier to live a neat compartmentalized life. Expose a little bit of yourself to one person and some other small portion to someone else, but never give total access to anyone. Well, as you may have guessed, that's not my style. I'm not saying that I converted Frank, nor was I trying to, but when someone's being completely open with you it's contagious. Makes it difficult to sit behind the wall you've built round yourself and simply observe. Besides, all of us, even the most reluctant ones, have a secret desire to explain ourselves, to point out our most attractive and marvellous features. What I'm saying is that Frank, in the years we've been together, has told me a great deal about himself. And in the process he's told me a lot about you.'

'Should I hold my napkin over my face and slip out of here?'

'No. Nothing like that. What I mean to say is that the times when Frank talked about you were the times when he told me the most about himself.' She took out a cigarette case, offered one to Helen, who refused, then lit one herself. 'I take it you don't smoke these evil weeds.'

'It's not a matter of character,' Helen said. 'And I'm not a fanatic about my health. It's just that I never got started. That doesn't mean I've never smoked a cigarette because I have. But I've never been addicted.'

'That's the right word. It's an addiction, no doubt about it. But in my case it takes a strange form. Sometimes I go for weeks without smoking, but with a cigarette case all the while in my bag. Then, for no reason that I understand, I'll smoke four packs in one day.

403

You've heard of binge drinkers, I'm sure. I'm a binge smoker.' She inhaled deeply and said, 'Where were we?'

'I'm not sure.'

'As I recall, you'd asked me how Frank reacted when I told him we'd agreed to meet.'

'That's right. Did he ask you why?'

Connie nodded. 'At last he did and at last I was able to tell him. You see, Frank has never been contented with me. Not really. And I know he was miserable with that odd woman he married after the two of you were divorced. So I told him it was very important for me to meet the only woman who had ever made him happy.'

'What did he say to that?'

'He said nothing.'

'Then he was simply being kind to me,' Helen said. 'The truth is I was something less than a wonderful wife. As you must know, our decision to get a divorce was mutual. And when we got together later, when he was still married to his second wife and later after he'd divorced her, that, too, was a period that didn't exactly give him divine contentment. In fact, I have a letter he wrote to me in which he lists all my flaws. He concluded, in no uncertain terms, that I would be no asset to any man. I still read that letter occasionally. It keeps me from getting too pleased with myself.'

'That surprises me,' Connie said. Then: 'Don't misunderstand me. If I've given the impression that Frank has gone off on long soliloquies to me about his marriage to you, then that's a false impression. Whatever else he is or is not, Frank is not cruel. He would never run the risk of hurting my feelings by comparing me, in any way whatsoever, with you. So my conclusions about you, or you and Frank together, are based on intuition rather than testimony from him.'

'I'm sure you have excellent intuition but in this instance it's caused you to draw an incorrect conclusion. When I say that Frank's assessment of me, assuming he still has one and it's knowable, is more negative than positive, that judgment is based on a great many years I spent with him, married and unmarried. And, of course, the letter I mentioned. I'm sorry I don't have it with me. I'd let you read it. It's all academic now in any case. I'm sure you didn't invite me to lunch to tell me that your husband is still in love with me.'

Connie smiled. 'When my youngest daughter was six years old

404

she came home from school one day and said, "Jeffrey got up in class today and said that love is a four-letter word. And the teacher scolded him for saying that. He was right, wasn't he?" I didn't have an answer for her but Chip did. He told her it didn't matter how many letters. He said the important thing is that any word is just a word. When I asked him later what he meant he said all the really good stuff can't be defined at all, let alone squeezed into one word. He said placing an order is one thing. Accepting delivery is another matter altogether.'

She sat silent for a moment. 'Don't get the idea that I'm comparing Frank with Chip. I'm not. There's no way to. They're as different as fresh water and salt water. I also don't mean to imply that my life with Chip was unadulterated joy. It wasn't. He was the kind of guy that most women turned to look at. They always had, so he was used to it. He didn't have to tumble into bed with anyone who was available to prove something to himself. But . . . during the first ten years of our marriage it seemed I was always pregnant. So I'm sure he slipped a few times. But it didn't matter. Because I knew it meant nothing to him and I wouldn't let it mean anything to me. What I'm saying . . . and I'm taking the long way round to say it . . . is that the thing I got from Chip, the *best* thing, the part that will always stay with me, was that every time I looked at him I was able to say to myself, "He's really having a good time. This is good for him. He feels good about himself. He feels good about us. There's no place he'd rather be. Nobody he'd rather be with." And when he looked at me he saw the same thing. So we didn't have to promise or swear or cry out in the night. Everything we wanted was there. It was all in place. Perfectly visible to the naked eye. What I mean is this: when you live with someone you don't have to ask. It's all there to be seen. Or it's not there. When I looked at Chip I knew he had everything he required to make him whole. When I look at Frank I know he needs something I can't give him.'

'And I'm sure he needed all sorts of things he didn't get from me,' Helen said.

'Perhaps he did. But he may have forgotten.'

'Are you and Frank breaking up? Is that what you're saying?'

'I'm not making any grand statement. I'm just trying to sort things through in my head and you're being nice enough to listen to me.'

405

'You're not suggesting that I should step in and take your place, I assume.'

Connie laughed. 'God, no. If I made a suggestion like that I'm sure you'd spill coffee in my lap. I'm not sure what I'm up to. Nothing self-serving, I assure you. I truly did want to see you. I feel like a dreadful failure in relation to Frank and I suppose I thought if I spent an hour or so with you I might understand that failure a little better.'

'You're not planning to leave him then?'

'Why do you ask that?'

'Because you sound very much like a woman who's preparing to pack her bags and call a taxi.'

'I've never thought of it as my leaving him or his leaving me. I just feel the water rising every day.'

'And there's nothing you can do?' Helen said.

'Oh, my, no. I've never imagined there was. I can watch and wait and be warm and decent, but there's certainly nothing I can do. Nothing that can be done.'

Connie called for the bill then and paid it. When the waiter moved away Helen said, 'You must have guessed that I almost didn't respond to your note.'

'I did guess. There was quite a delay before you called.'

'I wasn't being rude. I just couldn't imagine what you wanted to see me about, why you wanted to talk with me. Now that we've met and talked, I'm still not sure.'

'Well, perhaps we should leave it that way then,' Connie said.

As they walked through the lobby toward the taxi station on Walton Place, Helen said, 'I come into Chicago every few weeks. Next time I'm in I'll give you some advance notice and we'll have another lunch. My treat.'

'Thank you. I appreciate that. But I think perhaps it's best if we let things rest as they are.'

When Connie's taxi pulled away Helen walked slowly to the corner. She turned right and walked up Michigan Boulevard to the tunnel leading to Oak Street Beach. She sat there on a bench, her hands in her lap, looking out across the lake. It was late afternoon before she got up, walked back to the Drake to claim her car, and started home to Fort Beck.

Chapter Nine

[1]

Jesse did not deceive himself when he set out to examine Helen in the same way he had explored the true nature of himself and Raymond. He knew it was a complex and treacherous undertaking. But that very complexity kept him on course. If he was to continue his dissection of the Bradshaws, his relationship to them and theirs to him, there was no way to manoeuvre round the fact of Helen. She was a linchpin in the process. She had been a key player in the beginning and she was a key player now. In most of the major events of his life she had been either participant or witness.

As he tried to organize their history together, a listing of places and dates made clear to him how many different shadings and colours had been dominant at various times. Trying to orchestrate those differences into major and minor passages, trying to find a thematic core to a great mass of *objets trouvés* proved fruitless. Searching for a pattern he could follow and failing to find one, he concluded at last that he must let his hand activate his mind and simply write down the details he remembered most vividly:

Raymond had spoken to me at great length about Helen before I met her. He'd shown me photographs from her infancy till age twelve. Indeed there was a good-sized framed picture of her in every room in the house.

Even before she came to visit that first summer, when she was twelve or thirteen, before I had ever seen her, I resented her. When I looked at her photographs I found fault with every

407

feature of her face. I told myself that her expression showed vanity, self-absorption and cruelty. Her mouth, I concluded, was unquestionably the mouth of a cruel girl who would become a cruel woman.

Now of course I know, and I'm sure I knew it then, that I was fiercely jealous and envious. Having decided that Raymond, my new benefactor, was my private property, I was in no frame of mind to include someone else, daughter or no. My cheeks ached from smiling whenever he described some admirable attribute of his daughter.

When she came to visit the first time, I saw nothing about her that contradicted my original judgments. If anything she was more hateful in person. But she was very pretty. I couldn't quarrel with that. And she wasn't stupid as I'd hoped she would be. She was both intelligent and clever. These attributes, however, coupled with Raymond's obvious adoration of her, only intensified the antipathy I felt.

Most disturbing of all, whereas I saw her as a real threat to my relationship with Raymond, she accepted me as though I was truly her brother. I was not deceived by such behaviour but Raymond, I could see, was totally taken in. 'It's incredible,' he said to me after her first visit, 'she thinks of you as a brother. She told me so.'

Even before that revelation from Raymond I had decided that my best manoeuvre was to treat her with even more loving kindness than she was showing to me. Whether Raymond's eyes were on me or not I humoured her, escorted her, brought her flowers from the garden and drowned her in compliments. And when she had to leave to return to her mother in New York, I managed a huskiness in my voice when I said goodbye. It was intended as a display of repressed emotion and it was successful, I think.

My only consolation in the next two years was that she came to Fort Beck only for school holidays. So Raymond's house was occupied, in the main, by him, the housekeeper, and me. When Helen arrived I always managed a high level of enthusiasm and brotherly affection, but once we'd bundled her on the train and sent her east again, she vanished from my mind. When Raymond chose to talk about her at great length I simply smiled, nodded my head, and let my thoughts wander elsewhere. By then I was

408

convinced that he thought of me as a son, just as I thought of him as a father. From that premise it was easy for me to conclude that he was content, as I was, to have his daughter in the house only for occasional visits.

This was my frame of mind when Helen arrived, supposedly for a visit, in the summer of her fifteenth year, and announced that she had come to stay. It was impossible to misinterpret Raymond's reaction. He was overjoyed.

By this time I had finished my first year at Foresby and had a scholastic record that I knew had pleased Raymond. I had many friends at school, an active social life, and I would have expected that Helen's presence would no longer be a threat to me. But it was. She had suddenly become quite mature, both in appearance and attitude. She declared herself the lady of the house and took pride, it seemed, in having two men to look after. The housekeeper, who had always been smitten with her, now became her disciple. Helen became, in truth, the mistress of the house. She made decisions about the gardening, our meals, and interior decorating; and she selected most of the radio programmes we listened to. Having given herself a mandate to please Raymond and me, she set a course, or so it seemed to me, designed to please herself.

My own tactic, since I did not want, in any way, to disturb the new rhythms of the household, was to spend whatever time I could with Raymond, usually on campus or in town, away from the house, and to spend as little time as possible with Helen.

I don't know to this day if she knew at that time how I felt about her. But whether she knew or not she decided, apparently, to outmanoeuvre me. She made me her confidant. She told me everything she was thinking and doing and planning to do. She asked my advice about her studies, about clothes, about young men. For a long time she was unsuccessful in changing my opinion of her but she did a great deal to alter and embellish my opinion of myself. At any age it's difficult to ignore a person who thinks you are an authority on all subjects, someone who seeks your advice on the smallest details of her life. At the age of nineteen, it's impossible.

Having already persuaded myself that Raymond was, if not my blood father, my *true* father, it was an easy second step, under Helen's barrage of attention, to begin to accept a brother

409

role with her. She was not only shrewd enough to seek out my advice, she was careful to follow it. As I stubbornly insisted to myself that she was nothing in my life, except perhaps an obstacle, the Pygmalion effect did begin to take charge. I asked myself how anyone who was so totally under my control could in any way be a threat.

Raymond, of course, was delighted with any evidence that his daughter and I felt a family connection with each other. So that, too, prompted me to pay more attention to Helen than my inclinations would have otherwise allowed. Still I made no overtures to her. She seemed always to believe that any time I allowed her was time that I could have better used elsewhere. I denied that when she suggested it but I allowed her, all the same, to believe it.

Raymond once said to me, 'You have some lunatic instinct to go on fighting battles you've already won. That's your fatal flaw.' I was never sure what he meant. But long after he was dead it occurred to me that perhaps he was referring, in an oblique way, to our three-cornered household. His and Helen's and mine. A close-knit family, yet not quite a family. A surfeit of love, but spooned out in unequal portions. Did he know that I was competing always for my share, struggling to get much more than my share if that was possible? Did he sense that I carefully accommodated Helen but that I had no true affection for her? And no love for anyone except him and myself? I don't believe he did. Raymond was a master at selecting the best course and then following it. If he decided, from the moment when Helen came home to live, that the three of us would be a solid family unit then I'm sure that from then on he ignored or excised anything that seemed to contradict that decision.

Subsequent experience tells me that Helen was not deceived for a moment. Not by me. Like her father she had decided how things should be, what contributions each of us should make. And her chosen role, I suspect, was to make up for whatever I was unwilling or unable to supply. Did she know then that she and I would end up together as we are now? I don't think so. After Raymond's death, perhaps. But not before.

If I were writing a novel about all this I would use the war in a dramatic way, as some sort of turning-point in our three-way relationship. Exposure to death, coming of age, all that world-shaking stuff. As it happened, however, when I came back from France, apart from my stiff leg, the cane and the limp, things were not changed. All the things that had been unclear or unfinished before remained that way. When necessary, behaviour was substituted for emotion and forward movement was not slowed.

Then Raymond died. If he, in some way, had kept Helen and me apart, his death drew us together. We weren't free to give each other what we'd given him. It was not that simple. Rather, it was as though his death had somehow perfected us. Whatever we might think of each other, he had loved us both. Neither of us questioned that. So each of us felt quick-frozen, suddenly, with Raymond's perception of the other. This was not articulated, of course. It could not have been. But we seemed to believe, in those first hours after his death, that the two of us were the guardians now of what the three of us had been.

All this spiritual bonding could have vanished in the weeks following Raymond's death. But circumstances didn't allow it. When we accidentally learned the truth about his background, when we discovered that the person we both knew best had actually been another person altogether, that the perfect man had not been perfect after all, we were linked together again, not by love or grief but by a disturbing secret.

Nora used to say that Helen had always been in love with me, that she was certainly in love with me by the time the two of us arrived in England the summer following Raymond's death. Knowing what love means to Nora, I've always denied that this was true. But if it was true, if whatever Helen had always felt for me took a sudden turn, it would have happened most likely in those confusing weeks just after his death, when she was forced to consider her father and his memory in ways she was not prepared to do.

Did I see her differently as well? Of course I did. Without Raymond as an armature she was vulnerable suddenly in a way she hadn't been before. Her game of seeming to depend on me became real now. I felt truly connected to her and related to her. I had no sense of being her father but I did feel responsible for her. And some time later I began to feel something for her that was an abrupt surprise to me.

When I came home one winter afternoon the house seemed deserted. But as I walked through the first-floor reception hall, I

411

heard a fire crackling in the library fireplace. I thought Helen had probably gone in there to read or do her school work. When I walked to the head of the couch, however, I saw she was sleeping. She was lying on her back with one arm under her head, the other trailing off the couch to the floor. Her cheeks were flushed from the fireplace heat and her lips were parted. As I stood looking down at her, the room dead quiet except for the sounds of burning logs, she moaned suddenly. Her body turned slowly on the cushions and seem to tremble. Then she moaned again. Half pain, half joy, it seemed. I had a raw impulse then to lock the library door and lie down beside her in front of the fire. I moved quietly to the door. But when I got there I went through the doorway, walked quickly to the front entrance, and left the house.

[2]

Polly and Jack sat facing each other in the visitor's room in the prison. They were silent, confusion on her face, anger on his. 'I don't understand,' she said at last. 'What are you trying to do to me?'

'I'm not doing anything to you. I just said that if you come here just to find fault with me than you might as well not come at all.'

'But why would you say something like that? You know coming here means everything to me. I count the days from the time I leave till the time they allow me to come back.'

'That's just what I don't want you to do, damn it. I've told you that before. You can't build your life around two visits a month to this crummy joint.'

'I didn't plan it this way,' she said. 'I hate just seeing you for a few minutes each time in this gold-fish bowl. But I have to see you, one way or another, and this way is better than none.'

'It's not for me. If all you can do when you're here is tell me what a stupid jackass I am.'

'I didn't say anything like that and you know it. I said it looks as if you're trying to make things worse for yourself.'

'What is that supposed to mean?'

412

'You've had trouble with the guards, you don't eat half the time, and you've been getting into fights in the exercise yard.'

'Who told you that?' he said.

'What's the difference. It's true, isn't it?'

'Did they tell you I won all those fights? Two guys had to go to the infirmary for stitches. I guess you didn't know I was a fighter. Left hooks, that's my secret. Feint with the right and slice in there with a sharp left hook. Hay-makers, that's all these ass-holes know. I cut 'em up with the left.'

'You know all this goes on your record. You'll never get a parole.'

'I don't expect a parole. Never did. Twenty years, the man said. So that's what I'm geared for. In twenty years I could win a thousand fights. Maybe more.'

'Every time I see you you have a bruise on your cheek or a cut on your face. You've lost twenty pounds since you came here and you cough as if you're choking to death.'

'Cigarettes,' he said. 'Good old black tobacco cigarettes. One thing good in this hole is the cigarettes. One drag and your head starts to spin. Like smoking dope. If you smoke enough you lose your appetite and you don't have to look at that crap they call food. Looking at it is bad enough. Eating it will put you in bed for a week.'

'Are you trying to make yourself sick? Is that it?'

'Who told you that? Did somebody put that idea in your head?'

'Nobody had to. All I have to do is look at you.'

'I'll bet you thirty thousand dollars I can tell you who's been talking to you. That fat little pansy who calls himself a chaplain.'

'He's married and has two children. He showed me their pictures.'

'Don't let that fool you,' Jack said. 'One of these days when he's strolling around the exercise yard somebody's gonna plant him like a tree. Head first in a hole.'

'He said nice things about you. He said you're a great musician.'

'How the hell would he know? He probably thinks Scarlatti was a trapeze performer.'

'He told me his father taught violin and his wife plays the oboe,' Polly said.

'If she's married to him she probably plays Russian roulette and prays for the worst.'

'He asked me why you've stopped playing.'

413

'Tell him to go screw himself. How does he know whether I'm playing or not?'

'His office is just down the corridor from that room where they let you keep your cello. He used to hear you when you went there to play. Hasn't heard you for weeks, he says.'

'Who is this guy . . . St Francis . . . looking after the flowers and the animals? What did you do, go to his house for the weekend?'

'I didn't go anywhere. Last time I came to see you he followed me out to the parking area and we sat in my car and talked.'

'That's what he likes, the bugger. Loves to talk. Likes to sit and stare at people, and talk his brains out. But he doesn't talk to me. I steer clear of him. When he comes near my cell, I put a pillow over my head and pretend I'm dead. He didn't tell you he's been talking to me, did he?'

'No. He said you insult him whenever he tries to talk to you.'

'Well, that's progress. At least the bastard knows when he's been insulted.'

'Don't you know when somebody wants to help you?'

'Help? I don't need help. And if I did I wouldn't go to Brother Leon or whatever he calls himself. He doesn't want to give help, anyway. His big pitch is absolution and forgiveness. That's what he's selling. But I'm not buying. Absolution's the last thing in the world I want. I'd be happy with a strong dose of good old-fashioned guilt. But I can't even manage that. I have to settle for insomnia.'

'Why have you stopped eating?' She said.

'Not hungry. And I haven't stopped. Just slowed down. Want to keep my girlish figure.'

'Jack, you're so skinny your clothes flop on you when you walk.'

'Thin is beautiful. I read that in a copy of *Der Spiegel*.'

She sat silent, looking at him. Then: 'Do you remember how important it was for you to have your cello here? Do you remember how difficult it was for Dr Liebermann and me to get permission for you to play it twice a week?'

Jack nodded. 'It was a miracle. You performed a bloody miracle.'

'All the time I was by myself in Heidelberg, between visits here, it made things easier for me, thinking that you could . . . that you had your music.' She paused but he said nothing. 'And now you've decided not to play any longer. I don't understand that.'

'Since you have an open line to the chaplain and he has an open line to God I suggest you ask him.'

'I don't want to ask him. I'm asking you.'

'All right, I'll tell you. I was sitting there sawing away one day, locked in that storeroom without windows, boxes of office supplies and crates of canned meats and vegetables stacked all around me, and suddenly I thought, "What the hell am I doing here? I'm trying to mix two ingredients that won't mix." Music is freedom, and life in a cell is *no* freedom. So how could I pretend to have both at the same time? The more I thought about it, the more I realized I was kidding myself. So I decided to give up the cello and devote all my energies to being a prisoner.'

'That's nonsense, Jack, and you know it. I don't understand a word you're saying.'

'Another thing,' he went on. 'Since I became a fighter it's made a change in my hands.' He held his hands out, palms down, so she could see his swollen knuckles. 'Every guy I take on in the exercise yard seems to have a hard head.'

Suddenly, there were tears in her eyes.

'None of that stuff,' he said. 'That's our contract. No weeping during visiting hours.'

'What do you expect? You're starving yourself into a skeleton. You're doing your best to poison your lungs with cigarettes, and now you're wrecking your hands so you can't . . .'

'No tears, baby. Everything's all right here.'

'No, it's not. Nothing's all right.'

'I'm healthy as a hog. Happy as a lark. Good spirits. Full of goodwill towards my fellow man.'

'You're trying to drive me away, aren't you?'

'I love you, kid. Why would I do that?'

'Because you would. Because that's the way you are. Don't you think I know you? You think I'm giving up my life for you. You've told me that. But you're wrong. This *is* my life. I wouldn't have planned it this way but we have no choice so I'll take what I can get and be thankful for it. You have to accept that, Jack, because that's the way it's going to be. So stop trying to make me give up on you. It won't work, if you've decided to starve yourself to death that won't work either. It won't set me free, if that's what's in your head. Because the day you die, that's the day I'll die, too. That's not a threat. I just want you to understand the way things are.'

'Not you, Polly. You're not the type.'

'You can think what you like,' she said. 'I'm not trying to

415

convince you of anything. But don't think for one moment that I don't mean exactly what I'm saying.'

'Romeo and Juliet. Found dead together in the monastery.'

She shook her head. 'Not like that. There's nothing theatrical or romantic about what I'm saying. I'm not saying I can't live without you. I'm saying I won't. So don't imagine you'll be doing me a favour by starving yourself to death.'

He reached across the table and put his hand on hers. 'I've really wrecked you, haven't I?' he said. 'When I met you, you were all sweet innocence with roses in your cheeks. Now you've gone tough and mean and hard-headed.'

'That's true. I have. And don't you forget it.'

[3]

After her visit to Jack, after she had discussed it in detail with Bill, she said, 'I feel as if I've gone through major surgery. This is worse than when he first went to prison. Then I was faced with twenty years of life without him. Now I don't know when the phone will ring and tell me . . .'

'I think you're going overboard on this thing. Just because he . . .'

'You don't know him, Bill. I *know* him. When he gets a crazy notion in his head it takes over his body and brain and everything else. And right now he has such a notion. I'm not sure exactly what it is but I have a very good idea. And it scares me to death.'

Later that evening, after dinner, she said, 'I don't want you to misunderstand what I'm about to say. I mean, I really appreciate your having been here all these weeks, but I . . .'

'If you're planning to throw me out, save your breath. I'm not going.'

'Of course I'm not throwing you out. You know that. It's just that I see some dreary days ahead and I don't want to subject you to them.'

'Don't worry about me,' Bill said. 'If you start crying and carrying on I'll go out to the cinema till you've finished.'

'It won't help to make jokes. I'm serious. As I said, it's been splendid having you here but now I think it's best for me to be by myself.'

'I disagree.'

'I thought you might. But I think it's a decision that I have to make.'

'I disagree about that, too. You're too screwed up to make any sort of sensible decision.'

After a moment she said, 'I want to be alone, Bill.'

'I understand that. But I don't want you to be alone.'

'You're very sweet but . . .'

'There's nothing sweet about it. I came here because I thought you were in a bad patch. You've just told me that the situation is worse now than it was at the start. So you can't expect me to accept that announcement as an exit cue.'

'I don't expect anything. I just hope you'll understand what I think is best for me. And accept it.'

'I do understand,' Bill said, 'but I don't accept it.'

'This is starting to remind me of arguments we had when I was eight years old and you were seven. You remember how cross I used to get with you?'

'Indeed I do. Are you about to get cross with me again?'

'I hope not,' Polly said.

'So do I. because it won't do you a particle of good.'

'Are you saying you have no respect for what I want?'

'Not at all. I love you and respect you even when you're wrong. But I don't respect you enough to pack up my ditty bag and move out.'

'I seem to remember your saying once that under certain circumstances you might move to a flat down the street.'

'I did say that. And when I said it I meant it. But circumstances have changed since then.'

'That's correct,' she said, 'and because of those circumstances I think I should be by myself.'

'Because of those circumstances I think you should not.'

'You're hopeless, Bill. I can always move out myself and leave you here.'

'I don't think you'd do that but if you did I would simply trail along after you.'

'But I would give you no key to my new home,' she said.

He smiled. 'Love finds a way.'

417

[4]

One night, quite late, Nora went with friends to have a late dinner at La Coupole. As they crossed the terrace and entered the restaurant through the revolving doors, Nora saw Karina at a table near the front. She was sitting with two blonde young men in dinner-jackets. As her friends went towards the centre of the restaurant to claim their table, Nora walked over to say hello to Karina. Neither of the young men stood up as she approached the table and Nora did not offer her hand in the French manner.

'You're back in Paris,' Nora said. 'What a nice surprise.'

Karina looked up at her, did not smile, and did not reply.

'How long will you be here?' Nora said.

'I'm not sure.'

'Shall we have lunch?'

'That would be nice.'

'Is Wednesday good for you?'

'I'm afraid not. Thursday, perhaps.'

'Excellent,' Nora said. 'Fouquet's at one o'clock.'

As Nora walked away towards her own table she heard Karina say something in French. And the two young men laughed.

'Wasn't that Karina?' One of Nora's friends said as she sat down.

'Yes, it was.'

'I heard she'd gone off to Brazil.'

'She did. But it seems she's back,' Nora said.

'You and she are old friends, aren't you?'

Nora smiled. 'Let's just say I've known her for a long time.'

On Thursday, Nora arrived at Fouquet's just before one. She sat at a table secluded from the rest of the restaurant by potted ferns, and sipped Campari and soda. At one-fifteen she asked for the wine list and studied it. At one-thirty she began to look over the menu. At ten to two she called the waiter over, told him she would not be ordering lunch after all, and left the restaurant.

Two days later she had a letter from Karina, written in purple ink on the writing paper of the Hotel Lancaster. There was no date and no greeting. Karina's message simply started at the top, rambled on for two pages, and stopped.

I trust you did not go to Fouquet's as we discussed at La Coupole.

I tried to make it clear by my manner that I was simply being polite, that I had no intention of meeting you on Thursday or any other time. I did not want to embarrass you in front of my two Swedish escorts so I pretended a politeness I do not feel.

Although I had assumed, after our last meeting, that we would not meet again, I was almost pleased to see you as I did. I think it was necessary that you should look in my eyes and see that I am not your friend.

Perhaps you think I was never your friend. Perhaps you prefer to think that. But I was, Nora. I was your friend, then your lover, but always your friend. I have always believed that friendships between women survived longer than any others and I certainly believed that about us. But I was mistaken.

Since I told you so much about my husband's problems the last time we talked I will take a moment to finish the tale. He has beautifully established himself in a fine old estate in the mountains north-west of Rio. We have a new name and Austrian passports and many old friends from Germany living nearby. We also have a lovely house on the beach at Ipanema. I will spend most (or all) of my time there and my husband will lurk behind the walls of his estate enjoying himself in whatever ways he can at his age. Not only do I accept this new life that was forced on me, I relish it. There is great energy in Rio and I have began to make my mark.

I tell you these details so you will not grieve for me, so you will not say, 'Poor Karina', to yourself. Having been a recipient of your love (if one dares to call it that), I have no desire to experience your sympathy. And God deliver me from your pity.

There was a time when I believed I could never possibly write to you as I'm writing now. I loved you, as you know, and I was also in awe of you. My own ego has always been a healthy one. I know that I was blessed when natural gifts were passed round. But my self-esteem shrank quickly when I measured myself beside you. I admired you too much to envy you. I considered myself fortunate to be your intimate friend. And when time passed and things changed in your life and we became more than friends, I counted myself as a fortunate woman indeed. For the first time in my life I thought only of what I might give and not what I might get in return. It was a dazzling, almost frightening experience for me. I didn't allow myself to hope that our

419

time together would last. I didn't dare consider the fact that it might end. I was tortured by my feeling that I wasn't good enough for you, dreading the day when you might discover that fact.

I am aware of how people regard me. They call me promiscuous, and I am. Morality as a concept has never been clear to me, so being labelled immoral or amoral has never disturbed me in any way. If there is such a thing as morality it must have a thousand definitions. If I had one of my own, which I don't, I'm sure it would have something to do with honesty, with consistency, with being what one seems to be, with delivering what one promises, with not trying to reclaim gifts that were freely given. In short, I have never wanted to feel sorry for things I've done. And I don't.

How does all this apply to you? In your mind maybe it doesn't. But in my mind, now that I know you well, now that I have seen facets of you that I didn't or couldn't see before, I realize that you are capable of countless things that I, for all of my cloudy reputation, could never do.

The love that I gave you I am both unable and unwilling to take back. The admiration is another matter altogether. That I take back. I could never call you hard or cold or brittle or unfeeling, but there is something of all these things buried somewhere inside you. Love can never be detached, can it? Isn't that what love is, a passionate inability to be detached, to look at a beloved person with detachment, to be anything less than involved? Love is a condition that invites pain. The risk is always there. The pain is always there. Every time I've felt it I've told myself 'never again'. But that's a promise that can't be kept.

Having loved and admired and worshipped you, I now feel sorry for you. You have everything except what you really want. And the saddest part of all . . . you have no idea what you have to give up in order to get it.

All these years I thought Jesse was a fool and a bastard for leaving you. Now I know *why* he left.

Oscar Mullet flew to London five times in three weeks. Each time he returned to Madrid, a chartered plane met him at the airport and flew him directly to the film location at Montehormoso. On his last trip, however, he called Dorsey at their Madrid apartment and said, 'I have to talk to you. I'll be there in an hour.'

'I have an appointment at the dressmaker . . .'

'Cancel it.'

'It's all right. I'll be home by five.'

'No, it's not all right,' he said. 'Cancel it. I'll see you in an hour.'

When he walked into their drawing-room she said, 'What's happened to you? You look awful.'

'No sleep. And a lot of grief.'

'What do you mean?'

'I mean I'm in major trouble. I could end up broke. I could end up in jail.'

'For what? What are you talking about?'

'Business stuff. I won't tell you the details because in the first place it wouldn't mean anything to you and in the second place I don't want you to know, just in case they drag you up on the witness stand.'

'Why would they do that?'

'Because you're my wife. Because you're a principal in half a dozen corporations I control. They won't believe you, no matter what you say, but at least if you don't know anything you won't have to lie.'

'Lie about what?'

'About me. About my business. About bank accounts. About everything with a dollar sign on it. The income tax bastards in London have decided to go after me. They're trying to build a case that will drown me.'

'But you pay your taxes. I've seen how much you pay. You pay a fortune every year.'

'It's not that simple. There's a ton of money involved. A lot of cash being moved around. It's easy to make mistakes. I'm involved in Switzerland and Italy and Spain. In a big way. And Britain and America besides. I mean, you have to be a financial wizard to keep your finger on everything that's going on. I have the best bookkeepers I can buy and even they're confused half of the time.'

'I don't understand what you're saying.'

'I'm saying that if somebody decides you're crooked, that your company's money is being mishandled, there's always some piece of evidence that seems to prove it. You know how the movie business is. Nobody's hands are completely clean. Everybody's on the arm. Putting promises in the bank. Borrowing against an indication of a hint of interest in a maybe property that's not even on paper yet. We're all blowing smoke. That's the way the business works. We steal from one project to keep another one from going under. We steal from John Huston to pay Henry Fonda and next time around we lift a little something from Dick Widmark to pay back Huston.'

'But you're talking about *jail*.'

'I don't know what I'm talking about. Not yet. I just know we've got accountants and bureaucrats crawling all over us. And it looks as if they have my tail in a crack.'

'But you have lawyers,' Dorsey said. 'You have more lawyers than anybody alive.'

Oscar nodded. 'I've had lawyers who could get me out of trouble but I've never had one yet who could keep me out of trouble. I've got something good going over here. I don't want to be indicted and wreck it all. Those London tabloids would have me looking like Jesse James.'

'What can you do?'

'America, I'm not worried about. We've got people over there who have the Internal Revenue Service in their pocket. And we've got friends in London, too. But they say the Exchequer can't be scared and it can't be bought. So we're trying to come up with something else. That's where you can help. You and Rab Bradshaw.'

'He won't even talk to me,' she said.

'Sure he will. He talked to you last time he was in Madrid.'

'I don't know what gave you that idea.'

'Save your breath, Dorsey. I know he came here to see you. He told me and the servants told me. Nobody's questioning your virginity. We're talking about important stuff. Did he say anything to you about my business, about a possible investigation into my affairs?'

422

'No. What does he know about it?'

'I'm not sure,' Oscar said.

'Even if he did know something, he wouldn't tell me about it.'

'He might. You see, I have a notion that there might be a connection between you and Rab . . .'

'I told you. That's all over.'

'Is that why he came to see you? To kiss you goodbye?'

'No. He doesn't want it to be over. He still wants me to divorce you so I can marry him.'

'That part checks out at least. That's what he told me.'

'What else did he tell you?' she said.

'Don't you know?'

'I haven't seen him since he talked to you. He just wrote me a note and said he'd told you everything about everything.'

'That's right. He did.'

'He told you what happened in Virginia?'

Oscar nodded. 'Showed me the cast on his wrist. He said you thought I was responsible for that.'

'I didn't know what to think,' Dorsey said. 'I was so crazy and frightened I didn't know what I was saying.'

'I told him you said you wanted a divorce so you could marry him. But when you came down here to Madrid, all smiles and conversation, I decided you'd changed your mind.'

'You know I changed my mind. I told you that.'

'Did you tell him?'

She nodded. 'He knows.'

'I think maybe he forgot. That's why I think you might be able to help me out of this financial mess the Brits are trying to put me in.'

'How? I don't see how.'

'I've been thinking about the talk I had with Bradshaw when he came out to Montehormoso. He wanted to talk about you and that didn't surprise me. But first of all we talked some business. Mostly he talked and I listened. The truth is the first hint I had that I might be in some trouble with the Exchequer came from Rab. He said he had a friend in the department, he wouldn't tell me his name – most of those birds are knights or lords or something – and this gentleman mentioned that they were starting a look-see at my operation. Just thought he should warn me about what was happening, Rab said. Damned nice of him, I thought, and I told him

423

so. But a little surprising in the situation where we find ourselves. Because the next topic we discussed was you. He explained to me in some detail that the only reason you're staying with me is because you're scared not to.'

'I didn't tell him to say . . .'

'Let me finish,' Oscar said. 'He said you were afraid I might get custody of Charlie if you sued me for divorce and I said I would certainly try to do that. He also said that you think those photographs of you that were taken in a motel room in Virginia are now in my hands and that you're afraid of what I might do with them.'

'Of course I'm nervous about those pictures. No matter who has them.'

'Well, since you're my wife, even if someone did send the pictures to me, I certainly wouldn't want them passed around any more than you do.'

'But what if I weren't your wife?'

Oscar smiled. 'That's a hypothetical question, isn't it, since you've made it very plain that you've broken it off with Bradshaw and no longer want to divorce me.' When she didn't answer he said, 'Am I right?'

'Yes.'

'Let's get back to my talk with Rab at Montehormoso. When I went to London and found out that the investigation he'd mentioned was already beginning to take place I sat down by myself one evening in the Dorchester Grill and tried to figure out what part, if any, Rab had played in this investigation of my business. Slowly a scenario began to shape up in my head. Suppose the investigation was not what it seemed to be. Suppose it was a sham. Rab had admitted to me that he had news of it from a personal friend at the Exchequer. I assume his friend has a high position there. So what if Rab had suggested to his friend not that he break the laws of his department but that he actually set in motion a routine inspection of my business? Many of those are begun, I'm told, and quickly abandoned. By telling me beforehand, Rab would see that I knew what was going on, he would demonstrate that he was willing to violate a friend's confidence to warn me. So in one stroke he could tell me I was in trouble and imply that he was my ally. At the same time he tells me that the only thing that is preventing him from marrying my wife is her fear of the consequences. Do you see a bargaining position being set up here?'

'My mind doesn't work that way,' she said. 'You know that.'

'All right. Let's see how this plays out. Suppose I go to Rab and talk to him as I've been talking to you. Suppose I said that I see desperate days ahead, that I could be bankrupt, or in prison, or both. What do you think his reaction might be?'

'I don't know. Since he'd warned you it might happen, I guess I'd expect . . . I'm not sure how he'd feel.'

'Neither am I. But suppose I said to him that he's the only person I can turn to, what if I asked him to go this friend at Exchequer and see if there was some way the audit of my records could be called off? I assume he'd say that he did not have the power to do that. What do you think?'

'I don't think he'd do it. I don't imagine he could.'

'Probably true. But not necessarily. Remember, he knows the investigation is a phoney anyway.'

'I don't believe he'd set that up,' she said. 'Even if he could.'

'Maybe not. But I don't disbelieve it either. So I say to him that I'm desperate and he's my last hope. I can't bribe him or give him anything because he has more money than God. But there is something I have that he wants. He knows it and so do I. Suppose I say to him that if he intercedes for me, if he's successful in getting me out of the jam I'm in, that I'll agree to a divorce and sign papers granting you custody rights to Charlie . . . how do you think he'd react to that?'

'I don't know.'

'How would you react to it?'

'I don't like this whole conversation. I'm not a screenplay or an actor's contract that you can hustle on the open market.'

'Of course not. But let's be honest about it. If you could be free to marry Bradshaw and have custody of Charlie and do me a favour at the same time, wouldn't you at least consider it?'

'This is like some fairy-tale. A word game. I'm not good at these things and you know it.'

'All right. Let's look at it this way. If you don't divorce me and I end up broke, you'll be broke too. If I go to prison, you'll be broke and married to a jailbird. But if Rab can get me out of this, you'll have him and your kid and champagne at every meal. Or if you have a change of heart and decide you want to stay with me, you can do that, too.'

425

'You mean you'd promise Rab that you'd divorce me and then change your mind?'

'I couldn't do that. I told you . . . I'd be willing to sign a separation agreement and a custody agreement beforehand.'

'Then how could I come back to you?'

'Why not? Just because I've signed papers doesn't mean you have. No one can force you to divorce me. No one can force you to marry Bradshaw. I'm not assuming you'd want to stay with me, but the way would be open.'

'You really have a sick mind, Oscar. You can't tell the difference between movies and real life.'

He shook his head. 'You're wrong about that, Dorsey. What we're talking about *is* real life. And if you don't use your head, you could be a big loser.'

'You talk as if I have some decision to make. I don't. You're going to do whatever you think is best, no matter what I say.'

'No, I'm not. As far as Rab's concerned, I'm not going to do anything. I can't do anything.'

'Didn't you just tell me he may be the only person who can help you?'

'That's right. But even so, I can't approach him. I can't promise him anything because he doesn't trust me.'

'Then what have we been talking about?'

'He trusts you,' Oscar said. 'You're the only one who can explain the situation to him.'

'I could never do that, Oscar. I'd fall apart in the middle of a sentence.'

'No, you wouldn't. Because when you think it over you'll see that you have everything to gain and absolutely nothing to lose.'

'I can't and I won't. I can't do it.'

'Of course you can,' Oscar said.

'You don't even know if he can do anything. You don't even know if he'll try.'

'That's true. But unless something else turns up, it's the best shot we have.'

'Not in my hands,' she said. 'I've never been able to persuade anybody about anything.'

Oscar smiled. 'Bradshaw's not just anybody. He's a receptive audience. You'll be able to persuade him.'

426

[6]

One black night in Larvik, between two and three in the morning, Floyd had a telephone call from Betsy.

'I know it's the middle of the night there. I'm sorry I woke you up.'

'That's all right. I can barely hear you. This is a rotten connection. Where are you?'

'I'm at the airport in Mexico City. I'm leaving Taylor.'

'When did this happen?'

'Today. We drove down from Santa Barbara and took a plane from LA this afternoon.'

'Who's *we?*'

'I'm travelling with a friend,' she said.

'How about the girls?'

'They're with me, too. Listen, I have to get off now. They're calling my flight. We're going to a little town on the west coast. I'll call you from there. And if Taylor gets in touch with you, you haven't heard from me . . . OK?'

She didn't call him the following day. Nor the day after that. Six days after they'd talked on the telephone he had a letter from her, the envelope encrusted with Orozco postage stamps.

Hope you haven't been worried because you haven't heard from me. The telephone service from here is almost non-existent. On a clear day you can call Taxco or Mexico City and local legend has it that someone once got through to Tucson, but beyond that, nothing. So I'm writing.

I need help, Floyd. All kinds of help. Money and encouragement and advice. Most of all I need to see you. Is there any chance that you and Valerie could come here? I hope you can.

The friend I mentioned to you on the phone is Dan Wilhoyt. He's a builder from Santa Barbara and I want to marry him. But first I have to figure a way to disentangle myself from Taylor. Thank God, I have Jennifer and Julie with me. At least I managed *that*. But now I'm scared to death he'll trace me and show up here with twenty lawyers.

As soon as he read her letter through, Floyd called his bank and asked them to cable her a draft for ten thousand dollars. Then he made plane reservations for himself and Valerie to fly to Mexico. When he told her what he'd done she said, 'I can't go there, Floyd. We talked about it before. You go and do whatever has to be done and I'll watch over things here. Where is this place? I've never heard of it.'

'It's north of Acapulco on the Pacific coast. It's called Tocalan. There's still no road through from Mexico City. You have to fly in. Or you can take a boat from Acapulco or Zihuatanejo.'

'Have you been there?'

'No. But my friend, Abe Rettberg has. He lived there in a shack on the beach for a year.'

'I hope Betsy's not in a shack on the beach.'

Floyd shook his head. 'She's at the Papagallo. It's a good hotel. Very fancy, Abe said. I think you'd like it. You've never been to Mexico.'

'I know. I want to go with you some time. But Dr Fjeldstad thinks I should . . .'

'You know what I think of Dr Fjeldstad.'

'Yes, I do. But all the same I'm sure he's helped me. I feel much calmer since I've been seeing him.'

'You can calm down a hungry crocodile if you give him enough tranquillizers.'

'It's not just that. It's very peaceful here in Larvik. I think that's the best thing for me just now.'

'Listen, kid, I've said this to you a dozen times before but I think it's worth saying again. I know you've had some upsetting experiences, with Polly especially, but no matter how much you'd like to fix everything, some things can't be fixed. They have to fix themselves.'

'I know that,' she said. 'I hate it but I know it.'

'You're a healthy woman. You know that and so does everyone else. I'd just hate to see you get into a frame of mind where you might . . . I mean I hope you don't feel dependent on Fjeldstad or any other doctor. You're not sick, Val. Your body works fine and so does your head. You've been dealing with problems and tough situations all your life. You can still do that. Don't let some jackass Norwegian quack tell you that you have to be tranquillized to get through the day.'

428

Valerie smiled. 'It's not like that, sweetheart. It's nothing like that. This is just a temporary stress situation . . .'

'I hate those bloody clinical terms. Stress and tension and anxiety. Most people never even know about those things till some idiot doctor explains them. He says, "You seem to be suffering from anxiety" and the patient says, "That's it. That's what wrong with me." And from that moment on it's true.'

'That's not me you're describing,' Valerie said. 'You know I'm not that way.'

'That's right. I do know that. That's why I don't want you to start depending on things you don't need.'

'I won't. I promise. I just depend on you and our lovely cocktails every evening at six.'

It was late at night when Floyd's plane cut through the purple clouds of poisoned air that cover Mexico City and landed at the airport at the eastern edge of Distrito Federal. He slept in a hotel nearby and flew in a small plane the next morning to Tocalan.

Since leaving Oslo, Floyd's thoughts had been totally occupied with Betsy. Time telescoped and looped and doubled back in his mind, and Betsy's mother's problem seemed as fresh and new to him suddenly as those of her daughter. Since his marriage to Valerie, and even before that, almost since the day of Jeannette's death, he had disciplined himself, had tried very hard to train himself, not to relive those agonizing years, not to attempt to piece together a jagged puzzle that resisted assemblage. When he and Betsy, just the two of them, had stood beside Jeannette's grave in a country graveyard in the Nevada mountains he had put his arms round his stepdaughter and said, 'We have to put it behind us, kid.' By saying that to her he had tried to tattoo it on his own brain, tried to position himself in a way that would permit him to remember the sweet and good and wild and lovely things about Jeannette, and wipe out as much as possible the smears of deception and accusation and shrill anger. Now, however, in the cool cocoon of a throbbing airliner he found that all sorts of words and movements and sounds and scents filtered back, bringing Jeannette vividly to life.

After her mother's death, as Betsy matured, Floyd had studied her carefully for evidence of genetic inheritance from Jeannette. He had found none, or almost none. Betsy, at twenty-one, seemed more solidly at home in the world, more at peace with herself, than

429

Jeannette had ever been. Her children, her pets, everyone except her husband, seemed to warm and unfold their petals in her presence. Whereas Jeannette darted with sudden bursts of speed and changes of direction like a chickadee, Betsy flew directly from nest to feeder, from branch to bird-bath. While Jeannette sling-shotted between laughter and tears, maniacal joy and black anger, Betsy's days were free of strong colours or high decibels. She seemed, from an early age, to have come to terms with everything. As much as Floyd detested her husband, Taylor Brill, as difficult as it was for him to imagine what had brought them together, it never occurred to him that they might not stay together. He believed strongly that Betsy, either by nature or guided by some childhood memory of her mother's erratic rhythms, would stick by any choice that she made. He had never envisioned her being forced to explain to her own daughters why she felt compelled to leave their father. Whatever shortcomings existed in her marriage to Taylor, and in Floyd's eyes those shortcomings were grave and manifold, there was no possibility, he felt, that they would ever separate.

Yet, here he was on his way to help her, to bandage her and tend to her as he'd tended to her mother, in one way or another, every day they'd been together. Betsy, the constant wife, had redefined herself, it seemed. Not only had she abandoned her bizarre husband, she had light-heartedly selected his successor and carried him with her, along with her daughters and other pieces of baggage.

Would he encounter a new Betsy now? Had she discovered new facets of herself, found new ways to think and move and react? Or had she, at least in her own mind, simply thrown off the cerebral and arbitrary rhythms of her robot husband and reclaimed the self she had been before she met him and was devoured by him?

Floyd's first impression, when she met him at the jungle-surrounded airport in the hills just east of Tocalan, was that she had indeed returned to what she had once been. In her white trousers and loose shirt and sandals, her hair falling down her back, she looked very much as she had when he'd visited her at school.

'Dan's taken the girls to the beach and I'm taking you for a sexy lunch at El Padrino. A lovely view of the sea and lots of pretty ladies to look at.'

430

'Were you surprised?' she said when they were seated in the restaurant, cantilevered from a cliff edge high over the ocean.

'At first I was. Very. But as I thought about it, I wasn't. And I wasn't sad about it either.'

'I know. When you came to visit us in Santa Barbara, I knew you were . . . how shall I say it . . . I could see that you didn't exactly respond . . .'

'I didn't like him,' Floyd said. 'I don't like him. When you were with him I saw no reason for me to be brutally honest about it. But now that things have changed . . .'

'I think I knew what you were thinking,' she said, 'and I thought it was very classy of you not to put me in the position of defending him. The funny thing is that I wouldn't have defended him. Not to you. I've known for a long time that I'd dialled a wrong number but I suppose I was hoping for the best, trying to consider what was best for the children, waiting for some revelation. I probably would have welcomed some support from you about them. But all the same I was glad we didn't spoil your visit by picking Taylor's bones.'

'I kept thinking that he must have changed a lot since you met him in school. I was trying to see what had attracted you in the first place.'

'You think I haven't hashed that over in my head? Constantly. For more than a year now. The easy answer is that I've changed but he hasn't. But that's not true. He's changed more than I have, I think. What did I see in him at first? All kinds of things. He was a good athlete but he wasn't like the other athletes at school. He was a super student but he wasn't a fanatic about it. He was a pleasant-looking masculine guy, and girls always noticed him, but he didn't seem to be in love with himself. He appeared to have all sorts of nice ingredients. Looking back, I guess that's what attracted me. Balance. You know what I mean? Not so common in a young man twenty-one or twenty-two years old. There was nothing unpredictable or volatile about him. He just seemed to *be* there. Growing up, I hadn't known so many people like that, especially Mom and Dad. Maybe I told myself that anybody as different from them as Taylor was had to be somebody special. Does any of this make sense?'

Floyd nodded.

'Also I had a big crush on his body. No use kidding about that.

431

He looked very cute in his skimpy little running-suit. He was so thin you could see every muscle in his frame. I wasn't exactly a sheltered little flower when I met him – I mean, I wasn't a virgin, and I had a remarkable yen for him. And he for me. He was relentless. He truly overwhelmed me. "Ardent" is the word they use to describe young men like Taylor. So I tumbled off the branch like a ripe peach. And I wasn't sorry. I was glad. And he was glad. So we told each other how much in love we were, he set a couple of school running records that spring, and we graduated, me *cum laude* and Taylor *magna cum laude*. And we got married.

'We moved to Santa Barbara then, Taylor started making a great deal of money, Julie was born, then Jennifer, and everything was gorgeous. Or so I told myself. But gradually the veils fell away from my eyes. Every day I saw new evidence of what he had become, of how far he had drifted from what he had been. He was programmed. Once I'd labelled it, I saw it in every area of his behaviour. In the way he ate, the way he slept, even the way he swam. And I could see he had begun to program Julie and Jennifer. And me, of course. At first I thought it was a stage he had to go through, some idiotic rite of passage connected with his work. But slowly I realized it was more than a programme. It was a condition. And every day it became more rigid and formalized and permanent. It seemed that everything he did, everything we did together, was accompanied by the faint sound of a snare drum playing double time.'

'Did you talk to him about it?'

'Not like I'm talking to you now. I tried to talk around it a few times but I got nowhere. Taylor reacts badly to anything that borders on criticism and what I was trying to get at was something vital to his whole nervous system. The only constructive thing I could have said was, "For Christ's sake, stop what you're doing." He wouldn't have understood that, of course, and if he had understood it, he wouldn't have accepted it. I couldn't bring myself to say it, in any case. So I did what a lot of married women do. I kept my focus on my children, tried to count my blessings like beads on a string, and I had two or three stiff drinks every afternoon before he came home from his office. I guess I thought I was in a situation I would never get out of. When I was really depressed I told myself that things would get better some place along the line. And all the while, Taylor was insisting that we should have more children.'

432

'And then you met your friend,' Floyd said.

'Dan. That's right. He's a builder, I think I told you that, but he and his wife got a divorce and he's been trying to dig out financially ever since. The judge gave her half his business, good old California community property laws, so Dan had to sell his assets to settle with her. She really cleaned him out. Ever since then, he's been working as a master carpenter trying to get on his feet again. So that's how I met him. Taylor decided to put a new cedar deck around our pool, build a guest-house at the back of the garden, and double the size of our kitchen. All together, it was six or eight months' work. But Dan only got as far as replacing the deck and enlarging the kitchen. Actually, there was about a week's work left on the kitchen when we picked up the girls one day, drove to Los Angeles, and took a plane from there to Mexico. That was the day I called you from the Mexico City airport.'

[7]

Dan Wilhoyt looked like a poster advertising the benefits of orange juice and California sunshine. He was not tall or handsome but his thirty-eight-year old body looked as though it had been deprived and tortured to keep it in twenty-year-old condition. His teeth were irregular but chalk-white, his pale blue eyes seemed bleached by sea water, and his hair was yellow from the sun. He wore faded cut-off jeans, a sweat-shirt with no sleeves, and stained white sneakers without socks. 'He always dresses like that,' Betsy told Floyd, 'or almost always. I love that look. He says he's never worn a necktie in his life, and I believe him. I can't wait for you two to sit down by yourselves and have a couple drinks together. You'll love Dan. I know you will.'

The day after Floyd arrived in Tocalan, he and Dan did have a talk together in a cantina on the beach not far from their hotel. In a letter to Valerie he wrote, 'He couldn't stop talking about his failures. It seems he's failed at everything he's tried, including marriage. He's been married three times, divorced three times. But with all that he seems to be bursting with self-confidence. The things that most of us try to hide he seems to be proud of.'

433

'Talk about a screw-up,' Dan said, as soon as they sat down in the cool cantina and ordered drinks, 'if I told you the story of my life you'd think I was making it up. Wanda, my second wife, used to say they should make a movie about me. Starring Steve McQueen. She always thought I looked like Steve, or he looked like me, one of the two. I competed against him a couple times in the dirt-bike races, once in Paso Robles, and another time down at El Centro. I was dynamite on a dirt bike till I broke my leg one Sunday on the Malibu Canyon road. My dad bought me my first bike when I was eleven. He was a decent guy. Made a lot of money in plastics. I didn't see much of him when I was growing up but he was damned generous with me. I always had a good car from the time I was old enough to drive. Dad saw to that. And plenty of pocket money. He always said, "What's the use of making money if somebody doesn't enjoy it." Well, I enjoyed it all right. But when Arthur died – that was my Dad's name – everything blew up in my face. My mother, who'd never said three words to me when Dad was alive, suddenly came to life. She took charge of the money and everything else. Told me she'd support me if I went to school, but if I didn't go to school and make something of myself – that was her favourite expression – she'd cut me off and I'd have to go to work. She knew damn well I wouldn't go to school. I'd never liked school from the time I was five years old. But I also didn't want to be out there in the slam-bang world beating my brains out to pay the rent. So I found a lawyer who took her to court. My mother and I said a lot of mean things to each other in front of the judge and the judge said some pretty tough things to me. But when it was all over I had a couple hundred thousand in the bank in my own name and my mother had a piece of paper signed by me saying I'd been paid in full from Arthur's estate and I wasn't supposed to come to her for money any time in the future. And I never have. Mostly because I've never seen her or heard from her since that day we walked out of the courtroom. She went back to Rhode Island where her family lived and married some rich old bird twice her age, and as far as I know she's still there. But I didn't give a damn then and I don't give a damn now. I'd beaten her in court, which was what I wanted to do, and I had plans to run that two hundred thousand into a couple million. But I screwed that up, too.'

'What happened?' Floyd asked.

434

'Actually, looking back on it, it wasn't my fault. It was either bad timing or bad luck. I've had my share of that. What I did was, I invested in a vineyard in the Sonoma Valley and a tomato canning plant in the high desert just outside of a town called Pear Blossom. On paper, they both looked fool-proof. I mean, if I still had the money I think I'd make the same investments today. But, as I said, bad luck hit me. California had the rainiest year in history and all those expensive grape-vines rotted in the ground. So that took care of the vineyard. And that summer all the tomatoes went bad in the fields because there was a picker's strike and a trucker's strike. Both at the same time. So less than a year after the judge awarded me two hundred grand I'd lost it all. I was broke. I borrowed a couple thousand from my first wife's mother and went to Reno. I figured with a little luck at the slot machines I could go home with ten grand in my pocket. But the machines were cold that weekend so I went back to Ventura – that's where we were living then – with my pockets empty.'

'Betsy tells me you're a builder.'

Dan smiled and signalled to the waiter for another round of drinks. 'By default,' he said. 'That certainly wasn't what I had in mind for myself. There was a lot of real estate development going on around Oxnard and Ventura and Santa Barbara, and what I wanted to do was get hold of a big tract of land not too far from the ocean and put forty or fifty homes on it. But . . . I had no money and no credit. I spent a few months trying to hustle some start-up money from the banks, from my friends, from anybody who might have cash to put in. But I came up dry. Instead of being a developer I ended up with a hammer and saw, putting up houses for somebody else. I was always handy with tools. That was the only thing I liked in school. So that's what I did for a few years till I could put together a crew and start doing sub-contracting work. From there I moved up to contracting, making bids on the whole job, from foundations all the way through to finish work inside. I got to the point where I was doing bigger jobs, time and material, where I got ten percent for myself out of every dollar that went into labour and construction materials. So I was riding high. Money in the bank, pretty good credit, and sniffing around for a nice piece of land I could buy and develop. Then the roof fell in again. My third wife divorced me and took me for every cent I had. Then, as soon as we'd signed the final papers, she married some jackass

435

petroleum engineer who'd been working in Ojai and they ran off to Venezuela. And they took my four-year-old boy with them. Talk about drunk..I was drunk for six weeks after that happened. I was happy to get rid of Sally but I sure hated to lose that kid.'

'Nothing you could do about it?'

Dan shook his head. 'She had custody.'

'But you had visitation rights, didn't you?'

'Sure I did. I figured she'd go on living in Santa Barbara. Or in Ventura maybe. So I planned to see him a lot. Then, *bang*, he was gone. If I'd known what she was planning I could have gone to court and stopped her, but once she was gone I was a dead duck. Even then, maybe I could have done something if I'd had all the money in the world to spend on lawyers. But like I told you, I was strapped. Talk about a rotten break. Right about then, I decided that any luck I'd ever had had run out. I was a sad sack of potatoes, let me tell you. Didn't care if I ate, didn't care if I worked, didn't give a damn about anything. Then little by little, about a year ago, I started to work again. No big jobs. Doing cabinet work mostly. Remodelling, adding rooms. That sort of thing. Not beating the bushes, just taking whatever jobs came my way. Word of mouth, recommendations. If you can do a good carpenter's job, there's always plenty of people willing to hire you. That's how I met Taylor Brill. He got in touch with me because I'd worked for a lawyer friend of his in Montecito. I met him at his house on Saturday, and we talked about what he needed to have done, and we made a deal. Betsy and the girls weren't there that day so I didn't meet her till I came to work two or three weeks later, after I'd finished another job I'd been working on. You want another drink?'

'Sure, why not,' Floyd said, and signalled to the waiter.

'You probably think I'm going to say it was love at first sight. But it wasn't. At first I didn't see her much because I was working outside on the pool deck. But when I moved inside to start on the kitchen, there she was. She'd offer me some coffee every once in a while and sometimes she'd sit down and have a cup with me. We talked about her two daughters and I told her about my son, Eric, and little by little we found out quite a bit about each other. She talked about you and her parents. She told me some of the things that happened to them and the crazy way it all ended. So we became friends. We talked to each other the way people do sometimes because they know that when the job's over or the vacation, or whatever it is, they'll never see each other again. I mean, neither of us knew *anybody* that the other one knew. I enjoyed seeing her every day but when I left her house and went home at five o'clock I didn't think about her at all till I saw her the next day. I mean, if I'd been looking for a woman, which I wasn't, because I was still trying to get over the shafting I'd taken from Sally, even so, I would never have zeroed in on Betsy. She was off limits as far as I was concerned. I'd never heard her say a bad thing about her husband and I knew she was crazy about Jennifer and Julie. I mean, she was a happily married woman if I'd ever seen one. You know what I'm saying?'

Floyd nodded and Dan went on. 'Then one day, the walls came tumbling down. Usually when I got to their house in the morning, Taylor was already gone, but this particular day I saw his car was still in the garage when I drove into the parking area. When I came into the back of the house, where I was working on the kitchen, there was no one there, but I heard the two little girls banging around upstairs getting ready to leave for school and I could hear Taylor's voice from the living room in the front of the house. A few minutes later he and the children went into the garage, got in the car, and left. The house was dead quiet then but after a while I heard an odd sound I didn't recognize coming from the front. I walked through the hallway till I came to the living room. Betsy was standing with her back to me, looking out the window towards the garden. She was standing as stiff as a board but I could tell she was crying. I walked across the room and stopped a few feet behind her. I asked her if there was anything I could do and she said, "There's nothing anybody can do. I wish I was dead." After that day everything was different between us. In three weeks we began to make plans to go away together. And when the time came, when we'd made all the arrangements, we took the girls and left.'

'What are your plans now?' Floyd said.

'We don't have any plans. We can't make any plans. We just knew she had to get away from that bastard. We had to get Jennie and Julie away from him.'

'What do you mean by that?'

'I'd better let Betsy tell you that. I get so steamed up I can't talk about it.'

Just as Betsy had made herself busy during the afternoon so that

437

Floyd and Dan could spend some time together, so did Dan absent himself that evening.

'What do you think of him?' Betsy said.

'He's a good guy. I like him,' Floyd said.

'He's a wonderful man. I can't tell you how important he is to me. He's human. He has flaws. He laughs too loud and he cries sometimes and smokes too much and gets drunk. But he can do things with his hands. He can make things and fix things. I never really understood how rotten Taylor is till I met Dan. I love the way he is with Julie and Jennie, and I dearly love the way he is with me. He's not well educated and, God knows, he's not a lucky man. I'm sure you know that by now.'

'He tells me he feels very lucky now.'

'I know. He tells me that all the time. He thinks I'm the answer to everything for him and that's what I want to be. He feels terribly guilty because I had to ask you for money but I told him it was no problem for you. I'm sure I'll be all right financially once I get things squared away with Taylor.'

'That may be tougher than you think. Taylor's not going to be easy to deal with. But you're not to fret about money. I'll take care of that end of it.'

'I know you will. And that means a lot to me. I was just telling you that it makes Dan feel strange that he can't pay for everything. I told him I'm married to a money machine *now*. That's not what I'm looking for the second time around.'

They sat up very late, talking details. Dan came back to the hotel and went to his own room to bed, and still they went on talking. At last, just before Floyd left to go to his room, he said, 'Did you leave Taylor a note when you left?'

'Yes. I told him I was leaving him and I wanted a divorce, and I'd be in touch with him later.'

'Do you think he has any idea where you are?'

'I don't think so,' she said.

'If he puts a private detective on it and they start checking airline passenger lists he could find out. So let's do a manoeuvre. I want you to write him a letter. Tell him you're in Norway visiting me but you'll only be there for a few days. From Norway you and the girls will be going to France. And tell him your California lawyer will be in touch with him.'

'I don't have a lawyer.'

438

'You will have. I'm going to New York to work that out tomorrow.'

'What about the letter? How do we . . . ?'

'Put it in an envelope addressed to Taylor. I'll send it along to Valerie in a larger envelope. She'll put Norwegian stamps on your letter and mail it to him from Larvik.'

'You're cute.'

'It should buy us some time. We don't want him showing up here and trying to run away with Jennie and Julie. And another thing, before I leave here I'll rent an apartment in my name so you and the kids can move in there. That way your names won't show up on any hotel register.'

'You always fix things for me,' she said.

'This is the first time I can remember when you needed something fixed.'

'I hope it will be the last time.'

[8]

After two days in New York meeting with Mike Rosenthal Floyd flew to Chicago to see Helen. She met him at the airport and they drove together to Fort Beck. After he had told her the details of Betsy's situation, Helen said, 'Her husband sounds awful. I'm surprised she's stayed with him as long as she has. He'll make a divorce difficult, won't he?'

Floyd nodded. 'No doubt about it. That's why we have to stop him before he gets started. That's why I spent two days with Rosenthal. He put me on to the best divorce lawyer in California. At least, Mike says she's the best, and if he says it, I believe it. The lawyer, it turns out, is a lady. Ruth Berquist is her name. Mike and I were on the phone to her for several hours planning a strategy. She's flying to Mexico tomorrow morning to take depositions from Betsy and the two children. Then I'll meet her in California when I leave here, and if all goes well we'll go after Taylor and give him an idea of what he's up against.'

'I'm not an authority on divorce procedures,' Helen said, 'But

439

hasn't she put herself in a bad position by running away with another man? Don't they consider that desertion?'

'Usually. But there are extenuating circumstances here. The lawyers are going to say she turned to Dan in desperation, that she needed a friend, an ally, a defender. Also, they've played it cool in Mexico. They were in the same hotel but she and the girls were on one floor and Dan was two floors down. Now she's in an apartment with Jennie and Julie, and Dan's still in a hotel.'

'What's he like?' Helen asked.

'I don't know him very well yet. But one thing I'm sure of . . . he's as different from Taylor as anyone can be.'

'Do you like him?'

'She likes him, Helen. That's all that concerns me. Betsy's no fool. If she sees something good in him then it must be there.'

'Not necessarily, my dear. Love steers us all down mean streets. Remember . . . Betsy also saw something good in Taylor.'

'Don't remind me,' Floyd said.

'What does he do, the new man?'

'He's a builder.'

'That's a lucrative profession.'

'Not in his case. He's broke. I think they'll be living on Betsy's money.'

'Can she handle that?'

'She has some money of her own but she's going to have a lot more. I'm going to adopt her. You adopted me and made me a Bradshaw. Angus adopted Jesse and made him a Bradshaw. Now I'm going to do the same thing for Betsy.'

'What a fine idea. She's always been like a daughter to you. Why not make it legal?'

'That's the way I feel. Rosenthal's having the adoption papers drawn up now and we'll make it official as fast as we can.'

'Wonderful. I'll have a granddaughter after all.'

'And some great grandchildren. I'm not sure how you'll feel about that.'

'I'll feel fine about it. The more, the merrier.'

Jesse's reaction, when Helen told him that evening at the dinner table, was considerably more restrained than hers had been. 'Well,' he said, 'that's a surprise.'

'A lovely surprise,' Helen said.

'You don't seem overjoyed,' Floyd said to Jesse.

440

'As I said, I'm surprised. As you know, I don't know Betsy very well. Haven't met her more than twice, it seems to me.'

'That doesn't matter, darling,' Helen said. 'I haven't had a chance to spend much time with her either. But she's Floyd's stepdaughter. Or at least she has been. Now she'll be his daughter.'

'Adopted,' Jesse said.

'Of course. But it's all the same. She'll be a Bradshaw now.'

'I have the feeling you're thinking something you don't want to say,' Floyd said.

'Don't mind Jesse,' Helen said. 'He's always this way. Has to consider everything very carefully before he gives his approval.'

'But Floyd's not asking for my approval, are you, Floyd? He's not asking for anyone's approval.'

'That's right. I'm not.'

'Then we can drop the whole subject,' Jesse said.

'I don't think I want to drop it,' Floyd said. 'Let's pretend I am asking for your approval. Let's pretend I couldn't adopt Betsy if you objected.'

'A hypothetical case?' Jesse said.

'If you like.'

'All right. We'll make it a little parlour game. If you came to me for approval, and the approval was mine to give, I suppose I'd wonder why you've chosen to adopt her now. I'd probably ask you why you didn't adopt her when you were married to her mother.'

'Because her real father was alive then.'

'Then I think my second question would be: why didn't you adopt her after both her parents died?'

'Her grandparents were alive then and she didn't want to hurt their feelings. Now they're all dead except for the grandmother on her father's side, and she and Betsy are not in touch with each other. Haven't been for years.'

'But now she's married, with children of her own. Seems like an unusual time for adoption.'

'What are you trying to say, Jesse?'

'I have no viewpoint. I'm just trying to look at the matter objectively. And I keep coming back to the same place. I think a disinterested observer might conclude that Betsy would like a firm financial foundation for herself now that she's getting a divorce.'

'What's wrong with that?' Floyd asked.

'Nothing, I suppose. As long as we're all candid about what's going on. If Betsy needs money or wants money, then there's no question that the simple act of becoming a Bradshaw will provide her with a great deal of money for herself and her children.'

'As it has the rest of us.'

'Exactly,' Jesse said.

'Maybe I didn't make myself clear. This isn't something that Betsy asked for. She doesn't even know it's about to happen. It's something I want for her.'

'That's not difficult to understand,' Helen said.

'Jesse understands,' Floyd said. 'He just doesn't approve.'

'What's the matter with you, Jesse? You act as if you're wearing a white wig and you're trying a federal case,' Helen said.

'Not at all. Since we've established that I have no right of approval or disapproval, we're simply having a philosophical discussion. The point I'm making is that there is a substantial difference between being adopted and discovering you're wealthy, and being adopted because you *want* to be wealthy.'

'Oh, for Christ's sake, Jesse,' Floyd said.

'I'm ashamed of you,' Helen said. 'That's a nasty thing to say.'

'I'm casting no aspersions against Betsy. We're talking about appearances. At least, I am.'

'Since Betsy knows nothing about this adoption, the only motives you can question are mine. And I freely admit I want Betsy to have the money and the independence she'll have when I adopt her. I don't want her to have to come to me. She's always known she could do that. I don't want her to go into this divorce proceeding with her hat in her hand, not knowing how Taylor will behave and how that behaviour will affect her future life and that of her daughters. I want her to feel secure.'

'That's what everybody wants,' Jesse said, 'but most of us aren't fortunate enough to . . .'

'You were,' Floyd said. 'I'm sure you don't tell yourself that your life would have been the same if Angus hadn't adopted you.'

'If you're implying that I agreed to become a Bradshaw because of the money involved . . .'

'I'm not implying anything,' Floyd said. 'I'm asking you. If you're taking a lofty position about other people's motives, let's talk about yours.'

'Why don't we drop this subject?' Helen said. 'Floyd wants to

442

adopt Betsy and there's no reason why he shouldn't. Why don't we let it rest there?'

'No, Jesse said. 'Floyd deserves an answer to his question. In case I haven't made it clear, I don't think anyone should be taken into the family just to solve their financial problems. Nor do I think we should all embark on a programme of indiscriminate adoption. This is, after all, a family of blood-lines and tradition. We mustn't think of it as a club where one can simply apply for membership and be taken in . . .'

'What are you saying, darling?' Helen said. 'This is Betsy we're talking about. Her mother was a Bradshaw by marriage. Her step-father, Floyd, has more Bradshaw blood that I do.'

'Let me finish,' Jesse said. 'Floyd seems to believe that I was motivated by the prospect of wealth. Let me put it this way – and I'm sure Helen will bear me out: I was joined to the Bradshaws, I saw myself as a Bradshaw, long before I became aware of the family in England. The only Bradshaws I knew were Helen and Raymond. When I met Raymond he seemed to be a moderately successful university professor. When he died that status hadn't changed. If he had asked to adopt me I would have been delighted. But that question never came up. Because I'm sure he already thought of me as a son, just as I felt he was my father. So my adoption by Angus was merely a formality to me. I had thought of myself as a Bradshaw since I was sixteen years old.'

'And Betsy has thought of me as her father since she was ten years old.'

Later that night, when Floyd was in his robe and pyjamas, Helen came to his room. 'I'm sorry about that discussion at the dinner table. I don't know what he was trying to say.'

'It's not your fault,' Floyd said. 'He's a self-righteous bastard and he always has been.'

'I wish you wouldn't say things like that. I can't stand the thought of you two not being nice to each other.'

'And I'm sorry to see you in the middle, but if you think the situation between us is going to change, you'd better not get your hopes up. Jesse and I have resented each other from the beginning. He resented me as your son and now he resents me as Valerie's husband. And I certainly resented him when he was married to Valerie. That's what this whole discussion tonight was about. Jesse was trying to score some points against me. Maybe it was all for your benefit. I don't know. But it's not something I'd like to repeat.'

'I'm sure it won't come up again.'

'I wish I believed that, but I don't. Jesse and I are never going to fall into each other's arms.'

'I don't expect that. But I'm sure you'll manage to be civil to each other for the few days while you're here.'

'I've decided not to stay,' Floyd said. 'I was really looking forward to spending some time with you but I can't hack it with Jesse. I used up all my patience and civility tonight. One more session and I would really unload on him. I don't want to put that pressure on you.'

'I'll talk to him first thing in the morning. He'll behave. I promise you.'

Floyd shook his head. 'Sorry, Mom, it just won't work. It wouldn't be any fun for me or for you either. We'd be sitting on a powder keg. Why don't you drive up to Chicago with me tomorrow morning? We'll spend the day together and I'll take a late flight to California.'

After a long moment she said, 'I feel terrible. Is this the way it's going to be now? Won't I ever be able to see you and spend time with you? You're the most important person in the world to me and you're unavailable. I don't mean it's your fault. But is this something that can't be fixed? Isn't there something we can work out so we don't have to meet in airports, and nowhere else?'

'I don't know. I don't like it any better than you do. I came because I thought things could be pleasant for a few days and . . . well, it didn't work out that way, did it?'

'I hope you don't blame me.'

'I don't blame anybody. If I were in Jesse's shoes, maybe I'd act the same way he does.'

'He's not always the way he was tonight.'

'I'm sure he's not,' Floyd said. 'But when he sees me, he sees red. So I guess it's better if he doesn't see me. I know it's better if I don't see him.'

'But where does that leave me?'

'I don't know. I'm sure Jesse loves you and you know I love you. But he and I certainly don't love each other.' He bent down and kissed her. 'So I guess we'll go on meeting in airports. That's better than nothing.'

Ruth Berquist, the lawyer Mike Rosenthal had recommended, was a stout grey-haired woman in her sixties. In a white apron, she would have seemed at home behind the counter of a pastry shop. But her voice, when she spoke, was rich with authority. As she and Floyd drove to Santa Barbara from Los Angeles he said, 'How did Taylor react when you spoke to him on the telephone?'

'Very calm. No histrionics. I told him his wife had asked me to represent her and suggested that we should have a preliminary meeting. He asked if Betsy would be with me and I said no, but you would.'

'What did he say to that?'

'No reaction. When I suggested that he might like to bring his lawyer to the meeting he said he didn't think that was necessary at this point.'

'Very matter of fact.'

'Exactly. He sounds like a man who's holding four aces and a king.'

'That's Taylor. He's shrewd and stubborn. Thinks he's a match for anyone.'

'Good. I'd rather deal with tough guys than weak sisters. It's boring to see a man cry.'

'Where are we meeting him?'

'He suggested that we came to his office but I told him I preferred more neutral ground. I booked a suite at the Biltmore. He'll meet us there.'

Taylor was waiting for them in the hotel lobby when they arrived. He was even more pencil-thin than Floyd remembered. His dark linen suit was neatly pressed and buttoned, and his shoes had a high polish. He was perfectly composed and was extravagantly polite to Mrs Berquist. As soon as they were sitting at a table in their third-floor suite Taylor said, 'Let me tell you what I already know. Then we'll go on from there. When Mrs Brill left our home I found a note from her saying she was planning to ask me for a divorce and that her lawyer would contact me. I know that she and my daughters flew from Los Angeles to Mexico City. Enquiries were made. I also know she is travelling with a man. It's almost impossible for me to believe that she's gone off with the carpenter who was remodelling our kitchen but since he's no longer in Santa Barbara and since his name appeared on the passenger list of her flight to Mexico, it seems to be more than a coincidence. I was unable to trace her after she arrived in Mexico City. In fact, I was preparing to go there myself to look for her when I had a letter from her mailed in Norway. The letter said she would be leaving there and going to France with Julie and Jennifer. Unless she's simply trying to throw me off the track I assume that's where they are now. Is that true?'

'Mrs Brill has asked us not to disclose her present address,' Mrs Berquist said.

'Does that mean I'm to be prevented from seeing my children?'

'Not at all. That's one reason we're having this meeting. To try to work out those details. As soon as we can report to Mrs Brill that we've made substantial progress toward a separation agreement, I believe she expects to return to America. At that time the final details of custody and visitation rights will be worked out.'

'You seem to be assuming that I'll agree to a divorce.'

'We assume nothing. Your wife has told us that she no longer wishes to live with you and be married to you. Since she cannot be forced to sustain a marriage that isn't satisfactory to her, since no one can be forced to live with another person if they choose not to, and since divorce is the legal instrument to end a failed marriage . . .'

'I don't believe it's a failed marriage.'

'I understand that,' Mrs Berquist said, 'but it seems that your wife feels differently about it.'

'Once we've had a chance to talk, when I've had a chance to spend some time with her, I guarantee you she'll change her mind about that. We're a family. We have two lovely daughters. Betsy doesn't want to give that up.'

'Are you saying that you're unwilling to discuss any aspects of a divorce procedure until after you've talked with your wife?'

'That's exactly what I'm saying.'

'You realize that your wife can start the proceedings whether you agree or not, don't you?'

'I don't think she'll do that.'

Ruth Berquist referred to her portfolio, which lay open on the table in front of her. 'I have written authorization from Mrs Brill to start a divorce action as soon as possible. The proper papers are in my office now waiting to be filed.'

'I will file a counter-suit.'

'That's your privilege, of course. But if I may say so, that seems like an unnecessary complication. If you plan to cross-file, we will simply let you file the original suit. Mrs Brill has no objection to that. And it will save a great deal of time and expense.'

'But I don't want a divorce.' Taylor said. 'We have a perfectly fine marriage and I want it to continue.'

'But your wife doesn't. So we're back where we began,' Mrs Berquist said. She looked at Floyd. After a moment he turned to Taylor and said, 'If you think she'll change her mind and come back to you, I think you'll be disappointed. I believe she expects to live in Europe. Those are her plans, whether you agree to a divorce or not.'

'I can stop her from running away with my children.'

'They're her children, too,' Floyd said.

'As I said before,' Mrs Berquist said, 'no court can force her to live with you. And it's a problem to sue for child custody when you're still married. If you start such an action, divorce would inevitably be a part of the package. You'd be in the same position you're in now.'

'If you're trying to convince me that I have no alternatives, I don't accept that. I think I'm in a strong position. I didn't leave Betsy. She left me.'

'That's true. But whatever you imagine your legal position to be, your practical situation is quite different. Your wife has gone, she's taken the children with her, and you don't know where she is.'

'Anyone can be found. And once I know where she is, I will use whatever legal means are available to have her and the children brought back here.'

'Assuming that you were able to do that,' Mrs Berquist said, 'what would be your next step?'

'Once she's back home she'll come to her senses.'

'But what if she doesn't? You can't keep her locked up.'

'I don't think Betsy wants to give up her children. And that's what she'll have to do if she decides to go away again.'

'That, of course, is for the courts to decide.'

'If it came to that, I'd welcome the opportunity to make my case in court. Mothers don't automatically get custody these days. I'm

447

the one who can give the girls a fine home and a proper life. If Betsy insists on flying around the world with a carpenter I can't imagine any court awarding the children to her.'

'Since none of us knows the precise plans Mrs Brill has for her children, I think it's pointless to speculate about that.'

'I'm a Christian man, Mrs Berquist. I believe in decency and morality. If Betsy thinks that I will support her in some pagan European lifestyle, she is gravely mistaken.'

'Betsy doesn't need your support,' Floyd said. 'She has a great deal of money in her own name.'

'She'll need it,' Brill said, 'if she plans to get into a custody battle with me. I also have a great deal of money and I'll spend it all if that's what it takes to have my two daughters here with me.'

Mrs Berquist smiled. 'I think we're making some progress. At first you said you would not consider a divorce under any circumstances. Now we're discussing who will have custody of the children. Does that indicate a change in your position?'

'No. I am morally opposed to any divorce. I believe that marriage is a lifetime contract.'

'I respect your views. But we must remember that a marriage contract involves two people with equal rights.'

'No one has the right to break up a happy family.'

'If Betsy was happy,' Floyd said, 'I don't think we'd be sitting here like this. Do you think she's happy?'

'I don't want to discuss that with you,' Taylor said.

'Let's be clear about this, Mr Brill,' Mrs Berquist said, 'you don't have to discuss anything with us. We've gone to a great deal of trouble to come here and have this meeting because we thought it might simplify matters for both you and Mrs Brill. But if it doesn't appear that way to you, then we're all wasting our time. I will simply drive back to Beverly Hills, file the divorce papers and let the court answer all the questions you seem to have.'

'I don't think Betsy will go ahead with a divorce till she and I have had a chance to talk it over.'

'If she wanted to talk to you,' Floyd said, 'she wouldn't be out of the country.'

'As I told you,' Mrs Berquist said, 'she's already made up her mind. She's left the timing to me. If we can't reach some civilized understanding today, she wants me to start proceedings at once.'

'What do you mean by "a civilized understanding"?'

448

'Just that. An acceptance by both parties that if one person wants a marriage to end, then the other person must sooner or later accept that. If it can be sooner rather than later, a lot of anger and frustration can usually be avoided.'

'You make it sound like a real estate transaction,' Taylor said.

'That is certainly not my intention. The difficult part of my law practice is that two people never decide in unison to end a marriage. Almost always, one person wants it and the other one doesn't. There's a lot of pain involved. But once a firm decision has been made, by either one partner or both, then the details must be orchestrated in the fairest possible way. If I can do that job and make you feel good about it, I will certainly handle it that way. But I must do it in any case. As far as you and Mrs Brill are concerned, I would be less than candid if I didn't tell you that she is very hurt and very angry. And I think she's afraid of you. She not only wants to divorce you, she feels she must. But for the children's sake, she hopes it can be done as simply and quietly as possible. She has no desire to humiliate you.'

'I don't know what you're talking about,' Brill said.

'Of course you do. I prefer not to go into it in detail but if you force me to, I will.'

He sat looking at her, no visible change in his expression or his demeanour. But all the same the combative edge that was such a prominent part of him seemed suddenly blunted.

'What do you expect me to say?' he asked finally.

'That's up to you, of course. If you see any benefit to this meeting, if you think we can make some progress in resolving matters between you and your wife, then we can proceed. Otherwise . . .'

'I've told you I don't want a divorce.'

'I understand that. But since you know now that Mrs Brill insists on going forward with the proceedings, I think we have to try to move ahead. Try to tell me exactly what you want, Mr Brill, and I will tell you what she wants, and we'll go on from there.'

'I want my family together,' he said, 'the way we've always been. Everything I've accomplished here in Santa Barbara has been for Betsy and the girls. I need my children. I need to see them and take care of them,' He paused, 'If I can't have that, if there's no way that Betsy can be persuaded to come to her senses and be a proper wife and mother, then I suppose I'll have to go along with a divorce. But if I do, it will be on my terms. I see no reason why

449

I should make life easy for her and whatever beach bum she decides to pick up with.'

'Be careful what you say, Taylor,' Floyd said.

'I mean it. If she wants to get along without me, then she'll have to do without the things I've given her. The house is in my name, it's a part of my company, and both cars as well, so if she thinks she's going to move back into the house and move me out, she's very mistaken. Either she's my wife or she's not. Since she's decided to leave, it's my Christian duty to keep the lives of Julie and Jennifer as unchanged as possible. Children depend on familair surroundings, things they're accustomed to. That doesn't mean that I plan to cut Betsy off without a cent. But I don't expect to provide her with a life of luxury. From now on, whatever I'm able to accumulate will be for the benefit of my daughters.'

Floyd and Mrs Berquist exchanged a glance and she said to Taylor, 'I'm sure you're aware that division of community property as well as amounts of money that Mrs Brill would receive for herself and for child support . . .'

'There's no question of child support. The girls will live with me and I'll support them.'

'In any case,' Berquist went on, 'all those financial questions will be settled between your lawyers and me, with the court as final arbiter.'

'No court will sympathize with a woman who deserted her husband and children for no reason.'

'She didn't desert her children,' Floyd said. 'The girls are with her now.'

'She left me,' Brill said. 'I didn't leave her.'

'I think you've given us a clear picture of what your position is. Now I'll try to give you an idea of our objectives in the matter. Regarding the financial aspects of the separation agreement, Mrs Brill has made no specific requests. She tells me she is content to leave all those details in the hands of counsel. As you know, there are statutory guidelines about community property here in California. Since I have only a very general idea about your assets it would be inappropriate to try to go into those details at this time. Any lump-sum payments or schedule of alimony to Mrs Brill would be hinged to those financial figures as well as to the quality of life she has enjoyed as your wife. The thing we are particularly concerned with, of course, is the economic security and well-being of the two children. Where they live and how they live.'

'I'll take care of that, I assure you,' Brill said. 'If I don't have custody of the children there'll be no divorce.'

'You may not like to hear this, Mr Brill, but those matters are outside your control. There's going to be a divorce. And the issue of child custody was the main thing that Mrs Brill wanted us to discuss here today.'

'There's nothing to discuss.'

'We think there is. You remember that I suggested you bring your attorney with you today?'

Brill nodded. 'Not necessary. I know when I need a lawyer and when I don't. This morning I don't need one.'

'I must be blunt with you now,' Berquist said. 'You must not expect to retain custody of your two daughters. It's out of the question. Mrs Brill insists on having sole and undisputed custody of the children. If you are not willing to grant her that custody she has authorized me to bring an action that will declare you morally unfit.'

'What?'

'Your wife is prepared to testify that you are a threat to your own children.'

'Do you realize what you're saying to me?'

'I'm an attorney, Mr Brill. I know all the implications of what I'm saying. Your wife and other witnesses are prepared to say these things in court, so I have no hesitation about saying them to you in private.'

'I have no idea what you're talking about. If this is some device you've fixed on to frighten me, I assure you it won't work.'

'It's not a device. In fact, we are trying to make things easier for you. Your wife has no desire to air these matters before a judge if it can be avoided. But she's prepared to do so if you are unco-operative.'

'If Betsy thinks she can get what she wants by lying about me to a judge, let her do it. She'll only make a fool of herself.'

Mrs Berquist sat upright and absolutely motionless in her chair. At last she opened her briefcase and took out a thick file-folder. 'I have five notarized depositions here, three of them taken in Mexico and two in Santa Barbara. They represent the sworn statements of Dr Karen Applegate, a child psychologist, and Rosita Guzman, a teacher at the school your daughters attend. There is also extensive testimony from Mrs Brill and from each of your children. I won't attempt to summarize their statements for you. I suggest that you read them carefully. Then, I'm sure you'll understand why we're having this meeting.'

The three of them sat silently as Brill slowly read each page of the five documents. When he looked up finally, he said, 'It's easy to see what happened. Someone poisoned their minds. Someone coached them to say those things. They're practically babies still. They don't know what they're saying. They don't know anything about such things. Someone told them what to say.'

'Who do you think would do that?'

'How would I know? California attracts a lot of crazy people. Or the children may have seen something on television. The papers are full of these stories. And little girls have wild imaginations.'

'I spoke with Dr Applegate myself,' Berquist said. 'She said the same things you're saying. Until she'd questioned Julie and Jennie. She spoke to them separately. On separate days. She asked them all the trick questions a doctor asks when she's trying to get the truth. Each of the girls told the same stories they'd told their teacher and their mother. And each of them said she didn't want her sister to know what she'd told. Each of them believed that what she was describing had happened only to her. Dr Applegate found absolutely no evidence that they'd made up the story together. She believes they're telling the truth. So does Miss Guzman, so does your wife, and so do I.'

'You can believe what you like,' he said. He touched the folder with his fingertips. 'But that doesn't make it true. None of this is true.'

'Then you have nothing to be concerned about. If I were your attorney I would advise you to counter-sue and to fight for custody of your children.'

'I have to do that,' he said. 'I have no choice. Julie and Jennifer would never sit in the same room with me and say things like that. They wouldn't make up stories about their father.' He took a silk handkerchief out of the breast pocket of his jacket and carefully dried his upper lip. 'They know how much I love them. There's no fooling a child. As soon as you touch a baby they know if you love them or not. Even at night, when you turn them over or cover them up or pat them to make them go to sleep, they know whose

452

hand it is. They know. *Raison de peau*, the French call it. That means your skin knows things your brain has forgotten or never knew. Animals know. They all sleep in a great warm lump.' He looked down at the folders again. 'It's disgusting, reading cold words on a page like this. They don't explain anything, don't prove anything. No man living loves his children as much as I do. I'm proud of the way I feel. I'm proud of the way they feel about me. They love me. I've never doubted that. And I don't doubt it now.'

As he and Mrs Berquist drove south on the coast highway toward Los Angeles, Floyd said, 'What's going to happen now?'

'I'm not sure. Not a great deal, I would imagine. Mr Brill is a strange young man but he's not stupid and he's not insensitive. Nor is he self-destructive. He may hate to lose . . . who doesn't? . . . but he's shrewd enough to know when he's outgunned. My guess is that he'll show those depositions to his lawyer. Or maybe he'll read them over a few times and decide not to show them to anybody. Either way, the result will be the same. His wife will have her divorce and she'll have full custody of the children. And their father's visitation rights will be very strict indeed.'

'I think he's an impossible bastard,' Floyd said, 'but he really is crazy about his kids.'

'No doubt about it.'

'Do you think there's a chance they made up those stories about him?'

She smiled. 'Of course there's a chance. Girls that age can be frightful little wretches sometimes. But my instinct tells me they're telling the truth.'

Book Four

Chapter Ten

[1]

It was three weeks, a month perhaps, after Floyd left Fort Beck before Jesse sat down at his desk to continue the piece he had begun to write about Helen, a further building-block in his attempt to structure the Bradshaws, their relations to him and to each other. He told himself he would not allow Floyd's recent visit to colour what he would write, told himself that a single evening could not be regarded as significant, that however he felt about Helen's behaviour that night he mustn't interpret it as anything other than what it had been. She had been witness to a tiresome argument and had tried to intercede in some sensible and civilized way. At least, that had seemed to be her intention. The fact that she had interceded each time on the side of her son should not be held against her, Jesse concluded. Since he himself was prone to behave in terms of his convictions, he could not hold such behaviour against her. Or so he believed. But he did hold it against her. Jagged scraps of that evening and that discussion and Helen's uneven participation in it stayed with him.

Some years later, when almost everything in his life had changed, when he reread the piece he had written those short weeks after the evening with Floyd, he saw very clearly, in the language and the attack of his prose, that he had failed in his attempt to blot out that unpleasant experience, that the resentment he felt had been sharpened, dipped in acid, and directed towards Helen.

Was the love I felt for Helen after Raymond's death only, in fact,

457

a thin residue of what I had felt for him? More and more that seems to me to be true. And perhaps it's not unusual. My love for the family unit that the three of us represented could easily have been transferred to her, could have been defined then, for many years, as something it wasn't.

Perhaps the fact that we related to each other for most of our lives as brother and sister was an indication not of love, as we've told ourselves in recent years since we've lived together, but of an absence of that feeling; a willingness to accept something else: the garden variety family love we had shared with Raymond.

I remember how surprised I was, in those first months after the two of us went to England to meet Raymond's family, when Nora assumed that Helen and I were lovers. It was not the jolt of having a secret revealed, or having one's midnight desires made public. It was a sense of genuine disbelief that anyone might see Helen and me in that light. Because – and this is the salient point – I had never seen myself in that light. This is not to say that I was blind to Helen's startling physical beauty. I had watched her move from girlhood to womanhood, and those changes had not, by any means, been lost on me. I saw her as someone who was, and would always be, appealing to men. When she began to go out with boys her age, I had the classic male relative's reaction. None of those loud awkward boys, heavily scented with shaving lotion, was good enough for her. They were a bit too young or a bit too old, I felt, too ugly or suspiciously handsome, too timid or far too sexually self-confident. But as I judged and criticized, I felt no impulse to substitute myself for Helen's imperfect swains. Does that mean something? I think it does. I have never been jealous of her, never felt possessive. I am not tortured by visions of her erotic life with another man. When I learned, many years after the fact, about her affair with Hugh, I felt a twinge, certainly, but it had no element of jealousy in it. I was simply annoyed and offended that, while she had confided so much in me through the years, she had chosen not to tell me about Hugh.

And what are Helen's true feelings towards me? I've never known that, of course, nor will I ever, but I suspect that they are similar to mine towards her. She would like to be in love with me but she is not. Because we have been constants in each other's lives she has chosen to label that condition as 'love'. Perhaps she

458

has truly persuaded herself. But I think not. She feels pride of ownership, just as I do with her. The fact that we have come together at last in Raymond's house, where we first met, satisfies her sense of order, I'm sure, as it does mine. But the calm and comfortable, patient and tolerant, kind and considerate life we share has almost nothing to do with the storms of the heart, the gut-wrenching pain and lunatic joy that chain a man and woman to each other, that torture and tantalize and define them.

Perhaps we waited too long. But I think that is not the explanation. We came together, in truth, not just when it was convenient, but when it at last seemed inevitable, when all other trails had been wandered and explored. We came back to each other, as we returned to Raymond's house: there was no place else to go.

If these conclusions are true, how do I explain what happened to us that first summer at Wingate Fields? After it was announced that Angus Bradshaw had adopted me as his son and that Nora and I were engaged to be married, why did Helen immediately return alone to America? And why did I follow her there? For Nora, the explanation was simple. We were in love with each other, Helen and I, as Nora had suspected. Helen had left Wingate Fields in a fit of anger and jealousy, and I had followed her because I felt guilty.

I did feel guilty, of course. Perhaps that's why I returned to America. But why did I stay there, postponing my marriage to Nora and postponing it a second time, until at last she toddled off to Scotland and married Edmund Bick? A credible explanation is not easy to find. Since Helen was not in Fort Beck when I got there, since she was having a baby, giving birth to Floyd in Maine, since she then chose to travel from place to place for the next three or four years till she met Frank Wilson and married him, what kept me from returning to England? It's a question I've asked myself many times. And I've considered many answers. The darkest one of all I have come to accept as the true one. I left, not for Helen's sake, but for my own.

I no longer deceive myself, haven't deceived myself for many years, about my motivations as a very young man. When I left my family in Chicago, I was not sure what I wanted. But I told myself I would know it when I saw it. And I did. When I first set foot in Raymond Bradshaw's house, some small voice inside me said, 'I want to stay here. I want to belong here. I want to become the sort of man who lives like this.' I've always felt that I was born, not in a hospital in Oklahoma City, but in Raymond's house that first day I arrived. I loved Raymond more than any person I've ever known, but before I loved him I loved what he represented.

In addition to the wrenching sadness I felt when he died, I was panic-stricken about the future. Raymond's house without Raymond in it was a changed place. Even before I knew that I would lose my job as an instructor at Foresby, I questioned my future. After I discovered that I would be terminated there, I knew there was no possibility of my staying in Fort Beck.

My only hope, I decided, certainly my best and most promising hope, was in England. By then I was corresponding with Raymond's relatives. The photo they'd sent of Wingate Fields was tucked in my desk drawer, where I could look at it several times a day. I was determined to go there, whether Helen went or not. She agreed to go at last only because she knew that I would go alone if she didn't come along.

From the first moment I saw Wingate Fields I was determined to stay there. Everything I did or said, everyone I befriended, all my actions and attitudes were directed toward that course, to serve that purpose.

Because of Raymond, because of Helen, because of my close association with them, and because I schemed and planned like a field marshal, things moved into place more quickly than I had hoped. Nora was my original target. The fact that she was already engaged to Edmund Bick was a consideration but in no way a deterrent. I quickly realized, however, that Nora could not be pursued. One could only make oneself available. Or, if you really wanted to pique her interest, you could contrive to seem unavailable. Since she had already concluded that Helen and I had chosen each other, this latter course, with no effort on my part, became the most desirable one.

Angus, on the other hand, was an unexpected windfall. When I met him, he seemed to be an impregnable fortress, subject to neither attack nor infiltration. And that original assessment was correct, I think. But he too, because of Raymond, chose to pursue me. Within weeks I realized that Nora wanted to marry me and Angus was determined to adopt me. Just then, shortly after those

460

announcements were made at a festive dinner, Helen sailed for America, and I, a few days later, followed her.

When I say there is a dark answer to why I did not return to Wingate Fields till after Nora had given up on me and married someone else, I suspect – more than that I believe – that I expected her to do that, perhaps wanted her to do that. Did I feel that my adoption by Angus, my full and triumphant entry into the Bradshaw circle by that means, made a marriage to Nora unnecessary? I am willing to accept the fact that those *were* my feelings. If that is true, should I feel guilty about it? I don't think so. After all, it didn't affect my life with Nora when we came together and stayed together at last. Nor did it redirect Helen, who had made other choices for herself that seemed not, in any way, to include me.

If I am peaceful about these past decisions, why do I continue to examine them? Why, after all these years, do they linger in my mind? God knows. Perhaps it's the enigma of Helen, seeing her every day, lying in bed beside her every night, remembering, whether I wish to or not, all the years that have passed, how our relationship, hers and mine, has changed and how it seems to have remained the same. Perhaps I feel no guilt because I am sure that she feels none. When I was quite young, when I first knew Helen, I was put off somehow, in some secret way that I never revealed, by the cavalier way in which she had chosen to leave her mother, to board a train in New York, travel to Fort Beck and, except for short visits, never go back. The fact that I had left my entire family in much the same way did not help me to understand or accept Helen's action. There was a fundamental difference between what she did and what I did. Whereas I had always felt like a stranger in my parents' home, with only a faint connection with my mother, none with my father, and a brother and sister to whom I felt no link whatsoever, Helen truly loved her mother, spoke of her with affection, and kept framed photos of her on the bureau in her room. It was not a pretence. Both Raymond and I were convinced that her feelings for her mother were deep and lasting. But she felt, apparently, no need to demonstrate them. She almost never wrote a letter to Anna, and the weekly letter to Helen from Anna sometimes lay on the hall table for days before she opened it and read it. Odd.

When Floyd was born I understand very clearly her rationale

461

for doing what she did. I understand it but still it's difficult for me to accept. The fact that she herself was unable at last to live with what she had done only supports the feelings I have that she was primarily concerned with what was best for her. Less concerned with the child.

Is it possible that inside the creature she presents to the world, a warm and vulnerable, intelligent and attractive woman, pleasant and flexible and accommodating, there lives quite a different kind of animal, one that is altogether different from what the exterior suggests, a night-feeding carnivore perhaps, a soft and furry creature that burrows in the earth and lives, for all its beauty, very much to itself? Is the nun truly kind and virtuous or does her starched habit conceal decay?

Is it possible that Nora, whose character has redefined and adjusted itself to fit all circumstances and whose morals are non-existent, has, in truth, a depth of feeling that is totally foreign to Helen?

I realize that by asking such questions, if only of myself, I suggest, in each instance, an affirmative answer. And the most disturbing and frequently recurring question of all is this one: has Helen ever loved anyone except Raymond? Is she capable of it? Has she even tried? Or did she simply close off some dark and private area of herself the morning we found him dead and confine herself from that day on to indications and manifestations, to geniality and *politesse* and being safe? Was she Raymond's property and no one else's? As long as I leave that question unanswered perhaps I'll be able to avoid asking it about myself.

[2]

One morning, Rosalind Dillworth, Rab's secretary, came into his office and said, 'You'll never guess who pursued me in the street yesterday evening after work.'

'I'm sure there's a long list of men who pursue you in the streets.'

'Not normally. I'm adept at discouraging that sort of thing. But

462

not last night. It was that American screenwriter, Robert Gingrich, the one who came here to see you some months ago.'

'Is he still in London?'

'Very much so, it seems. I think he's become attached to our public houses. As I was strolling across to Park Lane to take my bus, he bounced out of a wine bar on South Audley Street and invited me in for a glass of hock. Or claret, he said, if I should prefer that.'

'Which did you prefer?'

'Neither. I told him I had to hurry home because I'd invited a cousin to have a meal with me.'

'Not true, of course,' Rab said.

'Actually, it was true. But I would have invented a story in any case. Even if I liked crowded wine bars, which I don't, I am not attracted to Mr Gingrich. There's a kind of sogginess about him. Soft pink hands. Thighs that rub together when he walks. Perspiration on the upper lip. You know what I'm saying?'

Rab nodded. 'So he accosted you in the street and you fought him off.'

'Not exactly. He trailed along beside me to the bus stop, talking a mile a minute. And when I boarded the bus, he got on too. Sat beside me all the way to King's Road. And when I got off he walked along with me to my little mews house.'

'And you invited him in to spend the night.'

'Not quite. We chatted a bit at the gate and then I sent him off.'

The fact was that although Rosalind had no interest whatsoever in Gingrich she was very much interested in the things he had to say. Not in his detailed evaluations of the pubs and wine bars of Mayfair, nor in his tales of deceit and dishonesty among British film-makers, but once they were seated on the bus his conversation took a more tantalizing turn.

'That's a decent young man you work for,' he said. 'Several cuts above the producers I've been exposed to. They're all of a piece, those lice, here as well as in America. And Cinecitta in Rome is like a community of cannibals. Everyone at risk. Blood flowing in all the urinals. I hope I don't offend you.'

'I have three brothers,' she said. '*Nothing* offends me.'

'At first I was afraid that your friend, Rab Bradshaw, had fallen in with bad companions. I mean, I thought he'd been sucked into some business dealings with Oscar Mullet. I wanted to warn him but I wasn't sure that I should. You have to be careful about

463

carrying bad news to people. Also, I didn't want to foul my own nest, so to speak. I have no respect for Mullet. I think he's a bastard. I know he's a bastard. But I profit from him. I can count on him for fifty or sixty thousand a year, sometimes more. So I hold my nose, take the money, and order another drink. The first director I ever worked with, when I was a dewy-eyed young playwright just come to California from New York, said to me, "This is a whore's business, Gingrich. Just paste that in your head and remember it. It won't keep you from getting stabbed in the back but at least you won't bleed to death." '

'Are you saying that Mr Mullet is no worse than any of the others?'

'No, I'm not saying that. He is worse. Most producers are just dumb hustlers trying to steal a few dollars or a few million dollars. They're playing the game the way they learned it, and telling themselves they're honest businessmen. But Mullet's another case altogether, a totally different scrap of cheese. He knows what he's doing. He's not brilliant but he's shrewd and he's smart. He's a crook and he knows it. He set out to be a crook and he succeeded. He steals the way most of us breathe air. He wakes up in the morning, brushes his teeth and says, "Who can I screw today? How much can I steal before dinner time?" You're smiling. You think I'm exaggerating. But I'm not. Not me. I know that sucker. And he knows me. I may be the only guy in the film business who has him over a barrel. And I'll *always* have him over a barrel. If all of my fingers fall off and I can't type a single line of dialogue, that fifty or sixty thousand a year will still keep trickling in. You know what I'm saying?'

'No, I don't. Are you sure you want to tell me all this?'

'No secrets involved. I'm just telling you that Mullet's not a man to be trusted. And everybody who's ever met him knows that. So I'm glad to find out that Bradshaw isn't having any truck with him. At least, that's the way I hear it. Am I right?'

'You'd have to ask Mr Bradshaw about that. I don't discuss his activities with anyone.'

'Of course you don't. And I respect that. But I wasn't trying to pick your brain. I'm telling you things, as a man who respects your employer, not seeking information. I guess you've probably heard that Mullet's in big trouble with the tax people here in England. Did you hear that?'

464

Rosalind smiled. 'I can't remember.'

'OK. I get it. So I'll just keep on talking and we'll pretend you know what I'm talking about. The thing is, they've got him dead to rights but they're not going to do anything about it. I mean they're going to invite him to leave the country and take his business with him but there won't be any talk of fraud, no fines, and no publicity. That's because some American congressman paid a visit to the Internal Revenue department and Internal Revenue sent a man here to schmooze with the Exchequer folks. Everybody became convinced that Mullet's money shenanigans could be dealt with better in America. That may be true but the fact is they won't be dealt with at all. Do you follow me? When Mr Mullet emigrated to America his first job was managing a bowling alley and roller-skating rink in New Jersey. After that he ran a chain of theatres in New England that showed dirty movies. And the next thing anybody knew, he owned those theatres. Arranged a big loan with a bank in Bimini and paid cash for all those bloody theatres. Are you starting to get the picture? Of course you are. Mr Mullet is *connected*. But that still won't keep him in England. The Brits are co-operative but not crazy. They know there'll be another oddball here to take Mullet's place but they'll deal with that when it happens. For now, they need to save some face. So Mullet has to go, taking his wife with him. Do you know Dorsey Mullet?'

'I've seen her picture in the papers. I've never met her.'

'You realize that your boss knows her, don't you?'

'Mr Bradshaw knows a lot of people.'

'You're really cute. Maybe I'll hire you myself. How would you like an easy job working for a writer who hardly ever writes?'

'I wouldn't like that. I prefer to keep busy.'

'Good for you. Let's get back to Dorsey Mullet. The interesting thing about Dorsey is that she could have been a first-class lady. But she made careless choices. I mean, she came from Nebraska but so did Monty Clift and Brando and Hank Fonda. Being from Nebraska didn't screw her up. The fact is she screwed herself up. But not for any of the classic reasons. She wasn't man-crazy, she wasn't greedy, and she wasn't in love with herself. She was *scared*. Scared of everything. I mean she never found herself in any situation that didn't scare hell out of her. So she was always looking for something to hide behind. She's spent her whole life trying to protect herself. And finally she convinced herself that Mullet could protect her from everything, that if she married him she'd never have to be scared again. Can you imagine that? Can you believe that anybody would see a son-of-a-bitch like him as a safe haven? Well, she did. And sure enough, he helped her build a wall around herself. But then a strange thing happened. She found out she was scared to death of what was happening inside that wall. Now there's no way on God's earth she can fix that except to leave him.'

'Why doesn't she do that?'

'Ahh, that's a good question, one I've asked myself a thousand times. And I've asked her as well.'

'What did she say?'

'Pretends not to know the answer. But she knows, all right. It's the same old story. She's scared of what might be lurking round the next corner. The Dorsey Syndrome, I call it. She knows she's miserable with Mullet but she's grown accustomed to it. Without him, she's not sure what sort of problems she might encounter. So she's chosen the devil she knows over the devil she doesn't know. Dorsey didn't invent that attitude, of course. The world's bedrooms are filled with women who would love to be somewhere else. But they're too frightened or too dilatory to kiss the old man goodbye and strike out on their own. Even misery can give you a certain sense of security.'

Rosalind smiled. 'You should be a writer.'

'I know. That's what I used to think. Then I decided to be a hack instead. But mostly I just follow the Mullets around from one place to another.'

'Why is that?'

'We complement each other. Oscar has no more respect for me than I have for him but he likes to have me around. For all his chutzpah, he's not too proud of himself. I think I'm one of the few men he knows that he feels superior to. He bought me once and now he thinks he owns me for life. And he's probably right. Dorsey's another matter altogether. She and I have been joined at the forehead for a lot of years. I'm the only human being in the world she can trust and she knows it. So I'm the family pet. No real love among us but we depend on each other. Dorsey and I know a secret that Oscar doesn't know, and Oscar and I have a secret from Dorsey. It's your regular, home-grown family relationship. Power on one side, fear on the other. I'm half-chamberlain, half-jester, but vitally necessary for the particular sort of unhappi-

466

ness the Mullets have chosen for themselves. I'm their security blanket. When they leave England they know I'll be dragging along after them. And they're right, of course.'

'Where will they be going?'

'For the present, they'll stay in Madrid. Till Oscar finishes the work he's doing there. Then he'd like to go back to California but she doesn't go for that idea. His second choice would be Italy but Dorsey hates Rome as much as she hates Beverly Hills. He has a couple of projects on the fire in Australia but the people who shovel money at him, his friends in the mob, aren't too keen about that part of the world. And neither is Dorsey. So my guess would be that he'll stay in Madrid. So far, Dorsey's not afraid of Spain. She will be later, of course, but for now, since she can't bury herself in the Cotswolds, I think she'll insist on Madrid.'

'So you'll be leaving London, too.'

Gingrich nodded. 'I hate to give up the pubs and wine bars but I'm told that Madrid has its own sort of saloon society. So I'll make an adjustment.' Then: 'I don't suppose I could interest you in relocating to Madrid.'

'I don't think so. I'm fully occupied here.'

'I'm sure you are. But all the same I thought it might be something you'd like to consider. I clean up pretty good once I put my mind to it. I've been accused of all sorts of things in my life but no one has ever said I don't know how to treat a lady. With the proper inspiration, I might even write another play.'

'I'm flattered by your offer but as I said . . .'

'I understand. You're fully occupied.'

After she finished telling Rab in detail about her conversation with Gingrich, he said, 'I think I may be standing in the way of some fine opportunities for you. As much as I need you here . . .'

'You'll not get rid of me that easily. I can't stand the thought of your having to make do with some voluptuous eighteen-year-old secretary-bird who'd type your letters in a messy way and create havoc in your files. I feel responsible for you.'

'But couldn't you feel responsible for poor old Gingrich?'

'I think not.'

'Had he ever rung you up before to offer himself as a gift?'

She shook her head. 'Not at all. This was a chance meeting. I'm sure of it.'

'But why would he tag along after you and give you all that information?'

'Perhaps he expected me to pass it along to you.'

'Why wouldn't he come to me directly? He knows I'm accessible.'

'I don't know.'

'Did he say anything about me and Dorsey?'

'Not much. Just what I told you.'

'Odd fellow. Let's see how accurate his information is. See if you can get me Alfred Hinson on the telephone.'

Rosalind picked up the receiver on her side of the desk and dialled a number. She talked to an operator and two secretaries. At last she pointed to Rab's telephone and said, 'He's coming right on.'

After a few pleasantries with Hinson, Rab said, 'You remember, we've had two or three discussions about Oscar Mullet. I'm asking you this in strict confidence, of course, but can you tell me how his situation is developing?'

Rab sat comfortably in his chair, listening. Occasionally he interjected, 'I see,' or 'I understand,' or 'Yes, of course.' At last he said, 'Thank you very much, Alfred. I appreciate your trusting me with this information and I assure you it will go no further. But in fairness I must tell you that some of the things you've just told me are already being circulated in certain quarters here in London.' He paused. Then: 'Good. I'm glad you're aware of that.'

As he hung up the receiver Rab said to Rosalind, 'It seems your friend Gingrich, has at least some of his facts straight.'

'What did Lord Hinson say?'

'It seems the American tax people did take an interest in the case. Persuaded the Exchequer that any action they might take could prejudice or weaken the United States case against Oscar. But, all the same, Britain has withdrawn his right to do business or own property here. There'll be no public announcement of this but he's been quietly requested to leave the country.'

'How does that . . .' Rosalind began and then stopped.

'How does what?'

'I started to ask you a question, then I realized it's none of my business.'

Rab smiled. 'If you're curious as to how all this will affect his wife, so am I. Since I haven't heard from her since my trip to Madrid, I may have to rely on Gingrich as my principal source of information. Now that we know he has the facts I may have to buy him a few gins and see what more he has to say. Am I free to offer *you* in exchange for information?'

Rosalind made a face. 'I think I have demonstrated my love and loyalty on many occasions. I'm sure you'll understand if I draw the line just this side of Robert Gingrich.'

[3]

Dr Klaus Hofer was slender and clean-shaven. He moved with the grace of a downhill skier, which he was. He had sinewy capable hands and friendly blue-green eyes and he wore his hair slicked back from his broad forehead. He sat quietly in his chair studying Polly who sat across the desk from him. Her face was pale and she looked as though she'd been crying. At last she looked up. 'You're a doctor,' she said. 'I'm sure you're a good one. I'm not a doctor, of course, but I've read a lot about physiology and medicine. I simply can't believe there's nothing you can do. That there's nothing to be done for Jack.'

'If I said there was nothing to be done,' he said, 'I didn't express myself clearly. There are always medical alternatives – but in Jack's case . . .'

'You said yourself he has no serious physical problems.'

'That's correct. Or so it seems. We have an excellent staff here at Wurzburg. This is the best prison hospital in Western Germany, perhaps in all of Europe, but none of my colleagues have been any more successful than I have in diagnosing Jack's illness. If we knew why he's losing strength, as he seems to be doing, then we would certainly know how to treat him. But he's a mystery to us as he is to you.'

'He's so thin. He never had much extra weight. But in the past weeks he seems to have lost at least a stone. I know he hasn't eaten properly since he's been here at Wurzburg . . .'

'Now he doesn't eat at all,' Hofer said. 'The past ten days he has turned back all of his food.'

'Can't you do something about that? Can't you force him?'

'Medical science hasn't found a way to cure the common cold, bad breath, or snoring. And we've found no way to feed strong-minded patients who don't want to eat.'

'Of course you have. Can't you feed him intravenously?'

He shook his head. 'That only works with patients who want to eat but can't. Stubborn people, like Jack, can only be fed intravenously if they're fully sedated and under constant surveillance. Otherwise they simply pull the tubes out of their veins.'

'But that's suicidal. Jack has no impulse to do that.'

'Have you talked to Dr Schlossberg?'

'Twice,' she said. 'But not today. I came straight to your office as soon as I got here this afternoon, as soon as they told me Jack was in hospital again.'

'Did Schlossberg have any answers for you?'

'Clinical ones. But you realize that no psychologist or psychiatrist could ever make sense out of Jack. He used to say "Science of the mind is science of the blind." '

'Do you agree with that?'

'Of course not. I'm just pointing out that if Dr Schlossberg approached Jack with the notion that he was suffering from a minor psychological maladjustment, the doctor would surely come away from that meeting convinced that he had just interviewed an incurable lunatic. Jack would make sure of that.'

'But that's a problem in itself, isn't it?'

'Not at all. Jack likes to shoot people down for fun, not because he can't help himself. There is no theory, no philosophy, no absolute that he can't rip to shreds. And the more seriously it's presented to him, the smaller pieces he'll make of it.'

'I brought up Dr Schlossberg because he's published some interesting articles about the effects of prison life on normal men. He concludes that self-destruction is a common pattern. Not suicide. There are surprisingly few suicides among our prisoners. But all the same, odd habits and rhythms develop that can be extremely damaging. It's as though there's an effort to intensify, by their own efforts, the punishment the state has dealt them. And the more intelligent the prisoner, the more he seems susceptible to such behaviour.'

'Are you saying that's Jack's problem?'

Hofer shook his head. 'I don't know what his problem is. That's what we're trying to find out. That's why you and I are talking. As late as this morning, when I examined him, there was no

470

evidence of a treatable illness but, as I said, he seems to be getting steadily weaker. We don't like to conclude that he's deliberately starving himself but the effect is the same, whether it's deliberate or not. The body must be nourished. If it's not, all of its systems gradually deteriorate.'

'Last time we talked, you said you were giving him vitamin shots.'

'I said we were trying. And we are. But in spite of his condition he's very strong. We need three attendants and a doctor to give him an injection. Even then, he usually manages somehow to abort it. The best treatment any physician has is his patient's desire to get better. Without such desire there are problems. Take it one step further, when a patient actively struggles against treatment, medical science can become very feeble indeed.'

When Polly left Hofer's office, an attendant led her through a maze of corridors till they arrived at Jack's room. He was sitting by his bed in a chair, the window behind him covered on the outside by a heavy iron grating. As soon as she came through the door Jack said, 'Don't have a long face. Nobody loves a girl with a long face.'

Dr Hofer had warned her that Jack's appearance had changed markedly in the short time since she'd seen him last. Even so, she was shocked when she saw him. His eyes seemed to rest in dark hollows, the skin was drawn tight over his cheekbones, and his teeth when he smiled seemed very long, like the teeth of an old man. And his face when she kissed him felt soft and cool like an old man's face.

'I'm living like a king here,' he said. 'I should have figured out this dodge months ago. Clean sheets, no labour detail, no waiting in line to take a shower or use the can. I mean, this is like a bloody hotel. Nurses and orderlies looking after you, a doctor dropping by once or twice a day. And the joke is, I'm not even sick. I'm healthy as a hog. I feel like I broke out of jail and moved into the Waldorf-Astoria. I might even get them to haul my cello up here so I can entertain my fellow patients. That's what they call us. We used to be prisoners and now all of a sudden we're patients. Isn't that a kick in the ass?'

'Why won't you eat, Jack?'

'What do you mean?'

'You know what I mean. I mean why won't you eat anything?'

'Boy, are you dumb. That's my gimmick. Don't you get it? I have to do something to qualify as a patient. Otherwise they take away my night-gown and turn me into a yard-bird again. I mean, my mother didn't raise a dumb kid. If I'm not a problem for all these smart doctors they've got here then the next thing I know they'll lost interest in me. If that happens, I'm cooked. Back in the chicken-house. Four in a cell. The whole place smelling like three hundred men took a leak, all at the same time. Do I need that? Hell, no. I like it better here.'

'But you have to eat or you'll make yourself sick.'

'That's it. That's the idea. You have to be a little bit sick or they won't let you stay here. My problem is I'm so bloody healthy I can't make myself sick. I'm breaking my chops trying to create a few symptoms and they keep shaking their heads and saying to each other, "His vital signs are very good." Of course they're good. I'm one healthy bastard.'

'Oh, God, Jack. What are you up to?'

'Survival in an alien world. That's my game.'

'I used to think we were like one person. I thought I knew you better than anyone else in the world.'

'You do. When my authorized biography is written I want you to do it.'

She went on as though she hadn't heard him. 'Now that I can't see you every day and every night, now that these little visits are all the time we can spend together, I sit at home by myself and sometimes I think I don't know you at all.'

'At home by yourself. Is that what you said? What's become of brother Bill?'

'I didn't mean that. I meant when I'm not with you I always feel as if I'm by myself.'

'You didn't answer my question. Is your brother still standing by? Is he still in residence?'

'Yes, thank God. I don't know what I'd do without him.'

'Is he handy with a mop and pail?'

She smiled and shook her head. 'Not Bill. He's useless around the house. But still the people who do the work do it better since he's there.'

'That's the key to the German psyche. Fear of the schoolmaster. On the other hand maybe the housekeeper and the laundress

472

believe that Bill's truly the man of the house. Perhaps they think he's taken my place in your bed.'

'They think nothing of the kind. They know he's my brother.'

'Ah, but this is the land of legend and folklore and forbidden love. You're a student of German literature. The Romans didn't invent incest, they just gave it a name. The Germans had known about it all along.'

'I assure you, the ladies who take care of my house have never even heard the word and if they had they certainly wouldn't associate it with Bill and me. And neither would you if you didn't have a perverse mind.'

'Neither a borrower nor a lender be.'

'Don't think you're getting me off the subject, Jack. I was talking with your doctor for an hour.'

'The head doctor or the body doctor?'

'Dr Hofer.'

'Very cute man, Doc Hofer. Don't you think he's cute?'

'Damn it, Jack, this is serious. Don't you know what you're doing to yourself?'

'You bet I do. I just told you. I conned these zoo-keepers into putting me in the hospital and thereby I improved my lot in life..'

'Do you really think you're fooling people? Don't you think I know what you're doing? Have you looked at yourself in a mirror lately?'

He nodded. 'Bad colour. I have the grey pallor of a prison inmate. Otherwise, not bad.'

'If you don't care about yourself, please think about me. I can't sleep or read or think or do anything since you started this idiotic starvation routine. All I see in my mind is your sad skinny body and your bony cheeks. You're driving me crazy. You're going to make yourself very sick. The doctors think you're trying to kill yourself.'

'What do they know? In the first place I'm too self-centred to commit suicide and in the second place, if I did want to kill myself, I can think of much better ways to do it. And besides, I'm not starving. I must drink a gallon of coffee a day and there's an orderly here who smuggles me all the cigarettes I want. Nothing like a dynamite shot of caffeine and nicotine to kill your appetite.'

'Have you given up on everything? Is that it? Have you given up on me?'

473

'Why would you say that? You've made me famous in this joint. None of these other dog-faces has a woman like you who comes to visit them. Once the word got around about what you look like I became an important man in this bug house.'

'You know what I mean. Have you decided there's no future for us? Is this the only way you can figure out that will keep me from waiting around till you get out of prison?'

'You've been dipping into those cheap novels again. Whatever else I am, I'm not a romantic fellow, and you know it. If I wanted to get rid of you, do you think the only way I could work that out is by getting rid of myself?'

She sat looking at him, a heavy industrial clock ticking loudly on the wall behind her. At last she said, 'When I'm not with you, which is most of the time, I think of all the things I'll say to you when I see you. I fantasize about what we'll talk about, things we'll remember, plans we'll make. Then I see you and it all dries up. You say you're glad to see me but I feel, every time I come here, as if you're searching for ways to make me angry or hurt my feelings. When I leave and get in my car to drive home, I start to cry as soon as I turn on the ignition key. It's a reflex now. I don't want to do it but I can't help it. Every time I'm here with you I feel as if you're trying to drive me away. I mean, I try not to be all sad and serious and gloomy when I see you but each time there's something, some new trick you've found, that makes me feel like an outsider. And when I try to get you to help me, you laugh it off and make a joke. You laugh everything off. Even now, when I tell you I'm afraid you'll die if you don't start taking care of yourself, if you don't get away from this starvation game you're playing, you laugh it off.'

'Why not?' he said. 'There nothing funnier than death. Did I ever tell you I used to work for a mortician? When I was in college in Iowa. Worked for a man named Cutler who'd bought an old schoolhouse and turned it into an undertaking parlour. I lived there, too. Slept in a back bedroom behind the coffin storage room. Cutler was a decent guy. He had a nervous wife but he was all right. He used to sing to himself and eat an apple or a liverwurst sandwich while he was embalming his customers. People in the town liked him. When he passed the collection plate in church on Sundays people would say, "There's Harry Cutler, looking for his next victim." Interesting thing about a corpse. Once it's embalmed it's light as a feather and stiff as a board. You can lift it up and carry it, with one hand. But when they're first dead, when they're still warm, they're heavy as sandbags. Another thing, I got the idea that everybody dies in the middle of the night. At least, they did in Iowa, that year I worked for old man Cutler. One night there was a bad train wreck at a crossing just outside of town. Two trains, head-on. We were picking up arms and legs and pieces of bodies in wicker baskets. Then we matched them up when we got back to the funeral home. A year or so of stuff like that and you can't take death too seriously. Cutler always said that he'd decided to die in bed in his own house but it didn't work out that way. He was helping to load a heavy coffin on a flat-bed truck one day but it slid off, pinned him to the driveway, and crushed his skull.'

'You're hopeless,' she said. 'I never know when you're telling the truth and when you're not.'

'I always tell the truth. I only lie when my country and my President are in jeopardy.'

When the guard signalled it was time for her to leave, Jack said, 'Goodbye, kid.'

This time the tears didn't wait till she was in the car. She stood with her arms at her sides, the heavy wooden table between them and said, 'Please use your head. Please be good. Don't make yourself sick.'

'I'll be good,' he said. 'A clean mind in a clean body.'

'Promise?'

'I promise.'

[4]

When Nora telephoned Valerie in Norway and asked her to spend a few days with her in London, Floyd urged her to go.

'I can't do that,' she said. 'We don't fly off on separate little vacations, you and I. If we both can't go, we both stay home.'

'Not true. When I had to go to Mexico and California you didn't go with me. One of the reasons you gave when I asked you was . . .'

'I remember. I said it would be nice if you could spend some time alone with Betsy.'

'Exactly. Now I'm saying it would be nice if you could spend some days with Nora.'

'But you know Nora,' she said. 'Aren't you afraid we'll zip down to Southampton and find ourselves two naughty sailors?'

'I'm afraid but optimistic. Since I make such excellent coffee in the morning I expect that to pull you back.'

The two women stayed in a house on Eaton Place that Rab had arranged for them. They had dinner with him at the Savoy their first night in London.

'Should we count ourselves lucky that you found time for us?' Nora asked him.

'Extremely fortunate,' he said. 'I have to fly to Rome tomorrow and I'll be there for five days.'

'When you're back, we'll be gone,' Valerie said.

'Exactly. That's why we had to work it out for tonight.'

'Are you devoting all your time to your career as a producer,' Nora asked, 'or are you a full-time womanizer doing just a bit of work on the side.'

'I've tried to emulate you, grandmother. I believe there's time for all things.'

'If you call me "grandmother" once more you may find that you have the time but not the capability.'

Rab told them in detail then about some of his projects, long-term and short-term. When he'd finished, Valerie explained as well as she could about Floyd's trip to Mexico and Betsy's divorce. 'Her husband turned out to be a peculiar fellow, indeed,' she said. 'I don't know all the facts but whatever they were it was quite impossible for Betsy to stay with him. At first Floyd thought it would be a long drawn-out affair – the divorce proceedings – but as it turned out, she was permitted to get a divorce in Mexico and I believe she plans to marry again very soon.'

'So Bill told me,' Rab said. 'He also said that we now have a new half-sister, or stepsister, or foster sister.'

'That's true,' Valerie said. 'Floyd adopted her.'

'The family's growing,' he said.

'No thanks to you and your brother,' Nora said. 'Young men of my generation were married and had fathered two or three children by the time they were your age.'

'Times have changed. Now young men my age father two or three children and don't get married.'

476

'If you're hinting that you have some undernourished foundlings tucked in dark corners somewhere, I have, as you know, a large house in Paris and another in the country and I would be happy to take as my own any stray Bradshaw children you may have scattered about.'

'Don't encourage him,' Valerie said.

'It's a serious offer,' Nora said to Rab. 'A standing offer, I might add. Since I can't seem to find a live-in man who pleases me, I may as well mother a few children.'

'Sorry to disappoint you,' Rab said, 'but I have nothing to offer you at the moment. I will keep you in mind, however, in future.'

Turning to Valerie then, Nora said, 'What about this new young man Betsy's chosen?'

'Not a champion, I'm afraid. Or so Floyd seemed to feel. On the other hand he's a prize, apparently, compared to the husband she just discarded. He's wild about Betsy and very fond of her children. He has no resources, none at all, but now Betsy will have an adequate income . . .'

'Adequate is hardly the word,' Nora said.

' . . . so they'll be able to have a comfortable life.'

'Will they stay in Mexico?'

'I think not,' Valerie said. 'Floyd mentioned Montana. I think they plan to live in a place called Great Falls. Betsy's new man is a builder. He wants to build them a house there.'

'Young love in springtime,' Rab said.

Nora waggled a forefinger at him. 'Don't be cynical, you brute. Love still makes the world revolve, you know.'

'But you must admit the axis has fallen a bit out of line. Bumpy and uneven revolutions.'

'Does all this cynicism mean that you have no plans to settle down and raise a brood?'

'No current plans of that kind.'

Later, during their dinner, Valerie asked Rab if there was any chance that he might stop off in Germany to see Polly on his way home from Italy.

'Not this trip. I was there only three weeks ago when I had to go to Munich. Have you seen her?'

'I've tried to invite myself several times but there always seems to be some problem. Polly used to write me religiously once a week.

477

Now I hardly ever hear from her. I know she's going through a tough patch but all the same . . .'

'What about Bill? Do you hear from him?'

'Not often. How did things seem when you were there?'

'They always put on a bit of a show for me, I suspect. Go into great detail about everything the two of them have been doing. But this last time the show was pretty thin. Polly seemed not to be listening to anything that was said and Bill seemed totally focused on Polly. So I was dancing all by myself.'

'What did they say about Jack?'

'Routine answers. Pretty much what Polly always says. Looking for the bright side. Talking about the future. Always before I've been impressed by her conviction about what she was saying. This time the conviction was missing. The words barely got past her lips.'

'God, what a terrible fix she's in,' Valerie said. 'How wretched it must be to wake up every morning and have nothing to look forward to.'

'She seems to look forward to her visits to Jack,' Rab said, 'and nothing else.'

'All the same, it must be a comfort to her having Bill there,' Nora said.

Rab nodded. 'No question about that. She's very dependent on him. When we were growing up she made all Bill's decisions for him. Now it's just the reverse.'

'It's a blessing he's with her,' Valerie said.

'It's a blessing for Polly. I'm not sure it's good for Bill.'

'How do you mean?' Nora said.

'Whatever he'd planned to do with his life, he seems to have postponed it. They don't discuss it with me but the impression I get is that he and Polly have some sort of emotional contract between them. As long as she's there in Heidelberg waiting for Jack to be released from prison, Bill will stay with her. That bothers me but I don't know what to do about it. I'm as concerned about Polly as he is, but I'm also concerned about him.'

Later that evening, when she and Valerie were alone together in the house on Eaton Place, Nora said, 'Does it upset you, discussing Polly's situation?'

'Of course it does. But it also upsets me if I don't talk about it. It just seems to hover there, waiting to be examined and fussed

478

about or fretted over. It never occurred to me when the children were small that there would ever be a time, whatever their ages, when I wouldn't be able to help them if they were in trouble. But now I realize that I can't help them at all. And even if I could, they don't ask for help.'

'And that upsets you?'

'Of course it does. How can it not?'

'When you were younger than they are,' Nora said, 'you made it very clear to me that you were grown-up, that you were able to deal with your own problems.'

'And was I?'

'Naturally, I didn't think so. But since you made it quite clear that I didn't have a vote in the matter, I stood aside and let you take charge of your life. And I was surprised to see that you did quite well. With no help or advice from me.'

'Are you saying I should look the other way and let Rab and Polly and Bill deal with things as best they can?'

'I'm not saying you should. I'm saying you must.'

'Floyd tells me the same thing. And I believe him. I also believe you. But I can't seem to turn off my head. It keeps sending me messages.'

'What sort of messages?'

'I keep telling myself that this is not simply the case of a mother's refusal to let go of her children. Actually, I feel that I let them go too soon, before they were ready to be turned loose, and now they're getting even with me.'

'How strange to hear you say that. Your mind doesn't work that way. At least, it never has before.'

'I'm not paranoid, if that's what you mean. I truly believe what I'm saying. I always told myself that the children were not disturbed in any way when Jesse and I separated. I also told myself that they were happy for me when I married Floyd, that they wanted me to be contented and have a good life. But now I know that I believed those things because I wanted to believe them. I needed to believe them. Thinking that Rab and Polly and Bill would be unaffected and undamaged gave me the freedom to do what I wanted to do and not feel guilty. But the pendulum swung back.'

'How do you think they're "getting even"? In what way? I don't understand that.'

'It's a subtle thing. And looking back, I realize it's gone on for a long time. Since Jesse and I first told them we'd decided to separate. Somewhere along the line, they redefined me. They decided I was undependable. They decided to pull away. And that's what they've done.'

'If you want my opinion,' Nora said. 'I think you've stayed in gloomy Norway too long. You and Floyd should go back to the Algarve. Or take a house in Tuscany. The Norwegians still believe in trolls, you know. Anyone who stays there too long grows morbid and starts to drink aquavit at breakfast time.'

Valerie smiled. 'I don't expect you to take me seriously. But you asked me, so I told you.'

'I do take you seriously. But I certainly don't read your relationship with your children the way you do.'

'I told you . . . it's a subtle thing. I'm sure they would disagree with me, just as you do. And I understand that. Because they have not failed *me*. That's not what I'm saying. Instead, all of them have failed themselves. Each of them has gone off on an odd course, one that's counter-productive and inconsistent with their backgrounds. Even Rab, who has become dramatically successful, seems to approach his work and his career in an almost vengeful way, as though he feels that life must be attacked. Bill and Polly, on the other hand, have chosen to withdraw from life. You say I'm not responsible for those choices they've made, and maybe you're right. But I can't help thinking that I am.'

'If that's true, then Jesse is equally to blame.'

'In theory, yes. In practice, no. He and Rab, of course, have never worked things out. I've never understood that and I don't understand it now. But in any case that's a separate situation from the one I've been talking about. If Jesse and I were still married, he and Rab would still be at loggerheads, I'm sure. But Polly and Bill are another matter. They were always close to me and close to each other. They're still close to each other but not to me.'

'I thought they treated you beautifully at the time of the trial, when we were in Heidelberg.'

'Of course they did. I taught them good manners and they haven't forgotten them. They would never do anything obvious or deliberate to hurt me. They've simply pulled away from me. Don't misunderstand me . . . I don't see it as a conspiracy. I don't imagine they discuss it between themselves. But it's a fact nonetheless. And as they've withdrawn from me, they've grown closer to Jesse.

480

They've chosen *him*. I feel guilty and sick about it and I can't make that feeling go away.'

The tone of their first evening did not carry over through their four days together in London. The weather was pleasant and clear, the streets were not clogged with travellers, and they enjoyed the city like two schoolgirls on holiday. They shopped extravagantly on Jermyn Street and Bond Street and in all the new boutiques in Mayfair. They strolled arm in arm through the National Gallery and the Tate, attended a matinée performance of a comedy with Alec Guinness at the Haymarket, heard Claudio Arrau in concert, saw Edith Evans and Wendy Hiller at the Garrick and Ralph Richardson at the Aldwych. They ate rich meals and drank wine without wisdom or bad conscience. They were together and in true contact with each other in a way they hadn't experienced in a long time, or perhaps ever. Their mother-and-daughter relationship, which had always had unusual guidelines and configurations became almost totally inoperative. They were simply two attractive women who had chosen to meet in London, to enjoy themselves and indulge themselves.

Only on their last evening together did they catch up the threads of that first evening and examine conditions rather than activities. As they lingered over a long dinner at Chez Ma Cousine on Sloane Square, Nora said, 'May I ask a question that's none of my business?'

'There is no such question.'

'We'll see about that. This is a question about you and Floyd.'

'If I can answer it, I will. If I can't, I won't.'

'When I was your age, young married women used to say to each other that when they had no problems with their husbands, their other difficulties didn't seem important. But when they did have problems at home, everything else seemed to be a problem also.'

'It makes sense, doesn't it? What's your question?'

'I've been thinking about the things you said a few days ago, the first night we were in London, about your children and how things haven't seemed to work out the way you might have hoped between yourself and them. And I couldn't help wondering if perhaps there might be something you weren't saying, something you may not be admitting to yourself, about you and Floyd.'

Valerie smiled. 'The only thing wrong with Floyd and me is me.

481

Nothing's missing in my life with him. It never occurred to me at the beginning that I could ever come to love him more than I did then. But I do. He thrills me and excites me and drives me crazy. I never get tired of touching him and looking at him. He's the most interesting man I've ever met. He may be the only truly interesting man I've met. I thought, after we'd been together a month, that I'd memorized every single thing about him. Every trait, every taste, every characteristic. But each day, even now, after all this time, I find out something new. The basic things about him never change, I suppose, but apart from those, he's loose and fluid, like a stag swimming in a stream. He's not locked in. Things happen to him. He hears sounds and see objects. Everything about him is sensory. He's not afraid to draw a new conclusion, not afraid to be wrong. To me, he seems to know everything. The important things, I mean. The things that really matter. What I'm trying to say is that he's very new to me. And I guess he always will be. So the real answer to your question is this: Am I in any way to him what he is to me?'

'I'm sure you are.'

'I hope you're right but I doubt it. I don't see how I can be. With all the contentment I have with Floyd, with all the love I feel for him, I still can't deal with the guilt and self-doubt I feel. I'm not sure if it gets worse each year but it certainly seems more deep-rooted. I try to keep it from Floyd but I can't. He knows I take tranquillizers during the day and sleeping-pills at night. He blames my doctors. He thinks I don't need that kind of medication. I'm afraid to tell him that I would never sleep at all if I didn't take pills. He knows the things that disturb me are not his fault but all the same I sense that he feels to blame. It's human nature, isn't it? When you live with someone and you see that they're smiling and happy and feeling good about themselves, you like to think that you're responsible, at least in small part, for all that contentment. But the other side of the coin isn't so encouraging. When that same person develops a poor self-image, when they stare into space and lie awake at night, there's no way not to feel responsibility for that too.'

'Do you stare into space?'

Valerie smiled. 'Not intentionally. Not on purpose. But guilt is a strange little creature. It never sleeps. It's always available. Always willing to take up your total concentration.'

'Are your children really on your mind all the time?'

'It's not just the children. It's me in relation to them. It's me in relation to myself. And it's me in relation to Floyd. In the beginning I thought that nothing could be more perfect than our life together. At that time I believed that Rab and Polly and Bill had taken control of their own lives, that I'd given them everything I was able to give. Not only did they not need my constant attention, I decided they wouldn't want it if I offered it. So that meant that Floyd and I were free to squander ourselves on each other. We had scads of money, we were young and energetic, so we could devote ourselves to a life of self-indulgence.'

'And that's what you've done,' Nora said, 'if I can judge from the exotic postcards and snap-shots you've sent me.'

'Yes, we have.'

'Are you saying you have regrets?'

'Not at all. No regrets at all. I've had a lovely time. Perfect.' She paused. 'Too perfect, maybe.'

'Nothing can be too perfect, Nora said.

'I know. That's what I've always told myself. But in the past year or so, I've begun to wonder if it's been as perfect for Floyd as it has for me.'

'Has he complained?'

'No.'

'Is he taking tranquillizers and sleeping-pills?'

'No.'

'Then let's not worry about Floyd.'

'But I do.' Valerie said. 'I look at him sometimes and I think, "He's invested everything in me. He has no children, he has no profession. Everything he does is connected to me." '

'My God, Valerie, what's wrong with that? That's what most women pray for before they go to sleep at night.'

'Don't misunderstand. I'm not complaining for myself. I just can't help wondering if that's enough for him, if I'm enough for him. If he's truly content to lead the sort of nomadic sybaritic life we live, will he still feel the same ten years from now?'

'What in the world has come over you?' Nora said. 'Forget about ten years from now. Forget about next year. Don't you know when you're well off? It's a screwed-up, imperfect world, Valerie. Don't waste time trying to fix it. When it's working for you, put it in a bowl and eat it with a spoon. God forbid that anything should

483

really go wrong for you and Floyd. But if it ever does you'll realize then what you don't seem to realize now. The gods are smiling on you and you're looking the other way. Being lucky is knowing you're lucky. If you don't appreciate what you have till after it's gone, then you deserve to lose it.' She smiled. 'I may not have learned much in my life but I've certainly learned that.'

Valerie picked up her wine glass and studied the colour in the candlelight. She took a sip, set the glass down, and said, 'You're talking about Jesse, aren't you?'

Nora smiled. 'We don't want to get into that, do we?'

'Why not? We've been talking about *my* man. Why can't we talk about yours?'

'He's not *my* man. Hasn't been for a long time. In any case, you and I talked this through before. Before you married Floyd, as I remember. We decided that neither of us should feel remorse.'

'And I don't,' Valerie said.

'That's good. Neither do I.'

'Are you saying that you didn't realize what you and Jesse had together till after it was over?'

'The first time I didn't. The second time I *did* but I didn't handle things right. So I let him get away.'

'What about the next time?' Valerie said.

'The trees are on fire. There probably won't be a next time.'

'What if there is?'

'If there is, and I wouldn't wager a great deal of money on it, if there is, I promise you that I will take whatever measures are necessary to keep him where he belongs.'

'With you,' Valerie said.

'That's correct. With me.'

[5]

For three days and nights in Madrid it had rained steadily. The bright flowers along the garden path below Dorsey's window hung heavy on their stems. The city itself seemed sodden, as grey as stone. On the third wet afternoon, she sat at a delicate table just beside the glass doors leading to a wide balcony and wrote a letter to Rab.

My Darling,

Did you assume that I'm dead? If so, I'm not surprised. Many days I assume that I'm dead.

The weather is hateful here. Very unlike Madrid, which is usually dry and cold, or dry and hot, depending on the time of year. But now it's suddenly cold and damp and miserable. Days to match my mood.

I have postponed writing to you or calling you in London because I was hoping I would be able to tell you that I have dealt with all my problems and slain all the dragons in my garden. Unfortunately I must report that both the problems and the dragons are still very much with me. On days like this, with the rain punishing the windows, it's hard for me to have positive hopes or thoughts about anything.

Mostly I sit here and dream about my heavenly cottage in the Cotswolds. I think about what it was like being there with you and I ask myself why we can't go there, you and I, put our car in the garage, order in a great supply of food and wine, and just stay, like two voluntary prisoners, cut off from the world and insanely happy. A simple act, I tell myself. So why can't we do it? Is it only because I lack courage. God knows, I lack the courage for most things I'd like to do. I hate myself for that. I feel like a starving woman at a banquet who for some reason refuses to eat.

As if my own problems, our problems, were not painful and difficult enough, everything is intensified now by what's happening with Oscar. I know nothing about his business. I know nothing about anybody's business, including my own, but I know catastrophe when I see it, and that's what's about to hit us. A direct hit on Oscar and a glancing blow to me. Unless some miracle takes place, Oscar will have to leave London, stop doing business in England and sell the two houses we own there, including the Cotswold cottage. How this will affect my life, and Charlie's life, God only knows. I'm trying not to think that far ahead. I can't think ahead because I see no solutions. All I want to think about is you, how we can get out of this tight corner we're in, how we can be together. I wish I could forget everything and everybody else, fly to London, drag you off to the country,

485

and stay there. But I can't do that. And I guess you wouldn't like me much if I could do that, if I were that kind of carefree person.

So where are we? Are we worse off, you and I, than when we saw each other last, here in Madrid? I'm afraid so. If you've decided by now that I'm more trouble than I'm worth, that wouldn't surprise me. I hope you haven't decided that, but if you have, I wouldn't blame you. I'm a helpless cow, and I know it, but still I'm trying every way I can to straighten things out. I can't ask you to be patient but I hope you will be. However it may seem to you, nothing is so important to me as being with you. We'll work things out, won't we? I hope you miss me half as much as I miss you. I love you and I need you.

All my love

D.

When she finished the letter she took it into the library, where Oscar was working at his desk, and handed it to him. He read it through, then handed it back to her and said, 'Very good. How could anybody fail to respond to a touching letter like that?'

[6]

Jesse's writing habits were orderly and systematic. When he was working in the library, his notes and reference materials were carefully positioned on the broad desk-top, easy to see and easy to reach. When he finished each day, these papers were placed in their proper folders, the pages he had typed were slipped into another folder labelled 'Work in Progress', and all were stored in a file drawer of his desk that contained nothing except the relevant material he was working on. When Jesse was not sitting in his chair, when no work was being done, the desk-top was always bare and clean.

One blustery spring morning, however, when he had gone off to Springfield for the day, Helen, when she went into the library to close the windows, saw that there was a file folder lying on his desk. Just as she reached the window and began to crank it shut, a gust of wind swirled in from the west, picked up the folder, and scattered pages across the library carpet.

Jesse's desk was not forbidden territory to Helen, any more than it had been when it was Raymond's desk. Jesse had never instructed her to leave his papers unread and undisturbed. Although he was orderly, he was not secretive. There were keys to the desk drawers but he never locked them.

Helen's own rules, however, were quite specific, and the staff observed them just as she did. No papers on Jesse's desk, or any place else, were to be disturbed, rearranged, or read. The fact that he seldom, if ever, left papers lying about did not lessen the specificity of her orders. She would never permit herself to look at his work without permission, any more than she would have opened a letter addressed to him.

As she gathered together the pages that had blown about the room, as she put them back in their folder, she had no intention of reading them or putting them in order. The top page as she put them back on the desk was not the first page of the group. As she shuffled them together one last time to fit them neatly in the folder, it was sheer chance that kept that particular page still jutting out as she closed the folder; sheer chance, also, that the line on the exposed top page had the name Nora in it. Helen closed the folder, weighted it with a brass ink-well, and left it on the desk. Then she went back upstairs to resume what she'd been doing before the sudden weather change had caused her to assist the housekeeper in closing the windows.

Jesse had driven off at nine, just after breakfast, the window-closing had taken place perhaps an hour later, in mid-morning. It was two-thirty in the afternoon before Helen succumbed at last to something stronger and more disturbing than mere curiosity. She walked deliberately downstairs to the library, sat at Jesse's desk, and opened the folder. Each page had a red-pencilled page number in the lower right-hand corner. She quickly put the pages in order, positioned herself comfortably in the desk chair, and began to read. She turned the pages quickly. When she finished, her face had gone quite pale. Sitting up straight in the chair, she turned and looked out through the leaded window at the garden. Then she picked up the folder, carried it to a chair by the window, and read through the pages again. Slowly this time.

Upstairs later, soaking in her tub, she tried to erase what she'd read from her memory. But neither the central thrust of what Jesse had written nor the specific details could be pushed away. Certain passages and descriptions and conclusions played back, word for word, in her memory as though they had been recorded there.

Was the love I felt for Helen after Raymond's death only, in fact, a thin residue of what I had felt for him..she would like to be in love with me but she is not . . . we came back to each other, as we returned to Raymond's house: there was no place else to go . . . from the first moment I saw Wingate Fields I was determined to stay there . . . a soft creature that burrows in the earth and and lives, for all its beauty, very much to itself . . . is it possible that Nora has, in truth, a depth of feeling that is totally foreign to Helen . . . has she ever loved anyone except Raymond . . . is she capable of it?

That evening when she was having cocktails in the library with Jesse, she asked him if he'd driven through a windstorm that morning on the way to Springfield.

'It didn't turn out to be much but it got off to a good start,' he said. 'Black sky, rain spattering the car windows, and gusts of wind that made it hard to steer. How was it here?'

'Pretty much what you described. More wind than anything else. We had to scurry through the house closing the windows.' She gestured towards the folder on his desk. 'You left that folder out and there were pages scattered all over the room.'

'How did I manage that? I usually have everything tucked away in drawers.'

'You just overlooked it, I suppose. I picked up the pages and put them back in the folder.'

Jesse put his drink down, walked around the desk, and picked up the folder. He riffled quickly through the pages and said, 'You even got the pages back in order. You're a good custodian.'

'Thank you. I do my best.'

He opened his lower desk drawer and slipped the folder in among the others. 'Were you tempted to read it?'

'Not at all. Raymond trained me well. I'm not a snoop.'

'I write for the public,' Jesse said. 'I have no secrets.'

'I didn't know what it was. I wouldn't have read it in any case.

488

I keep hearing that privacy is a thing of the past but I hope that's not true.'

'So do I.'

They sat there smiling at each other in the cool dim-lit room. He realized that she had read the pages in his folder and she realized that he had wanted her to.

[7]

When Nora returned to Paris after her visit to London with Valerie she felt vital and rejuvenated. In a letter to Karina she wrote:

How wonderfully alive and full of energy I feel. Clear and bright as a Mondrian. I have no explanation for all these primary colours that seem to have spattered themselves on my psyche but I'm enormously grateful for them.

At first I thought it was probably London that had stimulated me. But that ugly and sloven old harridan of a city has never had such powers attributed to it, even by its uncritical admirers. I used to be one of those, incidentally. Did I ever tell you that? When I was married to (or imprisoned by) Edmund Bick, Valerie's unbelievably handsome father, I thought there was no problem in life that could not be eliminated by simply stepping on a train and speeding down to London. How we change. How our standards change. Look at yourself, for example. There was a time when you were convinced your life would end if you left Paris. Now you're a wild enthusiast about the splendours of Brazil. There was a time also when you had decided that I was not deserving of your friendship. I still have the nasty letter you wrote to me. But if I am to judge from your letters since then, you have forgiven me (and yourself, perhaps) and find me, if not lovable, at least acceptable. And why not? Hate takes more energy than love.

Enough about you, let's talk about me for a while. Why do you suppose I feel so good? So positive and alert and eager to see the sun in the morning? My daughter, of course, deserves a lot of the credit. We had a lovely London adventure together.

Up early, staying up late at night, feeding and wining ourselves and trying to miss none of the pleasure the West End has to offer. And we talked, of course, like magpies. Like fond sisters. Not like mother and daughter at all.

I would like to tell you that Valerie's youth and good spirits brought on these feelings that I have. But the sad truth is that she is suffering from a persistent but nameless angst that gives her no peace. Her health is robust, she is more beautiful than she was at twenty, and she and her husband adore each other. So what's the problem? She doesn't know, but the problem persists.

As the days passed after her return home from London, as she continued to feel indescribably complete, Nora at first rejected, then gradually came to accept, the proposition that there was a connection between Valerie's nameless anxieties and her own contentment. The first had stimulated the second. At first she told herself that Valerie's confusion, her inability to enjoy her exceptionally good fortune, had merely made Nora conscious of how fortunate she herself was. But that rationale didn't entirely satisfy her for long. At last she lay on her back in her bed one night and admitted to herself that she felt good *because* her daughter felt bad. After years of saying, and pretending to believe, that Valerie was blameless when Jesse married her after living for twenty years with her mother, after years of putting the blame at her own door, Nora admitted to herself at last that she had always blamed her daughter, and had blamed her even more in some ways, after she discarded Jesse later and married Floyd. Some small voice inside Nora had insisted that retribution was a prime tenet of life. When she left Edmund Bick he had said, 'Some day someone will do to you what you've done to me.' And it had happened, of course. Now, in a very different way, it was happening to Valerie.

Nora did not rejoice in her daughter's pain. Nothing like that. But it did, somehow, make her feel better about herself. She felt vindicated. She sensed a pattern of fairness and order she hadn't recognized before. A perfect daughter and an imperfect mother were subject to the same laws and the same punishments. For the first time in many years she had a feeling she was loath to put a label on. She didn't allow herself to call it innocence.

Chapter Eleven

[1]

The last time Polly saw Jack alive she was encouraged by the way he looked. He was painfully thin, of course, and the grey streaks in his hair were more prominent, but his colour was better, she told herself. 'Very handsome today,' she said to him. 'I almost didn't recognize you.'

'I thought I'd give you a treat. I took a bath and the orderly gave me a shave and a haircut. I'm like brand-new merchandise. The nurses can't keep their hand off me.'

'Did you tell them you're in bondage to me?'

He nodded. 'Those were the exact words I used.'

There was a book on the night-stand by his bed, reproductions of paintings by Degas. The text about his life and work. 'Doc Hofer brought me that. He's a Degas freak. Thinks Degas is the greatest modern painter. He got all excited when I told him Degas isn't a modern painter at all.'

'I like Degas,' Polly said.

'So do I. Everybody likes Degas. That's his problem.'

'He painted beautiful pictures. What more do you want?'

'I want a lot more than that. Boudin and Tiepolo painted beautiful pictures too, but who cares? You look at those paintings and there's nobody home. Louis Armstrong would have looked at Degas' work and said, "*Head* music".'

'What does that mean?'

'You're not dumb. You know what it means.'

'Tell me, anyway,' she said.

'It means the musical notes are all correct but there's nothing behind them.'

'Why do you say Degas isn't modern?'

'Because he's not. That doesn't mean he's not gifted. He's gifted as hell. But he's a classicist. He's traditional. And his biggest problem is facility. His hand couldn't draw a line that wasn't graceful and beautiful.'

'What's wrong with that?'

'Everything. Life's not like that and art's not like that. You have to smell the man who did it. We're all stumbling fools, you know that. So some evidence of that condition has to be present in the painting. New forms and new techniques aren't the answer. If the painter is really *inside* the work then it's something that nobody's ever seen before. It has to be. Beauty came too easy to Degas. And it was somebody's else's definition of beauty. He carried it with him in his head. When he painted in New Orleans he did Parisian paintings. There's a lot of terrific ugly stuff in New Orleans but he missed it. Too bad. It could have changed his way of working. All of us have something ugly in us. A serious painter's job is to use that and make it visible. Otherwise he might as well be designing fabrics for ladies' dresses.'

'Did you convince Hofer?'

'No. He still loves Degas. He'll love him till he dies because he feels safe with him. I told him to take a chance and fall in love with Max Beckmann but he wasn't buying it. He hates Beckmann. Doesn't like Münch or Kirchner either.'

'Neither do I.'

'Of course you do. If you didn't like those painters you wouldn't like me. If all of us turned into paintings overnight, I'd be a Beckmann.'

'What would I be?'

'You probably think you'd be an Ingres or a Vermeer but I say you'd turn into an early Kandinsky. And when you grow up you'll be a Beckmann too. Just like me.'

'You're not a Beckmann. That's too tame for you. You're like a picture somebody paints in an asylum.'

'You think I'm insulted by that?' he said. 'Well, I'm not. It makes me think you're paying attention after all, not letting Goethe and Thomas Mann make all your judgments for you. I think you've got a future, pal.'

'And I think you're a crazy man.'

'That's why you love me,' he said. 'All you sheltered English girls are helpless in the hands of lunatics. When I'm old and cautious, puttering around in the garden, you'll detest me. You'll take up with a lorry driver.'

Before she left home that morning, Polly had made a promise to herself that she would not admonish him or plead with him to take care of himself. As she drove to Wurzburg she repeated that pledge. When she saw him in the hospital, hair trimmed and clean-shaven, it was easy for her to tell herself that he looked better, that his colour and his attitude were better. She welcomed the presence of the Degas book, the opportunity it gave them to talk as they'd done hundreds of time before, to get outside themselves, to forget, or seem to forget, for those moments, that Jack was being restrained where he was, that he had no freedom of choice or movement.

When he tired of Degas and Beckmann, he rambled on at length about Mahler and Haydn and Bartok, about Bach, whom he loved, and Wagner, whom he detested. Not once did she break her pledge to herself, either by a word or a look. She allowed him to choose the subjects and expound on them at length. It reminded her of the evenings they'd spent together in the apartment in Heidelberg. Those times came to life for her again.

When she left the hospital and drove out through the gate in the prison wall, she felt an exhilaration that she hadn't experienced in all the time she'd been coming there. She knew there was no rational explanation for the way she felt. Nor did she search for one. She simply revelled in the warm and good feeling. Trying to explain it to Bill that evening, she said, 'Do you ever wake up in the morning and say to yourself, "My God, but I feel smashing today." You realize there's no reason for it but it doesn't matter. You feel as though nothing can possibly go wrong and even if it does you can handle it, or correct it, or even put it out of your mind if necessary. Indestructible. That's how you feel. That's what it was like seeing Jack today. And he felt it too, I think. He looked so marvellous and he talked so well. We had a lovely time.'

'Is he really better? Did you see his doctor?'

She shook her head. 'I wanted to stay with what I saw and the way I felt. I wanted no clinical talk or medical reservations today. I simply wanted to spoon the frosting off the top of the cake and eat it, and that's what I did. After all these months I've finally

493

found a way to deal with this situation. I'm sure of it. And I think Jack has, too. Now we can stop trying to fix things that can't be fixed and simply make the best of it till the time comes when we can put it behind us.'

Two days later Jack died at three in the morning of a ruptured aorta. Dr Hofer telephoned Polly as soon as he left the operating room. 'I know there's nothing I can say to make it easier for you,' he said, 'but I didn't want you to hear the news from anyone but me.'

As soon as she hung up the receiver, Polly went into Bill's bedroom and told him what had happened. 'He died in the operating room,' she said, 'Before they even had time to give him an anaesthetic.'

'My God, Poll . . . I can't tell you how sorry I am. What can I do?'

'Right now the best thing you can do is try to go back to sleep. That's what I'm going to do. I don't feel like talking.'

'Are you all right?' Bill said.

'I'm as all right as I can be.'

'Are you sure?'

She nodded. 'I'm glad you're here. That helps.'

She went back to her room then, closed her door and locked it. Crossing to the bathroom, she took out a bottle of barbiturates she'd kept hidden behind stacks of clean towels in the linen cabinet. Pouring the capsules out in her hand, she swallowed them all, two or three at a time, and rinsed them down with water.

[2]

From the day he arrived in Heidelberg to stay with his sister, perhaps even before that day, Bill had sensed that he would have a critical role to play. He felt that a time would come when his presence would be absolutely vital. During the following months, as the quiet days and weeks crawled by, the pattern broken only by Polly's visits to Wurzburg, it would have been easy for him to conclude that he'd been mistaken, that he, in fact, had nothing whatsoever to offer her. He was a companion of sorts, a benevolent

494

distraction, but beyond that he was able to contribute nothing. He refused to accept such conclusions, however. He stubbornly insisted to himself that a moment would come when he would be indispensable, when things would have to be done that only he could do.

When Hofer called, Bill had heard the telephone ring and he was instantly awake. From Polly's room he could hear the faint sound of her voice as she spoke. And he heard the clicking sound when she hung up the receiver a few minutes later. Before he could get out of bed to go to her room, he heard her footsteps coming along the hallway.

After they talked in his room, after she'd told him about Jack, Bill was reassured by her calmness. He heard her move back to her room, heard her door softly close. Then, like a sharp signal in the stillness, he heard the dead-bolt snap into place. Polly had often joked about that second lock. 'Who would want a lock like that on the bedroom door? Unless there's a gorilla in the next room who would ever use such a lock?'

Bill got up, put on his robe, and walked down the corridor to Polly's room. Standing outside her door, he heard the water running in her bathroom sink. It shut off then and he heard nothing more. He gently tried the door but it was solidly locked. Still he waited by the door and listened. At last the tiny ribbon of light at the bottom of her door went dark and he heard her get into bed. He eased away then and turned to go back to his room but something pulled him back. He tapped lightly on her door and said, 'Are you all right, Polly?'

'Just going to sleep.'

'Why did you lock the door?'

There was a pause. Then she said, 'I didn't realize I did.'

'I wish you'd unlock it. I don't like the idea of your being all bolted in.'

'It's all right. Go to sleep, Bill.'

'I need to ask you something,' he said then. 'Let me in. It will just take a minute.'

'I'm going to sleep. We'll talk in the morning.'

'This won't wait till morning.'

'Don't be a pest, Billy.'

'I'm serious, Polly. Open the door.'

When she didn't answer he said, 'Please, Polly. Let me in.' He

495

stood with his ear against the door. There was no sound from inside. He turned and picked up a heavy oak chair that sat against the wall in the corridor. Holding it like a battering ram, he began to pound it against the door just by the latch. At last the lock pulled loose, there was a jagged rending of the wood frame, and the door swung open. He crossed to Polly's bed and switched on the light. Her speech was blurred as she tried to pull herself up in the bed. 'What're you doing . . . what's the matter with you..?'

Bill turned away from her and went into the bathroom. The empty prescription bottle was sitting on the edge of the sink. He put it in the pocket of his robe and went back to the side of Polly's bed. She tried to push him away but she was too weak to resist. He wrapped a blanket round her, picked her up and carried her out to his car. Ten minutes later she was being treated in the emergency room of Heidelberg's university hospital.

[3]

As soon as he knew Polly was out of danger, when she was sleeping in her room with a private nurse watching over her, Bill went back to the apartment, bathed and dressed, and drove to Wurzburg. It was late in the afternoon when he got back to Heidelberg. He went straight to the hospital. Before going to Polly's room, he spoke to the supervisor on her floor.

'The private nurses have been with her all day, as you instructed, and she's been under mild sedation. Medically, there seems to be no problem. She's a healthy young woman.'

'Does she seem upset? Have you talked with her?'

'I stopped in to see her late this morning and again about an hour ago. She's exhausted but apart from that I saw nothing alarming in her behaviour. She asked about you. I'm sure she'll be glad you're here.'

The private nurse, a substantial Bavarian woman with ginger hair, waited outside in the corridor while Bill and Polly talked.

'Is she my bodyguard?' Polly said.

Bill shook his head. 'Just a private nurse. I wanted somebody with you in the room.'

'That's what I mean. Somebody to protect me against myself. Did you think that as soon as I woke up I'd try to kill myself again?'

'I don't want to talk about that. I'm just happy to see you feeling better.'

'I'm not feeling better. I feel bloody awful. If you think you did me a favour by bringing me here and having those beautiful drugs pumped out of my stomach, you're mistaken. I wanted to die. I still want to die.'

'I don't believe that,' he said.

'You'll see.'

'Is that a threat?'

'Not at all. I'm just telling you how I feel.'

'And here's how I feel. Since this was your first attempt I thought it made sense to give you a chance to reconsider.'

'All I wanted to do was go to sleep and not wake up again. That's still all I want.'

'Then I suppose you'll manage to do it. But not while I'm living with you.'

'What does that mean?'

'Seems clear to me. You may be anxious to kill yourself but I'm just as eager to prevent that. You may think you don't want to live but I very much want you to live. I'm going to eat with you, sleep in the same room with you, and take you to the bathroom if I have to. But you're not going to kill yourself. Not unless you kill me first.'

[4]

They kept her in the hospital for three days. When Bill took her home she found a letter there, a prison envelope addressed in Jack's handwriting. 'When did this come?' she asked.

'The day after you went into the hospital. He must have sent it the day before he died. I almost burned it.'

'Maybe you should have,' she said.

'Too late now. I didn't.'

'Maybe I should burn it.'

Bill shook his head. 'I don't think so. I think you should read it.'

497

She stood there in the hallway of her apartment holding the envelope in her hand. 'Why don't you read it first? Then if you think I should . . .'

'Nothing doing, Polly. You've been through the hardest part. You don't have to back away now.'

'Can I read it out loud to you then? Maybe that will make it easier.'

'It's not my business, Polly.'

'Yes, it is. Everything's your business now.'

She tore open the envelope, took out the letter, and began to read. After the first sentences she started to cry. But she didn't stop reading till she came to the end.

I'm not gonna make it, kid. I know you think I've been slowly trying to kill myself but you're wrong. Suicide's not my game. But all the same I know it's going to happen. Is that possible? I mean is it possible for somebody to know when they're about to bow out. I would say no. You know me. I'm a super-realist. No fantasy in my life. Just meat and potatoes and down-home talk. On the other hand, a guy I knew in the Army said his sister hadn't been feeling too well and one day she said to him, 'You know something . . . I've had enough.' That night she took a bubble bath, shampooed her hair, went out with her husband for a couple drinks, came home and went to bed, turned her face to the wall, and died in her sleep.

You always accuse me of kidding around too much. Too many jokes. Well, I'll tell you, I'm not light-hearted about this whole matter. But I'm not heavy-hearted either. In spite of all my bitching and moaning through the years, I've had a lot of fun. Still nobody but an idiot gets up and leaves the table when there are several more courses still to be served. But . . . what the hell.

The other side of the coin is that you and I both know that I wasn't meant to be locked up. Not for a day even, not for a week and certainly not for twenty years. So if there was a God in Heaven, which there ain't, or if I had a guardian angel, which I don't, maybe those two old souls, who were looking the other way when I was sent here to Wurzburg, finally looked my way and said, 'We've got to get that poor sad-assed creature out of there.' Judging from the bongo beats and rim-shots inside my chest, they've got me scheduled, or somebody's got me scheduled, for an early release.

If you were going to die, it would wreck me. I mean it. I count on your living for ever. But since it's me who's making the trip, you mustn't expect me to take it seriously, at least not for very long. (See above.) The secret of my success (and the ill-kept secret of all my failures) is that I take almost nothing seriously, certainly not myself. There was a time when I considered myself a dedicated musician. I thought my heart and my guts lived inside my cello. But I was wrong about that too. I just live inside my skin like everybody else. At last I walked away from music as easily as I walked away from my wife and kid.

Speaking of my wife and kid, I want you to do me a favour. When the doctors finally decide I'm dead instead of just drunk or sleeping, please ask them to put me in a nice box and fly me back to Wisconsin. Does that surprise you? It surprises *me*. But since I wasn't worth much to those people when I was alive, maybe they'll get some kind of a weird thrill from burying me. Also, when the Army sees that I'm dead, maybe they'll cough up my insurance for my daughter to help her buy a donut shop, or a fancy man, or whatever she decides she wants. I know you're a generous soul and you won't mind being stuck for whatever it costs to ice me down and ship me home. But if you think I owe you something, I promise you I'll pay you back in gold doubloons the next time I see you.

I'm not stupid, kid. I know you're gonna feel bad. And that's all right. Feel as bad as you want to but don't let it wreck you. If you do, I'll come back and haunt you. Just think about the good stuff, because that's what I'm doing. All the sweet-smelling, idle and wonderful hours. The mornings and the afternoons and the soft nights. The bright-red summers and the silver snows. We had a feast, Polly. Nobody ever had it so fine, and nobody will again. But who says the good stuff has to last for ever? It's not even supposed to. It just lasts as long as it lasts. And if you're paying attention, that's long enough. I love you, kid. I owe you a lot.

She stopped reading then, looked up from the letter, and said, 'That's it. That's the end of it.'

Helen was sitting in Frank Wilson's apartment overlooking Lake Michigan on the south side of Chicago. Frank sat in a leather chair facing her. There was a vacuum in the room as though all the air had been abruptly sucked away. Finally he said, 'I'm not trying to hurt your feelings. You asked me a question and I tried to tell you the truth. I don't know what you expected me to say.'

'I don't know either. In any case it's not your fault. I made the mistake. I needed to talk to someone and I thought . . .'

'Don't give me that,' he said. 'The first thing you said when we talked on the phone yesterday was that you wanted to talk to my wife. You were trying to reach Connie.'

'Let's forget it, Frank.'

'It's true, isn't it? I got you by default. When you found out that Connie and I are divorced, *then* you decided to bring your troubles to me.'

'I was surprised when I called her office and they said the number had been disconnected. They gave me the number here as a referral number.'

'And much to your surprise, I answered the phone.'

'I was surprised. I told you that,' she said.

'You mean you didn't remember this phone number?'

'No, I didn't. I just copied it down from the operator and dialled it.'

'Good health and a bad memory,' Frank said. 'They say that's the formula for happiness.'

'Even if I had recognized the number I wouldn't have expected you to be here. I assumed you'd given this place up.'

'Not me. I like it here. This is where I hibernate.'

'Your wife said you were living on Lake Shore Drive.'

'We were. But when she left, I sold the place. Never liked it anyway. All glass and aluminium. Not a piece of wood in the whole damn building. No, that's not right. I guess we had a little cutting-board in the kitchen. But that was it.'

'When the operator told me her number had been disconnected, it never occurred to me that she'd left Chicago.'

'All my ex-wives leave town. Sometimes I think about that when I'm sitting here having a drink. But I don't think about it often.'

'Did you think it was odd that she and I had lunch together that day?'

'To tell you the truth, I don't remember what I thought. It wouldn't have mattered anyway. Connie and I didn't ask each other's permission to do whatever we wanted to do. Did you ask Jesse's permission?'

'I didn't ask him exactly. He knew I'd had a note from Connie saying she'd like to meet me some time.'

'So what did he say?'

'Not much. I think it amused him.'

'Did it amuse him when you told him you were coming up here today to see me?'

'I didn't tell him.'

'Ah-ha,' he said.

'He's not tolerant where you're concerned. He's never quite figured out how you fit into my life.'

'I'm easy to explain. I was your first and only husband. You know what they say. If you keep getting married to different people that means you were happy in your first marriage. If you divorce the first time and never get married again that's a pretty good sign you were miserable, that the whole institution doesn't appeal to you.'

'You're really trying to shoot me down, aren't you?'

'Not at all,' he said. 'I was trying to make the point that if I'd been a better husband you wouldn't have avoided marriage after we gave it up.'

'Do you think that's what I did?'

'Maybe avoided is not the right word. But the record seems to indicate that one marriage was plenty for you.'

'And so far you've had three,' she said.

'That's correct.'

'I'm surprised it didn't work with Connie. I thought she was terrific.'

'She was,' Frank said. 'And it did work. It just didn't last.'

'Doesn't make sense.'

'Most things don't make sense. Sometimes the marriages that work best don't seem to make any sense at all.'

'You and I made sense, didn't we?'

'Seemed so to me,' he said, 'but we didn't stay together. Connie and I made sense too. At least we thought we did.'

501

'So what happened? Or shouldn't I ask?'

'No secrets here,' he said. 'But I thought maybe you already knew.'

'How would I know?'

'After your ladies' lunch, I mean. It wasn't too long after that when Connie headed west. I thought she might have confided in you.'

Helen shook her head. 'As a matter of fact, you got high marks from both of us.'

'She didn't drop a hint that she was bored with me?'

'Not at all. Now that you mention it, I seem to remember that she thought you might be bored with her.'

'Not me. She was so damned busy I didn't see enough of her to get bored. And when I did see her she was full of energy and information and ideas. Her brain never stopped crackling. Nothing boring about Connie. But when she left, it was as if she'd never been here. I didn't miss her.'

'Did you miss me when we broke up?'

'Which time?'

'When we got a divorce.'

He nodded. 'Sure I missed you. I was vulnerable then.'

'But not now?'

'Nope. Not now. It's all a matter of glands. The better they function, the more you get hurt.'

'I've never stopped getting hurt,' she said.

'Then you must have sensational glands.'

After a long moment she said, 'When you've loved someone, do you think it's possible to become friends later?'

'Not a chance.'

'Don't you think of me as a friend?'

'Never in a million years.'

'Why not?' she said.

'Because it doesn't work that way.'

'Then why do I think you're my friend?'

'Because that's what you want to think, I suppose. And because you're sentimental. All females are sentimental. They don't like things to end. When you don't like something, when it's out of style or doesn't fit any longer, you'd rather store it in the attic than burn it or throw it away. Even if you know damned well you'll never use it again. Most men either hate their ex-wives or they

502

want to sleep with them. The women, on the other hand, want to maintain some kind of civilized relationship. Just in case they need a friend.'

'You think I'm that way?'

'I don't draw conclusions about you. I never did.'

'I wouldn't be here today, would I, crying on your shoulder about Jesse, if I didn't think of you as a friend?'

'That's hard to say. Bartenders hear sad stories twenty times a day. From people they've never seen before.'

'It would be a good joke on me, wouldn't it, after all these years, if it turned out that you're my best friend?'

'You have lots of friends.'

'I'm not so sure,' she said. 'But even if I do, I didn't call them.'

'You didn't call me, either. You called Connie.'

'But then I called you.'

'You said you didn't recognize the number.'

'I lied.'

'Then it was desperation.'

'I don't think so. I thought I could talk to you. I wanted to talk to you. I thought you could straighten me out if anybody could.'

'But I can't. And I don't want to try. I'm not interested in Jesse's opinion of you. I don't care what he said, or what he wrote down in his diary or his memory book. If you have a problem with him, then *you* settle it. Don't come to me for advice.'

'I didn't ask you for advice. I just know that you know me better than anyone does. I still have that letter you wrote me when I took Floyd to England the first time. You remember what you wrote?'

'No.'

'I don't believe you,' she said.

'It's true. I guess I wrote whatever was in my head at the time. But I didn't keep a copy of it.'

'I've practically memorized it. Do you want to hear what you wrote?'

'No. What's the point?' he said.

'The point is that what Jesse wrote about me bears a sharp resemblance to what you wrote in that letter. If two people as different as you and Jesse see the same flaws in me I can't just kick up my heels and say you're both crazy, can I?'

'Sure you can. Why not?'

'Because I care about what I'm doing. It matters to me how I affect people. When I see myself one way and people who know me best see me in an entirely different way then I feel as if I have to do something about it. I'm not an eighty-year-old woman. I can change if I want to.'

'No, you can't. None of us can. After age six, the important stuff is already locked into place. Ask any psychologist.'

'I don't want to ask any psychologist. I'm asking myself and I'm asking you. You may not be my friend but I'm yours and I'm asking you for help.'

'And I'm telling you I can't solve my own figure-eights, let alone yours. I'm not a writer like your friend, Jesse. If his opinions of you seem to coincide with mine then my first reaction is that mine must have been wrong. I've never passed judgment on you. At least, I never tried to. All I tried to do in that letter was to tell you how I felt. When we were married you had me hypnotized. I didn't know where in hell I was. So when we got together later I just tried to stay afloat. One day at a time. I knew it wasn't going to last for ever. But that didn't make things any better when you sashayed off to England with your son. I figured you were trying to send me a message. Was I right?'

'I guess you were. I was very upset after that automobile accident we had. I didn't think we had much of a future. Even later . . .'

'You were right. As it turned out, we didn't have a future.'

She got up and walked to the window that looked out across the lake. When she turned back she said, 'I know I'm not stupid. But is it possible that I've drawn a blank for all these years? When I look in the glass am I seeing someone who's really not there?'

'I don't know.'

'Yes, you do. If you don't know, who does? Do I have to put together what you wrote and what Jesse wrote and just say to myself, "That's you, Helen, whether you like it or not." '

'You don't have to do anything you don't want to do.'

'Oh, yes, I do. Do you think it was easy for me to come here and tell you that somebody else has signed in with an opinion of me that's as low as yours? I'm not asking for compliments or reassurance. I need someone to tell me the truth.'

'I can't do that, Helen, and I wouldn't do it if I could. I'm too close to you. We've been too close to each other. That letter I wrote you . . . I couldn't send you a letter like that today. I don't feel old but I know I'm older than I was then. I'm not so cocksure now,

504

not so confident about my opinions. Everything between you and me is subjective. Always has been and always will be. All we were good at was loving each other. We weren't running a mutual character-building programme and we're not doing that now. We can't do that. I've never laid eyes on Jesse. If he was sitting where you're sitting, however, I could give him some great objective advice. But I can't do that with you. I can't advise you or direct you or evaluate you. And I don't want to.'

She came back to her chair and sat down. 'Suppose Jesse was sitting here, instead of me, suppose he said, "You know her, Frank. Tell me what I'm doing wrong." What would you say?'

'You mean if I thought he was crazy about you and wanted to find a way to stay with you?'

'Yes.'

'That's easy. Let's pretend I'm Jesse. I'll tell you what I want you to do. First of all, I want you to sell that house in Fort Beck. I don't want you to forget you ever lived there but I want you to put it in the past where it belongs. That whole life there with your father and Jesse is ancient history. You're not your father's daughter, you're not a member of the Bradshaw family, you're not a fixture or a part of anything. You're just yourself. I want you to go some place new with me, some place neither one of us has ever been. We'll build a house and make a life and that will be where we'll live. Not Fort Beck and not Wingate Fields, not any place we've ever lived before. We'll get to *start* something for a change instead of joining something. Instead of repeating something.'

'Is that what you think I need?' she said. 'Is that what you think I want?'

'I don't know what you want. You just asked me what advice I'd give Jesse.'

'It's so strange,' she said then. 'I can't imagine Jesse ever saying those things to me. He's the last person in the world who would want me to cut myself off from the past like that.'

'But what if he did take my advice? What if he asked you to do that?'

She smiled. An uncomfortable smile. 'I could never do it,' she said. 'Those things you're talking about leaving behind are the things I count on, the things I need. It's never occurred to me to sell Raymond's house in Fort Beck. All those lovely things, all the memories. I'm sure I'd feel as though I'd sold myself. I'm a Brad-

505

shaw. Raymond's house and his home at Wingate Fields are a part of me. You understand that, don't you?'

'Of course I do,' he said. 'I understand it very well. That's why I'd never try to give you advice.'

[6]

Late one morning, Rosalind spoke to Rab on the office intercom. 'There's a lady on the telephone for you. I think it's Oscar Mullet's wife.'

When Rab picked up the receiver Dorsey said, 'I'm at Heathrow. Just flew up from Madrid.'

'Good. I'll buy you lunch at Benjamin's.'

'I'm afraid not. I've just hired a car. I'm driving out to the cottage. Can you meet me there?'

'Yes, I can. I'll be there about five.'

'Wonderful,' she said. 'And I promise not to talk about problems. We'll pretend I don't have any problems.'

Just before he left for a meeting at the Dorchester, Rosalind came into his office and said, 'Can you spare me five minutes?'

'Any time.'

When she sat down he said, 'This isn't some catastrophe, I hope. You're not resigning, are you?'

She smiled. 'You may decide to discharge me but I'm not resigning.'

'That's good news.'

'I've never meddled in your personal life, have I?'

'God, no. I wish you would. I need all the help I can get.'

'But you haven't had it from me. Correct?'

'Correct. Somebody trained you well.'

'I trained myself,' she said. 'Made up my own rules. Hands off the boss. Do the work and go home. If he's married, don't become best friends with his wife. If he's single, don't become best friends with him. Don't gossip. Don't ask questions. Don't meddle. Now I'm going to break my own rules. I'm talking about that telephone call you had this morning. Am I out of bounds?'

'Not yet.'

'After my talk with Gingrich I assumed she was out of the picture. But now she's back. Is she back?'

'I don't know,' Rab said.

'When you start having whisky with your coffee in the morning and four gins at lunch, when you come back from America with a fractured wrist, you mustn't be surprised if I'm concerned about you.'

For a moment Rab said nothing. Then: 'How old are you?'

'How old do you want me to be?'

'Are you older than I am?'

'Everyone's older than you are. I'm twenty-eight.'

'We're practically twins. Except you're smarter.'

'No, I'm not,' she said. 'You're smart and I'm practical. And you're trying to get me off the subject, aren't you?'

'Am I?'

'I'll come straight to the point,' Rosalind said. 'I don't think she's good enough for you. In fact, if I'm any judge of such matters, I believe she's very bad for you. And I don't mean because she's married. I made an absolute fool of myself with a married bloke when I was only twenty years old. I'm sure you two have a jolly time in bed together and I know from her photographs in the papers that she's smashing to look at but I didn't like the expression in Gingrich's face when he talked about her. Something smarmy about him whenever she was the subject. Do you know what I'm trying to say?'

Rab smiled. 'I think you want me for yourself.'

'Of course I do,' she said, 'But that's not what I'm talking about. I am making what you might call a selfless gesture. In fact, I have now finished making it. If you think I've gone bonkers and intruded on your personal life just tell me so and I will slink away, back to my files.'

'Don't slink away. I'm glad you intruded.'

'But all the same, I should mind my own business,' she said.

'Not at all. I wish I were better at minding my business. When you ask me what's going on with Dorsey, I honestly don't know. But I hope to find out in the next day or so. When I do I'll give you a full report.'

'I don't want a full report,' Rosalind said. 'That's not what I'm talking about. I just want you to look out for yourself. Stay out of the choppy water.'

When Rab arrived at Dorsey's cottage later that day it was almost
six o'clock. When she met him at the door she was wearing her
night-dress. She put her arms around him and kissed him and
pulled him down to the floor of the parlour just past the entryway.
'Don't make me wait,' she said. 'Please don't make me wait.'

[7]

It was nearly midnight when they had supper.
'Do you think I'm a strumpet?' She said as they sat down opposite
each other. 'Am I lascivious and predatory?'
'All those things. You should be ashamed of yourself.'
'But I'm not. I missed you so much I thought I'd die. I felt as
though I was about to shrivel up and disappear.'
'You may have died but you didn't shrivel up.'
'I got fat, didn't I?'
'Just in the right places,' he said.
'When I feel terrible and lost and helpless I eat too much. Some
people drink or smoke hundreds of cigarettes. Not me. I eat pasta
and ham and eggs and sinful desserts drowned in whipped cream.
You stayed thin and interesting, as brown as a piece of mahogany,
and I became a well-padded señora.'
She kept the promise she had made him on the telephone. She
did not talk about Oscar or her son. She did not present herself as
a helpless creature without alternatives. They talked and laughed
as they had when they first knew each other, when they'd spent
long afternoons in Rab's apartment in the building on Grantham
Place.
They slept late the morning of the second day, walked along the
stream and through the woods after breakfast, drove to the nearby
village, browsed in the local book store, drank lager in a pub
called the Careless Maiden, and generally squandered the day and
evening like two people who had spent many years together and
expected to spend many more. Not until very late that night as
they lay in the upstairs bedroom together, a fresh breeze fluttering
the window curtains, not until then did she say, 'Is there something
you can do to help Oscar?'

As he'd driven west from London the previous afternoon, Rab had decided to pretend that his most recent and detailed knowledge of Oscar's predicament had come to him in Dorsey's letter. He saw no advantage in discussing his talks with Lord Hinson or Gingrich's revelations to Rosalind.

'What's his current situation?' Rab asked.

'Colour it black. Nothing much new since I wrote to you. That means there's been no improvement. Unless some miracle takes place, unless someone intercedes on his behalf, it looks as if we'll be drummed out of the country.'

'What sort of intercession are you talking about?'

'Oscar says the first news he had of this whole mess came from you. He said a friend of yours at the Exchequer had told you about it.'

'That was some time ago. It sounds as though things have moved ahead quite a lot since then.'

'Oscar got the impression that this friend you spoke about was an important man. He thought perhaps you could . . . I don't know . . . don't ask me precisely what Oscar has in mind. I think he believes there's always a way to approach someone, to try to negotiate a compromise. But since he's not British, since he doesn't really know any influential people here, he wanted me to ask you if . . . you know what I'm trying to say.'

'Is that why you flew up here from Madrid? Because Oscar asked you to?'

'No. You know better than that. I needed to see you. I was dying to see you.'

'But this business with the Exchequer gave you a reason for coming, something to tell Oscar.'

'You're the reason I came. And I don't have to explain anything to Oscar. He doesn't own me.'

'What you're saying is that it's as important to you as it is to him that he gets out of these financial difficulties he finds himself in.'

'Of course it is. You must see that. I have a lot at stake. How can I possibly persuade Oscar to sit down like a civilized person and agree to a divorce when he has all this other business hanging over his head? How can I hope to win him over when we discuss Charlie's future? He's very angry about what's happening. If he turns all that anger against me, I'm lost.'

'All this has a familiar ring. Are we back to where we started?'

'I hope not. Once his business troubles are solved, I think maybe he'll listen to reason.'

'What if he won't?' Rab said. 'What if his troubles aren't solved? What if he's forced to leave England and go back to America?'

'Then I'm sunk.'

'This is the part I don't understand. You're not in the film business. You're not having financial problems with the Crown. No one's suggesting that you leave England.'

'Of course they are. Or they will. I'm his wife. I'm an officer in his corporations.'

'Then you simply resign. Turn everything back to him. That's something a good solicitor can manage straight away. You disengage yourself from his business affairs and commence a divorce action. Next year at this time you'll be married to me.'

'And I'll never see my son again.'

'I don't believe that.'

'That's because you don't know Oscar as well as I do. He may not be able to win his fight with the British government but he can certainly win any fight with me. He knows that and so do I.'

'But I don't know it. I don't accept that at all. How can he keep you with him if you convince him you want to leave.'

'Charlie. *Charlie*. We always come back to Charlie. That's why I was hoping you might have some influence with the Exchequer. That would give me a card to play with Oscar. If I could offer him something, then maybe I could get what I want in return. Doesn't that make sense?'

'It makes sense. But that doesn't mean it can be done.'

'Who is this man you know?' she asked. 'Is he just a business friend or is he a real friend?'

'He's a real friend. I've known him all my life.'

'Have you ever asked for a favour before?'

'No.'

'Then isn't it worth a try?'

'I wouldn't know where to begin. If Oscar had some new evidence that proves he hasn't been involved in the irregularities the Exchequer's accusing him of, that would be one thing. But from what you say, I assume that Oscar is not an innocent victim. Is that correct?'

'I'm sure he's not innocent.'

'Then there's nothing I could present on his behalf. I could only

510

say he's a friend of mine, which he isn't, or maintain that he deserves better treatment because he's a decent hard-working chap. If everything you say is true, I'm afraid it's too late for such arguments. It would seem that the officials have specific evidence to support their conclusions about Oscar.'

'I'm not talking about evidence or whether Oscar deserves what he's getting. I'm talking about asking a favour from a friend. People do it all the time, don't they?'

'I don't know. Perhaps they do. But I can't do it. I don't have friends who can deliver that kind of favour.'

'Then I'm finished,' she said.

'No, you're not. You're not finished and we're not finished. I can't solve Oscar's problems but I can solve yours. You'll see.'

When he woke up the next morning she was gone. Downstairs on the kitchen table he found a note from her.

Oscar's problems are my problems. I don't like it but that's the way it is. Since I met you I've deceived myself into believing I have choices. But I don't. I made my choice a long time ago and I'm stuck with it. If you're ever in California look me up. I'll buy you lunch at the Polo Lounge. You can eat while I drink. I expect to do a lot of that from now on.

[8]

If Helen had believed that talking with Frank would in some way temper the distress that reading Jesse's notes had caused, and she had indeed expected some such relief, the actual result was a sharp disappointment. As she drove home to Fort Beck after seeing Frank, her thoughts were even more blurred than before. Seeing herself in the rear-view mirror, she marked something unfamiliar in her eyes, a subtle shading, to be sure, but one she could not ignore. She was unable to put a name to it, this new and tentative thing she saw, but its lack of definition in no way lessened its negative impact. She quickly slipped on her tinted driving glasses so she would no longer be face to face with whatever she had become or was in the process of becoming.

For the next few days she filled the hours with activity. She fussed and fretted over household details, held detailed meetings with the housekeeper, the cook, and the gardener. She sent chairs to be recovered and draperies to be relined. A roofer and a tree surgeon were called in for estimates, an oriental rug shipped to Chicago for repair. She shopped for gifts for Betsy and the children, mailed a book about Pechstein to Polly in Heidelberg, and wrote a long and rambling letter to Bill. From breakfast till bedtime, every moment was scheduled and filled with activity. But it didn't work. Sharp memories of Jesse's words and observations irritated her like thistles. She ricocheted back and forth between two positions. If Jesse was being self-serving and vengeful, simply trying to hurt her, then there was no escaping the conclusion that he had turned abruptly cruel and hateful. If, on the other hand, he saw things in her which she had never seen in herself, if his judgments of her were correct, then she had no choice but to detest herself. Either choice sickened her.

At last she concluded that she had to go to the source. She must talk it out with Jesse. One evening after dinner she told him she'd read the contents of the folder he'd left on his desk.

'I suspected that,' he said. 'You're not a good liar.'

'Neither are you. You expected me to read it, didn't you? You wanted me to read it.'

'No. Not specifically. If I'd truly wanted you to read it, I'd have given it to you. But once I realized I'd left it out, once you told me you'd seen it, the possibility that you might have read it didn't upset me.'

'Didn't you think it would upset *me*? Is that what you really think of me . . . those things I read?'

'It's not a question of that . . .'

'Oh, yes, it is,' she said. 'That's exactly what it is.'

Jesse shook his head. 'I wasn't making final judgments of you, or me, or anybody else. I was exploring some ideas, some history, some relationships.'

'Are you saying you didn't mean those things?'

'No. I'm not saying that. But none of it was meant personally. As I said, it's an exploration, an attempt to understand, to put people and experiences in perspective.'

'That won't work, Jesse. The words are yours, the ideas are yours, the names are real. The people are real. You are you, Nora

512

is Nora, and Helen is me. It's not a short story. Those are real conclusions about you and me, about us.'

When he didn't answer she said, 'At first I was hurt. Now I simply don't understand. Either something strange and terrible is happening to you or something worse has already happened to me without my knowing it.'

'I'm a writer, Helen. I have to try new things. That's just something I wrote. It's nothing to get excited about.'

'I'm not excited,' she said. 'I'm very calm. But I'm mystified. I don't have to quote little pieces of what I read. You know it all as well as I do. You do know what you wrote, don't you? You do remember?'

'Yes, I do. I reread it a couple of days ago.'

'What was your reaction?'

'I don't think it's the best thing I've ever written.'

'I don't mean that. I'm not talking about style. I'm talking about content. Did you change things as you read it, did you cross out lines and write new words in, did you make notes in the margin when you read something that didn't seem accurate to you?'

'No, I didn't.'

'In other words, you stand behind it as it is.'

'I haven't given it that much thought. I don't take it as seriously as you do.'

'No, I guess you don't.'

After a moment Helen said, 'Let me ask you another question. Is this some sophisticated device you've hit on to let me know you're moving on?'

'What gave you that idea?'

'I will quote one little morsel for you. I believe you wrote that you and I ended up together here in Fort Beck because there was nowhere else to go. Let's stop dancing around and deal with that. Is that why we're here? Is that why you're here?'

'There were many other times we could have come here together. What I meant to say, I suppose, is that the circumstances had something to do with our coming here and staying together when we did.'

'As far as I'm concerned, there was only one circumstance,' she said. 'I was in love with you and I believed you were in love with me. Nothing intricate or involved. Nothing fancy. Just that. I wanted to spend the rest of my life with you.'

513

'Are you saying you don't want that now?'

'I'm saying I don't know where I am. I'm trying to make some sense out of all this but you're not helping me. If you really meant those things you wrote, if that's the way you think of me, then I can't imagine that you're planning to stay with me. And surely you can't believe that I would want you to. If I'm to believe what you wrote, then there's no place on earth for you except Wingate Fields. And whether you admit it to yourself or not . . .' she stopped.

'What were you about to say?'

'Nothing. I decided against it.'

Helen slept in the downstairs bedroom that night. More accurately, she lay in bed in the darkness, looked up at the ceiling, and tried to sleep. If she'd been upset and distraught before talking with Jesse, she now felt drained. If the things he'd written had bewildered her, their conversation had been even more baffling. He had seemed either unable to unwilling to engage himself, to deal with the subject, to deal with her. The stuff he was made of appeared to have gone diaphanous.

Lying there in the dead quiet of her house, trying to find something solid to refer to, her mind kept carrying her back to that far-off summer in England, the night when she'd learned that Angus would adopt Jesse and that Jesse and Nora were engaged to be married. That night, too, she had lain awake long after dinner was finished and the house was dark, trying to piece things together in her mind, trying to make a joining of the Jesse she knew and the seemingly new person she had heard new facts about at the dinner table that evening. She had felt betrayed then and she felt betrayed now, as though she'd participated in an uneven contest with two sets of rules.

Betrayed. The word kept reappearing. Was it a part of Jesse's behaviour pattern? He had left his parents when he was sixteen and so far as she knew had seen them only one time after that. He had never seen his brother and sister again. After becoming engaged to Nora, he had returned to America and caused their wedding to be postponed. At last it was cancelled when she married Edmund Bick. Later, after her divorce, he and Nora had lived together in Paris for twenty years. When they separated he had married Nora's daughter, Valerie. How long had that alternative existed in his mind? No one could answer that question. Nor could anyone say what had prompted him to take up his life with Nora

514

again while he was still married to Valerie. Did Valerie feel betrayed by that? She must have. And did Nora feel betrayed when Jesse, after his divorce from Valerie, suddenly returned to America and Helen? And what about now? Has he planned his next move?

These questions Helen asked herself had multiple answers. But there was a pattern of events that could not be denied. Even when she told herself that no person's lifetime behaviour would hold up under the close scrutiny she was giving to Jesse's, when she questioned the fairness of passing judgment from such a synopsis, even then she could not ignore what her senses told her. This most stalwart and dependable and permanent person in her life either had never been, or had gradually ceased to be, what she thought he was, what she wanted and needed him to be. Was he subconsciously emulating Raymond, who after his death was revealed as a different person than he had pretended to be? Was he trying to tell her that she must not depend on him? Was he trying to put her in a position where she would be forced to do what he himself was unable to do? Did he want to be rejected? Did he want her to dissolve the binding medium, however one might define it, that had held them together for so many years?

All these questions and their tiny tributaries trickled through her mind. She would lie for long moments finding no answer to anything. Then, in a rush, a thousand answers would crowd into place, each more final and compelling than the previous one and all, at last, meaningless and confusing. It was nearly dawn before she slept. When she woke up it was almost noon. The housekeeper brought her breakfast on a tray and tried to pretend that it was normal for Helen to sleep in the downstairs bedroom and take her breakfast there. Just before she left the room, Helen asked her if Jesse had gone out.

'Yes, he did. Early this morning. Had a cup of coffee and went right along. Left before eight.'

'He mentioned that he might be going to Champaign this week. Perhaps he drove over there.'

'I don't think so. He didn't take his car. He just walked out the front door carrying his raincoat and turned north on Locust Street.'

After she'd bathed and dressed, Helen went upstairs to the bedroom suite she shared with Jesse. Aside from the fact that only one side of their bed had been slept in, the room looked the same as it did every morning. The book Jesse had been reading was on his bedside table, his pyjamas were draped across a chair at the foot of the bed. In the bathroom his toilet articles were all in their normal place and his robe hung on the back of the door.

It was mid-afternoon before Helen had occasion to go into the library. When she did, as though it had lured her there, the first thing she noticed was a file folder on top of Jesse's desk. She sat in the desk chair, opened the folder, and found a hand-written note inside. There was no salutation at the top but it was clearly meant for her.

> I know you want me to leave so you'll forgive me, I'm sure, if I don't wait around to be dismissed. You and Raymond have always been the foundation stones of my life. That fact won't change.
>   Since I came to this house empty-handed, I think it's appropriate that I leave the same way.

[9]

Before the doctor released Polly from the hospital in Heidelberg he discussed her condition with Bill. 'She has no clinical problems, none whatsoever,' he said, 'and she seems remarkably calm and under control. But we mustn't be deceived by that. She's had two major shocks. The death of her friend and her own attempt at suicide. She has every reason to be an emotional wreck but she's not. That could be a good sign. It might also be a discouraging sign. If she's decided to keep everything inside herself, that could mean she's in for some difficulties in the future. I know you two live in the same house but I know nothing about your schedule. Will you be able to spend time with her?'

'I have no schedule. I plan to spend all my time with her for as long as she needs me.'

'That's good. She may pretend that she wants to be alone but don't be deceived by that. She needs someone with her, not because she's likely to try suicide again, but because she simply needs someone. She'll have some ups and downs, rather radical ones perhaps, but if you stick with her she'll gradually get stronger and

516

better and come back to life again. Just now she's in a kind of emotional limbo but she'll get over it.'

Just before Bill left his office the doctor said, 'There's one more thing you should be aware of. The more supportive you are of your sister, the more successful you are in helping her to put this unhappiness behind her, the more dependent she'll become.'

'That's all right. I depend on her too, we've always depended on each other.'

Having prepared himself for all sorts of aberrant behaviour, Bill was totally unprepared for what happened once they were back in the house. When he'd sat with Polly in her room at the hospital she'd been, as the doctor had described her, calm and under control. She and Bill had talked together, not about Jack, but about Rab and their parents and things they remembered about growing up at Wingate Fields. She made no effort to pretend that nothing had happened but on the other hand she did not seem determined to dwell on her misfortunes. She appeared to feel that it was desirable for her to bandage her wounds and move forward.

Once they were at home, however, she changed abruptly, seemed to retreat inside herself and become almost totally silent. As though she was trying to emulate Jack, she drank a great deal of coffee but ate almost nothing. After two weeks of this, when she did try to eat, her stomach rejected the food. She lost weight and because she was filled with caffein she couldn't sleep. The weather was cold and nasty just then, and she decided suddenly that her bedroom window must be open all night. A week later she was back in hospital with pneumonia.

When she came home from the hospital this time she was as silent as before but her appetite had returned. She developed a passion for cream custards and nut meats, gained back all the weight she had lost and another half-stone as well.

'Am I terribly fat and ugly?' she said to Bill.

'Not at all. You look fine.'

'Why do I ask you? You're not an objective observer. I'm your splendid older sister and you're crazily in love with me.'

Such bright outbursts were followed by long periods of silence. She sat, seemingly catatonic, staring out the window at the black skeletons of winter trees. A cot had been brought into her bedroom and Bill slept there as he had told her he would. During the day he sat in a chair by the wide window reading or drawing detailed stage designs for imaginary plays in a large linen-covered sketch book. One afternoon he said, 'You must get tired of looking at me. If you promise me you won't do anything silly, maybe I'll do you a great favour and move back to my own bedroom across the hall.'

She had an art book open on her lap, reproductions of drawings by Leonardo. It was as though she hadn't heard what Bill said. She didn't answer or look up from her book. Every few minutes she deliberately turned a page.

A few days later, however, when she was eating her lunch off a tray on her lap and Bill was having a sandwich and a glass of lager at a table in the corner of her bedroom, she said, 'I'm glad you spend so much time with me. I like it when I wake up at night and see you sleeping on your funny cot. It reminds me of when we were little, when we all took our naps together in Nanny's apartment. We each had our own little brass bed. My quilt had ducks on it and yours had chickens. And Rab's was a crazy quilt of many colours.'

One afternoon she began to cough. Bill gave her a codeine syrup the doctor had prescribed when she had pneumonia, and though she woke up twice during the night and had to take two more doses of the cough mixture, by the following morning her coughing had stopped. That afternoon, however, she began to run a fever. Bill sent out to the chemist for medication to lower her temperature, he bathed her wrists and forehead regularly with cold cloths, and by ten o'clock that night her cheeks felt cool and she went to sleep.

In the middle of the night, however, she began to chill. Bill put more blankets on the bed and turned up the thermostat in the room but she was cold, still, and shivering, and her lips were blue. 'I'm freezing,' she said. 'What's the matter with me? I've never been so cold.' He put his hand on her cheek and she said, 'Oh, that feels better. How can you be so warm when I'm so cold? Put your other hand on my face. Let me put my hands on your face. Oh, God, why can't I stop shivering? Why can't I get warm?'

He lay down beside her then, on top of the blankets, wearing his robe and pyjamas. He put his arms around her and she burrowed against him. 'I'm freezing, Bill. I'm really freezing.'

The room was very warm now from the hot air blowing through the heating system but she shook so much the frame of the bed and the metal springs squeaked in the dark silence. He held her against him with her cold cheek against his. Slowly, very slowly, her body stopped trembling. He could feel her hands and her body

518

begin to get warm. At last she relaxed, went heavy in the bed, and went to sleep. He lay very still, afraid to move, afraid he'd waken her, and at last, with the hot air continuing to blow into the room, he went to sleep too.

[10]

As Helen sat in her library reading the last note she would ever receive from Jesse, as she reviewed in detail their conversation of the night before, her assessment of him was not a generous one. Under the circumstances even Jesse would not have expected it to be. On the other hand, that assessment must not, in fairness, be accepted as definitive. Nor should Jesse's assessment of himself, as he took the train from Fort Beck to Chicago that morning, be so accepted. Because his was, in fact, no more generous than hers. If he seemed dispassionate and careless and self-serving to her, he saw himself the same way.

Although Jesse was not accustomed to dwelling on his own motivations and behaviour, it was clear from the things he had written about the Bradshaws that the principal target of his criticism was himself. Under his own probing and dissection, his life-long pattern of self-doubt took on gradually the features, first of guilt, then of contempt. The list of his transgressions that Helen ticked off to herself was short and incomplete indeed when measured beside his own count. His judgements were more informed and more cruel than hers. Having built a writing career on his critical perceptions, he now turned those skills against himself, considered all the evidence available to him, and concluded that he had developed, when he was still quite young, long before he left his parents and went to live with Raymond, a system of transferral that worked consistently in his favour. Any shortcoming or inadequacy he detected in himself was quickly passed along to someone else. Or he attributed it to a particular circumstance or a specific place and thus shucked the burden from his own shoulders. How simple and beautifully effective it is, when one senses dissatisfaction with oneself, to change course, to move to a new address, to choose new friends, to abandon old lovers.

He realized that he had once done all this instinctively, had somewhere along the line begun to do it systematically, and had at last reached a level of cynicism and sophistication that prompted him to take no action himself but to stimulate others to do what he himself was unable or unwilling to do. But even as he told himself, as he had told Helen in his note, that he was leaving only because he knew she wished it, he was not deceived. He knew that his most recent hiding-place, in Fort Beck, inside Raymond's house, with Helen, had ceased at last to conceal him from himself. A new location was needed, or a benevolent old location, a change of rhythm, fresh surroundings, new voices, new responses.

He thought of Wingate Fields, not as his best choice, but perhaps as his only choice. Ignoring the fact that all his previous periods of residence there had ended somehow on an unsatisfactory note, he forged ahead, dwelt on his first impressions rather than subsequent ones, and repeatedly assured himself that those failures had been caused by other people, people who no longer lived there. Apart from the staff, of course, there was no one at all in residence at Wingate. It had become a home for absent Bradshaws. If he went there to live, when he went there to live, he would be the only family member on the premises. He did not admit to himself that this was his principal reason for going there but he knew all the same that it was.

And there was Angus. Angus, in life, had been the energy centre of Wingate. His presence there had been a lure. After his death, the memory of that presence continued to be a lure. Certainly it was for Jesse. He felt always as he came up the long driveway, walked across the meadows, or sat in the great rooms, that something of the power and electricity of Angus remained, that contact could be made with it, that the brain would then quicken and the heart-beat get stronger. 'I always sleep well here,' he had often said to Valerie. 'The food tastes better. The claret has a better perfume.'

As a critic, he had built his early reputation as a scourge of the romantics. Romantic literature, romantic painting, romantic music were all anathema to him. 'Any romantic artist, from his first brushstroke, his first line of poetry, his first note of music, brands himself as a child-man, someone who feeds on dreams and spun sugar. Art must the stuff of life, not the scent of bath oil. Romantic art is a bird without wings, a bloodless woman, an empty wine glass.'

He was attacking himself, of course. The deficiencies he decried were his own. The people and places he selected were carefully chosen to compensate for those hateful shortcomings. Each time it became clear to him that he was the same imperfect creature he'd always been, he was forced to find new places and new people. When his train arrived in Chicago the morning he left Fort Beck his itinerary was clear in his mind. He would fly to Paris first and go from there to Wingate Fields.

[11]

After Floyd was born, when Helen was just nineteen years old, when she was upset still by her decision to give him up for adoption, when the disturbing experiences of Raymond's death and her visit to his family in England were not far behind her, she chose not to go back to school at Foresby. She decided instead to educate herself, to travel at random around America, to stop in whatever towns or cities caught her fancy, and to stay there for as long as she remained interested, to read and work and make new friends, to make use of herself, to learn about herself, to find her way as the solitary person she seemed destined now to be.

Just as Jesse had in some way triggered that original period of travel and self-examination, so did his most recent departure stimulate her to leave Fort Beck. Three days later she was staying at the Fairmont Hotel in San Francisco. From there, she wrote a letter to Frank.

Surprise. I'm in San Francisco. I didn't sell my house and burn my bridges, as you suggested, but I did decide to spend some days on the move. I haven't been to San Francisco in years, so here I am.

You may be surprised to hear that Jesse has wandered off somewhere and he won't be back. Because I don't want him back. So maybe you're a fortune-teller. Maybe, at long last, Raymond and Jesse are going to take a back seat in my life. Ancient history . . . was that the expression you used? We'll see.

I feel all young and strange, like a one-legged lady who went to a revival meeting and threw away her crutches. I sit here

521

looking out the window and realize that nobody in the world is trying to reach me. No one is wondering where I am. A few years ago such a realization would have destroyed me. Now I revel in it. Do you think it's possible that at last I'm coming of age? Whatever it is that I'm doing, it feels good. It feels very good.

On the plane coming out here I thought about the talk we had in Chicago. You said people who were once in love can never become friends. I've decided you're right. I've also decided it doesn't matter. I don't mean that you don't matter. It just doesn't matter whether we call each other friends or not. Perhaps it doesn't matter if we never see each other again either, but I hope we do. If we do, I promise I won't ask you for advice. I've stopped looking – after all these years – for people I can depend on. I think I will just depend on myself from now on.

[12]

'I can't believe you two broke up,' Nora said. 'A double coffin together, buried beneath a cornfield in Illinois . . . that's where I thought you and Helen would end up.'

'We didn't break up exactly. I just left,' Jesse said.

'Another broken heart. Poor Helen. She's probably crying her eyes out.'

Jesse shook his head. 'Not likely. I think she knew I'd be leaving. She wanted me to leave.'

'I'm astonished. Are you telling me she waited most of her life for you and then had a change of heart?'

'Nothing so romantic as that, I suspect. We just came to a fork in the road.'

'Is that an old cowboy expression?'

'If you like.'

'When a cowboy gets tired of his horse does he say they just came to a fork in the road?'

'I suppose,' Jesse said.

'Yippee! Is *that* what the cowboys say?'

'You're in good spirits, aren't you?'

522

'Of course. I am now what the French call 'a woman of a certain age'. I no longer dine out every night with handsome men. So this is an occasion. Guaranteed to lift the spirits.' She sipped from her glass. Then: 'Let's be serious for a moment. Is this a permanent thing with you and Helen, or are you just taking a vacation from each other?'

'We didn't sign a separation agreement, if that's what you mean. There was no contract, so there was nothing to dissolve. But I don't expect to go back to Fort Beck and I'm sure she has no plans to join me at Wingate Fields.'

'Is that where you're going?'

'Not this minute. But I expect I'll end up there eventually.'

'You're just stopping off here in Paris, then. Renewing old acquaintances, so to speak?'

'So to speak.'

'Will we have the pleasure of your company for a few weeks or only a few days?'

'I haven't drawn up an itinerary. It might be a few months.'

'Will you be staying at my luxurious house or in an unpleasant hotel?'

'I plan to sleep in your bed unless you've made other arrangements,' he said.

'In that case you'll certainly be here longer than a few days.'

'I see you still have no self-confidence.'

'*Au contraire*. In certain areas I'm bursting with self-confidence.'

[13]

Nora had sold *Icarus*, the magazine she and Jesse had founded together several years before. 'I also sold the art gallery. I am now an idle hussy. A woman of leisure. We'll explore Paris in a way we never had time to do before. You'll be stunned by how expensive everything has become. But I will treat you to everything while you're here. The waiters will adore it. They love to see an attractive man being entertained by a wealthy woman. They will whisper about us and the kitchen workers will come to the door and stare.

523

I will send a magnum of champagne to the chef, and when we get up to leave the restaurant the waiters and busboys will applaud.'

For several weeks they celebrated the weather, the food, the wine, and their good fortune. They made no plans, kept to no schedule, and respected no deadlines or closing hours. They stayed up late, slept late, and took their meals when the impulse seized them. *Petit déjeuner* often took place at one in the afternoon, *déjeuner* at six, and *dîner* at midnight.

One morning between three and four, when they were eating eggs at a café for *routiers* on the south edge of Paris, Nora said, 'We've been stepping on tiptoe around the subject of Wingate Fields. So let's talk about it. Now that you've seduced me again for the five thousandth time, do you plan to abandon me and go off to be a country squire in Northumberland?'

'I don't know. That's what I was planning but it's hard to think of leaving this fine wine and excellent food you've been buying for me.'

'Perfect. That's exactly what you're meant to say.'

Jesse spoke often of Wingate Fields. He told her about changes that had taken place and of further changes that needed to be made. 'Last time I was there I hired a man named Jenkins to manage the estate. He grew up on a farm in Cumberland and worked for many years as a civil engineer in Newcastle. He knows how to handle people and he knows how to handle himself. We're lucky to have him, I think. At the same time I hired a man named Norman Whitehead and his wife, Esther. She's a fine cook, and he'll manage the staff and the house. They're not a cheerful pair. Bible-thumpers, Jenkins calls them. But they came highly recommended and they're hard workers. And there's no question in my mind that Whitehead will keep a close watch on the house accounts. I'm sure he still believes that a petty thief should have one hand cut off.'

'In that atmosphere of high morality you'll never be able to take me to Wingate,' Nora said.

'That's true. I may have to make an honest woman of you.'

'That seems awfully extreme. Perhaps the best solution would be for you to make extended visits here in Paris when you're tired of stomping about the stables in your boots.'

'I seem to remember your saying that the thought of spending your declining years at Wingate appealed to you.'

'Did I say that?'

'That's the way I remember it,' Jesse said.

'Is that why it appeals to you . . . as a setting for your declining years?'

'Not at all. My declining years are behind me. My concern now is how best to spend my indolent years.'

'How about a few months each year in Paris, followed by a few months at Wingate, followed by a few months in Paris, et cetera? How does that sound to you?'

'Sounds quite nice, actually. How does it sound to you?'

'Sounds nice to me also.'

They were careful to avoid firm choices or decisions in these talks. They spoke always of possibilities rather than plans. No one took the lead. No one followed. Their structures were built of striped candy covered with sugar frosting. Tentative and unsure of the terrain, both of them, they proceeded cautiously, one step forward, two steps back, until gradually a pattern began to become visible. Bit by bit, Wingate Fields changed from a possibility to a probability and their mutual acceptance of it cemented their acceptance of each other. They spoke now, not of whether they would go to Northumberland, but when. Carefully considering the seasons, they discussed how they would apportion the months. They agreed that summer in Paris was impossible and winter in Northumberland was too cruel. From October to April, they agreed, they should be in France, except for the holiday time when they would spend two or three weeks at Wingate. May, June, July, August, and September also would be spent in Northumberland. 'But we won't be rigid about it, will we?' Nora asked. 'Won't we allow ourselves the freedom to hop back and forth once in a while?'

'I'm sure we will,' Jesse said. 'That seems reasonable to me.'

They had these discussions during February and March. Some time in April, they concluded, they would get married in a tidy ceremony at the local *mairie*. They then would go along to Wingate Fields for the spring and summer and begin the life they had cautiously laid out for themselves.

On April 6th, however, a letter came from Bill that changed their plans. At first they thought it would be a temporary change but as the events of summer and early fall unfolded, they accepted the fact that circumstances had caused the compass needle to spin and the clock to keep imperfect time.

525

Dear Nora,

I'm trying to locate my father. Do you know where he is? I wrote him a letter in Fort Beck but it came back stamped 'No longer at this address'. When I tried to ring him, the housekeeper told me Helen was in San Francisco but she didn't know where Jesse was. Rab doesn't know either.

I don't mean to alarm you. There's no catastrophe here in Heidelberg. In fact, things are quite marvellous here. Big changes afoot. Polly and I have decided to leave Germany and go home to Wingate Fields. I've had some correspondence with Whitehead and he's having the rooms in the west wing put in order and freshened up for us. Both Polly and I are excited about the prospect of going back there.

I'm anxious to pass on the good news to Dad. If you know how to reach him, please tell him to get in touch with me at Wingate. By the time you get this letter we'll be on our way.

We hope to see you soon in Northumberland. Polly and I are planning to bring the house to life again. You must come for a long visit.

When both she and Jesse had read the letter, Nora said, 'That's awfully good news about Polly, isn't it?'

Jesse nodded. 'I'm delighted that she's got out of Heidelberg. It always disturbed me that she was hanging on there, telling herself . . . God knows what she was telling herself.'

'But now she'll be isolated at Wingate. Is that the best place for her?'

'Not the best,' Jesse said. 'At least, it's not the choice I would have made for her. But it's not my choice to make. And in spite of what I'm saying, I'm sure it will have a positive effect on her, being able to spend some time in the house where she grew up. If she still needs to convalesce a bit, I can't imagine a better rest home than Wingate Fields.'

'You see this as a temporary move, then?'

'No question about it. It's one thing for you and me to talk about the kind of life we can make for ourselves in Northumberland. It's quite another matter for two young people like Polly and Bill. There are all sorts of things they want to do, I'm sure, all sorts of people and places they want to see. They're bright and energetic. They want to test themselves, and they will. Give them six months at

526

Wingate and they'll be eager to break away and get on with their lives.'

'Does that mean you'll have to postpone your plans for six months.'

'That doesn't matter,' he said. 'I'm happy to do it.'

'Does that mean I have to put up with you here in Paris?'

'I'm afraid it does.'

[14]

When Bill and Polly called Rab's office in London to tell him they'd moved back to Wingate Fields, he was away on a trip to Canada. As soon as he was back in England he came to Northumberland to see them.

'You're full of surprises,' he said when they were sitting in the west wing parlour. 'Last time I saw you in Germany I thought you were both there for life.'

Polly smiled. 'Now we're here for life.'

'Well, we'll see about that,' Rab said. 'I'd hate to make a bet on where you'll be a couple years from now, Polly.' He turned to Bill, 'Or you either, squirrel.'

'We made up our minds,' Bill said. 'We're going to breathe new life into this ancient pile. Till the fields, polish the silver, and preserve the traditions.'

'You'd better wait till you're married before you lock yourself into a long-term plan. Your wife may have ideas of her own about where she wants to live.'

'That's what I told him,' Polly said, 'But he says he has no plans to get married.'

'Nobody has plans,' Rab said. 'You can't plan to get married till you find somebody who wants to marry you.'

'Since when are you a marriage expert?' Bill said. 'I don't see a ring on your finger. You're the oldest of all three of us. Maybe we just decided to let you go first.'

'Don't wait for me,' Rab said. 'I'm a wastrel, a philanderer. I may never get married.'

'That's precisely the way Bill and I feel,' Polly said. 'He'll be my

527

bachelor brother and I'll be his spinster sister. We'll grow old together here at Wingate Fields.'

'Oh, for God's sake,' Rab said. 'That's the most pathetic thing I've ever heard.'

When he was alone with Bill later Rab said, 'How is she?'

'Polly? You saw her. She looks bloody great.'

'I can see how she looks. But how is she?'

'She's a different woman. She's like she used to be. Better than she used to be.'

'Does she still talk about Jack?'

'All the time. I guess she always will. But she can handle it now. She can talk about how good it was and how rotten it was and she can live with it both ways.'

'That's terrific,' Rab said. 'You really helped her, I think. Remember how I tried to talk you out of staying with her in Heidelberg after they sent Jack to prison? Well, I was mistaken. You made a good choice.'

'I didn't do anything. I was just there.'

'What could be better than that?'

'I don't know,' Bill said.

'Nothing could. That's what I'm saying. You were around when she needed someone and you deserve a lot of credit for that.'

'I don't want credit.'

'I know you don't. But you know what I mean. And now comes the tough part. You helped her the way you did because she knew she could depend on you. Now you have to force her to depend on herself.'

'I'm not forcing her to do anything.'

'I didn't mean that the way it sounded,' Rab said. 'I meant that you have to allow her to depend on herself. That's the next stage.'

'There isn't any next stage. This isn't some sort of business deal. I'm not developing a piece of real estate. This is something between Polly and me.'

'But you're not doing her a favour when you allow her to become totally dependent on you, when you promise her you're never going to get married.'

'I'm not allowing her to do anything, Rab. She's doing what she wants to do. And we haven't promised each other anything. A long time before Jack died, Polly said she never wanted to get married. And I'd made up my mind to the same thing.'

'But that's stupid, Bill. Of course you'll get married. All of us will. But even if you don't, it's still a bad thing to tell Polly. It makes her think she never has to come out of her shell, that you'll always be around to look after her.'

'She's right. I always will be.'

'Oh, for Christ's sake, you sound like some sort of religious zealot. Jesus freaks, they call them in America. Are you telling me that you and Polly have made lifetime commitments to each other?'

'We haven't made any commitment. I told you that. She just knows she can depend on me and I know I can depend on her.'

'We're a family,' Rab said. 'Everybody knows that. I like to think we can all depend on each other.'

'That's a fairy-tale. We can't depend on Jesse and he can't depend on us. We can't depend on Valerie. We can't depend on Nora. Do you think you can depend on me?'

'Of course I do.'

'No, you don't,' Bill said. 'And I can't depend on you.'

'Ask me a favour some time and you'll find out you're wrong.'

'We're not talking about favours. We're talking about being there.'

Rab lit a cigarette. 'Do you know what this reminds me of? When I was at Cambridge we used to drink gin and sit up half the night discussing the great indestructible verities. Fairness, equity, love, truth. What do they all mean? Do they exist in human relationships. Are there such things as real loyalty, true devotion, unshakable honour? We said the same things over and over to each other. We always concluded that we lived in a world without values but that we, the few of us in that room, would light a beacon that would make the world ashamed of itself. Do you know what happened to all those enlightened idealistic young men? One of them went to prison for embezzlement and one was cashiered out of the Foreign Office under suspicion of turning over documents to the Turks. A third one runs a gambling ship in Malta, and all the rest of them are grubbing and swindling their way through life, trying to accumulate as much money as they can before they die of alcoholism or a bleeding ulcer.'

'I'm not interested in your bloody friends. What do they have to do with me?'

'Quite a lot. They all deceived themselves and you're doing the

529

same thing. One of these days you'll turn round, look at a calendar, and discover you're thirty years old.'

'And fifty years later I'll discover I'm eighty years old. What's your point?'

'My point is that it's not selfish or mean to think of yourself sometimes, to consider your own needs, to plan ahead a bit for your own future and your own family.'

'Is that what you're doing? What kind of a future do you see for yourself? And since you don't need money any more than I do, I'm not interested in learning how much money you made last year.'

'You're right. But at least I haven't painted myself into a corner. And that's what I'd like to keep you from doing. I'd hate to see you and Polly stumble into some sort of emotional contract. It's unwise and unnecessary, and it could do you both a great deal of harm.'

'What a sanctimonious bastard you are. You're so busy analysing things that you can't see anything. So let me put it to you simply. Polly and I love each other. She cares what happens to me and I care what happens to her. As I told you before we don't have any contract, emotional or otherwise. We don't want one and we don't need one.'

Chapter Twelve

[1]

In the months following Polly and Bill's return to Wingate Fields, an action which in Polly's mind signalled an end to the torment she had suffered in Germany, during those months the other members of the Bradshaw family seemed to slip into a period as pleasant and peaceful as the one Polly was experiencing.

Floyd and Valerie discovered ocean travel. Emerging from the chill gloom of a particularly black Norwegian winter, they booked themselves on a Belgian freighter leaving from Antwerp, calling at Le Havre, Tenerife in the Canary Islands, Dakar, Abidjan and Zaire, then returning leisurely to Antwerp. Before leaving Antwerp, they signed up for a subsequent voyage scheduled to leave Bremen in July with stops in Rotterdam, Livorno, the Suez Canal, Singapore, Hong Kong, Keeling Island, Pusan, Yokohama, and Oakland, California. 'Fifty days at sea,' Valerie said, 'what a lovely prospect. And from California perhaps we'll find a ship that will take us lazily to Fiji and Tahiti and New Zealand.'

Helen's new-found distractions were similar but on a smaller scale. She had hired a car and driver in San Francisco and was exploring the splendours or Northern California, Oregon, and Washington. Whereas during her travels round America as a young woman she had taken pains to conceal her wealth, had supported herself in each town or city where she'd stopped with the wages from whatever job she could find, now she indulged herself. She stayed in elegant hotels and ate in the finest restaurants her travel books could provide. Her driver, a retired policeman named

McGovern from Sausalito, was booked into hotel accommodation as luxurious as her own.

If Valerie and Floyd believed they had discovered a continuing and rewarding life-style, Helen knew that she was simply in a holding pattern, constructing round herself a cushion of time killed and miles travelled until some impulse, or revelation, or dissatisfaction, prompted her to return to her nest, to build a new nest or inhabit someone else's nest. For the moment she was content to have her road maps and travel folders provide her with a daily structure. On the road early each morning, she slept in a different bed every night. Everything was new. Nothing was familiar.

If she had written out a master plan, which she had not, Helen might very well have concluded that when she finished this period of wandering she would be content to stay home and wander no more. Or she might have concluded that she felt most at home now when she was away from home, that she slept best in a fresh new bed, that she felt very strong and free indeed to be where no one knew her, to be where nobody who did know her knew how to reach her.

Nora and Jesse might have been expected to be disappointed that their cautious plans about returning to Wingate had been derailed or at best postponed. But the process they'd gone through in making those plans had been as beneficial to them, it seemed, as carrying them out might have been. Finding themselves deprived of a summer in Northumberland, they rented a lodge in the mountains near Chamonix, sent Nora's cook and her houseman ahead to stock the kitchen and wine cellar, and spent a quiet green summer in the country.

'Were we so happy before when we were together?' Nora said.

'I don't think so. We were too busy arming ourselves, building up our defences, mounting counter-attacks.'

'What a fool I was,' she said.

'Maybe not. A year from now, you may look back on this summer and say, "What a fool I was then." '

'Not bloody likely, my darling.'

Rab, who, compared with the other family members, seemed sanguine and trouble-free, was in fact still entangled with Dorsey. Not with her presence; he had not seen her since the night they'd spent together at her cottage in the Cotswolds, but with the unanswered questions, the sense of incompleteness, the lack of truth, that seemed still to characterize the months they had spent together, planning a future he knew now would not come to pass.

Since he'd awakened that last morning and discovered she was gone he'd had no illusions about what could be reclaimed from the ruins. Failing to understand any of it, he stopped trying to understand. 'When there's nothing to be done, do nothing,' he kept telling himself. Logic told him also that he and Dorsey came from different planets. They differed in almost every way. The unlikeness that had drawn them together would surely at last have pulled them apart. She had brought him nothing except her physical self. But the memories of that sensual lunacy they'd shared was what kept her stingingly alive, even after common sense told him she was dead and buried. At night, alone in his bed, he expected to be haunted by the sounds, the scents, the words, and touches he could not forget. But she followed him about by day also. She appeared, disconcertingly, visible to no eyes but his, in pubs and theatres and restaurants, in offices, on tennis courts, in board rooms, wherever he happened to be.

He tried hating her. And he was able to do that. He listed flaws in her character and the list became quite long. He branded her as a deceitful and self-deceiving. She was a failed mother, he concluded, and would be a hopeless discontented wife no matter who she was married to. He told himself time after time that he was fortunate to be rid of her and he believed it. He knew it was true. He told himself he didn't love her and never had done. He also believed that. But he never tried to tell himself he didn't want her. He never regretted any moment, or any hour, or any night he'd spent with her. However black he managed to paint her, he never for a second wished he hadn't met her.

One morning in October, when he came into the office, Rosalind said, 'Guess who rang me up last night?'

'No games today. I drank eight gins and three brandies last night.'

'Robert Gingrich. He said to say hello to you.'

'Is that why he called?' Rab asked.

'Not actually. He wanted me to visit a few night-spots with him.'

'Did you go?'

She shook her head.

'You'll die a spinster,' Rab said.

'Impossible. I'm a divorced woman.'

533

'Did he make you a nasty proposal?'

'Not nasty. Just tiresome. He's staying at Brown's. He thought I might like to come over and spend the night with him.'

'They serve fine tea at Brown's. Maybe you should have gone.'

'Not interested. He said he'll be here till Friday. Told me to tell you he'll buy you a drink if you have time.'

'Not a bad idea. Ring him up and tell him I'll take him to dinner tonight. Dining room of the Stafford at eight o'clock. Drinks at my club at seven.'

'You're not serious, are you?'

'Of course I'm serious. Why not?'

'He's a bloody bore. If you have nowhere to go for dinner come to my house.'

'That's also not a bad idea. If Gingrich is busy, I will.'

After a moment she said, 'If you just want to find out about your lady friend I can save you a tiresome dinner with Gingrich. She's back in California. You know a place called Bel Air?'

'That's where the rich folks live.'

'It figures.' She stood up and said, 'I take back my offer. I don't want you to come to my house.' A few minutes later she rang through from her office and said, 'Mr Gingrich would love to have dinner with you. I hope you get a bad clam and suffer through the night.'

[2]

Responding apparently to the honour of having cocktails at an exclusive club on St James's and dinner later at the Stafford, Gingrich appeared in a dark well-tailored suit. He seemed freshly barbered and scented, cologne on his cheeks and gin on his breath. He had decided apparently to behave as a proper English gentleman. Though he failed at that, he did manage not to attract undue attention to himself.

As soon as they were seated in one of the reception rooms at Rab's club Gingrich said, 'As your secretary may have told you, I'm only in London for a few days, so I'm happy you found time to have dinner with me.'

534

'Have you just come from America?'

'No, I haven't. I've been in Spain with the Mullets. After they left for California I spent some time in Seville. A screenwriter I used to know retired down there. Living like a king, but he hates it. All he wanted to talk about was California gossip. Can't stand prosperity, I guess. He's got a nice wife, number four, but he can't stop yapping about a woman he was married to ten years ago. She was a real tramp. Slept with anybody who asked her. But she had great legs and that's all this poor bastard friend of mine remembers. I said to him, 'You don't love *her*, for Christ's sake. You just miss that daily shot of humiliation she gave you.' And you know what he said? He said, 'No doubt about it. I'd rather be crapped on any day than bored to death.' Can you believe that? That's the Hollywood credo. Any action is better than no action. And that's where I'm heading. Back to the sleaze mills.' He took a long drink from his glass, lit a cigarette, and said, 'Listen, let's not kid ourselves. I know you're not having dinner with me because I'm intelligent and good-looking. You want to know what's happening with Dorsey . . . am I right?'

'I understand she's back in California, and I assume she and Oscar plan to stay there.'

'That's the back plot. You've got that much straight. But it doesn't tell you anything about the real story. She's an unhappy woman, Mr Bradshaw. She's miserable. She hates California like a snake. Hated it ten years ago. Hates it now.'

'Then why did she go back there?'

'That's what I asked her. I knew what was going on between you two. I was hoping she'd have the guts to do something about it. When the three of us had drinks at Claridge's that day I thought, 'By God, she's gonna shake herself loose.' But I was wrong. She wanted to but she didn't. I guess she can't. I saw how lousy she felt when they were packing up to leave Madrid and I told her she was crazy. I told her to get the hell away from Oscar and go back to you, and she said, 'Don't you think I want to? That's all I want to do.' But the next day she was still packing. And when the plane left, she was on it. We had a drink at the airport while Oscar was screwing around at the exchange bank, buying and selling money, and I said to her, 'If you don't leave him now, you'll never leave him.' But she didn't say anything. She just sat there with tears in her eyes and didn't say a word.'

535

'It's her son,' Rab said. 'Isn't that the problem? That's what she can't deal with.'

'I'm not sure. I know that's what she tells herself. But I think there's more to it than that. She says she's scared she'll lose the kid but I think she's just plain scared of everything. Scared of any kind of change, scared of herself. That kid of hers is no prize, either, you know. He knows he's got her over a barrel. He plays her like a slot machine. I told her that if she's willing to give him up she'll never have to but she feels so fucking guilty every time his name comes up that she can't breathe. It's a damned shame. She's a woman who has everything. Only one tiny little ingredient missing. But that's the one thing she needs in order to function. Oscar knows that about her, and her son knows it too. So she's helpless when she tries to deal with them. I hope I'm not bringing you bad news. For all I know, you might be able to turn her around. Maybe you think there's still a chance for the two of you.'

Rab shook his head. 'For a long time I thought there *was* a chance. I kept seeing things the way I wanted them to be instead of the way they are. But finally I had to admit to myself that the problem isn't Oscar or her son. The real problem is . . . well, I don't have to tell you. You just described it.'

They had several drinks before they went along to the Stafford for dinner. Rab steered the conversation from Dorsey to the motion picture business, a subject that seemed to stimulate Gingrich. With each drink he seemed to find a new plateau of gossip and scandal and anecdote. Through the Sancerre and claret, he concentrated on production mistakes and major betrayals of clients by their lawyers and agents. Through dessert, coffee and cognac, he dwelt on sexual escapades, seductions and adulteries. As Rab listened, as he felt himself growing more sober while Gingrich got drunk, he remembered something he'd once said to Rosalind. 'I may have to rely on Gingrich as my principal source of information. I may have to buy him a few gins some night and listen to what he has to say.'

When Gingrich's third Remy-Martin was brought to the table Rab said, 'You remember Rosalind, the young woman in my office, don't you?'

'Of course I do. Remember her very well. I made a couple of indecent proposals to her but I was rejected.'

'She told me the two of you spent a pleasant evening together some time ago.'

536

'Not an evening exactly.' Gingrich said. 'I walked her to the bus and then I rode along home with her. But she didn't ask me in. Entertaining her cousin that evening. I believe that's what she said.'

'She said you talked quite a lot about Mullet.'

'I probably did. There's always something to say about Oscar.'

'You told her that you and Oscar have a secret that Dorsey doesn't know.'

'That's true.'

'And you and Dorsey have a secret that Oscar doesn't know. Did Rosalind get it right?'

'Yes, she did. She must be an excellent secretary. I hope to hire her away from you some day.'

'I warn you, she's an expensive item. I pay her a handsome salary.'

'In that case, maybe I'll just shanghai her in the street some night. Abduct her and take her down to Brighton.'

'I think she's fond of Brighton. She has an aunt there.'

Gingrich took a sip of cognac. Then: 'You think I'm a stupid-assed drunk, don't you?'

'No, I don't.'

'Yes, you do. But I don't mind. You think if I get drunk enough I'll tell you some things you don't know about Dorsey.'

'If that's what you think,' Rab said, 'I'd better sign the bill and leave you here for a pleasant evening of drinking. Then you won't have to worry about my prying information out of you.' He signalled to the waiter, who came at once to the table. 'If you bring me the bill I'll sign it. But please don't total it. My guest, Mr Gingrich, will be staying on.'

'Wait a minute,' Gingrich said as the waiter moved away. 'Don't get pissed off at me. I think you're a good guy. I didn't mean to take a potshot at you. If I said something out of line, I apologize.'

'No apology necessary,' Rab said. The waiter returned with the bill then and Rab signed it.

'Have another drink,' Gingrich said. 'I'm buying. I've had a nice evening. I don't want to end it by sitting here and getting pissed by myself.'

In the profession he had chosen, Rab was in constant contact with performers. He admired many of them, suffered through his dealings with some, and absolutely avoided any exposure, social or otherwise, to certain others. With actors, however, he was fascinated by their mastery of craft, their ability to glide from one emotion to another, to transform themselves, to bring an audience to tears or laughter with a look or a gesture. He knew that he himself had none of those skills. Although young women, from time to time, had accused him of being less than candid in his utterances of fidelity, he was seldom caught in a deliberate lie because he seldom told one. He had once said to Bill, 'I suppose I'd lie like a thief if I were better at it, but I have no gift for it at all.'

Thus, when Gingrich accused him of getting him drunk in order to prise information out of him, Rab felt doubly guilty. In the first instance for being caught out, and in the second for having handled himself so clumsily. His false indignation and his calling for the bill seemed to him like clear self-indictments. Therefore, when Gingrich asked him not to leave, Rab capitulated at once and ordered another drink.

Gingrich responded as though he had heard a prearranged signal. Seeming to discard the cynical trappings that normally distinguished his stories, he began to talk about Dorsey in a different tone than Rab had heard him use before.

'There are a lot of unqualified fools who cast films. I've always said that a sure-fire way to wreck a movie is to put the wrong actor in a key role. But it happens all the time. Because the people making the decisions don't know a good actor any more than they know a good script when they see it. So they make a set of rules for themselves, these casting directors. Or they memorize a set of rules that someone else has made. An actor does well if they tell themselves he has "balls", or if they call him an "animal". Monty Clift and Leslie Howard got away with being "sensitive", but those days are over. Sensitive is the kiss of death today. Even for women. Now they talk about women having balls. An actress is great because she's a "bitch", or because she has a "slutty" quality, or because she looks like someone who can "really get down in the dirt". A producer I worked for last year wanted an actress who looked like "she'd just taken on five guys in the back seat of a car".

'There's only one human quality they still talk about that's not connected with the bed or the toilet. They all admit that it's rare but the fact is they don't really know what it is and don't recognize it when they see it. All they know is the word. And they recite it to each other with reverence. "Vulnerability," they say. "Bring me

538

an actress who's truly vulnerable and I'll make her a star." The truth is that all actors are vulnerable. That's why they become actors. Casting people and producers and directors meet vulnerable actors every day. And they turn them into dog meat. Sometimes it only takes one interview to turn a vulnerable kid into a wife-beater, or to put a young girl on the bus heading back to Arkansas. The sad part about all this crap is that for once the bubbleheads are right. Nobody ever makes it all the way unless they have that quality. At least, they didn't used to when movies were good, when they had more than one dimension. Gable, Cooper, Garbo, Brando, Lombard, Jimmy Stewart – they all had it. Tracy had it. And Bogart. The only big star who didn't have it at all was Chaplin. And he knew it. So he put on make-up and baggy clothes, and spent his entire career pretending he was vulnerable. And he fooled the world. The closest he ever came to playing himself was *Monsieur Verdoux*. People hated the film and they hated him in it.'

Gingrich excused himself then and went to the lavatory. When he came back he said, 'Did you notice that's the first time I went to the can. A couple years ago I used to pee twenty times a day. And I'd get up four or five times during the night. Then a make-up man I know who drinks even more than I do told me about zinc tablets. Very good for the prostate, he said. So I started taking one or two a day and they changed my whole life.' He finished the cognac in his glass and signalled the waiter for another one.

'I was talking about vulnerability,' he said. 'But mostly I was talking about Dorsey. If somebody asked me if she's vulnerable, I'd say, "She's nothing *but* vulnerable." They say our bodies are ninety percent water. Not Dorsey. She's ninety percent vulnerability. Always has been. Always will be. Everything else about her has changed in the years I've known her but that part is unchangeable.'

Gingrich lit a cigarette. Finally he said, 'You asked me about what I said to Rosalind that evening, about the secrets I have with Oscar and Dorsey. They really are secrets and I shouldn't have brought them up at all. But I was in the bag and trying to make some time with your fancy secretary. I had no intention, however, of telling her any more than that. But I think maybe I'm going to tell you.'

'Perhaps it's better if you don't,' Rab said. 'It's none of my affair now. Nothing's going to work out for me and Dorsey. I don't expect I'll ever see her again.'

'I don't think you will either. That's why I don't mind telling you a couple things. You and Dorsey got a bad shuffle. I saw you together. I liked what I saw. I'm sure you're a tough guy but all of us bleed when we're cut. And sometimes not knowing what the hell is going on is the roughest part of all. You keep trying to fill in the blank spaces and there's no way to do it.'

Gingrich paused then as though he expected an answer but Rab said nothing.

'I don't know what Dorsey told you about me,' he said then, 'but whatever it was, this is the truth. We were in love with each other and we wanted to get married. I was already married but my wife and I were separated; she had an eye on another guy and there was nothing keeping us from getting a divorce except a shortage of money. Money, that was the killer. I was a poor dope from New Jersey. My dad was a great guy but he was a victim. He never made ten thousand dollars a year in his whole life. But it tickled him to death that I'd managed to work my way through college. To him and my mom that meant I'd be able to get myself a decent job, buy a house, and get married. They were right about that part of it. I got married a few times. But I've never owned a house and I've never had what my folks thought of as a decent job. I didn't want that stuff. I wanted to write plays and get rich and have my name in the paper. Most of all I wanted to get rich but I didn't admit that to myself. Not then. I just wanted to get a divorce, marry Dorsey, and have a good life. Finally, after six years of trying, I got my first play produced. It got some good reviews, I got my name in the New York papers, and a good agent latched on to me. And then I met Oscar Mullet. We had a meeting in his office and he said he might be interested in making a movie out of my play. But when we left the office my agent said, 'Don't get your hopes up. I've dealt with him before. He's just blowing smoke.' A couple weeks went by and we heard no more from Mullet so I figured that was the end of it. Then one night Dorsey and I were sitting in a coffee house on MacDougal Street and Mullet came wheeling in with a slick-looking guy in a shiny suit and two dames who looked like strippers. He spotted me and came over to our table. I introduced him to Dorsey and we all schmoozed for a few minutes and then he went back to his friends. He sat facing our table and every time I glanced that way he was staring at Dorsey. When we got up to leave he followed us out to the sidewalk and told me he was still interested in my play. He asked us to have lunch with him the next day. So we did. It wasn't much of a lunch. I wanted to talk business and he wanted to talk about me and Dorsey. She was used to having guys go to pieces over her and I was accustomed to watching it. On the way home she said, 'What was that all about?' and I said, 'That was all about some dumb bastard trying to make an impression on you.' She smiled and said, 'He missed the boat.'

'Later that night my agent called and said, "Mullet's ready to talk turkey. He wants to see us in his office at ten o'clock in the morning." So that's how it happened. I got the snow job of all time. Oscar had two lawyers and a vice-president of William Morris with him in his office. He offered me a firm picture deal for my play, including a contract for me to write the screenplay. He also was willing to take an option on my next play. Then came the hook. He had a picture getting ready to shoot in the Philippines. But the writer was a drunk. Oscar needed a stand-by writer who could stick with the production through five or six months of shooting. "It's a tough location," he told me. "In the jungle, middle of nowhere. But Rollie Burton's a good director. You'll learn a lot from him." Well, to make a long story short, I went to the Philippines. I left three days later. I told the agent and I told myself that I wouldn't go unless Dorsey thought it was a good idea.'

'Did she think it was a good idea?' Rab asked.

'She hated it. Hated the idea of my being stuck in some God-forsaken jungle for all those months. But she knew how important it was for me to make a film deal for my play. And how important it was for us to get hold of some money so my wife and I could get a divorce. I didn't have a choice, you see. The Philippine deal was all wrapped up inside the other offer. All or nothing. If I turned down part of it, I turned down all of it.'

'So you accepted.'

Gingrich nodded. 'Dorsey talked me into it. Or at least that's what I told myself. And she believed that, too. She's convinced that I never would have left New York if she hadn't persuaded me it was a good idea. So . . . when I came back to America more than six months later and found out she was married to Oscar, she was the one who felt guilty. She still feels guilty. What she doesn't know . . . she didn't know it then and she doesn't know it now . . . is that I knew what was going on. Even before I left. I sensed what

541

Oscar was up to. And Oscar knew I knew it. I sold Dorsey to him just as surely as if he'd handed me a cheque and I'd handed him the key to her bedroom. The sick part is that he's still making payments and I'm still accepting them.'

'And Dorsey doesn't know?'

'Not only that. She wouldn't believe it if somebody told her. She made up her mind that she's to blame. And if she lives to be a hundred she'll still feel that way. She knows that Oscar manipulated her and manipulated me. He found out what our weaknesses were and he played on them. I wanted money and Dorsey wanted a combination daddy and bodyguard. And she wanted a safe life for Charlie. She wanted him to have everything.

'And there was the problem of my divorce that never seemed to get settled. Dorsey and I had been together for three years. All that time I'd been trying to get a divorce but there was always something in the way. Two days before I left for the Philippines my wife broke up with her boyfriend. She called up Dorsey and told her she wanted me to come home. She loved me and didn't want a divorce. So Dorsey was walking around on ping-pong balls. She was a sitting duck for Oscar. He was a friend of the family. He told her that every day. Saw that she was taken care of. Had my salary cheques deposited in her account. Told her what a smart and talented fellow I was. Went to the zoo with her and Charlie. Took care of everything when Charlie got sick. You know Dorsey. So do I. She's scared of her shadow. Oscar picked up on that straight away. And bit by bit he convinced her that anything she was afraid of could be fixed. By him. That did it. Next thing she knew, she was married. They wrote me a Dear John letter together. Later she told me they both cried while they were writing it. Isn't that a lot of crap? But I believe it. In any case, it's worked out OK for me. Both of them have been trying to make it up to me ever since. Sometimes I think that's what keeps them together. Like two people who committed a crime and they're bound together for ever. Me and Charlie. We're the glue that keeps their idiotic marriage on the rails. That, as they used to say, is a hot one. What did she tell you about Charlie? Did she say his father was that pretty-boy rich kid from Florida?'

Rab nodded and Gingrich went on. 'That's the official story. Sometimes I think she's started to believe it herself. Just like Oscar has convinced himself that Charlie's *his* kid. And Charlie would

542

probably like to be Oscar's son. The kid's as much of a whore as I am. Blood will tell. The apple doesn't fall far from the tree and all that stuff.'

'What does that mean?' Rab asked. 'Am I missing something?'

'I doubt it. You're a smart guy. I'm telling you that I'm Charlie's old man. He's my kid. That's our vengeance on Oscar, Dorsey's and mine. He can live with the idea that Dorsey had a fling with some good-looking kid from a rich family but it would wreck him if he knew I'm Charlie's dad. I think he's probably convinced himself that Dorsey and I never even slept together. I mean, to Oscar I'm a second-rate Jew that he keeps on the payroll because it makes him feel better about himself. He wouldn't feel good at all if he found out the kid he's so proud of is really mine.'

'Who knows about this?'

'Nobody. Just Dorsey and me. And now you know.'

'Charlie doesn't know?'

'No. And he never will.'

'Do you ever see him?'

Gingrich nodded. 'I saw him a lot when he was growing up. When we were all living in California.'

'Do you like him?'

'Not much. And he doesn't like me at all. Maybe Oscar talked to him about me. In any case he looks at me like I'm a bug. He doesn't seem too crazy about Dorsey either. Oscar didn't create him but he's done a thorough job of producing him. Dorsey and I made the kid but Oscar owns him.'

[3]

When Bill and Polly were still in Heidelberg, from the moment they first began to talk about going home to Wingate Fields, the physical dimensions of the Bradshaw estate had seemed to be the dominant lure. Bill had used it first as a point of persuasion and at last Polly had begun to see what he saw and repeat what he said.

'Heidelberg's a beautiful place,' he said. 'It's intricate and ancient and crumbling and moss-covered. Scars from French cannon-balls that have been on the walls for two hundred years. I mean you

Their rhythm those first weeks was not frenetic but relentless. They seemed to feel that a great deal had to be accomplished and that full energy was required to make it all happen. They were particularly intent on putting the far end of the west wing into the order they desired. That was the section of the house they had chosen for their living quarters. There were two reception rooms there, three bedrooms, three baths, a butler's pantry with a breakfast room, and a small library fitted out as a study. Outside entrances led directly to the west gardens and the stables beyond.

Both of them, Polly particularly, had specific notions as to how these rooms they'd chosen should be arranged. There were busy days of carting pieces of furniture, mirrors, carpets and bric-à-brac from one end of the house to the other till at last the two of them were satisfied that the living quarters they'd envisioned when they were still in Heidelberg had in fact been provided.

All through this process of preparation they used the house fully, as they had promised themselves they would. An elaborate breakfast early in the morning, a bit of lunch in the conservatory, high tea in the drawing room, and a sumptuous dinner for two at nine each evening in the dining hall. After dinner, Polly played Schumann on the piano in the music room and they often shot billiards together till well past midnight. They renewed relationships with older members of the staff, and made an effort to acquaint themselves with those who had entered service at Wingate since they'd left home. They established themselves in short order as the brother-sister master and mistress of a house that had survived without family direction through the years since Clara's death.

Suddenly they then switched from this pattern of involvement and activity and high visibility to another sort of life together. In a period of a few days, it seemed, they became reclusive. They went outside in the daytime, of course, walked and rode together, and drove Bill's roadster through the rock-bordered lanes and roads of the county. But when they were in the house they were seldom seen outside their rooms in the west wing.

One evening Polly had said, 'Why don't we have dinner brought here to our drawing room? That might be a pleasant change.'

The change had been pleasant indeed, it seemed. In a few weeks' time they were taking all their meals in the west wing. Their breakfast room was refitted and refurnished to make a proper dining room and their butler's pantry was fully stocked. Although it was an arrangement the staff had never seen before, either at Wingate or in other homes where they had served, they seemed to adjust to it smoothly. Only the cook, Esther Whitehead, complained to her husband, Norman, and to other members of the kitchen staff. 'It's an insult to a person's work. When a fine meal is prepared it should be eaten properly. In appropriate surroundings. Every time I see those trays and trolleys leaving for the west wing it makes me angry. We might just as well convert the breakfast room and the dining hall to storerooms.'

Her husband, perhaps to demonstrate his own dissatisfaction with the new system as well as his wife's, made a point of enquiring each morning where the master and mistress would like their meals served that day. At last Polly told him, 'Unless we tell you otherwise, we'll have all our meals here in the west wing.'

After Whitehead turned and left the room Bill said, 'You wounded him. It makes him very uncomfortable that we don't put on our best clothes and go to the dining hall every evening.'

'He's an odd man,' Polly said. 'But his discomfort does not concern me. Does it concern you?'

'Not at all.'

'Then we simply won't be concerned.'

[4]

During the following months all the Bradshaw family members, having been aware of Polly's tragic situation during her time in Heidelberg, wrote to her and Bill at Wingate Fields to say how delighted they were that the Bradshaws – more important, two of the *younger* Bradshaws – were in residence again on the family estate. Suggestions were made that all the family should gather there soon, on Angus's birthday perhaps, or at Christmas, Twelfth Night, or Easter.

The female Bradshaws, particularly, Helen and Valerie and Nora, even if they didn't say it in so many words, seemed to believe that a rebirth of the clan was about to take place. Everyone hoped that Polly would soon find a husband and Bill a wife, and some even harboured a dream that the unpredictable Rab would then follow suit. And at last all, or some, of this youngest generation of Bradshaws would live together at Wingate Fields. Wives and husbands and children and dogs.

Polly and Bill answered all these letters and expressions of goodwill in the same spirit in which they'd been written. To all suggestions of family gatherings, however, to all hints that one or more of their relatives might soon be coming to visit, they composed a persuasive list of reasons why such plans should be postponed.

'We'd love to see you, of course,' Polly wrote, 'but give us a bit of time first. When you do arrive, you'll understand why. We have so many plans for this magnificent old treasure of a house, all of which will delight you, but we fondly hope that we can give you a surprise as well. So indulge us, *s'il vous plaît*, and you'll be glad you did. Nothing you have loved will be discarded or modernized but everything will be cleaned and polished and sensibly refurbished. When you see what we're doing you'll all want to move back here.'

Even Jesse, who considered himself the absent master of Wingate Fields and was so considered by both staff and family (with the exception of Rab who considered himself the master) resisted making his occasional visits to Northumberland after reading these letters of entreaty from his son and daughter. Nora, who had reasons of her own for wanting him to stay in Paris, was quick to side with Polly and Bill. 'Thank God Polly has found a new enthusiasm. It's the best possible therapy for her, to become involved with our old mausoleum of a birth-place. Until she's married, with children to look after, it will occupy her totally. You have to be careful, I think, not to do or say anything that might push her back into that gloomy corner she's occupied for so long.'

Although Jesse did not accept most of Nora's romantic notions, they did coincide comfortably with some of his own reasons for staying away from Wingate. He was afraid he might discover that Polly was not so fully recovered from Jack's death as her letters made it seem. He did not believe that his own presence might trigger a bad reaction in his daughter, that an unsettling memory of the days and weeks he had spent with her in Heidelberg before Jack's trial might come back to her, but he entertained that thought, all the same, as a possibility.

Even when the children were small, Valerie had always cautioned him about showing too obviously his preference for Polly. So he had tried to give equal time and affection to all three. But no one, particularly the children, had been deceived. Polly was Jesse's favourite. It was an accepted fact. So, as much as he longed to see her, he wanted to feel sure that the pain he had seen in her eyes those times he'd visited her in Germany was gone for good.

There was resentment at work, also, much of it directed towards Bill. Just as Valerie had been upset by Polly and Bill's turning towards their father and away from her, so did Jesse feel that Bill had managed in some way to redefine Jesse's role in relation to his daughter. He had been disturbed by Bill's willingness to look after Polly in Heidelberg. He had been even more unsettled by Polly's acceptance of that help from her brother. He felt diminished and discarded, and the feeling stubbornly refused to be reasoned away.

Jesse had also resented, and he continued to resent, the fact that his own carefully made plans had been frustrated by Bill's sudden decision to make his home at Wingate Fields. He never questioned that it was Bill's decision and that Polly had simply been conscripted. The fact that Wingate had been, historically, the simultaneous home of three or four generations of Bradshaws, that the whole design of the rambling stone building actually provided for that sort of life, had no effect on Jesse's frame of mind. As the years had gone by, as one circumstance or another had kept him away from Northumberland, all his dreams about returning there had featured himself as the solitary master in residence. He would undoubtedly have defended himself by saying that no other family member had been rejected, they had simply not been included.

Since returning to Paris, he had gradually opened the gates wide enough for Nora to slip through, but no others, not even his children, not even Polly, were a part of his vision for the final years of his life. In the pattern of fantasy that had been triggered the first moment he saw Wingate Fields it was not enough for him to replace Angus, to rule the lands, the family and the staff. It was not his goal to be first among equals, to be the dominant and ruling figure. He needed to be the only person in the mansion, the only one at table – not just the final and decisive voice but the only voice.

These feelings did not cause him to mope about in Paris and spit in the Seine. On the contrary. For a resentful man, he seemed surprisingly content and fulfilled. But the baby fox inside his shirt feasted every day on his entrails. Knowing of nothing he could do that would advance his purpose, he concluded that he must wait and hope that some incident might occur that would transform an impossibility into a possibility.

The letter he received from Jenkins, therefore, in the late spring brought him hope rather than dismay.

I do not wish to alarm you, Mr Bradshaw, but there is a situation here that I think only you can properly deal with. I would call it disturbing rather than dangerous but I do think it requires your prompt attention. There is a possibility that much of the house staff could leave us at any moment. Please advise me when I can expect to see you here.

[5]

Jenkins met Jesse at Newcastle airport and drove him to Wingate Fields. He was a well-conditioned grey-haired man, his face and hands brown from the sun. Something military about his bearing. But today, even before they began to discuss the reasons for his letter to Jesse, he seemed ill at ease.

When they were in the car, slowly making their way out of the airport complex, Jesse said, 'What's all this about the staff threatening to leave?'

'It's Whitehead who's behind it, I believe. He and his wife. They're religious people, you know. I'm not quite sure what denomination it is that they're attached to. I've heard it mentioned but it's not a sect I'm familiar with.'

'Yes, I remember,' Jesse said. 'They both made a point of their church beliefs when we hired them.'

'Don't misunderstand me. Their religious ideas are not the central problem here. I mentioned that fact only because I think it's a part of what we're dealing with. They're quirky people, sir. No doubt of that. Rigid, I suppose you might say. But no one could accuse them of being anything less than proficient in their line of work. They set a fine example for the rest of the staff. They're industrious and conscientious workers.'

'Are they well liked?'

'I'd say they're respected. And I expect that's the way they want it. They tend to keep to themselves. Don't jolly about much with the others. Or so I'm told. But in these matters that I have to discuss with you, they've taken the lead. When Whitehead spoke to me, he made it clear that he was speaking for the others as well.'

'He told you they're threatening to leave?'

Jenkins nodded. 'Not the entire staff perhaps. I've made some inquiries – since it's a delicate matter I haven't gone into detail with anyone except Whitehead – and I think certain older members are willing to stay on. But if the Whiteheads go I think a number of other people will follow.'

'If Whitehead's a troublemaker,' Jesse said, 'I want him to leave. I will tell him that, and the rest of the staff as well. I know it's not easy to replace good people but we've done it before. And we'll do it now if it's necessary.'

'I'm in a difficult position here,' Jenkins said. 'It's not one that I relish. You see, Whitehead is not the problem. Or so it seems to me. As I mentioned a moment ago there is a certain delicate matter at the centre of all this . . .'

'Yes, I heard that. What's that all about?'

'It seems to concern your son and daughter.'

'If you're saying that Whitehead and other staff members refuse to take direction from either Polly or Bill, then those people should not be working here. And I'm surprised that they are. If Whitehead has complaints he should take them to Bill, not to you. What does Bill have to say about all this staff dissension?'

'I don't think he's aware of it,' Jenkins said.

'You haven't told him about your discussion with Whitehead?'

'No, sir.'

'Why not?'

'I couldn't. I didn't think it was my place. That's why I asked you to put in an appearance.'

'Is there some mystery here that I know nothing about? I'm convinced that you are perfectly capable of managing this estate. You've proved that. I also know that my son and daughter are able to make any necessary decisions as regards staff. So I'm not at all sure why I'm here. Why did you ask me to come?'

'As you know, I'm a family man myself, Mr Bradshaw. I have two fine daughters and five grandchildren. If there's a mystery here, as you say, then it's simply because I don't know how to tell

550

you what you must be told. If this was simply a matter of replacing staff, of course I wouldn't have called you here . . .'

'Just tell me in plain words what's bothering Whitehead. Why has he threatened to leave?'

'I don't want you to associate what I'm going to tell you with me. So I will tell you precisely what Whitehead said to me.'

'That's what I want to know,' Jesse said.

'He believes that your son and daughter are living together as man and wife.'

'He *said* that to you?'

'Yes, he did.'

'I'm surprised you didn't discharge him on the spot.'

'If he's wrong I thought it was important for you to discredit him before any other steps are taken.'

'What does that mean . . . "*if* he's wrong"?'

'I told him I didn't want to discuss it with him but he insisted on giving me details anyway. I was quite sharp with him but he wouldn't stop talking. He said his own honour was in question if he wasn't allowed to substantiate what he'd told me.'

'And what did the bastard say?'

'I'm sorry, sir, but I'm not willing to repeat what he told me. You're my employer. I refuse to invade your privacy in that way. I will simply say that other staff members are able to give the same first-hand reports that he was giving me. Or so he says.'

'I can't beleive what I'm hearing. Does that mean that Whitehead and other staff members have been exchanging stories about my son and daughter?'

'If what he says is true,' Jenkins said, 'there was a great deal of information being passed round.'

For the remainder of the drive home Jesse sat silent, looking out the window, his face grim and unusually pale. When they arrived at Wingate Fields, when Polly and Bill greeted him at the east entrance to the house, he said, 'It's wonderful to see you both. Jenkins and I have a little estate business to handle, then I'll come find you and we'll have a good visit.'

He went directly to the library and then closed the door behind him. A few minutes later Jenkins came in with Whitehead. When Whitehead said, 'Good afternoon, sir,' Jesse said, 'That's the last sound I want to hear from you.' He got up, walked round the desk, and stood directly in front of Whitehead. 'If I hear one word from your foul mouth I've instructed Jenkins to keep you quiet. If he's not able to, I assure you that I am. If you understand me, nod your head.'

Whitehead's face and neck coloured a deep pink suddenly and his lips trembled. But he nodded and said nothing, and Jesse looked at his watch. 'At twenty minutes past four,' he said, 'exactly one hour from now, a car will be waiting for you at the kitchen entrance. You have that much time to pack whatever clothes and belongings you and your wife want to take with you. Anything you leave behind will be shipped to whatever address you specify. I have instructed Mr Jenkins to give both you and your wife two months' wages. The car will take you to Newcastle and the driver will pay for your tickets to whatever destination you select in England. After I've spoken to the rest of the staff and consulted my solicitor I will decide whether or not to bring an action against you and your wife for slander. That will be all.'

Ten minutes later, while Jenkins supervised the Whiteheads' preparations for departure, the entire staff filed into the seldom-used banquet room. When they were ranged in front of him Jesse said, 'I have just discharged Mr Whitehead and his wife for improper conduct. For reasons known only to themselves they saw fit to make slanderous statements about members of my family. I have been told there are other staff members who may believe the false statements that were being gossiped about by the Whiteheads. If there are such people here in this room I urge you to turn in your resignations at once. Anyone who makes the error the Whiteheads have made will be dismissed promptly and will be subject to prosecution as well. All of you who live here in our home are thought of as friends. We expect the same loyalty from you that we give to you. Just as we do not make judgements of you, we will certainly not permit you to make judgements of us. We will not conduct an inquisition to determine if any of you have allied yourself with the Whiteheads, but we expect those of you who listened sympathetically to their fabrications to submit your resignations. There has never been dissension in this house between family and staff, and I am determined that there never shall be. We offer you respect and goodwill. We expect no less from you.'

Jesse and his son and daughter all dressed for dinner that evening. They met in the drawing room for cocktails and had their dinner later in the dining hall.

Jesse had feared some residue of anxiety, particularly in Polly, left over from her time in Germany. He had prepared himself for a change in her. But there was none. Certainly there was no discernible change. Nor did Bill seem to have undergone any remarkable transformation since he'd left Fort Beck to go to Germany.

Jesse had told himself that he would give no credence whatsoever to the report he'd had from Jenkins. He saw Whitehead's dismissal and the lecture to the staff as an end to that matter. He would not study Bill and Polly when they were together to see what note of familiarity or family affection could have been misconstrued and taken for something other than what it was.

When they appeared together in the drawing room, however, he could not keep himself from trying to see behind the screen of teasing banter that had characterized their relationship for as long as he could remember. But there was no detectable nuance, no glance, no gesture that indicated anything new, or intimate, or remarkable. He saw, as he always did when he looked at them, two attractive young people who were informed, articulate and entertaining. Polly had once said to him, 'You love us more when we're dressed up.' He had denied that, of course, but if he had been completely honest with himself he would have conceded that paternal pride came easier when your children were pleasant to look at.

As their dinner progressed, and they stayed at table for the entire evening, he concluded, and considering the circumstances that had brought him there it was a surprising conclusion, that it was the warmest, most pleasant time he'd spent with any of his children since they'd grown up. On other occasions he'd always been aware of the barriers of restraint and mistrust that are said to exist between one generation and another, particularly between a father and his children. But this night there was no such obstruction. They all spoke freely of Valerie and Floyd, or Nora and Rab, and Bill told funny stories about his adventures in Fort Beck, when he'd been living with Jesse and Helen and attending Foresby. Toward the end of dinner, misled perhaps by claret and champagne, Jesse was able to envision a life wherein evenings like this would be common. Members of the family assembled at the end of the day from their various wings and rooms and apartments in the complexity of Wingate, their individual and group activities all moulded together in a warm and rewarding way.

553

It was almost midnight when they left the dining hall. Polly, burlesqueing a sort of music hall intoxication, waved her chiffon scarf in the air and tottered off to the west wing. But Bill joined his father for a brandy in the library. When they sat down facing each other in soft leather chairs, the decanter on a low table between them, Jesse said, 'I assume you noticed that Whitehead wasn't with us tonight.'

'Yes, indeed. I did notice that.'

'Did you know I sacked him?'

'Yes, I did. And his wife along with him.'

'Who told you?'

Bill smiled. 'It's a big old barn we live in but there are no secrets here.'

'Were you told why I discharged the Whiteheads?'

'I assumed it was because they're tiresome and boring, or perhaps because they're such bloody Christers. Actually, I didn't hear the reason.'

Jesse sipped from his snifter. Then he said, 'I wasn't planning to discuss it with you but since you're the master here now, and since my reasons for dismissing them do concern you and Polly, perhaps I should.'

'I'm always interested in a bit of gossip.'

'I would prefer that you did not pass it along to Polly, however.'

'Ahhh,' Bill said. 'Then I think you'd best not tell me. I don't keep secrets from Poll. We tell each other everything.'

Polly, as she was being discussed, was studying herself very seriously in the looking-glass of her dressing room as she removed her make-up with cold cream. While she prepared herself for bed, her father and Bill were talking earnestly in the library. When she fell asleep in the bed that had belonged to her great-grandmother, the two men were still together in the book-lined room at the other end of the house.

[6]

By mid-afternoon the following day Jesse was back in Paris. When he explained to Nora everything that had transpired at Wingate, starting with the information Jenkins had given him and ending

with his late-night conversation with Bill, she said, 'I can't believe
it. What dreadful people those Whiteheads must be. Don't they
realize what Polly has gone through? Can't they see how dependent
she's become on her brother, how she relies on him? I think Bill
saved her. I'm convinced that she couldn't have pulled it off by
herself. Don't you agree?'

'I certainly do.'

'And to think that small-minded people could misinterpret a
relationship like that. Between a brother and sister. But how were
they able to influence other people?'

'I suppose we'll never know the answer to that. I wasn't about
to dignify the gossip by quizzing members of the staff. But
according to Jenkins, Whitehead told him he hadn't influenced the
others. He said they'd come to their own conclusions.'

'What rot! Bill must have been furious when you told him.'

'I expected him to be but he wasn't.'

'What did he say?'

'He was remarkably tolerant, I thought. He wasn't fond of the
Whiteheads. He admitted that. But he said it didn't surprise him
that people had misinterpreted his dependence on Polly and hers
on him. He said people were not accustomed to a brother and sister
who would rather be together than with anyone else.'

'Of course they're not accustomed to it,' Nora said, 'because it
almost never happens. And it won't continue with them either.
Once Polly's put right again, it won't be long till she's looking over
her brother's shoulder at other young men. And the same with
Bill. They're both healthy young colts and they'll behave as we all
did at that age.'

'I said something very like that to Bill but he just nodded his
head. No more than that. He seems to feel that he and his sister
have signed some sort of blood contract. Like he and Rab used to
do when they played pirates on the pond.'

'And you didn't discuss any of this with Polly?'

Jesse shook his head. 'I hadn't planned to discuss it with Bill
either. Not beyond telling him the reason I'd sacked Whitehead.
But Bill's reaction to my explanation was so strange – almost a non-
reaction – that I stayed with it a bit longer than I'd expected to.'

'In what way? How do you mean?'

'I just couldn't believe that he wasn't surprised by what I said. I
expected him to be mad as hell. But he wasn't. So I kept trying to.

get some sort of reaction from him. I told him that if anyone ever said things like that about me and my sister I'd be angry enough to kill him. I said there was almost nothing uglier a person could accuse you of.'

'What did he say to that?'

'Nothing. Just sat there listening to me with an odd little smile on his face. I told him about growing up on the south side of Chicago with all those Italian and Polish kids. It was a rough bunch. Tough talk. Dirty language. But you never said anything about another kid's family. Any mention of his mother or his sister and you'd better be ready for a fight.'

'Still no reaction from Bill?'

Jesse shook his head. 'Zero. I could have been talking about ten other people for all the difference it seemed to make to him.'

'Did you see him this morning before you left?'

'Bright and early. We had breakfast together.'

'Polly, too?'

'No. He said she was still asleep. Not feeling too well. Too much champagne last night.'

'Do you think he told her about the conversation the two of you had?'

'I doubt if he told her last night. It was quite late. But I'm certain he's told her by now. As I mentioned before, he says he tells her everything.'

'God, it all sounds dreadful. I'm glad I wasn't there.'

'So am I. It was hard to get things in focus. I felt as if I was punching balloons with my fist.'

'Something's still bothering you,' she said.

'Several things.'

'Like what?'

'I keep remembering something Bill said when I asked him how he found out I'd discharged Whitehead. He said, "It's a big old barn we live in but there are no secrets here." '

'Why does that bother you?'

'I'm not sure. It just does.'

In the weeks just after Jesse's visit to Wingate, Bill and Polly once again began to take charge of the affairs of the estate. They hired a new cook and house manager to replace the Whiteheads, they discharged half a dozen other staff members and took on replacements, and they put into motion once more the programme of refurbishing they had begun when they first returned to Wingate. A first priority would be the redecorating of the suite of rooms in the east wing that Bill had once occupied with his brother.

'I was quite ill before we left Germany,' Polly told the decorator as they discussed work plans, 'and I was extremely dependent on my brother. But now I'm all well and I want to give him some freedom to take up his own life again. He's quite keen on those rooms in the east wing so we must make him comfortable and at home there.'

While the work was being done, Bill moved his things to a second-floor guest suite at the front of the house, overlooking the long approach from the road and the old coach entrance. He also spent more time than before with Jenkins, driving or riding horseback across the moors, consulting with the tenant farmers and going over estate accounts with the bookkeeper.

It seemed that Bill and Polly saw each other now only at breakfast and dinner. Bill was often absent at midday but more often than not they met each morning in the breakfast room and said goodnight after dinner in the dining hall. 'We're all delighted you're feeling better now,' the housekeeper said to Polly. 'It's a pleasure to see you busy about the house and playing the piano after dinner.'

'I'm pleased to hear you say that,' Polly said. 'Wingate Fields means a great deal to me. I'm happy to pitch in and help it function.'

God knows what sort of suffering they endured during those few short weeks when they tried, Bill and Polly, to restructure their lives, as they attempted to obey rules they no longer believed in, to ignore their feelings and their memories. Long after they realized that they could not undo what had already been done, they continued to try. But at last she could not sit across from him at table without weeping and he could do nothing at all unless he was fortified with brandy.

One night, well past midnight, the housekeeper was awakened

by one of the other servants. 'I'm sorry to disturb you, mum, but I couldn't sleep. I was reading in my bed when I heard sounds from the west wing. It sounded like gun shots.'

Polly and Bill were found lying in her bed with their arms round each other. There was a bullet hole in his temple and one in hers. The small dark revolver was in Polly's hand.

[8]

They were buried in the family cemetery just beside the chapel at Wingate Fields. Only Jesse and Rab and Nora were there for the burial. The Bishop of Newcastle, who normally presided over Bradshaw funerals, was not notified. Jesse read a passage from the Scriptures at the graveside. Apart from that there was no ceremony. By mid-afternoon Rab was back in London. Nora and Jesse were on a plane returning to Paris.

During the following months there was at first an effort by the remaining family members to communicate with each other, but those efforts gradually ended. When Rab and Rosalind Dilworth were married, her sister was a witness but no Bradshaws were there. And when they spent a month in the north of England after their wedding, they stayed at Bick House in Cumbria, the home of Valerie's father.

After months of travelling through northern California and Washington and Oregon, Helen bought a house on an island in the bay west of Seattle. She had sold her home in Fort Beck a few weeks before. She had not seen Frank Wilson since she'd left Illinois but they had begun to talk on the telephone at least once a week, usually on Sunday mornings.

In the weeks just following the burial at Wingate, Nora and Jesse told themselves that soon they would begin to go to Northumberland again and eventually they would live there, as they had planned. Jesse studied the monthly reports that Jenkins sent along and shared them with Nora. Little by little, however, they found they were spending less time in Paris and a great deal more time at Nora's house in the forest north of the city. Jenkins's reports about the estate were hastily read and put aside. Or not read at all.

When Bill and Polly died, Valerie and Floyd had been on a vagabond freighter somewhere between Bali and the east coast of Africa. The news reached them at last three weeks later. Not long after that they discovered a ship that made regular trips between Oakland and Auckland, stopping at Fiji, Tahiti and New Caledonia.

After their first round trip, when the ship returned to Oakland, they booked a passage on the next voyage, leaving five days later. After three such trips they reserved the same stateroom for an indefinite period.

They did not become acquainted with the various groups of passengers they sailed with. They did nothing to attract attention to themselves. But they were noticed all the same. People observed that Valerie almost never appeared on the upper decks and her husband seldom went below.

Angus had predicted that Jesse would live to see the winds blowing through the broken windows and empty rooms of Wingate Fields. That prediction did not come true. Or perhaps it did. In any case, there were no Bradshaws there to witness it.

The Bradshaw Trilogy
Volume I

NO PLACE TO CRY

When Helen Bradshaw's father dies she is shocked to discover that he was not the man she thought she knew. Raymond Bradshaw had always been close to his daughter yet he concealed from her the fact that an unhappy love affair had driven him away from his own parents and out of his native England.

Twenty years after his disappearance, news of Raymond's death in America reaches his family in Yorkshire. And though their grief is deep and painful, they are delighted to learn that they have a grandchild – Helen.

Though at first reluctant to meet the family her father had so emphatically rejected, Helen nonetheless sails from New York in June 1919 to make their acquaintance.

The Bradshaw Trilogy
Volume II

THE FIRES OF SUMMER

The Fires of Summer continues the dramatic story of the Bradshaw family, a story that began in 1919 when the young Helen Bradshaw sailed from New York to England to meet the family her father had so bitterly and mysteriously rejected.

Now it is 1941 and another young stranger is about to return to the Bradshaw fold, crossing the Atlantic to confront a long-buried past and discover a lost inheritance. After twenty years of fruitless searching, Helen has at last tracked down her illegitimate son, Floyd, whose existence she had kept a painful secret since his adoption and whom she feared she would never see again.

can't help feeling like a part of history when you walk through these old grey streets every day. It ennobles you and makes you feel insignificant all in one stroke. I'm trying to say I wouldn't trade the time I've spent here for anything. But it's not a place to spend your life. Not a place to spend our lives. It's too heavy, too compartmentalized. The place is more important than the people. Eventually you feel dehumanized.'

Polly had come round slowly. But a day came when she said to Bill, 'You've mesmerized me. I have images in my head that I didn't invite. I lie in bed at night and see the moors of Northumberland. I dream that I'm walking through the deer park in my night-dress. I see meadows and hills, and horses galloping in the early morning, their ears up and their tails flying. Then I wake up and look out at the grey streets of Heidelberg and wonder why I'm here.'

After weeks had passed, when they'd decided they would indeed leave Heidelberg and return to Wingate, the size, the grandeur, the openness of their family home were the intoxicants that swept them ahead. The plans they made were all of scope and movement and space. They would use and explore and investigate the far-flung and rich possibilities of that great house and its almost endless expanse of land. They would learn about it, roam across it, smell it and touch it in an intimate way they had never ventured before. They would relish the high-ceilinged rooms, the extended gardens and the groves of ancient trees. 'We'll become expansive,' Polly said. 'No more hushed voices and small gestures. We will grow tall and wide and free so that we'll fit in our fine house. We'll become huge in our spirit and giant in our joy. We'll have boundless tolerance and gargantuan generosity. We will fill that empty house, you and I, in every way. We'll use every room.'

For two weeks after their return, more than two, they had forged ahead busily from breakfast till bed-time. They examined the house from cellar to attic, with Whitehead, and suggested changes they would like made. They also had extended meetings with key members of the staff regarding details of the service they would require. They both rode out with Jenkins to meet new tenant farmers and to reacquaint themselves with other tenants they had known since childhood. Once these opening formalities were completed, the two of them walked and rode, by car and on horseback, for many miles, refreshing their memories about places that had been half-forgotten.